65
Great
Murder
Mysteries

65
Great Murder Mysteries

Edited by
Mary Danby

This edition published in Great Britain
in 1983 by

Octopus Books Limited
59 Grosvenor Street
London W1

in collaboration with

William Heinemann Limited
10 Upper Grosvenor Street
London W1

and

Martin Secker & Warburg Limited
54 Poland Street
London W1

The arrangement of this collection is
copyright © 1983 Mary Danby

Second impression, reprinted 1984

ISBN 0 86273 083 X

Printed and bound in Great Britain by Collins, Glasgow

Contents

Contents

Evidence in Camera

Margery Allingham

There are people who might consider Chippy Wager unethical and others who go a great deal further. At the time I am telling you about he was on the *Cormorant*, which is not that paper's real name, but why make enemies if you don't have to? He was, and is of course, a photographer; one of those boys who shoot through a cop's legs and jump on to the running-board of the limousine so that you can see the society bride in tears as she takes her first cold look at the man she's got. They pay those lads plenty, but Chippy had uses for money, mainly liquid, and he made another income on the side by taking photographs privately of practically everything from the Mayor and Corporation to the local beauty queen. He made time for these activities when there was none, and used the *Cormorant*'s excellent equipment, but, as he said, he had to drink.

We both went down to St Piers for the fifth murder. I was on the old *Post* at the time, and when I say 'we' went I mean among others. The Southern Railway put on one excursion train for the Press and another for the police.

The story was simple and, if you like that sort of thing, good. You probably remember it. It rated about as much space as an election and by the time the body of the fifth victim, Mrs Lily Clarke, was found at St Piers it was practically the one subject of conversation in the bars. Briefly, someone was killing off middle-aged redheads in seaside towns. There had been a summer of it. In May Mrs Wild was killed in Whichborne, in June Mrs Garrard at Turnhill Bay, and by July the murderer had got round to Southwharf and had attended to a Mrs Jelf. In August he chose a fashionable resort and strangled Mrs Ginger Hollis, just outside the polo ground at Prinny's Plage, and in September there was this latest affair at St Piers.

In all five instances the details were astonishingly similar. Each victim was respectable, homely in appearance, in the habit of letting rooms to visitors, and either naturally or artificially auburn-haired. Each woman was found strangled in a secluded place in the open-air, with her untouched handbag beside her. Each woman lost some trifling ornament, such as a cheap earring, a gold clasp from a chain bracelet, a locket containing edelweiss, and once, in Mrs Hollis's case, a small silver button with a regimental crest on it.

Not once was any trace of the murderer seen either before or after the crime, and by the time the St Piers news came through the police were savage while the Press were on the verge of being bored. There was still plenty to write about but nothing new. The *Cormorant* and its sisters, who had worked themselves up to screaming hysterics in July, were showing signs of exhaustion, and even the heavies, like ourselves and the *World*, were back on such items as the slayer's preference for the new moon.

From my own purely personal point of view the thing was becoming a nightmare and the principal reason for that was Chippy. I had first met him when I travelled down to Whichborne in May. On that occasion there were seventeen of us in a carriage which might have held ten without active inconvenience, and although he was the last to arrive he was in a corner seat with only myself atop of him before the journey was half way over. I do not know how he did this. My impression is that there was a jolt in a tunnel and that when we came out into the light there he was, slung with cameras, sitting just underneath me.

I suppose I must bring myself to describe him. He is a small thin rag of a man with a surprisingly large square head in which, somewhere low down in front, has been inserted the bright predatory face of an evil child. Whenever I think of him, which is as seldom as possible, I receive a mental picture of white lashes on red lids and a row of widely spaced uneven teeth barred in a 'Have you got anything *I* want?' smile.

His is hardly one of the dressy professions but I have seen even his confrères blench when confronted by some of his ensembles. Peterson, my opposite number on the *World*, who interests himself in these matters, insists that the man finds his clothes lying about in hotel bedrooms. It may be so. At any rate, when I first saw him he was certainly wearing jodhpurs, carefully tailored for a larger and even more curiously shaped leg, a green cardigan buttoning on the wrong side, and a new cheap sports coat adorned by a single gigantic beer-stain. Every pocket, one frankly marsupial, bulged strangely rather than dangerously, and he carried as much gear as a paratrooper.

I remember my conversation with him on that occasion. I had pulled back my sleeve to glance at the time and he prodded me in the back.

'That's a good watch,' he said. 'Ever had it photographed?'

I said that strange as it might seem to him such a notion had never entered my head.

'It's wise,' he assured me seriously. 'In case you ever have it pinched, see? Gives the busies something to go on? I'll do it for you when we get in. It won't cost you more than half a bar. You're married, of course. Got any kids?'

I told him no, and he seemed hurt.

'Kids make good pictures,' he explained. 'Kids and dogs. Got a dog?'

Again I had to disappoint him.

'Pity,' he said. 'What a pal, eh? What a pal. You might pick one up down here. There's a chap only five miles out who breeds Irish wolf-hounds. I'll put you on to him and we'll take a spool. Surprise the wife, eh?'

I escaped from him as soon as I could but everything was against me. The news, what there was of it, broke late and the town was packed. By the time I realized that I should have to stay there was no accommoda-tion in the place. I was resigning myself to a bench on the front when I ran into Chippy just before closing time in the back bar of the Queen's. He was in the same predicament, having, so he said, had to waste time photographing a cotton magnate and his fifth wife who were having their second honeymoon in the King's Suite at the Grand. He was not worrying, however, and when they turned us out he produced an old friend who was the manager of a flea-ridden little pub in a back street. He fixed us up with two cots in an attic, for which I paid, and I let Chippy take a photograph of my watch, rewarding him, as far as I re-member, with fourteen shillings and sixpence in cash for three excellent prints.

After that I was doomed. The man became an incubus, haunting me as I drank furtively in corners or hunted our murderer with one eye, so to speak, behind me lest I myself should be waylaid. I do agree with Peterson that I am free, adult, and a member of a profession which ought at least to be able to look after itself, and I could once I suppose have got rid of him with brutality and the fishy eye, but I could not bring myself to do it. He was so fearful, so unmitigatedly awful that he fascinated me. Some unsuspected masochism in my nature compelled me to be at least half civil to him, and then of course he was often so infuriatingly useful. There was a rumour that he was lucky, but that explanation did him less than justice. He was indefatigable and his curious contacts and side jobs sometimes provided him with most useful breaks, as for instance when he nipped down to Whichborne station to oblige a man who wanted a shot of his greyhound and got instead a very fine one of the Yard's Chief Inspector Tizer getting off the train at a time when no one was sure if the local police had appealed to H.Q. and if so who was going to be sent.

By the time the murderer had got round to St Piers Chippy was most anxious that the homicidal nut should be apprehended and the case finished. His reason was personal and typical and I happened to know about it because he had confided it to me one night at Prinny's Plage, when he had hounded me down to a hostelry which I felt fairly confident not even he had heard of. I can see him now, pointing to the brewer's almanac which hung on the varnished match-boarding of the bar wall.

'Look, chum,' he said, his filthy forefinger tracing out the dates, 'next new moon is September sixteen, isn't it? Don't think I'm complaining about that. It'll still be summer then and the seaside suits me. But what about the month after? New moon October fourteen. I don't want anything awkward to happen then, do I?'

I made a point of never giving him encouragement and I said nothing, knowing perfectly well I should not silence him.

'October fourteen.' He was indignant. 'The Distillers Livery Company conference begins on the fourteenth. Fancy missing that. What a tragedy, eh? What a tragedy!'

That was in August. We were all expecting the September murder, although naturally there was no way of telling where it was going to crop up. When the news broke just too late for the edition which everybody was holding for it in a shamefaced way, it was very nearly anticlimax. As Peterson said, there would have been almost more news value in the story if it hadn't occurred. No one was pleased. The livelier dailies had planted men at most of the larger southern watering places but no one had thought of St Piers, cheap and respectable, out on the mud-flats of the estuary. We had a local correspondent there, as we had in every town in the country. The last thing he had sent us, according to the book, was an account of a stork which a coachload of machine-shop operatives had seen flying inland one evening in June the previous year. According to his story, the phenomenon had caused wild excitement in the town. It appeared to be that sort of place.

I managed to avoid Chippy going down but I saw his back disappearing into the Railway Tavern as I picked up a taxi at the station. I was glad of the respite, for the newsflash which had come in was so familiar in its wording – 'Body of well-nurtured woman found strangled. Lonely woodland. Auburn-haired. Chief Inspector Tizer hurrying to scene' – that I felt a wave of pure nausea at the prospect of having to deal with him as well.

St Piers was much as I had feared. At first it is only the light and the faint smell of iodine which warns the newcomer that the coast is at hand, but towards the front, where the architecture veers towards Victorian Moorish, a faded ocean licks a dun-coloured strand and the shops sell coloured buckets and sticks of sweet rock and crested china to take home.

I found our local correspondent, a tobacconist called Cuffley, in his shop on the parade. He was waiting for me on the step, every hair in his moustache electrified with excitement. He had leapt to the job, had been on the spot soon after the body had been discovered, and had had a word with the inevitable small boy who had given the first alarm. He had even written a short piece which began, as I remember, '*Mad Killer Visits St Piers at Last*. A baleful sun rose early this morning over the municipally maintained woodland behind the Kursaal and must have shone down unheeding for quite a space on the ghastly, blue, contorted lips of a respected local resident …' However, he had got the victim's name and address for me and had written it down in block caps on the back of one of his trade cards: MRS LILY CLARKE, KNOLE, SEAVIEW AVENUE. It was the same sort of name and the same sort of address as all the others in the long weary business, and when he told me with delight that he had recognised a relation of the dead woman among his customers, and had gone to the length of having her waiting for me in the little room behind the shop, I knew before I saw her exactly the kind of gal I was going to find. The sameness of all five cases was slightly unnerving. I recognised at once both the horror and the dreadful secret enjoyment she was finding in it. I had seen it often that summer.

Her story, too, was a fifth variation of a tale I had heard four times already. Like her predecessors, Mrs Clarke had been a widow. She had not dyed her hair exactly but she had touched it up. She had not taken in lodgers in the ordinary way, being much too refined. But yes, on occasions she had obliged. The idea of her going for a walk at night with a man she did not know! Well, if the situation had not been so tragic the relation would have had to laugh, she would really.

I asked the question I had grown used to asking. 'Was she a nice woman? Did you like her?' I was prepared for the girl's hesitation and the faint uneasiness, the anxiety to speak well of the dead. I remembered comments on the other women. 'She had a temper.' 'You would not call her exactly generous.' 'She liked her own way.' 'She could be very nice when she wanted to.'

This time Mr Cuffley's customer, in speaking of Mrs Clarke, said something which seemed to me to sum up them all.

'Oh, she was all for herself,' she said grimly and shut her mouth like a vice.

At Sub-Divisional Police Headquarters there was no information of a startling character. Mrs Clarke had met her death at some time before midnight and in the process she had not been robbed. Fifteen pounds in treasury notes had been found in the mock-crocodile handbag which still hung from her arm. The sergeant in charge spoke of the negligence of the criminal in this respect with an amazement which bordered upon indignation. The only blessed thing she had lost, he said regretfully, was a silver tassel which had hung from the old-fashioned silver brooch she wore in her lapel, and of course, her life.

As in all the earlier crimes there was absolutely no suspect. There were no visitors staying at Knole, Seaview Avenue, and so far no one had come forward to report having seen the woman out with a stranger.

I sent my story off and took a tram to the Kursaal. Half the town appeared to have the same idea and I joined a stream of consciously casual strollers advancing purposefully up a threadbare path between ragged ill-used trees. The body had been found in a dusty glade where cartons and little scraps of paper grew instead of anemones. The spot needed no signpost. The police had got their screens up and I could see Tizer's hunched shoulders appearing above one of them.

The sightseers stood around at a police-prescribed distance and here again nothing was new. In the last few months reams had been written about the avid, open-mouthed defectives who had come to stare at the last couch of each of the victims, and here as far as I could see they all were once more. I felt certain I had seen the dreary man with the fascinated blue eyes and the watch-chain full of darts medals at every road accident, case of illness in the street, or mere surface reconstruction at which I had had the misfortune to be present. The adolescent girl with the weeping baby brother was familiar, too, and as for the plump middle-aged man with the broad smile he could not possibly have known he was wearing, I was sure I had seen him, or someone darned like him, grinning at the scene of every catastrophe in my experience. They were all standing about, looking and hoping, God knew what for. One group, which contained at least one collapsible perambulator, appeared to be thinking of picnicking.

I had a word with Tizer, who was not pleased to see me and had nothing to tell me. He is never sanguine and by this time his gloom was painful. I came away feeling nearly as sorry for him as I was for myself.

The Press was there in force and I walked down the hill with Peterson. We came on Chippy at the turning where the path divides. He was busy, as usual, and appeared to be taking a photograph of a holiday trio, two plump blondes in tight slacks and brassieres, with a flushed lout wriggling between them. There could be only one explanation of the performance and I was gratified if surprised to see he had the grace not to notice me.

'Grafters and buskers on fairgrounds call it "mug-faking", I believe,' observed Peterson as we turned into the White Lion. 'What does he charge them? Half a dollar? It's an interesting comment on the price of whisky.' He has an acid little voice.

For the rest of the week the case dragged on. We had our hopes raised by several false alarms. Tizer thought he had a lead and went scampering to St Leonards with a trail of us behind him, but the chase led nowhere. Everybody did what they could. The *Cormorant* tried to start a stink against the police. The tame psychiatrists wrote more articles for the Sundays. Somebody asked a question in the House and the Yard sent a second Chief Inspector down. Middle-aged women everywhere began to give themselves airs.

From our point of view it was all very dull. The weather turned cold and three of the best hotels ran out of scotch. I saw Chippy now and again but he did not worry me. He was picking up plenty of work, I gathered, and, if his glazed eyes in the evenings were any guide, appeared to find it profitable.

He had a new friend, I was interested to see. So far I have not mentioned Chippy's friends. A natural distaste and embarrassment has prevented me from enlarging on them. It is one of his major dis-advantages that he always seems to discover a local drinking companion who matches, if not exceeds, the man himself in pure unpresentableness. On this occasion he had chummed up with the fat man I had seen grinning at the scene of the crime, or if it was not he it was someone very like him. God knows what he was by profession, a bookmaker's tout perhaps, or a traveller in something unmentionable. I had nothing against him save that if I had seen but the soles of his feet through a grating, or the top of his hat from a bus, I should have known unerringly that he was a fellow for whom I should never have the slightest possible use. He had crumbs in the creases of his blue serge waistcoat, he dribbled his beer when he drank, his voice was hoarse and coarse and negligible, and the broad vacant grin never left his face.

Chippy went about with him most of the time and I was grateful for my release. I was agitating the office for my recall by the Saturday and should have left, I think, by the Sunday had not I made a sudden startling discovery. Chippy was trying to avoid not only me but every other newspaperman in the town. At first I could not bring myself to believe it, but having ceased to hide from him I suddenly found I saw very little of him, and then that Sunday morning we met face to face on the steps of the Grand. In the normal way it would have been I who had become wooden-faced and evasive and he who pursued me to insist on the morning snifter, but today he slunk from me and for the first time in my life I thought I saw him discomposed. I even stood looking after him as he shuffled off, his harness clumping round his shanks, but it was not until I was drinking with Peterson and one or two others some fifteen minutes later that the truth occurred to me. Some-one had asked if Chippy had gone since he had not seen him lately, while somebody else observed that he too had noticed a singular freshness in the atmosphere.

Peterson defended him at once with all that charity of his which is far more lethal than straight attack, and I stood quite still looking at the big calendar over the bar.

Of course. I could not think why I had not realized it before. For Chippy, time was growing pretty short.

I was so anxious that Peterson, whom I love like a brother and who knows me nearly as well, should not cotton on to my idea that I wasted several valuable minutes in what I hope was misleading casualness before I drifted off, ostensibly to phone my wife. From that moment I hunted Chippy as he had never hunted me and it was not too easy an undertaking, since, as I have said, the place was stiff with pressmen and I was more than anxious not to raise any general hue and cry. Anything he had I was willing to share, but, until my wire was safely sent, not with the world.

I hunted carefully and systematically like a peasant woman going through a shawl for a flea, and for the best part of the day I was fighting a conviction that he had vanished into air. But just before six, when I was growing desperate, I suddenly saw him, still festooned with cameras, stepping ashore from a so-called pleasure steamer which had been chugging a party round the bay for the best part of three hours. The other people looked to me like the same crowd who had tramped up to the wood behind the Kursaal the day after the body was found. The adolescent girl with the baby brother was certainly there, and so was Chippy's buddy of the moment, the man with the smile.

From that moment I do not think I lost sight of him or them either. Shadowing them was comparatively simple. The whole party moved, it seemed by instinct, to the nearest hostelry and from there in due course they moved to the next. So it went on throughout the whole evening, when the lights first came out yellow in the autumn haze and, too, when they shone white against the quickening dark.

I do not know when he first became aware that I was behind him. I think it was on the second trip up the Marine Boulevard, where the bars are so thick that no serious drinking time is lost in transit. I met his eyes once and he hesitated but did not nod. He had a dreadful group round him. The man with the smile was still there and so was a little seedy man with a cap and a watch-chain, and two plump blondes in slacks. I recognised them all and none of them, if I make myself clear. After that I could feel him trying to shake me off, but he was hampered and I was, I think, a fraction more sober than he. There must have been a bar on the boat.

After a while I realised that he was going somewhere in particular, heading somewhere definitely if obliquely, like a wasp to its nest. His red eyes wandered to the clock more and more often, I noticed, and his moves from pub to pub seemed quicker and more frequent.

Then I lost him. The party must have split. At any rate I found myself following one of the blondes and a sailor who I felt was new to me, unless of course it was not the same blonde but another just like her. I was in the older and dirtier part of the town and closing time, I felt with dismay, could not possibly be far off. For some time I searched in a positive panic, diving into every lighted doorway and pushing every swinging door. As far as I remember I neglected even to drink and it may be it was that which saved me.

At any rate I came finally to a big ugly old-fashioned drinking house on a corner. It was as large and drab and inviting as a barn and in the four-ale bar, into which I first put my head, there was no one at all but a little blue-eyed seedy man wearing a flat cap and a watch-chain weighted with medals. He was sitting on a bench close to the counter, drinking a pint with the quiet absorption of one who has been doing just that for the last two hours. I glanced at him sharply but there was no way of telling if he had been the same man who had been with Chippy's party. It was not that I am unobservant, but such men exist not in hundreds but in thousands in every town on or off the coast, and there was nothing distinctive about this one. Also, he was alone.

I turned away and would have passed on down the street, when I noticed that there was a second frontage to the building. I put my head in the first door I came to and saw Chippy's back. He was leaning on the bar, which was small and temporarily unattended, the landlord having moved further along it to the adjoining room. At first I thought he was alone, but on coming into the room I saw his smiling friend reclining on a narrow bench which ran along the inner wall. He was still beaming but the vacancy of his broad face was intensified, if one can say such a thing, and I knew he must have ceased to hear anything Chippy was telling him long ago. Chippy was talking. He always talks when he's drunk, not wandering nor thickly but with the low intensity some people find unnerving. He was in full flight now. Soft incisive words illustrated by the sharp gestures of one hand – the other, after all, was supporting him – flowed from him in a steady forceful stream. I had to go very close up behind him to hear what he was saying.

'Trapped,' he whispered to his friend's oblivion. 'Trapped for life by a woman with a sniff and a soul so mean – so *mean* – so *MEAN* ...' He turned and looked at me. 'Hullo,' he said.

I remember I had some idea that in that condition of his I could fool him that I'd either been there all the time or was not there at all, I forget which. Anyway I certainly stood looking at him in surprise without speaking. The thing that surprised me was that he had his old Rolleiflex, the thing he used for close inside work, hanging round his neck with the sight-screens, or whatever they call them, up ready for action.

He returned my stare with friendliness at first, but I saw caution creep across his eyes, tomcat fashion, and presently he made an effort.

'Goodbye,' he said.

The barman saved me answering him by bustling back, wiping the wood and thrusting a can at me all in one motion. He rattled the money

I gave him in the till and waddled off again after nodding to Chippy in a secret important way I entirely misunderstood.

'She was mean, was she?' I ventured, mumbling into my beer.

'As hell,' Chippy agreed and his red eyes wandered up to look over my shoulder. 'Come in, son,' he said softly.

A pallid youth was hesitating in the doorway and he came forward at once, a long cardboard roll held out before him like a weapon. He was white with excitement, I thought, and I did not suppose it was at the sight of us.

'Dad said you was to have these and he'd see you tomorrow.'

I could see by the way Chippy took the parcel that it was important, but he was so casual, or so drunk, that he almost dropped it, and did scatter some of the coins that he gave the boy. He carried them in handfuls in his jacket pocket, apparently.

As soon as the kid had gone, Chippy tore the paper off the roll and I could see it consisted of four or five huge blown-up prints, but he did not open them out, contenting himself with little squints at each corner, and I could see nothing.

The smiling man on the bench moved but did not rise. His eyes were tightly shut but he continued to grin. Chippy looked at him for some time before he suddenly turned to me.

'He's canned,' he said. 'Canned as a toot. I've been carting him round the whole week to have someone safe to talk to, and now look at him. Never mind. Listen to me. Got imagination?'

'Yes,' I assured him flatly.

'You'll need it,' he said. 'Listen. He was young, a simple ordinary friendly kid like you or I were, and he came to the seaside on his holiday. Only one week's holiday in the year.' He paused for the horror to sink in. 'One week, and she caught him. God! Think of it!'

I looked at the smiling man on the bench and I must have been a little whistled myself, for I saw no incongruity in the tale.

'He was *ordinary*!' shouted Chippy suddenly. 'So ordinary that he might be you or me.'

I did not care for that and I spoke sharply.

'His wife caught him, you say?'

'No.' He lowered his voice to the intense stage again. 'Her mother. The landlady. She worked it. Twisted him.' He made a peculiar bending movement with his two hands. 'You know, said things. Made suggestions. Forced it. He had to marry the girl. Then he had hell. Couldn't afford it. Got nagged night and day, day and night. Got him down.'

He leant towards me and I was aware of every one of his squat uneven teeth.

'He grew old,' he said. 'He lost his job. Got another, buying old gold. Used to go round buying old gold for a little firm in the Ditch who kept him skint. It went on for years. Years and years. And more years. A long time. Then it happened. He began to see her.'

'Who?' I demanded. 'His wife?'

'No, no.' Chippy was irritated. 'She'd left him, taken all he had, sold the furniture and scarpered with another poor mug. That was years ago. No, he began to see the mother.'

'Good God,' I said, 'and she was red-haired, I suppose?'

'And mean,' he told me solemnly. 'Mean as hell.'

I was trembling so much I had to put my beer down.

'Look here, Chippy,' I began, 'why wasn't he spotted? Why didn't *she* spot him?'

He took me by the coat collar.

'Imagination,' he whispered at me. 'Use it. Think. He married the girl in nineteen-twelve, but this year he began to see the mother as she used to be.'

Our heads were very close together over the bar and his soft urgent voice poured the story at me.

'He's been travelling round the coast for years buying old gold. Everybody knows him and nobody notices him. Millions of women recognize him when he taps at their doors and very often they sell him little things. But he was ill last winter, had pleurisy, had to go into hospital. Since he's been out he's been different. The past has come back to him. He's been remembering the tragedy of his life.' He wiped his mouth and started again.

'In May he saw her. At first she looked like a woman he knew called Mrs Wild, but as they were talking her face changed and he recognized her. He knew just what to do. He told her he'd had a bargain he didn't feel like passing on to his firm. Said he'd got a ring cheap and if she'd meet him he'd show it to her and maybe sell it to her for the same money he paid for it. He knew it was a tale she would fall for because he knew just how mean she was. She went because she'd known him for years coming round to the door, and she didn't tell anybody because she thought she was doing something shady, see?'

'And when he got her alone he killed her?' I whispered.

'Yes.' Chippy's voice held an echoed satisfaction. 'Paid her out at last. He went off happy as an old king and felt freed and content and satisfied until June, when he went to Turnhill Bay and knocked all unsuspecting at a door in a back street and – *saw her again.*'

I wiped my forehead and stood back from him.

'And at Southwharf, and at Prinny's Plage?' I began huskily.

'That's right. And now St Piers,' said Chippy. 'Whenever there's a new moon.'

It was at this precise moment that the smiling drunk on the bench opened his eyes and sat straight up abruptly, as drunks do, and then with a spurt set out at a shambling trot for the door. He hit the opening with a couple of inches to spare and was sucked up by the night. I yelled at Chippy and started after him, pausing on the threshold to glance back.

Chippy leant there against the bar, looking at me with fishlike un-intelligence. I could see he was hopeless and the job was mine. I plunged out and saw the smiling man about fifty yards down the street. He was conspicuous because he kept to the middle of the road and was advancing at a perfectly extraordinary trot which had a skip or a gallop in it at every two or three yards, as if he were jet-propelled. I was not in sprinting form myself, but I should certainly have caught him and broken my heart if I had not tripped over a grating thirty feet from the pub door.

It was as I was getting up that I looked over my shoulder and saw Chief Inspector Tizer and the local Super, together with a couple of satellites, slip quietly across the road. It was just enough to make me stone-cold sober and I slid back in behind the police just before they closed the door.

Chippy was standing at the bar with Tizer on one side of him and the local man on the other. The five blown-up prints were spread out on the wood and everyone was so engrossed in them that I came quietly up behind and saw everything over Chippy's own head.

They were five three-quarter length portraits of the same man. Each one had been take out of doors in a gaping crowd, and on each print a mid-section was heavily circled with process-white. In each case, within the circle was a watch-chain hung with darts medals and other small decorations, which might easily have been overlooked had not attention thus been called to them. In the first portrait the watch-chain carried two medals and a cheap silver earring. In the second a gold clasp from a chain bracelet had been added. In the third a small locket. In the fourth a silver button. And in the fifth there hung beside the rest an ugly little tassel from an old-fashioned brooch.

Tizer, who is one of those men who look as if they have been designed by somone who was used to doing bison, put a fist as big as a ham on Chippy's little shoulder.

'You're trying to tell me you only noticed this yesterday and you had the astounding luck to find the earlier photographs in your file?' His tone was pretty ugly, I thought, but Chippy shrugged himself free. Like myself he was sober enough now.

'I *am* lucky,' he said coldly, 'and observant.' He glanced at the bar-tender who was fidgeting in the archway where the counter ran through into the other room. 'Ready, George?'

'Yes, he's still there, Mr Wager. I've slipped round and shut the doors on him. He's sitting very quiet, just drinking his beer.'

He lifted the flap and the police moved forward in a body. Chippy turned to me.

'Poor little blob,' he said. 'He's quite happy now, you see, till next new moon.'

'When you will be otherwise engaged, I seem to remember,' I said acidly.

He glanced at me with a sudden smile and adjusted his camera.

'That's right,' he said. 'There's sympathy in this business but no senti-ment. Wait just a minute while I get the arrest.'

The Case of the Emerald Sky

Eric Ambler

Assistant Commissioner Mercer of Scotland Yard stared, without speaking, at the card which Sergeant Flecker had placed before him. There was no address, simply:

DR. JAN CZISSAR
Late Prague Police

It was an inoffensive-looking card. An onlooker, who knew only that Dr Czissar was a refugee Czech with a brilliant record of service in the criminal investigation department of the Prague police, would have been surprised at the expression of dislike that spread slowly over the assistant commissioner's healthy face.

Yet, had the same onlooker known the circumstances of Mercer's first encounter with Dr Czissar, he would not have been surprised. Just one week had elapsed since Dr Czissar had appeared out of the blue with a letter of introduction from the mighty Sir Herbert at the home office, and Mercer was still smarting as a result of the meeting.

Sergeant Flecker had seen and interpreted the expression. Now he spoke.

'Out, sir?'

Mercer looked up sharply. 'No, sergeant, In, but too busy,' he snapped.

Half an hour later Mercer's telephone rang.

'Sir Herbert to speak to you from the Home Office, sir,' said the operator.

Sir Herbert said, 'Hello, Mercer, is that you?' And then without waiting for a reply: 'What's this I hear about your refusing to see Dr Czissar?'

Mercer jumped but managed to pull himself together. 'I did not refuse to see him, Sir Herbert,' he said with iron calm. 'I sent down a message that I was too busy to see him.'

Sir Herbert snorted. 'Now look here, Mercer; I happen to know that it was Dr Czissar who spotted those Seabourne murderers for you. Not blaming you, personally, of course, and I don't propose to mention the matter to the commissioner. You can't be right every time. We all know that as an organization there's nothing to touch Scotland Yard. My point is, Mercer, that you fellows ought not to be above learning a thing or two from a foreign expert. Clever fellows, these Czechs, you know. No question of poaching on your preserves. Dr Czissar wants no publicity. He's grateful to this country and eager to help. Least we can do is to let him. We don't want any professional jealousy standing in the way.'

If it were possible to speak coherently through clenched teeth, Mercer would have done so. 'There's no question either of poaching on preserves or of professional jealousy, Sir Herbert. I was, as Dr Czissar was informed, busy when he called. If he will write in for an appointment, I shall be pleased to see him.'

'Good man,' said Sir Herbert cheerfully. 'But we don't want any of this red tape business about writing in. He's in my office now. I'll send him over. He's particularly anxious to have a word with you about this Brock Park case. He won't keep you more than a few minutes. Goodbye.'

Mercer replaced the telephone carefully. He knew that if he had replaced it as he felt like replacing it, the entire instrument would have been smashed. For a moment or two he sat quite still. Then, suddenly, he snatched the telephone up again.

'Inspector Cleat, please.' He waited. 'Is that you, Cleat? Is the commissioner in? . . . I see. Well, you might ask him as soon as he comes in if he could spare me a minute or two. It's urgent. Right.'

He hung up again, feeling a little better. If Sir Herbert could have words with the commissioner, so could he. The old man wouldn't stand for his subordinates being humiliated and insulted by pettifogging politicians. Professional jealousy!

Meanwhile, however, this precious Dr Czissar wanted to talk about the Brock Park case. Right! Let him! He wouldn't be able to pull that to pieces. It was absolutely watertight. He picked up the file on the case which lay on his desk.

Yes, absolutely watertight.

Three years previously, Thomas Medley, a widower of 60 with two adult children, had married Helena Merlin, a woman of 42. The four had since lived together in a large house in the London suburb of Brock Park. Medley, who had amassed a comfortable fortune, had retired from business shortly before his second marriage, and had devoted most of his time since to his hobby, gardening. Helena Merlin was an artist, a landscape painter, and in Brock Park it was whispered that her pictures sold for large sums. She dressed fashionably and smartly, and was disliked by her neighbours. Harold Medley, the son aged 25, was a medical student at a London hospital. His sister, Janet, was three years younger, and as dowdy as her stepmother was smart.

In the early October of that year, and as a result of an extra heavy meal, Thomas Medley had retired to bed with a bilious attack. Such attacks had not been unusual. He had had an enlarged liver, and had been normally dyspeptic. His doctor had prescribed in the usual way. On his third day in bed the patient had been considerably better. On the fourth day, however, at about four in the afternoon, he had been seized with violent abdominal pains, persistent vomiting, and severe cramps in the muscles of his legs.

These symptoms had persisted for three days, on the last of which there had been convulsions. He had died that night. The doctor had certified the death as being due to gastro-enteritis. The dead man's estate had amounted to, roughly, £110,000. Half of it went to his wife. The remainder was divided equally between his two children.

A week after the funeral, the police had received an anonymous letter suggesting that Medley had been poisoned. Subsequently, they had received two further letters. Information had then reached them that several residents in Brock Park had received similar letters, and that the matter was the subject of gossip.

Medley's doctor was approached later. He had reasserted that the death had been due to gastro-enteritis, but admitted that the possibility of the condition having been brought by the wilful administration of poison had not occurred to him. The body had been exhumed by licence of the home secretary, and an autopsy performed. No traces of poison had been found in the stomach; but in the liver, kidneys and spleen a total of 1.751 grains of arsenic had been found.

Inquiries had established that on the day on which the poisoning symptoms had appeared, the deceased had had a small luncheon consisting of breast of chicken, spinach (canned), and one potato. The cook had partaken of spinach from the same tin without suffering any ill effects. After his luncheon, Medley had taken a dose of the medicine prescribed. for him by the doctor. It had been mixed with water for him by his son, Harold.

Evidence had been obtained from a servant that, a fortnight before the death, Harold had asked his father for £100 to settle a racing debt. He had been refused. Inquiries had revealed that Harold had lied. He had been secretly married for some time, and the money had been needed not to pay racing debts but for his wife, who was about to have a child.

The case against Harold had been conclusive. He had needed money desperately. He had quarrelled with his father. He had known that he was the heir to a quarter of his father's estate. As a medical student in a hospital, he had been in a position to obtain arsenic. The poisoning that appeared had shown that the arsenic must have been administered at about the time the medicine had been taken. It had been the first occasion on which Harold had prepared his father's medicine.

The coroner's jury had boggled at indicting him in their verdict, but he had later been arrested and was now on remand. Further evidence from the hospital as to his access to supplies of arsenical drugs had been forthcoming. He would certainly be committed for trial.

Mercer sat back in his chair. A watertight case. Sentences began to form in his mind. 'This Dr Czissar, Sir Charles, is merely a time-wasting crank. He's a refugee and his sufferings have probably unhinged him a little. If you could put the matter to Sir Herbert in that light . . .'

And then, for the second time that afternoon, Dr Czissar was announced.

Mercer was angry, yet, as Dr Czissar came into the room, he became conscious of a curious feeling of friendliness towards him. It was not entirely the friendliness that one feels towards an enemy one is about to destroy. In his mind's eye he had been picturing Dr Czissar as an ogre. Now, Mercer saw that, with his mild eyes behind their thick spectacles, his round, pale face, his drab raincoat and his unfurled umbrella, Dr Czissar was, after all, merely pathetic. When, just inside the door, Dr Czissar stopped, clapped his umbrella to his side as if it were a rifle, and said loudly: "Dr Jan Czissar. Late Prague Police. At your service,' Mercer very nearly smiled.

Instead he said: 'Sit down, doctor. I am sorry I was too busy to see you earlier.'

'It is so good of you . . .' began Dr Czissar earnestly.

'Not at all, doctor. You want, I hear, to compliment us on our handling of the Brock Park case.'

Dr Czissar blinked. 'Oh, no, Assistant Commissioner Mercer,' he said anxiously. 'I would like to compliment, but it is too early, I think. I do not wish to seem impolite, but . . .'

Mercer smiled complacently. 'Oh, we shall convict our man, all right, doctor. I don't think you need to worry.'

Dr Czissar's anxiety became painful to behold. 'Oh, but I do worry. You see—' he hesitated diffidently, '—he is not guilty.'

Mercer hoped that the smile with which he greeted the statement did not reveal his secret exultation. He said blandly, 'Are you aware, doctor, of all the evidence against him?'

'I attended the inquest,' said Dr Czissar mournfully. 'But there will be more evidence from the hospital, no doubt. This young Mr Harold could no doubt have stolen enough arsenic to poison a regiment without the loss being discovered.'

The fact that the words had been taken out of his mouth disconcerted Mercer only slightly. He nodded. 'Exactly.'

A faint, thin smile stretched the doctor's full lips. He settled his glasses on his nose. Then he cleared his throat, swallowed hard and leaned forward. 'Attention, please,' he said sharply.

For some reason that he could not fathom, Mercer felt his self-confidence ooze suddenly away. He had seen that same series of actions, ending with the peremptory demand for attention, performed once before, and it had been the prelude to humiliation, to ... He pulled himself up sharply. The Brock Park case was watertight. He was being absurd.

'I'm listening,' he said.

'Good.' Dr Czissar wagged one solemn finger. 'According to the medical evidence given at the inquest, arsenic was found in the liver, kidneys and spleen. No?'

Mercer nodded firmly. 'One point seven five one grains. That shows that much more than a fatal dose had been administered. Much more.'

Dr Czissar's eyes gleamed. 'Ah, yes. Much more. It is odd, is it not, that so much was found in the kidneys?'

'Nothing odd at all about it.'

'Let us leave the point for the moment. Is it not true, Assistant Commissioner Mercer, that all post-mortem tests for arsenic are for arsenic itself and not for any particular arsenic salt?'

Mercer frowned. 'Yes, but it's unimportant. All arsenic salts are deadly poisons. Besides, when arsenic is absorbed by the human body, it turns to the sulphide. I don't see what you are driving at, doctor.'

'My point is this, assistant commissioner, that usually it is impossible to tell from a delayed autopsy which form of arsenic was used to poison the body. You agree? It might be arsenious oxide, or one of the arsenates or arsenites, copper arsenite, for instance; or it might be a chloride, or it might be an organic compound of arsenic.'

'Precisely.'

'But,' continued Dr Czissar, 'what sort of arsenic should we expect to find in a hospital, eh?'

Mercer pursed his lips. 'I see no harm in telling you, doctor, that Harold Medley could easily have secured supplies of either salvarsan or neosalvarsan. They are both important drugs.'

'Yes, indeed,' said Dr Czissar. 'Very useful in one-tenth of a gram doses, but very dangerous in larger quantities.' He stared at the ceiling. 'Have you seen any of Helena Merlin's paintings, assistant commissioner?'

The sudden change of subject took Mercer unawares. He hesitated. Then: 'Oh, you mean Mrs Medley. No, I haven't seen any of her paintings.'

'Such a chic, attractive woman,' said Dr Czissar. 'After I had seen her at the inquest I could not help wishing to see some of her work.

I found some in a gallery near Bond St.' He sighed. 'I had expected something clever, but I was disappointed. She paints what she thinks instead of what is.'

'Really? I'm afraid, doctor, that I must . . .'

'I felt,' persisted Dr Czissar, bringing his cowlike eyes once more to Mercer's, 'that the thoughts of a woman who thinks of a field as blue and a sky as emerald green must be a little strange.'

'Modern stuff, eh?' said Mercer shortly. 'I don't much care for it, either. And now, doctor, if you've finished, I'll ask you to excuse me. I . . .'

'Oh, but I have not finished yet,' said Dr Czissar kindly. 'I think, assistant commissioner, that a woman who paints a landscape with a green sky is not only strange, but also interesting, don't you? I asked the gentlemen at the gallery about her. She produces only a few pictures – about six a year. He offered to sell me one of them for 15 guineas. She earns £100 a year from her work. It is wonderful how expensively she dresses on that sum.'

'She had a rich husband.'

'Oh, yes. A curious household, don't you think? The daughter Janet is especially curious. I was so sorry that she was so much upset by the evidence at the inquest.'

'A young woman probably would be upset at the idea of her brother being a murderer,' said Mercer dryly.

'But to accuse herself so violently of the murder. That was odd.'

'Hysteria. You get a lot of it in murder cases.' Mercer stood up and held out his hand. 'Well, doctor, I'm sorry you haven't been able to upset our case this time. If you'll leave your address with the sergeant as you go, I'll see that you get a pass for the trial,' he added with relish.

But Dr Czissar did not move. 'You are going to try this young man for murder, then?' he said slowly. 'You have not understood what I have been hinting at?'

Mercer grinned. 'We've got something better than hints, doctor – a first-class circumstantial case against young Medley. Motive, time and method of administration, source of the poison. Concrete evidence, doctor! Juries like it. If you can produce one scrap of evidence to show that we've got the wrong man, I'll be glad to hear it.'

Dr Czissar's back straightened, and his cowlike eyes flashed. He said, sharply, 'I, too, am busy. I am engaged on a work on medical jurisprudence. I desire only to see justice done. I do not believe that on the evidence you have you can convict this young man under English law; but the fact of his being brought to trial could damage his career as a doctor. Furthermore, there is the real murderer to be considered. Therefore, in a spirit of friendliness, I have come to you instead of going to Harold Medley's legal advisers. I will now give you your evidence.'

Mercer sat down again. He was very angry. 'I am listening,' he said grimly; 'but if you . . .'

'Attention, please,' said Dr Czissar. He raised a finger. 'Arsenic was found in the dead man's kidneys. It is determined that Harold Medley could have poisoned his father with either salvarsan or neosalvarsan. There is a contradiction there. Most inorganic salts of arsenic, white arsenic, for instance, are practically insoluble in water, and if a quantity of such a salt had been administered, we might expect to find traces of it in the kidneys. Salvarsan and neosalvarsan, however, are compounds of arsenic and are very soluble in water. If either of them had been administered through the mouth, we should *not* expect to find arsenic in the kidneys.'

He paused; but Mercer was silent.

'In what form, therefore, was the arsenic administered?' he went on. 'The tests do not tell us, for they detect only the presence of the element, arsenic. Let us then look among the inorganic salts. There is white arsenic, that is arsenious oxide. It is used for dipping sheep. We would not expect to find it in Brock Park. But Mr Medley was a gardener. What about sodium arsenite, the weed-killer? But we heard at the inquest that the weed-killer in the garden was of the kind harmful only to weeds. We come to copper arsenite. Mr Medley, was, in my opinion, poisoned by a large dose of copper arsenite.'

'And on what evidence,' demanded Mercer, 'do you base that opinion?'

'There is, or there has been, copper arsenite in the Medley's house.' Dr Czissar looked at the ceiling. 'On the day of the inquest, Mrs Medley wore a fur coat. I have since found another fur coat like it. The price of the coat was 400 guineas. Inquiries in Brock Park have told me that this lady's husband, besides being a rich man, was also a very mean and unpleasant man. At the inquest, his son told us that he had kept his marriage a secret because he was afraid that his father would stop his allowance or prevent his continuing his studies in medicine. Helena Medley had expensive tastes. She had married this man so that she could indulge them. He had failed her. That coat she wore, assistant commissioner, was unpaid for. You will find, I think, that she had other debts, and that a threat had been made by one of the creditors to approach her husband. She was tired of this man so much older than she was – this man who did not even justify his existence by spending his fortune on her. She poisoned her husband. There is no doubt of it.'

'Nonsense!' said Mercer. 'Of course we know that she was in debt. We are not fools. But lots of women are in debt. It doesn't make them murderers. Ridiculous!'

'All murderers are ridiculous,' agreed Dr Czissar solemnly; 'especially the clever ones.'

'But how on earth . . . ?' began Mercer.

Dr Czissar smiled gently. 'It was the spinach that the dead man had for luncheon before the symptoms of poisoning began that interested me,' he said. 'Why give spinach when it is out of season? Canned vegetables are not usually given to an invalid with gastric trouble. And then, when I saw Mrs Medley's paintings, I understood. The emerald sky, assistant commissioner. It was a fine, rich emerald green, that sky – the sort of emerald *green that the artist gets when there is aceto-arsenite of copper in the paint!* The firm which supplies Mrs Medley with her working materials will be able to tell you when she bought it. I suggest, too, that you take the picture – it is in the Summons Gallery – and remove a little of the sky for analysis. You will find that the spinach was prepared at her suggestion and taken to her husband's bedroom by her. Spinach is *green* and *slightly bitter* in taste. *So is copper arsenite.*' He sighed. 'If there had not been anonymous letters . . .'

'Ah!' interrupted Mercer. 'The anonymous letters! Perhaps you know . . .'

'Oh, yes,' said Dr Czissar simply. 'The daughter Janet wrote them. Poor child! She disliked her smart stepmother and wrote them out of spite. Imagine her feelings when she found that she had – how do you say? – put a noose about her brother's throat. It would be natural for her to try to take the blame herself.'

The telephone rang and Mercer picked up the receiver.

'The commissioner to speak to you, sir,' said the operator.

'All right. Hello . . . Hello, Sir Charles. Yes, I did want to speak to you urgently. It was——' He hesitated. ' – it was about the Brock Park case. I think that we will have to release young Medley. I've got hold of some new medical evidence that . . . Yes, yes, I realize that, Sir Charles, and I'm very sorry that . . . All right, Sir Charles, I'll come immediately.'

He replaced the telephone.

Dr Czissar looked at his watch. 'But it is late and I must get to the museum reading-room before it closes.' He stood up, clapped his umbrella to his side, clicked his heels and said loudly: Dr Jan Czissar. Late Prague Police. At your service!'

Acid Test

Margot Arnold

It was exactly three months after she murdered her husband that Mrs Waddell decided that she really ought to do something about the body. It had been such an enjoyable experience *not* having Mr Waddell around that time had somehow just slipped by, and now she had only three months left before her period of safety was up. This six-month breathing-spell was supposedly the duration of her late Herbert's fact-finding tour in South America – for he was a freelance writer of unenviable reputation but enviable sales. And when he did not show up brim-full of facts and only too eager to recount the most scurrilous of them, she was quite sure that questions would be asked by some right-minded busybody. And this would be a great nuisance, she reflected, if not downright dangerous.

Anyway, she had begun to think that the nice deep hole in the cellar full of quick-lime and Herbert was, to say the least of it, a little trite, in view of all the more complicated methods propounded in the crime fiction she had absorbed since her own successful sally into the field.

Although it had really done the trick of disposing of the more dis-posable parts of Mr Waddell remarkably well, a recent trip to the cellar had confirmed her fears that, while very good on the softer parts of Herbert, the lime was not making much headway on the bony structure, and she was therefore faced with the problem of liquidating the not inconsiderable skeleton of her late unlamented.

She had briefly toyed with the idea of taking out the lime and substi-tuting sulphuric acid which, she recalled, Mr Haigh had found very practical for body liquidation. But after experimenting with a small bottleful, she found to her dismay that, as *her* pit was not lined, the acid just sank out of sight in no time at all; and on further reflection she could see that a procession of large carboys full of sulphuric acid coming into the house might occasion a flurry of interest among her generally torpid neighbours.

She was still searching diligently through the crime section of the public library for a really bright idea, when a feature article in the local paper handed her the solution on a plate – or, to be exact, a deep dish. The article dealt with the local museum and, more specifically, with the activities of its star attraction, Dr Globbi, who had discovered a new kind of ape-man and was busy unveiling his precious find to the world. This unveiling, however, was rather an arduous process, because the ape-men had very irritatingly got themselves encased in limestone breccia, which had to be dissolved away before the specimens could be examined.

The learned doctor described his techniques of doing this, which apparently involved vast quantities of some kind of acid, and in so doing used a sentence that immediately caught Mrs Waddell's anxious eye. 'The crux of the problem,' said Dr Globbi, 'lies in using the acid in such a way that it dissolves the surrounding rock before it can attack the bone itself and reduce it to unrecognizable fragments.' Since the phrase 'unrecognizable fragments' had been beating on Mrs Waddell's mind like a tom-tom, she began to feel that Dr Globbi's problem and her own were so nearly akin that a closer acquaintanceship with that learned man was indicated. Being a methodical kind of woman, she thought her plans through and began at once to implement them, step by cautious step.

First, she spread it around her few cronies that she was bored with housekeeping for just herself and was thinking of getting an amusing job. She then 'cased' the museum several times, even penetrating into the basement where, as everyone knows, museums usually store their experts. She did this by gathering up some fossils obtained by the ex-Herbert on another fact-finding tour and taking them in to be identified by the museum's geologist. In the course of this – for museum people are notoriously a gossipy lot – she ascertained to her great relief that Dr Globbi (a) had no assistant, and (b) was always complaining that his 'real' work was being slowed down by the constant outside demands on his time, and that he did need an assistant, which the museum was either too mean or too impecunious to give him. Feeling definitely more at ease with this knowledge under her stylish hat, Mrs Waddell hastily perused a few tomes on palaeontology and archaeology, picking out the terms she felt might come in handy, and, armed with these and a copy of the newspaper article, sallied forth to see Dr Globbi.

The doctor turned out to be little, old, and extremely fat, peering myopically through double-lensed spectacles under a remarkable thatch of white, straw-like hair that gave him the air of an intelligent Yorkshire terrier. In her present state of mind, Mrs Waddell would not have cared if he had had three heads and barked, so she was at her most charming; and, given the right occasion, Mrs Waddell could be *very* charming.

She had, she said, flourishing the paper, read this thrilling article about his great work. From a child she had been fascinated by archaeology – and here she clearly enunciated all the other ologies she had conned – and she wondered if by any miraculous chance he could possibly use her as an assistant, however unskilled but oh, so willing, to further this great work. Before he could open his mouth to say he had no money to pay one, she hurried on to say that of course she would like to earn just a *little* pin-money, but it was really the thrill of working for such an eminent scientist on things of such great import that mattered most.

Mrs Waddell, who was extremely handsome in a 'Snow Queen' kind of way, had dressed for the interview in what she mentally termed her 'sexily unobtrusive' style, and she thought that from the outset she had caught a gleam of non-scientific interest in the beady eyes behind the double lenses. She felt a pang of pique, nonetheless, when the interest seemed redoubled after she had mentioned that she was not interested in the money, but she ploughed gamely on in the same vein.

After she had finished her little speech, a trifle breathless from anxiety and all those long words, Dr Globbi erupted into a series of alarming throat clearings and snufflings, which made her wonder if he was having a fit; however, he eventually managed to get his gears meshed and rolled on pontifically. He would be delighted to have such a charming and interested person working with him; that, ahem, he was not sure she realized how long and tedious the work would be, but that, harrumph, ahem, he did not doubt that sufficient funds could be found to give her a small salary for at least a few months, and if she was still interested would she like to see the laboratory and discuss the nature of the work? Mrs Waddell said she would be delighted.

The door, marked importantly: 'Palaeontological Lab. Strictly Private', opened into a long, high, narrow room. It was rather like the entrance to an Egyptian tomb, thought Mrs Waddell, who had absorbed more of her required reading than she realized. On one side, open racks crowded with unappetizing hunks of rock reached the ceiling; on the other, a long narrow bench ran the length of the room, ending in a large, deep sink fitted with three rubber-nozzled taps. On the bench sat a series of deep, white porcelain bowls, full of a substance that bubbled murkily and let off a peculiarly powerful smell.

Dr Globbi led her to a work bench concealed in a little nook that ran off at right angles to the main room, grabbing a large hunk of rock from the shelves in passing. Out of it stuck a spiky and very tattered-looking bone – the pelvis of an ape-man, confided the doctor in a hushed and reverent whisper as he commenced to demonstrate his technique. Mrs Waddell listened with an absorption that did justice to the build-up she had given herself, particularly when he started the practical demonstration.

First, squeaked the doctor, the bone in the specimen had to be painted with many coats of glyptal and allowed to dry. Then a final, thicker coating was applied. When this had dried, the specimen was ready for the bath in acetic acid solution. It was kept in the acid until it had stopped bubbling, washed off in running water – sometimes for days – and then the whole business was repeated until the bone was completely free of the rock.

'What if the glyptal was not put on the bone?' Mrs Waddell enquired faintly.

'Then, pouf!' Dr Globbi replied, gesturing wildly. 'The bone would dissolve into unrecognizable fragments in twenty-four hours.'

Mrs Waddell gave a satisfied sigh. 'How very fascinating,' she said softly.

Two days later, Mrs Waddell, resplendent in a white lab coat that practically swept the floor ('To protect your pretty clothes,' said Dr Globbi skittishly), and thick rubber gloves ('To protect those dainty hands,' said he, even more skittishly), began as a full-time lab assistant on a minuscule salary and a six-month contract.

For the first week, she concentrated on proving to him what a first-rate bone-getter-outer she was. He tended to hover anxiously at first, but when all her specimens survived he was lulled into a sense of security, and at the beginning of the second week his visits tended to be more for social than business purposes. So, on the Wednesday of the second week (Mrs Waddell having paid a visit to the cellar the previous evening), the first bits of Mr Waddell journeyed to the museum in his widow's fashionable and very commodious handbag, and were deposited, unglyptalized, beneath the specimens bubbling happily in their bath. On Thursday, the first fragments of Mr Waddell were duly washed down the drain with great thoroughness. This process was repeated with increasing tempo, for time was running short. Starting with ten acid baths, Mrs Waddell gradually worked up to forty, and, as the ape-men came out gleaming, white and whole, so Mr Waddell departed, soggy, grey and unrecognizable, into the sewers.

The process was not without its alarms. Dr Globbi would occasionally appear, squint myopically into some of the bowls and poke at the murkily bubbling breccia under which a piece of Herbert was lurking, but she invariably managed to distract him with some well-aimed query, and he would depart unsuspecting, with a fond squeeze, or, on more light-hearted days, a fond pinch.

There was one terrible day when he arrived while she was coating a piece of ancient jaw-bone and said absently, 'Don't bother coating the teeth, the acid doesn't attack them.' She had literally gone stone cold, for Herbert had had a very fine set of teeth – rather like a horse's, she had always thought – and the idea of being stuck with thirty-two of these shining headstones made her blood run cold.

That difficulty was solved before the day was out. Dr Globbi, seeing her trying to fit a particularly large lump of rock into a bowl, had taken it out of her hands with a maniacal giggle and beckoned her mysteriously to follow him. 'This is where we cheat a little,' he gasped between giggles. 'I know we should preserve *all* the micro-faunal material in the rock, but with the acid being *such* a price and equipment being so limited, I do this occasionally.'

He led her to what looked like a medieval instrument of torture. 'This is a press used for the preparation of geological specimens. If you put the rock in carefully and clamp it down, you can crush off all the bits of limestone except that around the bone itself – see!' And he expertly nipped off a few inches as easily as cutting a dead flower off a stalk.

'Will it work on small rocks too?' Mrs Waddell asked hopefully.

'Oh, anything at all! Crushes it to powder, if you wish,' was the gleeful reply.

So, one lunch-time when the museum was duly deserted by the carnivorous descendants of the ape-men, all thirty-two of Herbert's perfect teeth were neatly arrayed in rows on sheets of grease-proof paper, and their granulated dust duly followed in the wake of his more perishable parts down the drain.

The home end of things was not entirely without its bad moments either. Mrs Waddell had found herself a little queasy at the start; she told herself that it was the all-pervasive scent of the acetic acid which even followed her home and clung fondly to her clothes, but dismantling Herbert was undoubtedly a contributory cause. She had managed to remove the teeth without a qualm – one of the things she had so disliked about Herbert was that he sucked those items noisily both during and after meals – but when it came to breaking up the skull she found the job definitely distasteful. It was through no sentimental remembrances of Herbert's better qualities, for, as far as she was able, she could not recollect that he'd had any. No, it was simply that she had always had a dislike for breaking anything, and the ape-men had made her even more breakage conscious than usual. When the time came, therefore, she turned away her head and lashed out wildly with a spade until a resounding crunch told her the deed was done. She felt a whole lot better when the last fragment of the skull had in due course slipped away, because now there was no trace of the depressed fractures that had resulted that last morning when she had bashed Herbert over the head in his bath with his best niblick, carefully wrapped in a face-cloth.

There was one other bad incident towards the end of the dissolution period that had given her a great shock and had made her more careful for the remainder of the process. She had been travelling to work on the bus as usual, when some clumsy oaf knocked against her, upsetting her handbag and sending the contents – including a leg-bone of Herbert's wrapped in a sheet of *The News of the World* (an appropriate touch, she felt) – rolling down the aisle. She had retrieved the contents with as much presence of mind as she could muster, and, with a rather ghastly smile at her neighbour, had waved the bone and confided, albeit a trifle hoarsely, 'For my Great Dane – he won't eat anything smaller.'

But all went very smoothly, by and large, and three months and one week after Mrs Waddell had first really studied the problem, the last of Herbert oozed soggily down the drain. She felt a new woman, and when Dr Globbi came in for his morning squeeze she almost squeezed him back, recalling only just in time that his giggle was almost as infuriating as Herbert's teeth-sucking had been.

On the home front, she had been free from anxiety for a week. The lime, its duty done in the pit, she had carefully taken out and spread on the freshly-dug garden as fertilizer, wondering idly as she did so if its bone-meal content would improve its performance. She scraped down the sides and bottom of the pit to allow for possible Herbert-seepage and spread that out, too. Finally, she bought several sacks of seed potatoes and deposited them in the hole to sprout in peace.

By the time the police got around to making inquiries about the missing Herbert, the lime had sunk in, the potatoes had sprouted and Mrs Waddell was at peace with the world.

She had long since laid the ground-work for his disappearance by hinting to her friends that she was sorely afraid 'something had happened to Herbert'. His few surviving relatives had given him up as a bad job long before even she had, and so, being peculiarly prone to believe anything bad about him, were easy to fix. Therefore, when the police duly arrived, she was all set to carry off the part of the brave little woman keeping a good face to the world and trying to bear her cross of trouble in private.

The police were suspicious, as indeed they are paid to be, and the local inspector at one point got most excited when he found the hole in the cellar, only to be cast down to find nothing there but potatoes waving eerie, green-white fingers at him. He did, however, surreptitiously take some soil samples, which Mrs Waddell considered very sneaky, and she remained thereafter distinctly stiff with him, even when the samples yielded no information whatsoever.

For the sake of appearances, she continued to work at the museum until Dr Globbi started visiting her work bench even more frequently than usual, with heavy hints that a scientist, however eminent, needed an understanding help-mate. She then withdrew gracefully but firmly, leaving him bereft but several hundred specimens the richer.

The police continued their diligent work until, at the total absence of evidence as to whether Mr Waddell did or did not still ungrace the earth, even they threw up their collective hands in despair and abandoned the project.

Mrs Waddell continued to live quietly on the proceeds of the various strong-boxes her husband had lovingly tucked away in various quarters to cheat the Inland Revenue, and the keys of which she had removed from his waistcoat pocket the day she murdered him. When seven years had gone by, she collected fifty thousand pounds of insurance – for Mr Waddell had been a very careful man. Indeed, he had liked to talk about how thoughtful he was of his wife's future – though he kept the said wife sadly short of money in the present. No longer being in such dire straits, Mrs Waddell settled back to enjoy his thoughtfulness.

Alas for morality! In this instance, justice does not triumph. No drains inspector emerges clutching a vital piece of Herbert to bring Mrs Waddell at last to her deserts. Nor does Dr Globbi reappear, publishing in a spasm of unrequited love one of Herbert's teeth, overlooked in the crushing, and proving that ape-men used dentifrice. All that is left to be said is that Mrs Waddell and the fifty thousand pounds eventually met and married a young dance instructor, and – I am delighted to relate – lived unhappily ever after.

Eyewitness

Robert Arthur

Los Angeles, 1940

Outside it was raining – raining in hard black lines of water that slanted down out of the sky the way they had the night the girl vanished.

She was out there now, out there somewhere in the black wet night, just as she had been every night now for the last four weeks. Out there where her husband had left her, cold, crumpled, dead, all the warmth and love gone out of her, all the colour gone from her cheeks, all the light from her eyes. Out there in the night that had hidden her murder under a pall of blackness, and the rain that had been pouring down from the heavens when her husband hid her body.

Davis knew she had been murdered – knew it as well as he knew the alphabet, or his name, or the day of the week, all those things so familiar a man never has to think of them. Davis knew it, but he couldn't prove it; and desperately, doggedly, he wanted to prove it, as he had never wanted to prove anything in fourteen years on the Force.

He parked his car and trudged through the acute angle of the falling rain, water dripping down his shapeless felt hat, down his square rugged face, down his old ulster, down his legs, over his shoes. Trudged through the alley and turned in the stage door of the theatre, where he slapped the rain from his hat and from his ulster before he asked to speak to Master.

With his hat off, his forehead beamed where the hair was going back, and grey showed up in the hair that was left. He wasn't old, not even middle-aged, but his face looked old and tired tonight, like the face of a man who has been too long trying to do something he desperately wants to do and cannot.

The doorman showed Davis into the little dressing-room where Master sat, quietly smoking, while his Negro dresser bustled about. Master was a big man, broad-shouldered, with a mane of blond hair and bright blue eyes that stared unwinkingly – stared as if they never blinked, so that a man might become nervous merely from the impact of their moveless gaze.

It was almost an hour before the evening curtain rose on Master's act. Davis took a gingerly seat on the edge of a chair, the water running across the floor below him from his shoes, and began, choosing his words with great care, like a man anxious to hew exactly to the line of fact and err not a hair on either side.

'There's a lot of talk about perfect murders going around,' Davis said harshly. 'And if such a thing is possible, this may be it.'

Master nodded, as if he understood all that had not been said – understood, that Davis had heard of him somehow, somewhere, had heard of some murder he had brought his efforts to bear upon in the past, had come to him now for help and was trying desperately to interest him in the case he had brought; understood that Davis desperately, fiercely wanted help, but would not ask for it.

'We think she's dead, but we don't know,' Davis went on. 'We think he killed her; but we don't know that either. If she's dead, we can't find the body. If we could find the body, we might not be able to prove it was murder. If we could prove it was murder, still we might have trouble proving *he* did it. And yet we're sure she's dead, it's murder, and he did it. That's the only explanation that fits the facts.'

Master nodded again, understanding that it was Davis who was sure it was murder, and Davis was sure *he*, whoever *he* might be, had done it.

Master helped himself to a cigar from a box at hand, and passed one to the detective. Davis took it, but forgot to light it; merely put it in his mouth and chewed on it as he spoke.

'She died in the darkness,' Davis went on, still speaking carefully. 'Died in the complete blackness of a city without lights. It was the night of the big flood – Wednesday, the second of March – and all the lights went out for more than half an hour. There were no lights at all, except candles indoors and automobile headlights out, and the headlights cut only thin, pale paths of light through the rain and the darkness.'

He paused, as if suddenly feeling the words coming out too fast, too expressively for a Headquarters detective ten years in plainclothes.

But Master still nodded, still understanding the emotion behind what Davis was telling him, and after a moment of sucking hard on the unlighted cigar to collect his thoughts, Davis continued:

'She was young, she was pretty, she was loving. She was always laughing, always gay. She had been married three years, and her husband was an actor – a young leading man in pictures. But he had been only a carhop at a drive-and-eat before the movies, and she had been the same, making twelve dollars a week and living on it. They met, they got married – and then the movies found him and he began to make money and still more money.

'Began to see a big future ahead of him.'

Davis paused long enough to light the cigar with a hand that trembled a bit.

'You see, he's tall and smooth – that's the only word to describe him. Inside he's yellow, rotten; but outside he's big, tanned, with even white teeth and eyes that seem to promise something to every woman he meets. And he's been rising in pictures because of women – stars who have taken an interest in him. Lately there's been one in particular. She's getting old, but she's still powerful and can do a lot for him. But won't as long as he's married.

'So you see, he wants to get rid of his wife. He can't get a divorce. He has no grounds. But he feels that she's holding him back, keeping him from rising to the top, keeping him from becoming a big star; she's dead weight around his neck. He does not love her; he's too selfish to love anyone but himself. Now all he thinks of is getting rid of her. He even thinks of murder; or if somehow she would only disappear.

'Well, a month ago the lights went out, and she disappeared.'

The detective stopped again; his voice was becoming hoarse.

'They lived in Hollywood, off Beachwood Drive, in the hills above Hollywood Boulevard. Not as fashionable a place as he wanted, but the best he could afford yet. Besides, it kept her and her mother, who stayed with them, out of sight, behind the scenes.

'She kept house while he worked; she stayed at home while he was out, sometimes all night, making "contacts" and being seen in fashionable places. Many of his associates didn't know he was married.

'She never complained, never chided him. She never even guessed he was sorry he had ever married her. She was loyal – loyal all the way through.'

Davis stopped, then went on more calmly.

'To amuse herself, she went for long walks in the hills or went to the movies alone. On this night, this Wednesday night, she went to an early show at the Pantages Theatre. Her mother was out playing bridge, and he was working.

'He came home around eight, just after her mother. A few minutes later she phoned him. It was raining. It had been raining for days. There were floods all through the San Fernando Valley. A bridge in Long Beach washed out, drowning a dozen or more. But Hollywood saw only the rain. The floods scarcely touched Hollywood.

'So she phoned him that because of the rain she couldn't get a taxi. Would he come for her and pick her up in front of the theatre?

'He said he would. His mind was full of hot, bright, ambitious schemes that night. She – the movie star – had been talking to him that day, we've learned. She'd promised him the lead in her next picture. If – well, you know what that *if* was.

'No doubt he'd often thought of killing her before that night. But that night the opportunity came. Ten minutes after he left the house, every light in the city went out.'

Davis let his words sink in. He leaned forward and tapped the big blond man on the knee for extra emphasis.

'Every light in the city went out. It's a strange feeling when that happens, when the power fails, when the lights go off and the radios go silent, and all the street corners are as dark as the inside of a grave. A candle flickers here, a match there, and they only make the darkness darker. Well, that's what happened that night.

'He wasn't gone long. He came back to the house within forty-five minutes, before the lights came on again. And she wasn't with him.

'He said he couldn't find her. That he had parked the car and searched for her in front of the Pantages. He thought she must have gotten panicky when the lights went out, and found a taxi, or started walking or something. He thought she'd be home ahead of him. But she wasn't. She never came home. So presently he called us. Called us and told us his story. That he had missed her in the darkness, and now she had vanished.

'Well, we took down his story and promised to broadcast an alarm. A lot of people vanished that night, in the flood, and we had our hands full. Some of them are still missing too. Possibly he figured on that.

'After taking down his story, we left; of course our investigation that night was only the sketchiest. It was several days before we got around to making any thorough investigations. And then it was too late.

'So there it was. She had vanished. Where? God knows. What can happen on the streets of a darkened city? Anything.

'Around midnight her husband went out in the car again. He was gone for hours, until almost morning, in the pouring rain. The lights were on again, but because of the weather the streets were deserted. No one could be found who had seen him or his car. Where had he gone? What had he done? He said he had been driving around in a half-crazy condition, hunting for her, calling her name, driving aimlessly, hoping to find her wandering in a daze, perhaps, but unhurt.

'Well, perhaps. But you know what we think?'

Davis tapped the Master's knee again.

'We think that he found her in the darkness in front of the Pantages and she got in the car with him. In the darkness, no one would notice what car stopped, or who got in. No one saw her get in. He drove part way home, and still the lights didn't come on. He was burning with resentment of her.

'And suddenly, impulsively, there on a side street, unseen in the night, the windows of the car fogged by the driving rain, he throttled her. Throttled her and hid her body in the baggage trunk of the car, where it was when he returned home and called us.

'Where it was until he went out on that long drive, in which he claimed he was searching for her. But when he was really hiding her body – hiding it so well we've never found it.'

There was bitterness in the detective's voice, and Master understood that this case meant something personal to him; not just a routine assignment.

'Do you know Los Angeles?' the detective asked, and Master shook his head. 'Well,' Davis told him, 'Los Angeles is a big place. There are arroyos and caves in the hills, old quarries, parks, lakes, rivers, right inside the county limits.

'Suppose he had previously picked a place, had had it in mind all along. Suppose he had done that, you can see how difficult it would be for us to find her. In the end, we might never find her, unless chance stepped in.'

Davis sagged suddenly, like a tired man.

'If we could only find her,' he said quietly. 'That's all I hope to do. There's almost no chance to prove guilt against him under the circumstances. Though I'd like to. God knows how I'd like to!'

For the first time, though the fact had escaped the detective's attention, Master spoke.

'I think we will find her,' he said.

'But he'll go free!' Davis said harshly.

Master shook his head slowly.

'Perhaps not,' he said sombrely. 'You forget the eyewitness.'

'The eyewitness!' the detective exclaimed. 'There was no eyewitness!'

'To every murder there is an eyewitness,' the big blond man rumbled.

'Poppycock!' the detective snapped irritably. 'It would be a big help if there were. Don't you suppose more murderers would go to the chair if such a thing were true? Unless you mean God, who can't help us any.'

'There is always an eyewitness,' Master said quietly, but his words carried force and conviction. 'Sometimes it is hard to make him speak.'

He seemed to withdraw from the room for a moment into some inward meditation. Then:

'But tonight, I think, from what you have told me, we will be able to make him speak. We will find the body. And I think the one who saw the murder will give you the evidence needed to convict.'

Davis opened his mouth, to protest, to argue; then he shut it again. He did not know what the big man meant, but he was at the end of his own rope. And somehow Master's words carried conviction.

'First,' Master instructed, 'call the husband and tell him you are going to come tonight to take him to his wife's body. Say that an eyewitness to her disappearance knows where she is. Say that she was murdered, and her murder was seen, her murderer followed when he hid the body. Tell him nothing more. Let him think over your words until we come. No I have a show to do. I will be with you later.'

Davis did as the big man told him. Then, with a growing sense of awe and wonder, he watched Master's performance. After that, just before midnight, when Master had changed into rough tweeds and an ulster, they took Davis's car and drove out towards Hollywood.

His name was Harold Murney, and at midnight they found him waiting for them, alone in a small house in the Hollywood hills, where from his living-room window the blue and red neons of Hollywood gleamed faintly through the pouring rain.

He was tall and broad-shouldered, as Davis had described him, and hard. Amazingly hard. It was in his voice, in his eyes. Hard and evil.

But Davis was hard too. His square face, dripping water from the rain blown into their faces as he and Master came up the long footpath from the drive to the house, glistened in the light. His eyes gleamed too, a peculiar blue gleam of hope and hatred. Murney was the man he wanted to convict, and Murney knew it. But he knew, the detective did, that there was no shadow of evidence against the younger man, and so did the actor.

So, whether guilty or innocent, Murney could easily stare back insolently at Davis without flinching, without showing any alarm.

'You said you'd found my wife?' Murney asked suspiciously, glancing from Master to Davis and back to the big blond man, whose presence the detective had not bothered to explain.

'I said we'd take you to her,' Davis replied dully.

Murney stared at him suspiciously, his eyes green beneath half-lowered lids.

'Where?' he asked.

'Where her murderer hid her,' Davis told him evenly.

'Murderer?'

Murney's voice indicated only what it should have – shock and surprise. If he was guilty, as a murderer he was a good actor too.

'Are you sure you're not mistaken?' the young man asked then, coolly, and Davis shook his head. 'No,' the actor answered himself, after a moment, 'I suppose it's your business to be sure. All right, you say you've found her and she was murdered. Have you got her murderer?'

'We'll have him shortly after we've taken you to the body,' he answered. 'The murder, as well as the concealment of the body, was seen by an eyewitness, fortunately.'

This time Murney's breath did suck in perceptibly.

'It seems incredible,' he said, and now he let amusement creep into his voice. 'Frankly, I don't believe you've found my wife, that she was murdered or that there is any such eyewitness. If there is, why didn't he speak up sooner?'

'He had his reasons.' Davis said, and his voice was suddenly harsh. 'But he will speak now. I suppose, Murney, you've no objection to coming with us to identify your wife and help us nab her killer?'

Murney hesitated for an instant. Some of the ruddy colour had gone from his cheeks. But when he spoke his voice was still easy, still confident.

'Of course not,' he said loudly. 'You know how much I want to help you.'

All this time Master had not spoken, had only stood there, his face wet with rain because he had worn no hat, his bright blue eyes staring unwinkingly at Murney. The actor took his eyes off Master now with an effort.

'I'll get my coat and be right with you,' he said roughly. 'Though I'm convinced it's a wild-goose chase.'

He got dressed for the weather, and Davis led the way down the footpath.

'We'll take my car,' he said. 'Too bad, it's a coupé. We'll be a bit crowded.'

His words were regretful, but his voice was not. He slid in behind the wheel and Harold Murney, after a moment's hesitation, got in beside him. Last of all Master squeezed himself in and closed the car door.

Davis started the motor and let in the clutch. They were jammed tightly together, but none of the men commented on the fact. Davis and Master stared straight ahead, the detective seeming intent on his driving. Murney glanced quickly from one face to the other, but could read nothing in them. Jammed between the two, he sat stiffly, as if he found the space too small in which to relax.

'We are going to retrace the murderer's path,' Davis said quietly, as the car rolled silently downhill and into Beachwood Drive, the only direction in which it could go.

Murney started to speak, and then thought better of it. But he shifted a little uneasily as they coasted downward towards Franklin Avenue, and he almost jumped when Master, for the first time, spoke.

'Turn here,' he said suddenly. 'Right.'

Davis braked and turned into Scenic Drive, after almost over-running the narrow entrance of the street. Momentary surprise showed on Harold Murney's face; then his lips tightened, and he said nothing as they crossed Gower and came to Vista Del Mar, a crooked, hilly street lined with houses almost European in their picturesqueness.

'Left,' Master said abruptly.

They turned left, drifted down Vista Del Mar, and came out on Franklin. At Master's order they turned right on Franklin, crossed Argyle, Vine and Ivar, climbed the hill, dropped down a steep slope and pulled up at broad Cahuenga Boulevard.

'Right,' Master said here, as Harold Murney stirred again, and an instant later ordered them sharply left at the traffic light on to Wilcox, and then quickly right again on the continuation of Franklin.

From time to time Murney had shifted uneasily, wedged between the two men, at all this manoeuvring. When presently they pulled up for the stop light at Highland Avenue, and Master ordered them left, he burst out in a voice gone a little shrill:

'Where are we going with all this nonsensical driving?' he demanded. 'What kind of a game are you playing? There's no police station in this direction, no hospital, no morgue. I demand to know where you are taking me!'

'Along the path of a murderer,' Master told him, deeply, 'and that route is always twisted.'

They swung left, then right at the next light, and straight ahead until they came to a dead end. Then left, and drifted downward a hundred yards or so to stop where La Brea and Hollywood crossed, having reached the point by a devious and twisting route for whose choosing there seemed little reason.

Harold Murney seemed to be losing his self-control.

'I demand you let me out!' he said shrilly, his voice higher still. 'This is fantastic. This is some sort of plot. You haven't found my wife and you don't know where she is. I think you're trying to shake me down!'

'We are showing you the route a murderer took,' Master told him quietly. 'The devious, back-street route he took in the rainy night that was like this night, the winding route he took to obviate every possible chance of being seen and noticed.'

Murney gulped and swallowed hard.

'That's nonsense!' he cried. 'That's ridiculous! How do you know my wife's murderer came this way – if she was murdered? You don't. You couldn't.'

But his voice held a note that seemed to indicate he was trying to convince himself, not them. Davis did not even turn to look at him, merely guided the car straight ahead down La Brea Boulevard, past Sunset and past Santa Monica.

But as they swung right on Melrose at Master's orders, Murney tried to reach across the big blond man and open the car door.

'I demand that you let me out!' he gasped, almost sobbingly. 'You've no legal right to keep me if I want to get out.'

Master stretched out an arm and pinned him into his seat. Biting his lips and seeming to shake a little, as if from rage, Murney sat back.

Then they were turning northward again, the windshield wiper clicking busily, sweeping aside the water that filmed the glass between each downward swing of the arm. The rain beat down on the steel top of the coupé, and the motor purred with a soft, even beat.

*

They rolled along for block after block and then, in response to a quiet word from Master, their course changed. They turned, and presently they were climbing a long slope that led them away from Hollywood and its rain-haloed lights, towards the darkness of the valley beyond.

Murney was sitting rigidly between the two men. But he jumped when Master's voice rang out, almost accusingly.

'Right!'

Davis swung them into a side street, dark, deserted. They idled along, and no house lights showed, only dim street lights at long intervals. Presently their lights reflected from the rain-wet boards of a high fence. Master turned his head a little, from right to left. Between them Murney sat in wire-tight tenseness.

'Stop!' The word was like a pistol shot. Even Davis jumped a bit. Then he pulled to the kerb and cut the motor. It expired with a little cough, and for a moment they sat there in complete silence, broken only by the persistent beating of the rain.

'Apex Pictures' storage lot,' Davis said aloud, though as if to himself. 'Where they store all their old scenery and sets, stuff that hasn't any value.'

Master nodded.

'Let us get out here,' he suggested, and, opening the car door, descended.

He stood on the pavement until Murney reluctantly, it seemed, descended, though only a few minutes before he had been anxious to get out of the car. The actor tried to light a cigarette, cupping the match in his hand and bending over; but the flame wavered and shook and went out. With a curse he flung the wet cigarette into the gutter.

'I don't know why you've brought me here,' he said wildly. 'But I'm going home, do you hear? You can't keep me! You can't!'

Master linked an arm through his and held him.

'What are you afraid of?' Davis sneered. 'You haven't done anything, have you? You didn't murder her, did you?'

'No, no, you know well enough I didn't!' Harold Murney cried.

'Then come on,' Davis said, 'before you make us think different.'

'I think we will go inside,' Master said evenly, and, beaten, shaking, the actor fell into step with him.

With Davis on the other side, they walked slowly along the high fence. The rain still fell, wetly and insistently, and there was no one to see them. They could have been taking the actor to murder him, and no one would have noticed.

After fifty yards they came to a high gate, and Master stopped.

'Gate,' Davis said. 'It's locked. I'll get tools.'

He went back to the car, returned with a flashlight and a tyre iron. A twist of the tyre iron burst the staples that held the padlock; that gate creaked open.

'Now we will go in,' Master said.

'No!' Murney cried, squirming but unable to break free. 'I won't go in with you! You have no right to bring me here! What do you want, anyway, what do you want?'

'Only for you to identify your wife,' Davis said. 'Come along. We're almost there.'

With the flashlight cutting a wedge out of the darkness in front of them they entered, their feet crunching loud on gravelled paths. Davis fanned the flashlight about, and the rays glinted off the peeling surface of a plaster mosque, off a Norman castle made of wood and paper, off the squat shape of an Egyptian pyramid.

Master led them down one of the dark paths, moving slowly, slowly, as if on the verge of stopping at any moment. They passed mouldering scenery flats, and the wreck of an entire Western town that consisted only of false building fronts, ragged and tattered. The path curved; they came back towards the Egyptian pyramid. Abruptly Master halted.

'Shine your light about,' he said to Davis. The detective did so.

'A pyramid made out of wood and plaster,' he said aloud. 'A model of the Sphynx with the head fallen off. A big, imitation Egyptian sarcophagus. Some artificial rocks. A—'

'The sarcophagus,' Master interrupted. 'Yes, the sarcophagus – an imitation of an ancient burial place; a fitting spot to find the body of a murder victim. Open it, and let us see if our eyewitness spoke the truth.'

'No!' Murney screamed now, and his lunge to break free was maddened, desperate. 'She's not here! You must be crazy, thinking she is. How could she be here? This is a trick, a trick!'

The two men held him until his struggles ceased and he stood, shaken by dry, gasping sobs. They did not speak. When the actor was quiet again, Davis released his arm. He strode forward, played his flashlight briefly over the scaling paint of the wooden sarcophagus. Then he thrust in the tyre iron. A push, and the lid of the sarcophagus lifted. Davis let it crash to the ground. He turned his flashlight into the interior.

She was there. She lay stretched out, one arm flung up across her face as if to shut out the light. But no light would trouble her eyes again. She had been there for a month, and she was no longer beautiful.

'She's here,' Davis said, and the words could hardly be heard above the soft sound of the rain.

'I know,' Master answered. 'I know. Our eyewitness told us the truth. Look at her, Murney. Look at her and identify her.'

'No!' the actor cried. 'No! You knew! You knew all along! You had to know. You couldn't have brought me here, couldn't have retraced the exact route I drove to get here that night, if you didn't know. Someone told you. Someone saw me and told you. Oh God, why did they have to see me?'

Davis had a pair of handcuffs. As the actor fell to his knees in the gravel path, breathing heavily, his mouth and eyes and face all loose, slack, twisted, Davis used them.

He pulled and Harold Murney rose shudderingly to his feet.

'But I couldn't have been followed!' he screamed. 'Couldn't have! I'd have known if I had been. Nobody could have followed me through all those twists and turns without my seeing them. Tell me! Tell me! How did you bring me here over the same route I used? How? How?'

He beat with his handcuffed wrists on the detective's chest, and Davis caught his arms and held them. Master moved over and fastened his bright gaze on the actor's face.

'You brought us here,' he said. 'Your guilty conscience brought us here. It was a trick, if you will. Nevertheless, it was you who guided us every inch of the way to this spot.'

'No! I didn't! I didn't!'

'You brought us here just as anyone who has hidden something, and has that hidden thing much on his mind, will inevitably lead one who knows the secret to the hiding-place.

'I said it was your conscience. Call it, if you want to be more technical, your involuntary muscular responses to mental commands that were not quite given. We passed a corner where you had turned that night. You did not want us to know you had turned there. Your brain thought of the turn, thought that we must not know of it. So you twitched. You jerked slightly in that direction. As your mind thought, your body moved – not much, but enough for me.

'For I was wedged tightly beside you, remember, and I knew how to read these little movements your body could not keep from making. I learned the trick from Harry Houdini, who was the master of us all. At your leisure you can learn more about it, for it is written in one of his books.

'It is always easy when the subject is nervous, and you were nervous. That is why we called you earlier in the evening, told you we would lead you to her body. To make you nervous.'

'Who – who are you?' Harold Murney whispered. 'You're not a detective. Who—'

'His name is Master.' Davis answered the question. 'He is a professional stage magician and prestidigitator. Too bad you'll never see him work. His act is a sensation. Especially when he has a member of the audience take something and hide it, and then, walking beside the hider, finds the hidden object without fail, every time.'

'Then who're you?' Murney screamed at Davis. 'You're not a detective either! No detective would have hounded me like this. No detective would have thought of it. Who're you?'

'I'm a detective,' Davis told him, 'but I'm also the fellow she was going to marry until you came along. That's who I am.'

'Oh – you – then you – you—'

The breath gasped and bubbled in Harold Murney's throat.

'Then you lied!' he choked out. 'You lied. There was no eyewitness. There was no one to give evidence. There was no witness and you couldn't have convicted me!'

Davis shook his head.

'No,' he said, 'I didn't lie. There was an eyewitness. He led us here and gave us the evidence we needed. The eyewitness who is always present at every murder. The one who always sees the crime – the one who commits it. In this case you, Murney, you – you were the eyewitness we meant!'

The Murder of the Mandarin

Arnold Bennett

'What's that you're saying about murder?' asked Mrs Cheswardine as she came into the large drawing-room, carrying the supper-tray.

'Put it down here,' said her husband, referring to the supper-tray, and pointing to a little table which stood two legs off and two legs on the hearthrug.

'That apron suits you immensely,' murmured Woodruff, the friend of the family, as he stretched his long limbs into the fender towards the fire, farther even than the long limbs of Cheswardine. Each man occupied an easy-chair on either side of the hearth; each was very tall, and each was forty.

Mrs Cheswardine, with a whisk infinitely graceful, set the tray on the table, took a seat behind it on a chair that looked like a toddling grand-nephew of the arm-chairs, and nervously smoothed out the apron.

As a matter of fact, the apron did suit her immensely. It is astounding, delicious, adorable, the effect of a natty little domestic apron suddenly put on over an elaborate and costly frock, especially when you can hear the rustle of a silk petticoat beneath, and more especially when the apron is smoothed out by jewelled fingers. Every man knows this. Every woman knows it. Mrs Cheswardine knew it. In such matters Mrs Cheswardine knew exactly what she was about. She delighted, when her husband brought Woodruff in late of a night, as he frequently did after a turn at the club, to prepare with her own hands – the servants being in bed – a little snack of supper for them. Tomato sandwiches, for instance, miraculously thin, together with champagne or Bass. The men preferred Bass, naturally, but if Mrs Cheswardine had a fancy for a sip of champagne out of her husband's tumbler, Bass was not forthcoming.

To-night it was champagne.

Woodruff opened it, as he always did, and involuntarily poured out a libation on the hearth, as he almost always did. Good-natured, ungainly, long-suffering men seldom achieve the art of opening champagne.

Mrs Cheswardine tapped her pink-slippered foot impatiently.

'You're all nerves to-night,' Woodruff laughed, 'and you've made me nervous.' And at length he got some of the champagne into a tumbler.

'No, I'm not,' Mrs Cheswardine contradicted him.

'Yes, you are, Vera,' Woodruff insisted calmly.

She smiled. The use of that elegant Christian name, with its faint suggestion of Russian archduchesses, had a strange effect on her, particularly from the lips of Woodruff. She was proud of it, and of her surname too – one of the oldest surnames in the Five Towns. The syllables of 'Vera' invariably soothed her, like a charm. Woodruff, and Cheswardine also, had called her Vera during the whole of her life; and she was thirty. They had all three lived in different houses at the top end of Trafalgar Road, Bursley. Woodruff fell in love with her first, when she was eighteen, but with no practical result. He was a brown-haired man, personable despite his ungainliness, but he failed to perceive that to worship from afar off is not the best way to capture a young woman with large eyes and an emotional disposition. Cheswardine, who had a black beard, simply came along and married the little thing. She fluttered down on to his shoulders like a pigeon. She adored him, feared him, cooed to him, worried him, and knew that there were depths of his mind which she would never plumb. Woodruff, after being best man, went on loving, meekly and yet philosophically, and found his chief joy in just these suppers. The arrangement suited Vera; and as for the husband and the hopeless admirer, they had always been fast friends.

'I asked you what you were saying about murder,' said Vera sharply, 'but it seems—'

'Oh! did you?' Woodruff apologized. 'I was saying that murder isn't such an impossible thing as it appears. Any one might commit a murder.'

'Then you want to defend Harrisford? Do you hear what he says, Stephen?'

The notorious and terrible Harrisford murders were agitating the Five Towns that November. People read, talked, and dreamt murder; for several weeks they took murder to all their meals.

'He doesn't want to defend Harrisford at all,' said Cheswardine, with a superior masculine air, 'and of course any one might commit a murder. I might.'

'Stephen! How horrid you are!'

'You might, even!' said Woodruff, gazing at Vera.

'Charlie! Why, the blood alone—'

'There isn't always blood,' said the oracular husband.

'Listen here,' proceeded Woodruff, who read variously and enjoyed philosophical speculation. 'Supposing that by just taking thought, by just wishing it, an Englishman could kill a mandarin in China and make himself rich for life, without anybody knowing anything about it! How many mandarins do you suppose there would be left in China at the end of a week?'

'At the end of twenty-four hours, rather,' said Cheswardine grimly.

'Not one,' said Woodruff.

'But that's absurd,' Vera objected, disturbed. When these two men began their philosophical discussions they always succeeded in disturbing her. She hated to see life in a queer light. She hated to think.

'It isn't absurd,' Woodruff replied. 'It simply shows that what prevents wholesale murder is not the wickedness of it, but the fear of being found out, and the general mess, and seeing the corpse, and so on.'

Vera shuddered.

'And I'm not sure,' Woodruff proceeded, 'that murder is so very much more wicked than lots of other things.'

'Usury, for instance,' Cheswardine put in.

'Or bigamy,' said Woodruff.

'But an Englishman *couldn't* kill a mandarin in China by just wishing it,' said Vera, looking up.

'How do we know?' said Woodruff, in his patient voice. 'How do we know? You remember what I was telling you about thought-transference last week. It was in *Borderland*.'

Vera felt as if there was no more solid ground to stand on, and it angered her to be plunging about in a bog.

'I think it's simply silly,' she remarked. 'No, thanks.'

She said 'No, thanks' to her husband, when he tendered his glass.

He moved the glass still closer to her lips.

'I said "No, thanks,"' she repeated dryly.

'Just a mouthful,' he urged.

'I'm not thirsty.'

'Then you'd better go to bed,' said he.

He had a habit of sending her to bed abruptly. She did not dislike it. But she had various ways of going. To-night it was the way of an archduchess.

II

Woodruff, in stating that Vera was all nerves that evening, was quite right. She was. And neither her husband nor Woodruff knew the reason.

The reason had to do most intimately with frocks.

Vera had been married ten years. But no one would have guessed it, to watch her girlish figure and her birdlike ways. You see, she was the only child in the house. She often bitterly regretted the absence of offspring to the name and honour of Cheswardine. She envied other wives their babies. She doted on babies. She said continually that in her deliberate opinion the proper mission of women was babies. She was the sort of woman that regards a cathedral as a place built especially to sit in and dream soft domestic dreams; the sort of woman that adores music simply because it makes her dream. And Vera's brown studies, which were frequent, consisted chiefly of babies. But as babies amused themselves by coming down the chimneys of all the other houses in Bursley, and avoiding her house, she sought comfort in frocks. She made the best of herself. And it was a good best. Her figure was as near perfect as a woman's can be, and then there were those fine emotional eyes, and that flutteringness of the pigeon, and an ever-changing charm of gesture. Vera had become the best-dressed woman in Bursley. And that is saying something. Her husband was wealthy, with an increasing income, though, of course, as an earthenware manufacturer, he joined heartily in the general Five Towns lamentation that there was no longer any money to be made out of 'pots.' He liked to have a well-dressed woman about the house, and he allowed her an incredible allowance, the amount of which was breathed with awe among Vera's friends; a hundred a year, in fact. He paid it to her quarterly, by cheque. Such was his method.

Now a ball was to be given by the members of the Ladies' Hockey Club (or such of them as had not been maimed for life in the pursuit of this noble pastime) on the very night after the conversation about murder. Vera belonged to the Hockey Club (in a purely ornamental sense), and she had procured a frock for the ball which was calculated to crown her reputation as a mirror of elegance. The skirt had – but no (see the columns of the *Staffordshire Signal* for the 9th November 1901). The mischief was that the gown lacked, for its final perfection, one particular thing, and that particular thing was separated from Vera by the glass front of Brunt's celebrated shop at Hanbridge. Vera could have managed without it. The gown would still have been brilliant without it. But Vera had seen it, and she *wanted* it.

Its cost was a guinea.

Well, you will say, what is guinea to a dainty creature with a hundred a year? Let her go and buy the article. The point is that she couldn't, because she had only six and sevenpence left in the wide world. (And six weeks to Christmas!) She had squandered – oh, soul above money! – twenty-five pounds, and more than twenty-five pounds, since the 29th of September. Well, you will say, credit, in other words, tick? No, no, no! The giant Stephen absolutely and utterly forbade her to procure anything whatever on credit. She was afraid of him. She knew just how far she could go with Stephen. He was great and terrible. Well, you

will say, why couldn't she blandish and cajole Stephen for a sovereign
or so? Impossible! She had a hundred a year on the clear understanding that it was never exceeded nor anticipated. Well, you will
discreetly hint, there are certain devices known to housewives.... Hush!
Vera had already employed them. Six and sevenpence was not merely
all that remained to her of her dress allowance; it was all that remained
to her of her household allowance till the next Monday.

Hence her nerves.

There that poor unfortunate woman lay, with her unconscious tyrant
of a husband snoring beside her, desolately wakeful under the night-light
in the large, luxurious bedroom – three servants sleeping overhead,
champagne in the cellar, furs in the wardrobe, valuable lace round her
neck at that very instant, grand piano in the drawing-room, horses in
the stable, stuffed bear in the hall – and her life was made a blank
for want of fourteen and fivepence! And she had nobody to confide in.
How true it is that the human soul is solitary, that content is the only
true riches, and that to be happy we must be good!

It was at that juncture of despair that she thought of mandarins. Or
rather – I may as well be frank – she had been thinking of mandarins
all the time since retiring to rest. There *might* be something in Charlie's
mandarin theory.... According to Charlie, so many queer, inexplicable
things happened in the world. Occult – subliminal – astral – thought-
waves. These expressions and many more occurred to her as she recollected Charlie's disconcerting conversations. There *might*.... One
never knew.

Suddenly she thought of her husband's pockets, bulging with silver,
with gold, and with bank-notes. Tantalizing vision! No! She could not
steal. Besides, he might wake up.

And she returned to mandarins. She got herself into a very morbid
and two-o'clock-in-the-morning state of mind. Suppose it was a dodge
that *did* work. (Of course, she was extremely superstitious; we all are.)
She began to reflect seriously upon China. She remembered having
heard that Chinese mandarins were very corrupt; that they ground the
faces of the poor, and put innocent victims to the torture; in short, that
they were sinful and horrid persons, scoundrels unfit for mercy. Then
she pondered upon the remotest parts of China, regions where Europeans
never could penetrate. No doubt there was some unimportant mandarin,
somewhere in these regions, to whose district his death would be a
decided blessing, to kill whom would indeed be an act of humanity.
Probably a mandarin without wife or family; a bachelor mandarin whom
no relative would regret; or, in the alternative, a mandarin with many
wives, whose disgusting polygamy merited severe punishment! An old
mandarin already pretty nearly dead; or, in the alternative, a young
one just commencing a career of infamy!

'I'm awfully silly,' she whispered to herself. 'But still, if there *should* be anything in it. And I must, I must, I must have that thing for my dress!'

She looked again at the dim forms of her husband's clothes, pitched anyhow on an ottoman. No! She could not stoop to theft!

So she murdered a mandarin; lying in bed there; not any particular mandarin, a vague mandarin, the mandarin most convenient and suit-able under all the circumstances. She deliberately wished him dead, on the off-chance of acquiring riches, or, more accurately, because she was short of fourteen and fivepence in order to look perfectly splendid at a ball.

In the morning when she woke up – her husband had already departed to the works – she thought how foolish she had been in the night. She did not feel sorry for having desired the sudden death of a fellow-creature. Not at all. She felt sorry because she was convinced, in the cold light of day, that the charm would not work. Charlie's notions were really too ridiculous, too preposterous. No! She must reconcile herself to wear-ing a ball dress which was less than perfection, and all for want of fourteen and fivepence. And she had more nerves than ever!

She had nerves to such an extent that when she went to unlock the drawer of her own private toilet-table, in which her prudent and fussy husband forced her to lock up her rings and brooches every night, she attacked the wrong drawer – an empty unfastened drawer that she never used. And lo! the empty drawer was not empty. There was a sovereign lying in it!

This gave her a start, connecting the discovery, as naturally at the first blush she did, with the mandarin.

Surely it couldn't be, after all.

Then she came to her senses. What absurdity! A coincidence, of course, nothing else! Besides, a mere sovereign! It wasn't enough. Charlie had said 'rich for life.' The sovereign must have lain there for months and months, forgotten.

However, it was none the less a sovereign. She picked it up, thanked Providence, ordered the dog-cart, and drove straight to Brunt's. The particular thing that she acquired was an exceedingly thin, slim, and fetching silver belt – a marvel for the money, and the ideal waist decora-tion for her wonderful white muslin gown. She bought it, and left the shop.

And as she came out of the shop, she saw a street urchin holding out the poster of the early edition of the *Signal*. And she read on the poster, in large letters: 'DEATH OF LI HUNG CHANG.' It is no exaggeration to say that she nearly fainted. Only by the exercise of that hard self-control, of which women alone are capable, did she refrain from tumbling against the blue-clad breast of Adams, the Cheswardine coachman.

She purchased the *Signal* with well-feigned calm, opened it and read: '*Stop-press news. Pekin. Li Hung Chang, the celebrated Chinese statesman, died at two o'clock this morning. – Reuter.*'

III

Vera reclined on the sofa that afternoon, and the sofa was drawn round in front of the drawing-room fire. And she wore her fluffiest and languidest *peignoir*. And there was a perfume of eau-de-Cologne in the apartment. Vera was having a headache; she was having it in her grand, her official manner. Stephen had had to lunch alone. He had been told that in all probability his suffering wife would not be well enough to go to the ball. Whereupon he had grunted. As a fact, Vera's headache was extremely real, and she was very upset indeed.

The death of Li Hung Chang was heavily on her soul. Occultism was justified of itself. The affair lay beyond coincidence. She had always *known* that there was something in occultism, supernaturalism, so-called superstitions, what not. But she had never expected to prove the faith that was in her by such a homicidal act on her own part. It was detestable of Charlie to have mentioned the thing at all. He had no right to play with fire. And as for her husband, words could give but the merest rough outline of her resentment against Stephen. A pretty state of things that a woman with a position such as she had to keep up should be reduced to six and sevenpence! Stephen, no doubt, expected her to visit the pawnshop. It would serve him right if she did so – and he met her coming out under the three brass balls! Did she not dress solely and wholly to please him? Not in the least to please herself! Personally she had a mind set on higher things, impossible aspirations. But he liked fine clothes. And it was her duty to satisfy him. She strove to satisfy him in all matters. She lived for him. She sacrificed herself to him completely. And what did she get in return? Nothing! Nothing! Nothing! All men were selfish. And women were their victims.... Stephen, with his silly bullying rules against credit and so forth.... The worst of men was that they had no sense.

She put a new dose of eau-de-Cologne on her forehead, and leaned on one elbow. On the mantelpiece lay the tissue parcel containing the slim silver belt, the price of Li's death. She wanted to stick it in the fire. And only the fact that it would not burn prevented her savagely doing so. There was something wrong, too, with the occultism. To receive a paltry sovereign for murdering the greatest statesman of the Eastern hemisphere was simply grotesque. Moreover, she had most distinctly not wanted to deprive China of a distinguished man. She had expressly stipulated for an inferior and insignificant mandarin, one that could be spared and that was unknown to Reuter. She supposed she ought to have looked up China at the Wedgwood Institution and selected a definite mandarin with a definite place of residence. But could she be expected to go about a murder deliberately like that?

With regard to the gross inadequacy of the fiscal return for her deed, perhaps that was her own fault. She had not wished for more. Her brain had been so occupied by the belt that she had wished only for the belt. But, perhaps, on the other hand, vast wealth was to come. Perhaps something might occur that very night. That would be better. Yet would it be better? However rich she might become, Stephen would coolly take charge of her riches, and dole them out to her, and make rules for her concerning them. And besides, Charlie would suspect her guilt. Charlie understood her, and perused her thoughts far better than Stephen did. She would never be able to conceal the truth from Charlie. The conversation, the death of Li within two hours, and then a sudden fortune accruing to her – Charlie would inevitably put two and two together and divine her shameful secret.

The outlook was thoroughly black anyway.

She then fell asleep.

When she awoke, some considerable time afterwards, Stephen was calling to her. It was his voice, indeed, that had aroused her. The room was dark.

'I say, Vera,' he demanded, in a low, slightly inimical tone, 'have you taken a sovereign out of the empty drawer in your toilet-table?'

'No,' she said quickly, without thinking.

'Ah!' he observed reflectively, 'I knew I was right.' He paused, and added coldly, 'If you aren't better you ought to go to bed.'

Then he left her, shutting the door with a noise that showed a certain lack of sympathy with her headache.

She sprang up. Her first feeling was one of thankfulness that that brief interview had occurred in darkness. So Stephen was aware of the existence of the sovereign! The sovereign was not occult. Possibly he had put it there. And what did he know he was 'right' about?

She lighted the gas, and gazed at herself in the glass realizing that she no longer had a headache, and endeavouring to arrange her ideas.

'What's this?' said another voice at the door. She glanced round hastily, guiltily. It was Charlie.

'Steve telephoned me you were too ill to go to the dance,' explained Charlie, 'so I thought I'd come and make inquiries. I quite expected to find you in bed with a nurse and a doctor or two at least. What is it?' He smiled.

'Nothing,' she replied. 'Only a headache. It's gone now.'

She stood against the mantelpiece, so that he should not see the white parcel.

'That's good,' said Charlie.

There was a pause.

'Strange, Li Hung Chang dying last night, just after we had been talking about killing mandarins,' she said. She could not keep off the subject. It attracted her like a snake, and she approached it in spite of the fact that she fervently wished not to approach it.

'Yes,' said Charlie. 'But Li wasn't a mandarin, you know. And he didn't die after we had been talking about mandarins. He died before.'

'Oh! I thought it said in the paper he died at two o'clock this morning.'

'Two a.m. in Pekin,' Charlie answered. 'You must remember that Pekin time is many hours earlier than our time. It lies so far eastward.'

'Oh!' she said again.

Stephen hurried in, with a worried air.

'Ah! It's you, Charlie!'

'She isn't absolutely dying, I find,' said Charlie, turning to Vera: 'You are going to the dance after all – aren't you?'

'I say, Vera,' Stephen interrupted, 'either you or I must have a scene with Martha. I've always suspected that confounded housemaid. So I put a marked sovereign in a drawer this morning, and it was gone at lunch-time. She'd better hook it instantly. Of course I shan't prosecute.'

'Martha!' cried Vera. 'Stephen, what on earth are you thinking of? I wish you would leave the servants to me. If you think you can manage this house in your spare time from the works, you are welcome to try. But don't blame me for the consequences.' Glances of triumph flashed in her eyes.

'But I tell you—'

'Nonsense,' said Vera. 'I took the sovereign. I saw it there and took it, and just to punish you, I've spent it. It's not at all nice to lay traps for servants like that.'

'Then why did you tell me just now you hadn't taken it?' Stephen demanded crossly.

'I didn't feel well enough to argue with you then,' Vera replied.

'You've recovered precious quick,' retorted Stephen with grimness.

'Of course, if you want to make a scene before strangers,' Vera whimpered (poor Charlie a stranger!), 'I'll go to bed.'

Stephen knew when he was beaten.

She went to the Hockey dance, though. She and Stephen and Charlie and his young sister, aged seventeen, all descended together to the Town Hall in a brougham. The young girl admired Vera's belt excessively, and looked forward to the moment when she too should be a bewitching and captivating wife like Vera, in short, a woman of the world, worshipped by grave, bearded men. And both the men were under the spell of Vera's incurable charm, capricious, surprising, exasperating, indefinable, indispensable to their lives.

'Stupid superstitions!' reflected Vera. 'But of course I never believed it really.'

And she cast down her eyes to gloat over the belt.

Nemesis

Phyllis Bentley

Furnivall was, quite frankly, in search of a subject. His latest novel (he had no idea, of course, that it was to prove his last) had appeared at the turn of the year, and settled, as all Furnivall's fervent gushing fictions seemed to settle, with a regularity as pleasing to his publishers as it was irritating to his critics, into a steady best-seller. Now he was on the look-out for a plot for the next.

On a delicious summer's evening, as he was on his way to a railway junction from a lecture at a north-country school, he came upon Trith-in-Allerdale. The road bends sharply through a thick copse here as it descends to the river, so that the whole enchanting picture of Trith, one of the loveliest villages of a lovely dale, is revealed suddenly to the traveller's eyes as he reaches the bridge-head, perfect and complete, like a work of art. The swift peaty river Allert, sparkling darkly gold as it foams through the rocky gorge below; the steep bluffs smothered in a tangle of rich fresh green; the graceful single arch of the high bridge, the grey village built of the same honest dale stone as its sturdy little Norman church, the towering green fell behind, across which slow-moving clouds drew shadows of brown velvet – Furnivall, seeing them all for the first time in the clear warm sunshine as the taxi bumped round the bend, exclaimed with pleasure. For Furnivall had, you know, plenty of aesthetic perception, which it was his crime to vulgarize and exploit. A dip in the bank which the years had not been able to obliterate, and some piles of moss-covered masonry facing each other across the stream, seemed to hint at an earlier bridge. On the right, rather withdrawn, as if it had originally flanked the older road, thought Furnivall shrewdly, stood a honey-coloured inn, turning a very plain but spotless face proudly to the afternoon light. Between the building and the cliff lay an agreeable little lawn, surrounded by thick beds of flowers – Furnivall knew the names of very few flowers, but liked a herbaceous border when he saw one. As the taxi crossed the bridge, a perfectly stunning girl came from the house and shook out a table-cloth over the lawn. Oh, a perfectly stunning girl! Smooth, dark hair, a perfect oval face, eyes like sloes, a skin as darkly golden as the sparkling Allert, rich red lips – 'Stop here!' commanded Furnivall, rapping the glass sharply. He paid off the taxi, not without a slight wrangle, and went in for a pint.

The landlord, proclaimed above the lintel as Harry Armboth, a stolid, gingerish person in middle life, a widower, father of the stunning Etta, proved rather dull, and Furnivall did not linger in the bar, but wandered up the road toward the village.

Now it was Furnivall's habit to look into graveyards as opportunity offered, especially country graveyards, in order to collect a few local names for future use in novels. A good round country name, two or three hundred years old, added a kind of bloom, an authenticity, to a character otherwise a little weak; while for comic 'characters' a rustic surname was almost indispensable. So, conscientious, as ever, in search of material, Furnivall luckily swung the little gate which served to keep out four-footed wanderers, and entered the Trith-in-Allerdale churchyard. Luckily, or unluckily; at any rate it was here he made his grand find.

And what a find it was! A neglected, greenish, tumbledown stone, quite plain, curved at the top, not very old, put in fifty or sixty years ago at the most, thought Furnivall; standing, or rather leaning, apart from the rest in a little triangular patch to itself on the very edge of the river cliff. The stone's inscription – incredible good fortune! marvellous story! – read:

> THIS STONE WAS ERECTED
> BY THE SUBSCRIPTION
> OF HIS FELLOW-WORKMEN
> TO THE WELL-LOVED MEMORY OF
> A YOUNG MAN
> THOUGHT TO BE A NATIVE OF ITALY
> KNOWN BY THE NAME OF
> JOHN BAPTIST
> WHO WAS DROWNED IN THE ALLERT
> WHILE ENGAGED IN THE EXECUTION OF HIS
> DUTY
> ON

The date was defaced by lichen.

Marvellous, thought Furnivall, every fibre of his novelist's mind aquiver. Marvellous! *A young man, thought to be a native of Italy*. What romance! How had he wandered to this far northern dale? All kinds of exciting and picturesque hypotheses to explain the presence of this southern humming-bird in Trith at once darted through Furnivall's mind. *John Baptist* – that was Gian' Battist', of course. *Erected to the well-loved memory* – a charming person, our Giovanni. He probably played on

the guitar – or sang in his soft southern tenor, decided Furnivall com-
posing rapidly, beneath the harsh northern moon. *Drowned in the Allert*
– poor lad, poor lad. In the execution of his duty, too. Oh, it was a gift,
a gift! What a romance he would make of it! *What* a romance! Colourful,
tender, soul-stirring – already he read the adjectives in his publisher's
blurb. *What* a gift of a plot! What period should he set it in? Better find
out the real date first, perhaps. Hot on the scent, he returned eagerly to
the Bridge Inn.

On the stone seat outside sat a fine antique figure of a man – a spare
but solid ancient, with a tanned, much-wrinkled face, beaked nose,
bright grey eyes, square bald head and a fringe of well-brushed whisker,
brindled white and ginger. He was well dressed in the country fashion –
tweeds and cloth gaiters, noted Furnivall mechanically – and seemed
very much at home; from his look, and the way the men passing in and
out of the bar greeted him: 'Evening, William!' 'Evening, Mr Armboth!'
Furnivall judged he was perhaps the landlord's father. Sitting down
beside him, Furnivall hazarded this suggestion.

'Father-in-law, sir,' snapped old William Armboth.

His tone indicated that he thought it no business of Furnivall's, and
he continued to sit erect and gaze in front of him, his hands clasped on
the knob of his fine ashplant, in a manner discouraging to conversation.
But Furnivall was not easily discouraged; he opined that William's
daughter had married her cousin, that the lovely Etta was William's
grand-daughter, that Armboth was a frequent name in those parts, that
the weather was fine and the Allert swift, and having broken down the
old man's outer defences, as it were, by securing his assent to all these
propositions, he came to the matter near his heart, and remarked:

'Interesting stone that, up in the graveyard yonder.' As old Armboth
offered no comment, Furnivall was obliged to enlarge. 'The young man
thought to be a native of Italy. A story there, perhaps?'

At this old Armboth turned his gaze on Furnivall, who found it rather
uncomfortably piercing and prolonged.

'Be you kin to him?' he said at length.

'To whom?' said Furnivall, slightly taken aback. 'Oh, to Gian' Battist'?
No. I am a novelist, you see,' explained Furnivall with a modest titter.
'So naturally I am interested in these old tales.'

'Ah,' said Armboth. There seemed a kind of contempt in his tone, and
he withdrew his gaze.

'I think I shall go up after dinner and call on the Vicar – you have
a vicar here, I suppose?' said Furnivall. 'And get him to show me the
burial register – there may be some details of Gian' Battist's demise.'

'Aye, we've a vicar,' agreed old Armboth.

Furnivall went in, arranged for a bed and dined. The Allerdale lamb
was admirable, and he was waited on by the beautiful Etta, to whom he

behaved with grave respect. That kind of beauty demanded a grave respect, thought Furnivall smugly; whatever the critics said, he, Furnivall, had fine perceptions and knew qualities when he saw them. A plump, white little man, with town-dweller's muscles, softened by easy living, Furnivall had no desire to walk the half-mile up to the village again, but his curiosity about Gian' Battist' – or rather, not exactly his curiosity, his feeling that he was on to a good thing – triumphed, and he set off for the village. Old Armboth, who was still sitting before the door in the golden evening light, pointed him out a short cut across the fields.

But Furnivall must have mistaken his directions, for somehow he found himself away beyond the village, right up on the slope of the fell. How on earth he had got there he couldn't imagine, and he had a good deal of difficulty in making his way back to the inn. He must see the Vicar tomorrow, thought Furnivall crossly.

Breakfast next morning was rather disappointing; there was something the matter with the milk, which Furnivall thought inexcusable, considering the number of brown and white cows which dotted the fields around. He went to the kitchen hatchway at the close of the meal to lodge a complaint – oh, a very jovial, humorous complaint; Furnivall believed in keeping on the right side of his inferiors; but still, a complaint; he rapped on the old wood sharply. The hatch glided back, and he found himself confronting the most charming pair of blue eyes he had ever seen; faded but still sweet; matched by a delicate pure profile, a clear cheek, a cloud of creamy hair. Furnivall stammered, disconcerted; the little lady, so old, so tiny, so delicately made, was somehow not at all the kind of person to whom one complained about the milk. To gain time he asked if she were Mrs Armboth; in a soft sweet tone which held echoes of now muted bells she said, Yes, she was wife to William Armboth. Etta now came up and bent her dark glowing grace above the fragile Dresden prettiness of her grandmother, putting an arm about the old lady's charming little waist. Furnivall, bowing, flustered, made a complimentary reference to the delicious contrast of beauties thus provided.

'You wished something, sir?' Mrs Armboth rebuffed him in her pretty tones.

It was impossible to mention milk; Furnivall, pleased with his resource, asked for another indication of the short cut to the vicarage. Mrs Armboth led him to the rear of the house – where a green track still hinted the course of the old road – and stretching out her wrinkled but shapely little hand, pointed out stiles and gave him a few instructions.

These, for the rest of the morning, Furnivall strove to follow. He followed them at first along clear paths; later through trackless fields; he followed them over mortarless stone walls which collapsed when mounted and bit his ankles, through miry ponds, beneath scratchy bushes, along precipitous paths on the verge of the river bank. He sweated, he swore, he bruised and scratched himself, he puffed and panted, he walked and climbed and slithered and even rolled, but he never at any time came near the vicarage garden gate.

Upon my word, he thought, when at last he reached a road and found himself five miles from Trith, if I were one of those supernatural ghost-story fellers, I should begin to think Gian' Battist' meant to prevent me finding out anything about his death ... At once his novelist's faculty began to work on this idea. Was there a short story in it? *The Angry Ghost. The Jealous Ghost.* No, that's been used before ... Well ... he trudged back to the Bridge Inn morosely.

He ate a late lunch in silence, slept heavily till the cool of the evening, then without mentioning his destination to anybody – for he felt a fool about his inability to cross a couple of fields without losing himself – he trotted pompously up the road to Trith. The vicarage was perfectly easy to find; a kindly square house beside the church. A neat old housekeeper opened the door, and Furnivall asked for the Vicar.

'The Vicar's away judging a fishing competition, sir,' replied the housekeeper.

'When did he leave?' gulped Furnivall hoarsely.

'This morning, sir, by the noon train,' replied the housekeeper. 'He won't be back till late tonight. Are you ill, sir?' she added solicitously, seeing Furnivall suddenly shudder.

'No – just a ghost over my grave,' smiled Furnivall. But he thought: 'A very powerful ghost, Gian' Battist'!' And the thought was somehow an uneasy one.

But in the morning the sun shone, his secretary had forwarded a letter from his publisher asking about his next novel, his courage revived and he found the vicarage easily.

Furnivall introduced himself to the Vicar – a mild white-haired old man with a scholarly stoop – as a writer.

'Indeed?' said the Vicar mildly. 'On what subject? How unfortunate for you to have the same name as the vulgar romancer fellow. No relation, I hope? No, no.'

'Have you been in Trith long?' asked Furnivall hurriedly.

'Forty-five years. Trith is my first and my only cure of souls.'

'Were you here when Gian' Battist' was drowned?' exclaimed Furnivall, delighted.

'Yes. I came here that very year. I helped to pull his body from the stream. I was young then,' said the Vicar with a smile.

'What date was it exactly? On the grave it isn't visible – lichen, you know.'

'I cannot recall the date with accuracy,' said the Vicar. 'We can find it in the Burials Register if you really wish to know. But may I inquire—'

'It's a question of an old man's inheritance in Italy,' lied Furnivall. 'I was out there during the war, you see, and—'

'Oh, in that case let us go over to the vestry at once,' cried the Vicar, beaming happily. He took down a large old key and led the way across his garden to the church.

'The young man you are interested in, Mr Furnivall,' he began: 'lost his life during the building of the present bridge. He was one of the gang of navvies who built the bridge, you know. They were camped on the south bank, just opposite the Bridge Inn. It was their custom to leave one of their number on guard at the head of the bridges on that side, the old bridge being in process of demolition and the new one of erection; and on a winter's night of wind and storm, while on guard, the Italian fell into the Allert and was drowned. The river is deep at any time in the gorge, and was then in spate; the current swept him against the piers of the new bridge, smashed in his head and drowned him. But your present hosts can tell you far more of John Baptist than I can,' concluded the Vicar. 'Lucy Armboth – old Mrs William – was the daughter of the then landlord of the Bridge Inn. (She married her cousin, you know; it's an Armboth habit; her daughter Harriet did the same and died in childbirth producing Etta.) Yes, Lucy must have seen the navvies many a time, as a young girl.'

'Really!' exclaimed Furnivall. 'Was she living at the inn at the time?'

'Undoubtedly,' replied the Vicar. 'She did not marry William till some months later. On her father's death, William took over the licence of the inn.'

'Old William told me nothing of all this when I mentioned John Baptist to him,' grumbled Furnivall.

'Ah well,' said the Vicar, stooping to examine the row of black leather registers on the lowest shelf: 'Trust none save kith is the troth of Trith – it's a local saying, you know, Mr Furnivall. That's odd, now. That's very odd.'

'What's odd?' demanded Furnivall.

'The volume for the year of the drowning isn't here,' said the Vicar. 'Very odd. Are you ill, Mr Furnivall? You look quite pale.'

'No. But he's a very powerful ghost, your Gian' Battist',' gasped Furnivall.

The Vicar promised to find the volume by the afternoon if Furnivall could wait in Trith so long. But Furnivall did not pledge himself, for he felt sure the register would not be found.

Leaving the Vicar somewhat more rapidly than courtesy dictated, Furnivall hurried down to the Bridge Inn – at a great speed, as if the ghost were chasing him and might be outdistanced if he made haste. On the lawn between the river bank and the house Mrs Armboth was sitting, a rug over her knees, her pretty fingers busy with some fine crochet lace.

'Mrs Armboth,' began Furnivall fervently, drawing one of the basket chairs to her side. 'Lucy Armboth!' (The old lady started.) 'I beg you, I implore you to tell me all you know of the young man thought to be a native of Italy, drowned in the Allert and buried in Trith churchyard five and forty years ago. You must have known him. I beg of you to give me all the personal details you can of him – his appearance, manners, speech, everything. Even details which may not seem to you important, Mrs Armboth, when worked upon by the creative imagination will serve to bring him vividly to life. He will be enshrined,' raved Furnivall, letting himself go: 'in – er – in short, in my best novel.'

He mopped his forehead – his own eloquence always heated him – and gazed at Mrs Armboth imploringly. She returned his gaze from eyes dilated by some strong emotion which, if Furnivall had not known such feelings irrelevant, he would have judged to be mingled fear and rage.

'What do you want to know about John Baptist, Mr Furnivall?' said Mrs Armboth in a low, intense tone.

'Well – his appearance, to begin with,' urged Furnivall, delighted to find her yield. 'What was he like?'

'He was like Etta,' whispered Lucy Armboth.

'What!' cried the startled Furnivall, bounding in his chair.

'He was like Etta, like Etta, don't you see?' urged Lucy. 'You said yourself how unlike Etta is to all the rest of us around. Etta is his living image, and what more natural? She's his grand-daughter, after all. Her mother was like him too, to my mind, but by a bit of luck she had the Armboth red hair.'

'You mean,' gasped Furnivall, overwhelmed, 'that Gian' was – your lover?'

The old woman nodded. 'You fool, of course,' she said. 'When he was drowned I married Will Armboth to give the child a name. He'd been my lad before Giovanni came and made me love him.'

'Your husband – knows – all this?' gulped Furnivall.

'No. No one knows. All these years I've kept the secret, and now you come to dig it all up and bring dishonour on me, just to make a tale. I did my best to keep you back from learning aught of it. I tried to drive you away. But there's no teaching such as you,' said Mrs Armboth contemptuously.

Furnivall swallowed. 'I'll go at once,' he said.

'That will be best,' said Lucy Armboth, her blue eyes flashing fire.

Furnivall crept away.

What a fool he had been! What a blind, unperceptive, crassly blundering fool!

But, as he packed, and his mind roamed over the incident of his disastrous stay in Trith, he began to doubt whether after all he had been quite such a fool as he had feared. The checks and hindrances imposed between himself and Gian', which it had been amusing to consider supernatural, were now explained as due to Lucy's hostility; but was that really so? That first evening, how had he been kept from the vicarage? It was old William Armboth who had given him the wrong route. Why? If William Armboth knew the old story, there was reason enough for him to wish to hide it; but Lucy affirmed he did not know. Ah, but he did know, decided Furnivall, and his whole body was flooded with the delicious tide of returning self-satisfaction; yes, yes, William knew his wife's secret, had always known, perhaps always believed she knew he knew; after all these years, it was Furnivall's mission to reveal this, and set Lucy's heart at rest. It needed a writer of delicate perception, like Furnivall, to see into these rugged hearts, to bring the perfect close to this long dramatic tale. (And what a story it was, now! Better than ever; really grand!) Tears of happy sentiment actually filled Furnivall's eyes as he saw himself playing the *deus ex machina*, bringing peace to the dear old Armboths. He hurried downstairs and out into the garden, eager to conclude this perfect *dénouement* and drive dramatically away.

To his disappointment, Lucy was gone; old William Armboth, firm, erect, with well-brushed whiskers and well-polished stick, sat in her place.

'Ah – I wanted to speak to Mrs Armboth,' Furnivall panted.

Old William turned his head and looked at him, but did not speak.

'I'm just leaving,' enlarged Furnivall eagerly. 'And it's really important that I should speak to Mrs Armboth before I go.'

The old man continued to gaze at him in silence.

'Tell her – tell her it's about Gian' Battist',' urged Furnivall.

Something flickered in the old man's eyes and passed.

'You seem to find that Eyetalian very interesting, Mester,' he observed.

'Well, yes I do,' admitted Furnivall. 'Interesting and pathetic, Mr Armboth.'

'Ah,' said William. He withdrew his gaze from Furnivall's and stared ahead. After a pause he spoke again. 'I reckon I can show you t'very spot where he fell in t'river, if you'd care to see,' he offered in a reluctant but yielding tone.

'Can you indeed? I should be delighted,' said Furnivall with enthusiasm, eager, as always, for authentic local colour.

'Come this way, then,' said the old man. He heaved himself up and set off slowly down the garden, crossed a flower-bed and plunged into the wooded slope beyond.

Furnivall followed. After a few sharp encounters with branch and bush, he found himself in a broad green path descending towards the river. It was an uncomfortable progress; the paths were smothered in nettles and docks, and crossed by great trails of ropy weed and prickly bramble calculated to trip up any town-bred author. Furnivall was soon hot and sweating, and he noticed that William panted too.

'Here we are, you see,' said William slowly at last. 'We've been walking what's left of the old road. This here' – he struck a mound of green with his stick and the concealed stone rang – 'is the old bridgehead. Look over, Mester – you'll see the bank falls sheer to the stream.'

Furnivall, stepping forward and bending over, one hand on the mossy stone to support himself, saw the Allert, looking very dark and deep and swift, rushing directly below.

'But what was he doing?' began Furnivall – and halted. He had been about to ask what Gian' was doing this side the Allert, when the navvies' camp lay on the other bank, but of course the answer to that was plain enough; he had been visiting Lucy Armboth. What did old William really think of that, he wondered; it was an unrivalled opportunity for discovering the answer in the old man's face.

'So that's what happened to him, he slipped in the dark and fell,' began Furnivall, turning.

He gaped. Old Armboth stood towering above him, his lips drawn back in a ferocious snarl, his eyes fixed in a bloodshot glare, his face crimson, congested with rage. His gnarled hands, raised high above his head, grasped a huge rough stone. He took a step forward.

Too late, Furnivall understood what had happened to Gian' Battist'. 'I shan't be missed for hours – if only I had promised to see the Vicar – what a fool I've been,' he thought. He thought: 'My perceptions are as dull as the critics say.' It was the bitterest moment of his life – and the last.

The Avenging Chance

Anthony Berkeley

Roger Sheringham was inclined to think afterwards that the Poisoned Chocolates Case, as the papers called it, was perhaps the most perfectly planned murder he had ever encountered. The motive was so obvious, when you knew where to look for it – but you didn't know; the method was so significant, when you had grasped its real essentials – but you didn't grasp them; the traces were so thinly covered, when you had realized what was covering them – but you didn't realize. But for a piece of the merest bad luck, which the murderer could not possibly have foreseen, the crime must have been added to the classical list of great mysteries.

This is the gist of the case, as Chief Inspector Moresby told it one evening to Roger in the latter's rooms in the Albany a week or so after it happened:

On Friday morning, the fifteenth of November, at half-past ten in the morning, in accordance with his invariable custom, Sir William Anstruther walked into his club in Piccadilly, the very exclusive Rainbow Club, and asked for his letters. The porter handed him three and a small parcel. Sir William walked over to the fire-place in the big lounge hall to open them.

A few minutes later another member entered the club, a Mr Graham Beresford. There were a letter and a couple of circulars for him, and he also strolled over to the fire-place, nodding to Sir William, but not speaking to him. The two men only knew each other very slightly, and had probably never exchanged more than a dozen words in all.

Having glanced through his letters, Sir William opened the parcel and, after a moment, snorted with disgust. Beresford looked at him, and with a grunt Sir William thrust out a letter which had been enclosed in the parcel. Concealing a smile (Sir William's ways were a matter of some amusement to his fellow-members), Beresford read the letter. It was from a big firm of chocolate manufacturers, Mason & Sons, and set forth that they were putting on the market a new brand of liqueur-chocolates designed especially to appeal to men; would Sir William do them the honour of accepting the enclosed two-pound box and letting the firm have his candid opinion on them?

'Do they think I'm a blank chorus-girl?' fumed Sir William. 'Write 'em testimonials about their blank chocolates, indeed! Blank 'em! I'll complain to the blank committee. That sort of blank thing can't blank well be allowed here.'

'Well, it's an ill wind so far as I'm concerned,' Beresford soothed him. 'It's reminded me of something. My wife and I had a box at the Imperial last night. I bet her a box of chocolates to a hundred cigarettes that she wouldn't spot the villain by the end of the second act. She won. I must remember to get them. Have you seen it – *The Creaking Skull*? Not a bad show.'

Sir William had not seen it, and said so with force.

'Want a box of chocolates, did you say?' he added, more mildly. 'Well, take this blank one. I don't want it.'

For a moment Beresford demurred politely and then, most unfortunately for himself, accepted. The money so saved meant nothing to him for he was a wealthy man; but trouble was always worth saving.

By an extraordinarily lucky chance neither the outer wrapper of the box nor its covering letter were thrown into the fire, and this was the more fortunate in that both men had tossed the envelopes of their letters into the flames. Sir William did, indeed, make a bundle of the wrapper, letter, and string, but he handed it over to Beresford, and the latter simply dropped it inside the fender. This bundle the porter subsequently extracted and, being a man of orderly habits, put it tidily away in the waste-paper basket, whence it was retrieved later by the police.

Of the three unconscious protagonists in the impending tragedy, Sir William was without doubt the most remarkable. Still a year or two under fifty, he looked, with his flaming red face and thick-set figure, a typical country squire of the old school, and both his manners and his language were in accordance with tradition. His habits, especially as regards women, were also in accordance with tradition – the tradition of the bold, bad baronet which he undoubtedly was.

In comparison with him, Beresford was rather an ordinary man, a tall, dark, not unhandsome fellow of two-and-thirty, quiet and reserved. His father had left him a rich man, but idleness did not appeal to him, and he had a finger in a good many business pies.

Money attracts money, Graham Beresford had inherited it, he made it, and, inevitably, he had married it, too. The daughter of a late ship-owner in Liverpool, with not far off half a million in her own right. But the money was incidental, for he needed her and would have married her just as inevitably (said his friends) if she had not had a farthing. A tall, rather serious-minded, highly cultured girl, not so young that

her character had not had time to form (she was twenty-five when Beresford married her, three years ago), she was the ideal wife for him. A
bit of a Puritan perhaps in some ways, but Beresford, whose wild oats,
though duly sown, had been a sparse crop, was ready enough to be a
Puritan himself by that time if she was. To make no bones about it,
the Beresfords succeeded in achieving that eighth wonder of the modern
world, a happy marriage.

And into the middle of it there dropped with irretrievable tragedy,
the box of chocolates.

Beresford gave them to her after lunch as they sat over their coffee,
with some jesting remark about paying his honourable debts, and she
opened the box at once. The top layer, she noticed, seemed to consist
only of kirsch and maraschino. Beresford, who did not believe in spoiling
good coffee, refused when she offered him the box, and his wife ate the
first one alone. As she did so she exclaimed in surprise that the filling
seemed exceedingly strong and positively burnt her mouth.

Beresford explained that they were samples of a new brand and then,
made curious by what his wife had said, took one too. A burning taste,
not intolerable but much too strong to be pleasant, followed the release
of the liquid, and the almond flavouring seemed quite excessive.

'By Jove,' he said, 'they are strong. They must be filled with neat
alcohol.'

'Oh, they wouldn't do that, surely,' said his wife, taking another. 'But
they are very strong. I think I rather like them, though.'

Beresford ate another, and disliked it still more. 'I don't,' he said with
decision. 'They make my tongue feel quite numb. I shouldn't eat any
more of them if I were you, I think there's something wrong with them.'

'Well, they're only an experiment, I suppose,' she said. 'But they do
burn. I'm not sure whether I like them or not.'

A few minutes later Beresford went out to keep a business appointment
in the City. He left her still trying to make up her mind whether she
liked them, and still eating them to decide. Beresford remembered that
scrap of conversation afterwards very vividly, because it was the last
time he saw his wife alive.

That was roughly half-past two. At a quarter to four Beresford arrived
at his club from the City in a taxi, in a state of collapse. He was helped
into the building by the driver and the porter, and both described him
subsequently as pale to the point of ghastliness, with staring eyes and
livid lips, and his skin damp and clammy. His mind seemed unaffected,
however, and when they had got him up the steps he was able to walk,
with the porter's help, into the lounge.

The porter, thoroughly alarmed, wanted to send for a doctor at once,
but Beresford, who was the last man in the world to make a fuss, refused
to let him, saying that it must be indigestion and he would be all right

in a few minutes. To Sir William Anstruther, however, who was in the lounge at the time, he added after the porter had gone:

'Yes, and I believe it was those infernal chocolates you gave me, now I come to think of it. I thought there was something funny about them at the time. I'd better go and find out if my wife—' He broke off abruptly. His body, which had been leaning back limply in his chair, suddenly heaved rigidly upright; his jaws locked together, the livid lips drawn back in a horrible grin, and his hands clenched on the arms of his chair. At the same time Sir William became aware of an unmistakable smell of bitter almonds.

Thoroughly alarmed, believing indeed that the man was dying under his eyes, Sir William raised a shout for the porter and a doctor. The other occupants of the lounge hurried up, and between them they got the convulsed body of the unconscious man into a more comfortable position. Before the doctor could arrive a telephone message was received at the club from an agitated butler asking if Mr Beresford was there, and if so would he come home at once as Mrs Beresford had been taken seriously ill. As a matter of fact she was already dead.

Beresford did not die. He had taken less of the poison than his wife, who after his departure must have eaten at least three more of the chocolates, so that its action was less rapid and the doctor had time to save him. As a matter of fact it turned out afterwards that he had not had a fatal dose. By about eight o'clock that night he was conscious; the next day he was practically convalescent.

As for the unfortunate Mrs Beresford, the doctor had arrived too late to save her, and she passed away very rapidly in a deep coma.

The police had taken the matter in hand as soon as Mrs Beresford's death was reported to them and the fact of poison established, and it was only a very short time before things had become narrowed down to the chocolates as the active agent.

Sir William was interrogated, the letter and wrapper were recovered from the waste-paper basket, and, even before the sick man was out of danger, a detective inspector was asking for an interview with the managing director of Mason & Sons. Scotland Yard moves quickly.

It was the police theory at this stage, based on what Sir William and the two doctors had been able to tell them, that by an act of criminal carelessness on the part of one of Mason's employees, an excessive amount of oil of bitter almonds had been included in the filling mixture of the chocolates, for that was what the doctors had decided must be the poisoning ingredient. However, the managing director quashed this idea at once: oil of bitter almonds, he asserted, was never used by Mason's.

He had more interesting news still. Having read with undisguised astonishment the covering letter, he at once declared that it was a forgery. No such letter, no such samples had been sent out by the firm at all;

a new variety of liqueur-chocolates had never even been mooted. The fatal chocolates were their ordinary brand.

Unwrapping and examining one more closely, he called the inspector's attention to a mark on the underside, which he suggested was the remains of a small hole drilled in the case, through which the liquid could have been extracted and the fatal filling inserted, the hole afterwards being stopped up with softened chocolate, a perfectly simple operation.

He examined it under a magnifying-glass and the inspector agreed. It was now clear to him that somebody had been trying deliberately to murder Sir William Anstruther.

Scotland Yard doubled its activities. The chocolates were sent for analysis, Sir William was interviewed again, and so was the now conscious Beresford. From the latter the doctor insisted that the news of his wife's death must be kept till the next day, as in his weakened condition the shock might be fatal, so that nothing very helpful was obtained from him.

Nor could Sir William throw any light on the mystery or produce a single person who might have any grounds for trying to kill him. He was living apart from his wife, who was the principal beneficiary in his will, but she was in the South of France, as the French police subsequently confirmed. His estate in Worcestershire, heavily mortgaged, was entailed and went to a nephew; but as the rent he got for it barely covered the interest on the mortgage, and the nephew was considerably better off than Sir William himself, there was no motive there. The police were at a dead end.

The analysis brought one or two interesting facts to light. Not oil of bitter almonds but nitrobenzine, a kindred substance, chiefly used in the manufacture of aniline dyes, was the somewhat surprising poison employed. Each chocolate in the upper layer contained exactly six minims of it, in a mixture of kirsch and maraschino. The chocolates in the other layers were harmless.

As to the other clues, they seemed equally useless. The sheet of Mason's notepaper was identified by Merton's, the printers, as of their work, but there was nothing to show how it had got into the murderer's possession. All that could be said was that, the edges being distinctly yellowed, it must be an old piece. The machine on which the letter had been typed, of course, could not be traced. From the wrapper, a piece of ordinary brown paper with Sir William's address hand-printed on it in large capitals, there was nothing to be learnt at all beyond that the parcel had been posted at the office in Southampton Street between the hours of 8.30 and 9.30 on the previous evening.

Only one thing was quite clear. Whoever had coveted Sir William's life had no intention of paying for it with his or her own.

*

'And now you know as much as we do, Mr Sheringham,' concluded Chief Inspector Moresby, 'and if you can say who sent those chocolates to Sir William, you'll know a good deal more.'

Roger nodded thoughtfully.

'It's a brute of a case. I met a man only yesterday who was at school with Beresford. He didn't know him well because Beresford was on the modern side and my friend was a classical bird, but they were in the same house. He says Beresford's absolutely knocked over by his wife's death. I wish you could find out who sent those chocolates, Moresby.'

'So do I, Mr Sheringham,' said Moresby gloomily.

'It might have been any one in the whole world,' Roger mused. 'What about feminine jealousy, for instance? Sir William's private life doesn't seem to be immaculate. I dare say there's a good deal of off with the old light-o'-love and on with the new.'

'Why, that's just what I've been looking into, Mr Sheringham, sir,' retorted Chief Inspector Moresby reproachfully. 'That was the first thing that came to me. Because if anything does stand out about this business it is that it's a woman's crime. Nobody but a woman would send poisoned chocolates to a man. Another man would send a poisoned sample of whisky, or something like that.'

'That's a very sound point, Moresby,' Roger meditated. 'Very sound indeed. And Sir William couldn't help you?'

'Couldn't,' said Moresby, not without a trace of resentment, 'or wouldn't. I was inclined to believe at first that he might have his suspicions and was shielding some woman. But I don't think so now.'

'Humph!' Roger did not seem quite so sure. 'It's reminiscent, this case, isn't it? Didn't some lunatic once send poisoned chocolates to the Commissioner of Police himself? A good crime always gets imitated, as you know.'

Moresby brightened.

'It's funny you should say that, Mr Sheringham, because that's the very conclusion I've come to. I've tested every other theory, and so far as I know there's not a soul with an interest in Sir William's death, whether from motives of gain, revenge, or what you like, whom I haven't had to rule quite out of it. In fact, I've pretty well made up my mind that the person who sent those chocolates was some irresponsible lunatic of a woman, a social or religious fanatic who's probably never even seen him. And if that's the case,' Moresby sighed, 'a fat chance I have of ever laying hands on her.'

'Unless Chance steps in, as it so often does,' said Roger brightly. 'and helps you. A tremendous lot of cases get solved by a stroke of sheer luck, don't they? *Chance the Avenger*. It would make an excellent film-title. But there's a lot of truth in it. If I were superstitious, which I'm not, I should say it wasn't chance at all, but Providence avenging the victim.'

'Well, Mr Sheringham,' said Moresby, who was not superstitious
either, 'to tell the truth, I don't mind what it is, so long as it lets me
get my hands on the right person.'

If Moresby had paid his visit to Roger Sheringham with any hope
of tapping that gentleman's brains, he went away disappointed.

To tell the truth, Roger was inclined to agree with the chief inspector's
conclusion, that the attempt on the life of Sir William Anstruther and
the actual murder of the unfortunate Mrs Beresford must be the work
of some unknown criminal lunatic. For this reason, although he thought
about it a good deal during the next few days, he made no attempt
to take the case in hand. It was the sort of affair, necessitating endless
inquiries that a private person would have neither the time nor the
authority to carry out, which can be handled only by the official police.
Roger's interest in it was purely academic.

It was hazard, a chance encounter nearly a week later, which translated this interest from the academic into the personal.

Roger was in Bond Street, about to go through the distressing ordeal
of buying a new hat. Along the pavement he suddenly saw bearing down
on him Mrs Verreker-le-Flemming. Mrs Verreker-le-Flemming was
small, exquisite, rich, and a widow, and she sat at Roger's feet whenever
he gave her the opportunity. But she talked. She talked, in fact, and
talked, and talked. And Roger, who rather liked talking himself, could
not bear it. He tried to dart across the road, but there was no opening
in the traffic stream. He was cornered.

Mrs Verreker-le-Flemming fastened on him gladly.

'Oh, Mr Sheringham! *Just* the person I wanted to see. Mr Sheringham, *do* tell me. In confidence. Are you taking up this dreadful business
of poor Joan Beresford's death?'

Roger, the frozen and imbecile grin of civilized intercourse on his face,
tried to get a word in; without result.

'I was horrified when I heard of it – simply horrified. You see, Joan
and I were such *very* close friends. Quite intimate. And the awful thing,
the truly *terrible* thing is that Joan brought the whole business on herself.
Isn't that *appalling*?'

Roger no longer wanted to escape.

'What did you say?' he managed to insert incredulously.

'I suppose it's what they call tragic irony,' Mrs Verreker-le-Flemming
chattered on. 'Certainly it was tragic enough, and I've never heard anything so terribly ironical. You know about that bet she made with her
husband, of course, so that he had to get her a box of chocolates, and
if he hadn't Sir William would never have given him the poisoned ones
and he'd have eaten them and died himself and good riddance? Well,
Mr Sheringham—' Mrs Verreker-le-Flemming lowered her voice to a
conspirator's whisper and glanced about her in the approved manner.

'I've never told anybody else this, but I'm telling you because I know you'll appreciate it. *Joan wasn't playing fair.*'

'How do you mean?' Roger asked, bewildered.

Mrs Verreker-le-Flemming was artlessly pleased with her sensation.

'Why, she'd seen the play before. We went together, the very first week it was on. She *knew* who the villain was all the time.'

'By Jove!' Roger was as impressed as Mrs Verreker-le-Flemming could have wished. 'Chance the Avenger! We're none of us immune from it.'

'Poetic justice, you mean?' twittered Mrs Verreker-le-Flemming, to whom these remarks had been somewhat obscure. 'Yes, but Joan Beresford of all people! That's the extraordinary thing. I should never have thought Joan *would* do a thing like that. She was such a *nice* girl. A little close with money, of course, considering how well off they are, but that isn't anything. Of course it was only fun, and pulling her husband's leg, but I always used to think Joan was such a *serious* girl, Mr Sheringham. I mean, ordinary people don't talk about honour and truth, and playing the game, and all those things one takes for granted. But Joan did. She was always saying that this wasn't honourable, or that wouldn't be playing the game. Well, she paid herself for not playing the game, poor girl, didn't she? Still, it all goes to show the truth of the old saying, doesn't it?'

'What old saying?' said Roger, hypnotized by this flow.

'Why, that still waters run deep. Joan must have been deep, I'm afraid.' Mrs Verreker-le-Flemming sighed. It was evidently a social error to be deep. 'I mean, she certainly took me in. She can't have been quite so honourable and truthful as she was always pretending, can she? And I can't help wondering whether a girl who'd deceived her husband in a little thing like that might not – oh, well, I don't want to say anything against poor Joan now she's dead, poor darling, but she can't have been *quite* such a plaster saint after all, can she? I mean,' said Mrs Verreker-le-Flemming, in hasty extenuation of these suggestions, 'I do think psychology is so very interesting, don't you, Mr Sheringham?'

'Sometimes, very,' Roger agreed gravely. 'But you mentioned Sir William Anstruther just now. Do you know him, too?'

'I used to,' Mrs Verreker-le-Flemming replied, without particular interest. 'Horrible man! Always running after some woman or other. And when he's tired of her, just drops her – biff! – like that. At least,' added Mrs Verreker-le-Flemming somewhat hastily, 'so I've heard.'

'And what happens if she refuses to be dropped?'

'Oh dear, I'm sure I don't know. I suppose you've heard the latest?'

Mrs Verreker-le-Flemming hurried on, perhaps a trifle more pink than the delicate aids to nature on her cheeks would have warranted.

'He's taken up with that Bryce woman now. You know, the wife of the oil man, or petrol, or whatever he made his money in. It began about three weeks ago. You'd have thought that dreadful business of being responsible, in a way, for poor Joan Beresford's death would have sobered him up a little, wouldn't you? But not a bit of it; he—'

Roger was following another line of thought.

'What a pity you weren't at the Imperial with the Beresfords that evening. She'd never have made that bet if you had been.' Roger looked extremely innocent. 'You weren't, I suppose?'

'I?' queried Mrs Verreker-le-Flemming in surprise, 'Good gracious, no. I was at the new revue at the Pavilion. Lady Gravelstroke had a box and asked me to join her party.'

'Oh, yes. Good show, isn't it? I thought that sketch *The Sempiternal Triangle* very clever. Didn't you?'

'*The Sempiternal Triangle?*' wavered Mrs Verreker-le-Flemming.

'Yes, in the first half.'

'Oh! Then I didn't see it. I got there disgracefully late, I'm afraid. But then,' said Mrs Verreker-le-Flemming with pathos, 'I always do seem to be late for simply everything.'

Roger kept the rest of the conversation resolutely upon theatres. But before he left her he had ascertained that she had photographs of both Mrs Beresford and Sir William Anstruther and had obtained permission to borrow them some time. As soon as she was out of view he hailed a taxi and gave Mrs Verreker-le-Flemming's address. He thought it better to take advantage of her permission at a time when he would not have to pay for it a second time over.

The parlour-maid seemed to think there was nothing odd in his mission, and took him up to the drawing-room at once. A corner of the room was devoted to the silver-framed photographs of Mrs Verreker-le-Flemming's friends, and there were many of them. Roger examined them with interest, and finally took away with him not two photographs but six, those of Sir William, Mrs Beresford, Beresford, two strange males who appeared to belong to the Sir William period, and, lastly a likeness of Mrs Verreker-le-Flemming herself. Roger liked confusing his trail.

For the rest of the day he was very busy.

His activities would have no doubt seemed to Mrs Verreker-le-Flemming not merely baffling but pointless. He paid a visit to a public library, for instance, and consulted a work of reference, after which he took a taxi and drove to the offices of the Anglo-Eastern Perfumery Company, where he inquired for a certain Mr Joseph Lea Hardwick and seemed much put out on hearing that no such gentleman was known to the firm and was certainly not employed in any of their branches. Many questions had to be put about the firm and its branches before he consented to abandon the quest.

After that he drove to Messrs Weall & Wilson, the well-known institution which protects the trade interests of individuals and advises its subscribers regarding investments. Here he entered his name as a subscriber, and explaining that he had a large sum of money to invest, filled in one of the special inquiry-forms which are headed Strictly Confidential.

Then he went to the Rainbow Club, in Piccadilly.

Introducing himself to the porter without a blush as connected with Scotland Yard, he asked the man a number of questions, more or less trivial, concerning the tragedy.

'Sir William, I understand,' he said finally, as if by the way, 'did not dine here the evening before?'

There it appeared that Roger was wrong. Sir William had dined in the club, as he did about three times a week.

'But I quite understood he wasn't here that evening?' Roger said plaintively.

The porter was emphatic. He remembered quite well. So did a waiter, whom the porter summoned to corroborate him. Sir William had dined, rather late, and had not left the dining-room till about nine o'clock. He spent the evening there, too, the waiter knew, or at least some of it, for he himself had taken him a whisky-and-soda in the lounge not less than half an hour later.

Roger retired.

He retired to Merton's in a taxi.

It seemed that he wanted some new notepaper printed, of a very special kind, and to the young woman behind the counter he specified at great length and in wearisome detail exactly what he did want. The young woman handed him the books of specimen pieces and asked him to see if there was any style there which would suit him. Roger glanced through them, remarking garrulously to the young woman that he had been recommended to Merton's by a very dear friend, whose photograph he happened to have on him at that moment. Wasn't that a curious coincidence? The young woman agreed that it was.

'About a fortnight ago, I think, my friend was in here last,' said Roger, producing the photograph. 'Recognize this?'

The young woman took the photograph, without apparent interest.

'Oh, yes. I remember. About some notepaper, too, wasn't it? So that's your friend. Well, it's a small world. Now this is a line we're selling a good deal of just now.'

Roger went back to his rooms to dine. Afterwards, feeling restless, he wandered out of the Albany and turned up Piccadilly. He wandered round the Circus, thinking hard, and paused for a moment out of habit to inspect the photographs of the new revue hung outside the Pavilion. The next thing he realized was that he had got as far as Jermyn Street and was standing outside the Imperial Theatre. Glancing at the advertisements of *The Creaking Skull*, he saw that it began at half-past eight.

Glancing at his watch, he saw that the time was twenty-nine minutes past that hour. He had an evening to get through somehow. He went inside.

The next morning, very early for Roger, he called on Moresby at Scotland Yard.

'Moresby,' he said without preamble, 'I want you to do something for me. Can you find me a taximan who took a fare from Piccadilly Circus or its neighbourhood at about ten past nine on the evening before the Beresford crime, to the Strand somewhere near the bottom of Southampton Street, and another who took a fare back between those points. I'm not sure about the first. Or one taxi might have been used for the double journey, but I doubt that. Anyhow, try to find out for me, will you?'

'What are you up to now, Mr Sheringham?' Moresby asked suspiciously.

'Breaking down an interesting alibi,' replied Roger serenely. 'By the way, I know who sent those chocolates to Sir William. I'm just building up a nice structure of evidence for you. Ring up my rooms when you've got those taximen.'

He strolled out, leaving Moresby positively gaping after him.

The rest of the day he spent apparently trying to buy a second-hand typewriter. He was very particular that it should be a Hamilton No. 4. When the shop-people tried to induce him to consider other makes he refused to look at them, saying that he had had the Hamilton No. 4 so strongly recommended to him by a friend, who had bought one about three weeks ago. Perhaps it was at this very shop? No? They hadn't sold a Hamilton No. 4 for the last three months? How odd!

But at one shop they had sold a Hamilton No. 4 within the last month, and that was odder still.

At half-past four Roger got back to his rooms to await the telephone message from Moresby. At half-past five it came.

'There are fourteen taxi-drivers here, littering up my office,' said Moresby offensively. 'What do you want me to do with 'em?'

'Keep them till I come, Chief Inspector,' returned Roger with dignity.

The interview with the fourteen was brief enough, however. To each man in turn Roger showed a photograph, holding it so that Moresby could not see it, and asked if he could recognize his fare. The ninth man did so, without hesitation.

At a nod from Roger, Moresby dismissed them, then sat at his table and tried to look official. Roger seated himself on the table, looking most unofficial, and swung his legs. As he did so, a photograph fell unnoticed out of his pocket and fluttered, face downwards, under the table. Moresby eyed it but did not pick it up.

'And now, Mr Sheringham, sir,' he said, 'perhaps you'll tell me what you've been doing?'

'Certainly, Moresby,' said Roger blandly. 'Your work for you. I really have solved the thing, you know. Here's your evidence.' He took from his note-case an old letter and handed it to the Chief Inspector. 'Was that typed on the same machine as the forged letter from Mason's, or was it not?'

Moresby studied it for a moment, then drew the forged letter from a drawer of his table and compared the two minutely.

'Mr Sheringham,' he said soberly, 'where did you get hold of this?'

'In a second-hand typewriter shop in St Martin's Lane. The machine was sold to an unknown customer about a month ago. They identified the customer from that same photograph. As it happened, this machine had been used for a time in the office after it was repaired, to see that it was O.K., and I easily got hold of that specimen of its work.'

'And where is the machine now?'

'Oh, at the bottom of the Thames, I expect,' Roger smiled. 'I tell you, this criminal takes no unnecessary chances. But that doesn't matter. There's your evidence.'

'Humph! It's all right so far as it goes,' conceded Moresby. 'But what about Mason's paper?'

'That,' said Roger calmly, 'was extracted from Merton's book of sample notepapers, as I'd guessed from the very yellowed edges might be the case. I can prove contact of the criminal with the book, and there is a page which will certainly turn out to have been filled by that piece of paper.'

'That's fine,' Moresby said more heartily.

'As for that taximan, the criminal had an alibi. You've heard it broken down. Between ten past nine and twenty-five past, in fact during the time when the parcel must have been posted, the murderer took a hurried journey to that neighbourhood, going probably by bus or underground, but returning as I expected, by taxi, because time would be getting short.'

'And the murderer, Mr Sheringham?'

'The person whose photograph is in my pocket,' Roger said unkindly. 'By the way, do you remember what I was saying the other day about Chance the Avenger, my excellent film-title? Well, it's worked again. By a chance meeting in Bond Street with a silly woman I was put, by the merest accident, in possession of a piece of information which showed me then and there who had sent those chocolates addressed to Sir William. There were other possibilities, of course, and I tested them, but then and there on the pavement I saw the whole thing, from first to last.'

'Who was the murderer, then, Mr Sheringham?' repeated Moresby.

'It was so beautifully planned,' Roger went on dreamily. 'We never grasped for one moment that we were making the fundamental mistake that the murderer all along intended us to make.'

'And what was that?' asked Moresby.

'Why, that the plan had miscarried. That the wrong person had been killed. That was just the beauty of it. The plan had *not* miscarried. It had been brilliantly successful. The wrong person was *not* killed. Very much the right person was.'

Moresby gaped.

'Why, how on earth do you make that out, sir?'

'Mrs Beresford was the objective all the time. That's why the plot was so ingenious. Everything was anticipated. It was perfectly natural that Sir William should hand the chocolates over to Beresford. It was foreseen that we should look for the criminal among Sir William's associates and not the dead woman's. It was probably even foreseen that the crime would be considered the work of a woman!'

Moresby, unable to wait any longer, snatched up the photograph.

'Good heavens! But Mr Sheringham, you don't mean to tell me that ... Sir William himself!'

'He wanted to get rid of Mrs Beresford,' Roger continued. 'He had liked her well enough at the beginning, no doubt, though it was her money he was after all the time.

'But the real trouble was that she was too close with her money. He wanted it, or some of it, pretty badly; and she wouldn't part. There's no doubt about the motive. I made a list of the firms he's interested in and got a report on them. They're all rocky, every one. He'd got through all his own money, and he had to get more.

'As for the nitrobenzine which puzzled us so much, that was simple enough. I looked it up and found that beside the uses you told me, it's used largely in perfumery. And he's got a perfumery business. The Anglo-Eastern Perfumery Company. That's how he'd know about it being poisonous, of course. But I shouldn't think he got his supply from there. He'd be cleverer than that. He probably made the stuff himself. And schoolboys know how to treat benzol with nitric acid to get nitrobenzine.'

'But,' stammered Moresby, 'but Sir William ... He was at Eton.'

'Sir William?' said Roger sharply. 'Who's talking about Sir William? I told you the photograph of the murderer was in my pocket.' He whipped out the photograph in question and confronted the astounded chief inspector with it. 'Beresford, man! Beresford's the murderer of his own wife.

'Beresford, who still had hankerings after a gay life,' he went on more mildly, 'didn't want his wife but did want her money. He contrived this plot, providing as he thought against every contingency that could possibly arise. He established a mild alibi, if suspicion ever should arise, by taking his wife to the Imperial, and slipped out of the theatre at the first interval. (I sat through the first act of the dreadful thing myself last night to see when the interval came.) Then he hurried down to the

Strand, posted his parcel, and took a taxi back. He had ten minutes, but nobody would notice if he got back to the box a minute late.

'And the rest simply followed. He knew Sir William came to the club every morning at ten-thirty, as regularly as clockwork; he knew that for a psychological certainty he could get the chocolates handed over to him if he hinted for them; he knew that the police would go chasing after all sorts of false trails starting from Sir William. And as for the wrapper and the forged letter he carefully didn't destroy them because they were calculated not only to divert suspicion but actually to point away from him to some anonymous lunatic.'

'Well, it's very smart of you, Mr Sheringham,' Moresby said, with a little sigh, but quite ungrudgingly. 'Very smart indeed. What was it the lady told you that showed you the whole thing in a flash?'

'Why, it wasn't so much what she actually told me as what I heard between her words, so to speak. What she told me was that Mrs Beresford knew the answer to that bet; what I deduced was that, being the sort of person she was, it was quite incredible that she should have made a bet to which she knew the answer. *Ergo*, she didn't. *Ergo*, there never was such a bet. *Ergo*, Beresford was lying. *Ergo*, Beresford wanted to get hold of those chocolates for some reason other than he stated. After all, we only had Beresford's word for the bet, hadn't we?

'Of course he wouldn't have left her that afternoon till he'd seen her take, or somehow made her take, at least six of the chocolates, more than a lethal dose. That's why the stuff was in those meticulous six-minim doses. And so that he could take a couple himself, of course. A clever stroke, that.'

Moresby rose to his feet.

'Well, Mr Sheringham, I'm much obliged to you sir. And now I shall have to get busy myself.' He scratched his head. 'Chance the Avenger, eh? Well, I can tell one pretty big thing Beresford left to Chance the Avenger, Mr Sheringham. Suppose Sir William hadn't handed over the chocolates after all? Supposing he'd kept 'em, to give to one of his own ladies?'

Roger positively snorted. He felt a personal pride in Beresford by this time.

'Really, Moresby! It wouldn't have had any serious results if Sir William had. Do give my man credit for being what he is. You don't imagine he sent the poisoned ones to Sir William, do you? Of course not! He'd send harmless ones, and exchanged them for the others on his way home. Dash it all, he wouldn't go right out of his way to present opportunities to Chance.

'If,' added Roger, 'Chance really is the right word.'

Sweets to the Sweet

Robert Bloch

Irma didn't look like a witch.

She had small, regular features, a peaches-and-cream complexion, blue eyes, and fair, almost ash-blonde hair. Besides, she was only eight years old.

'Why does he tease her so?' sobbed Miss Pall. 'That's where she got the idea in the first place – because he calls her a little witch.'

Sam Steever bulked his paunch back into the squeaky swivel chair and folded his heavy hands in his lap. His fat lawyer's mask was immobile, but he was really quite distressed.

Women like Miss Pall should never sob. Their glasses wiggle, their thin noses twitch, their creasy eyelids redden, and their stringy hair becomes disarrayed.

'Please, control yourself,' coaxed Sam Steever. 'Perhaps if we could just talk this whole thing over sensibly—'

'I don't care!' Miss Pall sniffled. 'I'm not going back there again. I can't stand it. There's nothing I can do, anyway. The man is your brother and she's your brother's child. It's not my responsibility. I've tried—'

'Of course you've tried.' Sam Steever smiled benignly, as if Miss Pall were foreman of a jury. 'I quite understand. But I still don't see why you are so upset, dear lady.'

Miss Pall removed her spectacles, and dabbed at her eyes with a floral-print handkerchief. Then she deposited the soggy ball in her purse, snapped the catch, replaced her spectacles, and sat up straight.

'Very well, Mr Steever,' she said. 'I shall do my best to acquaint you with my reasons for quitting your brother's employ.'

She suppressed a tardy sniff.

'I came to John Steever two years ago in response to an advertisement for a housekeeper, as you know. When I found that I was to be governess to a motherless six-year-old child, I was at first distressed. I know nothing of the care of children.'

'John had a nurse the first years,' Sam Steever nodded. 'You know Irma's mother died in childbirth.'

'I am aware of that,' said Miss Pall, primly. 'Naturally, one's heart goes out to a lonely, neglected little girl. And she was so terribly lonely, Mr Steever – if you could have seen her, moping around in the corners of that big, ugly old house—'

'I have seen her,' said Sam Steever, hastily, hoping to forestall another outburst. 'And I know what you've done for Irma. My brother is inclined to be thoughtless, even a bit selfish at times. He doesn't understand.'

'He's cruel,' declared Miss Pall, suddenly vehement. 'Cruel and wicked. Even if he is your brother, I say he's no fit father for any child. When I came there, her little arms were black and blue from beatings. He used to take a belt—'

'I know. Sometimes, I think John never recovered from the shock of Mrs Steever's death. That's why I was so pleased when you came, dear lady. I thought you might help the situation.'

'I tried,' Miss Pall whimpered. 'You know I tried. I never raised a hand to that child in two years, though many's the time your brother has told me to punish her. "Give the little witch a beating" he used to say. "That's all she needs – a good thrashing". And then she'd hide behind my back and whisper to me to protect her. But she wouldn't cry, Mr Steever. Do you know, I've never seen her cry.'

Sam Steever felt vaguely irritated and a bit bored. He wished the old hen would get on with it. So he smiled and oozed treacle. 'But just what is your problem, dear lady?'

'Everything was all right when I came there. We got along just splendidly. I started to teach Irma to read – and was surprised to find that she had already mastered reading. Your brother disclaimed having taught her, but she spent hours curled up on the sofa with a book. "Just like her," he used to say. "Unnatural little witch. Doesn't play with the other children. Little witch". That's the way he kept talking, Mr Steever. As if she were some sort of – I don't know what. And she so sweet and quiet and pretty!

'Is it any wonder she read? I used to be that way myself when I was a girl, because – but never mind.

'Still, it was a shock that day I found her looking through the *Encyclopaedia Britannica*. "What are you reading, Irma?" I asked. She showed me. It was the article on Witchcraft.

'You see what morbid thoughts your brother has inculcated in her poor little head?

'I did my best. I went out and bought her some toys – she had absolutely nothing, you know; not even a doll. She didn't even know how to *play*! I tried to get her interested in some of the other little girls in the neighbourhood, but it was no use. They didn't understand her and she didn't understand them. There were scenes. Children can be cruel, thoughtless. And her father wouldn't let her go to public school. I was to teach her—

'Then I brought her the modelling clay. She liked that. She would spend hours just making faces with clay. For a child of six Irma displayed real talent.

'We made little dolls together, and I sewed clothes for them. That first year was a happy one, Mr Steever. Particularly during those months when your brother was away in South America. But this year, when he came back – oh, I can't bear to talk about it!'

'Please,' said Sam Steever. 'You must understand. John is not a happy man. The loss of his wife, the decline of his import trade, and his drinking – but you know all that.'

'All I know is that he hates Irma,' snapped Miss Pall, suddenly. 'He hates her. He wants her to be bad, so he can whip her. "If you don't discipline the little witch, I shall," he always says. And then he takes her upstairs and thrashes her with his belt – you must do something, Mr Steever, or I'll go to the authorities myself.'

The crazy old biddy would at that, Sam Steever thought. Remedy – more treacle. 'But about Irma,' he persisted.

'She's changed, too. Ever since her father returned this year. She won't play with me any more, hardly looks at me. It is as though I failed her, Mr Steever, in not protecting her from that man. Besides – she thinks she's a witch.'

Crazy. Stark, staring crazy. Sam Steever creaked upright in his chair.

'Oh you needn't look at me like that, Mr Steever. She'll tell you so herself – if you ever visited the house!'

He caught the reproach in her voice and assuaged it with a deprecating nod.

'She told me all right, if her father wants her to be a witch she'll be a witch. And she won't play with me, or anyone else, because witches don't play. Last Halloween she wanted me to give her a broomstick. Oh, it would be funny if it weren't so tragic. That child is losing her sanity.

'Just a few weeks ago I thought she'd changed. That's when she asked me to take her to church one Sunday. "I want to see the baptism," she said. Imagine that – an eight-year-old interested in baptism! Reading too much, that's what does it.

'Well, we went to church and she was as sweet as can be, wearing her new blue dress and holding my hand. I was proud of her, Mr Steever, really proud.

'But after that, she went right back into her shell. Reading around the house, running through the yard at twilight and talking to herself.

'Perhaps it's because your brother wouldn't bring her a kitten. She was pestering him for a black cat, and he asked why, and she said,

"Because witches always have black cats". Then he took her upstairs.

'I can't stop him, you know. He beat her again the night the power failed and we couldn't find the candles. He said she'd stolen them. Imagine that – accusing an eight-year-old child of stealing candles!

'That was the beginning of the end. Then today, when he found his hairbrush missing—'

'You say he beat her with his hairbrush?'

'Yes. She admitted having stolen it. Said she wanted it for her doll.'

'But didn't you say she has no dolls?'

'She made one. At least I think she did. I've never seen it – she won't show us anything any more; won't talk to us at table, just impossible to handle her.

'But this doll she made – it's a small one, I know, because at times she carries it tucked under her arm. She talks to it and pets it, but she won't show it to me or to him. He asked her about the hairbrush and she said she took it for the doll.

'Your brother flew into a terrible rage – he'd been drinking in his room again all morning, oh don't think I don't know it! – and she just smiled and said he could have it now. She went over to her bureau and handed it to him. She hadn't harmed it in the least; his hair was still in it, I noticed.

'But he snatched it up, and then he started to strike her about the shoulders with it, and he twisted her arm and then he—'

Miss Pall huddled in her chair and summoned great racking sobs from her thin chest.

Sam Steever patted her shoulder, fussing about her like an elephant over a wounded canary.

'That's all, Mr Steever. I came right to you. I'm not even going back to that house to get my things. I can't stand any more – the way he beat her – and the way she didn't cry, just giggled and giggled and giggled – sometimes I think she *is* a witch – that he made her into a witch—'

Sam Steever picked up the phone. The ringing had broken the relief of silence after Miss Pall's hasty departure.

'Hello – that you Sam?'

He recognized his brother's voice, somewhat the worse for drink.

'Yes, John.'

'I suppose the old bat came running straight to you to shoot her mouth off.'

'If you mean Miss Pall, I've seen her, yes.'

'Pay no attention. I can explain everything.'

'Do you want me to stop in? I haven't paid you a visit in months.'

'Well – not right now. Got an appointment with the doctor this evening.'

'Something wrong?'

'Pain in my arm. Rheumatism or something. Getting a little diathermy. But I'll call you tomorrow and we'll straighten this whole mess out.'

'Right.'

But John Steever did not call the next day. Along about supper time, Sam called him.

Surprisingly enough, Irma answered the phone. Her thin, squeaky little voice sounded faintly in Sam's ears.

'Daddy's upstairs sleeping. He's been sick.'

'Well don't disturb him. What is it – his arm?'

'His back, now. He has to go to the doctor again in a little while.'

'Tell him I'll call tomorrow, then. Uh – everything all right, Irma? I mean, don't you miss Miss Pall?'

'No, I'm glad she went away. She's stupid.'

'Oh. Yes. I see. But you phone me if you want anything. And I hope your Daddy's better.'

'Yes. So do I,' said Irma, and then she began to giggle and then she hung up.

There was no giggling the following afternoon when John Steever called Sam at the office. His voice was sober – with the sharp sobriety of pain.

'Sam – for God's sake, get over here. Something's happening to me!'

'What's the trouble?'

'The pain – it's killing me! I've got to see you, quickly.'

'There's a client in the office, but I'll get rid of him. Say, wait a minute. Why don't you call the doctor?'

'That quack can't help me. He gave me diathermy for my arm and yesterday he did the same thing for my back.'

'Didn't it help?'

'The pain went away, yes. But it's back now. I feel – like I was being crushed. Squeezed, here in the chest. I can't breathe.'

'Sounds like pleurisy. Why don't you call him?'

'It isn't pleurisy. He examined me. Said I was sound as a dollar. No, there's nothing organically wrong. And I couldn't tell him the real cause.'

'Real cause?'

'Yes. The pins. The pins that little fiend is sticking into the doll she made. Into the arm, the back. And now heaven only knows how she's causing *this*.'

'John you mustn't—'

'Oh what's the use of talking? I can't move off the bed here. She has me now. I can't go down and stop her, get hold of the doll. And nobody else would believe it. But it's the doll all right, the one she made with the candle-wax and the hair from my brush. Oh – it hurts to talk – that cursed little witch! Hurry, Sam. Promise me you'll do something – anything – get that doll from her – get that doll—'

Half an hour later, at four-thirty, Sam Steever entered his brother's house.

Irma opened the door.

It gave Sam a shock to see her standing there, smiling and unperturbed, pale blonde hair brushed immaculately back from the rosy oval of her face. She looked just like a little doll. A little doll. . . .

'Hello, Uncle Sam.'

'Hello, Irma. Your Daddy called me, did he tell you? He said he wasn't feeling well—'

'I know. But he's all right now. He's sleeping.'

Something happened to Sam Steever; a drop of ice-water trickled down his spine.

'Sleeping?' he croaked. 'Upstairs?'

Before she opened her mouth to answer he was bounding up the steps to the second floor, striding down the hall to John's bedroom.

John lay on the bed. He was asleep, and only asleep. Sam Steever noted the regular rise and fall of his chest as he breathed. His face was calm, relaxed.

Then the drop of ice-water evaporated, and Sam could afford to smile and murmur 'Nonsense' under his breath as he turned away.

As he went downstairs he hastily improvised plans. A six-month vacation for his brother; avoid calling it a 'cure'. An orphanage for Irma; give her a chance to get away from this morbid old house, all those books . . .

He paused halfway down the stairs. Peering over the banister through the twilight he saw Irma on the sofa, cuddled up like a little white ball. She was talking to something she cradled in her arms, rocking it to and fro.

Then there was a doll, after all.

Sam Steever tiptoed very quietly down the stairs and walked over to Irma.

'Hello,' he said.

She jumped. Both arms rose to cover completely whatever it was she had been fondling. She squeezed it tightly.

Sam Steever thought of a doll being squeezed across the chest. . . .

Irma stared up at him, her face a mask of innocence. In the halflight her face did resemble a mask. The mask of a little girl covering – what?

'Daddy's better now, isn't he?' lisped Irma.

'Yes, much better.'

'I knew he would be.'

'But I'm afraid he's going to have to go away for a rest. A long rest.'

A smile filtered through the mask. 'Good,' said Irma.

'Of course,' Sam went on, 'you couldn't stay here all alone. I was wondering – maybe we could send you off to school, or to some kind of a home—'

Irma giggled. 'Oh, you needn't worry about me,' she said. She shifted about on the sofa as Sam sat down, then sprang up quickly as he came close to her.

Her arms shifted with the movement, and Sam Steever saw a pair of tiny legs dangling down below her elbow. There were trousers on the legs, and little bits of leather for shoes.

'What's that you have, Irma?' he asked. 'Is it a doll?' Slowly, he extended his pudgy hand.

She pulled back.

'You can't see it,' she said.

'But I want to. Miss Pall said you made such lovely ones.'

'Miss Pall is stupid. So are you. Go away.'

'Please, Irma. Let me see it.'

But even as he spoke, Sam Steever was staring at the top of the doll, momentarily revealed when she backed away. It was a head all right, with wisps of hair over a white face. Dusk dimmed the features, but Sam recognized the eyes, the nose, the chin. . . .

He could keep up the pretence no longer.

'Give me that doll, Irma!' he snapped. 'I know what it is. I know *who* it is—'

For an instant, the mask slipped from Irma's face, and Sam Steever stared into naked fear.

She knew. She knew he knew.

Then, just as quickly, the mask was replaced.

Irma was only a sweet, spoiled, stubborn little girl as she shook her head merrily and smiled with impish mischief in her eyes.

'Oh Uncle Sam,' she giggled. 'You're so silly! Why, this isn't a *real* doll.'

'What is it, then?' he muttered.

Irma giggled once more, raising the figure as she spoke. 'Why, it's only – candy!' Irma said.

'Candy?'

Irma nodded. Then, very swiftly, she slipped the tiny head of the image into her mouth.

And bit it off.

There was a single piercing scream from upstairs.

As Sam Steever turned and ran up the steps, little Irma, still gravely munching, skipped out of the front door and into the night beyond.

Nightmare in Yellow

Fredric Brown

He awoke when the alarm clock rang, but lay in bed awhile after he'd shut it off, going a final time over the plans he'd made for embezzlement that day and for murder that evening.

Every little detail had been worked out, but this was the final check. Tonight at forty-six minutes after eight he'd be free, in every way. He'd picked that moment because this was his fortieth birthday and that was the exact time of day, of the evening rather, when he had been born. His mother had been an astrology fanatic, which was why the moment of his birth had been impressed on him so exactly. He wasn't superstitious himself but it had struck his sense of humour to have his new life begin at forty, to the minute.

Time was running out on him, in any case. As a lawyer who specialized in handling wills, a lot of money passed through his hands – and some of it had passed into them. A year ago he'd 'borrowed' five thousand dollars to put into something that looked like a sure-fire way to double or triple the money, but he'd lost it instead. Then he'd 'borrowed' more to gamble with, in one way or another, to try to recover the first loss. Now he was behind to the tune of over thirty thousand; the shortage couldn't be hidden more than another few months and there wasn't a hope that he could replace the missing money by that time. So he had been raising all the cash he could without arousing suspicion, by carefully selling property, and by this afternoon he'd have running-away money to the tune of well over a hundred thousand dollars, enough to last him the rest of his life.

And they'd never catch him. He'd planned every detail of his trip, his destination, his new identity, and it was foolproof. He'd been working on it for months.

His decision to kill his wife had been relatively an afterthought. The motive was simple: he hated her. But it was only after he'd come to the decision that he'd never go to jail, that he'd kill himself if he was ever picked up, that it came to him that – since he'd die anyway if caught – he had nothing to lose in leaving a dead wife behind him instead of a living one.

He'd hardly been able to keep from laughing at the appropriateness of the birthday present she'd given him (yesterday, a day ahead of time); it had been a new suitcase. She'd also talked him into celebrating his birthday by letting her meet him downtown for dinner at seven. Little did she guess how the celebration would go after that. He planned to have her home by eight forty-six and satisfy his sense of the fitness of things by making himself a widower at that exact moment. There was a practical advantage, too, in leaving her dead. If he left her alive but asleep, she'd guess what had happened and call the police when she found him gone in the morning. If he left her dead, her body would not be found that soon, possibly not for two or three days, and he'd have a much better start.

Things went smoothly at his office; by the time he went to meet his wife everything was ready. But she dawdled over drinks and dinner and he began to worry whether he could get her home by eight forty-six. It was ridiculous, he knew, but it had become important that his moment of freedom should come then and not a minute earlier or a minute later. He watched his watch.

He would have missed it by half a minute if he'd waited till they were inside the house. But the dark of the porch of their house was perfectly safe, as safe as inside. He swung the cosh viciously once, as she stood at the front door, waiting for him to open it. He caught her before she fell and managed to hold her upright with one arm while he got the door open and then got it closed from the inside.

Then he flicked the switch and yellow light leaped to fill the room, and, before they could see that his wife was dead and that he was holding her up, all the assembled birthday party guests shouted 'SURPRISE!'

The Hands of Mr Ottermole

Thomas Burke

At six o'clock of a January evening Mr Whybrow was walking home through the cobweb alleys of London's East End. He had left the golden clamour of the great High Street to which the tram had brought him from the river and his daily work, and was now in the chess-board of byways that is called Mallon End. None of the rush and gleam of the High Street trickled into these byways. A few paces south – a flood-tide of life, foaming and beating. Here – only slow shuffling figures and muffled pulses. He was in the sink of London, the last refuge of European vagrants.

As though in tune with the street's spirit, he too walked slowly, with head down. It seemed that he was pondering some pressing trouble, but he was not. He had no trouble. He was walking slowly because he had been on his feet all day, and he was bent in abstraction because he was wondering whether the Missis would have herrings for his tea, or haddock; and he was trying to decide which would be the more tasty on a night like this. A wretched night it was, of damp and mist, and the mist wandered into his throat and his eyes, and the damp had settled on pavement and roadway, and where the sparse lamplight fell it sent up a greasy sparkle that chilled one to look at. By contrast it made his speculation more agreeable, and made him ready for that tea – whether herring or haddock. His eye turned from the glum bricks that made his horizon, and went forward half a mile. He saw a gas-lit kitchen, a flamy fire and a spread tea-table. There was toast in the hearth and a singing kettle on the side and a piquant effusion of herrings, or maybe of haddock, or perhaps sausages. The vision gave his aching feet a throb of energy. He shook imperceptible damp from his shoulders, and hastened towards its reality.

But Mr Whybrow wasn't going to get any tea that evening – or any other evening. Mr Whybrow was going to die. Somewhere within a hundred yards of him another man was walking: a man much like Mr Whybrow and much like any other man, but without the only quality that enables mankind to live peaceably together and not as madmen in a jungle. A man with a dead heart eating into itself and bringing forth the foul organisms that arise from death and corruption. And that thing in man's shape, on a whim or a settled idea – one cannot know – had said within himself that Mr Whybrow should never taste another herring. Not that Mr Whybrow had injured him. Not that he had any dislike of Mr Whybrow. Indeed, he knew nothing of him save as a familiar figure about the streets. But, moved by a force that had taken possession of his empty cells, he had picked on Mr Whybrow with that blind choice that makes us pick one restaurant table that has nothing to mark it from four or five other tables, or one apple from a dish of half a dozen equal apples; or that drives Nature to send a cyclone upon one corner of this planet, and destroy five hundred lives in that corner, and leave another five hundred in the same corner unharmed. So this man had picked on Mr Whybrow, as he might have picked on you or me, had we been within his daily observation; and even now he was creeping through the blue-toned streets, nursing his large white hands, moving ever closer to Mr Whybrow's tea-table, and so closer to Mr Whybrow himself.

He wasn't, this man, a bad man. Indeed, he had many of the social and amiable qualities, and passed as a respectable man, as most successful criminals do. But the thought had come into his mouldering mind that he would like to murder somebody, and, as he held no fear of God or man, he was going to do it, and would then go home to *his* tea. I don't say that flippantly, but as a statement of fact. Strange as it may seem to the humane, murderers must and do sit down to meals after a murder. There is no reason why they shouldn't, and many reasons why they should. For one thing, they need to keep their physical and mental vitality at full beat for the business of covering their crime. For another, the strain of their effort makes them hungry, and satisfaction at the accomplishment of a desired thing brings a feeling of relaxation towards human pleasures. It is accepted among non-murderers that the murderer is always overcome by fear for his safety and horror at his act; but this type is rare. His own safety is, of course, his immediate concern, but vanity is a marked quality of most murderers, and that, together with the thrill of conquest, makes him confident that he can secure it, and when he has restored his strength with food he goes about securing it as a young hostess goes about the arranging of her first big dinner – a little anxious, but no more. Criminologists and detectives tell us that *every* murderer, however intelligent or cunning, always makes one slip in his tactics – one little slip that brings the affair home to him. But that is only half true. It is true only of the murderers who are caught. Scores of murderers are not caught: therefore scores of murderers do not make any mistake at all. This man didn't.

As for horror or remorse, prison chaplains, doctors, and lawyers have told us that of murderers they have interviewed under condemnation and the shadow of death, only one here and there has expressed any contrition for his act, or shown any sign of mental misery. Most of them display only exasperation at having been caught when so many have gone undiscovered, or indignation at being condemned for a perfectly reasonable act. However normal and humane they may have been before the murder, they are utterly without conscience after it. For what is conscience? Simply a polite nickname for superstition, which is a polite nickname for fear. Those who associate remorse with murder are, no doubt, basing their ideas on the world-legend of the remorse of Cain, or are projecting their own frail minds into the mind of the murderer, and getting false reactions. Peaceable folk cannot hope to make contact with this mind, for they are not merely different in mental type from the murderer: they are different in their personal chemistry and construction. Some men can and do kill, not one man, but two or three, and go calmly about their daily affairs. Other men could not, under the most agonizing provocation, bring themselves even to wound. It is men of this sort who imagine the murderer in torments of remorse and fear of the law, whereas he is actually sitting down to his tea.

The man with the large white hands was as ready for his tea as Mr Whybrow was, but he had something to do before he went to it. When he had done that something, and made no mistake about it, he would be even more ready for it, and would go to it as comfortably as he went to it the day before, when his hands were stainless.

Walk on, then Mr Whybrow, walk on; and as you walk, look your last upon the familar features of your nightly journey. Follow your jack-o'-lantern tea-table. Look well upon its warmth and colour and kindness; feed your eyes with it, and tease your nose with its gentle domestic odours; for you will never sit down to it. Within ten minutes' pacing of you a pursuing phantom has spoken in his heart, and you are doomed. There you go – you and phantom – two nebulous dabs of mortality, moving through green air along pavements of powder-blue, the one to kill, the other to be killed. Walk on. Don't annoy your burning feet by hurrying, for the more slowly you walk, the longer you will breathe the green air of this January dusk, and see the dreamy lamplight and the little shops, and hear the agreeable commerce of the London crowd and the haunting pathos of the street-organ. These things are dear to you, Mr Whybrow. You don't know it now, but in fifteen minutes you will have two seconds in which to realize how inexpressibly dear they are.

Walk on, then, across this crazy chess-board. You are in Lagos Street now, among the tents of the wanderers of Eastern Europe. A minute or so, and you are in Loyal Lane, among the lodging-houses that shelter

the useless and the beaten of London's camp-followers. The lane holds
the smell of them, and its soft darkness seems heavy with the wail of
the futile. But you are not sensitive to impalpable things, and you plod
through it, unseeing, as you do every evening, and come to Blean Street,
and plod through that. From basement to sky rise the tenements of an
alien colony. Their windows slit the ebony of their walls with lemon.
Behind those windows strange life is moving, dressed with forms that
are not of London or of England, yet, in essence, the same agreeable
life that you have been living, and tonight will live no more. From high
above you comes a voice crooning *The Song of Katta*. Through a window
you see a family keeping a religious rite. Through another you see a
woman pouring out tea for her husband. You see a man mending a
pair of boots; a mother bathing her baby. You have seen all these things
before, and never noticed them. You do not notice them now, but if
you knew that you were never going to see them again, not because
your life has run its natural course, but because a man whom you have
often passed in the street has at his own solitary pleasure decided to
usurp the awful authority of nature, and destroy you. So perhaps it's
as well that you don't notice them, for your part in them is ended. No
more for you these pretty moments of our earthly travail: only one
moment of terror, and then a plunging darkness.

Closer to you this shadow of massacre moves, and now he is twenty
yards behind you. You can hear his footfalls, but you do not turn your
head. You are familiar with footfalls. You are in London, in the easy
security of your daily territory, and footfalls behind you, your instinct
tells you, are no more than a message of human company.

But can't you hear something in those footfalls – something that goes
with a widdershins beat? Something that says: *Look out, look out. Beware,
beware*. Can't you hear the very syllables of *murd-er-er, murd-er-er*? No;
there is nothing in footfalls. They are neutral. The foot of villainy falls
with the same quiet note as the foot of honesty. But those footfalls, Mr
Whybrow, are bearing on to you a pair of hands, and there *is* something
in hands. Behind you that pair of hands is even now stretching its muscles
in preparation for your end. Every minute of your days you have been
seeing human hands. Have you ever realized the sheer horror of hands
– those appendages that are a symbol of our moments of trust and affection and salutation? Have you thought of the sickening potentialities
that lie within the scope of that five-tentacled member? No, you never
have; for all the human hands that you have seen have been stretched
to you in kindness or fellowship. Yet, though the eyes can hate, and
the lips can sting, it is only that dangling member that can gather the
accumulated essence of evil, and electrify it into currents of destruction.
Satan may enter into man by many doors, but in the hands alone can
he find the servants of his will.

Another minute, Mr Whybrow, and you will know all about the horror of human hands.

You are nearly home now. You have turned into your street – Caspar Street – and you are in the centre of the chess-board. You can see the front window of your little four-roomed house. The street is dark, and its three lamps give only a smut of light that is more confusing than darkness. It is dark – empty, too. Nobody about; no lights in the front parlours of the houses, for the families are at tea in their kitchens; and only a random glow in a few upper rooms occupied by lodgers. Nobody about but you and your following companion, and you don't notice him. You see him so often that he is never seen. Even if you turned your head and saw him, you would only say 'Good evening' to him, and walk on. A suggestion that he was a possible murderer would not even make you laugh. It would be too silly.

And now you are at your gate. And now you have found your door key. And now you are in, and hanging up your hat and coat. The Missis has just called a greeting from the kitchen, whose smell is an echo of that greeting (herring!) and you have answered it, when the door shakes under a sharp knock.

Go away, Mr Whybrow. Go away from that door. Don't touch it. Get right away from it. Get out of the house. Run with the Missis to the back garden, and over the fence. Or call the neighbours. But don't touch that door. Don't, Mr Whybrow, don't open . . .

Mr Whybrow opened the door.

That was the beginning of what became known as London's Strangling Horrors. Horrors they were called because they were something more than murders: they were motiveless, and there was an air of black magic about them. Each murder was committed at a time when the street where the bodies were found was empty of any perceptible or possible murderer. There would be an empty alley. There would be a policeman at its end. He would turn his back on the empty alley for less than a minute. Then he would look round and run into the night with news of another strangling. And in any direction he looked nobody to be seen and no report to be had of anybody being seen. Or he would be on duty in a long quiet street, and suddenly be called to a house of dead people whom a few seconds earlier he had seen alive. And, again, whichever way he looked nobody to be seen; and although police whistles put an immediate cordon around the area, and all houses were searched, no possible murderer to be found.

The first news of the murder of Mr and Mrs Whybrow was brought by the station sergeant. He had been walking through Caspar Street on his way to the station for duty, when he noticed the open door of No. 98. Glancing in, he saw by the gaslight of the passage a motionless

body on the floor. After a second look he blew his whistle, and when
the constables answered him he took one to join him in a search
of the house, and sent others to watch all neighbouring streets, and make
inquiries at adjoining houses. But neither in the house nor in the streets
was anything found to indicate the murderer. Neighbours on either side,
and opposite, were questioned, but they had seen nobody about, and
had heard nothing. One had heard Mr Whybrow come home – the
scrape of his latchkey in the door was so regular an evening sound, he
said, that you could set your watch by it for half-past six – but he had
heard nothing more than the sound of the opening door until the sergeant's whistle. Nobody had been seen to enter the house or leave it,
by front or back, and the necks of the dead people carried no finger-
prints or other traces. A nephew was called in to go over the house,
but he could find nothing missing; and anyway his uncle possessed
nothing worth stealing. The little money in the house was untouched,
and there were no signs of any disturbance of the property, or even
of struggle. No signs of anything but brutal and wanton murder.

Mr Whybrow was known to neighbours and work-mates as a quiet,
likeable, home-loving man; such a man as could not have any enemies.
But, then, murdered men seldom have. A relentless enemy who hates
a man to the point of wanting to hurt him seldom wants to murder
him, since to do that puts him beyond suffering. So the police were
left with an impossible situation: no clue to the murderer and no motive
for the murders; only the fact that they had been done.

The first news of the affair sent a tremor through London generally,
and an electric thrill through all Mallon End. Here was murder of two
inoffensive people, not for gain and not for revenge; and the murderer,
to whom, apparently, killing was a casual impulse, was at large. He
had left no traces, and, provided he had no companions, there seemed
no reason why he should not remain at large. Any clear-headed man
who stands alone, and has no fear of God or man, can, if he chooses,
hold a city, even a nation, in subjection; but your everyday criminal
is seldom clear-headed, and dislikes being lonely. He needs, if not the
support of confederates, at least somebody to talk to; his vanity needs
the satisfaction of perceiving at first hand the effect of his work. For
this he will frequent bars and coffee-shops and other public places. Then,
sooner or later, in a glow of comradeship, he will utter the one word
too much; and the nark, who is everywhere, has an easy job.

But though the doss-houses and saloons and other places were
'combed' and set with watches, and it was made known by whispers
that good money and protection were assured to those with information,
nothing attaching to the Whybrow case could be found. The murderer
clearly had no friends and kept no company. Known men of this type
were called up and questioned, but each was able to give a good account

of himself; and in a few days the police were at a dead end. Against the constant public gibe that the thing had been done almost under their noses, they became restive, and for four days each man of the force was working his daily beat under a strain. On the fifth day they became still more restive.

It was the season of annual teas and entertainments for the children of the Sunday Schools, and on an evening of fog, when London was a world of groping phantoms, a small girl, in the bravery of best Sunday frock and shoes, shining face and new-washed hair, set out from Logan Passage of St Michael's Parish Hall. She never got there. She was not actually dead until half-past six, but she was as good as dead from the moment she left her mother's door. Somebody like a man, pacing the street from which the Passage led, saw her come out; and from that moment she was dead. Through the fog somebody's large white hands reached after her, and in fifteen minutes they were about her.

At half-past six a whistle screamed trouble, and those answering it found the body of little Nellie Vrinoff in a warehouse entry in Minnow Street. The sergeant was first among them, and he posted his men to useful points, ordering them here and there in the tart tones of repressed rage, and berating the officer whose beat the street was. 'I saw you, Magson, at the end of the lane. What were you up to there? You were there ten minutes before you turned.' Magson began an explanation about keeping an eye on a suspicious-looking character at that end, but the sergeant cut him short; 'Suspicious characters be damned. You don't want to look for suspicious characters. You want to look for *murderers*. Messing about ... and then this happens right where you ought to be. Now think what they'll say.'

With the speed of ill news came the crowd, pale and perturbed; and on the story that the unknown monster had appeared again, and this time to a child, their faces streaked the fog with spots of hate and horror. But then came the ambulance and more police, and swiftly they broke up the crowd; and as it broke the sergeant's thought was thickened into words, and from all sides came low murmurs of 'Right under their noses.' Later inquiries showed that four people of the district, above suspicion, had passed that entry at intervals of seconds before the murder, and seen nothing and heard nothing. None of them had passed the child alive or seen her dead. None of them had seen anybody in the street except themselves. Again the police were left with no motive and with no clue.

And now the district, as you will remember, was given over, not to panic, for the London public never yields to that, but to apprehension and dismay. If these things were happening in their familiar streets, then anything might happen. Wherever people met – in the streets, the markets and the shops – they debated the one topic. Women took to bolting their windows and doors at the first fall of dusk. They kept their children closely under their eye. They did their shopping before dark, and watched anxiously, while pretending they weren't watching, for the return of their husbands from work. Under the Cockney's semi-humorous resignation to disaster, they hid an hourly foreboding. By the whim of one man with a pair of hands the structure and tenor of their daily life were shaken, as they always can be shaken by any man con-temptuous of humanity and fearless of its laws. They began to realize that the pillars that supported the peaceable society in which they lived were mere straws that anybody could snap; that laws were powerful only so long as they were obeyed; that the police were potent only so long as they were feared. By the power of his hands this one man had made a whole community do something new: he had made it think, and left it gasping at the obvious.

And then, while it was yet gasping under his first two strokes, he made his third. Conscious of the horror that his hands had created, and hungry as an actor who has once tasted the thrill of the multitude, he made fresh advertisement of his presence; and on Wednesday morning, three days after the murder of the child, the papers carried to the breakfast-tables of England the story of a still more shocking outrage.

At 9.32 on Tuesday night a constable was on duty in Jarnigan Road, and at that time spoke to a fellow-officer named Peterson at the top of Clemming Street. He had seen this officer walk down that street. He could swear that the street was empty at that time, except for a lame boot-black whom he knew by sight, and who passed him and entered a tenement on the side opposite that on which his fellow-officer was walking. He had the habit, as all constables had just then, of looking constantly behind him and around him, whichever way he was walking, and he was certain that the street was empty. He passed his sergeant at 9.33, saluted him, and answered his inquiry for anything seen. He reported that he had seen nothing, and passed on. His beat ended at a short distance from Clemming Street, and, having paced it, he turned and came again at 9.34 to the top of the street. He had scarcely reached it before he heard the hoarse voice of the sergeant: 'Gregory! You there? Quick. Here's another. My God, it's Peterson! Garrotted. Quick, call 'em up!'

That was the third of the Strangling Horrors, of which there were to be a fourth and a fifth; and the five horrors were to pass into the unknown and unknowable. That is, unknown as far as authority and the public were concerned. The identity of the murderer *was* known, but to two men only. One was the murderer himself; the other was a young journalist.

This young man, who was covering the affairs for his paper, the *Daily Torch*, was no smarter than the other zealous newspaper men who were hanging about these byways in the hope of a sudden story. But he was patient, and he hung a little closer to the case than the other fellows, and by continually staring at it he at last raised the figure of the murderer like a genie from the stones on which he had stood to do his murders.

After the first few days the men had given up any attempt at exclusive stories, for there was none to be had. They met regularly at the police station, and what little information there was they shared. The officials were agreeable to them, but no more. The sergeant discussed with them the details of each murder; suggested possible explanations of the man's methods; recalled from the past those cases that had some similarity; and on the matter of motive reminded them of the motiveless Neil Cream and the wanton John Williams, and hinted that work was being done which would soon bring the business to an end; but about that work he would not say a word. The inspector, too, was gracefully garrulous on the theme of murder, but whenever one of the party edged the talk towards what was being done in this immediate matter, he glided past it. Whatever the officials knew, they were not giving it to newspaper men. The business had fallen heavily upon them, and only by a capture made by their own efforts could they rehabilitate themselves in official and public esteem. Scotland Yard, of course, was at work, and had all the station's material; but the station's hope was that they themselves would have the honour of settling the affair; and however useful the co-operation of the Press might be in other cases they did not want to risk a defeat by a premature disclosure of their theories and plans.

So the sergeant talked at large, and propounded one interesting theory after another, all of which the newspaper men had thought of themselves.

The young man soon gave up these morning lectures on the Philosophy of Crime, and took to wandering about the streets and making bright stories out of the effect of the murders on the normal life of the people. A melancholy job was made more melancholy by the district. The littered roadways, the crestfallen houses, the bleared windows – all held the acid misery that evokes no sympathy: the misery of the frustrated poet. The misery was the creation of the aliens, who were living in this makeshift fashion because they had no settled homes, and would neither take the trouble to make a home where they *could* settle, nor get on with their wandering.

There was little to be picked up. All he saw and heard were indignant faces and wild conjectures of the murderer's identity and of the secret of his trick of appearing and disappearing unseen. Since a policeman himself had fallen a victim, denunciations of the force had ceased, and the unknown was now invested with a cloak of legend. Men eyed other men, as though thinking: It might be *him*. It might be *him*. They were no longer looking for a man who had the air of a Madame

Tussaud murderer; they were looking for a man, or perhaps some harridan woman, who had done these particular murders. Their thoughts
ran mainly on the foreign set. Such ruffianism could scarcely belong
to England, nor could the bewildering cleverness of the thing. So they
turned to Rumanian gipsies and Turkish carpet-sellers. There, clearly,
would be found the 'warm' spot. These Eastern fellows – they knew
all sorts of tricks, and they had no real religion – nothing to hold them
within bounds. Sailors returning from those parts had told tales of con-
jurors who made themselves invisible; and there were tales of Egyptian
and Arab potions that were used for abysmally queer purposes. Perhaps
it *was* possible to them; you never knew. They were so slick and cunning,
and they had such gliding movements; no Englishman could melt away
as they could. Almost certainly the murderer would be found to be one
of that sort – with some dark trick of his own – and just because they
were sure that he *was* a magician, they felt that it was useless to look
for him. He was a power, able to hold them in subjection and to hold
himself untouchable. Superstition, which so easily cracks the frail shell
of reason, had got into them. He could do anything he chose; he would
never be discovered. These two points they settled, and they went about
the streets in a mood of resentful fatalism.

They talked of their ideas to the journalist in half-tones, looking right
and left, as though *HE* might overhear them and visit them. And though
all the district was thinking of him and ready to pounce upon him, yet,
so strongly had he worked upon them, that if any man in the street – say,
a small man of commonplace features and form – had cried '*I* am the
monster!' would their stifled fury have broken into flood and have borne
him down and engulfed him? Or would they not suddenly have seen
something unearthly in that everyday face and figure, something unearthly about his hat, something that marked him as one whom none of
their weapons could alarm or pierce? And would they not momentarily
have fallen back from this devil, as the devil fell back from the cross made
by the sword of Faust, and so have given him time to escape? I do not
know; but so fixed was their belief in his invincibility that it is at least
likely that they would have made this hesitation, had such an occasion
arisen. But it never did. Today this commonplace fellow, his murder-lust
glutted, is still seen and observed among them as he was seen and
observed all the time; but because nobody then dreamt, or now dreams,
that he was what he was, they observed him then, and observe him now,
as people observe a lamp-post.

Almost was their belief in his invincibility justified; for five days after
the murder of the policeman Petersen, when the experience and
inspiration of the whole detective force of London were turned towards
his identification and capture, he made his fourth and fifth strokes.

At nine o'clock that evening, the young newspaper man, who hung about every night until his paper was away, was strolling along Richards Lane. Richards Lane is a narrow street, partly a stall-market, and partly residential. The young man was in the residential section, which carries on one side small working-class cottages, and on the other the wall of a railway goods yard. The great wall hung a blanket of shadow over the lane, and the shadow and the cadaverous outline of the now deserted market stalls gave it the appearance of a living lane that had been turned to frost in the moment between breath and death. The very lamps, that elsewhere were nimbuses of gold, had here the rigidity of gems. The journalist, feeling this message of frozen eternity, was telling himself that he was tired of the whole thing, when in one stroke the frost was broken. In the moment between one pace and another silence and darkness were racked by a high scream and through the scream a voice: 'Help! help! *He's here!*'

Before he could think what movement to make, the lane came to life. As though its invisible populace had been waiting on that cry, the door of every cottage was flung open, and from them and from the alleys poured shadowy figures bent in question-mark form. For a second or so they stood as rigid as the lamps; then a police whistle gave them direction, and the flock of shadows sloped up the street. The journalist followed them, and others followed him. From the main street and from surrounding streets they came, some risen from unfinished suppers, some disturbed in their ease of slippers and shirt sleeves, some stumbling on infirm limbs, and some upright, and armed with pokers or the tools of their trade. Here and there above the wavering cloud of heads moved the bold helmets of policemen. In one dim mass they surged upon a cottage whose doorway was marked by the sergeant and two constables; and voices of those behind urged them on with 'Get in! Find him! Run round the back! Over the wall!' and those in front cried: 'Keep back! Keep back!'

And now the fury of a mob held in thrall by unknown peril broke loose. He was here – on the spot. Surely this time he *could not* escape. All minds were bent upon the cottage; all energies thrust towards its doors and windows and roof; all thought was turned upon one unknown man and his extermination. So that no one man saw any other man. No man saw the narrow, packed lane and the mass of struggling shadows, and all forgot to look among themselves for the monster who never lingered upon his victims. All forgot, indeed, that they, by their mass crusade of vengeance, were affording him the perfect hiding-place. They saw only the house, and they heard only the rending of woodwork and the smash of glass at back and front, and the police giving orders or crying with the chase; and they pressed on.

But they found no murderer. All they found was news of murder and a glimpse of the ambulance, and for their fury there was no other object than the police themselves, who fought against this hampering of their work.

The journalist managed to struggle through to the cottage door, and to get the story from the constable stationed there. The cottage was the home of a pensioned sailor and his wife and daughter. They had been at supper, and at first it appeared that some noxious gas had smitten all three in mid-action. The daughter lay dead on the hearthrug, with a piece of bread and butter in her hand. The father had fallen sideways from his chair, leaving on his plate a filled spoon of rice-pudding. The mother lay half under the table, her lap filled with the pieces of a broken cup and splashes of cocoa. But in three seconds the idea of gas was dismissed. One glance at their necks showed that this was the Strangler again; and the police stood and looked at the room and momentarily shared the fatalism of the public. They were helpless.

This was his fourth visit, making seven murders in all. He was to do, as you know, one more – and to do it that night; and then he was to pass into history as the unknown London horror, and return to the decent life that he had always led, remembering little of what he had done, and worried not at all by the memory. Why did he stop? Impossible to say. Why did he begin? Impossible again. It just happened like that; and if he thinks at all of those days and nights, I surmise that he thinks of them as we think of foolish or dirty little sins that we committed in childhood. We say that they were not really sins, because we were not then consciously ourselves: we had not come to realization; and we look back at that foolish little creature that we once were, and forgive him because he didn't know. So, I think, with this man.

There are plenty like him. Eugene Aram, after the murder of Daniel Clark, lived a quiet, contented life for fourteen years, unhaunted by his crime and unshaken in his self-esteem. Dr Crippen murdered his wife, and then lived pleasantly with his mistress in the house under whose floor he had buried his wife. Constance Kent, found Not Guilty of the murder of her young brother, led a peaceful life for five years before she confessed. George Joseph Smith and William Palmer lived amiably among their fellows untroubled by fear or by remorse for their poisonings and drownings. Charles Peace, at the time he made his one unfortunate essay, had settled down into a respectable citizen with an interest in antiques. It happened that, after a lapse of time, these men were discovered, but more murderers than we guess are living decent lives today, and will die in decency, undiscovered and unsuspected. As this man will.

But he had a narrow escape, and it was perhaps this narrow escape that brought him to a stop. The escape was due to an error of judgment on the part of the journalist.

As soon as he had the full story of the affair, which took some time, he spent fifteen minutes on the telephone, sending the story through, and at the end of the fifteen minutes, when the stimulus of the business had left him, he felt physically tired and mentally dishevelled. He was not yet free to go home; the paper would not go away for another hour; so he turned into a bar for a drink and some sandwiches.

It was then, when he had dismissed the whole business from his mind, and was looking about the bar and admiring the landlord's taste in watch-chains and his air of domination, and was thinking that the landlord of a well-conducted tavern had a more comfortable life than a newspaper man, that his mind received from nowhere a spark of light. He was not thinking about the Strangling Horrors; his mind was on his sandwich. As a public-house sandwich, it was a curiosity. The bread had been thinly cut, it was buttered, and the ham was not two months stale; it was ham as it should be. His mind turned to the inventor of this refreshment, the Earl of Sandwich, and then to George the Fourth, and then to the Georges, and to the legend of that George who was worried to know how the apple got into the apple-dumpling. He wondered whether George would have been equally puzzled to know how the ham got into the ham sandwich, and how long it would have been before it occurred to him that the ham could not have got there unless somebody had put it there. He got up to order another sandwich, and in that moment a little active corner of his mind settled the affair. If there was ham in his sandwich, somebody must have put it there. If seven people had been murdered, somebody must have been there to murder them. There was no aeroplane or automobile that would go into a man's pocket; therefore that somebody must have escaped either by running away or standing still; and again therefore –

He was visualizing the front page story that his paper would carry if his theory were correct, and if – a matter of conjecture – his editor had the necessary nerve to make a bold stroke, when a cry of 'Time, gentlemen, please! All out!' reminded him of the hour. He got up and went out into a world of mist, broken by the ragged disks of roadside puddles and the streaming lightning of motor buses. He was certain that he had *the* story, but, even if it were proved, he was doubtful whether the policy of his paper would permit him to print it. It had one great fault. It was truth, but it was impossible truth. It rocked the foundations of everything that newspaper readers believed and that newspaper editors helped them to believe. They might believe that Turkish carpet-sellers had the gift of making themselves invisible. They would not believe this.

As it happened, they were not asked to, for the story was never written. As his paper had by now gone away, and as he was nourished by his refreshment and stimulated by his theory, he thought he might put in an extra half-hour by testing that theory. So he began to look about for the man he had in mind – a man with white hair, and large white hands; otherwise an everyday figure whom nobody would look twice at. He wanted to spring his idea on this man without warning, and he was going to place himself within reach of a man armoured in legends of dreadfulness and grue. This might appear to be an act of supreme courage – that one man, with no hope of immediate outside support, should place himself at the mercy of one who was holding a whole parish in terror. But it wasn't. He didn't think about the risk. He didn't think about his duty to his employers or loyalty to his paper. He was moved simply by an instinct to follow a story to its end.

He walked slowly from the tavern and crossed into Fingal Street, making for Deever Market, where he had hope of finding his man. But his journey was shortened. At the corner of Lotus Street he saw him – or a man who looked like him. This street was poorly lit, and he could see little of the man; but he *could* see white hands. For some twenty paces he stalked him; then drew level with him; and at a point where the arch of a railway crossed the street, he was sure that this was his man. He approached him with the current conversational phrase of the district: 'Well, seen anything of the murderer?' The man stopped to look sharply at him; then, satisfied that the journalist was not the murderer, said:

'Eh? No, nor's anybody else, curse it. Doubt if they ever will.'

'I don't know. I've been thinking about them, and I've got an idea.'

'So?'

'Yes. Came to me all of a sudden. Quarter of an hour ago. And I'd felt that we'd all been blind. It's been staring us in the face.'

The man turned again to look at him, and the look and the movement held suspicion of this man who seemed to know so much. 'Oh? Has it? Well, if you're so sure, why not give us the benefit of it?'

'I'm going to.' They walked level, and were nearly at the end of the little street where it meets Deever Market, when the journalist turned casually to the man. He put a finger on his arm. 'Yes, it seems to me quite simple now. But there's still one point I don't understand. One little thing I'd like to clear up. I mean the motive. Now, as man to man, tell me, Sergeant Ottermole, just *why* did you kill those inoffensive people?'

The sergeant stopped, and the journalist stopped. There was just enough light from the sky, which held the reflected light of the continent of London, to give him a sight of the sergeant's face, and the sergeant's face was turned to him with a wide smile of such urbanity and charm that the journalist's eyes were frozen as they met it. The smile stayed for some seconds. Then said the sergeant: 'Well, to tell you the truth, Mister Newspaper Man, I don't know. I really don't know. In fact, I've been worried about it myself. But I've got an idea – just like you. Everybody knows that we can't control the workings of our minds. Don't they? Ideas come into our minds without asking. But everybody's supposed to be able to control his body. Why? Eh? We get our minds from lord-knows-where – from people who were dead hundreds of years before we were born. Mayn't we get our bodies in the same way? Our faces – our legs – our heads – they aren't completely ours. We don't make 'em. They come to us. And couldn't ideas come into our bodies like ideas come into our minds? Eh? Can't ideas live in nerve and muscle as well as in brain? Couldn't it be that parts of our bodies aren't really us, and couldn't ideas come into those parts all of a sudden, like ideas come into – into' – he shot his arms out, showing the great white-gloved hands and hairy wrists; shot them out so swiftly to the journalist's throat that his eyes never saw them – 'into *my hands.*'

Baby

Ramsey Campbell

When the old woman reached the shops Dutton began to lag farther
behind. Though his hands were as deep in his pockets as they could
go, they were shaking. It's all right, he told himself, stay behind. The
last thing you want is for her to notice you now. But he knew he'd
fallen behind because he was losing his nerve.

The November wind blundered out of the side streets and shook him.
As he hurried across each intersection, head trembling deep in his collar,
he couldn't help searching the doorways for Tommy, Maud, even old
Frank, anyone with a bottle. But nobody sat against the dull paint of
the doors, beneath the bricked-up windows; nothing moved except
tangles of sodden paper and leaves. No, he thought, trying to seize his
mind before it began to shake like his body. He hadn't stayed sober
for so long to lapse now, when he was so close to what he'd stayed sober
for.

She'd drawn ahead; he was four blocks behind now. Not far enough
behind. He'd better dodge into the next side street before she looked
back and saw him. But then one of the shopkeepers might see him hiding
and call the police. Or she might turn somewhere while he was hiding,
and he would lose her. The stubble on his cheeks crawled with sweat,
which clung to the whole of his body; he couldn't tell if it was boiling
or frozen. For a couple of steps he limped rapidly to catch up with the
old woman, then he held himself back. She was about to look at him.

Fear flashed through him as if his sweat were charged. He made himself gaze at the shops, at the stalls outside: water chestnuts, capsicums,
aubergines, dhal – the little notices on sticks said so, but they were alien
to him; they didn't help him hold onto his mind. Their price flags
fluttered, tiny and nerve-racking as the prickling of his cheeks.

Then he heard the pram. Its sound was deep in the blustering of the
wind, but it was unmistakable. He'd heard it too often, coming toward
the house, fading into the room below his. It sounded like the start of
a rusty metal yawn, abruptly interrupted by a brief squeal, over and
over. It was the sound of his goal, of the reason why he'd stayed sober

all night. He brought the pockets of his coat together, propping the iron bar more securely against his chest inside the coat.

She had reached the maze of marshy ground and broken houses beyond the shops. At last, Dutton thought, and began to run. The bar thumped his chest until it bruised. His trousers chafed his thighs like sandpaper, his calves throbbed, but he ran stumbling past the morose shoppers, the defiantly cheerful shopkeepers, the continuing almost ghostly trade of the street. As soon as she was out of sight of the shops, near one of the dilapidated houses, he would have her. At once he halted, drenched in sweat. He couldn't do it.

He stood laughing mirthlessly at himself as newspapers swooped at him. He was going to kill the old woman, was he? Him, who hadn't been able to keep a job for more than a week for years? Him, who had known he wasn't going to keep a job before he started working at it, until the social security had reluctantly agreed with him? Him, who could boast of nothing but the book he cashed weekly at the post office? He was going to kill her?

His mind sounded like his mother. Too much so to dishearten him entirely: it wasn't him, he could answer back. He remembered when he'd started drinking seriously. He'd felt then that if the social security took an interest in him he would be able to hold down a job; but they hadn't bothered to conceal their indifference, and soon after that they'd given him his book. But now it was different. He didn't need anyone's encouragement. He'd proved that by not touching a drink since yesterday afternoon. If he could do that, he could do anything.

He shoved past a woman wheeling a pramful of groceries, and ran faster to outdistance the trembling that spread through his body. His shoes crackled faintly with the plastic bags in which his feet were wrapped. He was going to kill her, because of the contemptuous way she'd looked at him in the hall, exactly as his mother had used to; because while he was suffering poverty, she had chosen worse and flaunted her happiness; because, although her coat had acquired a thick hem of mud from trailing, though the coat gaped like frayed lips between her shoulders, she was always smiling secretly, unassailably. He let the thoughts seep through his mind, gathering darkly and heavily in the depths. He *was* going to kill her – because she looked too old for life, too ugly and wizened to live; because she walked as if to do so were a punishment; because her smile must be a paralysed grimace of pain, after all; because her tuneless crooning often kept him awake half the night, though he stamped on her ceiling; because he needed her secret wealth. She had turned and was coming back toward him, past the shops.

His face huddled into his collar as he stumbled away, across the road. That was enough. He'd tried, he couldn't do more. If circumstances hadn't saved him he would have failed. He would have been arrested, and for nothing. He shifted the bar uneasily within his coat, anxious to be rid of it. He gazed at the burst husk of a premature firework, lying trampled on the pavement. It reminded him of himself. He turned hastily as the old woman came opposite him, and stared in a toy-shop window.

An orange baby with fat wrinkled dusty joints stared back at him. Beside it, reflected in a dark gap among the early Christmas toys and fireworks for tomorrow night, he saw the old woman. She had pushed her pram alongside the greengrocer's stall; now she let it go. Dutton peered closer, frowning.

He was sure she hadn't pushed the pram before letting go. Yet it had sped away, past the greengrocer's stall, then halted suddenly. He was still peering when she wheeled it out of the reflection, into the depths full of toys. He began to follow her at once, hardly shaking. Even if he hadn't needed her wealth to give him a chance in life, he had to know what was in that pram.

What wealth? How did he know about it? He struggled to remember. Betty, no, Maud had told him the day she hadn't drunk too much to recall. She'd read about the old woman in the paper, years ago: about how she'd been swindled by a man whom nobody could trace. She'd given the man her money, her jewels, her house, and her relatives had set the police on him. But then she had been in the paper herself, saying she hadn't been swindled at all, that it was none of their business what she'd gained from the trade; and Maud supposed they'd believed her, because that was the last she had seen of the woman in the paper.

But soon after that Maud had seen her in town, wheeling her pram and smiling to herself. She'd often seen her in the crowds, and then the old woman had moved into the room beneath Dutton, older and wearier now but still smiling. 'That shows she got something out of it,' Maud said. 'What else has she got to smile about? But where she keeps it, that's the thing.' She'd shown Dutton a bit she had kept of the paper, and it did look like the old woman, smiling up from a blot of fluff and sweat.

The old woman had nearly reached home now. Dutton stumbled over a paving stone that had cracked and collapsed like ice on a pool. The iron bar nudged his chest impatiently, tearing his skin. Nearly there now. He had to remember why he was doing this. If he could hold all that in his mind he would be able to kill her. He muttered; his furred tongue crawled in his mouth like a dying caterpillar. He must remember.

He'd gone into her room one day. A month ago, two? Never mind! he though viciously. He'd been drunk enough to take the risk, not too drunk to make sense of what he'd found. He'd staggered into the house and straight into her room. Since he knew she didn't lock the door, he'd expected to find nothing; yet he was astonished to find so little. In the strained light through the encrusted window, stained patches of wallpaper slumped and bulged. The bed knelt at one corner, for a leg had given way; the dirty sheets had slipped down to conceal the damage. Otherwise the room was bare, no sign even of the pram. The pram. Of course.

He had tried to glimpse what was in the pram. He'd pressed his cheek against his window whenever he heard her approaching, but each time the pram's hood was in the way. Once he'd run downstairs and peered into the pram as she opened her door, but she had pulled the pram away like a chair in a practical joke, and gazed at him with amazement, amusement, profound contempt.

And last week, in the street, he'd been so drunk he had reeled at her and wrenched the pram's handle from her grasp. He'd staggered around to look beneath the hood – but she had already kicked the pram, sending it sailing down a canted side road, and had flown screaming at him, her nails aimed straight for his eyes. When he'd fallen in the gutter she had turned away, laughing with the crowd. As he had pushed himself unsteadily to his feet, his hand deep in sodden litter, he was sure he'd glimpsed the pram halting inches short of crashing into a wall, apparently by itself.

He had decided then, as his hand slithered in the pulp. In his mind she'd joined the people who were laughing inwardly at him: the social security, the clerks in the post office. Only she was laughing aloud, encouraging the crowd to laugh. he would kill her for that. He'd persuaded himself for days that he would. She'd soon have no reason to laugh at his poverty, at the book he hid crumpled in his hand as he waited in the post office. And last night, writhing on his bed amid the darkly crawling walls, listening to her incessant contented wailing, he'd known that he would kill her.

He would kill her. Now.

He was running, his hands gloved in his pockets and swinging together before him at the end of the metal bar, running past a shop whose windows were boarded up with dislocated doors, past the faintly whistling waste ground and, beneath his window in the side of the house, a dormant restlessly creaking bonfire taller than himself. She must have reached her room by now.

The street was deserted. Bricks lay in the roadway, unmoved by the tugging of the wind. He wavered on the front steps, listening for sounds in the house. The baby wasn't crying in the cellar, which meant those people must be out; nobody was in the kitchen; even if the old man in the room opposite Dutton's were home, he was deaf. Dutton floundered into the hall, then halted as if at the end of a chain.

He couldn't do it here. He stared at the smudged and faded whorls

of the wallpaper, the patterns of numbers scribbled above the patch
where the telephone had used to be, the way the stairs turned sharply
in the gloom just below the landing. The bar hung half out of his coat.
He could have killed her beyond the shops, but this was too familiar.
He couldn't imagine a killing here, where everything suffocated even
the thought of change – everything, even the creaking of the floorboards.

The floorboards were creaking. She would hear them. All at once
he felt he was drowning in sweat. She would come out and see the iron
bar, and know what he'd meant to do. She would call the police. He
pulled out the bar, tearing a buttonhole, and blundered into her room.

The old woman was at the far end of the room, her back to him.
She was turning away from the pram, stooped over as if holding an
object against her belly. From her mouth came the sound that had kept
him awake so often, a contented lulling sound. For the first time he
could hear what she was saying. 'Baby,' she was crooning, 'baby.' She
might have been speaking to a lover or a child.

In a moment she would see him. He limped swiftly forward, his
padding footsteps puffing up dust to discolour the dim light more, and
swung the iron bar at her head.

He'd forgotten how heavy the bar was. It pulled him down toward
her, by his weakened arms. He felt her head give, and heard a muffled
crackling beneath her hair. Momentarily, as he clung to the bar as it
rested in her head against the wall, he was face to face with her, with
her eyes and mouth as they worked spasmodically and went slack.

He recoiled, most of all because there was the beginning of a wry
smile in her eyes until they faded. Then she fell with a great flat thud,
shockingly heavy and loud. Dust rolled out from beneath her, rising
about Dutton's face as he fought a sneeze, settling on the dark patch
that was spreading over the old woman's colourless hair.

Dutton closed his eyes and gripped the bar, propping it against the
wall, resting his forehead on the lukewarm metal. His stomach writhed,
worse than in the mornings, sending convulsions through his whole body.
At last he managed to open his eyes and look down again. She lay with
one cheek in the dust, her hair darkening, her arms sprawled on either
side of her. They had been holding nothing to her belly. In the dim
light she looked like a sleeping drunk, a sack, almost nothing at all.
Dutton remembered the cracking of her head and found himself giggling
hysterically, uncontrollably.

He had to be quick. Someone might hear him. Stepping over her,
he unbuttoned the pram's apron and pulled it back.

At first he couldn't make out what the pram contained. He had to
crane himself over, holding his body back from obscuring the light. The
pram was full of groceries – cabbage, sprouts, potatoes. Dutton shook
his head, bewildered, suspecting his eyes of practical joking. He pulled

the pram over to the window, remembering only just in time to disguise his hand in the rag to keep as a handkerchief.

The windowpanes looked like the back of a fireplace. Dutton rubbed them with his handkerchief but succeeded only in smudging the grime. He peered into the pram again. It was still almost packed with groceries; only, near the head of the pram, there was a clear space about a foot in diameter. It was empty.

He began to throw out the vegetables. Potatoes trundled thundering over the floorboards, a rolling cabbage scooped up dust in its leaves. The vegetables were fresh, yet she had entered none of the shops, and he was sure he hadn't seen her filching. He was trying to recall what in fact he had seen when his wrapped hand touched something at the bottom of the pram: something hard, round, several round objects, a corner beneath one, a surface that struck cold through his handkerchief – glass. He lifted the corner and the framed photograph came up out of the darkness, its round transparent cargo rolling. They almost rolled off before he laid the photograph on the corner of the pram, for his grip had slackened as the globes rolled apart to let the old woman stare up at him.

She was decades younger, and there was no doubt she was the woman Maud had shown him. And here were her treasures, delivered to him on her photograph as if on a tray. He grinned wildly and stooped to admire them. He froze in that position, hunched over in disbelief.

There were four of the globes. They were transparent, full of floating specks of light that gradually settled. He stared numbly at them. Close to his eyes threads of sunlight through the window selected sparkling motes of dust, then let them go. Surely he must be wrong. Surely this wasn't what he'd suffered all night for. But he could see no other explanation. The old woman had been wholly mad. The treasures that had kept her smiling, the treasures she had fought him for, were nothing but four fake snowstorm globes of the kind he'd seen in dozens of toy shops.

He convulsed as if seized by nausea. With his wrapped hand he swept all four globes off the photograph, snarling.

They took a long time to fall. They took long enough for him to notice, and to stare at them. They seemed to be sinking through the air as slowly as dust, turning enormously like worlds, filling the whole of his attention. In each of them a faint image was appearing: in one a landscape, in another a calm and luminous face.

It must be the angle at which you held them to the light. They were falling so slowly he could catch them yet, could catch the face and the landscape which he could almost see, the other images which trembled at the very edge of recognition, images like a sweet and piercing song, approaching from inaudibility. They were falling slowly – yet he was only making to move towards them when the globes smashed on the floor, their fragments parting like petals. He heard no sound at all.

He stood shaking in the dimness. He had had enough. He felt his trembling hands wrap the stained bar in his handkerchief. The rag was large enough; it had always made a companionable bulge in his pocket. He sniffed, and wondered if the old woman's pockets were empty. It was only when he stooped to search that he saw the enormous bulge in her coat, over her belly.

Part of his mind was warning him, but his fingers wrenched eagerly at her buttons. He threw her coat open, in the dust. Then he recoiled, gasping. Beneath the faded flowers of her dress she was heavily pregnant.

She couldn't be. Who would have touched her? Her coat hadn't bulged like that in the street, he was sure. But there was no mistaking the swelling of her belly. He pushed himself away from her, his hands against the damp wall. The light was so dim and thick he felt he was struggling in mud. He gazed at the swollen lifeless body, then he turned and ran.

Still there was nobody in the street. He stumbled to the waste ground and thrust the wrapped bar deep in the bonfire. Tomorrow night the blood would be burned away. As he limped through the broken streets, the old woman's room hung about him. At last, in a doorway two streets distant, he found Tommy.

He collapsed on the doorstep and seized the bottle Tommy offered him. The cloying wine poured down his throat; bile rose to meet it, but he choked them down. As the wind blustered at his chest it seemed to kindle the wine in him. There was no pregnant corpse in the settling dust, no room thick with dim light, no crackling head. He tilted his head back, gulping.

Tommy was trying to wrest the bottle from him. The neck tapped viciously against Dutton's teeth, but he held it between his lips and thrust his tongue up to hurry the last drops; then he hurled the bottle into the gutter, where it smashed, echoing between the blank houses. As he threw it, a police car entered the road.

Dutton sat inert while the policeman strolled towards him. Tommy was levering himself away rapidly, crutch thumping. Dutton knew one of the policemen: Constable Wayne. 'We can't pretend we didn't see that, Billy,' Wayne told him. 'Be a good boy and you'll be out in the morning.'

The wine smudged the world around Dutton for a while. The cell wall was a screen on which he could put pictures to the sounds of the police station: footsteps, shouts, telephones, spoons rattling in mugs. His eyes were coaxing the graffiti from beneath the new paint when, distant but clear, he heard a voice say, 'What about Billy Dutton?'

'Him knock an old woman's head in?' Wayne's voice said. 'I don't reckon he could do that, even sober. Besides, I brought him in around the time of death. He wasn't capable of handling a bottle, let alone a murder.'

Later a young policeman brought Dutton a mug of tea and some aging cheese sandwiches wrapped in greaseproof paper, then stood frowning with mingled disapproval and embarrassment while Dutton was sick. Yet though Dutton lay rocking with nausea for most of the night, though frequently he stood up and roamed unsteadily about the cell and felt as if his nausea were sinking deep within him like dregs, always he could hear Wayne's words. The words freed him of guilt. He had risked, and lost, and that was all. When he left the cell he could return to his old life. He would buy a bottle and celebrate with Tommy, Maud, even old Frank.

He could hear an odd sound far out in the night, separate from the musings of the city, the barking dogs, the foghorns on the Mersey. He propped himself on one elbow to listen. Now that it was coming closer he could make it out: a sound like an interrupted metal yawn. It was groaning toward him; it was beside him. He awoke shouting and saw Wayne opening his cell. It must have been the hinges of the door.

'It's about time you saw someone who can help you,' Wayne said.

Perhaps he was threatening to give Dutton's address to a social worker or someone like that. Let him, Dutton thought. They couldn't force their way into his room so long as he didn't do wrong. He was sure that was true; it must be.

Three doors away from the police station was a pub, a Wine Lodge. They must have let him sleep while he could; the Wine Lodge was already open. Dutton bought a bottle and crossed to the opposite pavement, which was an edge of the derelict area toward which he'd pursued the old woman.

The dull sunlight seemed to seep out of the ruined walls. Dutton trudged over the orange mud, past stagnant puddles in the shape of footprints; water welled up around his shoes, the mud sucked them loudly. As soon as there were walls between him and the police station he unstoppered the bottle and drank. He felt like a flower opening to the sun. Still walking, he hadn't lowered the bottle when he caught sight of old Frank sitting on the step of a derelict house.

'Here's Billy,' Frank shouted, and the others appeared in the empty window. At the edge of the waste land a police car was roving; that must be why they had taken refuge.

They came forward as best they could to welcome him. 'You won't be wanting to go home tonight,' Maud said.

'Why not? In fact there was no reason why he shouldn't know – he could have told them what he'd overheard Wayne discussing – but he wouldn't take that risk. They were ready to suspect anyone, these people; you couldn't trust them.

'Someone did for that old woman,' Frank said. 'The one in the room below you. Bashed her head in and took her pram.'

Dutton's throat closed involuntarily; wine welled up from his lips, around the neck of the bottle. 'Took her pram?' he coughed, weeping. 'Are you sure?'

'Sure as I was standing outside when they carried her out. The police knew her, you know, her and her pram. They used to look in to make sure she was all right. She wouldn't have left her pram anywhere, they said. Someone took it.'

'So you won't be wanting to go home tonight. You can warm my bed if you like,' Maud said toothlessly, lips wrinkling.

'What would anyone want to kill her for?' Betty said, dragging her grey hair over the scarred side of her face. 'She hadn't got anything.'

'She had once. She was rich. She bought something with all that,' Maud said.

'Don't care. She didn't have anything worth killing her for. Did she, Billy?'

'No,' Dutton said, and stumbled hurriedly on: 'There wasn't anything in that pram. I know. I looked in it once when she was going in her room. She was poorer than us.'

'Unless she was a witch,' Maud said.

Dutton shook the bottle to quicken the liquor. In a moment it would take hold of him completely, he'd be floating on it, Maud's words would drift by like flotsam on a warm sea. 'What?' he said.

'Unless she was a witch. Then she could have given everything she owned, and her soul as well, to that man they never found, and still have had something for it that nobody could see, or wouldn't understand if they did see.' She panted, having managed her speech, and drank.

'That woman was a witch right enough,' Tommy said, challenging the splintered floor with his crutch. 'I used to go by there at night and hear her singing to herself. There was something not right there.'

'I sing,' Frank said, standing up menacingly, and did so: "Rock of Ages." 'Am I a witch, eh? Am I a witch?'

'They weren't hymns she was singing, I'll be bound. If I hadn't seen her in the street I'd have said she was a darky. Jungle music, it was. Mumbo-jumbo.'

'She was singing to her baby,' Dutton said loosely.

'She didn't have a baby, Billy,' Maud said. 'Only a pram.'

'She was going to have one.'

'You're the man who should know, are you?' Frank demanded. 'She could have fooled me. She was flat as a pancake when they carried her out. Flat as a pancake.'

Dutton stared at Frank for as long as he could, before he had to look away from the deformed strawberry of the man's nose. He seemed to be telling the truth. Two memories were circling Dutton, trying to perch on his thoughts: a little girl who'd been peering in the old woman's window one day, suddenly running away and calling back – inappropriately, it had seemed at the time—'Fat cow'; the corpse on the dusty floor, indisputably pregnant even in the dim light. 'Flat as a pancake,' Frank repeated.

Dutton was still struggling to understand when Maud said, 'What's that?'

Dutton could hear nothing but the rushing of his blood. 'Sounds like a car,' Betty said.

'Too small for a car. Needs oiling, whatever it is.'

What were they talking about? Why were they talking about things he couldn't understand, that he couldn't even hear, that disturbed him? 'What?' Dutton yelled.

They all stared at him, focusing elaborately, and Tommy thumped his crutch angrily. 'It's gone now,' Maud said at last.

There was a silence until Betty said sleepily, 'If she was a witch where was her familiar?'

'Her what?' Dutton said, as the bottle blurred and dissolved above his eyes. She didn't know what she was talking about. Nor did he, he shouted at himself. Nor did he.

'Her familiar. A kind of, you know, creature that would do things for her. Bring her food, that kind of thing. A cat, or something. She hadn't anything like that. She wouldn't have been able to hide it.'

Nowhere to hide it, Dutton thought. In her pram – but her pram had been empty. The top of his head was rising, floating away; it didn't matter. Betty's hand wobbled at the edge of his vision, spilling wine toward him. He grabbed the bottle as her eyes closed. He tried to drink but couldn't find his mouth. Somehow he managed to stopper the bottle with his finger, and a moment later was asleep.

When he awoke he was alone in the dark.

Among the bricks that were bruising his chest was the bottle, still glued to his finger. He clambered to his feet, deafened by the clattering of bricks, and dug the bottle into his pocket for safety, finger and all. He groped his way out of the house, sniffing, searching vainly for his handkerchief. A wall reeled back from him and he fell, scraping his shoulder. Eventually he reached the doorway.

Night had fallen. Amid the mutter of the city, fireworks were already spluttering; distant chimneys sprang up momentarily against a spray of white fire. Far ahead, between the tipsily shifting walls, the lights of the

shops blinked faintly at Dutton. He took a draft to fend off the icy plucking of the wind, then he stuffed the bottle in his pocket and made for
the lights.

The mud was lying in wait for him. It swallowed his feet with an
approving sound. It poured into his shoes, seeping into the plastic bags.
It squeezed out from beneath unsteady paving stones, where there were
any. He snarled at it and stamped, sending it over his trouser cuffs. It
stretched glistening faintly before him as far as he see.

Cars were taking a short cut from the main road, past the shops.
Dutton stood and waited for their lights to sweep over the mud, lighting
up his way. He emptied the bottle into himself. Headlights swung
towards him, blazing abruptly in puddles, pinching up silver edges of
ruts from the darkness, touching a small still dark object between the
walls to Dutton's left.

He glared towards that, through the pale fading firework display on his
eyeballs. It had been low and squat, he was sure; part of it had been
raised, like a hood. Suddenly he recoiled from the restless darkness and
began to run wildly. He fell with a flat splash and heaved himself up, his
hands gloved in grit and mud. He stumbled towards the swaying lights
and glared about whenever headlights flashed between the walls. Around
him the walls seemed as unstable as the ground.

He was close enough to the shops for the individual sounds of the
street to have separated themselves from the muted anonymous roar of
the city, when he fell again. He fell into darkness behind walls, and
scrabbled in the mud, slithering grittily. When he regained his feet he
peered desperately about, trying to hold things still. The lights of the
street, sinking, leaping back into place and sinking, sinking; the walls
around him, wavering and drooping; a dwarfish fragment of wall close
to him, on his left. Headlights slipped passed him and corrected him. It
wasn't a fragment of wall. It was a pram.

In that moment of frozen clarity he could see the twin clawmarks its
wheels had scored in the mud, reaching back into darkness. Then the
darkness rushed at him as his ankles tangled and he lost his footing. He
was reeling helplessly toward the pram.

A second before he reached it he lashed out blindly with one foot. He
tottered in a socket of mud, but he felt his foot strike metal, and heard
the pram fall. He whirled about, running towards the whirling lights,
changing his direction when they steadied. The next time headlights
passed him he twisted about to look. The force of his movement spun
him back again and on, toward the lights. But he was sure he'd seen
the pram upturned in the mud, and shaking like a turtle trying to right
itself.

Once among the shops he felt safe. This was his territory. People were
hurrying home from work, children were running errands; cars laden

with packages butted their way towards the suburbs, honking. He'd stay here, where there were people; he wouldn't go home to his room.

He began to stroll, rolling unsteadily. He gazed in the shop windows, whose contents sank like a loose television image. When he reached a launderette he halted, frowning, and couldn't understand why. Was it something he'd heard? Yes, there was a sound somewhere amid the impatient clamour of the traffic: a yawn of metal cut short by a high squeal. It was something like that, not entirely, not the sound he remembered, only the sound of a car. Within the launderette things whirled, whirled; so did the launderette; so did the pavement. Dutton forced himself onward, cursing as he almost fell over a child. He shoved the child aside and collided with a pram.

Bulging out from beneath its hood was a swollen faceless head of blue plastic. Folds of its wrinkled wormlike body squeezed over the side of the pram; within the blue transparent body he could see white coils and rolls of washing, like tripe. Dutton thrust it away, choking. The woman wheeling it aimed a blow at him and pushed the pram into the launderette.

He ran helplessly forward, trying to retrieve his balance. Mud trickled through the burst plastic in his shoes and grated between his toes. He fell, slapping the pavement with himself. When someone tried to help him he snarled and rolled out of their reach.

He was cold and wet. His coat had soaked up all the water his falls had squeezed out of the mud. He couldn't go home, couldn't warm himself in bed; he had to stay here, out on the street. His mouth tasted like an abandoned bottle. He glared about, roaring at anyone who came near. Then, over the jerking segments of the line of car roofs, he saw Maud hurrying down a side street, carrying a bottle wrapped in newspaper.

That was what he needed. A ball of fire sprang up spinning and whooping above the roofs. Dutton surged toward the pedestrian crossing, whose two green stick figures were squeaking at each other across the path through the cars. He was almost there when a pram pushed at him from an alley.

He grappled with it, hurling it from him. It was only a pram, never mind, he must catch up with Maud. But a white featureless head nodded toward him on a scrawny neck, craning out from beneath the hood; a head that slipped awry, rolling loose on its neck, as the strings that tied it came unknotted. It was only a guy begging pennies for cut-price fireworks. Before he realized that Dutton had overbalanced away from it into the road, in front of a released car.

There was a howl of brakes, another, a tinkle of glass. Dutton found himself staring up from beneath a front bumper. Wheels blocked his vision on either side, like huge oppressive earmuffs. People were shouting at each other, someone was shouting at him, the crowd was chattering, laughing. When someone tried to help him to his feet he kicked out and clung to the bumper. Nothing could touch him now, he was safe, they wouldn't dare to. Eventually someone took hold of his arm and wouldn't let go until he stood up. It was Constable Wayne.

'Come on, Billy,' Wayne said. 'That's enough for today. Go home.'

'I won't go home!' Dutton cried in panic.

'Do you mean to tell me you're sending him home and that's all?' a woman shouted above the yapping of her jacketed Pekinese. 'What about my headlight?'

'I'll deal with him,' Wayne said. 'My colleague will take your statements. Don't give me any trouble, Billy,' he said, taking a firmer hold on Dutton's arm.

Dutton found himself being marched along the street, toward his room. 'I'm not going home,' he shouted.

'You are, and I'll see that you do.' A fire engine was elbowing its way through the traffic, braying. In the middle of a side street, between walls that quaked with the light of a huge bonfire, children were stoning firemen.

'I won't,' Dutton said, pleading. 'If you make me I'll get out again. I've drunk too much. I'll do something bad, I'll hurt someone.'

'You aren't one of those. Go home now and sleep it off. You know we've no room for you on Saturday nights. And tonight of all nights we we don't want to be bothered with you.'

They had almost reached the house. Wayne gazed up at the dormant bonfire on the waste ground. 'We'll have to see about that,' he said. But Dutton hardly heard him. as the house swayed toward him, a rocket exploded low and snatched the house forward for a moment from the darkness. In the old woman's room, at the bottom of the windowpane, he saw a metal bar: the handle of a pram.

Dutton began to struggle again. 'I'm not going in there!' he shouted, searching his mind wildly for anything. 'I killed that old woman! I knocked her head in, it was me!'

'That's enough of that, now,' Wayne said, dragging him up the steps. 'You're lucky I can see you're drunk.'

Dutton clutched the front door frame with both hands. 'There's something in there!' he screamed. 'In her room!'

'There's nothing at all,' Wayne said. 'Come here and I'll show you.' He propelled Dutton into the hall and switching on his flashlight, pushed open the old woman's door with his foot. 'Now, what's in here?' he demanded. 'Nothing.'

Dutton looked in, ready to flinch. The flashlight beam swept impatiently about the room, revealing nothing but dust. The bed had been pushed beneath the window during the police search. Its headrail was visible through the pane: a metal bar.

Dutton sagged with relief. Only Wayne's grip kept him from falling. He turned as Wayne hurried him toward the stairs, and saw the mouth of darkness just below the landing. It was waiting for him, its lips working. He tried to pull back, but Wayne was becoming more impatient. 'See me upstairs,' Dutton pleaded.

'Oh, it's the horrors, is it? Come on now, quickly.' Wayne stayed where he was, but shone his flashlight into the mouth, which paled. Dutton stumbled upstairs as far as the lips, which flickered tentatively toward him. He heard the constable clatter up behind him, and the darkness fell back farther. Before him, sharp and bright amid the darkness, was his door.

'Switch on your light, be quick,' Wayne said.

The room was exactly as Dutton had left it. And why not? he thought, confident all at once. He never locked it, there was nothing to steal, but now the familiarity of everything seemed welcoming: the rumpled bed; the wardrobe, rusted open and plainly empty; the washbasin; the grimy coin-meter. 'All right,' he called down to Wayne, and bolted the door.

He stood for a long time against the door while his head swam slowly back to him. The wind reached for him through the wide-open window. He couldn't remember having opened it so wide, but it didn't matter. Once he was steady he would close it, then he'd go to bed. The blankets were raised like a cowl at the pillow, waiting for him. He heard Constable Wayne walk away. Eventually he heard the children light the bonfire.

When blackening tatters of fire began to flutter toward the house he limped to close the window. The bonfire was roaring; the heat collided with him. He remembered with a shock of pleasure that the iron bar was deep in the blaze. He sniffed and groped vainly for his handkerchief as the smoke stung his nostrils. Never mind. He squinted at the black object at the peak of the bonfire, which the flames had just reached. Then he fell back involuntarily. It was the pram.

He slammed the window. Bright orange faces glanced up at him, then turned away. There was no mistaking the pram, for he saw the photograph within the hood strain with the heat, and shatter. He tested his feelings gingerly and realized he could release the thoughts he'd held back, at last. The pursuit was over. It had given up. And suddenly he knew why.

It had been the old woman's familiar. He'd known that as soon as Betty had mentioned the idea, but he hadn't dared think in case it heard him thinking; devils could do that. The old woman had taken it out in her pram, and it had stolen food for her. But it hadn't lived in the pram. It had lived inside the old woman. That was what he'd seen in her room, only it had got out before the police had found the body.

He switched off the light. The room stayed almost as bright, from the blaze. He fumbled with his buttons and removed his outer clothes. The walls shook; his mouth was beginning to taste like dregs. It didn't matter. If he couldn't sleep he could go out and buy a bottle. Tomorrow he could cash his book. He needn't be afraid to go out now.

It must have thrown itself on the bonfire because devils lived in fire. It must have realized at last that he wasn't like the old woman, that it couldn't live inside him. He stumbled toward the bed. A shadow was moving on the pillow. He baulked, then he saw it was the shadow of the blanket's cowl. He pulled the blanket back.

He had just realized how like the hood of a pram the shape of the blanket had been when the long spidery arms unfolded from the bed, and the powerful claws reached eagerly to part him.

A Note for the Milkman

Sidney Carroll

I sat in the parlour and waited until my wife was deeply and firmly in bed. I waited until I could hear the sound of her snoring, so rhythmic and so blissful. To myself I counted ten, as I always do when my heart is pounding. Then I got up from my casual chair and went into the kitchen.

Four little packets of white powder I took from my vest pocket while I hummed a happy song. There was no need for silence. Once my wife would bluster her way into slumberland nothing in the world could awaken her – except, perhaps, a dinner bell. I placed the little packets of powder side by side on the kitchen table. From another pocket I extracted the piece of paper from which I had copied my instructions.

For the hundredth time, with my head slightly to one side, my chin cupped in my free hand (it *is* a kittenish pose for a small man, I admit – but I can't help it) I read the words I had copied from the old book:

'This Essence, impervious to Heat, Ray of Sun, Ravage of Life or Time, can be devis'd, if with a true Deliberation, if the steps hereunto affix'd, are follow'd with a Physik's care...'

That part I knew by heart, as indeed I knew most of what followed. But I am an academic man. For the hundredth time I read every word on the paper, every step of the way:

'... utterly clean Vials and Flaggons are the first Necessity...'

Then I, who had gone over these motions time and time again in my mind's eye, finally went to work with my fingers.

I took bottles and glasses and two spoons. I took three test tubes I had purchased the week before at the Five and Ten. I cleaned all of these under the hottest water from the tap. I rinsed them over and over again and wiped them ferociously with a fresh towel. I held them under the naked light bulb overhead, wiped them again, held them under the light bulb again, wiped them until they dazzled. I have a slightly myopic eye, but when I was through cleaning those bottles and glasses they dazzled.

I took my white powders next, and my instructions, and I mixed the powders one with the other, and then over again with each other. In a brand new saucepan I had hidden for weeks at the back of one of the top shelves in the kitchen cabinet I cooked liquids made from the powders. I let the liquids simmer and cool and I poured them one into the other. I have steady hands. Only my eyes blinked needlessly and a tear would shimmy in the corner of the left one from time to time. An occupational disease. I dispose of these tears easily enough: I flick my head sharply; the tear is torn from the eye. You might say I have learned to expectorate with my eye. You might say it if you thought about it long enough.

Anyway:

I hummed my little song and I had certain little thoughts while I worked.

I was thinking of the time I had poisoned the pigeons in the park.

Why had I never been caught?, I asked myself, to tease myself. Of course I had the answer. Simple answer – so simple. I had never been caught because they could never guess where I would strike next. I had spread corn in an uptown park on a Monday morning. On Monday evening there were pictures in the papers of the scores of dead pigeons, like bodies on a beachhead. On Tuesday morning I would scatter peanuts in front of the library downtown, and that evening there would be more pictures of dead pigeons . . . downtown.

And what could the police do? How can the infantry know where the General is going to strike next? I had deployed, thrust, parried – tantalized them with my hitting and running. How could they capture such an enemy? When you leave tracks going in one direction they can follow you. But when one footprint falls here today, another ten miles away tomorrow, and on the third day the track falls behind your back, how can you follow – how can anybody follow? That was why they'd never caught me the time I'd had such fun poisoning the pigeons. *That* was my theory. That kind of track . . .

And so ran my thoughts (a few of them) when I mixed my powders and bitumens in the small yellow kitchen under the one bright bulb, with the shades tightly drawn, with the sounds of my wife's snoring coming from the bedroom.

At last I was finished. All of it was contained in the one test tube. I held it up to the light. The liquid in the test tube shone crystal clear. I smiled. One tear shimmied in the eye for joy. I flicked it. I knew I had kept faith with the old book in the library: I had made no mistakes.

'... one, only one common Deviation from our Ingredient, our Liquid will turn a brackish Hue. The final Sauce must be clear as the fresh rain Water ...'

My hand did not tremble though my poor heart was exulting. I had it. I stoppered the tube tightly with a cork, rested the vial full of my liquid clear as rain water in a glass, and went to work to clean up the kitchen. In five minutes the job was done, for – *ha!* – I am an old hand at the routine.

I wiped my hands. When they were bone dry I blew on them. A man who works in the stacks of a public library gets into the habit of blowing on his fingertips.

Now I read my secret paper once more:

'... no Thing on earth can blunt its Sting, no Thing can rend its Heart, nothing can still its corruptive Pulse; not Fire, not Water, not Air, not Earth. It is like Lucifer, unconquerable. Burn it, it will glow. Drown it, it will drink. Bury it, it will grow. When it touches, Doom. Skin will rot before its Stain dissolves ...'

I presented myself with one of my rare little jokes. 'It reads like old Bunyan writing an ad for varnish,' I told myself. I have my own sense of humour. Sly but fly, that's Henry Peters. And now I come to the vital part of the evening's entertainment.

Mrs Peters and I always used one bottle of milk and one of cream per day. Now, at night, the two clean and empty bottles, big and little brothers of vim, vigour and vitality, stood side by side on the sink. I regarded them. I cocked my head, as is my failing. I hesitated for just a second.

The milk bottle? The cream bottle? Both?

I thought about it, then I shrugged my shoulders. What difference did it make ... really? I picked up the milk bottle. I sniffed from the open neck of its lingering clean lactic fragrance. Then I poured one drop, exactly one drop (like a teardrop) of my fresh-as-rain-water liquid into the milk bottle. I swirled it around a bit, watched the drop run in circles at the bottom of the milk bottle until it spread and flattened and exhausted itself. 'It's alive,' I assured myself. I put the milk bottle and the cream bottle in the hallway just outside our front door, in the usual place, where the milkman would pick it up in the morning.

Two days later it happened. Of course it happened. Down on the lower west side of town. A family of five – father, mother, three children. Found dead at the breakfast table. Poisoned.

*

I read about it in the morning paper. After I read about it I folded the paper, ever so neatly, and allowed myself my chuckle for the morning. Golly whiskers! – this was going to be so easy! As easy as poisoning pigeons.

That night when the snores from the bedroom had begun to fill me with a sense of safety and assurance once more, I went back to the kitchen. I took the day's empty milk bottle and poured one drop of my liquid into it. The old book in the library had *told* me that nothing could kill this incredible thing, and the old book had not lied. Nothing *could* kill it – not heat, or light, or water, or fire – or Pasteurization. It would conquer any antidote. I dropped a new drop into the milk bottle and I put the bottle in its familiar place outside the front door.

I had results in two days. It was in the papers again in that fine bold type. A man in the Burbank district this time. Situation identical. Found at the breakfast table. Poisoned. He was slumped over and his face was in a bowl of cereal and he was stone cold dead.

That night I felt – well, restless. Like a spendthrift with a bulging wallet. Why play with pennies? I was in need of some sort of extravagant indulgence, so I poured *two* drops of my liquid into the milk bottle. In some manner (how explain these little fulfilments of the heart?) the extra drop gave me the extra tingle of the flesh I yearned for. Like giving a decapitated turkey an extra little whack with the axe – it's not necessary, but it's *so* satisfying! Educated people will know what I am talking about.

The next day it was an elderly couple in the North suburbs who got it. They were found dead over the coffee cups. The papers didn't say so, and certainly the police wouldn't say so, but *I* knew the one vital fact: Viz: that elderly couple took milk with their coffee.

Oh dear, oh dear! Why will people mix coffee with milk?

I had only one twinge of remorse. I knew in my heart of hearts I wasn't going to keep this up for ever. I could, you know, if I felt like it. Fun's fun and all that, but business is business and I had to keep the main piece of business uppermost in mind. It was getting time to close in. So I did it once more, just once more, for fun.

The clear drop falls into the milk bottle, the milk bottle is placed outside the door, the milkman picks it up in the morning, he takes it to the plant (or the dairy, or whatever they call it) and he drops it with the million other milk bottles into the chute, or the vat, or whatever it is, and all the bottles are boiled and cleansed with all the latest scientific methods, and all the bottles come out clear and fresh as fresh air. All but one. That one has a forgotten fluid in it that can not be destroyed by fire or flame or heat or light. And the day after that two ladies who live in the heart of town drop dead at the breakfast table.

Simple, wasn't it? Sly, wasn't it?

Perhaps others before me had toyed with the idea of a willy-nilly sort of slaughter, hitting hither and yon to confuse the police, then winding up with the one truly intended victim, so that the police would assume that the real victim was just another poor innocent selected on a willy-nilly basis. Maybe others before me had had that idea. Maybe. But one thing was certain: none before me had ever discovered the perfect weapon for such a campaign.

The milk bottle. The innocent milk bottle, which enters the homes of the rich and poor alike, uptown, downtown, midtown and in the suburbs. Can *you*, dear heart, think of a lethal weapon with such a democratic soul?

So far, the trail of my indiscriminate slaying was exactly to my liking. In succession the deaths had occurred once uptown, once downtown, once in Burbank and once in the North suburb. A perfect scattering of hits. Far and roundabout. On the maps in the police stations they were undoubtedly putting pins into a map of the city, endeavouring to make some kind of a pattern out of the design of these killings.

Let them go on looking for patterns! Let them go on breaking their heads questioning the neighbours for miles around about motives, and purported enemies of the deceased, and who in the name of God would be doing this thing. Let them look. Henry Peters had a design far above and beyond the little patterns that pins can make on a map. My design was in my head.

I drew the final stroke on the 18th of December, two weeks after I had commenced the campaign and the city was in a state of panic.

But first, on the night of the 17th, I sat down to dinner with Mrs Peters.

I did the serving. Mrs Peters' contribution to the evening ritual always ended with the cooking, if cooking it can be called. From then on the effort was all mine. I served the soup and the fish and the hot custard. When she finished each course she shoved the empty dish towards me, out from under the newspaper she was reading. When she was finished with the paper she let it drop to the floor.

'Well,' she asked, spooning the custard into her mouth with quick strokes.

'Well what, Rita?'

'What happened today?'

'Today? Oh, the usual. Nothing exciting. Old Mrs Canfield in the music stacks thinks she's got a tumour in her nose.'

'Long as she's got her health.'

Oh dear, I thought. In my youth I always thought she had such a pretty wit. I was ashamed for my youth.

'What else?' she asked.

'Nothing.'

Mrs Peters leaned back in her chair and looked at me with amusement. 'Mrs Canfield, Mrs Canfield ... you know, I got her up to here.' She drew one finger across her throat. Then – the danger signal: she smiled. 'Just how old *is* this Mrs Canfield?'

The tone of her voice was unmistakable; the leer in it; the filthy imputations. I dared not reply at once, for the old ailment suddenly creeping in – the choking sensation in my throat. But I did get it out, finally:

'Mrs Canfield is ... I should judge ... about seventy years old. She is ... a grandmother ... several times over ...' My small voice (I admit, it *is* a small voice) was almost boyish now because of the choking I could not prevent.

But how could she know the choking was my hatred for her? She was never aware of my more obvious emotions; she was sensitive only to the substrata of my thoughts. The *sewers* in me, she used to call them, mistaking my secrets for sewage. Uncanny she was about my hidden thoughts, always, but blind to the facts in my face staring into her face. She never understood how much I hated her.

She went on: 'So what? They're never too old for you, are they, Bunny? I've seen the looks you give some grandmothers I know.'

'Please ... Rita ...'

'Ha!' She pushed herself back from the table. I always found it hard to camouflage my disgust at this gross, unfeminine climax to her table manners – this shoving back from the table, this squeaking revolt of chair against floor. Her manners had not always been so utterly masculine. I thought: and in the springtime of her youth she was so graceful! What has changed her so? What turned her into a man-woman?

'Coffee,' she said. She put two fingers to her lips as her cheeks puffed out. 'Right away.'

I got up from the dining alcove and went back to the kitchen.

I have recorded the dinner conversation for your sake, to give you some notion of what strength of will it took not to kill her that night. She deserved it then and there – you agree? Well, you are more impetuous than I. I am an academic man and I did not kill her that night. Of course I was tempted. Two blue cups in two blue saucers were waiting for me. I filled them with the steaming coffee. In the hidden topmost shelf of the kitchen cabinet was the test tube ... all I had to do was reach upward. But I shook myself all over and gritted my teeth. Prudence ... *prudence!* I dared not upset my perfect plan with any impetuous improvisation that night. I brought her uncontaminated coffee, fresh and steaming and pure. She drank it and liked it and was at peace with the evening paper again. It was not until the following morning that I did it, the way I planned it.

I took my early breakfast alone, as usual. Then, as usual, I prepared the makings of breakfast for Rita. The batter for the waffles, the bread in the toaster, the spoonful of jam in the little pot. I filled the percolator and placed it on the gas range. When she would wake up at her usual hour and come shuffling into the kitchen, all she would have to do was to push pedals and levers. That was the sum total of her morning chores.

Then carefully, carefully, I removed the cap from the milk bottle, dropped three clear drops from the test tube into the milk, and carefully replaced the bottle cap. Rita, you see, always had a glass of milk *and* a cup of coffee for breakfast. Good for the digestion, she always said. I suppose it was; ailments aplenty she always had but alimentary congestion was never one of them. After the business with the milk bottle I left the apartment and went to work.

That was at 9:00 in the morning.

At 12:07 I came back to the apartment, as usual, for lunch. I came, as always, bearing gifts for myself – bundles of groceries for lunch under my arms. Any attentive neighbour could see that I was living up to my daily routine in every way. I walked the three flights up the hall stairway, put the key into the lock, opened the door, entered the apartment, and saw her. I closed the door carefully behind me before I took a good look. She lay in a heap beside the table. She must have grabbed the tablecloth as she fell. It covered her like a shroud up to the neck. Pieces of crockery were all over the floor. Good. All very good.

I set my bundles on the floor, as if I had dropped them at the awful sight that greeted me as I had come home for lunch. I walked into the kitchen, took the test tube from the topmost shelf and emptied the liquid down the sink. (I remember thinking that it would kill a lot of little fishes before it would dissolve in the unconquerable ocean.) I dropped all the paraphernalia, powders and test tubes, down the incinerator door. Then I walked seven steps to the telephone, dialled the operator, and when the usual soulless female voice whinnied 'Yes, pleeyuz?' into my ear, I said, as politely as possible, 'I want a policeman.'

So they came, and they performed their duties. They examined everything, asked many questions, kept the neighbours at bay, took pictures, measured things, and in a final burst of efficiency carried the body of the deceased away. I sat in a corner of the sofa in the parlour with a handkerchief to my nose.

To the questions, to the endlessly pointless questions, I merely nodded. Obviously, I was in a torpor of grief and bewilderment. I was in no condition to be intelligently interrogated. Two of the police detectives looked at one another, shook their heads in sympathetic vibration. *Better let the old guy alone . . .* they seemed to nod to one another. *This is too much of a shock to him* ... the nod seemed to say. I caught it all over the rim of the handkerchief.

There was one detective, name of Delaney, who came over and sat next to me on the sofa. He put one hand on my knee.

'Look, Mr Peters,' he said, 'this is no time to go into details. That I know. We'll get outa here and leave you alone. But first I want to explain one thing. You been reading the papers. You know we got a maniac loose somewheres – poisoning people all over the city. We don't know why – we don't know *what* the hell he's up to. All we know is he poisons people and he don't care *where* he does it. He done it here today. He's liable to do it on the west side tomorrow, or on the east side, or over on the island maybe – we don't know. We got no defence against this kind of thing – not yet, we haven't.'

I did not look at him as I removed the handkerchief from my mouth. 'But how,' I whispered. 'How did he get in? – and ... poor Rita. ...'

'Look now,' said Mr Delaney. 'Listen to me carefully. Maybe I'll make you understand a thing or two. The guy's crazy – whoever he is. He's got the finger on some of the citizens, and we don't know why. We got no connecting link. He picked your wife today. We don't know who he'll pick tomorrow. It's that kind of a deal, shows you why we got no defence against the guy. Against somebody with a system, we can fight. Against a guy who just *kills*, anywhere, anytime, just to kill – where do we stand? You heard of Jack the Ripper? Same thing. Never know where he's gonna hit next – 'cause – well, you see – this guy, whoever he is – he thought up the damnedest murder weapon you ever heard of in your whole life. I'm sorry I can't tell you what it is, Mr Peters. But I'll tell you this – !'

He stood up then and looked down at me with fire in his eye, with a set jaw in which there was all the omnipotence, all the majesty of the law. '*We* know what it is! And that's a good head start. We'll catch him, Mr Peters. You understand me?'

'I – I think so.'

'Just – please – keep what I'm telling you under your hat. Today, your wife. Tomorrow, somebody else's wife. Or kids. It's tough it had to be your wife this time, Mr Peters. Outa three million available people, he had to pick your wife. Well, that's life. We'll be goin' now.'

He patted me on the shoulder.

In my infinite grief then, they left me to the consolation of solitude.

So there it is, dear friends and gentle hearts. Seems there's a poisoner somewhere loose in the city and he strikes willy-nilly. Like lightning. Like a madman. He must be mad. Why else would he kill so many different people in so many different places? People who have nothing, but nothing at all, to do with one another. It makes no sense. The police say they don't even know how he gets in. Well then, citizens, lock your doors. Look under the beds at night. Don't forget to bar your windows – for who guarantees that madmen and lightning always use the front door?

My neighbours, in their passion for consolation, tell me that it's all the fault of the stupid police. All that bluster out of them all the time, so high and mighty with their parking tickets and their loud mouths when a man is minding his own business. But can you ever find one when you need one? Are they ever any good when it comes to an emergency, a real emergency?

I tell the neighbours that the police are not entirely to blame. Maybe they *do* know something. They can't tell *everything* they know.

To myself I say that they don't dare tell the public about the milk. They don't dare. Just picture to yourself what would happen. Nothing less than a calamity; everybody in town would stop drinking milk! All those babies would suffer! And the poor milk companies would surely go out of business. And all those milkmen would be out of work. And all those farmers who milk the cows … and the poor cows too, what would happen to them? No siree, you can't start *that* kind of a panic. No telling where that would lead to. It's much better if the police let a few people die every day until they can find the fiend who's responsible. Then they can tell the public everything. But not until then.

Mr Delaney told me to keep what he told me under my hat. I will, of course. I know how to keep a secret. I really do. I've kept the secret of my little book, haven't I? – I mean the old one in the library that contains the formula.

Formula, did I say? Let me tell *you* a secret. My little book contains *formulae*. Plural. There is one, for example, on page 137, the fifteenth chapter if you please. It tells how to make gold out of garbage. A simple process involving a few hours' work. Then on page 192 there is a perfume very easy to prepare. If a man anoints himself with a drop of it every morning he becomes irresistible to every female within an area of thirty square miles.

I propose to make the gold first, then the perfume.

I propose to have a lot of fun.

The Hammer of God

G. K. Chesterton

The little village of Bohun Beacon was perched on a hill so steep that the tall spire of its church seemed only like the peak of a small mountain. At the foot of the church stood a smithy, generally red with fires and always littered with hammers and scraps of iron; opposite to this, over a rude cross of cobbled paths, was 'The Blue Boar', the only inn of the place. It was upon this crossway, in the lifting of a leaden and silver daybreak, that two brothers met in the street and spoke; though one was beginning the day and the other finishing it. The Rev and Hon Wilfred Bohun was very devout, and was making his way to some austere exercises of prayer or contemplation at dawn. Colonel the Hon Norman Bohun, his elder brother, was by no means devout, and was sitting in evening dress on the bench outside 'The Blue Boar', drinking what the philosophic observer was free to regard either as his last glass on Tuesday or his first on Wednesday. The colonel was not particular.

The Bohuns were one of the very few aristocratic families really dating from the Middle Ages, and their pennon had actually seen Palestine. But it is a great mistake to suppose that such houses stand high in chivalric tradition. Few except the poor preserve traditions. Aristocrats live not in traditions but in fashions. The Bohuns had been Mohocks under Queen Anne and Mashers under Queen Victoria. But like more than one of the really ancient houses, they had rotted in the last two centuries into mere drunkards and dandy degenerates, till there had even come a whisper of insanity. Certainly there was something hardly human about the colonel's wolfish pursuit of pleasure, and his chronic resolution not to go home till morning had a touch of the hideous clarity of insomnia. He was a tall, fine animal, elderly, but with hair still startlingly yellow. He would have looked merely blond and leonine, but his blue eyes were sunk so deep in his face that they looked black. They were a little too close together. He had very long yellow moustaches; on each side of them a fold or furrow from nostril to jaw, so that a sneer seemed cut into his face. Over his evening clothes he wore a curious pale yellow coat that looked more like a very light dressing-gown than an overcoat, and on the back of his head was stuck an extraordinary broad-brimmed hat of a green colour, evidently some oriental curiosity caught up at random. He was proud of appearing in such incongruous attires – proud of the fact that he always made them look congruous.

His brother the curate had also the yellow hair and the elegance, but he was buttoned up to the chin in black, and his face was clean-shaven, cultivated, and a little nervous. He seemed to live for nothing but his religion; but there were some who said (notably the blacksmith, who was a Presbyterian) that it was a love of Gothic architecture rather than of God, and that his haunting of the church like a ghost was only another and purer turn of the almost morbid thirst for beauty which sent his brother raging after women and wine. This charge was doubtful, while the man's practical piety was indubitable. Indeed, the charge was mostly an ignorant misunderstanding of the love of solitude and secret prayer, and was founded on his being often found kneeling, not before the altar, but in peculiar places, the crypts or gallery, or even in the belfry. He was at the moment about to enter the church through the yard of the smithy, but stopped and frowned a little as he saw his brother's cavernous eyes staring in the same direction. On the hypothesis that the colonel was interested in the church he did not waste any speculations. There only remained the blacksmith's shop, and though the blacksmith was a Puritan and none of his people, Wilfred Bohun had heard some scandals about a beautiful and rather celebrated wife. He flung a suspicious look across the shed, and the colonel stood up laughing to speak to him.

'Good morning, Wilfred,' he said. 'Like a good landlord I am watching sleeplessly over my people. I am going to call on the blacksmith.'

Wilfred looked at the ground, and said: 'The blacksmith is out. He is over at Greenford.'

'I know,' answered the other with silent laughter; 'that is why I am calling on him.'

'Norman, said the cleric, with his eye on a pebble in the road, 'are you ever afraid of thunderbolts?'

'What do you mean?' asked the colonel. 'Is your hobby meteorology?'

'I mean,' said Wilfred, without looking up, 'do you ever think that God might strike you in the street?'

'I beg your pardon,' said the colonel; 'I see your hobby is folk-lore.'

'I know your hobby is blasphemy,' retorted the religious man, stung in the one live place of his nature. 'But if you do not fear God, you have good reason to fear man.'

The elder raised his eyebrows politely. 'Fear man?' he said.

'Barnes the blacksmith is the biggest and strongest man for forty miles round,' said the clergyman sternly. 'I know you are no coward or weakling, but he could throw you over the wall.'

This struck home, being true, and the lowering line by mouth and nostril darkened and deepened. For a moment he stood with the heavy sneer on his face. But in an instant Colonel Bohun had recovered his own cruel good humour and laughed, showing two dog-like front teeth under his yellow moustache. 'In that case, my dear Wilfred,' he said quite carelessly, 'it was wise for the last of the Bohuns to come out partially in armour.'

And he took off the queer round hat covered with green, showing that it was lined within with steel. Wilfred recognized it indeed as a light Japanese or Chinese helmet torn down from a trophy that hung in the old family hall. 'It was the first hat to hand,' explained his brother airily; 'always the nearest hat – and the nearest woman.'

'The blacksmith is away at Greenford,' said Wilfred quietly; 'the time of his return is unsettled.'

And with that he turned and went into the church with bowed head, crossing himself like one who wishes to be quit of an unclean spirit. He was anxious to forget such grossness in the cool twilight of his tall Gothic cloisters; but on that morning it was fated that his still round of religious exercises should be everywhere arrested by small shocks. As he entered the church, hitherto always empty at that hour, a kneeling figure rose hastily to its feet and came towards the full daylight of the doorway. When the curate saw it he stood still with surprise. For the early worshipper was none other than the village idiot, a nephew of the blacksmith, one who neither would nor could care for the church or for anything else. He was always called 'Mad Joe', and seemed to have no other name; he was a dark, strong, slouching lad, with a heavy white face, dark straight hair, and a mouth always open. As he passed the priest, his moon-calf countenance gave no hint of what he had been doing or thinking of. He had never been known to pray before. What sort of prayers was he saying now? Extraordinary prayers surely.

Wilfred Bohun stood rooted to the spot long enough to see the idiot go out into the sunshine, and even to see his dissolute brother hail him with a sort of avuncular jocularity. The last thing he saw was the colonel throwing pennies at the open mouth of Joe, with the serious appearance of trying to hit it.

This ugly sunlight picture of stupidity and cruelty of the earth sent the ascetic finally to his prayers for purification and new thoughts. He went up to a pew in the gallery, which brought him under a coloured window which he loved and always quieted his spirit; a blue window with an angel carrying lilies. There he began to think less about the half-wit, with his livid face and mouth like a fish. He began to think less of his evil brother, pacing like a lean lion in his terrible hunger. He sank deeper and deeper into those cold and sweet colours of silver blossoms and sapphire sky.

In this place half an hour afterwards he was found by Gibbs, the village cobbler, who had been sent for him in some haste. He got to his feet with promptitude, for he knew that no small matter would have brought Gibbs into such a place at all. The cobbler was, as in many villages, an atheist, and his appearance in church was a shade more extraordinary than Mad Joe's. It was a morning of theological enigmas.

'What is it?' asked Wilfred Bohun rather stiffly, but putting out a trembling hand for his hat.

The atheist spoke in a tone that, coming from him, was quite startlingly respectful, and even, as it were, huskily sympathetic.

'You must excuse me, sir,' he said in a hoarse whisper, 'but we didn't think it right not to let you know at once. I'm afraid a rather dreadful thing has happened, sir. I'm afraid your brother—'

Wilfred clenched his frail hands. 'What devilry has he done now?' he cried in involuntary passion.

'Why, sir,' said the cobbler, coughing, 'I'm afraid he's done nothing, and won't do anything. I'm afraid he's done for. You had really better come down, sir.'

The curate followed the cobbler down a short winding stair, which brought them out at an entrance rather higher than the street. Bohun saw the tragedy in one glance, flat underneath him like a plan. In the yard of the smithy were standing five or six men mostly in black, one in an inspector's uniform. They included the doctor, the Presbyterian minister, and the priest from the Roman Catholic chapel, to which the blacksmith's wife belonged. The latter was speaking to her, indeed, very rapidly, in an undertone, as she, a magnificent woman with red-gold hair, was sobbing blindly on a bench. Between these two groups, and just clear of the main heap of hammers, lay a man in evening dress, spread-eagled and flat on his face. From the height above Wilfred could have sworn to every item of his costume and appearance, down to the Bohun rings upon his fingers; but the skull was only a hideous splash, like a star of blackness and blood.

Wilfred Bohun gave but one glance, and ran down the steps into the yard. The doctor, who was the family physician, saluted him, but he scarcely took any notice. He could only stammer out: 'My brother is dead. What does it mean? What is this horrible mystery?' There was an unhappy silence; and then the cobbler, the most outspoken man present, answered: 'Plenty of horror, sir,' he said, 'but not much mystery.'

'What do you mean?' asked Wilfred, with a white face.

'It's plain enough,' answered Gibbs. 'There is only one man for forty miles round that could have struck such a blow as that, and he's the man that had most reason to.'

'We must not prejudge anything,' put in the doctor, a tall, black-bearded man, rather nervously; 'but it is competent for me to corroborate what Mr Gibbs says about the nature of the blow, sir; it is an incredible blow. Mr Gibbs says that only one man in this district could have done it. I should have said myself that nobody could have done it.'

A shudder of superstition went through the slight figure of the curate. 'I can hardly understand,' he said.

'Mr Bohun,' said the doctor in a low voice, 'metaphors literally fail me. It is inadequate to say that the skull was smashed to bits like an egg-shell. Fragments of bone were driven into the body and the ground like bullets into a mud wall. It was the hand of a giant.'

He was silent a moment, looking grimly through his glasses; then he added: 'The thing has one advantage – that it clears most people of suspicion at one stroke. If you or I or any normally made man in the country were accused of this crime, we should be acquitted as an infant would be acquitted of stealing the Nelson Column.'

'That's what I say,' repeated the cobbler obstinately; 'there's only one man that could have done it, and he's the man that would have done it. Where's Simeon Barnes, the blacksmith?'

'He's over at Greenford,' faltered the curate.

'More likely over in France,' muttered the cobbler.

'No; he is in neither of those places,' said a small and colourless voice, which came from the little Roman priest who had joined the group. 'As a matter of fact, he is coming up the road at this moment.'

The little priest was not an interesting man to look at, having stubbly brown hair and a round and stolid face. But if he had been as splendid as Apollo no one would have looked at him at that moment. Everyone turned round and peered at the pathway which wound across the plain below, along which was indeed walking, at his own huge stride and with a hammer on his shoulder, Simeon the smith. He was a bony and gigantic man, with deep, dark, sinister eyes and a dark chin beard. He was walking and talking quietly with two other men; and though he was never specially cheerful, he seemed quite at ease.

'My God!' cried the atheistic cobbler, 'and there's the hammer he did it with.'

'No,' said the inspector, a sensible-looking man with a sandy moustache, speaking for the first time. 'There's the hammer he did it with over there by the church wall. We have left it and the body exactly as they are.'

All glanced round, and the short priest went across and looked down in silence at the tool where it lay. It was one of the smallest and the lightest of the hammers, and would not have caught the eye among the rest; but on the iron edge of it were blood and yellow hair.

After a silence the short priest spoke without looking up, and there was a new note in his dull voice. 'Mr Gibbs was hardly right,' he said, 'in saying that there is no mystery. There is at least the mystery of why so big a man should attempt so big a blow with so little a hammer.'

'Oh, never mind that,' cried Gibbs, in a fever. 'What are we to do with Simeon Barnes?'

'Leave him alone,' said the priest quietly. 'He is coming here of himself. I know those two men with him. They are very good fellows from Greenford, and they have come over about the Presbyterian chapel.'

Even as he spoke the tall smith swung round the corner of the church, and strode into his own yard. Then he stood there quite still, and the hammer fell from his hand. The inspector, who had preserved impenetrable propriety, immediately went up to him.

'I won't ask you, Mr Barnes,' he said, 'whether you know anything about what has happened here. You are not bound to say. I hope you don't know, and that you will be able to prove it. But I must go through the form of arresting you in the King's name for the murder of Colonel Norman Bohun.'

'You are not bound to say anything,' said the cobbler in officious excitement. 'They've got to prove everything. They haven't proved yet that it is Colonel Bohun, with the head all smashed up like that.'

'That won't wash,' said the doctor aside to the priest. 'That's out of the detective stories. I was the colonel's medical man, and I knew his body better than he did. He had very fine hands, but quite peculiar ones. The second and third fingers were the same in length. Oh, that's the colonel right enough.'

As he glanced at the brained corpse upon the ground the iron eyes of the motionless blacksmith followed them, and rested there also.

'Is Colonel Bohun dead?' said the smith quite calmly. 'Then he's damned.'

'Don't say anything! Oh, don't say anything,' cried the atheist cobbler, dancing about in an ecstasy of admiration of the English legal system. For no man is such a legalist as the good Secularist.

The blacksmith turned on him over his shoulder the august face of a fanatic.

'It's well for you infidels to dodge like foxes because the world's law favours you,' he said; 'but God guards His own in His pocket, as you shall see this day.'

Then he pointed to the colonel and said: 'When did this dog die in his sins?'

'Moderate your language,' said the doctor.

'Moderate the Bible's language, and I'll moderate mine. When did he die?'

'I saw him alive at six o'clock this morning,' stammered Wilfred Bohun.

'God is good,' said the smith. 'Mr Inspector, I have not the slightest objection to being arrested. It is you who may object to arresting me. I don't mind leaving the court without a stain on my character. You do mind, perhaps, leaving the court with a bad set-back in your career.'

The solid inspector for the first time looked at the blacksmith with a lively eye; as did everybody else, except the short, strange priest, who was still looking down at the little hammer that had dealt the dreadful blow.

'There are two men standing outside this shop,' went on the blacksmith with ponderous lucidity, 'good tradesmen in Greenford whom you all know, who will swear that they saw me from before midnight till day-break and long after in the committee-room of our Revival Mission, which sits all night, we save souls so fast. In Greenford itself twenty people could swear to me for all that time. If I were a heathen, Mr Inspector, I would let you walk on to your downfall. But as a Christian man I feel bound to give you your chance, and ask you whether you will hear my alibi now or in court.'

The inspector seemed for the first time disturbed, and said, 'Of course I should be glad to clear you altogether now.'

The smith walked out of his yard with the same long and easy stride, and returned to his two friends from Greenford, who were indeed friends of nearly everyone present. Each of them said a few words which no one ever thought of disbelieving. When they had spoken, the innocence of Simeon stood up as solid as the great church above them.

One of those silences struck the group which are more strange and in-sufferable than any speech. Madly, in order to make conversation, the curate said to the Catholic priest:

'You seem very much interested in that hammer, Father Brown.'

'Yes, I am,' said Father Brown; 'why is it such a small hammer?'

The doctor swung round on him.

'By George, that's true,' he cried; 'who would use a little hammer with ten larger hammers lying about?'

Then he lowered his voice in the curate's ear and said: 'Only the kind of person that can't lift a large hammer. It is not a question of force or courage between the sexes. It's a question of lifting power in the shoulders. A bold woman could commit ten murders with a light hammer and never turn a hair. She could not kill a beetle with a heavy one.'

Wilfred Bohun was staring at him with a sort of hypnotized horror, while Father Brown listened with his head a little on one side, really interested and attentive. The doctor went on with more hissing emphasis:

'Why do these idiots always assume that the only person who hates the wife's lover is the wife's husband? Nine times out of ten the person who most hates the wife's lover is the wife. Who knows what insolence or treachery he had shown her – look there?'

He made a momentary gesture towards the red-haired woman on the bench. She had lifted her head at last and the tears were drying on her splendid face. But the eyes were fixed on the corpse with an electric glare that had in it something of idiocy.

The Rev Wilfred Bohun made a limp gesture as if waving away all desire to know; but Father Brown, dusting off his sleeve some ashes blown from the furnace, spoke in his indifferent way.

'You are like so many doctors,' he said; 'your mental science is really suggestive. It is your physical science that is utterly impossible. I agreed that the woman wants to kill the co-respondent much more than the petitioner does. And I agree that a woman will always pick up a small hammer instead of a big one. But the difficulty is one of physical impossibility. No woman ever born could have smashed a man's skull out flat like that.' Then he added reflectively, after a pause: 'These people haven't grasped the whole of it. The man was actually wearing an iron helmet, and the blow scattered it like broken glass. Look at that woman. Look at her arms.'

Silence held them all up again, and then the doctor said rather sulkily: 'Well, I may be wrong; there are objections to everything. But I stick to the main point. No man but an idiot would pick up that little hammer if he could use a big hammer.'

With that the lean and quivering hands of Wilfred Bohun went up to his head and seemed to clutch his scanty yellow hair. After an instant they dropped, and he cried: 'That was the word I wanted; you have said the word.'

Then he continued, mastering his discomposure: 'The words you said were, "No man but an idiot would pick up the small hammer".'

'Yes,' said the doctor. 'Well?'

'Well,' said the curate, 'no man but an idiot did.' The rest stared at him with eyes arrested and riveted, and he went on in a febrile and feminine agitation.

'I am a priest,' he cried unsteadily, 'and a priest should be no shedder of blood. I – I mean that he should bring no one to the gallows. And I thank God that I see the criminal clearly now – because he is a criminal who cannot be brought to the gallows.'

'You will not denounce him?' enquired the doctor.

'He would not be hanged if I did denounce him,' answered Wilfred with a wild but curiously happy smile. 'When I went into the church this morning I found a madman praying there – that poor Joe, who has been wrong all his life. God knows what he prayed; but with such strange folk it is not incredible to suppose that their prayers are all upside down. Very likely a lunatic would pray before killing a man. When I last saw poor Joe he was with my brother. My brother was mocking him.'

'By Jove!' cried the doctor, 'this is talking at last. But how do you explain—'

The Rev Wilfred was almost trembling with the excitement of his own glimpse of the truth. 'Don't you see; don't you see,' he cried feverishly;

'that is the only theory that covers both the queer things, that answers both the riddles. The two riddles are the little hammer and the big blow. The smith might have struck the big blow, but would not have chosen the little hammer. His wife would have chosen the little hammer, but she could not have struck the big blow. But the madman might have done both. As for the little hammer – why, he was mad and might have picked up anything. And for the big blow, have you never heard, doctor, that a maniac in his paroxysm may have the strength of ten men?'

The doctor drew a deep breath and then said, 'By golly, I believe you've got it.'

Father Brown had fixed his eyes on the speaker so long and steadily as to prove that his large grey, ox-like eyes were not quite so insignificant as the rest of his face. When silence had fallen he said with marked respect: 'Mr Bohun, yours is the only theory yet propounded which holds water every way and is essentially unassailable. I think, therefore, that you deserve to be told, on my positive knowledge, that it is not the true one.' And with that the old little man walked away and stared again at the hammer.

'That fellow seems to know more than he ought to,' whispered the doctor peevishly to Wilfred. 'Those popish priests are deucedly sly.'

'No, no,' said Bohun, with a sort of wild fatigue. 'It was the lunatic. It was the lunatic.'

The group of the two clerics and the doctor had fallen away from the more official group containing the inspector and the man he had arrested. Now, however, that their own party had broken up, they heard voices from the others. The priest looked up quietly and then looked down again as he heard the blacksmith say in a loud voice:

'I hope I've convinced you, Mr Inspector. I'm a strong man, as you say, but I couldn't have flung my hammer bang here from Greenford. My hammer hasn't any wings that it should come flying half a mile over hedges and fields.'

The inspector laughed amicably and said: 'No, I think you can be considered out of it, though it's one of the rummiest coincidences I ever saw. I can only ask you to give us all the assistance you can in finding a man as big and strong as yourself. By George! you might be useful, if only to hold him! I suppose you yourself have no guess at the man?'

'I may have a guess,' said the pale smith, 'but it is not at a man.' Then, seeing the scared eyes turn towards his wife on the bench, he put his huge hand on her shoulder and said: 'Nor a woman either.'

'What do you mean?' asked the inspector jocularly. 'You don't think cows use hammers, do you?'

'I think no thing of flesh held that hammer,' said the blacksmith in a stifled voice; 'mortally speaking, I think the man died alone.'

Wilfred made a sudden forward movement and peered at him with burning eyes.

'Do you mean to say, Barnes,' came the sharp voice of the cobbler, 'that the hammer jumped up of itself and knocked the man down?'

'Oh, you gentlemen may stare and snigger,' cried Simeon; 'you clergymen who tell us on Sunday in what a stillness the Lord smote Sennacherib. I believe that One who walks invisible in every house defended the honour of mine, and laid the defiler dead before the door of it. I believe the force in that blow was just the force there is in earthquakes, and no force less.'

Wilfred said, with a voice utterly undescribable: 'I told Norman myself to beware of the thunderbolt.'

'That agent is outside my jurisdiction,' said the inspector with a slight smile.

'You are not outside His,' answered the smith; 'see you to it,' and, turning his broad back, he went into the house.

The shaken Wilfred was led away by Father Brown, who had an easy and friendly way with him. 'Let us get out of this horrid place, Mr Bohun,' he said. 'May I look inside your church? I hear it's one of the oldest in England. We take some interest, you know,' he added with a comical grimace, 'in old English churches.'

Wilfred Bohun did not smile, for humour was never his strong point. But he nodded rather eagerly, being only too ready to explain the Gothic splendours to someone more likely to be sympathetic than the Presbyterian blacksmith or the atheist cobbler.

'By all means,' he said; 'let us go in at this side.' And he led the way into the high side entrance at the top of the flight of steps. Father Brown was mounting the first step to follow him when he felt a hand on his shoulder, and turned to behold the dark, thin figure of the doctor, his face darker yet with suspicion.

'Sir,' said the physician harshly, 'you appear to know some secrets in this black business. May I ask if you are going to keep them to yourself?'

'Why, doctor,' answered the priest, smiling quite pleasantly, 'there is one very good reason why a man of my trade should keep things to himself when he is not sure of them, and that is that it is so constantly his duty to keep them to himself when he is sure of them. But if you think I have been discourteously reticent with you or anyone, I will go to the extreme limit of my custom. I will give you two very large hints.'

'Well, sir?' said the doctor gloomily.

'First,' said Father Brown quietly, 'the thing is quite in your own province. It is a matter of physical science. The blacksmith is mistaken, not perhaps in saying that the blow was divine, but certainly in saying that it came by a miracle. It was no miracle, doctor, except in so far as a man is himself a miracle, with his strange and wicked and yet half-heroic heart. The force that smashed that skull was a force well known to scientists – one of the most frequently debated of the laws of nature.'

The doctor, who was looking at him with frowning intentness, only said: 'And the other hint!'

'The other hint is this,' said the priest. 'Do you remember the blacksmith, though he believes in miracles, talking scornfully of the impossible fairy tale that his hammer had wings and flew·half a mile across country?'

'Yes,' said the doctor, 'I remember that.'

'Well,' added Father Brown, with a broad smile, 'that fairy tale was the nearest thing to the real truth that has been said to-day.' And with that he turned his back and stumped up the steps after the curate.

The Reverend Wilfred, who had been waiting for him, pale and impatient, as if this little delay were the last straw for his nerves, led him immediately to his favourite corner of the church, that part of the gallery closest to the carved roof and lit by the wonderful window with the angel. The little Latin priest explored and admired everything exhaustively, talking cheerfully but in a low voice all the time. When in the course of his investigation he found the side exit and the winding stair down which Wilfred had rushed to find his brother dead, Father Brown ran not down but up, with the agility of a monkey, and his clear voice came from an outer platform above.

'Come up here, Mr Bohun,' he called. 'The air will do you good.'

Bohun followed him, and came out on a kind of stone gallery or balcony outside the building, from which one could see the illimitable plain in which their small hill stood, wooded away to the purple horizon and dotted with villages and farms. Clear and square, but quite small beneath them, was the blacksmith's yard, where the inspector still stood taking notes and the corpse still lay like a smashed fly.

'Might be the map of the world, mightn't it?' said Father Brown.

'Yes,' said Bohun very gravely, and nodded his head.

Immediately beneath and about them the lines of the Gothic building plunged outwards into the void with a sickening swiftness akin to suicide. There is that element of Titan energy in the architecture of the Middle Ages that, from whatever aspect it be seen, it always seems to be rushing away, like the strong back of some maddened horse. This church was hewn out of ancient and silent stone, bearded with old fungoids and stained with the nests of birds. And yet, when they saw it from below, it sprang like a fountain at the stars; and when they saw it, as now, from above, it poured like a cataract into a voiceless pit. For these two men on the tower were left alone with the most terrible aspect of the Gothic; the monstrous foreshortening and disproportion, the dizzy perspectives, the glimpse of great things small and small things great; a topsy-turvydom of stone in the mid-air. Details of stone, enormous by their proximity, were relieved against a pattern of fields and farms, pygmy in their distance. A carved bird or beast at a corner seemed like some vast walking or flying dragon wasting the pastures and villages below. The whole atmosphere was dizzy and dangerous, as if men were upheld in air amid the gyrating wings of colossal genii; and the whole of that old church, as tall and rich as a cathedral, seemed to sit upon the sunlit country like a cloud-burst.

'I think there is something rather dangerous about standing on these high places even to pray,' said Father Brown. 'Heights were made to be looked at, not to be looked from.'

'Do you mean that one may fall over?' asked Wilfred.

'I mean that one's soul may fall if one's body doesn't,' said the other priest.

'I scarcely understand you,' remarked Bohun indistinctly.

'Look at that blacksmith, for instance,' went on Father Brown calmly; 'a good man, but not a Christian – hard, imperious, unforgiving. Well, his Scotch religion was made up by men who prayed on hills and high crags, and learnt to look down on the world more than to look up at heaven. Humility is the mother of giants. One sees great things from the valley; only small things from the peak.'

'But he – he didn't do it,' said Bohun tremulously.

'No,' said the other in an odd voice; 'we know he didn't do it.'

After a moment he resumed, looking tranquilly out over the plain with his pale grey eyes. 'I knew a man,' he said, 'who began by worshipping with others before the altar, but who grew fond of high and lonely places to pray from, corners or niches in the belfry or the spire. And once in one of those dizzy places, where the whole world seemed to turn under him like a wheel, his brain turned also, and he fancied he was God. So that though he was a good man, he committed a great crime.'

Wilfred's face was turned away, but his bony hands turned blue and white as they tightened on the parapet of stone.

'He thought it was given to *him* to judge the world and strike down the sinner. He would never have had such a thought if he had been kneeling with other men upon a floor. But he saw all men walking about like insects. He saw one especially strutting just below him, insolent and evident by the bright green hat – a poisonous insect.'

Rooks cawed round the corners of the belfry; but there was no other sound till Father Brown went on.

'This also tempted him, that he had in his hand one of the most awful engines of nature; I mean gravitation, that mad and quickening rush by which all earth's creatures fly back to her heart when released. see, the inspector is strutting just below us in the smithy. If I were to toss a pebble over this parapet it would be something like a bullet by the time it struck him. If I were to drop a hammer – even a small hammer—'

Wilfred Bohun threw one leg over the parapet, and Father Brown had him in a minute by the collar.

'Not by that door,' he said quite gently; 'that door leads to hell.'

Bohun staggered back against the wall, and stared at him with frightful eyes.

'How do you know all this?' he cried. 'Are you a devil?'

'I am a man,' answered Father Brown gravely; 'and therefore have all devils in my heart. Listen to me,' he said after a short pause. 'I know what you did – at least, I can guess the great part of it. When you left your brother you were racked with no unrighteous rage to the extent even that you snatched up a small hammer, half inclined to kill him with his foulness on his mouth. Recoiling, you thrust it under your buttoned coat instead, and rushed into the church. You pray wildly in many places, under the angel window, upon the platform above, and on a higher platform still, from which you could see the colonel's Eastern hat like the back of a green beetle crawling about. Then something snapped in your soul, and you let God's thunderbolt fall.'

Wilfred put a weak hand to his head, and asked in a low voice: 'How did you know that his hat looked like a green beetle?'

'Oh, that,' said the other with the shadow of a smile, 'that was common sense. But hear me further. I say I know all this; but no one else shall know it. The next step is for you; I shall take no more steps; I will seal this with the seal of confession. If you ask me why, there are many reasons, and only one that concerns you. I leave things to you because you have not yet gone far wrong, as assassins go. You did not help to fix the crime on the smith when it was easy; or on his wife, when that was easy. You tried to fix it on the imbecile because you knew that he could not suffer. That was one of the gleams that it is my business to find in assassins. And now come down into the village, and go your own way as free as the wind; for I have said my last word.'

They went down the winding stairs in utter silence, and came out into the sunlight by the smithy. Wilfred carefully unlatched the wooden gate of the yard, and going up to the inspector, said: 'I wish to give myself up; I have killed my brother.'

Accident

Agatha Christie

'. . . And I tell you this – it's the same woman – not a doubt of it!'

Captain Haydock looked into the eager, vehement face of his friend and sighed. He wished Evans would not be so positive and so jubilant. In the course of a career spent at sea, the old sea captain had learned to leave things that did not concern him well alone. His friend, Evans, late C.I.D. inspector, had a different philosophy of life. 'Acting on information received—' had been his motto in early days, and he had improved upon it to the extent of finding out his own information. Inspector Evans had been a very smart, wide-awake officer, and had justly earned the promotion which had been his. Even now, when he had retired from the force, and had settled down in the country cottage of his dreams, his professional instinct was still active.

'Don't often forget a face,' he reiterated complacently. 'Mrs Anthony – yes, it's Mrs Anthony right enough. When you said Mrs Merrowdene – I knew her at once.'

Captain Haydock stirred uneasily. The Merrowdenes were his nearest neighbours, barring Evans himself, and this identifying of Mrs Merrowdene with a former heroine of a *cause célèbre* distressed him.

'It's a long time ago,' he said rather weakly.

'Nine years,' said Evans, accurately as ever. 'Nine years and three months. You remember the case?'

'In a vague sort of way.'

'Anthony turned out to be an arsenic eater,' said Evans, 'so they acquitted her.'

'Well, why shouldn't they?'

'No reason in the world. Only verdict they could give on the evidence. Absolutely correct.'

'Then that's all right,' said Haydock. 'And I don't see what we're bothering about.'

'Who's bothering?'

'I thought you were.'

'Not at all.'

'The thing's over and done with,' summed up the captain. 'If Mrs Merrowdene at one time of her life was unfortunate enough to be tried and acquitted for murder—'

'It's not usually considered unfortunate to be acquitted,' put in Evans.

'You know what I mean,' said Captain Haydock irritably. 'If the poor lady has been through that harrowing experience, it's no business of ours to rake it up, is it?'

Evans did not answer.

'Come now, Evans. The lady was innocent – you've just said so.'

'I didn't say she was innocent. I said she was acquitted.'

'It's the same thing.'

'Not always.'

Captain Haydock, who had commenced to tap his pipe out against the side of his chair, stopped, and sat up with a very alert expression.

'Hallo – allo – allo,' he said. 'The wind's in that quarter, is it? You think she wasn't innocent?'

'I wouldn't say that. I just – don't know. Anthony was in the habit of taking arsenic. His wife got it for him. One day, by mistake, he takes far too much. Was the mistake his or his wife's? Nobody could tell, and the jury very properly gave her the benefit of the doubt. That's all quite right and I'm not finding fault with it. All the same – I'd like to *know*.'

Captain Haydock transferred his attention to his pipe once more.

'Well,' he said comfortably. 'It's none of our business.'

'I'm not so sure . . .'

'But surely—'

'Listen to me a minute. This man, Merrowdene – in his laboratory this evening, fiddling round with tests – you remember—'

'Yes. He mentioned Marsh's test for arsenic. Said *you* would know all about it – it was in *your* line – and chuckled. He wouldn't have said that if he'd thought for one moment—'

Evans interrupted him.

'You mean he wouldn't have said that if he *knew*. They've been married how long – six years you told me? I bet you anything he has no idea his wife is the once notorious Mrs Anthony.'

'And he will certainly not know it from me,' said Captain Haydock stiffly.

Evans paid no attention, but went on:

'You interrupted me just now. After Marsh's test, Merrowdene heated a substance in a test-tube, the metallic residue he dissolved in water and then precipitated it by adding silver nitrate. That was a test for chlorates. A neat unassuming little test. But I chanced to read these words in a book that stood open on the table: "*H_2SO_4 decomposes chlorates with evolution of CL_4O_2. If heated, violent explosions occur; the mixture ought therefore to be kept cool and only very small quantities used.*"'

Haydock stared at his friend.

'Well, what about it?'

'Just this. In my profession we've got tests too – tests for murder. There's adding up the facts – weighing them, dissecting the residue when you've allowed for prejudice and the general inaccuracy of witnesses. But there's another test of murder – one that is fairly accurate, but rather – dangerous! *A murderer is seldom content with one crime.* Give him time, and a lack of suspicion, and he'll commit another. You catch a man – has he murdered his wife or hasn't he? – perhaps the case isn't very black against him. Look into his past – if you find that he's had several wives – and that they've all died shall we say – rather curiously? – then you *know*! I'm not speaking *legally*, you understand. I'm speaking of *moral* certainty. Once you *know*, you can go ahead looking for evidence.'

'Well?'

'I'm coming to the point. That's all right if there *is* a past to look into. But suppose you catch your murderer at his or her first crime? Then that test will be one from which you get no reaction. But suppose the prisoner acquitted – starting life under another name. Will or will not the murderer repeat the crime?'

'That's a horrible idea!'

'Do you still say it's none of our business?'

'Yes, I do. You've no reason to think that Mrs Merrowdene is anything but a perfectly innocent woman.'

The ex-inspector was silent for a moment. Then he said slowly:

'I told you that we looked into her past and found nothing. That's not quite true. There was a stepfather. As a girl of eighteen she had a fancy for some young man – and her stepfather exerted his authority to keep them apart. She and her stepfather went for a walk along a rather dangerous part of the cliff. There was an accident – the stepfather went too near the edge – it gave way, and he went over and was killed.'

'You don't think –'

'It was an accident. *Accident!* Anthony's over-dose of arsenic was an accident. She'd never have been tried if it hadn't transpired that there was another man – he sheered off, by the way. Looked as though he weren't satisfied even if the jury were. I tell you, Haydock, where that woman is concerned I'm afraid of another – accident!'

The old captain shrugged his shoulders.

'It's been nine years since that affair. Why should there be another "accident," as you call it, now?'

'I didn't say now. I said some day or other. If the necessary motive arose.'

Captain Haydock shrugged his shoulders.

'Well, I don't know how you're going to guard against that.'

'Neither do I,' said Evans ruefully.

'I should leave well alone,' said Captain Haydock. 'No good ever came of butting into other people's affairs.'

But that advice was not palatable to the ex-inspector. He was a man of patience but determination. Taking leave of his friend, he sauntered down to the village, revolving in his mind the possibilities of some kind of successful action.

Turning into the post office to buy some stamps, he ran into the object of his solicitude, George Merrowdene. The ex-chemistry professor was a small dreamy-looking man, gentle and kindly in manner, and usually completely absent-minded. He recognized the other and greeted him amicably, stooping to recover the letters that the impact had caused him to drop on the ground. Evans stooped also and, more rapid in his movements than the other, secured them first, handing them back to their owner with an apology.

He glanced down at them in doing so, and the address on the topmost suddenly awakened all his suspicions anew. It bore the name of a well-known insurance firm.

Instantly his mind was made up. The guileless George Merrowdene hardly realized how it came about that he and the ex-inspector were strolling down the village together, and still less could he have said how it came about that the conversation should come round to the subject of life insurance.

Evans had no difficulty in attaining his object. Merrowdene of his own accord volunteered the information that he had just insured his life for his wife's benefit, and asked Evans's opinion of the company in question.

'I made some rather unwise investments,' he explained. 'As a result my income has diminished. If anything were to happen to me, my wife would be left very badly off. This insurance will put things right.'

'She didn't object to the idea?' inquired Evans casually. 'Some ladies do, you know. Feel it's unlucky – that sort of thing.'

'Oh, Margaret is very practical,' said Merrowdene, smiling. 'Not at all superstitious. In fact, I believe it was her idea originally. She didn't like my being so worried.'

Evans had got the information he wanted. He left the other shortly afterwards, and his lips were set in a grim line. The late Mr Anthony had insured his life in his wife's favour a few weeks before his death.

Accustomed to rely on his instincts, he was perfectly sure in his own mind. But how to act was another matter. He wanted, not to arrest a criminal red-handed, but to prevent a crime being committed, and that was a very different and a very much more difficult thing.

All day he was very thoughtful. There was a Primrose League Fête that afternoon held in the grounds of the local squire, and he went to it, indulging in the penny dip, guessing the weight of a pig, and shying at coconuts all with the same look of abstracted concentration on his face. He even indulged in half a crown's worth of Zara, the Crystal Gazer, smiling a little to himself as he did so, remembering his own activities against fortune-tellers in his official days.

He did not pay very much heed to her sing-song droning voice – till the end of a sentence held his attention.

'. . . And you will very shortly – very shortly indeed – be engaged on a matter of life or death. . . . Life or death to one person.'

'Eh – what's that?' he asked abruptly.

'A decision – you have a decision to make. You must be very careful – very, very careful. . . . If you were to make a mistake – the smallest mistake—'

'Yes?'

The fortune-teller shivered. Inspector Evans knew it was all nonsense, but he was nevertheless impressed.

'I warn you – *you must not make a mistake*. If you do, I see the result clearly – a death. . . .'

Odd, damned odd. A death. Fancy her lighting upon that!

'If I make a mistake a death will result? Is that it?'

'Yes.'

'In that case,' said Evans, rising to his feet and handing over half a crown, 'I mustn't make a mistake, eh?'

He spoke lightly enough, but as he went out of the tent, his jaw set determinedly. Easy to say – not so easy to be sure of doing. He mustn't make a slip. A life, a valuable human life depended on it.

And there was no one to help him. He looked across at the figure of his friend Haydock in the distance. No help there. 'Leave things alone,' was Haydock's motto. And that wouldn't do here.

Haydock was talking to a woman. She moved away from him and came towards Evans and the inspector recognized her. It was Mrs Merrowdene. On an impulse he put himself deliberately in her path.

Mrs Merrowdene was rather a fine-looking woman. She had a broad serene brow, very beautiful brown eyes, and a placid expression. She had the look of an Italian madonna which she heightened by parting her hair in the middle and looping it over her ears. She had a deep rather sleepy voice.

She smiled up at Evans, a contented welcoming smile.

'I thought it was you, Mrs Anthony – I mean Mrs Merrowdene,' he said glibly.

He made the slip deliberately, watching her without seeming to do so. He saw her eyes widen, heard the quick intake of her breath. But her eyes did not falter. She gazed at him steadily and proudly.

'I was looking for my husband,' she said quietly. 'Have you seen him anywhere about?'

'He was over in that direction when I last saw him.'

They went side by side in the direction indicated, chatting quietly and pleasantly. The inspector felt his admiration mounting. What a woman! What self-command. What wonderful poise. A remarkable woman – and a very dangerous one. He felt sure – a very dangerous one.

He still felt very uneasy, though he was satisfied with his initial step. He had let her know that he recognized her. That would put her on her guard. She would not dare attempt anything rash. There was the question of Merrowdene. If he could be warned. . . .

They found the little man absently contemplating a china doll which had fallen to his share in the penny dip. His wife suggested going home and he agreed eagerly. Mrs Merrowdene turned to the inspector:

'Won't you come back with us and have a quiet cup of tea, Mr Evans?'

Was there a faint note of challenge in her voice? He thought there was.

'Thank you, Mrs Merrowdene. I should like to very much.'

They walked there, talking together of pleasant ordinary things. The sun shone, a breeze blew gently, everything around them was pleasant and ordinary.

Their maid was out at the fête, Mrs Merrowdene explained, when they arrived at the charming old-world cottage. She went into her room to remove her hat, returning to set out tea and boil the kettle on a little silver lamp. From a shelf near the fireplace she took three small bowls and saucers.

'We have some very special Chinese tea,' she explained. 'And we always drink it in the Chinese manner – out of bowls, not cups.'

She broke off, peered into a cup and exchanged it for another with an exclamation of annoyance.

'George – it's too bad of you. You've been taking these bowls again.'

'I'm sorry, dear,' said the professor apologetically. 'They're such a convenient size. The ones I ordered haven't come.'

'One of these days you'll poison us all,' said his wife with a half-laugh. 'Mary finds them in the laboratory and brings them back here, and never troubles to wash them out unless they've anything very noticeable in them. Why, you were using one of them for potassium cyanide the other day. Really, George, it's frightfully dangerous.'

Merrowdene looked a little irritated.

'Mary's no business to remove things from the laboratory. She's not to touch anything there.'

'But we often leave our teacups there after tea. How is she to know? Be reasonable, dear.'

The professor went into his laboratory, murmuring to himself, and with a smile Mrs Merrowdene poured boiling water on the tea and blew out the flame of the little silver lamp.

Evans was puzzled. Yet a glimmering of light penetrated to him. For some reason or other, Mrs Merrowdene was showing her hand. Was this to be the 'accident'? Was she speaking of all this so as deliberately to prepare her alibi beforehand? So that when, one day, the 'accident' happened, he would be forced to give evidence in her favour. Stupid of her, if so, because before that —

Suddenly he drew in his breath. She had poured the tea into the three bowls. One she set before him, one before herself, the other she placed on a little table by the fire near the chair her husband usually sat in, and it was as she placed this last one on the table that a little strange smile curved round her lips. It was the smile that did it.

He knew!

A remarkable woman – a dangerous woman. No waiting – no preparation. This afternoon – this very afternoon – with him here as witness. The boldness of it took his breath away.

It was clever – it was damnably clever. He would be able to prove nothing. She counted on his not suspecting – simply because it was 'so soon.' A woman of lightning rapidity of thought and action.

He drew a deep breath and leaned forward.

'Mrs Merrowdene, I'm a man of queer whims. Will you be very kind and indulge me in one of them?'

She looked inquiring but unsuspicious.

He rose, took the bowl from in front of her and crossed to the little table where he substituted it for the other. This other he brought back and placed in front of her.

'I want to see you drink this.'

Her eyes met his. They were steady, unfathomable. The colour slowly drained from her face.

She stretched out her hand, raised the cup. He held his breath. Supposing all along he had made a mistake.

She raised it to her lips – at the last moment, with a shudder, she leant forward and quickly poured it into a pot containing a fern. Then she sat back and gazed at him defiantly.

He drew a long sigh of relief, and sat down again.

'Well?' she said.

Her voice had altered. It was slightly mocking – defiant.

He answered her soberly and quietly:

'You are a very clever woman, Mrs Merrowdene. I think you understand me. There must be no – repetition. You know what I mean?'

'I know what you mean.'

Her voice was even, devoid of expression. He nodded his head, satisfied. She was a clever woman, and she didn't want to be hanged.

'To your long life and to that of your husband,' he said significantly, and raised his tea to his lips.

Then his face changed. It contorted horribly ... he tried to rise – to cry.... His body stiffened – his face went purple. He fell back sprawling over his chair – his limbs convulsed.

Mrs Merrowdene leaned forward, watching him. A little smile crossed her lips. She spoke to him – very softly and gently....

'You made a mistake, Mr Evans. You thought I wanted to kill George.... How stupid of you – how very stupid.'

She sat there a minute longer looking at the dead man, the third man who had threatened to cross her path and separate her from the man she loved.

Her smile broadened. She looked more than ever like a madonna. Then she raised her voice and called:

'George, George! ... Oh, do come here! I'm afraid there's been the most dreadful accident.... Poor Mr Evans....'

Coroner's Inquest

Marc Connelly

'What is your name?'

'Frank Wineguard.'

'Where do you live?'

'A hundred and eighty-five West Fifty-fifth Street.'

'What is your business?'

'I'm stage manager for *Hello, America*.'

'You were the employer of James Dawle?'

'In a way. We both worked for Mr Bender, the producer, but I have charge backstage.'

'Did you know Theodore Robel?'

'Yes, sir.'

'Was he in your company, too?'

'No, sir. I met him when we started rehearsals. That was about three months ago, in June. We sent out a call for midgets and he and Jimmy showed up together, with a lot of others. Robel was too big for us. I didn't see him again until we broke into their room Tuesday.'

'You discovered their bodies?'

'Yes, sir. Mrs Pike, there, was with me.'

'You found them both dead?'

'Yes, sir.'

'How did you happen to be over in Jersey City?'

'Well, I called up his house at curtain time Monday night when I found Jimmy hadn't shown up for the performance. Mrs Pike told me they were both out, and I asked her to have either Jimmy or Robel call me when they came in. Then Mrs Pike called me Tuesday morning and said she tried to get into the room but she'd found the door was bolted. She said all her other roomers were out and she was alone and scared.

'I'd kind of suspected something might be wrong. So I said to wait and I'd come over. Then I took the tube over and got there about noon. Then we went up and I broke down the door.'

'Did you see this knife there?'

'Yes sir. It was on the floor, about a foot from Jimmy.'

'You say you suspected something was wrong. What do you mean by that?'

'I mean I felt something might have happened to Jimmy. Nothing like this, of course. But I knew he'd been feeling very depressed lately, and I knew Robel wasn't helping to cheer him up any.'

'You mean that they had had quarrels?'

'No, sir. They just both had the blues. Robel had had them for a long time. Robel was Jimmy's brother-in-law. He'd married Jimmy's sister – she was a midget, too – about five years ago, but she died a year or so later. Jimmy had been living with them and after the sister died he and Robel took a room in Mrs Pike's house together.'

'How did you learn this?'

'Jimmy and I were pretty friendly at the theatre. He was a nice little fellow and seemed grateful that I'd given him his job. We'd only needed one midget for an Oriental scene in the second act and the agencies had sent about fifteen. Mr Gehring, the director, told me to pick one of them as he was busy and I picked Jimmy because he was the littlest.

'After I got to know him he told me how glad he was I'd given him the job. He hadn't worked for nearly a year. He wasn't little enough to be a featured midget with circuses or in museums, so he had to take whatever came along. Anyway, we got to be friendly and he used to tell me about his brother-in-law and all.'

'He never suggested that there might be ill-feeling between him and his brother-in-law?'

'No, sir. I don't imagine he'd ever had any words at all with Robel. As a matter of fact, from what I could gather I guess Jimmy had quite a lot of affection for him and he certainly did everything he could to help him. Robel was a lot worse off than Jimmy. Robel hadn't worked for a couple of years and Jimmy practically supported him. He used to tell me how Robel had been sunk ever since he got his late growth.'

'His what?'

'His late growth. I heard it happens among midgets often, but Jimmy told me about it first. Usually a midget will stay as long as he lives at whatever height he reaches when he's fourteen or fifteen, but every now and then one of them starts growing again just before he's thirty, and he can grow a foot or even more in a couple of years. Then he stops growing for good. But of course he don't look so much like a midget any more.

'That's what had happened to Robel about three years ago. Of course he used to talk about it all the time. Robel used to come over and see his agent in New York twice a week, but there was never anything for him. Then he'd go back to Jersey City. Most of the week he lived alone because after the show started Jimmy often stayed in New York with a cousin or somebody that lived uptown.

'Lately Robel hadn't been coming over to New York at all. But every Saturday night Jimmy would go over to Jersey City and stay till Monday with him, trying to cheer him up. Every Sunday they'd take a walk and go to a movie. I guess as they walked along the street Robel realized most the difference in their heights. And I guess that's really why they're both dead now.'

'How do you mean?'

'Well, as I told you, Jimmy would try to sympathize with Robel and cheer him up. He and Robel both realized that Jimmy was working and supporting them and that Jimmy would probably keep right on working, according to the ordinary breaks of the game, while Robel would always be too big. It simply preyed on Robel's mind.

'And then three weeks ago Monday Jimmy thought he saw the axe fall.

'I was standing outside the stage door – it was about seven-thirty – and Jimmy came down the alley. He looked down in the mouth, which I thought was strange, seeing that he usually used to come in swinging his little cane and looking pretty cheerful. I said, "How are you feeling, Jimmy?" and he said, "I don't feel so good, Mr Wineguard." So I said, "Why, what's the matter, Jimmy?" I could see there really was something the matter with him by this time.

' "I'm getting scared," he said, and I says, "Why?"

' "I'm starting to grow again," he says. He said it the way you just found out you had some disease that was going to kill you in a week. He looked like he was shivering.

' "Why, you're crazy, Jimmy," I says. "You ain't growing."

' "Yes, I am," he says. "I'm thirty-one and it's that late growth like my brother-in-law has. My father had it, but his people had money, so it didn't make much difference to him. It's different with me. I've got to keep working."

'He went on like that for a while and then I tried to kid him out of it.

' "You look all right to me," I said. "How tall have you been all along?"

' "Thirty-seven inches,' he says. So I says, "Come on into the prop-room and I'll measure you."

'He backed away from me. "No," he says, "I don't want to know how much it is." Then he went up to the dressing-room before I could argue with him.

'All week he looked awful sunk. When he showed up the next Monday evening he looked almost white.

'I grabbed him as he was starting upstairs to make up.

' "Come on out of it," I says. I thought he'd make a break and try to get away from me, but he didn't. He just sort of smiled as if I didn't understand. Finally, he says, "It ain't any use, Mr Wineguard."

' "Listen," I says, "You've been over with that brother-in-law of yours, haven't you?" He said yes, he had. "Well," I says, "that's what's bothering you. From what you tell me about him he's talked about his own tough luck so much that he's given you the willies, too. Stay away from him the end of this week."

'He stood there for a second without saying anything. Then he says, "That wouldn't do any good. He's all alone over there and he needs company. Anyway, it's all up with me, I guess. I've grown nearly two inches already."

'I looked at him. He was pretty pathetic, but outside of that there wasn't any change in him as far as I could see.

'I says, "Have you been measured?" He said he hadn't. Then I said, "Then how do you know? Your clothes fit you all right, except your pants, and as a matter of fact they seem a little longer."

' "I fixed my suspenders and let them down a lot farther," he says. "Besides they were always a little big for me."

' "Let's make sure," I says. "I'll get a yardstick and we'll make absolutely sure."

'But I guess he was too scared to face things. He wouldn't do it.

'He managed to dodge me all week. Then, last Saturday night, I ran into him as I was leaving the theatre. I asked him if he felt any better.

' "I feel all right," he says. He really looked scared to death.

'That's the last time I saw him before I went over to Jersey City after Mrs Pike phoned me Tuesday morning.'

'Patrolman Gorlitz has testified that the bodies were in opposite ends of the room when he arrived. They were in that position when you forced open the door?'

'Yes, sir.'

'The medical examiner has testified that they were both dead of knife wounds, apparently from the same knife. Would you assume the knife had fallen from Dawle's hand as he fell?'

'Yes, sir.'

'Has it been your purpose to suggest that both men were driven to despondency by a fear of lack of employment for Dawle, and that they might have committed suicide?'

'No, sir. I don't think anything of the kind.'

'What do you mean?'

'Well, when Mrs Pike and I went in the room and I got a look at the knife, I said to Mrs Pike that that was a funny kind of a knife for them to have in the room. You can see it's a kind of a butcher knife. Then Mrs Pike told me it was one that she'd missed from her kitchen a few weeks before. She'd never thought either Robel or Jimmy had taken it. It struck me as funny Robel or Jimmy had stolen it, too. Then I put two and two together and found out what really happened. Have you got the little broken cane that was lying on the bed?'

'Is this it?'

'Yes, sir. Well, I'd never been convinced by Jimmy that he was really growing. So when Mrs Pike told me about the knife I started figuring. I figured that about five minutes before that knife came into play Jimmy must have found it, probably by accident?'

'Why by accident?'

'Because Robel had gone a little crazy, I guess. He'd stolen it and kept it hidden from Jimmy. And when Jimmy found it he wondered what Robel had been doing with it. Then Robel wouldn't tell him and Jimmy found out for himself. Or maybe Robel did tell him. Anyway, Jimmy looked at the cane. It was the one he always carried. He saw where, when Jimmy wasn't looking, Robel had been cutting little pieces off the end of it.'

Banquo's Chair

Rupert Croft-Cooke

Sir William Brent was a man whom I respected for the whole-heartedness with which, for thirty years, he had applied himself to the one form of research in which he was interested. He had risen to the head of the English Criminal Investigation Department, and, I think, had enjoyed doing so.

In his quiet, pipe-smoking way, he had considered the innumerable problems which his work had presented to him, and although with no very spectacular performances he had succeeded in a vast proportion of the cases on which he worked.

Outwardly the typical Englishman, almost the refined English policeman, he used to be seen at Scotland Yard, his big, florid person unostentatiously bent on reaching his office and the matter in hand.

One quality in his methods was not mentioned in the eulogies with which the Press celebrated his retirement from office, although during my ten years' association with him I remarked it frequently. It was a sort of glinting mercilessness, a cruel, steely determination to outwit his culprits. I suppose that anyone in his position would tend to become callous. But towards the end it was plain to me that he regarded human nature as an abstract quantity, much as a scientist might regard a strange gas which it was his business to analyse. The motives of people, their arbitrary behaviour in peculiar circumstances, their weaknesses, only appealed to Brent as part of the intensely interesting game of detection.

After he retired I wondered what he would find to fill the place of all that had occupied him so long. I was not kept long in doubt, however. Within a short time of his leaving Scotland Yard, I received an invitation which could only mean that his former activities were not forgotten. 'Will you,' he wrote, 'come and dine with me at Turret House, Sydenham, on Thursday? Robert Stone will be there, and a third guest, and I can promise you an unforgettable evening.'

Naturally, I had no intention of missing such an intriguing invitation, and I wrote my acceptance immediately. Flippantly I added the postscript: 'Shall I come armed?' The answer came by telegram, and consisted of one word: 'Yes.'

On the appointed day I reached Turret House, in spite of a gusty November storm. I found it to be one of those red brick, sombre mansions, built here with ample gardens in the more spacious time of the late Queen. It stood back from the road behind tossed and dripping pine trees in the dejection of a district which had known better days. I did not like the house.

The door was opened by Lane, the man-servant whom I recognized from Sir William's more cheerful home in the West End. He took my coat, and I stepped into a hall, tiled, and having a florid stone staircase facing the door, and a dark conservatory leading out of it. Then, to my surprise, I was shown straight into the dining-room. Brent rose at once and greeted me over the corner of a large mahogany table laid for dinner. 'You will excuse this?' he said. 'As a matter of fact, it is the only room we use.'

'Oh, you don't live here?' I said with some relief.

He smiled towards the heavy cornice supporting stout curtains of faded crimson. 'Good Lord, no!' he said. 'But you shall hear everything in a moment, when Stone turns up. Meanwhile a Martini?'

We had not long to wait for Robert Stone, that humorous, wiry little writer who had travelled almost everywhere and was reputed to have fought a duel with a German ex-prince in the lavatory of the Café Royal. 'What the devil do you mean, Brent, by dragging me out to this red mausoleum?' he inquired almost as soon as he was in the room.

'My dear chap, I promised you something of an evening. If you can't trust me you can go straight home,' smiled Sir William soberly.

'Go home be damned! I want some dinner anyhow. But what a cow-house of a room!'

'Now just sit down there, Stone, and listen. We have not very much time before the arrival of . . . our third guest.' There was a pause, then Sir William continued in that rather emotionless voice of his: 'Perhaps you may remember a murder which took place in this suburb some time ago? It was called the Sydenham Murder, and caused considerable comment at the time because there was no arrest.'

Stone broke in. 'But it was perfectly obvious. I knew from the first who did it. The nephew.'

Sir William smiled. 'The police knew it, too.'

'Then why the hell . . .'

'Exactly. That was the common question. Unfortunately, the nephew had an absolute, an unimpeachable alibi. To have arrested him would have meant merely a waste of time and money, and a release in the end. Besides, a man discharged can never be arrested on the same murder charge. Anyway, I persuaded the people at the Yard to leave the matter to me and give me all the time I wanted. To-night, gentlemen, you are to see the last act in the – may I be permitted to say drama? You see,' he added quietly, 'it was in this house that the murder took place. But let me,' he hurried on as he saw my astonishment was about to cause an interruption, 'recall the circumstances to you.

'On November 17 last year – that is a year ago to-day – old Miss Fergusson, whose habits were as eccentric as any old lady's might be expected to be when she inhabits a house like this in solitude, gave her one maid the customary evening out and sat down alone to dinner in this room. She was a thin, sallow old lady, with those little soft reefs of old flesh which hang sometimes about the neck and cheeks of people of her age – sixty odd. She would sit very straight in that chair eating the cold meal which she had always in the evening, read for an hour or two, then go to sleep in an Arabian bedstead in the room over this. But on that night when her servant returned she found her mistress strangled.

'There seemed no doubt, at first, of the nephew's guilt. He was the old lady's sole heir; he was heavily in debt; he had a latchkey of the house; he had even been heard to threaten her on previous occasions. But when he was questioned, the result was a perfect alibi. It was one of those rare cases in which the police know their man but are powerless.'

Sir William paused and lit another cigarette. 'After my retirement I had every opportunity to think over the case, and at last I thought I saw a means by which, with infinite patience and devotion of time to the matter, I might bring the fellow to book.'

I shuddered a little at the 'infinite patience.' To think of this solid-looking Englishman with the queer kink in his nature, setting un-hurriedly about drawing his rat into the trap, had an aspect of the gruesome.

'Luck has favoured me,' he continued suavely. 'For instance, Bedford· (the nephew) decided to let this house furnished soon after the event. It was in taking it that I got to know him, and it was to my interests that the acquaintance should be fostered into a – friendship. He is a vain man, and can see nothing incongruous in my desire for his company. But it was another quality of his which led me to the plan I have adopted – his superstition.' Sir William laughed. 'It is a fault shared, almost without exception, by all criminals. To-night is the anniversary of the murder. And to-night Mr John Bedford will dine with us.'

'Well?' said Stone impatiently.

'I have enlisted the aid of Miss May Dacklethorpe,' said Sir William, 'undoubtedly our best tragic actress. During dinner she will enter the room in the precise likeness of the murdered woman. We, of course, shall remain outwardly unconscious of her – only Bedford will be aware of her presence. In this way I hope to wring some sort of confession from the man. You remember Macbeth and the ghost of Banquo?'

'But do you really imagine,' said little Stone, not without excitement, 'that he will come here on this night, in the circumstances?'

'Most certainly,' said Sir William. 'He has already dined with me four or five times, and to-night there is a special inducement – he is to meet you, Stone. His vanity is touched by the opportunity. There are one or two other points I must explain before he arrives – I have a number of police in the house, though somehow I do not anticipate violence. And during dinner the electric light will be switched off at the main and candles will be lit. We must have the correct atmosphere. Understand?'

Even before we had time to agree that we did, Lane announced Mr John Bedford.

A man in his late thirties hurried into the room, a tallish man, prematurely bald, with a weak droop to the corners of his mouth, and yet a curiously hard look in the eyes. A face which at first sight seemed precise appeared on scrutiny to be vicious.

We sat down almost at once to dinner, hurrying over the introductions to do so.

'How is the weather now?' asked Sir William when an excellent soup was before us.

'A beastly night,' said Bedford, 'but really, Sir William, you must allow me to congratulate you on your cook. This soup is a masterpiece.'

Unwittingly Bedford had given his host a cue. 'Ah, yes,' he answered in his chill voice. 'And thereby hangs a tale. My old cook had been with me twenty years. But she absolutely refused to stay in this house. She said it was haunted. Stone, this sort of thing amuses you; I should like you to have seen the silly old body giving me notice because she had seen the figure of an elderly lady with a scar on her neck walking about the passages! But it did no harm in a way – my cook is an artist. Why, Bedford, my dear chap, you don't look well. I expect you're a bit fagged out. It's a rotten journey down here.'

'Not – not a bit. Only, if you'll forgive me saying so, I find this room confoundedly hot.'

'Ah, I'm sorry. I had not noticed it at all. Lane, open a window, will you?'

As Lane threw open the window, the noise of the rain and wind was plainly audible outside. 'Isn't our climate vile?' remarked Stone. 'Really, I don't know why we stay in England for the winter. This time last year I was on the Riviera.'

'And I was in the East,' I added, feeling that I must add something to the conversation.

'Ah!' Sir William was thoughtful. 'Let me see, November 17. Yes.... This time last year I was in London, following the news ... watching the course of events. Lane, give Mr Bedford some more wine.'

The situation, even for me, was becoming intolerable. Bedford was mopping his brow. Then there was a flicker and our guest was shut out from our sight.

'Lane!' called Sir William sharply. 'What on earth is wrong with the lights?'

'I'll find out, sir,' said the butler and hurried out.

For a moment we were left in complete darkness, during which I think most of us drank, then Lane appeared with candles. 'The electric light is out of order, sir,' he said, 'and none of us understands it.'

'Then get the chauffeur in at once,' said Sir William.

Suddenly, as he spoke, I became aware of another figure in the room. Behind Sir William's chair was the image of an old lady with great suffering apparent in her forlorn face. I had seen May Dacklethorpe in some of her greatest successes, but this make-up I thought was a masterpiece. It gave one the impression of a lurid unreality. I scarcely dared look at the man opposite to me to see what impression the figure had made on his already distraught mind. But apparently he had not seen it. I turned to the food on my plate and as I did so I heard a low cry from Bedford.

'Why,' smiled Sir William, 'what's the matter, my dear chap?'

'Nothing, nothing. I wish we could have some light, Sir William. Half-darkness invariably gets on my nerves.'

'I can't say how sorry I am that this should have happened,' said Brent, 'but no doubt the chauffeur won't be long in setting the lights right. Meanwhile, another glass of champagne?'

'Thanks – thanks!'

He drank hurriedly, and then, setting down his glass with a crash, he burst out: 'Don't any of you see anything? You must! You must!'

'My dear Bedford!' Brent was all solicitation. 'You're unwell. Sit down. Is there anything I can do for you?'

It was painful to watch the effort Bedford took to get a grip on himself. 'I'm well enough, thanks,' he said, and I saw that his eyes were half-closed and he was trying to rivet them on his plate.

The strain was affecting us all. Conversation had dropped entirely. Then, very slowly, the woman whom we could not watch, except secretly, began to move towards him. That was too much. Consciousness of our presence, self-control, everything left him but fear. He became pitiably hysterical, tried to rise from his seat. 'Let me by!' he shouted. The figure stood between him and the door. 'Out of my way! Let me out of here.' One step more towards him the figure took and he screamed with a shrillness of which his voice was ordinarily incapable. 'I'll do it again,' he shouted. 'I'll do it again! Let me get by.'

We held our breath, not daring by the least word to call him back to actualities. 'I'll murder you again, you bitch!' he shrieked. 'I did it once and I'll do it again if you don't get out of my way.'

It was over. Sir William rose from his chair and rang a small pear-shaped electric bell which hung among the candelabra before him. Two police officials were in the room at once. 'I think you can arrest that man,' said Sir William. 'You have heard his confession.'

Bedford had sunk limply into his chair and was sobbing dementedly. The police almost lifted him from it as they handcuffed him, but he said nothing more as they led him from the room. I don't think he yet realized what had happened.

Stone was the first to break the silence. He spoke in a way which made me understand. 'Satisfied?' he said, almost sneering.

'Quite,' said Sir William. 'It has been a long job, but it has ended as I knew it would. I'm most grateful to you both. We'll continue our interrupted dinner.'

'I thought it was a pretty grim affair,' said Stone savagely. 'Your third degree methods repel me, Brent. But I suppose you know your job. Certainly May Dacklethorpe did. Her acting was superb.'

'And her make-up incredibly good,' I said.

'We must congratulate her,' Sir William agreed. 'I wonder where she has gone? Upstairs, perhaps. I had a room arranged for her. Lane!'

'Sir!'

'Just see where Miss Dacklethorpe is.'

'Miss Dacklethorpe, sir?'

'The lady who has been assisting us this evening.'

'I have not seen her, sir, but I will inquire.'

'Thank you. There were two policemen stationed at the door, Lane. They will know if she left.'

Lane left the room. He returned almost immediately with a salver in his hand. 'I have questioned the police, sir,' he said, 'but they know only of the arrival of Mr Stone and your friend. No lady has entered the house.' He paused. 'This telegram has arrived for you, sir.'

Brent tore open the envelope and read, and for the first time I saw Sir William Brent crumple up. 'Good God!' he whispered. 'Read it!'

We did.

'*Extremely sorry severe influenza quite unable to leave bed. May Dacklethorpe,*' the wire said.

Esmeralda

John Keir Cross

Mr Felix Broome lay on his back wide-eyed, unable to sleep. Beside him his wife, Nancy, snored raucously – a long complicated snore, starting with a sigh and ending with a staccato nasal grunt. Mr Broome, with a horrid fascination, followed the sound through all its convolutions, waiting desperately for some variation in the rhythm.

Mr Broome was forty-five. A small man, round-faced, with a little brunette moustache. His mouth was thin and loose. He had false teeth but never wore them – he found them uncomfortable; jam pips constantly lodged behind the plate, irritating him beyond endurance. He was bald; and, since Nancy hated him bald, he wore a toupee, slightly curled.

The room in which he and Nancy were lying was above the little newsagent and tobacconist shop he had. It was in a side street in Notting Hill – not far from the Portobello Road – a bright, neat shop that did good business. Mr Broome loved it dearly. He loved the smell of it – a smell all compact of newly printed paper, cheap sweets in cardboard boxes for the children (liquorice allsorts, wine gums, dolly mixtures, sensen cachous, chocolate macaroons and whipped cream snowballs) – and, above all, tobaccos: thick black plug for chewing, tangled shag for those who liked to roll their own cigarettes, sickly yellow curly-cut, artificially scented flake, and half-a-dozen goodly mixtures in brown earthenware jars with tops that were moulded in the shapes of Negro heads. Many a time, when the shop was empty, Mr Broome would lift the top of one of these jars and sniff lovingly at the richness within. Many a time, when no one was looking, he would slip a dolly mixture or a jelly baby into his little loose mouth and suck at it noisily and enjoyably. Or he would furtively bury himself in one of the serials in *Peg's Companion*.

He even, on one occasion, wrote a surreptitious letter to a character calling herself Wise Woman in one of the girl's papers he sold. He signed himself 'Worried' and said:

'Dear Wise Woman, – I have been married for fifteen years but am, I am afraid, very unhappy. It is not that my partner and I have any open differences, it is just that we do not seem suited to each other. We have no children. Our tastes are not dissimilar, but somehow we do not hit it off. Somehow we seem to have very little to say to each other, and so in the house there is often an atmosphere of strain and discomfort. What can I possibly do to relieve the situation? – my partner is a Roman Catholic, so divorce is out of the question, even indeed if there were any ground for divorce, which there certainly is not. Yours sincerely, etc . . .'

And next week, under a reproduction of his letter, he read Wise Woman's reply in small type:

'Dear Worried, – Alas, the sort of situation you describe is only too frequent nowadays. In so many lives I see Romance being supplanted by Boredom and Indifference. It is a pity you have no children – it is the tiny hands of children that more than anything else in the world smooth over the difficulties of married life and re-establish it in its full sanctity. They join together hearts that have drifted apart. Is it too late to think of adopting a child, if you cannot have one of your own? If this is not possible the only other thing I can suggest is that you should *try to find a common interest*. Are you fond of going to the Theatre or the Pictures? Make a habit of going once a week with your partner. I take it you yourself are not a Catholic? – try, nevertheless, to take an intelligent interest in your partner's religion. Make conversation, plan little surprises. And with luck and determination you will yet succeed, dear Worried, in salvaging your lives. Yours in sympathy – Wise Woman.'

Mr Broome remembered this advice with bitterness, as he lay listening to Nancy's snoring. 'Make conversation, plan little surprises.' As if it were possible to make conversation with Nancy! As if it were possible to plan little surprises for Nancy! He hated Nancy – the truth of the whole matter was simply that: he hated her. He hated everything about her – he hated her voice, he hated the way she dressed, he hated her vast podgy face with its sagging cheeks, he hated the smell of her. He who was so sensitive to smells – to the rich exotic smell of tobacco and the fresh clean smell of printed paper – how could he be expected to stomach the sweaty odour that came from Nancy? – all mingled with Woolworth's scent and pink gin? He hated every single thing that she said and did. He hated her very name. Nancy! Applied to the vast flabby hulk lying beside him it was grotesque. And names, he knew, were important – either directly or indirectly – ironically. There was his own name, for instance, Felix: meaning happy (there was an example of irony if you liked!). Or there was Miss Ickman upstairs – her first name was Cynthia, and Cynthia had been the Goddess of Chastity – could anything be more ironically suitable for that bleak and rigid virgin? Or there was – but here all irony vanished and Mr Broome sighed in the darkness

– a little sigh that was swallowed up and lost in the vast nasal sigh of Nancy's snoring – there was Esmeralda . . .

Nancy stirred and grunted. She heaved the bedclothes more firmly about her, and Mr Broome's right foot was uncovered. With a patient sigh he wriggled the blankets over it again.

He did not want to think quite yet of Esmeralda – not quite yet. There was a deliciousness in holding back – in savouring the moment when at last he would permit himself to think of her. There were many stages to be gone through before he could sink finally into the dream that began: 'If only . . .'

There came a creaking of a door from Miss Ickman's flat above. Lord, Lord – was she going to play the piano – at that time of night! He strained his ears, dreading to hear the familiar sound of the screwing up of the piano stool (Miss Ickman gave lessons, so the stool was never at the right height when she herself wanted to play). It came – and a moment later the sound of a Strauss waltz drifted down through the ceiling to him, the bass grotesquely magnified. Oh hell, oh hell! Now Nancy would waken – and Nancy awake was just one degree worse than Nancy asleep.

Yet, as the music went on, he found himself, in a way, welcoming it and enjoying it. The gay dancing rhythm brought into his mind a clear and exciting vision. Never mind if the vision was borrowed from a part of the dream that strictly speaking should come later. Esmeralda . . .

The snoring stopped suddenly in a long succession of short staccato grunts. Mr Broome held his breath. Nancy heaved herself over on her back.

'Felix,' she grunted. 'My God, is that bitch at it again! Stop her, Felix – knock on the ceiling.'

'It's only eleven o'clock, my love,' said Mr Broome quietly.

'It must be later than that. Besides, it's after half-past ten that you're not allowed to make a noise. Knock up, Felix – go on.'

He sighed. But he knew the routine too well. He got out of bed and, shivering, went over to the corner behind the door and picked up a long broom that lay against the wall there. Then he mounted on a chair and thumped with the end of it on the ceiling.

'Louder, Felix – louder,' hissed Nancy.

He thumped again, rhythmically. The playing stopped. The lid of the piano slammed shut angrily. Mr Broome stepped down, wearily returned the knocker to its place, and crawled into bed again.

'Thoughtless old bitch,' grunted Nancy.

'Go to sleep, my love,' said Mr Broome absently. 'Go to sleep . . .'

She snorted and turned over on her side. He had a sudden whiff of her loathsome smell. It made him feel sick. But with a curious meekness he lay still, waiting. Her breathing grew slower and heavier. Once more the snoring began.

Fifteen years of it, he thought – fifteen years of it! Why had he ever married her at all? (Yet he did know the answer to that – it belonged to the later part of the dream.) In any case, at the beginning she had been different. She had not been bulky, the way she was now. She was kinder in disposition, her voice was softer, she dressed quite passably well. On the honeymoon he had even been quite proud of her. He remembered once, as they came in from a bathe, he had overheard two men saying, as they looked at her wet figure up and down: 'A fine buxom body, that' – and he had thought: 'Yes, and it's mine – all mine . . .' He had thought that too, before, looking sideways at her as they knelt before the priest in the little Catholic Church in Notting Hill: 'A fine buxom body, and it's all mine . . . What if I do have to sign a paper and say that our children are to be brought up in the Catholic Faith? It doesn't really matter. The main thing is that we should have children – and with that fine buxom body belonging to me, that should be the easiest thing in the world . . . !'

And now for fifteen years the buxom body had belonged to him. It had steadily grown less attractive – he had wanted it less and less. But conversely, by an irony, he had wanted the fruits of it more and more. And now he knew, finally, that there never would be any fruits from it, he hated the vast bulk with all the vehemence he had. His letter to Wise Woman was the only outward expression his hatred had ever had – and heaven knows that timid effusion was a poor enough index to his feeling.

Mr Broome stretched out an arm and took a sip of water from the glass he kept beside his bed. A mouse stirred and scuttled in the quiet room. Outside he heard a late bus go slowly along the street. Nearer at hand a drunk man was singing mournfully, and a policeman's slow footsteps went clop-clop on the pavement. He closed his eyes. The moment had come at last – he had gone through all the preliminaries. if only . . .

If only, if only . . .

. . . She was exquisitely pretty. She was dressed in a diaphanous white frock. Her hair was fair – there was a little ribbon of pink silk in it. She was only thirteen, but not one member of the gigantic audience but was captivated and enchanted by her. She danced on and on, a small delicious figure in the glare of the footlights. A man in one of the boxes threw her a posy of flowers and she acknowledged it prettily, with a little curtsey woven into the dance. Some women behind Mr Broome in the dress circle put their heads together and began whispering. By straining his ears he could just make out an occasional word of what they said:

'Exquisite ... Enchanting ... Like a little fairy ...'

The dance ended. She swept one long and beautiful curtsey and the curtain slowly fell. The applause was enormous, terrifying. The curtain went up again and she was standing there, radiant in the light, blowing kisses to the audience. People were on their feet, cheering and clapping. The stage was covered with flowers. He felt like crying he was so moved.

And as he mingled with the crowd leaving the theatre, he heard again the two women talking behind him.

'Yes, dear – her name really is Esmeralda. Esmeralda Broome – the daughter of a little man who keeps a tobacconist's shop in Notting Hill somewhere. She's adorable, isn't she?'

Oh God, thought Mr Broome. Oh God! If only ...

The snoring went on remorselessly. Mr Broome was almost weeping. If he turned he could see, in the light that came in from the street, the dark shape of Nancy's head on the pillow. She lay on her back again, with her mouth wide open. Fifteen years!

He suddenly drew in his breath in a quick gasp. He lay perfectly still, staring with dilated eyes at the ceiling. Then he quietly raised himself to his knees. Still staring, he picked up the pillow he had been lying on. For a moment he stayed poised, holding it in his hands – then, with a small animal grunt, he lunged forward and crammed it on to Nancy's face.

The snoring stopped. He lay on the pillow, grunting and moaning, pressing it down with all his strength. She began to struggle – little inarticulate sounds came from beneath him. She heaved her enormous bulk on the bed – his nostrils were filled with the smell of the sweat and cheap scent. Still lying on her face, and grunting in little ecstatic gasps, he pushed his hands down under the pillow and fumbled for her throat. He felt the muscles of it twitching convulsively beneath his fingers. He squeezed with all his strength, and his fingers went deep into the flaccid flesh.

He lay like that for a long time. There was a mounting, rushing noise in his ears, like wind, or tumultuous applause. Outside he heard the clop of the feet again, as the policeman repassed the house. And he realized suddenly that all was quiet – there was no movement at all beneath him.

He rolled himself back into his own place in the bed. He listened to the silence. Then, exhausted, but with, somewhere inside him, the applause going on, he fell into a deep stupid sleep.

He opened his eyes at a quarter-past six. For a moment he lay looking at the creeping dawn light that came through the window. Then, quite quietly and detachedly, he remembered all that had happened the night before.

He turned and looked at Nancy. The pillow lay over her head. Curiously he lifted a corner of it – then replaced it with a shudder: the face beneath was swollen and ugly – the veins stood out in purple ridges, the teeth showed right through the upper lip, so great had been the pressure.

Mr Broome got out of bed. He went over to the window and stood there thoughtfully, scratching his backside. His striped flannel pyjamas hung from him loosely – he was a small and grotesque figure in the sick light.

A few people were astir in the street. A man with a bonnet and muffler passed briskly, a blue enamelled tea-bottle sticking out of his pocket. A little hawker's cart went by, the pony nodding dejectedly in the shafts, the driver half-asleep. A lean dog sniffed round the dustbins.

Mr Broome was surprised that he did not seem to have any feelings. According to the magazines in the shop downstairs, what he had done was spectacular – people wrote stories about murderers. And here was he, in real life, a murderer – and he felt nothing – nothing at all. He had even, he remembered, fallen asleep after killing Nancy. Fallen asleep! There was no end to mystery – things never worked out in life the way they did in books.

He dressed slowly and carefully, spending a long time in settling his tie at the mirror. Before him, on the dressing-table, was Nancy's array of scent bottles. He smiled wryly as he uncorked one of them and held it to his nose. But there was work to be done, he suddenly recollected, and he set the bottle down again and went briskly out of the room.

Underneath the shop there was a deep earth-floored cellar where Mr Broome kept old boxes and papers. Here he worked furiously for about an hour. At the end of that time there was a hole some three feet deep in a corner of the room. Mr Broome surveyed it with satisfaction, then he went upstairs to the bedroom again.

Nancy still lay quietly on the bed. This almost surprised him – he had half-expected to find her sitting at the dressing-table making herself up. But the enormous bulk was quite motionless – the pillow was still in position.

He stood surveying her for a little time. Then, bracing himself to the effort, he put his hands under her armpits and dragged her from the bed.

She was enormously heavy. He thought with irony, as he looked down along the bulging figure, swathed in a nightgown of pink chiffon, of the remark the two men had made on the beach: 'A fine buxom body, that . . .' Well, it was buxom no longer – mere clay and no more. Nancy could no longer demand his services for her body, when she had been drinking too much pink gin. There would be no more weeping agonies of resentment – no more vows of 'I won't give in to her, I won't, I *won't* – and then giving in to her, and regretting it, and feeling ashamed and weak next morning. It was all over now. He had beaten her at last, after fifteen long years.

Somehow he got the huge sagging lump down the stairs to the cellar. He dragged it heavily, walking backwards at an angle – Nancy resting on her heels, her huge yellow toes pointing to the ceiling. With a final heave he toppled it into the damp hole he had prepared, then stood back panting.

He went up into the shop to look at the time. It was a quarter to eight – in a quarter of an hour's time the shop should be open, if all was to seem normal. With a feverishness in his movements now, he rushed downstairs and shovelled the earth over the body. Then he replaced the boxes and papers he had cleared from the corner when he was digging the hole. A last look round to see that all was normal and he went upstairs, smoothing his jacket and straightening his tie as he climbed. By two minutes past eight the shutters were down and the shop was open.

'Good morning, Mr Broome,' said the van boy who delivered his bundle of papers. 'All right?'

'Couldn't be better, Bert,' said Mr Broome.

'And Mrs Broome OK?'

'Oh yes,' and he smiled his little loose toothless smile. 'She's in the pink, Bert – in the pink . . .'

Now all that day, as Mr Broome worked on in his shop, he was thinking. He began in the morning by thinking how strange it was that he was so calm. He, Felix Broome, forty-five, a man of no importance, had committed a murder. He who had never been able to make up his mind to do anything had at last done one supreme and dramatic thing. He had killed his wife and buried her in the cellar – yet behold, he was calmly going about his business as if nothing had happened.

Where was the sense of guilt that was supposed to overwhelm murderers? – where were the agonies of remorse that were said to assail them? If he felt anything at all it was a sense of relief – and occasionally, mingling with it, a sense of power and achievement. Later on in the day this feeling increased. Sometimes, as he handed a paper or some tobacco to a customer, he felt like leaning over the counter and saying:

'Excuse me, sir, but I thought I would just like to let you know that I have murdered my wife. We had been married for fifteen years and I hated her, sir – she stank. So I murdered her, sir – she's downstairs in the cellar now, under three feet of earth. Anything else, sir – some pipe-cleaners, matches?'

He pictured the sensation – the startled customer scuttling from the shop and calling a policeman. And, later on, the headlines in the papers – papers that would be sold over the very counter on which he leaned.

Wise Woman would get a shock if she knew that Worried, to whom she had given such excellent advice, had finished actually by murdering his partner; 'Plan little surprises' indeed! He had planned one of the biggest surprises in history – he, Felix Broome – a man of no account and a dreamer.

At this point, as he leaned on his counter, Mr Broome sighed deeply. It need never have happened. The fifteen years of misery need never have happened. If only – if only . . .

And there came into his mind a sudden image of a white whirling skirt. Esmeralda – she would have solved it.

At lunchtime he went to the little room at the back of the shop and cut himself some bread and cheese and boiled some tea on the gas-ring. And as he chewed his meal slowly (having put in his false teeth for the purpose), he began to think over a plan of campaign. One thing was clear – he had to get out of London. And in some way he had to disguise himself. If he left off his toupee and wore his false teeth continuously, that would make a considerable difference to his appearance. Then he could shave off his moustache. Fortunately, no photographs of him existed – he had always had a horror of cameras. And he had no relatives – at least, only one: a cousin in Canada – and she had not seen him for twenty years.

He would go, he decided, to the North of England – to Bradford, say, or Burnley: one of the vague black cities, on the top of the map, he had often heard of but never visited. Upstairs, in a hole in the mattress (the very mattress on which Nancy had died), he had almost three hundred pounds – his savings. With this sum it should be possible to start a little tobacconist's shop.

It was indeed curious, he reflected again, how calm he felt. He was quite confident that he would not be found out. As soon as it grew dark he would close the shop, gather together his few more precious belongings, and simply disappear. It would be some days before anyone got suspicious because the shop was closed – there was no one likely to call. If he put a card on the door – 'Closed till further notice' – that would satisfy Bert the van boy and Miss Ickman upstairs. Eventually, no doubt, there would be a search – an advertisement about the missing Mr and Mrs Broome would appear in the Sunday papers. Perhaps one day the police would discover Nancy's remains in the cellar – but what would it matter? By that time he would have started his new business in Blackburn or wherever it was – he would be comfortably established under a new name and with a different appearance. What could he call himself? Black? Thomson? Clarke? There was, he remembered, a significance in names. What about Nancy's maiden-name – Gilbert? Too obvious, perhaps – a clue that might give him away. Yet he could always use it as a first name. A sudden curious allusion came into his mind. A few days before, he had been reading an article in one of the cheaper and more spectacular weeklies – *The Real Bluebeard*, it had been called. And he remembered that the name of the famous wife-murderer had been Gilles de Rais. Why not call himself Gilbert Ray? A good name – and a significant one. Gilbert Ray, Tobacconist and Newsagent . . .

Chuckling to himself quietly, he took out his false teeth and went back into the shop. He popped a jelly baby into his mouth to suck by way of dessert. Then he sniffed lovingly at one of the earthenware tobacco jars. It was a pity, he thought, that he would have to leave his carefully-collected stock. But still – it was only for a little while. It would not take him long to gather more – when he started up again as Gilbert Ray.

There was little doing in the way of business during the afternoon. Mr Broome found himself looking forward to six o'clock, when he could put up the shutters and start disguising himself. He had a lot to do. He had checked in a time table that there was a train to Blackburn at 10.15 – everything had to be ready by then.

He started putting up the shutters at ten to six. Then he went into the back shop again and fried himself an egg. He was just on the point of going upstairs to the bedroom to start on his disguise, when he had a sudden uneasy thought. Had he bolted the shop door?

As he went through to examine the lock a sudden whiff of Nancy's perfume filled his nostrils. He paused – then shrugged and moved on to the door.

Surely enough, by an oversight, he had forgotten to fix the snib. With a little grunt of annoyance he stooped to remedy the mistake. And suddenly he had an overwhelming sense that someone was standing just outside. The feeling was powerful – ridiculous but powerful. A little ashamed of himself, he swung the door open – and then his little eyes grew round and his loose mouth sagged open stupidly.

A little girl in a white dress was standing facing him – a little girl whose long hair was tied charmingly in a bow of pink ribbon. And as he stared, she swept him a low and graceful curtsey.

'Esmeralda!' he gasped.

'How do you do, dear Father,' she said, with a smile. 'May I come in?'

Still smiling at him sweetly, she walked past him into the shop. He shivered – and again in his nostrils he felt a distant whiff of Nancy's Woolworth's perfume. He closed the door with a slam, locking it with trembling fingers. Then he turned and followed the little girl up the stairs in a daze.

And now they were sitting in the bedroom facing each other. She was exactly as he had pictured her so often – petite, exquisitely pretty, with small, quick gestures. She sat primly on the edge of a chair, her feet barely touching the ground – and all the time she smiled.

As for him, he did not know what to say or to do. He felt dazed – unable to comprehend what had happened – unwilling even to try to comprehend it. Was it a dream? Had he stupidly fallen asleep – at the very moment when he ought to be packing feverishly for his flight to Blackburn? He remembered how he had fallen asleep just after he had murdered Nancy – a curious, stupid thing to do. Was he perhaps a little bit mad? After all, there must, he thought, be something unusual in a man who suddenly murders his wife – who sets about covering up his tracks with the care and calmness he had given to the task that day. He did not know – he did not know anything: except that Esmeralda, about whom he had thought and dreamed so often, was now sitting in some unaccountable way before him, smiling at him. And she was lovely – she was only thirteen, but she was lovely. He almost felt like weeping.

He realized that she was speaking to him.

'Dear Father,' she was saying, 'don't be surprised that I have come to you at last. After all, there was only one thing ever that kept me away.'

He looked up at her. Her smile was rigid – in a way it was a little frightening. He almost wished that she would relax it – yet he realized that in his dreams she always had been smiling. He had never seen her with any other expression.

'You mean – ?' he said dazedly: and she nodded.

'Yes. Mother. But she's safely out of the way, isn't she? Oh I always hoped you'd do that to her someday, Father. She was such an ugly bitch!'

There was something hideous in the way she spoke – it alarmed him. She was only thirteen. His brain was in a whirl – things were growing wild and grotesque and somehow beyond his control. If only she wouldn't smile!

'You see, Father,' she went on, leaning forwards a little, 'I would only have been the same as her. You signed a paper, you know – do you remember? Fifteen years ago!... You said that any children you and Nancy had would be brought up to be like her. It might have been all right at the very beginning – she was quite presentable then, wasn't she? And she didn't stink.'

'I don't know what you mean,' he gasped.

'Oh you do – of course you do! Do you think I don't know you, after all these years? You liked her body a lot at the beginning. Do you remember the first time you saw her without her clothes on? That time when you went to Brighton for a day and missed the last train home? – and you went to a hotel and registered as Mr and Mrs Broome? It was before you were married, Father.'

Her tone was arch and horrible. He felt himself sweating slightly under the collar.

'I hated her body,' he said, in a muffled little whisper.

'Not at first, Father,' she said. 'You can't pretend that you hated it at first. It was only later, when she began to – well, Father,' (and she sank her voice to a low salacious whisper) *'when you began to grow old!'*

There was a long silence. Mr Broome felt a curious nightmare listlessness in all his limbs – he was weak and helpless. Things had suddenly turned inside out – it was not what he had ever meant – not it at all.

'Who are you?' he gasped at length. 'Are you a dream?'

'Father, dear!' she remonstrated. 'I'm your own dear daughter! Don't you recognize me? You've seen me a hundred times in your dreams – you've heard people talking about me. I'm Esmeralda, Father dear.'

'You're not,' he said, speaking thickly, with an effort. 'You aren't Esmeralda. Esmeralda is a little girl – I mean, I've always thought of her as a little girl – if I could have – I mean, if Nancy could have ...'

She laughed – a shrill, stagey, impersonal laugh.

'Oh Father, Father! You haven't known in the least bit what it's all been about, have you! You've thought it was all something else. You've sat in your shop and you've read the stories in the magazines, and you've thought it was all something else altogether! Poor old Father! Shall I tell you something, Father? Shall I tell you the story of your life? – the real story of your life?'

He stared at her, unable to speak. She went on smiling. And she got down from her chair and walked over towards him till she was only a yard away from him. Then she knelt down on the floor and leaned back on her heels – still smiling.

'Do you remember, Father, thirty years ago? You were fifteen – you had just left school. You were apprenticed to a draper in the Harrow Road – Carradine's. You were very shy. You used to blush if anyone spoke to you. And the girls called you baby-face, Father – do you remember that? Do you remember Miss Dobie, Father?'

'Stop it – stop it,' he groaned.

'Oh, Father – I'm only beginning! You can't stop me now – there's such a lot to say. Don't you remember – the ladies' combinations?'

She laughed again – her eyes bright and hard and glistening. He stared at her helplessly, in horror.

'Miss Dobie was twenty-eight, Father, and you were sixteen. She was a bitch, wasn't she? – all the men said so. The way she used to torture you – made you go into the underwear window and dress the dummies in Carradine's Special Line in Ladies' Combinations! – in full view of the public, too! Beastly, wasn't it. You hated her, Father. But you

couldn't help yourself, could you? – she was far too powerful for you.
That night when she had you to her room – smuggled you into the
ladies' hostel she lived in at Earl's Court – do you remember it, Father?
You were trembling all the time – it was all so new – you were only
sixteen ...'

'For Christ's sake, stop it!' he cried. 'It's filthy – it's filthy! Stop it!'

'It's the story of your life, Father. It's why you killed Mother. And
Father –' (and she lowered her voice to a whisper again) '– it's why
you created me!'

Mr Broome held his breath. He was aware of footsteps outside – they
came to him as from an enormous distance. It was the policeman beginning his evening beat – walking slowly and comfortably in a sane quiet
world.

'Poor Father, poor Father,' went on the crouching figure at his feet.
'You hardly knew all this, did you? You didn't ever have a real chance.
After Miss Dobie it was Alice. Do you remember Alice? You and she
at the Dance Palais, just after your twenty-first birthday? Learning the
Charleston. Do you remember that long spangly dress that she wore
– cut square at the neck and with a low waist? And when you danced
the last waltz, when the lights were low, and you were very close to
her – so close that your face was buried in her hair ... and it filled
your nostrils, Father – it was like a brown shag tobacco, all stringy,
but fragrant – you couldn't get enough of the scent of her ...'

'You devil, you devil!' said Broome, in a low sobbing voice.

'I'm only telling you, Father,' she said gently, and ironically. 'I'm
letting you know, that's all. It isn't what people imagine it to be, is
it, Father? Nothing is – not quite. People never do things for the reasons
they think they do – do they? It's always something else – something
nagging on in the background ... Oh, it was glorious last night – wasn't
it, Father? That magnificent moment!'

'What do you mean?' he gasped.

'You know what I mean – when you lay on the pillow and put your
hands round her throat. She was in your power, Father – at last it was
that way round: someone was in your power – instead of it being the
other way – you in someone else's power. That's what made it, wasn't
it, Father?'

Mr Broome raised his trembling hands to clasp his temples. Something
terrible and unutterably beastly had happened to him – out of the blue.
He had been so calm – so infinitely superior to things. He had worked
quietly in his shop all day, he had made his plans, he had been so sure
of himself. And now, from nowhere, came this foul and raging insanity.
He grew aware of the thin ironic voice going on and on.

'Yes – Miss Dobie, and Alice: and the strange girl you met when
you were on holiday that time at Weston-super-Mare – Margie her name

was – and Enid, that you met at your cousin's farewell party, when she went to Canada, and finally Nancy. It was always the same, wasn't it, Father? Life is always the same thing, happening over and over again. That's what none of them understands, isn't it? Wise Woman has no suspicion that that's the real truth about things, has she? Or she could never write such rubbish about Romance being supplanted by Boredom and Indifference, and the Tiny Hands of Children Reuniting Parted Hearts – now could she? It's all the same thing. I bet if you met Wise Woman herself, she'd stink of scent too – and she'd be like Nancy was when she had had too many pink gins. They wouldn't leave you alone, Father – not one of them. They're all the same.'

A terrible dry sob came out of the little man on the chair.

'Esmeralda!' he cried, 'for God's sake don't say any more – don't say it! Go away – leave me. You're different – it isn't you that has been saying these things. Something has happened to my brain – I'm imagining this – it's the strain – it's been too much. I'll go away – just let me get away from this bloody room. It'll be all right then. But don't go on about these things – for Christ's sake, don't say any more.'

He remained for a long time with his eyes closed. There was a rushing noise in his head. From infinitely far away he heard the footsteps of the policeman as they passed the house again. He did not dare to look up. Above all things in the world he did not dare to encounter the beastly rigid smile of the creature on the floor.

And then he realized that she was speaking again.

'Poor Father, poor Father,' she said: and it seemed that her tone was different – was quieter and less ironical. 'One illusion must be left – it's always the way, isn't it. The strongest man must always preserve at least *one* illusion – and you aren't a strong man, Father, are you – you're the weakest man in the world ... Ah, you don't remember, do you? You can't see far enough down, can you? And even if you could, you couldn't piece things together, could you? They wouldn't make sense, even if you did – things never make sense, not real things. It's all a jumble – it doesn't connect. Yet sometimes, if you look at it all quickly, there suddenly seems to be a sort of thread ...'

He still did not look up, and she went on quickly:

'The little girl, Father – the kernel of it all ... You were thirteen – it was at school. And do you remember you were made to sit beside her, as punishment? And she smiled at you when the teacher wasn't looking. And she had a little string of cheap glass beads round her throat – and they were green – and she told you they were emeralds. Do you remember that, Father, and mark it – *emeralds*? And you were reading a book in school that year – dreadfully dull, you thought, but they made you read it. *Notre-Dame de Paris*. It was about a hunchback.

And it seemed to you that there was something infinitely pitiable about that hunchback – there was something wrong with him, he was despised by everyone. He was just like you, Father.'

There was a long silence. Broome held his breath. The small voice went on.

'Yes, Father – they all despised him. Except ... there was the girl. Do you remember the girl in that book? She was all different. She was poetry, she was romance, she was all the warm and lovely things, she was beautiful – oh, beautiful! Do you remember her name, Father?'

He did not reply.

'Oh come, Father! You're bound to remember her name. It was – ?'

'Desdemona,' he said, in an almost inaudible whisper.

'*Father!* You always got those two mixed up! No – Desdemona was the *other* time. Don't you remember? – the other time you sat beside the little girl. It was when they took you all to the theatre that afternoon – and you were so tremendously excited. You had never been to a theatre at all before – though you had heard about them. You thought you were going to see dancing girls, didn't you, Father – but it wasn't anything like that at all. It was educational – it would be, since the school arranged it! – and it was a play – by Shakespeare. It was Desdemona who was the girl in that, Father. Her husband smothered her. You always got her mixed up with the other girl – the girl in the book – their names were so alike. Don't you remember? *She* was called—?'

'Esmeralda!' gasped Broome.

'Yes – Esmeralda! Clever Father! And the little girl sat beside you, Father – and she was dressed in white that day – and she had a little bag of sticky sweets, and she gave you some. And do you remember she wriggled in her seat, and her dress slipped up over her knees, and you sat there beside her, Father, and you looked at her, and you thought—'

She broke off. In the silence Broome heard, above him, in Miss Ickman's flat, the sound of the piano stool being screwed up. The girl spoke again, and this time all the terrible archness was back in her voice.

'Father – look at me. Look at me, Father.'

He slowly raised his head. His eyes were staring. She was regarding him with the hideous fixed smile still on her face. And as she knelt on the floor she was pulling her skirt lasciviously over her knees.

'Oh Christ!' cried Broome. 'No – no! It's abominable – it's hellish!'

He covered his eyes with his hands. There came an echo of the terrible impersonal laughter. And simultaneously, from above, there floated to his ears the strains of the Strauss waltz he had heard the night before.

An immense shudder shook him. He opened his eyes and rose wildly to his feet. The room was empty. But all about him – suffocating him – was the smell of Nancy.

The policeman, entering the little side-street near the Portobello Road, found Broome gibbering at the door of his shop. He went inside with him – Broome seized him and made him go inside. He looked on with stolid interest while the small sobbing figure tore at the loose earth on the floor of the cellar.

And he whistled through his teeth when he saw what the little man, with an expression of mixed terror and relief on his face, disclosed.

Later, when Broome had been taken away, the policeman and his sergeant made a search of the house.

'Blimey,' said the sergeant, as they opened the door of the bedroom – 'what a stink!'

'Someone's been mucking about with scent,' said the policeman.

They found that every bottle on the dressing-table had been smashed. The contents had been splashed over the room – the carpet, the walls, the bed – and then the bottles had been smashed.

'The little chap's hands were bleeding,' said the policeman. 'I thought it was the digging in the cellar – he went at it like a maniac. But it must have been this. Poor little devil – I couldn't help feeling sorry for him somehow . . .'

Lamb to the Slaughter

Roald Dahl

The room was warm and clean, the curtains drawn, the two table lamps alight – hers and the one by the empty chair opposite. On the sideboard behind her, two tall glasses, soda water, whisky. Fresh ice cubes in the Thermos bucket.

Mary Maloney was waiting for her husband to come home from work.

Now and again she would glance up at the clock, but without anxiety, merely to please herself with the thought that each minute gone by made it nearer the time when he would come. There was a slow smiling air about her, and about everything she did. The drop of the head as she bent over her sewing was curiously tranquil. Her skin – for this was her sixth month with child – had acquired a wonderful translucent quality, the mouth was soft, and the eyes, with their new placid look, seemed larger, darker than before.

When the clock said ten minutes to five, she began to listen, and a few moments later, punctually as always, she heard the tyres on the gravel outside, and the car door slamming, the footsteps passing the window, the key turning in the lock. She laid aside her sewing, stood up, and went forward to kiss him as he came in.

'Hullo, darling,' she said.

'Hullo,' he answered.

She took his coat and hung it in the closet. Then she walked over and made the drinks, a strongish one for him, a weak one for herself; and soon she was back again in her chair with the sewing, and he in the other, opposite, holding the tall glass with both his hands, rocking it so the ice cubes tinkled against the side.

For her, this was always a blissful time of day. She knew he didn't want to speak much until the first drink was finished, and she, on her side, was content to sit quietly, enjoying his company after the long hours alone in the house. She loved to luxuriate in the presence of this man, and to feel – almost as a sunbather feels the sun – that warm male glow that came out of him to her when they were alone together.

She loved him for the way he sat loosely in a chair, for the way he came in a door, or moved slowly across the room with long strides. She loved the intent, far look in his eyes when they rested on her, the funny shape of the mouth, and especially the way he remained silent about his tiredness, sitting still with himself until the whisky had taken some of it away.

'Tired, darling?'

'Yes,' he said. 'I'm tired.' And as he spoke, he did an unusual thing. He lifted his glass and drained it in one swallow although there was still half of it, at least half of it, left. She wasn't really watching him but she knew what he had done because she heard the ice cubes falling back against the bottom of the empty glass when he lowered his arm. He paused a moment, leaning forward in the chair, then he got up and went slowly over to fetch himself another.

'I'll get it!' she cried, jumping up.

'Sit down,' he said.

When he came back, she noticed that the new drink was dark amber with the quantity of whisky in it.

'Darling, shall I get your slippers?'

'No.'

She watched him as he began to sip the dark yellow drink, and she could see little oily swirls in the liquid because it was so strong.

'I think it's a shame,' she said, 'that when a policeman gets to be as senior as you, they keep him walking about on his feet all day long.'

He didn't answer, so she bent her head again and went on with her sewing; but each time he lifted the drink to his lips, she heard the ice cubes clinking against the side of the glass.

'Darling,' she said. 'Would you like me to get you some cheese? I haven't made any supper because it's Thursday.'

'No,' he said.

'If you're too tired to eat out,' she went on, 'it's still not too late. There's plenty of meat and stuff in the freezer, and you can have it right here and not even move out of the chair.'

Her eyes waited on him for an answer, a smile, a little nod, but he made no sign.

'Anyway,' she went on, 'I'll get you some cheese and crackers first.'

'I don't want it,' he said.

She moved uneasily in her chair, the large eyes still watching his face. 'But you *must* have supper. I can easily do it here. I'd like to do it. We can have lamb chops. Or pork. Anything you want. Everything's in the freezer.'

'Forget it,' he said.

'But, darling, you *must* eat! I'll fix it anyway, and then you can have it or not, as you like.'

She stood up and placed her sewing on the table by the lamp.

'Sit down,' he said. 'Just for a minute, sit down.'

It wasn't till then that she began to get frightened.

'Go on,' he said. 'Sit down.'

She lowered herself back slowly into the chair, watching him all the time with those large, bewildered eyes. He had finished the second drink and was staring down into the glass, frowning.

'Listen,' he said, 'I've got something to tell you.'

'What is it, darling? What's the matter?'

He had become absolutely motionless, and he kept his head down so that the light from the lamp beside him fell across the upper part of his face, leaving the chin and mouth in shadow. She noticed there was a little muscle moving near the corner of his left eye.

'This is going to be a bit of a shock to you, I'm afraid,' he said. 'But I've thought about it a good deal and I've decided the only thing to do is tell you right away. I hope you won't blame me too much.'

And he told her. It didn't take long, four or five minutes at most, and she sat very still through it all, watching him with a kind of dazed horror as he went further and further away from her with each word.

'So there it is,' he added. 'And I know it's kind of a bad time to be telling you, but there simply wasn't any other way. Of course I'll give you money and see you're looked after. But there needn't really be any fuss. I hope not anyway. It wouldn't be very good for my job.'

Her first instinct was not to believe any of it, to reject it all. It occurred to her that perhaps he hadn't even spoken, that she herself had imagined the whole thing. Maybe, if she went about her business and acted as though she hadn't been listening, then later, when she sort of woke up again, she might find none of it had ever happened.

'I'll get the supper,' she managed to whisper, and this time he didn't stop her.

When she walked across the room she couldn't feel her feet touching the floor. She couldn't feel anything at all – except a slight nausea and a desire to vomit. Everything was automatic now – down the stairs to the cellar, the light switch, the deep freeze, the hand inside the cabinet taking hold of the first object it met. She lifted it out, and looked at it. It was wrapped in paper, so she took off the paper and looked at it again.

A leg of lamb.

All right then, they would have lamb for supper. She carried it up-stairs, holding the thin bone-end of it with both her hands, and as she went through the living-room, she saw him standing over by the window with his back to her, and she stopped.

'For God's sake,' he said, hearing her, but not turning round. 'Don't make supper for me. I'm going out.'

At that point, Mary Maloney simply walked up behind him and without any pause she swung the big frozen leg of lamb high in the air and brought it down as hard as she could on the back of his head.

She might just as well have hit him with a steel club.

She stepped back a pace, waiting, and the funny thing was that he remained standing there for at least four or five seconds, gently swaying. Then he crashed to the carpet.

The violence of the crash, the noise, the small table overturning, helped bring her out of the shock. She came out slowly, feeling cold and surprised, and she stood for a while blinking at the body, still holding the ridiculous piece of meat tight with both hands.

All right, she told herself. So I've killed him.

It was extraordinary, now, how clear her mind became all of a sudden. She began thinking very fast. As the wife of a detective, she knew quite well what the penalty would be. That was fine. It made no difference to her. In fact, it would be a relief. On the other hand, what about the child? What were the laws about murderers with unborn children? Did they kill them both – mother and child? Or did they wait until the tenth month? What did they do?

Mary Maloney didn't know. And she certainly wasn't prepared to take a chance.

She carried the meat into the kitchen, placed it in a pan, turned the oven on high, and shoved it inside. Then she washed her hands and ran upstairs to the bedroom. She sat down before the mirror, tidied her face, touched up her lips and face. She tried a smile. It came out rather peculiar. She tried again.

'Hullo Sam,' she said brightly, aloud.

The voice sounded peculiar too.

'I want some potatoes please, Sam. Yes, and I think a can of peas.'

That was better. Both the smile and the voice were coming out better now. She rehearsed it several times more. Then she ran downstairs, took her coat, went out the back door, down the garden, into the street.

It wasn't six o'clock yet and the lights were still on in the grocery shop.

'Hullo Sam,' she said brightly, smiling at the man behind the counter.

'Why, good evening, Mrs Maloney. How're *you*?'

'I want some potatoes please, Sam. Yes, and I think a can of peas.'

The man turned and reached up behind him on the shelf for the peas.

'Patrick's decided he's tired and doesn't want to eat out tonight,' she told him. 'We usually go out Thursdays, you know, and now he's caught me without any vegetables in the house.'

'Then how about meat, Mrs Maloney?'

'No, I've got meat, thanks. I got a nice leg of lamb, from the freezer.'

'Oh.'

'I don't much like cooking it frozen, Sam, but I'm taking a chance on it this time. You think it'll be all right?'

'Personally,' the grocer said, 'I don't believe it makes any difference. You want these Idaho potatoes?'

'Oh yes, that'll be fine. Two of those.'

'Anything else?' The grocer cocked his head on one side, looking at her pleasantly. 'How about afterwards? What you going to give him for afterwards?'

'Well – what would you suggest, Sam?'

The man glanced around his shop. 'How about a nice big slice of cheesecake? I know he likes that.'

'Perfect,' she said. 'He loves it.'

And when it was all wrapped and she had paid, she put on her brightest smile and said, 'Thank you, Sam. Good night.'

'Good night, Mrs Maloney. And thank *you*.'

And now, she told herself as she hurried back, all she was doing now, she was returning home to her husband and he was waiting for his supper; and she must cook it good, and make it as tasty as possible because the poor man was tired; and if, when she entered the house, she happened to find anything unusual, or tragic, or terrible, then naturally it would be a shock and she'd become frantic with grief and horror. Mind you, she wasn't *expecting* to find anything. She was just going home with the vegetables. Mrs Patrick Maloney going home with the vegetables on Thursday evening to cook supper for her husband.

That's the way, she told herself. Do everything right and natural. Keep things absolutely natural and there'll be no need for any acting at all.

Therefore, when she entered the kitchen by the back door, she was humming a little tune to herself and smiling.

'Patrick!' she called. 'How are you, darling?'

She put the parcel down on the table and went through into the living-room; and when she saw him lying there on the floor with his legs doubled up and one arm twisted back underneath his body, it really was rather a shock. All the old love and loving for him welled up inside her, and she ran over to him, knelt down beside him, and began to cry her heart out. It was easy. No acting was necessary.

A few minutes later she got up and went to the phone. She knew the number of the police station, and when the man at the other end answered, she cried to him, 'Quick! Come quick! Patrick's dead!'

'Who's speaking?'

'Mrs Maloney. Mrs Patrick Maloney.'

'You mean Patrick Maloney's dead?'

'I think so,' she sobbed. 'He's lying on the floor and I think he's dead.'

'Be right over,' the man said.

The car came very quickly, and when she opened the front door, two policemen walked in. She knew them both – she knew nearly all the men at the precinct – and she fell right into Jack Noonan's arms, weeping hysterically. He put her gently into a chair, then went over to join the other one, who was called O'Malley, kneeling by the body.

'Is he dead?' she cried.

'I'm afraid he is. What happened?'

Briefly, she told her story about going out to the grocer and coming back to find him on the floor. While she was talking, crying and talking, Noonan discovered a small patch of congealed blood on the dead man's head. He showed it to O'Malley who got up at once and hurried to the phone.

Soon, other men began to come into the house. First a doctor, then two detectives, one of whom she knew by name. Later, a police photographer arrived and took pictures, and a man who knew about fingerprints. There was a great deal of whispering and muttering beside the corpse, and the detectives kept asking her a lot of questions. But they always treated her kindly. She told her story again, this time right from the beginning, when Patrick had come in, and she was sewing, and he was tired, so tired he hadn't wanted to go out for supper. She told how she'd put the meat in the oven – 'it's there now, cooking' – and how she'd slipped out to the grocer for vegetables, and come back to find him lying on the floor.

'Which grocer?' one of the detectives asked.

She told him, and he turned and whispered something to the other detective who immediately went outside into the street.

In fifteen minutes he was back with a page of notes, and there was more whispering, and through her sobbing she heard a few of the whispered phrases – '... acted quite normal ... very cheerful ... wanted to give him a good supper ... peas ... cheesecake ... impossible that she ...'

After a while, the photographer and the doctor departed and two other men came in and took the corpse away on a stretcher. Then the fingerprint man went away. The two detectives remained, and so did the two policemen. They were exceptionally nice to her, and Jack Noonan asked if she wouldn't rather go somewhere else, to her sister's house perhaps, or to his own wife who would take care of her and put her up for the night.

No, she said. She didn't feel she could move even a yard at the moment. Would they mind awfully if she stayed just where she was until she felt better? She didn't feel too good at the moment, she really didn't.

Then hadn't she better lie down on the bed? Jack Noonan asked.

No, she said, she'd like to stay right where she was, in this chair. A little later perhaps, when she felt better, she would move.

So they left her there while they went about their business, searching the house. Occasionally one of the detectives asked her another question. Sometimes Jack Noonan spoke to her gently as he passed by. Her husband, he told her, had been killed by a blow on the back of the head administered with a heavy blunt instrument, almost certainly a large piece of metal. They were looking for the weapon. The murderer may have taken it with him, but on the other hand he may've thrown it away or hidden it somewhere on the premises.

'It's the old story,' he said. 'Get the weapon, and you've got the man.'

Later, one of the detectives came up and sat beside her. Did she know, he asked, of anything in the house that could've been used as the weapon? Would she mind having a look around to see if anything was missing – a very big spanner, for example, or a heavy metal vase.

They didn't have any heavy metal vases, she said.

'Or a big spanner?'

She didn't think they had a big spanner. But there might be some things like that in the garage.

The search went on. She knew that there were other policemen in the garden all around the house. She could hear their footsteps on the gravel outside, and sometimes she saw the flash of a torch through a chink in the curtains. It began to get late, nearly nine she noticed by the clock on the mantel. The four men searching the rooms seemed to be growing weary, a trifle exasperated.

'Jack,' she said, the next time Sergeant Noonan went by. 'Would you mind giving me a drink?'

'Sure I'll give you a drink. You mean this whisky?'

'Yes, please. But just a small one. It might make me feel better.'

He handed her the glass.

'Why don't you have one yourself,' she said. 'You must be awfully tired. Please do. You've been very good to me.'

'Well,' he answered. 'It's not strictly allowed, but I might take just a drop to keep me going.'

One by one the others came in and were persuaded to take a little nip of whisky. They stood around rather awkwardly with the drinks in their hands, uncomfortable in her presence, trying to say consoling things to her. Sergeant Noonan wandered into the kitchen, came out quickly and said, 'Look, Mrs Maloney. You know that oven of yours is still on, and the meat still inside.'

'Oh *dear* me!' she cried. 'So it is!'

'I better turn it off for you, hadn't I?'

'Will you do that, Jack. Thank you so much.'

When the sergeant returned the second time, she looked at him with her large, dark, tearful eyes. 'Jack Noonan,' she said.

'Yes?'

'Would you do me a small favour – you and these others?'

'We can try, Mrs Maloney.'

'Well,' she said. 'Here you all are, and good friends of dear Patrick's too, and helping to catch the man who killed him. You must be terrible hungry by now because it's long past your supper time, and I know Patrick would never forgive me, God bless his soul, if I allowed you to remain in his house without offering you decent hospitality. Why don't you eat up that lamb that's in the oven? It'll be cooked just right by now.'

'Wouldn't dream of it,' Sergeant Noonan said.

'Please,' she begged. 'Please eat it. Personally I couldn't touch a thing, certainly not what's been in the house when he was here. But it's all right for you. It'd be a favour to me if you'd eat it up. Then you can go on with your work again afterwards.'

There was a good deal of hesitating among the four policemen, but they were clearly hungry, and in the end they were persuaded to go into the kitchen and help themselves. The woman stayed where she was, listening to them through the open door, and she could hear them speaking among themselves, their voices thick and sloppy because their mouths were full of meat.

'Have some more, Charlie?'

'No. Better not finish it.'

'She *wants* us to finish it. She said so. Be doing her a favour.'

'Okay then. Give me some more.'

'That's the hell of a big club the guy must've used to hit poor Patrick,' one of them was saying. 'The doc says his skull was smashed all to pieces just like from a sledge-hammer.'

'That's why it ought to be easy to find.'

'Exactly what I say.'

'Whoever done it, they're not going to be carrying a thing like that around them longer than they need.'

One of them belched.
'Personally, I think it's right here on the premises.'
'Probably right under our very noses. What you think, Jack?'
And in the other room, Mary Maloney began to giggle.

The Trial for Murder

Charles Dickens

I have always noticed a prevalent want of courage, even among persons
of superior intelligence and culture, as to imparting their own psychological experiences when those have been of a strange sort. Almost all
men are afraid that what they could relate in such wise would find no
parallel or response in a listener's internal life, and might be suspected
or laughed at. A truthful traveller, who should have seen some extraordinary creature in the likeness of a sea-serpent, would have no fear
of mentioning it; but the same traveller, having had some singular
presentiment, impulse, vagary of thought, vision (so-called), dream, or
other remarkable mental impression, would hesitate considerably before
he would own to it. To this reticence I attribute much of the obscurity
in which such subjects are involved. We do not habitually communicate
our experiences of these subjective things as we do our experiences of
objective creation. The consequence is that the general stock of experience in this regard appears exceptional, and really is so, in respect
of being miserably imperfect.

In what I am going to relate, I have no intention of setting up,
opposing, or supporting any theory whatever. I know the history of the
Bookseller of Berlin, I have studied the case of the wife of a late
Astronomer-Royal as related by Sir David Brewster, and I have followed
the minutest details of a much more remarkable case of Spectral Illusion
occurring within my private circle of friends. It may be necessary to
state as to this last, that the sufferer (a lady) was in no degree, however
distant, related to me. A mistaken assumption on that head might suggest
an explanation of a part of my own case – but only a part – which
would be wholly without foundation. It cannot be referred to my inheritance of any developed peculiarity, nor had I ever before any at
all similar experience, nor have I ever had any at all similar experience
since.

It does not signify how many years ago, or how few, a certain
murder was committed in England, which attracted great attention. We
hear more than enough of murderers as they rise in succession to their

atrocious eminence, and I would bury the memory of this particular brute, if I could, as his body was buried in Newgate Jail. I purposely abstain from giving any direct clue to the criminal's individuality.

When the murder was first discovered, no suspicion fell – or I ought rather to say, for I cannot be too precise in my facts, it was nowhere publicly hinted that any suspicion fell – on the man who was afterwards brought to trial. As no reference was at that time made to him in the newspapers, it is obviously impossible that any description of him can at that time have been given in the newspapers. It is essential that this fact be remembered.

Unfolding at breakfast my morning paper, containing the account of that first discovery, I found it to be deeply interesting, and I read it with close attention. I read it twice, if not three times. The discovery had been made in a bedroom, and, when I laid down the paper, I was aware of a flash – rush – flow – I do not know what to call it – no word I can find is satisfactorily descriptive – in which I seemed to see that bedroom passing through my room, like a picture impossibly painted on a running river. Though almost instantaneous in its passing, it was perfectly clear; so clear that I distinctly, and with a sense of relief, observed the absence of the dead body from the bed.

It was in no romantic place that I had this curious sensation, but in chambers in Piccadilly, very near to the corner of St James's Street. It was entirely new to me. I was in my easy-chair at the moment, and the sensation was accompanied with a peculiar shiver which started the chair from its position. (But it is to be noted that the chair ran easily on casters.) I went to one of the windows (there are two in the room, and the room is on the second floor) to refresh my eyes with the moving objects down in Piccadilly. It was a bright autumn morning, and the street was sparkling and cheerful. The wind was high. As I looked out, it brought down from the Park a quantity of fallen leaves, which a gust took and whirled into a spiral pillar. As the pillar fell and the leaves dispersed, I saw two men on the opposite side of the way, going from west to east. They were one behind the other. The foremost man often looked back over his shoulder. The second man followed him, at a distance of some thirty paces, with his right hand menacingly raised. First, the singularity and steadiness of this threatening gesture in so public a thoroughfare attracted my attention; and next, the more remarkable circumstance that nobody heeded it. Both men threaded their way among the other passengers with a smoothness hardly consistent even with the action of walking on a pavement; and no single creature, that I could see, gave them place, touched them, or looked after them. In passing before my windows, they both stared up at me. I saw their two faces very distinctly, and I knew that I could recognize them anywhere. Not that I had consciously noticed anything very remarkable in either face, except that the man who went first had an unusually lowering appearance, and that the face of the man who followed him was of the colour of impure wax.

I am a bachelor, and my valet and his wife constitute my whole establishment. My occupation is in a certain Branch Bank, and I wish that my duties as head of a Department were as light as they are popularly supposed to be. They kept me in town that autumn, when I stood in need of change. I was not ill, but I was not well. My reader is to make the most that can be reasonably made of my feeling jaded, having a depressing sense upon me of a monotonous life, and being 'slightly dyspeptic'. I am assured by my renowned doctor that my real state of health at that time justifies no stronger description, and I quote his own from his written answer to my request for it.

As the circumstances of the murder, gradually unravelling, took stronger and stronger possession of the public mind, I kept them away from mine by knowing as little about them as was possible in the midst of the universal excitement. But I knew that a verdict of Wilful Murder had been found against the suspected murderer, and that he had been committed to Newgate for trial. I also knew that his trial had been postponed over one Sessions of the Central Criminal Court, on the ground of general prejudice and want of time for the preparation of the defence. I may further have known, but I believe I did not, when, or about when, the Sessions to which his trial stood postponed would come on.

My sitting-room, bedroom, and dressing-room are all on one floor. With the last there is no communication but through the bedroom. True, there is a door in it, once communicating with the staircase; but a part of the fitting of my bath has been – and had then been for some years – fixed across it. At the same period, and as a part of the same arrangement, the door had been nailed up and canvassed over.

I was standing in my bedroom late one night, giving some directions to my servant before he went to bed. My face was towards the only available door of communication with the dressing-room, and it was closed. My servant's back was towards that door. While I was speaking to him, I saw it open, and a man look in, who very earnestly and mysteriously beckoned to me. That man was the man who had gone second of the two along Piccadilly, and whose face was the colour of impure wax.

The figure, having beckoned, drew back, and closed the door. With no longer pause than was made by my crossing the bedroom, I opened the dressing-room door, and looked in. I had a lighted candle already in my hand. I felt no inward expectation of seeing the figure in the dressing-room, and I did not see it there.

Conscious that my servant stood amazed, I turned round to him, and said: 'Derrick, could you believe that in my cool senses I fancied I saw a—' As I there laid my hand upon his breast, with a sudden start he trembled violently, and said, 'O Lord, yes, sir! A dead man beckoning!'

Now I do not believe that this John Derrick, my trusty and attached servant for more than twenty years, had any impression whatever of having seen any such figure, until I touched him. The change in him was so startling, when I touched him, that I fully believe he derived his impression in some occult manner from me at that instant.

I bade John Derrick bring some brandy, and I gave him a dram, and was glad to take one myself. Of what had preceded that night's phenomenon, I told him not a single word. Reflecting on it, I was absolutely certain that I had never seen that face before, except on the one occasion in Piccadilly. Comparing its expression when beckoning at the door with its expression when it had stared up at me as I stood at my window, I came to the conclusion that on the first occasion it had sought to fasten itself upon my memory, and that on the second occasion it had made sure of being immediately remembered.

I was not very comfortable that night, though I felt a certainty, difficult to explain, that the figure would not return. At daylight I fell into a heavy sleep, from which I was awakened by John Derrick's coming to my bedside with a paper in his hand.

This paper, it appeared, had been the subject of an altercation at the door between its bearer and my servant. It was a summons to me to serve upon a Jury at the forthcoming Sessions of the Central Criminal Court at the Old Bailey. I had never before been summoned on such a Jury, as John Derrick well knew. He believed – I am not certain at this hour whether with reason or otherwise – that that class of Jurors were customarily chosen on a lower qualification than mine, and he had at first refused to accept the summons. The man who served it had taken the matter very coolly. He had said that my attendance or non-attendance was nothing to him; there the summons was; and I should deal with it at my own peril, and not at his.

For a day or two I was undecided whether to respond to this call, or take no notice of it. I was not conscious of the slightest mysterious bias, influence, or attraction, one way or other. Of that I am strictly sure as of every other statement that I make here. Ultimately I decided, as a break in the monotony of my life, that I would go.

The appointed morning was a raw morning in the month of November. There was a dense brown fog in Piccadilly, and it became positively black and in the last degree oppressive east of Temple Bar. I found the passages and staircases of the Court-House flaringly lighted with gas, and the Court itself similarly illuminated. I *think* that, until I was conducted by officers into the Old Court and saw its crowded state, I did not know that the Murderer was to be tried that day. I *think* that, until I was so helped into the Old Court with considerable difficulty, I did not know into which of the two Courts sitting my summons would take me. But this must not be received as a positive assertion, for I am not completely satisified in my mind on either point.

I took my seat in the place appropriated to Jurors in waiting, and I looked about the Court as well as I could through the cloud of fog and breath that was heavy in it. I noticed the black vapour hanging like a murky curtain outside the great windows, and I noticed the stifled sound of wheels on the straw or tan that was littered in the street; also, the hum of the people gathered there, which a shrill whistle, or a louder song or hail than the rest, occasionally pierced. Soon afterwards the Judges, two in number, entered, and took their seats. The buzz in the Court was awfully hushed. The direction was given to put the Murderer to the bar. He appeared there. And in that same instant I recognized in him the first of the two men who had gone down Piccadilly.

If my name had been called then, I doubt if I could have answered to it audibly. But it was called about sixth or eighth in the panel, and I was by the time able to say 'Here!' Now observe. As I stepped into the box, the prisoner, who had been looking on attentively, but with no sign of concern, became violently agitated, and beckoned to his attorney. The prisoner's wish to challenge me was so manifest, that it occasioned a pause, during which the attorney with his hand upon the dock, whispered with his client, and shook his head. I afterwards had it from the gentleman, that the prisoner's first affrighted words to him were, '*At all hazards, challenge that man!*' But that, as he would give no reason for it, and admitted that he had not even known my name until he heard it called and I appeared, it was not done.

Both on the ground already explained, that I wish to avoid reviving the unwholesome memory of that Murderer, and also because a detailed account of his long trial is by no means indispensable to my narrative, I shall confine myself closely to such incidents in the ten days and nights during which we, the Jury, were kept together, as directly bear on my own curious personal experience. It is in that, and not in the Murderer, that I seek to interest my reader. It is to that, and not to a page of the Newgate Calendar, that I beg attention.

I was chosen Foreman of the Jury. On the second morning of the trial, after evidence had been taken for two hours (I heard the church clocks strike), happening to cast my eyes over my brother jurymen, I found an inexplicable difficulty in counting them. I counted them several times, yet always with the same difficulty. In short, I made them one too many.

I touched the brother juryman whose place was next to me, and I whispered to him, 'Oblige me by counting us.' He looked surprised by the request, but turned his head and counted. 'Why,' said he suddenly, 'we are thirt— but no, it's not possible. No. We are twelve.'

According to my counting that day, we were always right in detail, but in the gross we were always one too many. There was no appearance – no figure – to account for it; but I had now an inward foreshadowing of the figure that was surely coming.

The Jury were housed at the London Tavern. We all slept in one large room on separate tables, and we were constantly in the charge and under the eye of the officer sworn to hold us in safe keeping. I see no reason for suppressing the real name of that officer. He was intelligent, highly polite, and obliging, and (I was glad to hear) much respected in the City. He had an agreeable presence, good eyes, enviable black whiskers, and a fine sonorous voice. His name was Mr Harker.

When we turned into our twelve beds at night, Mr Harker's bed was drawn across the door. On the night of the second day, not being disposed to lie down, and seeing Mr Harker sitting on his bed, I went and sat beside him, and offered him a pinch of snuff. As Mr Harker's hand touched mine in taking it from my box, a peculiar shiver crossed him, and he said, 'Who is this?'

Following Mr Harker's eyes, and looking along the room, I saw again the figure I expected – the second of the two men who had gone down Piccadilly. I rose, and advanced a few steps; stopped, and looked round at Mr Harker. He was quite unconcerned, laughed, and said in a pleasant way. 'I thought for a moment we had a thirteenth juryman, without a bed. I see it is the moonlight.'

Making no revelation to Mr Harker, but inviting him to take a walk with me to the end of the room, I watched what the figure did. It stood for a few moments by the bedside of each of my eleven brother jurymen, close to the pillow. It always went to the right-hand side of the bed, and always passed out crossing the foot of the next bed. It seemed, from the action of the head, merely to look down pensively at each recumbent figure. It took no notice of me, or of my bed, which was the nearest to Mr Harker's. It seemed to go out where the moonlight came in, through a high window, as by an aerial flight of stairs.

Next morning at breakfast, it appeared that everybody present had dreamed of the murdered man last night, except myself and Mr Harker.

I now felt as convinced that the second man who had gone down Piccadilly was the murdered man (so to speak), as if it had been borne into my comprehension by his immediate testimony. But even this took place, and in a manner for which I was not at all prepared.

On the fifth day of the trial, when the case for the prosecution was drawing to a close, a miniature of the murdered man, missing from his bedroom upon the discovery of the deed, and afterwards found in a hiding-place where the Murderer had been seen digging, was put in evidence. Having been identified by the witness under examination, it was handed up to the Bench, and thence handed down to be inspected

by the Jury. As an officer in a black gown was making his way with
it across to me, the figure of the second man who had gone down
Piccadilly impetuously started from the crowd, caught the miniature
from the officer, and gave it to me with his own hands, at the same
time saying, in a low and hollow tone – before I saw the miniature,
which was in a locket – *'I was younger then, and my face was not then drained
of blood.'* It also came between me and the brother juryman to whom
I would have given the miniature, and the brother juryman to whom
he would have given it, and so passed it on through the whole of our
number, and back into my possession. Not one of them, however, detected this.

At table, and generally when we were shut up together in Mr Harker's
custody, we had from the first naturally discussed the day's proceedings
a good deal. On that fifth day, the case for the prosecution being closed,
and we having that side of the question in a completed shape before
us, our discussion was more animated and serious. Among our number
was a vestryman – the densest idiot I have ever seen at large – who
met the plainest evidence with the most preposterous objections, and
who was sided with by two flabby parochial parasites; all the three im-
panelled from a district so delivered over to Fever that they ought to
have been upon their own trial for five hundred Murders. When these
mischievous blockheads were at their loudest, which was towards midnight, while some of us were already preparing for bed, I again saw
the murdered man. He stood grimly behind them, beckoning to me.
On my going towards them, and striking into the conversation, he immediately retired. This was the beginning of a separate series of
appearances, confined to that long room in which *We* were confined.
Whenever a knot of my brother jurymen laid their heads together, I
saw the head of the murdered man among theirs. Whenever their comparison of notes was going against him, he would solemnly and irre-
sistibly beckon to me.

It will be borne in mind that down to the production of the miniature,
on the fifth day of the trial, I had never seen the Appearance in
Court. Three changes occurred now that we entered on the case for
the defence. Two of them I will mention together, first. The figure was
now in Court continually, and it never there addressed itself to me, but
always to the person who was speaking at the time. For instance: the
throat of the murdered man had been cut straight across. In the opening
speech for the defence, it was suggested that the deceased might have
cut his own throat. At that very moment, the figure, with its throat
in the dreadful condition referred to (this it had concealed before), stood
at the speaker's elbow, motioning across and across its windpipe, now
with the right hand, now with the left, vigorously suggesting to the
speaker himself the impossibility of such a wound having been self-

inflicted by either hand. For another instance: a witness to character, a woman, deposed to the prisoner's being the most amiable of mankind. The figure at that instant stood on the floor before her, looking her full in the face, and pointing out the prisoner's evil countenance with an extended arm and an outstretched finger.

The third change now to be added impressed me strongly as the most marked and striking of all. I do not theorize upon it; I accurately state it, and there leave it. Although the Appearance was not itself perceived by those whom it addressed, its coming close to such persons was invariably attended by some trepidation or disturbance on their part. It seemed to me as if it were prevented by laws to which I was not amenable, from fully revealing itself to others, and yet as if it could invisibly, dumbly, and darkly overshadow their minds. When the leading counsel for the defence suggested that hypothesis of suicide, and the figure stood at the learned gentleman's elbow, frightfully sawing at its severed throat, it is undeniable that the counsel faltered in his speech, lost for a few seconds the thread of his ingenious discourse, wiped his forehead with his handkerchief, and turned extremely pale. When the witness to character was confronted by the Appearance, her eyes most certainly did follow the direction of its pointed finger, and rest in great hesitation and trouble over the prisoner's face. Two additional illustrations will suffice. On the eighth day of the trial, after the pause which was every day made early in the afternoon for a few minutes rest and refreshment, I came back into Court with the rest of the Jury some little time before the return of the Judges. Standing up in the box and looking about me, I thought the figure was not there, until, chancing to raise my eyes to the gallery, I saw it bending forward, and leaning over a very decent woman, as if to assure itself whether the Judges had resumed their seats or not. Immediately afterwards the woman screamed, fainted, and was carried out. So with the venerable, sagacious, and patient Judge who conducted the trial. When the case was over, and he settled himself and his papers to sum up, the murdered man, entering by the Judges' door, advanced to his Lordship's desk, and looked eagerly over his shoulder at the pages of his notes which he was turning. A change came over his Lordship's face; his hand stopped; the peculiar shiver, that I knew so well, passed over him; he faltered, 'Excuse me, gentlemen, for a few moments I am somewhat oppressed by the vitiated air'; and did not recover until he had drunk a glass of water.

Through all the monotony of six of those interminable ten days – the same Judges and others on the bench, the same Murderer in the dock, the same lawyers at the table, the same tones of question and answer rising to the roof of the Court, the same scratching of the Judge's pen, the same ushers going in and out, the same lights kindled at the same hour when there had been any natural light of day, the same foggy

curtain outside the great windows when it was foggy, the same rain
pattering and dripping when it was rainy, the same footmarks of turnkeys and prisoner day after day on the same sawdust, the same keys
locking and unlocking the same heavy doors – through all the wearisome monotony which made me feel as if I had been Foreman of the
Jury for a vast period of time, and Piccadilly had flourished coevally
with Babylon, the murdered man never lost one trace of his distinctness
in my eyes, nor was he at any moment less distinct than anybody else.
I must not omit, as a matter of fact, that I never once saw the Appearance which I call by the name of the murdered man look at the
Murderer. Again and again I wondered, 'Why does he not?' But he
never did.

Nor did he look at me, after the production of the miniature, until
the last closing minutes of the trial arrived. We retired to consider, at
seven minutes before ten at night. The idiotic vestryman and his two
parochial parasites gave us so much trouble that we twice returned into
Court to beg to have certain extracts from the Judge's notes reread.
Nine of us had not the slightest doubt about those passages, neither,
I believe, had any one in the Court; the dunderhead triumvirate, however, having no idea but obstruction, disputed them for that very reason.
At length we prevailed, and finally the Jury returned into Court at ten
minutes past twelve.

The murdered man at that time stood directly opposite the Jury box,
on the other side of the Court. As I took my place, his eyes rested on
me with great attention; he seemed satisfied, and slowly shook a great
grey veil, which he carried on his arm for the first time, over his head
and whole form. As I gave in our verdict, 'Guilty', the veil collapsed,
all was gone, and his place was empty.

The Murderer, being asked by the Judge, according to usage, whether
he had anything to say before sentence of Death should be passed upon
him, indistinctly muttered something which was described in the leading
newspapers of the following day as 'a few rambling, incoherent, and
half-audible words, in which he was understood to complain that he
had not had a fair trial, because the Foreman of the Jury was pre-
possessed against him.' The remarkable declaration that he really made
was this: '*My Lord, I knew I was a doomed man when the Foreman of my
Jury came into the box. My Lord, I knew he would never let me off, because,
before I was taken, he somehow got to my bedside in the night, woke me, and
put a rope round my neck.*'

The Corpse Light

Dick Donovan

What I am about to relate is so marvellous, so weird and startling, that even now, as I dwell upon it all, I wonder why I of all men should have been subjected to the unnatural and unearthly influence. I no longer scoff when somebody reminds me that there is more in heaven and earth than is dreamt of in our philosophy.

It was about twenty years ago that I took up a medical practice in the old-fashioned and picturesque little town of Brinton-on-sea. At that time there was no railway into Brinton, the nearest station being some seven or eight miles away. The result was the town still retained a delightful old time air, while the people were as primitive and old-fashioned as their town. The nearest village was High Lea, about three miles away. Between the two places was a wide sweep of magnificent rolling down, delightful at all times, but especially so in the summer. Many an ancient farmhouse was dotted about, with here and there a windmill. The down on the seaside terminated in a high headland, from which a splendid lighthouse sent forth its warning beams over the fierce North Sea. Second only in conspicuousness to this lighthouse was an old and half ruined windmill, known all over the countryside as 'The Haunted Mill'.

When I first went to live in Brinton this mill soon attracted my attention, for it was one of the most picturesque old places of its kind I had ever seen; and as I had some artistic instincts, and could sketch, the haunted mill appealed to me. It stood on rising ground, close to the high-road that ran between Brinton and High Lea. I gathered that there had been some dispute about the ownership and for over a quarter of a century that disputed claim had remained unsettled; and during that long period the old mill had been gradually falling into ruin. The foundations had from some cause sunk, throwing the main building out of the perpendicular. Part of the roof had fallen in, and the fierce gales of a quarter of a century had battered the sails pretty well to matchwood. A long flight of wooden steps led up to the principal door, but these steps had rotted away in places, and the door itself had partly fallen inwards. Needless to say, this mill had become the home of bats and owls, and, according to the yokels, of something more fearsome than either. It was a forlorn and mournful-looking place, any way, even in the full blaze of sunshine; but seen in moonlight its appearance was singularly weird, and well calculated to beget in the rustic mind a feeling of horror, and to produce a creepy and uncanny sensation in anyone susceptible to the influence of outre appearances.

To me it did not appeal in any of these aspects. I saw in it only subject matter for an exceedingly effective picture, and yet I am bound to confess that even when transferred to board or canvas there was a certain grim suggestiveness of things uncanny, and I easily understood how the superstitious and unreasoning rustic mind was awed into a belief that this mouldering old mill was haunted by something more creepy and harrowing than bats and owls. Anyway, I heard wonderful tales, at which I laughed, and when I learned that the country people generally gave the mill a wide berth at night, I blamed them for their stupidity. But it was a fact that worthy, and in other respects intelligent, farmers and market folk coming or going between Brinton and High Lea after dark preferred the much longer and dangerous route by the sea cliffs, even in the wildest weather.

I have dwelt thus long on the 'Haunted Mill' because it bulks largely in my story, as will presently be seen, and I came in time to regard it with scarcely less awe than the rustics did.

It was during the second year of my residence in Brinton that a young man named Charles Royce came home after having been absent at sea for three years. Royce's people occupied Gorse Hill Farm, about two miles to the south of Brinton. Young Charley, a fine, handsome, but rather wild youngster, had, it appears, fallen desperately in love with Hannah Trowzell, who was a domestic in the employ of the Rector of the parish. But Charley's people did not approve of his choice, and, thinking to cure him, packed him off to sea, and after an absence of three years and a month the young fellow, bronzed, hearty, more rollicking and handsome than ever, returned to his native village. I had known nothing of Charles Royce or his history up to the day of his return; but it chanced on that very day I had to pay a professional visit to the Rectory, and the Rector pressed me to lunch with him. Greatly interested in all his parishioners, and knowing something of the private history of most of the families in his district, the rev. gentleman very naturally fell to talking about young Royce, and he told me the story, adding, 'Hannah is a good girl, and I think it's rather a pity Charley's people objected to his courting her. I believe she would have made him a capital wife.'

'Has she given him up entirely?' I asked.

'Oh, yes, and is engaged to Silas Hartrop, whose father owns the fishing smack the "North Sea Beauty". I've never had a very high opinion of Silas. I'm afraid he is a little too fond of skittles and beer. However, Hannah seems determined to have him in spite of anything I can say, so she must take her course. But I hope she will be able to reform him, and that the marriage will be a happy one. I really shouldn't be a bit surprised, however, if the girl took up with her old lover again, for I have reason to know she was much attracted to him, and I fancy Charley, if he were so minded, could easily influence her to throw Silas overboard.'

This little story of love and disappointment naturally interested me, for in a country town the affairs of one's neighbours are matters of greater moment than is the case in a big city.

So it came to pass that a few weeks after Charley's return it was generally known that, even as the Rector had suggested it might be, young Royce and pretty Hannah Trowzell were spooning again, and Silas virtually been told to go about his business. It was further known that Silas had taken his dismissal so much to heart that he had been seeking consolation in the beer-pot. Of course, folk talked a good deal, and most of them sympathized with Silas, and blamed Hannah. Very soon it began to be bruited about that Royce's people no longer opposed any objections to the wooing, and that in consequence Hannah and Charley were to become husband and wife at Christmas, that was in about seven weeks' time.

A month of the time had passed, and the 'askings' were up in the parish church, when one day there went forth a rumour that Charles Royce was missing. Rumour took a more definite shape a few hours later when it was positively stated that two nights previously Charles had left his father's house in high spirits and the best of health to visit Hannah, and walk with her, as she was going into the town to make some purchases. On his way he called at the 'Two Waggoners', a wayside inn, where he had a pint of beer and purchased an ounce of tobacco. From the time he left the inn, all trace of him was lost, and he was seen no more. Hannah waited his coming until long past the appointed hour, and when he failed to put in an appearance, she became angry and went off to the town by herself.

Next day her anger gave place to anxiety when she learnt that he had left his home to visit her, and had not since returned; and anxiety became alarm when two and three days slipped by without bringing any tidings of the truant. On the night that he left his home, the weather was very tempestuous, and it had been wild and stormy since. It was therefore suggested that on leaving the 'Two Waggoners' he might have got confused when he reached the common, which he had to cross to get to the Rectory; and as there were several pools and treacherous hollows on the common, it was thought he had come to grief; but the most diligent search failed to justify the surmise.

Such an event as this was well calculated to cause a sensation, not only in Brinton and its neighbourhood, but throughout the county. Indeed, for many days it was a common topic of conversation, and at the Brinton weekly market the farmers and the rustics dwelt upon it to the exclusion of other things; and, of course, everybody had some wonderful theory of their own to account for the missing man's disappearance. Despite wide publicity and every effort on the part of the rural and county police, to say nothing of a hundred and one amateur detectives, the mystery remained unsolved. Charles Royce had apparently disappeared from off the face of the earth, leaving not a trace behind.

In the process of time the nine days' wonder gave place to something else, and excepting by those directly interested in him, Charles Royce was forgotten. Hannah took the matter very seriously to heart, and for a while lay dangerously ill. Silas Hartrop, who was much affected by his disappointment with regard to Hannah, went to the dogs, as the saying is, and drank so heavily that it ended in an attack of delirium tremens. I was called in to attend him, and had hard work to pull him through. On his recovery his father sent him to an uncle at Yarmouth, who was in the fishing trade, and soon afterwards news came that young Hartrop had been drowned at sea. He was out in the North Sea in his uncle's fishing smack, and, though nobody saw him go, it was supposed that he fell overboard in the night. This set the local tongues wagging again for a time, but even the affairs of Brinton could not stand still because the ne'er-do-well Silas Hartrop was drowned. So sympathy was expressed with his people, and then the affair was dismissed.

About two years later I received an urgent message late one afternoon to hasten with all speed to High Lea, to attend to the Squire, who had been taken suddenly and seriously ill. I had had rather a heavy day of it, as there had been a good deal of sickness about for some time past, and it had taken me several hours to get through my list of patients. I had just refreshed myself with a cup of tea and was about to enjoy a cigar when the messenger came. Telling him to ride back as quickly as possible and say that I was coming, I busied myself with a few important matters which had to be attended to, as I might be absent for some hours, and then I ordered my favourite mare, Princess, to be saddled.

I set off from Brinton soon after seven. It was a November night, bitterly cold, dark as Erebus, while every now and then violent squalls swept the land from seaward. Princess knew the road well, so I gave the mare her head, and she went splendidly until we reached the ruined mill, when suddenly she wheeled round with such abruptness that, though I was a good horseman, I was nearly pitched from the saddle.

At the same moment I was struck in the face by something that seemed cold and clammy. I thought at first it was a bat, but remembered that bats do not fly in November; an owl, but an owl would not have felt cold and clammy. However, I had little time for thought, as my attention had to be given to the mare. She seemed disposed to bolt, and was trembling with fear. Then, to my intense astonishment, I noticed what seemed to be a large luminous body lying on the roadway. It had the appearnce of a corpse illuminated in some wonderful and mysterious manner. Had it not been for the fright of my mare I should have thought I was the victim of some optical delusion; but Princess evidently saw the weird object, and refused to pass it. So impressed was I with the idea that a real and substantial body was lying on the road, notwithstanding the strange unearthly light, that I slipped from the saddle, intending to investigate the matter, when suddenly it disappeared, and the cold and clammy *something* again struck me in the face.

I confess that for the first time in my life I felt a strange, nervous, unaccountable fear. Whatever the phenomenon was, there was the hard, stern fact to face that my horse had seen what I had seen, and was terrified. There was something strangely uncanny about the whole business, and when a terrific squall, bringing with it sleet and rain, came howling from the sea, it seemed to emphasize the uncanniness, and the ruined mill, looming gaunt and grim in the darkness, gave me an involuntary shudder. The next moment I was trying to laugh myself out of my nervousness. 'Princess and I', I mentally argued, 'have been the victims of some atmospheric delusion.' That was all very well, but the *something* cold and clammy that struck me in the face, and which *may* have struck the mare in the face also, was no atmospheric delusion. With an alacrity I did not often display, I sprang into the saddle, spoke some encouraging words to the mare, for she was still trembling, and when she bounded forward, and the haunted mill was behind me, I experienced a positive sense of relief.

I found my patient at High Lea in a very bad way. He was suffering from an attack of apoplexy, and though I used all my skill on his behalf he passed away towards midnight. His wife very kindly offered me a bed for the night, but as I had important matters to attend to early in the morning I declined the hospitality. It was half-past twelve when I left the house on my return journey. The incident by the haunted mill had been put out of my head by the case I had been called upon to attend, but as I mounted my mare the groom, who had brought her round from the stable, said, 'It be a bad night, doctor, for riding; the kind o' night when dead things come out o' their graves.'

I laughed, and replied:

'Tom, lad, I am surprised to hear you talk such rubbish. I thought you had more sense than that.'

'Well, I tell 'ee what, doctor; if I had to ride to Brinton tonight I'd
go by the cliffs and chance being drowned, rather than pass yon old
mill.'

These words for the moment unnerved me, and I honestly confess
that I resolved to go by the cliffs, dangerous as the road was in the
dark. Nevertheless, I laughed at Tom's fears, and ridiculed him, though
when I left the squire's grounds I turned the mare's head towards the
cliffs. In a few minutes I was ridiculing myself.

'John Patmore Lindsay,' I mentally exclaimed, 'you are a fool. All
your life you have been ridiculing stories of the supernatural, and now,
at your time of life, are you going to allow yourself to be frightened
by a bogey? Shame on you.'

I bucked up, grew bold, and thereupon altered my course, and got
into the high road again.

There had been a slight improvement in the weather. It had ceased
to rain, but the wind had settled down into a steady gale, and screeched
and screamed over the moorland with a demoniacal fury. The darkness,
however, was not so intense as it was, and a star here and there was
visible through the torn clouds. But it was an eerie sort of night, and
I was strangely impressed with a sense of my loneliness. It was absolutely
unusual for me to feel like this, and I suggested to myself that my nerves
were a little unstrung by overwork and the anxiety the squire's illness
had caused me. And so I rode on, bowing my head to the storm, while
the mare stepped out well, and I anticipated that in little more than
half an hour I should be snug in bed. As we got abreast of the haunted
mill the mare once more gibbed, and all but threw me, and again I
was struck in the face by the cold clammy *something*.

I almost think my hair rose on end as I observed that the illuminated
corpse was lying in the roadway again; but now it appeared to be surrounded by a lake of blood. It was the most horrible sight that ever
human eyes looked upon. I tried to urge Princess forward, but she was
stricken with terror, and, wheeling right round, was setting off towards
High Lea again. But once more I was struck in the face by the invisible
something, and its coldness and clamminess made me shudder, while there
in front of us lay the corpse in the pool of blood. The mare reared and
plunged, but I got her head round, determining to make a wild gallop
for Brinton and leave the horrors of the haunted mill behind. But the
corpse was again in front of us, and I shrank back almost appalled as
the *something* once more touched my face.

I cannot hope to describe what my feelings were at this supreme
moment. I don't believe anything human could have daunted me; but I
was confronted by a supernatural mystery that not only terrified me but
the mare I was riding. Whichever way I turned, that awful, ghastly object
confronted me, and the blow in the face was repeated again and again.

How long I endured the horrors of the situation I really don't know. Possibly the time was measured by brief minutes. It seemed to me hours. At last my presence of mind returned. I dismounted, and reasoned with myself that, whatever the apparition was, it had some import. I soothed the mare by patting her neck and talking to her, and I determined then to try and find a solution of the mystery. But now a more wonderful thing happened. The corpse, which was still made visible by the unearthly light, rose straight up, and as it did so the blood seemed to flow away from it. The figure glided past me, and a sense of extraordinary coldness made me shiver. Slowly and gracefully the shining corpse glided up the rotting steps of the old mill, and disappeared through the door-way. No sooner had it gone than the mill itself seemed to glow with phosphorescent light, and to become transparent, and I beheld a sight that took my breath away. I am disposed to think that for some moments my brain became so numbed that insensibility ensued, for I am conscious of a blank. When the power of thought returned, I was still holding the bridle of the mare, and she was cropping the grass at her feet. The mill loomed blackly against the night sky. It had resumed its normal appearance again. The wind shrieked about it. The ragged scud raced through the heavens, and the air was filled with the sounds of the raging wind. At first I was inclined to doubt the evidence of my own senses. I tried to reason myself into a belief that my imagination had played me a trick; but I didn't succeed, although the mystery was too profound for my fathoming. So I mounted the mare, urged her to her fastest pace, galloped into Brinton, and entered my house with a feeling of intense relief.

Thoroughly exhausted by the prolonged physical and mental strain I had endured, I speedily sank into a deep though troubled slumber as soon as I got into bed. I was unusually late in rising the next day. I found that I had no appetite for breakfast. Indeed, I felt ill and out of sorts; and, though I busied myself with my professional duties, I was haunted by the strange incidents of the preceding night. Never before in the whole course of my career had I been so impressed, so unnerved, and so dispirited. I wanted to believe that I was still as sceptical as ever, but it was no use. What I had seen might have been unearthly; but I *had seen it*, and it was no use trying to argue myself out of the fact. The result was, in the course of the afternoon I called on my old friend, Mr Goodyear, who was chief of the county constabulary. He was a strong-minded man, and, like myself, a hardened sceptic about all things that smacked of the supernatural.

'Goodyear,' I said, 'I'm out of sorts, and I want you to humour a strange fancy I have. Bring one of your best men, and come with me to the haunted mill. But first let me exact from you a pledge of honour that, if our journey should result in nothing, you will keep the matter secret, as I am very sensitive to ridicule.'

He looked at me in amazement, and then, as he burst into a hearty laugh, exclaimed:

'I say, my friend, you are over-working yourself. It's time you got a *locum tenens*, and took a holiday.'

I told him that I agreed with him; nevertheless, I begged him to humour me, and accompany me to the mill. At last he reluctantly consented to do so, and an hour later we drove out of the town in my dog-cart. There were four of us, as I took Peter, my groom, with me. We had provided ourselves with lanterns, but Goodyear's man and Peter knew nothing of the object of our journey.

When we got abreast of the mill I drew up, and giving the reins to Peter, I alighted, and Goodyear did the same. Taking him on one side, I said, 'I have had a vision, and unless I am the victim of incipient madness we shall find a dead body in the mill.'

The light of the dog-cart was shining full on his face, and I saw the expression of alarm that my words brought.

'Look here, old chap,' he said in a cheery, kindly way, as he put his arm through mine, 'you are not going into that mill, but straight home again. Come, now, get into the cart, and don't let's have any more of this nonsense.'

I felt disposed to yield to him, and had actually placed my foot on the step to mount, when I staggered back and exclaimed:

'My God! am I going mad, or is this a reality?'

Once again I had been struck in the face by the cold clammy *something*; and I saw Goodyear suddenly clap his hand to his face as he cried out – 'Hullo, what the deuce is that?'

'Aha,' I exclaimed exultantly, for I no longer thought my brain was giving way, 'you felt it too?'

'Well, something cold and nasty-like struck me in the face. A bat, I expect. Confound 'em.'

'Bats don't fly at this time of the year,' I replied.

'By Jove, no more they do.'

I approached him, and said in a low tone:

'Goodyear, this is a mystery beyond our solving. I am resolved to go into that mill.'

He was a brave man, though for a moment or two he hesitated; but on my insisting he consented to humour me, and so we lit the lantern, and leaving the groom in charge of the horse and trap, I, Goodyear, and his man made our way with difficulty up the rotting steps, which were slimy and sodden with wet. As we entered the mill an extraordinary scene of desolation and ruin met our gaze as we flashed the light of the lantern about. In places the floor had broken away, leaving yawning chasms of blackness. From the mouldering rafters hung huge festoons of cobwebs. The accumulated dust and dampness of years had given them the appearance of cords. And oh, how the wind moaned eerily through the rifts and crannies and broken windows! We advanced gingerly, for the floor was so rotten we were afraid it would crumble beneath our feet.

My companions were a little bewildered, I think, and were evidently at a loss to know what we had come there for. But some strange feeling impelled me to seek for something; though if I had been asked to define that something, for the life of me I could not have done it. Forward I went, however, taking the lead, and holding the lantern above my head so that its rays might fall afar. But they revealed nothing save the rotting floor and slimy walls. A ladder led to the upper storey, and I expressed my intention of mounting it. Goodyear tried to dissuade me, but I was resolute, and led the way. The ladder was so creaky and fragile that it was not safe for more than one to be on it at a time. When I reached the second floor and drew myself up through the trap, I am absolutely certain I heard a sigh. As I turned the lantern round so that its light might sweep every hole and corner of the place, I noticed what seemed to be a sack lying in a corner. I approached and touched it with my foot, and drew back in alarm, for touch and sound told me it contained neither corn nor chaff. I waited until my companions had joined me. Then I said to Goodyear, 'Unless I am mistaken there is something dreadful in that sack.'

He stooped and, whipping out his knife, cut the string which fastened up the mouth of the sack, and revealed a human skull with the hair and shrivelled mummified flesh still adhering to it.

'Great heavens!' he exclaimed, 'here is a human body.'

We held a hurried conversation, and decided to leave the ghastly thing undisturbed until the morrow. So we scuttled down as fast as we could, and went home. I did not return to the mill again myself. My part had been played. Investigation made it absolutely certain that the mouldering remains were those of poor Charley Royce, and it was no less absolutely certain that he had been foully murdered. For not only was there a bullet-hole in the skull but his throat had been cut. It was murder horrible and damnable. The verdict of the coroner's jury pronounced it murder, but there was no evidence to prove who had done the deed. Circumstances, however, pointed to Charley's rival, Silas Hartrop. Was it a guilty conscience that drove him to drink? And did the Furies who avenge such deeds impel him on that dark and stormy night in the North Sea to end the torture of his accursed earthly life? Who can tell?

The Veiled Lodger

Sir Arthur Conan Doyle

When one considers that Mr Sherlock Holmes was in active practice for twenty-three years, and that during seventeen of these I was allowed to co-operate with him and to keep notes of his doings, it will be clear that I have a mass of material at my command. The problem has always been, not to find, but to choose. There is the long row of year-books which fill a shelf, and there are the dispatch-cases filled with documents, a perfect quarry for the student, not only of crime, but of the social and official scandals of the late Victorian era. Concerning these latter, I may say that the writers of agonized letters, who beg that the honour of their families or the reputation of famous forbears may not be touched, have nothing to fear. The discretion and high sense of professional honour which have always distinguished my friend are still at work in the choice of these memoirs, and no confidence will be abused. I deprecate, however, in the strongest way the attempts which have been made lately to get at and to destroy these papers. The source of these outrages is known, and if they are repeated I have Mr Holmes' authority for saying that the whole story concerning the politician, the lighthouse and the trained cormorant will be given to the public. There is at least one reader who will understand.

It is not reasonable to suppose that every one of these cases gave Holmes the opportunity of showing those curious gifts of instinct and observation which I have endeavoured to set forth in these memoirs. Sometimes he had with much effort to pick the fruit, sometimes it fell easily into his lap. But the most terrible human tragedies were often involved in these cases which brought him the fewest personal opportunities, and it is one of these which I now desire to record. In telling it, I have made a slight change of name and place, but otherwise the facts are as stated.

One forenoon – it was late in 1896 – I received a hurried note from Holmes asking for my attendance. When I arrived, I found him seated in a smoke-laden atmosphere, with an elderly, motherly woman of the buxom landlady type in the corresponding chair in front of him.

'This is Mrs Merrilow, of South Brixton,' said my friend, with a wave of the hand. 'Mrs Merrilow does not object to tobacco, Watson, if you wish to indulge your filthy habits. Mrs Merrilow has an interesting story to tell which may well lead to further developments in which your presence may be useful.'

'Anything I can do—'

'You will understand, Mrs Merrilow, that if I come to Mrs Ronder I should prefer to have a witness. You will make her understand that before we arrive.'

'Lord bless you, Mr Holmes,' said our visitor; 'she is that anxious to see you that you might bring the whole parish at your heels!'

'Then we shall come early in the afternoon. Let us see that we have our facts correct before we start. If we go over them it will help Dr Watson to understand the situation. You say that Mrs Ronder has been your lodger for seven years and that you have only once seen her face.'

'And I wish to God I had not!' said Mrs Merrilow.

'It was, I understand, terribly mutilated.'

'Well, Mr Holmes, you would hardly say it was a face at all. That's how it looked. Our milkman got a glimpse of her once peeping out of the upper window, and he dropped his tin and the milk all over the front garden. That is the kind of face it is. When I saw her – I happened on her unawares – she covered up quick, and then she said, "Now, Mrs Merrilow, you know at last why it is that I never raise my veil."'

'Do you know anything about her history?'

'Nothing at all,'

'Did she give references when she came?'

'No, sir, but she gave hard cash, and plenty of it. A quarter's rent right down on the table in advance and no arguing about terms. In these times a poor woman like me can't afford to turn down a chance like that.'

'Did she give any reason for choosing your house?'

'Mine stands well back from the road and is more private than most. Then, again, I only take the one, and I have no family of my own. I reckon she had tried others and found that mine suited her best. It's privacy she is after, and she is ready to pay for it.'

'You say that she never showed her face from first to last save on the one accidental occasion. Well, it is a very remarkable story, most remarkable, and I don't wonder that you want it examined.'

'I don't, Mr Holmes. I am quite satisfied so long as I get my rent. You could not have a quieter lodger or one who gives less trouble.'

'Then what has brought matters to a head?'

'Her health, Mr Holmes. She seems to be wasting away. And there's something terrible on her mind. "Murder!" she cries. "Murder!" And once I heard her, "You cruel beast! You monster!" she cried. It was in the night, and it fair rang through the house and sent the shivers through me. So I went to her in the morning. "Mrs Ronder," I says, "if you have anything that is troubling your soul, there's the clergy," I says, "and there's the police. Between them you should get some help." "For God's sake, not the police!" says she, "and the clergy can't change what is past. And yet," she says, "it would ease my mind if someone knew the truth before I died." "Well," says I, "if you won't have the regulars, there is this detective man what we read about" – beggin' your pardon, Mr Holmes. And she, she fair jumped at it. "That's the man," says she. "I wonder I never thought of it before. Bring him here, Mrs Merrilow, and if he won't come, tell him I am the wife of Ronder's wild beast show. Say that, and give him the name Abbas Parva. Here it is as she wrote it, Abbas Parva. "That will bring him, if he's the man I think he is."'

'And it will, too,' remarked Holmes. 'Very good, Mrs Merrilow. I should like to have a little chat with Dr Watson. That will carry us till lunch-time. About three o'clock you may expect to see us at your house in Brixton.'

Our visitor had no sooner waddled out of the room – no other verb can describe Mrs Merrilow's method of progression – than Sherlock Holmes threw himself with fierce energy upon the pile of commonplace books in the corner. For a few minutes there was a constant swish of the leaves, and then with a grunt of satisfaction he came upon what he sought. So excited was he that he did not rise, but sat upon the floor like some strange Buddha, with crossed legs, the huge books all round him, and one open upon his knees.

'The case worried me at the time, Watson. Here are my marginal notes to prove it. I confess that I could make nothing of it. And yet I was convinced that the coroner was wrong. Have you no recollection of the Abbas Parva tragedy?'

'None, Holmes.'

'And yet you were with me then. But certainly my own impression was very superficial, for there was nothing to go by, and none of the parties had engaged my services. Perhaps you would care to read the papers?'

'Could you not give me the points?'

'That is very easily done. It will probably come back to your memory as I talk. Ronder, of course, was a household word. He was the rival of Wombwell, and of Sanger, one of the greatest showmen of his day. There is evidence, however, that he took to drink, and that both he and his show were on the down grade at the time of the great tragedy. The caravan had halted for the night at Abbas Parva, which is a small village in Berkshire, when this horror occurred. They were on their way to Wimbledon, travelling by road, and they were simply camping, and not exhibiting, as the place is so small a one that it would not have paid them to open.

'They had among their exhibits a very fine North African lion. Sahara King was its name, and it was the habit, both of Ronder and his wife, to give exhibitions inside its cage. Here, you see, is a photograph of the performance, by which you will perceive that Ronder was a huge porcine person and that his wife was a very magnificent woman. It was deposed at the inquest that there had been some signs that the lion was dangerous, but as usual, familiarity begat contempt, and no notice was taken of the fact.

'It was usual for either Ronder or his wife to feed the lion at night. Sometimes both, but they never allowed anyone else to do it, for they believed that so long as they were the food-carriers he would regard them as benefactors, and would never molest them. On this particular night, seven years ago, they both went, and a very terrible happening followed, the details of which have never been made clear.

'It seems that the whole camp was roused near midnight by the roars of the animal and the screams of the woman. The different grooms and *employés* rushed from their tents, carrying lanterns, and by their light an awful sight was revealed. Ronder lay with the back of his head crushed in and deep claw-marks across his scalp, some ten yards from the cage, which was open. Close to the door of the cage lay Mrs Ronder, upon her back, with the creature squatting and snarling above her. It had torn her face in such a fashion that it was never thought that she could live. Several of the circus men, headed by Leonardo, the strong man, and Griggs, the clown, drove the creature off with poles, upon which it sprang back into the cage, and was at once locked in. How it had got loose was a mystery. It was conjectured that the pair intended to enter the cage, but that when the door was loosed the creature bounded out upon them. There was no other point of interest in the evidence, save that the woman in a delirium of agony kept screaming, "Coward! Coward!" as she was carried back to the van in which they lived. It was six months before she was fit to give evidence, but the inquest was duly held, with the obvious verdict of death from misadventure.'

'What alternative could be conceived?' said I.

'You may well say so. And yet there were one or two points which worried young Edmunds, of the Berkshire Constabulary. A smart lad that! He was sent later to Allahabad. That was how I came into the matter, for he dropped in and smoked a pipe or two over it.'

'A thin, yellow-haired man?'

'Exactly. I was sure you would pick up the trail presently.'

'But what worried him?'

'Well, we were both worried. It was so deucedly difficult to reconstruct the affair. Look at it from the lion's point of view. He is liberated. What does he do? He takes half a dozen bounds forward, which brings him to Ronder. Ronder turns to fly – the claw-marks were on the back of his head – but the lion strikes him down. Then, instead of bounding on and escaping, he returns to the woman, who was close to the cage, and he knocks her over and chews her face up. Then, again, those cries of hers would seem to imply that her husband had in some way failed her. What could the poor devil have done to help her? You see the difficulty?'

'Quite.'

'And then there was another thing. It comes back to me now as I think it over. There was some evidence that, just at the time the lion roared and the woman screamed, a man began shouting in terror.'

'This man Ronder, no doubt.'

'Well, if his skull was smashed in you would hardly expect to hear from him again. There were at least two witnesses who spoke of the cries of a man being mingled with those of a woman.'

'I should think the whole camp was crying out by then. As to the other points, I think I could suggest a solution.'

'I should be glad to consider it.'

'The two were together, ten yards from the cage, when the lion got loose. The man turned and was struck down. The woman conceived the idea of getting into the cage and shutting the door. It was her only refuge. She made for it, and just as she reached it the beast bounded after her and knocked her over. She was angry with her husband for having encouraged the beast's rage by turning. If they had faced it, they might have cowed it. Hence her cries of "Coward!"'

'Brilliant, Watson! Only one flaw in your diamond.'

'What is the flaw, Holmes?'

'If they were both ten paces from the cage, how came the beast to get loose?'

'Is it possible that they had some enemy who loosed it?'

'And why should it attack them savagely when it was in the habit of playing with them, and doing tricks with them inside the cage?'

'Possibly the same enemy had done something to enrage it.'

Holmes looked thoughtful and remained in silence for some moments.

'Well, Watson, there is this to be said for your theory. Ronder was a man of many enemies. Edmunds told me that in his cups he was horrible. A huge bully of a man, he cursed and slashed at everyone who came in his way. I expect those cries about a monster, of which our visitor has spoken, were nocturnal reminiscences of the dear departed. However, our speculations are futile until we have all the facts. There is a cold partridge on the sideboard, Watson, and a bottle of Montrachet. Let us renew our energies before we make a fresh call upon them.'

When our hansom deposited us at the house of Mrs Merrilow, we found that plump lady blocking up the open door of her humble but retired abode. It was very clear that her chief preoccupation was lest she should lose a valuable lodger, and she implored us, before showing us up, to say and do nothing which could lead to so undesirable an end. Then, having reassured her, we followed her up the straight, badly-carpeted staircase and were shown into the room of the mysterious lodger.

It was a close, musty, ill-ventilated place, as might be expected, since its inmate seldom left it. From keeping beasts in a cage, the woman seemed, by some retribution of Fate, to have become herself a beast in a cage. She sat now in a broken arm-chair in the shadowy corner of the room. Long years of inaction had coarsened the lines of her figure, but at some period it must have been beautiful, and was still full and voluptuous. A thick dark veil covered her face, but it was cut off close at her upper lip, and disclosed a perfectly-shaped mouth and a delicately-rounded chin. I could well conceive that she had indeed been a very remarkable woman. Her voice, too, was well-modulated and pleasing.

'My name is not unfamiliar to you, Mr Holmes,' said she. 'I thought that it would bring you.'

'That is so, madam, though I do not know how you are aware that I was interested in your case.'

'I learned it when I had recovered my health and was examined by Mr Edmunds, the County detective. I fear I lied to him. Perhaps it would have been wiser had I told the truth.'

'It is usually wiser to tell the truth. But why did you lie to him?'

'Because the fate of someone else depended upon it. I know that he was a very worthless being, and yet I would not have his destruction upon my conscience. We had been so close – so close!'

'But has this impediment been removed?'

'Yes, sir. The person that I allude to is dead.'

'Then why should you not now tell the police anything you know?'

'Because there is another person to be considered. That other person is myself. I could not stand the scandal and publicity which would come from a police examination. I have not long to live, but I wish to die undisturbed. And yet I wanted to find one man of judgment to whom I could tell my terrible story, so that when I am gone all might be understood.'

'You compliment me, madam. At the same time, I am a responsible person. I do not promise you that when you have spoken I may not myself think it my duty to refer the case to the police.'

'I think not, Mr Holmes. I know your character and methods too well, for I have followed your work for some years. Reading is the only pleasure which Fate has left me, and I miss little which passes in the world. But in any case, I will take my chance to the use which you may make of my tragedy. It will ease my mind to tell it.'

'My friend and I would be glad to hear it.'

The woman rose and took from a drawer the photograph of a man.

He was clearly a professional acrobat, a man of magnificent physique, taken with his huge arms folded across his swollen chest and a smile breaking from under his heavy moustache – the self-satisfied smile of the man of many conquests.

'That is Leonardo,' she said.

'Leonardo, the strong man, who gave evidence?'

'The same. And this – this is my husband.'

It was a dreadful face – a human pig, or rather a human wild boar, for it was formidable in its bestiality. One could imagine that vile mouth champing and foaming in its rage, and one could conceive those small, vicious eyes darting pure malignancy as they looked forth upon the world. Ruffian, bully, beast – it was written on that heavy-jowled face.

'Those two pictures will help you, gentlemen, to understand the story. I was a poor circus girl brought up on the sawdust, and doing springs through the hoop before I was ten. When I became a woman this man loved me, if such lust as his can be called love, and in an evil moment I became his wife. From that day I was in hell, and he the devil who tormented me. There was no one in the show who did not know of his treatment. He deserted me for others. He tied me down and lashed me with his riding-whip when I complained. They all pitied me and they all loathed him, but what could they do? They feared him, one and all. For he was terrible at all times, and murderous when he was drunk. Again and again he was had for assault, and for cruelty to the beasts, but he had plenty of money and the fines were nothing to him. The best men all left us and the show began to go downhill. It was only Leonardo and I who kept it up – with little Jimmy Griggs, the clown. Poor devil, he had not much to be funny about, but he did what he could to hold things together.

'Then Leonardo came more and more into my life. You see what he was like. I know now the poor spirit that was hidden in that splendid body, but compared to my husband he seemed like the Angel Gabriel. He pitied me and helped me, till at last our intimacy turned to love – deep, deep, passionate love, such love as I had dreamed of but never hoped to feel. My husband suspected it, but I think that he was a coward as well as a bully, and that Leonardo was the one man that he was afraid of. He took revenge in his own way by torturing me more than ever. One night my cries brought Leonardo to the door of our van. We were near tragedy that night, and soon my lover and I understood that it could not be avoided. My husband was not fit to live. We planned that he should die.

'Leonardo had a clever, scheming brain. It was he who planned it. I do not say that to blame him, for I was ready to go with him every inch of the way. But I should never have had the wit to think of such a plan. We made a club – Leonardo made it – and in the leaden head he fastened five long steel nails, the points outwards, with just such a spread as the lion's paw. This was to give my husband his death-blow, and yet to leave the evidence that it was the lion which we would loose who had done the deed.

'It was a pitch-dark night when my husband and I went down, as was our custom, to feed the beast. We carried with us the raw meat in a zinc pail. Leonardo was waiting at the corner of the big van which we should have to pass before we reached the cage. He was too slow, and we walked past him before he could strike, but he followed us on tiptoe and I heard the crash as the club smashed my husband's skull. My heart leaped with joy at the sound. I sprang forward, and I undid the catch which held the door of the great lion's cage.

'And then the terrible thing happened. You may have heard how quick these creatures are to scent human blood, and how it excites them. Some strange instinct had told the creature in one instant that a human being had been slain. As I slipped the bars it bounded out, and was on me in an instant. Leonardo could have saved me. If he had rushed forward and struck the beast with his club he might have cowed it. But the man lost his nerve. I heard him shout in his terror, and then I saw him turn and fly. At the same instant the teeth of the lion met in my face. Its hot, filthy breath had already poisoned me and I was hardly conscious of pain. With the palms of my hands I tried to push the great steaming, blood-stained jaws away from me, and I screamed for help. I was conscious that the camp was stirring, and then dimly I remember a group of men, Leonardo, Griggs and others, dragging me from under the creature's paws. That was my last memory, Mr Holmes, for many a weary month. When I came to myself, and saw myself in the mirror, I cursed that lion – oh, how I cursed him! – not because he had torn away my beauty, but because he had not torn away my life. I had but one desire, Mr Holmes, and I had enough money to gratify it. It was that I should cover myself so that my poor face should be seen by none, and that I should dwell where none whom I had ever known should find me. That was all that was left to me to do – and that is what I have done. A poor wounded beast that has crawled into its hole to die – that is the end of Eugenia Ronder.'

We sat in silence for some time after the unhappy woman had told her story. Then Holmes stretched out his long arm and patted her hand with such a show of sympathy as I had seldom known him to exhibit.

'Poor girl!' he said. 'Poor girl! The ways of Fate are indeed hard to understand. If there is not some compensation hereafter, then the world is a cruel jest. But what of this man Leonardo?'

'I never saw him or heard from him again. Perhaps I have been wrong to feel so bitterly against him. He might as soon have loved one of the freaks whom we carried round the country as the thing which the lion had left. But a woman's love is not so easily set aside. He had left me under the beast's claws, he had deserted me in my need, and yet I could not bring myself to give him to the gallows. For myself, I cared nothing what became of me. What could be more dreadful than my actual life? But I stood between Leonardo and his fate.'

'And he is dead?'

'He was drowned last month when bathing near Margate. I saw his death in the paper.'

'And what did he do with this five-clawed club, which is the most singular and ingenious part of all your story?'

'I cannot tell, Mr Holmes. There is a chalk-pit by the camp, with a deep green pool at the base of it. Perhaps in the depths of that pool—'

'Well, well, it is of little consequence now. The case is closed.'

'Yes,' said the woman, 'the case is closed.'

We had risen to go, but there was something in the woman's voice which arrested Holmes' attention. He turned swiftly upon her.

'Your life is not your own,' he said. 'Keep your hands off it.'

'What use is it to anyone?'

'How can I tell? The example of patient suffering is in itself the most precious of all lessons to an impatient world.'

The woman's answer was a terrible one. She raised her veil and stepped forward into the light.

'I wonder if you would bear it,' she said.

It was horrible. No words can describe the framework of a face when the face itself is gone. Two living and beautiful brown eyes looking sadly out from that grisly ruin did but make the view more awful. Holmes held up his hand in a gesture of pity and protest, and together we left the room.

Two days later, when I called upon my friend, he pointed with some pride to a small blue bottle upon his mantelpiece. I picked it up. There was on it a red poison label. A pleasant almondy odour rose when I opened it.

'Prussic acid?' said I.

'Exactly. It came by post. "I send you my temptation. I will follow your advice." That was the message. I think, Watson, we can guess the name of the brave woman who sent it.'

Surprise! Surprise!

Roger F. Dunkley

When Dahlia Loom found the body, face down in its grey mackintosh, in her compost heap, she was, understandably, surprised. And annoyed. It had taken many months of laborious journeys with her potato peelings to organize and was just beginning to simmer nicely. She presumed he was a fugitive from 'The Duck and Orange', deep in his cups, who had stumbled one night against the Loom garden shed, ricocheted on to the compost heap and expired in an untidy heart attack. Such a combination of thoughtlessness and intemperance was difficult to condone, but Dahlia Loom was as charitable as her neighbour, and twice as inquisitive, being an ardent admirer of Dame Agatha Christie. Chins quivering, she approached the body more closely, saw the congealed blood, dark and sticky, around the holes in the neck, whimpered twice, and resolved to do everything she could to seek out the killer and see that justice was done.

Unable to contemplate more detailed investigation of the corpse at present, she retraced her steps slightly unsteadily up the garden path, glancing uneasily over her shoulder several times, and confronted her husband in the parlour.

'Herbert, there's a man on the compost heap.'

'Yes, dear,' said Herbert from somewhere inside a voluminous evening suit of mature vintage. He seemed bent on burying himself beneath the contents of the sideboard drawers.

'Dead,' said Dahlia Loom.

'Where's my rabbit?' said her husband. 'The collapsible one. And the bunting. The bazaar opens in half an hour.'

'Stabbed,' she said. 'We must do something about it.'

'Have a cup of tea and an aspirin,' said Mr Loom. He sighed – 'I'll have to manage with the pigeons again' – and left.

'We should contact the police, the Murder Squad,' called his wife.

A top-hat reappeared round the door. 'I should lie down if you've got another of those headaches,' advised Herbert Loom, 'like that chap from the hospital said.'

*

Frustrated, but hardly surprised, Mrs Loom donned her best coat – the
synthetic beaver lamb she had acquired from a recent jumble sale –
slipped a large magnifying-glass into her pocket, just in case, and, surmounted by a hat busy with plumes and trimmed with rabbit fur that
Herbert would have quickly recognized, she set out for the police station.
Since she passed her sister's front door *en route*, she knocked upon it and
disburdened herself to Lily of the morning's discovery.

'So something must be done,' she concluded. 'Justice,' she specified.

Lily's bosom sank, expelling a tired sigh. She peered into her sister's
shining eyes. 'Have a cup of tea,' she said. 'You'll feel better afterwards.'

'There's a body,' said Dahlia Loom, her voice rising shrilly, 'a corpse,
and you talk about tea. Clues, not tea bags.'

'Pardon, dear?'

'We should be hunting for clues. Finger-prints, murder weapons,
motives. That's what they always do. In the books. There's a murderer at large!' She produced her magnifying glass and flourished
it purposefully under her sister's nose. The nose withdrew in some
alarm.

'Harold should be back in a minute,' quavered Lily. 'He's got another
funeral on. He's been undertaking too much recently. There seems to
be quite a glut of them at the moment. I put it down to the hot summer
myself.' She fingered the beads on her meagre bosom, scrutinized her
sister's face for some moments, shook her head sadly, then leaned forward
and gently patted Dahlia's arm. 'You should tell that psychiatrist man
if you're still having the turns, dear, you know.'

Mrs Loom's frustration grew: her cheeks contrived to be ashen and
flushed simultaneously. Her lips trembled and parted to deliver her indignation, but the door opened and disclosed Harold.

'Thank goodness,' she exclaimed. 'Harold, I need help. What would
you do if you'd just found a body?'

Harold's moustache twitched slyly. 'Bury it,' he said.

The constable on duty held a sandwich in one hand and a pencil in
the other. He chewed the pencil.

Dahlia Loom pinged the bell again. The pencil crunched. She leaned
across the desk. 'I pinged,' she announced.

The policeman wiped the desiccated bits of pencil from his lips and
looked up. He saw the hat.

'I want a detective,' she told him; 'you know.'

'I know,' said the constable, unable to deploy his eyes any lower than
the plumes.

'Ostrich?' he said.

'*Detective*,' insisted Mrs Loom, puzzled.

The policeman breathed deeply. 'Burglary, is it?'

Dahlia glanced to each side and inclined her head conspiratorially. Their eyes locked. 'Murder,' she whispered, 'quite foul.'

There was a pause. 'Where?' he challenged.

'In our compost heap. It's become quite dishevellled. Cabbage leaves and grass cuttings in dreadful disarray.'

'Was the victim a gardening man?' suggested the constable. 'Someone in horticulture, perhaps?' He smirked behind the remains of his pencil. 'Tell me, do you enjoy the fictional works of Dame Agatha Christie, madam?' he asked.

Mrs Loom's pulse quickened. She felt her frustration glowing like a white pain behind her eyes. This wasn't the ruthless pursuit of justice she'd thrilled to in literature. He would be asking her to sit down and have a cup of tea next . . .

'Pull up a chair, madam,' said the policeman, baring his teeth in an official smile. 'Just a few questions.' He assembled a sheaf of forms. When they reached the third side, Dahlia Loom was pale with disenchantment and bureaucratic irrelevance.

'Any disabilities,' recited the constable tunelessly, 'physical' – he hesitated – 'or mental?'

Mrs Loom gnawed her lip and changed colour several times. 'Headaches. I used to see a man at the hospital,' she said. 'But the trouble went away. I don't see him any more. He wasn't very nice.'

The policeman finished his notes, laid down his pencil and opened a door behind him.

'Can I have the detective now?' She enunciated the words with exaggerated care and volume, her plumes trembling with suppressed anger. 'The killer must be brought to trial without further delay.'

The door closed and the constable disappeared. The air around the Loom hat vibrated. Minutes later the door opened and readmitted him.

'Yes. We'll be sending a man along presently, Mrs Doom.' He pushed a cup across the desk towards her.

'*Loom*,' said Dahlia. 'What's this?'

'For you. I thought you might like a cup of tea,' said the police constable.

'Are you sure you're a detective?' asked Mrs Loom, for the young man in her parlour was distinctly unpromising; he wore neither monocle nor cape. His left eye twitched. He pointed to the police car outside in which he'd just arrived.

'Are you sure *you* have a body, madam?' he replied.

Indignantly, Mrs Loom picked up the now empty teapot and led him past the late-flowering nasturtiums to the compost heap.

'There,' she said, and, sprinkling the soggy tea-leaves on the pile of vegetation with its four sprouting limbs, she retired deftly behind the detective.

The young man swooped professionally over the body, clicking first his tongue then his camera, and produced a variety of obscure instruments which he applied in even more eccentric ways.

Dahlia Loom offered him her magnifying-glass.

He raised an eyebrow and turned down the offer.

She hovered behind him, fluttering her hands with more zeal than helpfulness. When he next looked up she was tip-toeing beneath the over-hanging hedge, struggling to focus the ground through her glass. He lifted his eyes; the nervous tic returned.

'I'm scrutinizing,' she said, lowering her voice to a sepulchral whisper. 'Footprints.' She peered into the foliage. 'The murderer could be anywhere.' She turned her head and gasped. Frozen into horrified immobility she stood stiffly to attention, eyes wide. The detective pursed his lips and disentangled her from the predatory hedge which had just claimed her hairnet.

'Have you any hobbies, Mrs Broom?'

'*Loom.*' She nodded. 'I knit.'

'May I suggest you indulge yourself with some needles for a while – in the house?'

Dahlia Loom, offended by his independence and suspecting him of professional incompetence, returned to the house, sat down sullenly to knit, rose to search for the other number nine needle, failed to find it and sat down again, making do with a number ten. She clicked the needles savagely: there was a killer to be found, enquiries to be made, and here she was – knitting.

A shadow darkened the doorway; she jumped. It was the detective.

'I dropped a stitch,' she said accusingly. The man stared with interest and bewilderment at her handiwork. 'Bunting,' she explained. 'For Herbert.'

'Ah,' he said. 'Bunting. For Herbert.'

Indignation and doubt gnawed at Mrs Loom. This was no time to be talking of knitting. 'Have you found the murder weapon?' she demanded.

The detective took out a pencil and pad. 'Just a few questions, Mrs Tomb. Routine, I'm afraid.'

Dahlia Loom fidgeted angrily with her bunting. More questions? Action, not questions, was what was needed. She looked at the man with growing suspicion and parried his queries with ill-concealed impatience. They grew increasingly irrelevant: her age, her habits, her husband's age, her husband's habits, her health –

The colour mounted to Dahlia Loom's cheeks. She passed a hand over her brow.

'Headache?' asked the detective.

'Look,' said Mrs Loom, gesticulating belligerently with her needles, 'there's a killer on the loose. A brutal, unprincipled maniac. He may strike again at any moment. None of us is safe. We must hunt him down. Why are we wasting time with all these questions?'

'Routine,' murmured the man.

'Are you *sure* you're a detective?' She glared at him, her face puce.

'Would you like an aspirin?' he said.

The puce graduated to full-blown purple.

'Mrs Groom,' he said, 'do you know this man?' He flourished a card. 'Found in the wallet of the deceased.' She stared. 'Have you ever had occasion to undergo medical treatment? Did you sometimes receive visits of a professional nature from a Doctor Probe of the Sebastopol Road Hospital – Psychiatric Department?'

Dahlia Loom sprang trembling to her feet, her suspicions blossoming into certainty. Yes, he was just like the other one, asking all these irrelevant questions. That grey mackintosh and, doubtless, the white coat beneath. So many questions – and all she had was headaches!

'You psychiatrists,' she shrieked, 'you're all the same!'

The pain throbbed behind her eyes. She leapt at him, brandishing her knitting and, when he turned squeaking and twitching with fright, she pursued him out of the back door and down the path. The string of coloured bunting unwound and flapped ferociously behind her. He tripped and plunged headlong into the compost heap.

Dahlia Loom hovered over him, an avenging fury.

'All these empty questions,' she said. 'Find the answer, the truth. Who did it?'

The man tried to turn his head, his voice thick with fear and hedge-trimmings: 'Don't you see?' he spluttered. 'You did. With a knitting needle. Size ten!'

Mrs Loom, astonished, gazed through a mist at the knitting in her hand and then at the bodies, one dead, one trembling, in the vegetable perturbation at her feet. She had a moment of clarity. She remembered the needle, sticky with fresh blood. She remembered the brown stains caked on her palms and all that scrubbing with the Vim. She shook her head.

'It was a number nine,' she said.

The grey mackintosh whimpered. It squirmed and started to rise. 'Just like the other one,' she thought. The mist returned, the old frustration and resentment flashed in a sudden rage of pain in her temple and, with more thoroughness than skill, she stabbed at the mackintosh.

It heaved, scattering a flurry of groundsel and tea-leaves. 'Help,' it choked. She struck it again to make it go quiet. It made a gargling noise. She tugged, but the needle would not come out. The compost twitched again and a shoe jerked against her shin. 'Ouch,' said Dahlia Loom and, in a moment of inspiration, wound the gaily-hued bunting round the neck, and pulled. The throat made a messy, bubbling noise. Then, at last, the mackintosh went quiet. 'No more questions!' panted her frenzied brain.

She surveyed the remains of the compost heap and the tattered thread of stained bunting which triumphantly beribboned the second corpse. 'Herbert won't be pleased about all this,' she thought vaguely. 'He'll have to make do with the string of knotted hankies for a bit longer . . .'

When Dahlia Loom returned to the house – how much later she couldn't say – she heard the murmur of desultory conversation from her front parlour. She was delighted, for social intercourse was as rare as it was dull in the Loom household. Lily was there, and Harold. Herbert, too, was back, dunking his biscuit and his wilting bow-tie in the tepid tea he had just brewed for them all.

'We came to see what we could do, dear,' said Lily gently, turning a compassionate gaze on Herbert.

Dahlia gestured to them to follow her. 'Come and see,' she said, marching briskly outside. Moments later she reappeared, bearing the single knitting needle which had dropped from her bunting, discovered them debating in furtive whispers, and subsided into a chair. They nudged one another guiltily and lapsed into sheepish silence. Harold cleared his throat with unnecessary ostentation.

'Lily says you found a body,' he said. 'In the compost heap.'

'No,' she said faintly, 'I found – two!'

She glanced up at the open door, her eyes gleaming apprehensively.

'The murderer may yet be close at hand!' she whispered.

Unhappily they looked at one another. Her husband squeezed her arm and indicated the tea tray.

Then he noticed the groundsel. A moist sprig detached itself from somewhere behind her left ear and splashed on to the carpet.

They watched the stain materialize before them. It was rich and brown. Dahlia reached to retrieve the stray herbage, absently pressing her palm against her cheek and looking quizzically about her.

There was an appalled silence while the family studied the russet streaks now decorating her face. Mrs Loom broke it.

'Don't worry,' she said. 'They'll see the maniac's brought to trial in the end. They always do.' She beamed reassuringly at them.

'Now . . .' The quizzical look returned. 'Where did I put my knitting? And my needle. I seem,' observed Dahlia Loom vaguely, 'to have lost my number ten.' She frowned. 'Or was it a nine . . . ?'

The Two Bottles of Relish

Lord Dunsany

Smithers is my name. I'm what you might call a small man and in a small way of business.

I travel for Num-numo, a relish for meats and savouries – the world-famous relish I ought to say. It's really quite good, no deleterious acids in it, and does not affect the heart; so it is quite easy to push. I wouldn't have got the job if it weren't. But I hope some day to get something that's harder to push, as of course the harder they are to push, the better the pay. At present I can just make my way, with nothing at all over; but then I live in a very expensive flat. It happened like this, and that brings me to my story. And it isn't the story you'd expect from a small man like me, yet there's nobody else to tell it. Those that know anything of it besides me are all for hushing it up. Well, I was looking for a room to live in in London when first I got my job. It had to be in London, to be central; and I went to a block of buildings, very gloomy they looked, and saw the man that ran them and asked him for what I wanted. Flats they called them; just a bedroom and a sort of a cupboard. Well, he was showing a man round at the time who was a gent, in fact more than that, so he didn't take much notice of me – the man that ran all those flats didn't, I mean. So I just ran behind for a bit, seeing all sorts of rooms and waiting till I could be shown my class of thing. We came to a very nice flat, a sitting-room, bedroom and bathroom, and a sort of little place that they called a hall. And that's how I came to know Linley. He was the bloke that was being shown round.

'Bit expensive,' he said.

And the man that ran the flats turned away to the window and picked his teeth. It's funny how much you can show by a simple thing like. What he meant to say was that he'd hundreds of flats like that, and thousands of people looking for them, and he didn't care who had them or whether they all went on looking. There was no mistaking him, somehow. And yet he never said a word, only looked away out of the window and picked his teeth. And I ventured to speak to Mr Linley then; and I said, 'How about it, sir, if I paid half, and shared it? I wouldn't be in the way, and I'm out all day, and whatever you said would go, and really I wouldn't be no more in your way than a cat.'

You may be surprised at my doing it; and you'll be much more surprised at him accepting it – at least, you would if you knew me, just a small man in a small way of business. And yet I could see at once that he was taking to me more than he was taking to the man at the window.

'But there's only one bedroom,' he said.

'I could make up my bed easy in that little room there,' I said.

'The Hall,' said the man, looking round from the window, without taking his toothpick out.

'And I'd have the bed out of the way and hid in the cupboard by any hour you like,' I said.

He looked thoughtful, and the other man looked out over London; and in the end, do you know, he accepted.

'Friend of yours?' said the flat man.

'Yes,' answered Mr Linley.

It was really very nice of him.

I'll tell you why I did it. Able to afford it? Of course not. But I heard him tell the flat man that he had just come down from Oxford and wanted to live for a few months in London. It turned out he wanted just to be comfortable and do nothing for a bit while he looked things over and chose a job, or probably just as long as he could afford it. Well, I said to myself, what's the Oxford manner worth in business, especially a business like mine? Why, simply everything you've got. If I picked up only a quarter of it from this Mr Linley I'd be able to double my sales, and that would soon mean I'd be given something a lot harder to push, with perhaps treble the pay. Worth it every time. And you can make a quarter of an education go twice as far again if you're careful with it. I mean you don't have to quote the whole of the Inferno to show that you've read Milton; half a line may do it.

Well, about that story I have to tell. And you mightn't think that a little man like me could make you shudder. Well, I soon forgot about the Oxford manner when we settled down in our flat. I forgot it in the sheer wonder of the man himself. He had a mind like an acrobat's body, like a bird's body. It didn't want education. You didn't notice whether he was educated or not. Ideas were always leaping up in him, things you'd never have thought of. And not only that, but if any ideas were about, he'd sort of catch them. Time and again I've found him knowing just what I was going to say. Not thought-reading, but what they call intuition. I used to try to learn a bit about chess, just to take my thoughts off Num-numo in the evening, when I'd done with it. But problems I never could do. Yet he'd come along and glance at my problem and say, 'You probably move that piece first,' and I'd say, 'But where?' and he'd say, 'Oh, one of those three squares.' And I'd say, 'But it will be taken on all of them.' And the piece a queen all the time, mind you. And he'd say, 'Yes, it's doing no good there: you're probably meant to lose it.'

And, do you know, he'd be right.

You see, he'd been following out what the other man had been thinking. That's what he'd been doing.

Well, one day there was that ghastly murder at Unge. I don't know if you remember it. But Steeger had gone down to live with a girl in a bungalow on the North Downs, and that was the first we had heard of him.

The girl had £200, and he got every penny of it, and she utterly disappeared. And Scotland Yard couldn't find her.

Well, I'd happened to read that Steeger had bought two bottles of Num-numo; for the Otherthorpe police had found out everything about him, except what he did with the girl; and that of course attracted my attention, or I should have never thought again about the case or said a word of it to Linley. Num-numo was always on my mind, as I always spent every day pushing it, and that kept me from forgetting the other thing. And so one day I said to Linley, 'I wonder with all that knack you have for seeing through a chess problem, and thinking of one thing and another, that you don't have a go at that Otherthorpe mystery. It's a problem as much as chess,' I said.

'There's not the mystery in ten murders that there is in one game of chess,' he answered.

'It's beaten Scotland Yard,' I said.

'Has it?' he asked.

'Knocked them end-wise,' I said.

'It shouldn't have done that,' he said. And almost immediately after he said, 'What are the facts?'

We were both sitting at supper, and I told him the facts, as I had them straight from the papers. She was a pretty blonde, she was small, she was called Nancy Elth, she had £200, they lived at the bungalow for five days. After that he stayed there for another fortnight, but nobody ever saw her alive again. Steeger said she had gone to South America, but later said he had never said South America, but South Africa. None of her money remained in the Bank where she had kept it, and Steeger was shown to have come by at least £150 just at that time. Then Steeger turned out to be a vegetarian, getting all his food from the greengrocer, and that made the constable in the village of Unge suspicious of him, for a vegetarian was something new to the constable. He watched Steeger after that, and it's well he did, for there was nothing that Scotland Yard asked him that he couldn't tell them about him, except of course the one thing. And he told the police at Otherthorpe five or six miles away, and they came and took a hand at it too. They were able to say for one thing that he never went outside the bungalow and its tidy garden ever since she disappeared. You see, the more they watched him the more suspicious they got, as you naturally do if you're watching a man; so that very soon they were watching every move he made, but if it hadn't been for his being a vegetarian they'd never have started to suspect him, and there wouldn't have been enough evidence even for Linley. Not that they found out anything much against him, except that £150 dropping in from nowhere, and it was Scotland Yard that found that, not the police of Otherthorpe. No, what the constable of Unge found out was about the larch-trees, and that beat Scotland Yard utterly, and beat Linley up to the very last, and of course it beat me. There were ten larch-trees in the bit of garden, and he'd made some sort of an arrangement with the landlord, Steeger had, before he took the bunga-low, by which he could do what he liked with the larch-trees. And then from about the time that little Nancy Elth must have died he cut every one of them down. Three times a day he went at it for nearly a week, and when they were all down he cut them all up into logs no more than two foot long and laid them all in neat heaps. You never saw such work. And what for? To give an excuse for the axe was one theory. But the excuse was bigger than the axe; it took him a fortnight, hard work every day. And he could have killed a little thing like Nancy Elth without an axe, and cut her up too. Another theory was that he wanted firewood, to make away with the body. But he never used it. He left it all standing there in those neat stacks. It fairly beat everybody.

Well, those are the facts I told Linley. Oh yes, and he bought a big butcher's knife. Funny thing, they all do. And yet it isn't so funny after all; if you've got to cut a woman up, you've got to cut her up; and you can't do that without a knife. Then, there were some negative facts. He hadn't burned her. Only had a fire in the small stove now and then, and only used it for cooking. They got on to that pretty smartly, the Unge constable did, and the men that were lending him a hand from Otherthorpe. There were some little woody places lying round, shaws they call them in that part of the country, the country people do, and they could climb a tree handy and unobserved and get a sniff at the smoke in almost any direction it might be blowing. They did that now and then, and there was no smell of flesh burning, just ordinary cooking. Pretty smart of the Otherthorpe police that was, though of course it didn't help to hang Steeger. Then later on the Scotland Yard men went down and got another fact – negative, but narrowing things down all the while. And that was that the chalk under the bungalow and under the little garden had none of it been disturbed. And he'd never been outside it since Nancy disappeared. Oh yes, and he had a big file besides the knife. But there was no sign of any ground bones found on the file, or any blood on the knife. He'd washed them of course. I told all that to Linley.

Now I ought to warn you before I go any further. I am a small man myself and you probably don't expect anything horrible from me. But I ought to warn you this man was a murderer, or at any rate somebody was; the woman had been made away with, a nice pretty little girl too, and the man that had done that wasn't necessarily going to stop at things you might think he'd stop at. With the mind to do a thing like that, and with the long thin shadow of the rope to drive him further, you can't say what he'll stop at. Murder tales seem nice things sometimes for a lady to sit and read all by herself by the fire. But murder isn't a nice thing, and when a murderer's desperate and trying to hide his tracks he isn't even as nice as he was before. I'll ask you to bear that in mind. Well, I've warned you.

So I says to Linley, 'And what do you make of it?'

'Drains?' said Linley.

'No,' I says, 'you're wrong there. Scotland Yard has been into that. And the Otherthorpe people before them. They've had a look in the drains, such as they are, a little thing running into a cesspool beyond the garden; and nothing has gone down it – nothing that oughtn't to have, I mean.'

He made one or two other suggestions, but Scotland Yard had been before him in every case. That's really the crab of my story, if you'll excuse the expression. You want a man who sets out to be a detective to take his magnifying glass and go down to the spot; to go to the spot before everything; and then to measure the footmarks and pick up the clues and find the knife that the police have overlooked. But Linley never even went near the place, and he hadn't got a magnifying glass, not as I ever saw, and Scotland Yard were before him every time.

In fact they had more clues than anybody could make head or tail of. Every kind of clue to show that he'd murdered the poor little girl; every kind of clue to show that he hadn't disposed of the body; and yet the body wasn't there. It wasn't in South America either, and not much more likely in South Africa. And all the time, mind you, that enormous bunch of chopped larch-wood, a clue that was staring everyone in the face and leading nowhere. No, we didn't seem to want any more clues, and Linley never went near the place. The trouble was to deal with the clues we'd got. I was completely mystified; so was Scotland Yard; and Linley seemed to be getting no forwarder; and all the while the mystery was hanging on me. I mean if it were not for the trifle I'd chanced to remember, and if it were not for one chance word I said to Linley, that mystery would have gone the way of all the other mysteries that men have made nothing of, a darkness, a little patch of night in history.

Well, the fact was Linley didn't take much interest in it at first, but I was so absolutely sure that he could do it, that I kept him to the idea. 'You can do chess problems,' I said.

'That's ten times harder,' he said, sticking to his point.

'Then why don't you do this?' I said.

'Then go and take a look at the board for me,' said Linley.

That was his way of talking. We'd been a fortnight together, and I knew it by now. He meant to go down to the bungalow at Unge. I know you'll say why didn't he go himself; but the plain truth of it is, that if he'd been tearing about the countryside he'd never have been thinking, whereas sitting there in his chair by the fire in our flat there was no limit to the ground he could cover, if you follow my meaning. So down I went by train next day, and got out at Unge station. And there were the North Downs rising up before me, somehow like music.

'It's up there, isn't it?' I said to the porter.

'That's right,' he said. 'Up there by the lane; and mind to turn to your right when you get to the old yew-tree, a very big tree, you can't mistake it, and then ...' and he told me the way so that I couldn't go wrong. I found them all like that, very nice and helpful. You see, it was Unge's day at last. Everyone had heard of Unge now; you could have got a letter there any time just then without putting the county or post town; and this was what Unge had to show. I dare say if you tried to find Unge now ... well, anyway, they were making hay while the sun shone.

Well, there the hill was, going up into sunlight, going up like a song. You don't want to hear about the spring, and all the may rioting, and the colour that came down over everything later on in the day, and all those birds; but I thought, 'What a nice place to bring a girl to.' And then when I thought that he'd killed her there, well I'm only a small man, as I said, but when I thought of her on that hill with all the birds singing, I said to myself, 'Wouldn't it be odd if it turned out to be me after all that got that man killed, if he did murder her.' So I soon found my way up to the bungalow and began prying about, looking over the hedge into the garden. And I didn't find much, and I found nothing at all that the police hadn't found already, but there were those heaps of larch logs staring me in the face and looking very queer.

I did a lot of thinking, leaning against the hedge, breathing the smell of the may, and looking over the top of it at the larch logs, and the neat little bungalow the other side of the garden. Lots of theories I thought of, till I came to the best thought of all; and that was that if I left the thinking to Linley, with his Oxford-and-Cambridge education, and only brought him the facts, as he had told me, I should be doing

more good in my way than if I tried to do any big thinking. I forgot
to tell you that I had gone to Scotland Yard in the morning. Well,
there wasn't really much to tell. What they asked me was, what I
wanted. And, not having an answer exactly ready, I didn't find out
very much from them. But it was quite different at Unge; everyone was
most obliging; it was their day there, as I said. The constable let me
go indoors, so long as I didn't touch anything, and he gave me a look
at the garden from the inside. And I saw the stumps of the ten larch-trees,
and I noticed one thing that Linley said was very observant of me, not
that it turned out to be any use, but any way I was doing my best: I
noticed that the stumps had been all chopped anyhow. And from that
I thought that the man that did it didn't know much about chopping.
The constable said that was a deduction. So then I said that the axe
was blunt when he used it; and that certainly made the constable think,
though he didn't actually say I was right this time. Did I tell you that
Steeger never went outdoors, except to the little garden to chop wood,
ever since Nancy disappeared? I think I did. Well, it was perfectly true.
They'd watched him night and day, one or another of them, and the
Unge constable told me that himself. That limited things a good deal.
The only thing I didn't like about it was that I felt Linley ought to
have found all that out instead of ordinary policemen, and I felt that
he could have too. There'd have been romance in a story like that.
And they'd never have done it if the news hadn't gone round that the
man was a vegetarian and only dealt at the greengrocers. Likely as not
even that was only started out of pique by the butcher. It's queer what
little things may trip a man up. Best to keep straight is my motto. But
perhaps I'm straying a bit away from my story. I should like to do that
for ever – forget that it ever was; but I can't.

   Well, I picked up all sorts of information; clues I suppose I should
call it in a story like this, though they none of them seemed to lead
anywhere. For instance, I found out everything he ever bought at the
village, I could even tell you the kind of salt he bought, quite plain
with no phosphates in it, that they sometimes put in to make it tidy.
And then he got ice from the fishmongers, and plenty of vegetables, as
I said, from the greengrocer, Mergin & Sons. And I had a bit of a talk
over it all with the constable. Slugger he said his name was. I wondered
why he hadn't come in and searched the place as soon as the girl was
missing. 'Well, you can't do that,' he said. 'And besides, we didn't
suspect at once, not about the girl, that is. We only suspected there was
something wrong about him on account of him being a vegetarian. He
stayed a good fortnight after the last that was seen of her. And then we
slipped in like a knife. But, you see, no one had been inquiring about
her, there was no warrant out.'

   'And what did you find?' I asked Slugger, 'when you went in?'

'Just a big file,' he said, 'and the knife and the axe that he must have got to chop her up with.'

'But he got the axe to chop trees with,' I said.

'Well, yes,' he said, but rather grudgingly.

'And what did he chop them for?' I asked.

'Well, of course my superiors has theories about that,' he said, 'that they mightn't tell to everybody.'

You see, it was those logs that were beating them.

'But did he cut her up at all?' I asked.

'Well, he said that she was going to South America,' he answered. Which was really very fair-minded of him.

I don't remember now much else that he told me. Steeger left the plates and dishes all washed up and very neat, he said.

Well, I brought all this back to Linley, going up by the train that started just about sunset. I'd like to tell you about the late spring evening, so calm over that grim bungalow, closing in with a glory all round it as though it were blessing it; but you'll want to hear of the murder. Well, I told Linley everything, though much of it didn't seem to me to be worth the telling. The trouble was that the moment I began to leave anything out, he'd know it, and make me drag it in. 'You can't tell what may be vital,' he'd say. 'A tin-tack swept away by a housemaid might hang a man.'

All very well, but be consistent, even if you are educated at Eton and Harrow, and whenever I mentioned Num-numo, which after all was the beginning of the whole story, because he wouldn't have heard of it if it hadn't been for me, and my noticing that Steeger had bought two bottles of it, why then he said that things like that were trivial and we should keep to the main issues. I naturally talked a bit about Num-numo, because only that day I had pushed close on fifty bottles of it in Unge. A murder certainly stimulates people's minds, and Steeger's two bottles gave me an opportunity that only a fool could have failed to make something of. But of course all that was nothing at all to Linley.

You can't see a man's thoughts, and you can't look into his mind, so that all the most exciting things in the world can never be told of. But what I think happened all that evening with Linley, while I talked to him before supper, and all through supper, and sitting smoking afterwards in front of our fire, was that his thoughts were stuck at a barrier there was no getting over. And the barrier wasn't the difficulty of finding ways and means by which Steeger might have made away with the body, but the impossibility of finding why he chopped those masses of wood every day for a fortnight, and paid, as I'd just found out, £25 to his landlord to be allowed to do it. That's what was beating Linley. As for the ways by which Steeger might have hidden the body, it seemed to me that every way was blocked by the police. If you said

he buried it, they said the chalk was undisturbed; if you said he carried
it away, they said he never left the place; if you said he burned it, they
said no smell of burning was ever noticed when the smoke blew low,
and when it didn't they climbed trees after it. I'd taken to Linley
wonderfully, and I didn't have to be educated to see there was something big in a mind like his, and I thought that he could have done it.
When I saw the police getting in before him like that, and no way that
I could see of getting past them, I felt real sorry.

Did anyone come to the house, he asked me once or twice. Did
anyone take anything away from it? But we couldn't account for it that
way. Then perhaps I made some suggestion that was no good, or perhaps
I started talking of Num-numo again, and he interrupted me rather
sharply.

'But what would you do, Smithers?' he said. 'What would you do
yourself?'

'If I'd murdered poor Nancy Elth?' I asked.

'Yes,' he said.

'I can't ever imagine doing such a thing,' I told him.

He sighed at that, as though it were something against me.

'I suppose I should never be a detective,' I said. And he just shook
his head.

Then he looked broodingly into the fire for what seemed an hour.
And then he shook his head again. We both went to bed after that.

I shall remember the next day all my life. I was till evening, as usual,
pushing Num-numo. And we sat down to supper about nine. You
couldn't get things cooked at those flats, so of course we had it cold.
And Linley began with a salad. I can see it now, every bit of it. Well,
I was still a bit full of what I'd done in Unge, pushing Num-numo.
Only a fool, I know, would have been unable to push it there; but still,
I *had* pushed it; and about fifty bottles, forty-eight to be exact, are
something in a small village, whatever the circumstances. So I was
talking about it a bit; and then all of a sudden I realized that Num-numo
was nothing to Linley, and I pulled myself up with a jerk. It was really
very kind of him; do you know what he did? He must have known at
once why I stopped talking, and he just stretched out a hand and said,
'Would you give me a little of your Num-numo for my salad.'

I was so touched I nearly gave it him. But of course you don't take
Num-numo with salad. Only for meats and savouries. That's on the
bottle.

Though I just said to him, 'Only for meats and savouries.' Though
I don't know what savouries are. Never had any.

I never saw a man's face go like that before.

He seemed still for a whole minute. And nothing speaking about him
but that expression. Like a man that's seen a ghost, one is tempted to

write. But it wasn't really at all. I'll tell you what he looked like. Like a man that's seen something that no one has ever looked at before, something he thought couldn't be.

And then he said in a voice that was all quite changed, more low and gentle and quiet it seemed, 'No good for vegetables, eh?'

'Not a bit,' I said.

And at that he gave a kind of sob in his throat. I hadn't thought he could feel things like that. Of course I didn't know what it was all about; but, whatever it was, I thought all that sort of thing would have been knocked out of him at Eton and Harrow, an educated man like that. There were no tears in his eyes, but he was feeling something horribly.

And then he began to speak with big spaces between his words, saying, 'A man might make a mistake perhaps, and use Num-numo with vegetables.'

'Not twice,' I said. What else could I say?

And he repeated that after me as though I had told of the end of the world, and adding an awful emphasis to my words, till they seemed all clammy with some frightful significance, and shaking his head as he said it.

Then he was quite silent.

'What is it?' I asked.

'Smithers,' he said.

'Yes,' I said.

'Smithers,' said he.

And I said, 'Well?'

'Look here, Smithers,' he said, 'you must phone down to the grocer at Unge and find out from him this.'

'Yes?' I said.

'Whether Steeger bought those two bottles, as I expect he did, on the same day, and not a few days apart. He couldn't have done that.'

I waited to see if any more was coming, and then I ran out and did what I was told. It took me some time, being after nine o'clock, and only then with the help of the police. About six days apart they said; and so I came back and told Linley. He looked up at me so hopefully when I came in, but I saw that it was the wrong answer by his eyes.

You can't take things to heart like that without being ill, and when he didn't speak I said, 'What you want is a good brandy, and go to bed early.'

And he said, 'No. I must see someone from Scotland Yard. Phone round to them. Say here at once.'

But I said, 'I can't get an inspector from Scotland Yard to call on us at this hour.'

His eyes were all lit up. He was all there all right.

'Then tell them,' he said, 'they'll never find Nancy Elth. Tell one of them to come here, and I'll tell him why.' And he added, I think only for me, 'They must watch Steeger, till one day they get him over something else.'

And, do you know, he came. Inspector Ulton; he came himself.

While we were waiting I tried to talk to Linley. Partly curiosity, I admit. But I didn't want to leave him to those thoughts of his, brooding away by the fire. I tried to ask him what it was all about. But he wouldn't tell me. 'Murder is horrible,' is all he would say. 'And as a man covers his tracks up it only gets worse.'

He wouldn't tell me. 'There are tales,' he said, 'that one never wants to hear.'

That's true enough. I wish I'd never heard this one. I never did actually. But I guessed it from Linley's last words to Inspector Ulton, the only ones that I overheard. And perhaps this is the point at which to stop reading my story, so that you don't guess it too; even if you think you want murder stories. For don't you rather want a murder story with a bit of a romantic twist, and not a story about real foul murder? Well, just as you like.

In came Inspector Ulton, and Linley shook hands in silence, and pointed the way to his bedroom; and they went in there and talked in low voices, and I never heard a word.

A fairly hearty-looking man was the inspector when they went into that room.

They walked through our sitting-room in silence when they came out, and together they went into the hall, and there I heard the only words they said to each other. It was the Inspector that first broke that silence.

'But why,' he said, 'did he cut down the trees?'

'Solely,' said Linley, 'in order to get an appetite.'

The Kill

Peter Fleming

In the cold waiting-room of a small railway station in the West of England two men were sitting. They had sat there for an hour, and were likely to sit there long. There was a thick fog outside. Their train was indefinitely delayed.

The waiting-room was a barren and unfriendly place. A naked electric bulb lit it with wan, disdainful efficiency. A notice, 'No Smoking', stood on the mantelpiece: when you turned it round, it said 'No Smoking' on the other side, too. Printed regulations relating to an outbreak of swine fever in 1924 were pinned neatly to one wall, almost, but maddeningly not quite, in the centre of it. The stove gave out a hot, thick smell, powerful already but increasing. A pale leprous flush on the black and beaded window showed that a light was burning on the platform outside, in the fog. Somewhere water dripped with infinite reluctance on to corrugated iron.

The two men sat facing each other over the stove on chairs of an unswerving woodenness. Their acquaintance was no older than their vigil. From such talk as they had had, it seemed likely that they were to remain strangers.

The younger of the two resented the lack of contact in their relationship more than the lack of comfort in their surroundings. His attitude towards his fellow beings had but recently undergone a transition from the subjective to the objective. As with many of his class and age, the routine, unrecognized as such, of an expensive education, with the triennial alternative of those delights normal to wealth and gentility, had atrophied many of his curiosities. For the first twenty-odd years of his life he had read humanity in terms of relevance rather than reality, looking on people who held no ordained place in his own existence much as a buck in a park watches visitors walking up the drive: mildly, rather resentfully inquiring – not inquisitive. Now, hot in reaction from this unconscious provincialism, he treated mankind as a museum, gaping conscientiously at each fresh exhibit, hunting for the noncumulative evidence of man's complexity with indiscriminate zeal. To each magic circle of individuality he saw himself as a kind of free-lance tangent. He aspired to be a connoisseur of men.

There was undoubtedly something arresting about the specimen before him. Of less than medium height, the stranger had yet that sort of ranging leanness that lends vicarious inches. He wore a long black overcoat, very shabby, and his shoes were covered with mud. His face had no colour in it, though the impression it produced was not one of pallor; the skin was of a dark sallow, tinged with grey. The nose was pointed, the jaw sharp and narrow. Deep vertical wrinkles, running down towards it from the high cheekbones, sketched the permanent groundwork of a broader smile than the deep-set honey-coloured eyes seemed likely to authorize. The most striking thing about the face was the incongruity of its frame. On the back of his head the stranger wore a bowler hat with a very narrow brim. No word of such casual implications as a tilt did justice to its angle. It was clamped, by something at least as holy as custom, to the back of his skull, and that thin, questing face confronted the world fiercely from under a black halo of nonchalance. The man's whole appearance suggested *difference* rather than aloofness. The unnatural way he wore his hat had the significance of indirect comment, like the antics of a performing animal. It was as if he was part of some older thing, of which *homo sapiens* in a bowler hat was an expurgated edition. He sat with his shoulders hunched and his hands thrust into his overcoat pockets. The hint of discomfort in his attitude seemed due not so much to the fact that his chair was hard as to the fact that it was a chair.

The young man had found him uncommunicative. The most mobile sympathy, launching consecutive attacks on different fronts, had failed to draw him out. The reserved adequacy of his replies conveyed a rebuff more effectively than sheer surliness. Except to answer him, he did not look at the young man. When he did, his eyes were full of an abstracted amusement. Sometimes he smiled, but for no immediate cause.

Looking back down their hour together, the young man saw a field of endeavour on which frustrated banalities lay thick, like the discards of a routed army. But resolution, curiosity, and the need to kill time all clamoured against an admission of defeat.

'If he will not talk,' thought the young man, 'then I will. The sound of my own voice is infinitely preferable to the sound of none. I will tell him what has just happened to me. It is really a most extraordinary story. I will tell it as well as I can, and I shall be very much surprised if its impact on his mind does not shock this man into some form of self-revelation. He is unaccountable without being *outré*, and I am inordinately curious about him.'

Aloud he said, in a brisk and engaging manner: 'I think you said you were a hunting man?'

The other raised his quick honey-coloured, eyes. They gleamed with inaccessible amusement. Without answering, he lowered them again to contemplate the little beads of light thrown through the ironwork of the stove on to the skirts of his overcoat. Then he spoke. He had a husky voice.

'I came here to hunt,' he agreed.

'In that case,' said the young man, 'you will have heard of Lord Fleer's private park. Their kennels are not far from here.'

'I know them,' replied the other.

'I have just been staying there,' the young man continued. 'Lord Fleer is my uncle.'

The other looked up, smiled, and nodded, with the bland inconsequence of a foreigner who does not understand what is being said to him. The young man swallowed his impatience.

'Would you,' he continued, using a slightly more peremptory tone than heretofore, 'would you care to hear a new and rather remarkable story about my uncle? Its dénouement is not two days old. It is quite short.'

From the fastness of some hidden joke, those light eyes mocked the necessity of a definite answer. At length: 'Yes,' said the stranger, 'I would.' The impersonality in his voice might have passed for a parade of sophistication, a reluctance to betray interest. But the eyes hinted that interest was alive elsewhere.

'Very well,' said the young man.

Drawing his chair a little closer to the stove, he began:

As perhaps you know, my uncle, Lord Fleer, leads a retired, though by no means an inactive life. For the last two or three hundred years, the currents of contemporary thought have passed mainly through the hands of men whose gregarious instincts have been constantly awakened and almost invariably indulged. By the standards of the eighteenth century, when Englishmen first became self-conscious about solitude, my uncle would have been considered unsociable. In the early nineteenth century, those not personally acquainted with him would have thought him romantic. Today, his attitude towards the sound and fury of modern life is too negative to excite comment as an oddity; yet even now, were he to be involved in any occurrence which could be called disastrous or interpreted as discreditable, the press would pillory him as a 'Titled Recluse'.

The truth of the matter is, my uncle has discovered the elixir, or, if you prefer it, the opiate, of self-sufficiency. A man of extremely simple tastes, not cursed with overmuch imagination, he sees no reason to cross frontiers of habit which the years have hallowed into rigidity. He lives in his castle (it may be described as commodious rather than comfortable), runs his estate at a slight profit, shoots a little, rides a great deal, and hunts as often as he can. He never sees his neighbours except by accident, thereby leading them to suppose, with sublime but unconscious arrogance, that he must be slightly mad. If he is, he can at least claim to have padded his own cell.

My uncle has never married. As the only son of his only brother, I was brought up in the expectation of being his heir. During the war, however, an unforeseen development occurred.

In this national crisis my uncle, who was of course too old for active service, showed a lack of public spirit which earned him locally a good deal of unpopularity. Briefly, he declined to recognize the war, or, if he did recognize it, gave no sign of having done so. He continued to lead his own vigorous but (in the circumstances) rather irrelevant life. Though he found himself at last obliged to recruit his hunt-servants from men of advanced age and uncertain mettle in any crisis of the chase, he contrived to mount them well, and twice a week during the season himself rode two horses to a standstill after the hill-foxes which, as no doubt you know, provide the best sport the Fleer country has to offer.

When the local gentry came and made representations to him, saying that it was time he did something for his country besides destroying its vermin by the most unreliable and expensive method ever devised, my uncle was very sensible. He now saw, he said, that he had been standing too aloof from a struggle of whose progress (since he never read the paper) he had been only indirectly aware. The next day he wrote to London and ordered *The Times* and a Belgian refugee. It was the least he could do, he said. I think he was right.

The Belgian refugee turned out to be a female, and dumb. Whether one or both of these characteristics had been stipulated for by my uncle, nobody knew. At any rate, she took up her quarters at Fleer: a heavy, unattractive girl of twenty-five, with a shiny face and small black hairs on the backs of her hands. Her life appeared to be modelled on that of the larger ruminants, except, of course, that the greater part of it took place indoors. She ate a great deal, slept at will, and had a bath every Sunday, remitting this salubrious custom only when the house-keeper, who enforced it, was away on holiday. Much of her time she spent sitting on a sofa, on the landing outside her bedroom, with Prescott's *Conquest of Mexico* open on her lap. She read either exceptionally slowly or not at all, for to my knowledge she carried the first volume about with her for eleven years. Hers, I think, was the contemplative type of mind.

The curious, and from my point of view the unfortunate, aspect of my uncle's patriotic gesture was the gradually increasing affection with which he came to regard this unlovable creature. Although, or more probably because, he saw her only at meals, when her features were

rather more animated than at other times, his attitude towards her passed
from the detached to the courteous, and from the courteous to the
paternal. At the end of the war there was no question of her return
to Belgium, and one day in 1919 I heard with pardonable mortification
that my uncle had legally adopted her, and was altering his will in her
favour.

Time, however, reconciled me to being disinherited by a being who,
between meals, could scarcely be described as sentient. I continued to
pay an annual visit to Fleer, and to ride with my uncle after his big-boned
Welsh hounds over the sullen, dark-grey hill country in which – since
its possession was no longer assured to me – I now began to see a powerful,
though elusive, beauty.

I came down here three days ago, intending to stay for a week. I
found my uncle, who is a tall, fine-looking man with a beard, in his
usual unassailable good health. The Belgian, as always, gave me the
impression of being impervious to disease, to emotion, or indeed to
anything short of an act of God. She had been putting on weight since
she came to live with my uncle, and was now a very considerable figure
of a woman, though not, as yet, unwieldy.

It was at dinner, on the evening of my arrival, that I first noticed
a certain *malaise* behind my uncle's brusque, laconic manner. There was
evidently something on his mind. After dinner he asked me to come
into his study. I detected, in the delivery of the invitation, the first hint
of embarrassment I had known him to betray.

The walls of the study were hung with maps and the extremities of
foxes. The room was littered with bills, catalogues, old gloves, fossils,
rat-traps, cartridges, and feathers which had been used to clean his pipe
– a stale diversity of jetsam which somehow managed to produce an
impression of relevance and continuity, like the débris in an animal's
lair. I had never been in the study before.

'Paul,' said my uncle as soon as I had shut the door, 'I am very much
disturbed.'

I assumed an air of sympathetic inquiry.

'Yesterday,' my uncle went on, 'one of my tenants came to see me.
He is a decent man, who farms a strip of land outside the park wall
to the northward. He said that he had lost two sheep in a manner for
which he was wholly unable to account. He said he thought they had
been killed by some wild animal.'

My uncle paused. The gravity of his manner was really portentous.

'Dogs?' I suggested, with the slightly patronizing diffidence of one who
has probability on his side.

My uncle shook his head judiciously. 'This man had often seen sheep
which had been killed by dogs. He said that they were always badly
torn – nipped about the legs, driven into a corner, worried to death;

it was never a clean piece of work. These two sheep had not been killed like that. I went down to see them for myself. Their throats had been torn out. They were not bitten or nuzzled. They had both died in the open, not in a corner. Whatever did it was an animal more powerful and more cunning than a dog.'

I said, 'It could have been something that had escaped from a travelling menagerie, I suppose?'

'They don't come into this part of the country,' replied my uncle; 'there are no fairs.'

We were both silent for a moment. It was hard not to show more curiosity than sympathy as I waited on some further revelation to stake out my uncle's claim on the latter emotion. I could put no interpretation on those two dead sheep wild enough to account for his evident distress.

He spoke again, but with obvious reluctance.

'Another was killed early this morning,' he said in a low voice, 'on the Home Farm. In the same way.'

For the lack of any better comment, I suggested beating the nearby coverts. There might be some . . .

'We've scoured the woods,' interrupted my uncle brusquely.

'And found nothing?'

'Nothing. . . . Except some tracks.'

'What sort of tracks?'

My uncle's eyes were suddenly evasive. He turned his head away.

'They were a man's tracks,' he said slowly. A log fell over in the fireplace.

Again a silence. The interview appeared to be causing him pain rather than relief. I decided that the situation could lose nothing through the frank expression of my curiosity. Plucking up courage, I asked him roundly what cause he had to be upset? Three sheep, the property of his tenants, had died deaths which, though certainly unusual, were unlikely to remain for long mysterious. Their destroyer, whatever it was, would inevitably be caught, killed, or driven away in the course of the next few days. The loss of another sheep or two was the worst he had to fear.

When I had finished, my uncle gave me an anxious, almost a guilty look. I was suddenly aware that he had a confession to make.

'Sit down,' he said. 'I wish to tell you something.'

This is what he told me:

A quarter of a century ago, my uncle had had occasion to engage a new housekeeper. With the blend of fatalism and sloth which is the foundation of the bachelor's attitude to the servant problem, he took on the first applicant. She was a tall, black, slant-eyed woman from the Welsh border, aged about thirty. My uncle said nothing about her character, but described her as having 'powers'. When she had been at Fleer some months, my uncle began to notice her, instead of taking her for granted. She was not averse to being noticed.

One day she came and told my uncle that she was with child by him. He took it calmly enough till he found that she expected him to marry her, or pretended to expect it. Then he flew into a rage, called her a whore, and told her she must leave the house as soon as the child was born. Instead of breaking down or continuing the scene, she began to croon to herself in Welsh, looking at him sideways with a certain amusement. This frightened him. He forbade her to come near him again, had her things moved into an unused wing of the castle, and engaged another housekeeper.

A child was born, and they came and told my uncle that the woman was going to die; she asked for him continually, they said. As much frightened as distressed, he went through passages long unfamiliar to her room. When the woman saw him, she began to gabble in a pre-occupied kind of way, looking at him all the time, as if she were repeating a lesson. Then she stopped, and asked that he should be shown the child.

It was a boy. The midwife, my uncle noticed, handled it with a reluctance almost amounting to disgust.

'That is your heir,' said the dying woman in a harsh, unstable voice. 'I have told him what he is to do. He will be a good son to me, and jealous of his birthright.' And she went off, my uncle said, into a wild yet cogent rigmarole about a curse, embodied in the child, which would fall on any whom he made his heir over the bastard's head. At last her voice trailed away, and she fell back, exhausted and staring.

As my uncle turned to go, the midwife whispered to him to look at the child's hands. Gently unclasping the podgy, futile little fists, she showed him that on each hand the third finger was longer than the second. . . .

Here I interrupted. The story had a certain queer force behind it, perhaps from its obvious effect on the teller. My uncle feared and hated the things he was saying.

'What did that mean,' I asked; 'the third finger longer than the second?'

'It took me a long time to discover,' replied my uncle. 'My own servants, when they saw I did not know, would not tell me. But at last I found out through the doctor, who had it from an old woman in the village. People born with their third finger longer than their second become werewolves. At least' – he made a perfunctory effort at amused indulgence – 'that is what the common people here think.'

'And what does that – what is that supposed to mean?' I, too, found myself throwing rather hasty sops to scepticism. I was growing strangely credulous.

'A werewolf,' said my uncle, dabbling in improbability without self-consciousness, 'is a human being who becomes, at intervals, to all intents and purposes a wolf. The transformation – or the supposed transformation – takes place at night. The werewolf kills men and animals, and is supposed to drink their blood. Its preference is for men. All through the Middle Ages, down to the seventeenth century, there were innumerable cases (especially in France) of men and women being legally tried for offences which they had committed as animals. Like the witches, they were rarely acquitted, but, unlike the witches, they seem seldom to have been unjustly condemned.' My uncle paused. 'I have been reading the old books,' he explained. 'I wrote to a man in London who is interested in these things when I heard what was believed about the child.'

'What became of the child?' I asked.

'The wife of one of my keepers took it in,' said my uncle. 'She was a stolid woman from the North who, I think, welcomed the opportunity to show what little store she set by the local superstitions. The boy lived with them till he was ten. Then he ran away. I had not heard of him since then till' – my uncle glanced at me almost apologetically – 'till yesterday.'

We sat for a moment in silence, looking at the fire. My imagination had betrayed my reason in its full surrender to the story. I had not got it in me to dispel his fears with a parade of sanity. I was a little frightened myself.

'You think it is your son, the werewolf, who is killing the sheep?' I said at length.

'Yes. For a boast: or for a warning: or perhaps out of spite, at a night's hunting wasted.'

'Wasted?'

My uncle looked at me with troubled eyes.

'His business is not with sheep,' he said uneasily.

For the first time I realized the implication of the Welshwoman's curse. The hunt was up. The quarry was the heir to Fleer. I was glad to have been disinherited.

'I have told Germaine not to go out after dusk,' said my uncle, coming in pat on my train of thought.

The Belgian was called Germaine; her other name was Vom.

I confess I spent no very tranquil night. My uncle's story had not wholly worked in me that 'suspension of disbelief' which someone speaks of as being the prime requisite of good drama. But I have a powerful imagination. Neither fatigue nor common sense could quite banish the vision of that metamorphosed malignancy ranging, with design, the black and silver silences outside my window. I found myself listening for the sound of loping footfalls on a frost-baked crust of beech leaves. . . .

Whether it was in my dream that I heard, once, the sound of howling, I do not know. But the next morning I saw, as I dressed, a man walking quickly up the drive. He looked like a shepherd. There was a dog at his heels, trotting with a noticeable lack of assurance. At breakfast my uncle told me that another sheep had been killed, almost under the noses of the watchers. His voice shook a little. Solicitude sat oddly on his features as he looked at Germaine. She was eating porridge, as if for a wager.

After breakfast we decided on a campaign. I will not weary you with the details of its launching and its failure. All day we quartered the woods with thirty men, mounted and on foot. Near the scene of the kill our dogs picked up a scent which they followed for two miles and more, only to lose it on the railway line. But the ground was too hard for tracks, and the men said it could only have been a fox or a polecat, so surely and readily did the dogs follow it.

The exercise and the occupation were good for our nerves. But late in the afternoon, my uncle grew anxious; twilight was closing in swiftly under a sky heavy with clouds, and we were some distance from Fleer. He gave final instructions for the penning of the sheep by night, and we turned our horses' heads for home.

We approached the castle by the back drive, which was little used: a dank, unholy alley, running the gauntlet of a belt of firs and laurels. Beneath our horses' hoofs flints chinked remotely under a thick carpet of moss. Each consecutive cloud from their nostrils hung with an air of permanency, as if bequeathed to the unmoving air.

We were perhaps three hundred yards from the tall gates leading to the stableyard when both horses stopped dead, simultaneously. Their heads were turned towards the trees on our right, beyond which, I knew, the sweep of the main drive converged on ours.

My uncle gave a short, inarticulate cry in which premonition stood aghast at the foreseen. At the same moment something howled on the other side of the trees. There was relish, and a kind of sobbing laughter, in that hateful sound. It rose and fell luxuriously, and rose and fell again, fouling the night. Then it died away, fawning on society in a throaty whimper.

The forces of silence fell unavailingly on its rear; its filthy echoes still went reeling through our heads. We were aware that feet went loping lightly down the iron-hard drive . . . two feet.

My uncle flung himself off his horse and dashed through the trees. I followed. We scrambled down a bank and out into the open. The only figure in sight was motionless.

Germaine Vom lay doubled up in the drive, a solid, black mark against the shifting values of the dusk. We ran forward. . . .

To me she had always been an improbable cipher rather than a real person. I could not help reflecting that she died, as she had lived, in the livestock tradition. Her throat had been torn out.

The young man leant back in his chair, a little dizzy from talking and from the heat of the stove. The inconvenient realities of the waiting-room, forgotten in his narrative, closed in on him again. He sighed, and smiled rather apologetically at the stranger.

'It is a wild and improbable story,' he said. 'I do not expect you to believe the whole of it. For me, perhaps, the reality of its implications has obscured its almost ludicrous lack of verisimilitude. You see, by the death of the Belgian I am heir to Fleer.'

The stranger smiled: a slow, but no longer an abstracted smile. His honey-coloured eyes were bright. Under his long black overcoat his body seemed to be stretching itself in sensual anticipation. He rose silently to his feet.

The other found a sharp, cold fear drilling into his vitals. Something behind those shining eyes threatened him with appalling immediacy, like a sword at his heart. He was sweating. He dared not move.

The stranger's smile was now a grin, a ravening convulsion of the face. His eyes blazed with a hard and purposeful delight. A thread of saliva dangled from the corner of his mouth.

Very slowly he lifted one hand and removed his bowler hat. Of the fingers crooked about its brim, the young man saw that the third was longer than the second.

Something to Do with Figures

Miriam Allen de Ford

Outside was the California sunshine, but it did not penetrate to the little inside room where Wedderburn sat and thought – thought harder than ever before in his life.

His career for thirty years had been tied up with numbers, figures, arithmetical formulae. For twenty-seven of those years he had been book-keeper – for thirteen years, head book-keeper – in a wholesale dry goods house. He had never married. A little, thin, greying man with spectacles, he seemed the last person in the world to be intimately concerned with murder. And yet for a year past, most of his waking hours had been dedicated to solving the twisted story of Eric Scholl, of Lorina Brackett, and of her brother Willard.

Here he was, placed by fate or by accident, in a position where he alone of all human beings was *certain* that Lorina Brackett had been murdered, not by her brother who had been convicted and sentenced, but by young Eric Scholl, her next door neighbour in the Wyndham Hotel. Wedderburn himself lived at the Wyndham for years; he knew everybody concerned. He was morally certain of Scholl's motive, his opportunity, and he could make a shrewd guess at the method and weapon. But to prove it to the satisfaction of the police, to exonerate Willard in the face of the seemingly incontrovertible evidence, to take Willard out of the death chamber and put Scholl into it – that had been a very different matter, and one in which Wedderburn, straining every nerve, had been unable to succeed.

'It has something to do with figures – I always get back to that,' he had muttered to himself a thousand times. Perhaps it was natural that a man's mind should work that way when figures had made up most of his life. Figures meant time, for one thing, and time was of vital importance in the Brackett case. Lorina Brackett had come home to her room, No. 611, at about 3.00 o'clock on that fatal day. To her left was No. 610, her brother's room, with the common bathroom between. To her right, the last room at the end of the hall, was Scholl's, No. 612. Originally all the rooms had formed a suite, and 611 and 612 still communicated by a door which led to Scholl's bathroom, and which had been locked by the hotel and the key removed.

Scholl himself had been at home all afternoon, as usual; he was a shipyard worker on the graveyard shift, 4-F in the draft, but outwardly quite hale and sound. Willard had got home at precisely 5.18; his office was only four blocks away, which was the principal reason he had been a resident in a downtown hotel for so long. When his sister Lorina became a widow, she gave up her house and managed to get the room adjoining his, where she had lived ever since. Her brother could think of no valid objection, though he was not pleased. They had never been very good friends, and their constant quarrels, usually in shouted objurgations from one room to the other, through the two open bathroom doors between, were the common property of all the permanent guests on the sixth floor. Willard was not, perhaps, an admirable character; he was a fussy, pernickety man with fixed ways and a mean temper; nevertheless, Wedderburn thought, that was no reason he should be condemned to death for a murder he had not committed. Unfortunately, Wedderburn seemed to be the only person – except, presumably, Eric Scholl – who really believed in Willard's innocence; even his lawyer had given the impression of making the best of a bad case.

'I think he did it and I think it was a good job,' seemed to be the consensus of opinion around the Wyndham. For if her brother had been considered a grouchy eccentric, Mrs Brackett had been heartily disliked by everybody. She was, to be sure, fair, fat and forty. But her fairness was obviously synthetic; her fat was grotesque – she weighed over 200 pounds; and she seemed to have accumulated more bad manners, querulousness, curiosity, and selfishness than most people could have managed to collect in twice forty years. It was universally felt that the late Mr Brackett had been most fortunate in having died to escape her, and the only wonder was how she had ever corralled a husband at all.

Eric Scholl had not been one of the many to complain to the manager from time to time of the noise from 610 and 611, chiefly for the reason that in the daytime, when he had to sleep, the rooms were empty, and usually he was out in the evening, before he was due at the shipyard at midnight. However, he had growled more than once about Mrs Brackett's habit of keeping her door ajar whenever she was at home – 'snooping on when everybody in the wing comes and goes' was Scholl's description – and whenever he was in his bathroom he could hear distinctly, through the wood of the locked door, every movement of Mrs Brackett's heavy body and every word she exchanged with her brother or anyone else. On the afternoon of the day she was murdered, he had awakened earlier than usual, and about four o'clock he had come down to the lobby and hung around, having nothing better to do, reading a newspaper and chatting occasionally with the desk clerk, the girl at the cigar stand, and occasional guests who were doing the same thing. The Wyndham was that kind of hotel.

When Willard came in, at exactly 5.18, he and Scholl exchanged the curtest of greetings. Scholl pointedly let him go up in the elevator, and then as soon as Harry, the operator, came down again, Scholl got in to return to his own room; it was quite apparent that he desired none of Willard's company even for the time it takes an elevator to go up six stories.

About five minutes later, the desk got a phone call from Scholl's room. He sounded excited.

'Say, listen,' he said, 'you'd better send somebody up here. There's something going on in 611. The old lady's been screaming fit to burst your ears.'

'Aw, she's just having her regular fight with her brother,' answered the clerk.

'No, honest, I haven't heard a peep out of him, and she was screaming bloody murder. You'd better see what's wrong, Johnson.'

'Harry, take a run up to 611 and see what's eating Mrs Brackett,' the clerk ordered the elevator operator, who doubled as bellboy. 'If a bat's flown in her room or something, she'll be raising the roof.'

The door of 611 was not ajar when Harry got there. It was closed, and when he knocked there was no answer. He tried knocking at 610, Willard's room, but there was no answer there, either. He went back to 611 and knocked again. The door of 612 opened, and Scholl came out.

'Gee, Harry,' he said in a worried tone, 'I really think something's happened in there. Mrs Brackett was yelling her head off, and then all at once she stopped cold. And I haven't heard a word from Brother Willard. Better open up with your pass-key.'

Harry looked dubious, but another knock and a call brought only silence. He reached for the key. Scholl was right on his heels as he entered the room.

Lorina Brackett was lying in the middle of the floor, her shapeless bulk bulging grotesquely. She was face down, and all around her, from her chin to her vast bosom, was a thick, dark pool of blood.

And standing over her, looking white and dazed and paralysed was her brother. His right hand was bloody. Clutched in it was a short, sharp, heavy knife he used for his hobby of wood-carving.

Well, that was the set-up. The police found it easy to reconstruct the crime. Willard had gone into his room, taken off his hat and overcoat, perhaps settled down to finish a wooden wastebasket on which he had been working, before it was time to go out to dinner. His sister had heard him come in – the two doors to their bathroom were open – and doubtless had started at once to renew the bitter quarrel (the subject had been the disposition of their father's estate) which had been raging all the evening before, causing several annoyed calls to the desk from the sixth floor. Eric Scholl was not able to confirm this, since he had not been in his own bathroom but had been changing into his work clothes. The screams, however, he insisted, had come to him even through his closed bathroom door.

By the time Willard had recovered from his shock, he was in custody. The thing had gone through like clockwork. It was a pleasure to the police to get such an open-and-shut case. To his lawyer, when he got one, Willard had had nothing to offer in his own defence except to reiterate, in the irritated tone cf one who does not like being contradicted: 'I certainly didn't do it. I came home, and just as they say, I sat down for a spot of wood-carving before I went out again. I didn't hear Lorina moving about, and I thought that was funny, because she's practically always home when I get there. We were going to have dinner together, if she'd got over her mad from the night before. I hadn't seen her since; I suppose she was still asleep when I left in the morning.

'After a while I decided to find out if she was there. I guess it was only a minute or two at that; I know I'd just started to work on my carving. I got up, with the knife still in my hand, and went through the bathroom – no, the doors were closed till I opened them – and I remember that I called out, "Are you there, Lorina?"

'The minute I stepped into her room, I saw her. For a second I couldn't move – I felt sick. My heart's not too good lately, anyway; I had to hold on to the door-frame. Then I went and stood over her.

'She looked just the way she did when the others found her. I began to shake all over, and the knife dropped from my hand, right into that – right into the blood.

'I don't know why I stooped and picked it up – just automatic, I guess. Anyway, I did; and right then that knocking began. I couldn't talk, I couldn't even think. When Harry opened the door, all I could do was just stand there. But I swear to God, Mr Ellsworth,' and Willard would turn to his sceptical lawyer and his voice would shake with his earnestness, 'when I found her, there wasn't a sign of a knife or whatever her throat had been cut with. Sure, there were no fingerprints except mine on my knife – I'm the only person who ever handled it. But that knife didn't kill her. I don't know what did, but whatever it was I didn't use it. She was dead when I found her.'

The lethal weapon, wood-carving knife or not, had cut Lorina Brackett's jugular vein. It was venous blood that had been clotted in a pool around her.

'And she didn't scream – not while I was there,' her brother would add, in all the long conferences he held with Ellsworth, the lawyer, in the visitors' room of the city jail. 'That's why I suspect Scholl – one reason. He made that up so he could get them up there to discover me behind two locked doors with Lorina's body. It was just a piece of luck for him that I was holding the knife, and double luck that it had dropped on – that it had dropped down there and I had picked it up again. I believe he deliberately waited down in the lobby till I got home and then followed me up so as to give me just enough time to have been able to – to do it.

'Just as a matter of common sense, Mr Ellsworth, would any jury in the world think it was logical for a man to come home from the office, go to his room, and then march right in and cut his sister's throat? Do people do things like that – people who aren't crazy? And I'm not crazy, am I?'

'Of course not. But we've got to look at this from the outside, so to speak. You take the average man or woman on a jury. Of course they wouldn't think that any unpremeditated murder could take place that way. But they might think, a smart prosecutor could get them to think, that with this quarrel between you and all, you'd *planned* to do it just that way.'

'Then why didn't I beat it – get out before anybody discovered it – make a getaway? If I'd planned it, wouldn't I have my things all packed to get going the minute it was over?'

'They'd be told – I'm afraid I might as well put it that they *will* be told – that when it came to the point the excitement, with your bad heart and all, was too much for you; that you were caught before you could finish your plan.'

'But look, Mr Ellsworth, however he worked it, I'm sure it was Scholl who committed that murder. I don't know how he did it, though I can work it out. But I know why.'

'Why, then?'

'Lorina told me herself. You know, I kind of hate to say things like this about the dead, and about my own sister too. If I weren't in this fix I'd have kept it to myself forever. Lorina and I weren't ever fond of each other, even when we were kids, and we fought a lot over some fool ideas she had about how I'd handled the money our dad left us, but I'm ashamed to tell some of the things she wasn't ashamed to tell me about herself.

'Sure we quarrelled lots, but not all the time. There were times – when I didn't oppose her or answer her back – when we were friendly enough. And it was about a week before all this happened that she told me about it. She was proud of herself – she said she was just being patriotic. Being a sneak thief and a snooper was what I'd call it.

'You know the door between her room and Scholl's was supposed to be permanently locked. Lorina discovered she could open it and lock it again and he'd be none the wiser. She had too much time on her hands and too much curiosity, the way I look at it. Anyway, she told me whenever I was away and she knew that Scholl was out – she used to keep her door ajar, you know, and watch when everybody went by – she'd let herself into his room and snoop around.

'I don't mean she'd ever take money, or anything like that. Even Lorina wasn't that low. What ailed her was her curiosity. She'd read the man's private letters, for example; I guess it gave her a feeling of power to know, for instance, that he was having a hot affair with some girl when he didn't dream she had ever heard of it.

'Well, one evening she was rummaging around in his bureau drawers and she came across this bottle of pills and this letter. He's 4-F, you know – says he has something wrong with his insides, bad enough to keep him from fighting but not from welding. '

'Maybe you've read about this fellow they picked up, who was selling draft inductees some stuff that was supposed to give them palpitations and affect their sight and I don't know what all, so they couldn't pass their physical examinations. Well, what Lorina found was evidently some of this medicine and a letter – it wasn't signed – telling how to take it and what the results would be. I don't know why he kept the letter, unless he couldn't remember without it what dose to take, and when, and thought he might be called again some time and need it.

'Anyway, Lorina fished it and the bottle out from under his socks or something and took them away with her. She told me all about it, and she said she was going to turn Scholl in and use them for evidence.

'I'd have been for it – I have no more use than anyone else for a draft dodger – except that how could she go about it without confessing the way she'd got them? And then I wasn't any too sure she couldn't be had up for burglary; and I wasn't keen to have a scandal like that involving my own sister. I'd probably have lost my good job, for one thing.

'So I put the fear of God into her on that score, and I talked her out of it. The next was, she was going to send the stuff to the proper authorities with an anonymous letter. Since she'd already done what she had, that seemed to me to be the best solution. At first the idea pleased her – she'd get Scholl into trouble, and have the consciousness that she'd been the one who did it, but nobody could accuse her of it.

'But when I asked her a few days later if she'd done it, she said no. She said she had another idea. And about then she started harping on dad's money again, and the other subject never came up again.'

'Then what do you think happened?' Ellsworth asked.

'The way I figure it out is this. Lorina was awfully close with money. I think she worked out a scheme to blackmail Scholl.'

'There's no evidence of that.'

'No, because I don't think she'd got to the point yet. I think she was holding those things while she perfected the details of it. Mr Ellsworth, I wasn't there, but I'm morally certain that this is what actually occurred. I think Scholl woke up early that afternoon, and for some reason happened to think of the bottle and the letter. He looked where he'd hidden them and they were gone.

'Or maybe it happened another way. Maybe Lorina hadn't relocked that door properly the last time she'd been in his room, and maybe he was in the bathroom and noticed it. He disliked Lorina anyway, you know, and if he saw something funny about that lock he'd guess right away who had done it, and why. Then he'd naturally begin looking over his things to see if anything was missing or disarranged, and of course the first thing he'd think of would be the things he ought to have had sense enough to destroy. When he found they were gone, he'd be crazy mad and scared at the same time. His impulse would be to confront Lorina at once. If the door between their rooms was unlocked, he'd go in that way – she was practically always there in the afternoon. If it wasn't, then her door was always ajar, and he could lock it afterwards and go back by opening the bathroom door the way she did.

'Suppose he was shaving, getting ready to go out, when he noticed the lock. Nothing more natural than that he'd start hunting around to see if anything was wrong, while he still held the razor in his hand – look at the way I went in, myself, still holding the knife I'd been working with.

'Then, if I know Lorina, she might have been startled for a second, but she'd face him down. She'd say, yes, she'd taken the things and that she meant to turn him in, and how about it? She might even think that was an auspicious minute to try to sell the things back to him.

'Well, the rest is easy. She'd refuse to give him back his things, or suggest that if he wanted them badly enough he could pay for them – and Scholl would lose his head. He'd draw back to strike her, and then he'd realize he had a razor in his hand. Lorina'd throw back her head to scream – that's probably where he got that idea from – about her screaming. You give a hard edgewise blow at the right place with a sharp safety razor, and that's that.

'Mr Ellsworth, that's what must have happened. Eric Scholl ought to be here, not me. You tell them what I've told you, and get me out of here.'

Ellsworth tried, of course, but he was not convinced. His private belief was that Willard had murdered his sister, and that as his only way of extricating himself he had made up the rest. *If* Scholl had discovered his loss, *if* he had had a razor, things might very well have happened in just that way: only, Ellsworth thought, Lorina Brackett's brother *had* got there first, with a wood-carving knife.

However, Scholl was thoroughly investigated and questioned. There were points that confirmed the brother's story. The door between the rooms had been tampered with. The bottle and the letter were not found. If Willard was right, Scholl, after the murder, could have locked the door and hunted until he found them, and then destroyed them. Then he could have returned to his own room, washed his hands and the razor, dressed, and gone down to the lobby until Willard arrived, between 5.15 and 5.20, as always. Scholl, naturally, denied the whole story. His draft records were looked up, and it was true that he had been rejected because of an eye condition, but when he was re-examined by the police doctor his eyes were found still to be bad. He might perhaps have secured some of that medicine somehow, but there was no way of proving it.

That was the trouble with the whole situation. Nothing could be proved, and without proof Willard had no adequate defence. Scholl was not held, the case came to trial, and though Ellsworth tried conscientiously, he had nothing to offer except Willard's flat denial. He made as much as he could of the time factor, but unfortunately he could get nowhere. The body had still been warm when Harry and Scholl burst in; but Lorina Brackett had been a very heavy woman and fat corpses stay warm longer than thin ones. The blood had coagulated, but blood begins to coagulate as soon as shed, and blood from the veins, which flows out instead of jetting like arterial blood, probably coagulates that much faster. It was Mrs Brackett's jugular vein which had been cut.

So Lorina Brackett might have been dead only two minutes when found, or she might have been dead for two hours. Ellsworth had hoped that the uncertainty of so many points, and the fact that all the evidence against his client was circumstantial, might at least gain for him a manslaughter verdict. But there is no accounting for juries. Willard had been indicted on a first-degree murder charge, and it was of first-degree murder that he was convicted, with no recommendation for mercy. The judge had no alternative but to sentence him to death. An appeal for a new trial was denied, and the date of his execution was set. Twice he was reprieved by the governor, on Ellsworth's representation that new evidence was about to be revealed, but when the new evidence did not appear, further reprieve was denied.

It was at this point that Wedderburn began to be haunted by the thought that somehow Willard could be saved if only some point not obvious or hitherto brought out could be revealed – that some such point existed which would clear the condemned man and by implication involve Eric Scholl. Somewhere back in his subconscious mind the thought persisted, 'It has something to do with figures.'

And now suddenly, as he sat absorbed in the ramifications of the case, a spring was released. Something he had read or heard long ago jumped to the surface of his mind. It was the key to the whole thing, the solution he had sought so long.

The 'figure' which had haunted him was not a number, not a matter of time elapsed, or any phase of the arithmetic which was his second being. Suddenly he saw in his mind's eye the body of Lorina Brackett, lying on the floor of her hotel room – as numerous awed and horrified residents of the sixth floor of the Wyndham had seen it fleetingly through the open door before the police arrived. He saw the grotesque bulges, the spreading obesity – in a word, the 'figure' of the dead woman lying, fat arms thrust out, fat legs collapsed from her fall, her hair sticky from the pool of blood around her throat.

He recalled that she had lain *face downward on the floor*.

And now he recalled that odd, out-of-the-way fact. If a man dies suddenly from loss of blood he is nearly always found on his back. If a man bleeds to death gradually he will amost invariably be found with his *face towards the floor*.

Lorina Brackett lay face downward – so she had bled to death gradually. If her brother, who had gone upstairs *only a few minutes before*, had killed her, she would – 999,999 chances out of a million – have been found on her back. If Eric Scholl had killed her, between three and four o'clock, she would normally have been discovered just as she was discovered – face down.

In that one point, neglected and forgotten by everybody until Wedderburn suddenly stumbled upon it, lay the one chance for holding up Willard's execution and making another attempt to fasten the crime on Scholl.

But it was too late. Even as Wedderburn started at the sudden revelation, the cyanide tablets were being dropped into the hydrochloric acid. Almost instantly the poisonous gas spread through the death chamber, and the man within it strained against the straps which held him to his chair.

Fourteen minutes later the prison physician pronounced Willard Wedderburn dead.

The Turn of the Tide

C. S. Forester

'What always beats them in the end,' said Dr Matthews, 'is how to dispose of the body. But, of course, you know that as well as I do.'

'Yes,' said Slade. He had in fact, been devoting far more thought to what Dr Matthews believed to be this accidental subject of conversation than Dr Matthews could ever guess.

'As a matter of fact,' went on Dr Matthews, warming to the subject to which Slade had so tactfully led him, 'it's a terribly knotty problem. It's so difficult, in fact, that I always wonder why anyone is fool enough to commit murder.'

'All very well for you,' thought Slade, but he did not allow his thoughts to alter his expression. 'You smug, self-satisfied old ass! You don't know the sort of difficulties a man can be up against.'

'I've often thought the same,' he said.

'Yes,' went on Dr Matthews, 'it's the body that does it, every time. To use poison calls for special facilities, which are good enough to hang you as soon as suspicion is roused. And that suspicion – well, of course, part of my job is to detect poisoning. I don't think anyone can get away with it, nowadays, even with the most dunderheaded general practitioner.'

'I quite agree with you,' said Slade. He had no intention of using poison.

'Well,' went on Dr Matthews, developing his logical argument, 'if you rule out poison, you rule out the chance of getting the body disposed of under the impression that the victim died a natural death. The only other way, if a man cares to stand the racket of having the body to give evidence against him, is to fake things to look like suicide. But you know, and I know, that it just can't be done. The mere fact of suicide calls for a close examination, and no one has ever been able to fix things so well as to get away with it. You're a lawyer. You've probably read a lot of reports of trials where the murderer has tried it on. And you know what's happened to them.'

'Yes,' said Slade.

He certainly had given a great deal of consideration to the matter. It was only after long thought that he had, finally, put aside the notion of disposing of young Spalding and concealing his guilt by a sham suicide.

'That brings us to where we started, then,' said Dr Matthews. 'The only other thing left is to try and conceal the body. And that's more difficult still.'

'Yes,' said Slade. But he had a perfect plan for disposing of the body.

'A human body,' said Dr Matthews, 'is a most difficult thing to get rid of. That chap Oscar Wilde, in that book of his – *Dorian Grey*, isn't it? – gets rid of one by the use of chemicals. Well, I'm a chemist as well as a doctor, and *I* wouldn't like the job.'

'No?' said Slade, politely.

Dr Matthews was not nearly as clever a man as himself, he thought.

'There's altogether too much of it,' said Dr Matthews. 'It's heavy, and it's bulky, and it's bound to undergo corruption. Think of all those poor devils who've tried it. Bodies in trunks, and bodies in coal cellars, and bodies in chicken runs. You can't hide the thing, try as you will.'

'Can't I? That's all you know,' thought Slade, but aloud he said: 'You're quite right. I've never thought about it before.'

'Of course, you haven't,' agreed Dr Matthews. 'Sensible people don't unless it's an incident of their profession, as in my case.

'And yet, you know,' he went on, meditatively, 'there's one decided advantage about getting rid of the body altogether. You're much safer, then. It's a point which ought to interest you, as a lawyer, more than me. It's rather an obscure point of law, but I fancy there are very definite rulings on it. You know what I'm referring to?'

'No, I don't,' said Slade, genuinely puzzled.

'You can't have a trial for murder unless you can prove there's a victim,' said Dr Matthews. 'There's got to be a corpus delicti, as you lawyers say in your horrible dog-Latin. A corpse, in other words, even if it's only a bit of one, like that which hanged Crippen. No corpse, no trial. I think that's good law, isn't it?'

'By Jove, you're right!' said Slade. 'I wonder why that hadn't occurred to me before?'

No sooner were the words out of his mouth than he regretted having said them. He did his best to make his face immobile again; he was afraid lest his expression might have hinted at his pleasure in discovering another very reassuring factor in this problem of killing young Spalding. But Dr Matthews had noticed nothing.

'Well, as I said, people only think about these things if they're in-cidental to their profession,' he said. 'And, all the same, it's only a theoretical piece of law. The entire destruction of a body is practically impossible. But, I suppose, if a man could achieve it, he would be all right. However strong the suspicion was against him, the police couldn't get him without a corpse. There might be a story in that, Slade, if you or I were writers.'

'Yes,' assented Slade, and laughed harshly.

There never would be any story about the killing of young Spalding, the insolent pup.

'Well,' said Dr Matthews, 'we've had a pretty gruesome conversation, haven't we? And I seem to have done all the talking, somehow. That's the result, I suppose, Slade, of the very excellent dinner you gave me. I'd better push off now. Not that the weather is very inviting.'

Nor was it. As Slade saw Dr Matthews into his car, the rain was driving down in a real winter storm, and there was a bitter wind blowing.

'Shouldn't be surprised if this turned to snow before morning,' were Dr Matthews's last words before he drove off.

Slade was glad it was such a tempestuous night. It meant that, more certainly than ever, there would be no one out in the lanes, no one out on the sands when he disposed of young Spalding's body.

Back in his drawing-room, Slade looked at the clock. There was still an hour to spare; he could spend it in making sure that his plans were all correct.

He looked up the tide tables. Yes, that was right enough. Spring tides. The lowest of low water on the sands. There was not so much luck about that; young Spalding came back on the midnight train every Wednesday night, and it was not surprising that, sooner or later, the Wednesday night would coincide with a spring tide. But it was lucky that this particular Wednesday night should be one of tempest: luckier still that low water should be at one-thirty, the best time for him.

He opened the drawing-room door and listened carefully. He could not hear a sound. Mrs Dumbleton, his housekeeper, must have been in bed some time now. She was as deaf as a post, anyway, and would not hear his departure. Nor his return, when Spalding had been killed and disposed of.

The hands of the clock seemed to be moving very fast. He must make sure everything was correct. The plough chain and the other iron weights were already in the back seat of the car; he had put them there before old Matthews arrived to dine. He slipped on his overcoat.

From his desk, Slade took a curious little bit of apparatus: eighteen inches of strong cord, tied at each end to a six-inch length of wood so as to make a ring. He made a last close examination to see that the knots were quite firm, and then he put it in his pocket; as he did so, he ran through, in his mind, the words – he knew them by heart

– of the passage in the book about the Thugs of India, describing the method of strangulation employed by them.

He could think quite coldly about all this. Young Spalding was a pestilent busybody. A word from him, now, could bring ruin upon Slade, could send him to prison, could have him struck off the rolls.

Slade thought of other defaulting solicitors he had heard of, even one or two with whom he had come into contact professionally. He remembered his brother-solicitors' remarks about them, pitying or contemptuous. He thought of having to beg his bread in the streets on his release from prison, of cold and misery and starvation. The shudder which shook him was succeeded by a hot wave of resentment. Never, never, would he endure it.

What right had young Spalding, who had barely been qualified two years, to condemn a grey-haired man twenty years his senior to such a fate? If nothing but death would stop him, then he deserved to die. He clenched his hand on the cord in his pocket.

A glance at the clock told him he had better be moving. He turned out the lights and tiptoed out of the house, shutting the door quietly. The bitter wind flung icy rain into his face, but he did not notice it.

He pushed the car out of the garage by hand, and, contrary to his wont, he locked the garage doors, as a precaution against the infinitesimal chance that, on a night like this, someone should notice that his car was out.

He drove cautiously down the road. Of course, there was not a soul about in a quiet place like this. The few street-lamps were already extinguished.

There were lights in the station as he drove over the bridge; they were waiting there the arrival of the twelve-thirty train. Spalding would be on that. Every Wednesday he went over to his subsidiary office, sixty miles away. Slade turned into the lane a quarter of a mile beyond the station, and then reversed his car so that it pointed towards the road. He put out the side lights, and settled himself to wait; his hand fumbled with the cord in his pocket.

The train was a little late. Slade had been waiting a quarter of an hour when he saw the lights of the train emerge from the cutting and come to a standstill in the station. So wild was the night that he could hear nothing of it. Then the train moved slowly out again. As soon as it was gone, the lights in the station began to go out, one by one; Hobson, the porter, was making ready to go home, his turn of duty completed.

Next, Slade's straining ears heard footsteps.

Young Spalding was striding down the road. With his head bent before the storm, he did not notice the dark mass of the motor car in the lane, and he walked past it.

Slade counted up to two hundred, slowly, and then he switched on his lights, started the engine, and drove the car out into the road in pursuit. He saw Spalding in the light of the head lamps and drew up alongside.

'Is that Spalding?' he said, striving to make the tone of his voice as natural as possible. 'I'd better give you a lift, old man, hadn't I?'

'Thanks very much,' said Spalding. 'This isn't the sort of night to walk two miles in.'

He climbed in and shut the door. No one had seen. No one would know. Slade let in his clutch and drove slowly down the road.

'Bit of luck, seeing you,' he said. 'I was just on my way home from bridge at Mrs Clay's when I saw the train come in and remembered it was Wednesday and you'd be walking home. So I thought I'd turn a bit out of my way to take you along.'

'Very good of you, I'm sure,' said Spalding.

'As a matter of fact,' said Slade, speaking slowly and driving slowly, 'it wasn't altogether disinterested. I wanted to talk business to you, as it happened.'

'Rather an odd time to talk business,' said Spalding. 'Can't it wait till tomorrow?'

'No, it cannot,' said Slade. 'It's about the Lady Vere trust.'

'Oh, yes. I wrote to remind you last week that you had to make delivery.'

'Yes, you did. And I told you, long before that, that it would be inconvenient, with Hammond abroad.'

'I don't see that,' said Spalding. 'I don't see that Hammond's got anything to do with it. Why can't you just hand over and have done with it? I can't do anything to straighten things up until you do.'

'As I said, it would be inconvenient.'

Slade brought the car to a standstill at the side of the road.

'Look here, Spalding,' he said, desperately, 'I've never asked a favour of you before. But now I ask you, as a favour, to forgo delivery for a bit. Just for three months, Spalding.'

But Slade had small hope that his request would be granted. So little hope, in fact, that he brought his left hand out of his pocket holding the piece of wood, with the loop of cord dangling from its ends. He put his arm round the back of Spalding's seat.

'No, I can't, really I can't,' said Spalding. 'I've got my duty to my clients to consider. I'm sorry to insist, but you're quite well aware of what my duty is.'

'Yes,' said Slade. 'But I beg you to wait. I implore you to wait, Spalding. There! Perhaps you can guess why, now.'

'I see,' said Spalding, after a long pause.

'I only want three months,' pressed Slade. 'Just three months. I can get straight again in three months.'

Spalding had known of other men who had had the same belief in their ability to get straight in three months. It was unfortunate for Slade – and for Spalding – that Slade had used those words. Spalding hardened his heart.

'No,' he said, 'I can't promise anything like that. I don't think it's any use continuing this discussion. Perhaps I'd better walk home from here.'

He put out his hand to the latch of the door, and, as he did so, Slade jerked the loop of cord over his head. A single turn of Slade's wrist – a thin, bony, old man's wrist, but as strong as steel in that wild moment – tightened the cord about Spalding's throat. Slade swung round in his seat, getting both hands to the piece of wood, twisting madly. His breath hissed between his teeth with the effort, but Spalding never drew breath at all. He lost consciousness long before he was dead. Only Slade's grip of the cord round his throat prevented the dead body from falling forward, doubled up.

Nobody had seen, nobody would know. And what that book had stated about the method of assassination practised by Thugs was perfectly correct.

Slade had gained, now, the time in which he could get his affairs into order. With all the promise of his current speculations, with all his financial ability, he would be able to recoup himself for his past losses. It only remained to dispose of Spalding's body, and he had planned to do that very satisfactorily. Just for a moment Slade had felt as if all this were some heated dream, some nightmare, but then he came back to reality and went on with the plan he had in mind.

He pulled the dead man's knees forward so that the corpse lay back in the seat, against the side of the car. He put the car in gear, let in his clutch, and drove rapidly down the road – much faster than when he had been arguing with Spalding. Low water was in three-quarters of an hour's time, and the sands were ten miles away.

Slade drove fast through the wild night. There was not a soul about in those lonely lanes. He knew the way by heart – he had driven repeatedly over that route recently in order to memorize it.

The car bumped down the last bit of lane, and Slade drew up on the edge of the sands.

It was pitch dark, and the bitter wind was howling about him, under the black sky. Despite the noise of the wind, he could hear the surf breaking far away, two miles away, across the level sands. He climbed out of the driver's seat and walked round to the other door. When he opened it the dead man fell sideways, into his arms.

With an effort, Slade held him up, while he groped into the back of the car for the plough chain and the iron weights. He crammed the weights into the dead man's pockets, and he wound the chain round and round the dead man's body, tucking in the ends to make it all secure. With that mass of iron to hold it down, the body would never be found again when dropped into the sea at the lowest ebb of spring tide.

Slade tried now to lift the body in his arms, to carry it over the sands. He reeled and strained, but he was not strong enough – Slade was a man of slight figure, and past his prime. The sweat on his forehead was icy in the icy wind.

For a second, doubt overwhelmed him, lest all his plans should fail for want of bodily strength. But he forced himself into thinking clearly; he forced his frail body into obeying the vehement commands of his brain.

He turned round, still holding the dead man upright. Stooping, he got the heavy burden on his shoulders. He drew the arms round his neck, and, with a convulsive effort, he got the legs up round his hips. The dead man now rode him pick-a-back. Bending nearly double, he was able to carry the heavy weight in that fashion, the arms tight round his neck, the legs tight round his waist.

He set off, staggering down the imperceptible slope of the sands towards the sound of the surf. The sands were soft beneath his feet – it was because of this softness that he had not driven the car down to the water's edge. He could afford to take no chances of being embogged.

The icy wind shrieked round him all that long way. The tide was nearly two miles out. That was why Slade had chosen this place. In the depth of winter, no one would go out to the water's edge at low tide for months to come.

He staggered on over the sands, clasping the limbs of the body close about him. Desperately, he forced himself forward, not stopping to rest, for he only just had time now to reach the water's edge before the flow began. He went on and on, driving his exhausted body with fierce urgings from his frightened brain.

Then, at last, he saw it: a line of white in the darkness which indicated the water's edge. Farther out, the waves were breaking in an inferno of noise. Here, the fragments of the rollers were only just sufficient to move the surface a little.

He was going to make quite sure of things. Steadying himself, he stepped into the water, wading in farther and farther so as to be able to drop the body into comparatively deep water. He held to his resolve, staggering through the icy water, knee deep, thigh deep, until it was nearly at his waist. This was far enough. He stopped, gasping in the darkness.

He leaned over to one side, to roll the body off his back. It did not move. He pulled at its arms. They were obstinate. He could not loosen them. He shook himself, wildly. He tore at the legs round his waist. Still the thing clung to him. Wild with panic and fear, he flung himself about in a mad effort to rid himself of the burden. It clung on as though it were alive. He could not break its grip.

Then another breaker came in. It splashed about him, wetting him far above his waist. The tide had begun to turn now, and the tide on those sands comes in like a racehorse.

He made another effort to cast off the load, and, when it still held him fast, he lost his nerve and tried to struggle out of the sea. But it was too much for his exhausted body. The weight of the corpse and of the iron with which it was loaded overbore him. He fell.

He struggled up again in the foam-streaked, dark sea, staggered a few steps, fell again – and did not rise. The dead man's arms were round his neck, throttling him, strangling him. *Rigor mortis* had set in and Spalding's muscles had refused to relax.

The Blood on the Innocents

Celia Fremlin

For once, it was *Sally's* baby who was screaming, not hers. Tina raised her head from the pillow, the better to savour the delicious sounds. She wished that Colin, in the adjoining bed, would wake up too, and listen to the hideous racket, and be forced to admit, at last, how unfair he'd been, how unkind!

'*Other* mothers manage to keep their kids quiet,' he'd complained, angry and hollow-eyed, only a couple of nights ago. '*Other* mothers cope ... Look at Sally ... !'

Tina had looked at Sally a lot, naturally, ever since the night – nearly six months ago now – when the wretched girl had arrived, at past midnight, husband-less, her fair hair a-glitter with rain, and with her baby in her arms, to beg a night's lodging from Colin and Tina's land-lady. The night's lodging had extended to two ... to three ... to months and months, so that by now Sally and her 20-month-old Julie were accepted members of the household.

Accepted, that is, by the landlady, and by Colin, and by the silly old crone in the basement, and by the neat, bustling couple on the first floor. Not by Tina. No one had consulted Tina about any of it, right from the beginning. No one had asked *her* whether she minded another baby cluttering up the place, filling the clothes-line with nappies so that there was no space left for Edward's ... endlessly occupying the bath-room just at Edward's bedtime – adding insult to injury by the leisurely sounds of splashing and laughter that came through the door:

'Ooozi-woozie wuzz-wuzz!' she would hear Sally crooning idiotically, above the sound of delighted chuckles and sloshing water; 'Who's a wimsy-imsy oopsy, then!' – and Tina, outside on the landing, with teeth clenched, and one eye on the clock, would listen to this drivel, and to the sounds of splashing and laughter, and would fantasize about a sudden change of the sounds to a sinister 'glug-glug-glug' as the baby drowned. It was such daydreams as these, she sometimes felt, that kept her sane while Edward drearily howled, and Colin said, 'When's supper?' and the landlady called up the stairs, 'Whatever's the matter with that child, Tina? Do you want any help ...?'

Help, indeed! A fat lot they'd thought about helping *her* when they'd let in that promiscuous little bitch and her bastard!

Strong language, perhaps, for a respectable young matron, even in the privacy of her own head; but it was justified. Julie *was* a bastard – within hours of their arrival, Tina had made a point of ascertaining Sally's unmarried status; and within a week she had also discovered that Sally not only had a current boy-friend who came two or three evenings a week, but also an ex-boy-friend who kept ringing up and writing impassioned letters. Neither of them the child's father! Disgusting!

And what made it more disgusting still was that Julie did not seem to be suffering for it all in any of the proper ways. Tina had read lots of books about child-rearing, and it was clearly stated in all of them that lack of a stable father-figure did untold harm. Julie should, by rights, be backward, thumb-sucking, whiney; she should be withdrawn, negativistic, and difficult; she should throw tantrums, have feeding-problems ... and all the while it was *Edward* who was like this ... *Edward*, with his stable background, his two, attentive, properly-married parents! It was Edward, already turned two, who wouldn't sit on his potty, wouldn't say 'Please', and who threw tantrums in the hallway about taking off his red rubber boots before going upstairs. In the *hallway*, if you please, where the whole house could hear him!

The *unfairness* of it all! It was Julie – endlessly sucking sweets and lollies between meals – who ate a good dinner every day of meat and vegetables, whereas it was Edward – to the balancing of whose diet Tina had given so much study and forethought – who threw his greens on the floor, and beat with his fists on the kitchen table, and screamed.

'*You're* a good little girl, *you* are!' the landlady would say, lifting Julie down from her chair, and averting her eyes ostentatiously from the whining, fidgeting Edward on the other side of the table: '*You're* a good girl, *your* Mummy has taught you to eat up lovely, hasn't she ...?'

'Mummy has taught you ...!' What lying rubbish! As if Sally ever 'taught' her child anything – always humming, and telephoning, and making-up her face, and letting the child slop around in her night-things half the morning ... up and down the house, in and out of other people's rooms, feeding her teddy-bear biscuits on the stairs ...! No, it was *Tina* who believed in teaching; teaching manners, and considerate behaviour, and saying 'Please' and 'Thank you'. And after all this effort, what happened? It was *Julie* who was all smiles and sweetness and twisting the landlady round her little finger, while Edward just stared, and sucked his thumb, and said, 'I don't like you, you're an ugly lady!' when the landlady asked him if he'd like to watch television.

Unfair! Unfair! And the final, and bitterest, injustice of all was when
Colin began taking the landlady's side against his own child!

'I wish *Edward* would eat like that!' he would say, wistfully, as he
watched Julie polishing off her second sausage at tea in the landlady's
kitchen. 'What do you *do*, Sally, to get her to eat so well?' And Sally,
busy stirring some sort of foreign, messed-up stuff at the stove – no doubt
for her boy-friend of tonight! – would turn around, smiling and pre-
occupied, and say: 'What? Julie? Why, has she finished her sausage
already? – *Two* sausages? – Goodness, I hope there'll be some left for
me!' – and would turn back, humming, to her cookery.

Why, she didn't even *care* what the child ate or didn't eat – and here
was Tina, giving all this attention to Edward's needs in the way of protein
and carbohydrate and the rest: really studying the matter, and shopping
with vitamins and food-values in mind; putting the boy to bed at a
proper time, too, so that he should get the amount of sleep a two-year-old
needs, whereas Julie – four months younger – was allowed to stay up
till all hours, sitting on the lap of the current 'Uncle', being given
sips of Spanish wine, and tastes of prawn curry – *she* should have been
the one with the sallow, peaky little face and dark rings under her
eyes...!

'I wish he'd put on a bit of weight, Tina,' Colin had remarked, only
last night, glancing at the two children, one on each side of the kitchen
table; and added – with almost unbelievable tactlessness, even for a
husband – 'Why don't you get Sally to give you a few hints, darling?
– look at the gorgeous specimen *she's* produced!' He gave Julie's cheek
an approving little pinch; then turned to his own son, and in quite a
sharp voice ordered him to stop messing with his food and eat it up.

The ensuing howls, of course, brought the landlady back in – just
in time to see fragments of chopped liver flying all over the room as
Edward worked himself into a full-blown tantrum; and in the general
fluster and confusion no one specially looked at Tina, or bothered to
notice the look that had come into her face.

I hope she chokes, Tina was thinking to herself, watching Julie stuffing
half of a doughnut all at once into her rosy mouth. I hope she chokes,
right now, with that doughnut wedged in her lungs, blocking that merry
little laugh for ever. The rosy cheeks going blue, and then black ...
and everyone knowing, at last, what a careless, rotten mother Sally was,
letting her child choke to death unnoticed, while she giggled, and tossed
her head, and laughed into the telephone, saucepan still steaming in
one hand as she made an assignation (no doubt) with one of her
paramours.

Julie hadn't choked, of course: but never mind, this, tonight, was the next
best thing! With growing joy, Tina lay listening to the screams from

the next room, praying that the landlady would hear too, and would come up in her dressing-gown and hair curlers to complain. The way she did when it was *Edward* who was crying. How lovely it would be to hear *Sally* being told off and humiliated ('Whatever's the *matter* with that child? Can't you quieten her somehow? Pick her up? ... Take her into bed with you ...?').

This, actually, was the suggestion she'd had the nerve to make to Tina once – to *Tina*, who had read and studied the subject so thoroughly, and knew exactly what harm it did a child to be taken into bed with his parents – even *married* parents! And as for Sally ...! Tina here allowed her imagination to conjure up, and savour, the most disgusting possibilities imaginable: at this very moment, Sally might be lifting the screaming child out of its cot ... snuggling it, teddy-bear and all, down between herself and whoever happened to be co-habiting with her tonight ...! Loathsome ...! Revolting ...!

How the crying was going on! Tina began to feel a little uneasy: suppose no one was disturbed by it after all! Suppose they woke up too late, when the worst was over! After all, it couldn't go on for ever, and how awful it would be if it all subsided into hiccupping exhaustion without having annoyed anyone at all!

Particularly, of course, without having annoyed Colin. Leaning out of bed in the darkness, Tina was on the point of reaching across to the bed where her husband slept and shaking him, when it occurred to her that she would be giving herself away. There is no way of shaking a man awake without his realizing that it is the shake that has woken him; and then everything would be spoiled. It was the *screaming* that must wake him! Wake him, keep him awake, exhaust him and infuriate him, the way Edward's screams always did. Show him that *other* mothers couldn't always cope, either; that *other* children weren't always angels – not even the blue-eyed Julie, damn her to hell—

The screams must be made louder, that was the thing. Easy.

Creeping silently out of bed and across the floor, Tina cautiously opened the door.

That was better! The screams rang into the room gloriously now ... but even so, not loud *enough*! Gathering her nightdress around her, lest even the faintest rustle might give her away, Tina stepped softly through the open door and out on to the landing. Slowly, warily, her bare feet making no sound on the icy lino, she moved forwards through the darkness.

Crash! Scutter-scutter werr*oomph*! Tina almost fainted at the thunderous shock of sound, and at the sharp blow across her shins.

The pram! The blasted dolls' pram, which Julie had left, as always, slap in the middle of the landing! The blasted pram in which she endlessly trundled her blasted teddy-bear, in and out and up and down!

Tina could have screamed aloud in her shock and fury, she could have hurled curses to high heaven, but instead she stood absolutely still, not even breathing, while the pain in her shins gradually subsided, and the stillness of the sleeping house came rolling back.

Actually, the noise couldn't have been as loud as, in the moment of shock, she had imagined it. Just a dolls' pram, empty, knocking against the banisters. Certainly (she realized now) it couldn't have been anywhere near as loud as those screams still emanating from behind the closed door.

Wait, though, wait! Those screams were going to be louder yet! Wait, wait!

This was the hardest part – getting Sally's door open without being heard. Somewhere in there in the darkness, Sally would be rocking the child – leaning over the cot – something; and only if Tina was very slow, very cautious, could she fail to notice her door softly opening in the dark. . . .

Up and down the panel Tina's fingers played, until at last they encountered the door-handle . . . and below that the keyhole. Please God, don't let Sally have locked it . . . !

She hadn't. The knob turned smoothly under Tina's sweating hand, and the catch was released almost without a click.

What a glorious crescendo of screaming! Like this, with the door wide open, it was enough to wake the dead! Aglow with joy and triumph, Tina skimmed back across the landing and into bed. There she lay, hugging herself, all a-tremble with sheer happiness as she waited for Colin to be awakened by the awful din. Waited for him to stir, to moan, to start muttering, almost in his sleep: 'That *bloody* child . . . ! Tina, can't you *do* something? *Other* mothers . . .'

This would be her moment of glory. The moment for which she had been waiting, it sometimes seemed, for years and years.

'That bloody child,' she would explain sweetly, was not Edward this time, but Miss Sunshine-Blue-Eyes Julie. And as to the 'other mothers'. . . ! Already Tina was licking her lips in the darkness . . . it was like one of her daydreams come true!

But what was this? For a moment, she could not believe her ears. She jerked bolt upright in bed, and listened, appalled.

The crying had stopped! But when – how? So deep had she been in gleeful reverie that she had scarcely heard the *real* crying, and could not tell, now, whether it had stopped suddenly or bit by bit, hiccup after exhausted hiccup.

Anyway, stopped it had. Not a sound could be heard now, not a murmur.

And Colin had never woken up at all!

The disappointment was like nothing she had ever experienced in her life. He hadn't heard a thing! – and now it was too late! What use *now* to talk about it in the morning ... he wouldn't be interested ... wouldn't take it in. 'Give over!' he'd say, abstractedly, if she kept on about it – or perhaps even accuse her of being spiteful!

Oh, if *only* he had been woken by it – heard it with his own ears! Been kept awake by it, exhausted by it, maddened by it, as he was by Edward's crying! Or if only the landlady had come up and complained ... Making a commotion out there on the landing that he *couldn't* have slept through. ... And maybe Sally would have answered back like a fish-wife, hideous in curlers and face-cream, her voice shrill and shrewish. ...

Gradually, these dreams of the might-have-been turned to real dreams. Worn out by disappointment, and by futile regrets, Tina slept; and when she woke, it was morning.

Quite late morning, too, to judge by the piercing threads of sun-light that managed to make their way past the heavy, closely-drawn curtains. A good job it was Sunday, or Colin would have been late for work!

Funny, though, that Edward had allowed them to sleep in like this. Usually, Sunday or no Sunday, he'd be pestering around by seven or earlier, whining, grizzling, wanting to be amused. Asking for drinks of water and then not drinking them; asking for his potty, and then not using it. Never a minute's peace, normally, once it was daylight.

Funny he was so quiet. What could have made him sleep so late? Or what could he have found to play with that was so engrossing and so quiet? And just then, Tina heard the little pattering footsteps across the landing.

'Mummy!' came Edward's high little voice as he trotted into the darkened bedroom, 'Mummy, look at Teddy! Teddy's all wet ...!'

The thin, sallow little figure was right by the bedside now, thrusting a dark object at her ... sodden! ... Disgusting ...!

'Edward! Take it away!' she ordered; and at the same time switched on the bedside light.

He was smiling, and covered in blood – face, hands, pyjamas – every-thing and in his hands – thrust towards her like a birthday gift – was Julie's teddy-bear, soaked and dripping with blood.

How to prove that it wasn't *her* – that *she* hadn't done it? That her husband, in bed with Sally, must have been murdered by some person – most probably by that ex-boy-friend, who had written all those passion-ate letters, and must have come round last night to see what was going on? The murderer had tried to kill Sally as well as Colin – she had been found unconscious from loss of blood, but was expected to recover. Julie had been unharmed, and seemed already (under the care of the adoring landlady) to be recovering from the shock of whatever it was she had seen.

Tina was the one who hadn't recovered. They weren't giving her a chance. According to the other people in the house – including the landlady – a child had been screaming non-stop for the best part of two hours – but of course they had all thought it was Edward, and therefore nothing unusual.

But Tina – *she* must have known it wasn't Edward. *She* was right there, just across the landing from it all. How come she had just lain there, doing nothing, for two whole hours? Surely it must have occurred to her that something might be wrong? And how come, too, that her fresh fingerprints were all over the outside of Sally's door, up and down and all around the door-knob and the keyhole, as if she had been feeling her way in in the dark? And the marks of her bare feet, too, on the lino outside Sally's door? And besides all this was Tina *really* asking them to believe that she hadn't known – or guessed – that her husband might be in there with Sally? Hadn't realized that he had been growing fond of Sally all these weeks. . . . Hadn't even noticed that his bed was empty . . . ?

How could she convince them? How could she explain that the reason she had lain there doing nothing was that she was loving the sound of the child screaming, and wanted it to go on and on? That she had crossed the landing and opened Sally's door not with any evil intent, but just in order to hear the screams yet louder? And as to it occurring to her that something might be wrong – why, she had been lying there hoping that something *was*! Hoping, praying, daydreaming, as she had done for months . . . !

How *do* you explain this sort of thing, to people who don't understand? Explain that you are guilty merely of malice, cruelty, spite, and all-consuming desire to harm; but not of murder. That you are innocent, in fact?

The Squire's Story

Mrs Gaskell

In the year 1769 the little town of Barford was thrown into a state of great excitement by the intelligence that a gentleman (and 'quite the gentleman', said the landlord of the George Inn) had been looking at Mr Clavering's old house. This house was neither in the town nor in the country. It stood on the outskirts of Barford, on the roadside leading to Derby. The last occupant had been a Mr Clavering – a Northumberland gentleman of good family – who had come to live in Barford while he was but a younger son; but when some elder branches of the family died, he had returned to take possession of the family estate. The house of which I speak was called the White House, from its being covered with a greyish kind of stucco. It had a good garden to the back, and Mr Clavering had built capital stables, with what were then considered the latest improvements. The point of good stabling was expected to let the house, as it was in a hunting county; otherwise it had few recommendations. There were many bedrooms; some entered through others, even to the number of five, leading one beyond the other; several sitting-rooms of the small and poky kind, wainscoted round with wood, and then painted a heavy slate colour; one good dining-room, and a drawing-room over it, both looking into the garden, with pleasant bow-windows.

Such was the accommodation offered by the White House. It did not seem to be very tempting to strangers, though the good people of Barford rather piqued themselves on it, as the largest house in the town; and as a house in which 'townspeople' and 'county people' had often met at Mr Clavering's friendly dinners. To appreciate this circumstance of pleasant recollection, you should have lived some years in a little country town, surrounded by gentlemen's seats. You would then understand how a bow or a courtsey from a member of a county family elevates the individuals who receive it almost as much, in their own eyes, as the pair of blue garters fringed with silver did Mr Bickerstaff's ward. They trip lightly on air for a whole day afterwards. Now Mr Clavering was gone, where could town and county mingle?

I mention these things that you may have an idea of the desirability of the letting of the White House in the Barfodites' imagination; and to make the mixture thick and slab, you must add for yourselves the bustle, the mystery, and the importance which every little event either causes or assumes in a small town; and then, perhaps, it will be no wonder to you that twenty ragged little urchins accompanied the 'gentleman' aforesaid to the door of the White House; and that, although he was above an hour inspecting it under the auspices of Mr Jones, the agent's clerk, thirty more had joined themselves on to the wondering crowd before his exit, and awaited such crumbs of intelligence as they could gather before they were threatened or whipped out of hearing distance. Presently out came the 'gentleman' and the lawyer's clerk. The latter was speaking as he followed the former over the threshold. The gentleman was tall, well-dressed, handsome; but there was a sinister cold look in his quick-glancing, light blue eyes, which a keen observer might not have liked. There were no keen observers among the boys and ill-conditioned gaping girls. But they stood too near; inconveniently close; and the gentleman, lifting up his right hand, in which he carried a short riding-whip, dealt one or two sharp blows to the nearest, with a look of savage enjoyment on his face as they moved away whimpering and crying. An instant after, his expression of countenance had changed.

'Here!' said he, drawing out a handful of money, partly silver, partly copper, and throwing it into the midst of them. 'Scramble for it! fight it out, my lads! Come this afternoon, at three, to the George, and I'll throw you out some more.'

So the boys hurrahed for him as he walked off with the agent's clerk. He chuckled to himself, as over a pleasant thought. 'I'll have some fun with those lads,' he said; 'I'll teach 'em to be prowling and prying about me. I'll tell you what I'll do. I'll make the money so hot in the fire-shovel that it shall burn their fingers. You come and see the faces and the howling. I shall be very glad if you will dine with me at two; and by that time I may have made up my mind respecting the house.'

Mr Jones, the agent's clerk, agreed to come to the George at two, but, somehow, he had a distaste for his entertainer. Mr Jones would not like to have said, even to himself, that a man with a purse full of money, who kept many horses, and spoke familiarly of noblemen – above all, who thought of taking the White House – could be anything but a gentleman; but still the uneasy wonder as to who this Mr Robinson Higgins could be, filled the clerk's mind long after Mr Higgins, Mr Higgins's servants, and Mr Higgins's stud had taken possession of the White House.

The White House was re-stuccoed (this time of a pale yellow colour), and put into thorough repair by the accommodating and delighted land-lord; while his tenant seemed inclined to spend any amount of money on internal decorations, which were showy and effective in their character, enough to make the White House a nine days' wonder to the good people of Barford. The slate-coloured paints became pink, and were picked out with gold; the old-fashioned banisters were replaced by newly gilt ones; but, above all, the stables were a sight to be seen. Since the days of the Roman Emperor never was there such provision made for the care, the comfort, and the health of horses. But every one said it was no wonder, when they were led through Barford, covered up to their eyes, but curving their arched and delicate necks, and prancing with short high steps, in repressed eagerness.

Only one groom came with them; yet they required the care of three men. Mr Higgins, however, preferred engaging two lads out of Barford; and Barford highly approved of his preference. Not only was it kind and thoughtful to give employment to the lounging lads themselves, but they were receiving such a training in Mr Higgins's stables as might fit them for Doncaster or Newmarket.

The district of Derbyshire in which Barford was situated was too close to Leicestershire not to support a hunt and a pack of hounds. The master of the hounds was a certain Sir Harry Manley, who was *aut* a huntsman *aut nullus*. He measured a man by the 'length of his fork,' not by the expression of his countenance or the shape of his head. But, as Sir Harry was wont to observe, there was such a thing as too long a fork, so his approbation was withheld until he had seen a man on horseback; and if his seat there was square and easy, his hand light, and his courage good, Sir Harry hailed him as a brother.

Mr Higgins attended the first meet of the season, not as a subscriber but as an amateur. The Barford huntsmen piqued themselves on their bold riding; and their knowledge of the country came by nature; yet this new strange man, whom nobody knew, was in at the death, sitting on his horse, both well breathed and calm, without a hair turned on the sleek skin of the latter, supremely addressing the old huntsman as he hacked off the tail of the fox; and he, the old man, who was testy even under Sir Harry's slightest rebuke, and flew out on any other member of the hunt that dared to utter a word against his sixty years' experience as stable-boy, groom, poacher, and what not – he, old Isaac Wormeley, was meekly listening to the wisdom of this stranger, only now and then giving one of his quick, up-turning, cunning glances, not unlike the sharp o'er-canny looks of the poor deceased Reynard, round whom the hounds were howling, unadmonished by the short whip, which was now tucked into Wormeley's well-worn pocket.

When Sir Harry rode into the copse – full of dead brushwood and wet tangled grass – and was followed by the members of the hunt, as one by one they cantered past, Mr Higgins took off his cap and bowed – half deferentially, half insolently – with a lurking smile in the corner of his eye at the discomfited looks of one or two of the laggards.

'A famous run, sir,' said Sir Harry. 'The first time you have hunted in our country; but I hope we shall see you often.'

'I hope to become a member of the hunt, sir,' said Mr Higgins.

'Most happy – proud, I'm sure, to receive so daring a rider among us. You took the Cropper-gate, I fancy; while some of our friends here' – scowling at one or two cowards by way of finishing his speech. 'Allow me to introduce myself – master of the hounds.' He fumbled in his waistcoat pocket for the card on which his name was formally inscribed. 'Some of our friends here are kind enough to come home with me to dinner; might I ask for the honour?'

'My name is Higgins,' replied the stranger, bowing low. 'I am only lately come to occupy the White House at Barford, and I have not as yet presented my letters of introduction.'

'Hang it!' replied Sir Harry; 'a man with a seat like yours, and that good brush in your hand, might ride up to any door in the county (I'm a Leicestershire man!) and be a welcome guest. Mr Higgins, I shall be proud to become better acquainted with you over my dinner-table.'

Mr Higgins knew pretty well how to improve the acquaintance thus begun. He could sing a good song, tell a good story, and was well up in practical jokes; with plenty of that keen worldly sense, which seems like an instinct in some men, and which in this case taught him on whom he might play off such jokes, with impunity from their resentment, and with a security of applause from the more boisterous, vehement, or prosperous. At the end of twelve months Mr Robinson Higgins was, out-and-out, the most popular member of the Barford hunt; had beaten all the others by a couple of lengths, as his first patron, Sir Harry, observed one evening, when they were just leaving the dinner-table of an old hunting squire in the neighbourhood.

'Because, you know,' said Squire Hearn, holding Sir Harry by the button – 'I mean, you see, this young spark is looking sweet upon Catherine; and she's a good girl, and will have ten thousand pounds down, the day she's married, by her mother's will; and – excuse me, Sir Harry – but I should not like my girl to throw herself away.'

Though Sir Harry had a long ride before him, and but the early and short light of a new moon to take it in, his kind heart was so much touched by Squire Hearn's trembling, tearful anxiety, that he stopped and turned back into the dining-room to say, with more asseverations than I care to give:

'My good Squire, I may say I know that man pretty well by this time, and a better fellow never existed. If I had twenty daughters he should have the pick of them.'

Squire Hearn never thought of asking the grounds for his old friend's

opinion of Mr Higgins; it had been given with too much earnestness
for any doubts to cross the old man's mind as to the possibility of its
not being well founded. Mr Hearn was not a doubter, or a thinker,
or suspicious by nature; it was simply love for Catherine, his only
daughter, that prompted his anxiety in this case; and, after what Sir
Harry had said, the old man could totter with an easy mind, though
not with very steady legs, into the drawing-room, where his bonny,
blushing daughter Catherine and Mr Higgins stood close together on the
hearth-rug – he whispering, she listening with downcast eyes.

She looked so happy, so like what her dead mother had looked when
the Squire was a young man, that all his thought was how to please
her most. His son and heir was about to be married, and bring his wife
to live with the Squire; Barford and the White House were not distant
an hour's ride; and, even as these thoughts passed through his mind,
he asked Mr Higgins if he could not stay all night – the young moon
was already set – the roads would be dark – and Catherine looked up
with a pretty anxiety, which, however, had not much doubt in it, for
the answer.

With every encouragement of this kind from the old Squire, it took
everybody rather by surprise when one morning it was discovered that
Miss Catherine Hearn was missing; and when, according to the usual
fashion in such cases, a note was found, saying that she had eloped with
'the man of her heart', and gone to Gretna Green, no one could imagine
why she could not quietly have stopped at home and been married in
the parish church. She had always been a romantic, sentimental girl;
very pretty and very affectionate, and very much spoiled, and very much
wanting in common sense. Her indulgent father was deeply hurt at this
want of confidence in his never-varying affection; but when his son came,
hot with indignation from the Baronet's (his future father-in-law's house,
where every form of law and of ceremony was to accompany his own
impending marriage), Squire Hearn pleaded the cause of the young
couple with imploring cogency, and protested that it was a piece of
spirit in his daughter, which he admired and was proud of.

However, it ended with Mr Nathaniel Hearn's declaring that he and
his wife would have nothing to do with his sister and her husband.

'Wait till you've seen him, Nat!' said the old Squire, trembling with
his distressful anticipations of family discord; 'he's an excuse for any
girl. Only ask Sir Harry's opinion of him.'

'Confound Sir Harry! So that a man sits his horse well, Sir Harry
cares nothing about anything else. Who is this man – this fellow? Where
does he come from? What are his means? Who are his family?'

'He comes from the south – Surrey or Somersetshire, I forget which;
and he pays his way well and liberally. There's not a tradesman in Barford but says he cares no more for money than for water; he spends

like a prince, Nat. I don't know who his family are, but he seals with a coat of arms, which may tell you if you want to know – and he goes regularly to collect his rents from his estates in the south. Oh, Nat! if you would but be friendly, I should be as well pleased with Kitty's marriage as any father in the county.'

Mr Nathaniel Hearn gloomed, and muttered an oath or two to himself. The poor old father was reaping the consequences of his weak indulgence to his two children. Mr and Mrs Nathaniel Hearn kept apart from Catherine and her husband; and Squire Hearn durst never ask them to Levison Hall, though it was his own house. Indeed, he stole away as if he were a culprit whenever he went to visit the White House; and if he passed a night there, he was fain to equivocate when he returned home the next day; an equivocation which was well interpreted by the surly, proud Nathaniel. But the younger Mr and Mrs Hearn were the only people who did not visit at the White House.

Mr and Mrs Higgins were decidedly more popular than their brother and sister-in-law. She made a very pretty, sweet-tempered hostess, and her education had not been such as to make her intolerant of any want of refinement in the associates who gathered round her husband. She had gentle smiles for townspeople as well as county people; and unconsciously played an admirable second in her husband's project of making himself universally popular.

But there is some one to make ill-natured remarks, and draw ill-natured conclusions from very simple premises, in every place; and in Barford this bird of ill-omen was a Miss Pratt. She did not hunt – so Mr Higgins's admirable riding did not call out her admiration. She did not drink – so the well-selected wines, so lavishly dispensed among his guests, could never mollify Miss Pratt. She could not bear comic songs, or buffo stories – so, in that way, her approbation was impregnable. And these three secrets of popularity constituted Mr Higgins's great charm.

Miss Pratt sat and watched. Her face looked immovably grave at the end of any of Mr Higgins's best stories; but there was a keen, needle-like glance of her unwinking little eyes, which Mr Higgins felt rather than saw, and which made him shiver, even on a hot day, when it fell upon him. Miss Pratt was a dissenter, and, to propitiate this female Mordecai, Mr Higgins asked the dissenting minister whose services she attended, to dinner; kept himself and his company in good order; gave a handsome donation to the poor of the chapel.

All in vain – Miss Pratt stirred not a muscle more of her face towards graciousness; and Mr Higgins was conscious that, in spite of all his open efforts to captivate Mr Davis, there was a secret influence on the other side, throwing in doubts and suspicions, and evil interpretations of all he said or did. Miss Pratt, the little, plain old maid, living on eighty pounds a year, was the thorn in the popular Mr Higgins's side, although she had never spoken one uncivil word to him; indeed, on the contrary, had treated him with a stiff and elaborated civility.

The thorn – the grief to Mrs Higgins was this. They had no children! Oh! how she would stand and envy the careless busy motion of half a dozen children; and then when observed, move on with a deep, deep sigh of yearning regret. But it was as well.

It was noticed that Mr Higgins was remarkably careful of his health. He ate, drank, took exercise, rested, by some secret rules of his own; occasionally bursting into an excess, it is true, but only on rare occasions – such as when he returned from visiting his estates in the south, and collecting his rents. That unusual exertion and fatigue – for there were no stagecoaches within forty miles of Barford, and he, like most country gentlemen of that day, would have preferred riding if there had been – seemed to require some strange excess to compensate for it; and rumours went through the town that he shut himself up, and drank enormously for some days after his return. But no one was admitted to these orgies.

One day – they remembered it well afterwards – the hounds met not far from the town; and the fox was found in a part of the wild heath, which was beginning to be enclosed by a few of the more wealthy townspeople, who were desirous of building themselves houses rather more in the country than those they had hitherto lived in.

Among these the principal was a Mr Dudgeon, the attorney of Barford, and the agent for all the county families about. The firm of Dudgeon had managed the leases, the marriage-settlements, and the wills of the neighbourhood for generations. Mr Dudgeon's father had the responsibility of collecting the landowners' rents just as the present Mr Dudgeon had at the time of which I speak: and as his son and his son's son have done since. Their business was an hereditary estate to them; and with something of the old feudal feeling was mixed a kind of proud humility at their position towards the squires whose family secrets they had mastered, and the mysteries of whose fortunes and estates were better known to the Messrs Dudgeon than to themselves.

Mr John Dudgeon had built himself a house on Wildbury Heath – a mere cottage, as he called it; but though only two storeys high, it spread out far and wide, and workpeople from Derby had been sent for on purpose to make the inside as complete as possible. The gardens too were exquisite in arrangement, if not very extensive; and not a flower was grown in them but of the rarest species.

It must have been somewhat of a mortification to the owner of this dainty place when, on the day of which I speak, the fox, after a long race, during which he had described a circle of many miles, took refuge in the garden; but Mr Dudgeon put a good face on the matter when a gentleman hunter, with the careless insolence of the squires of those days and that place, rode across the velvet lawn, and tapping at the window of the dining-room with his whip-handle, asked permission – no! that is not it – rather, informed Mr Dudgeon of their intention – to enter his garden in a body, and have the fox unearthed. Mr Dudgeon compelled himself to smile assent with the grace of a masculine Griselda; and then he hastily gave orders to have all that the house afforded of provision set out for luncheon, guessing rightly enough that a six hour's run would give even homely fare an acceptable welcome.

He bore without wincing the entrance of the dirty boots into his exquisitely clean rooms; he only felt grateful for the care with which Mr Higgins strode about, laboriously and noiselessly moving on the tip of his toes, as he reconnoitred the rooms with a curious eye.

'I'm going to build a house myself, Dudgeon; and, upon my word, I don't think I could take a better model than yours.'

'Oh! my poor cottage would be too small to afford any hints for such a house as you would wish to build, Mr Higgins,' replied Mr Dudgeon, gently rubbing his hands nevertheless at the compliment.

'Not at all! not at all! Let me see. You have dining-room, drawing-room' – he hesitated, and Mr Dudgeon filled up the blank as he expected.

'Four sitting-rooms and the bedrooms. But allow me to show you over the house. I confess I took some pains in arranging it, and, though far smaller than what you would require, it may, nevertheless, afford you some hints.'

So they left the eating gentlemen with their mouths and their plates quite full, and the scent of the fox overpowering that of the hasty rashers of ham; and they carefully inspected all the ground-floor rooms. Then Mr Dudgeon said:

'If you are not tired, Mr Higgins – it is rather my hobby, so you must pull me up if you are – we will go upstairs, and I will show you my sanctum.'

Mr Dudgeon's sanctum was the centre room, over the porch, which formed a balcony, and which was carefully filled with choice flowers in pots. Inside, there were all kinds of elegant contrivances for hiding the real strength of all the boxes and chests required by the particular nature of Mr Dudgeon's business: for although his office was in Barford, he kept (as he informed Mr Higgins) what was the most valuable here, as being safer than an office which was locked up and left every night.

But, as Mr Higgins reminded him with a sly poke in the side, when next they met, his own house was not over-secure. A fortnight after the gentlemen of the Barford hunt lunched there, Mr Dudgeon's strong-box – in his sanctum upstairs, with the mysterious spring-bolt to the window invented by himself, and the secret of which was only known to the inventor and a few of his most intimate friends, to whom he had proudly shown it; – this strong-box, containing the collected Christmas rents of half a dozen landlords (there was then no bank nearer than Derby), was rifled; and the secretly rich Mr Dudgeon had to stop his agent in his purchases of paintings by Flemish artists, because the money was required to make good the missing rents.

The Dogberries and Verges of those days were quite incapable of obtaining any clue to the robber or robbers; and though one or two vagrants were taken up and brought before Mr Dunover and Mr Higgins, the magistrates who usually attended in the court-room at Barford, there was no evidence brought against them, and after a couple of nights' durance in the lock-ups they were set at liberty. But it became a standing joke with Mr Higgins to ask Mr Dudgeon, from time to time, whether he would recommend him a place of safety for his valuables; or if he had made any more inventions lately for securing houses from robbers.

About two years after this time – about seven years after Mr Higgins had been married – one Tuesday evening, Mr Davis was sitting reading the news in the coffee-room of the George Inn. He belonged to a club of gentlemen who met there occasionally to play whist, to read what few newspapers and magazines were published in those days, to chat about the market at Derby, and prices all over the country.

This Tuesday night it was a black frost; and few people were in the room. Mr Davis was anxious to finish an article in the *Gentleman's Magazine*; indeed, he was making extracts from it, intending to answer it, and yet unable with his small income to purchase a copy. So he stayed late; it was past nine, and at ten o'clock the room was closed.

But while he wrote, Mr Higgins came in. He was pale and haggard with cold; Mr Davis, who had had for some time sole possession of the fire, moved politely on one side, and handed to the new-comer the sole London newspaper which the room afforded.

Mr Higgins accepted it, and made some remark on the intense coldness of the weather; but Mr Davis was too full of his article, and intended reply, to fall into conversation readily. Mr Higgins hitched his chair nearer to the fire, and put his feet on the fender, giving an audible shudder. He put the newspaper on one end of the table near him, and sat gazing into the red embers of the fire, crouching down over them as if his very marrow were chilled. At length he said:

'There is no account of the murder at Bath in that paper?'

Mr Davis, who had finished taking his notes, and was preparing to go, stopped short, and asked:

'Has there been a murder at Bath? No! I have not seen anything of it – who was murdered?'

'Oh! it was a shocking, terrible murder!' said Mr Higgins, not raising his look from the fire, but gazing on with his eyes dilated till the whites were seen all round them. 'A terrible, terrible murder! I wonder what will become of the murderer? I can fancy the red glowing centre of that fire – look and see how infinitely distant it seems, and how the distance magnifies it into something awful and unquenchable.'

'My dear sir, you are feverish; how you shake and shiver!' said Mr Davis, thinking privately that his companion had symptoms of fever, and that he was wandering in his mind.

'Oh, no!' said Mr Higgins, 'I am not feverish. It is the night which is so cold.'

And for a time he talked with Mr Davis about the article in the *Gentleman's Magazine*, for he was rather a reader himself, and could take more interest in Mr Davis's pursuits than most of the people at Barford. At length it drew near to ten, and Mr Davis rose to go home to his lodgings.

'No, Davis, don't go. I want you here. We will have a bottle of port together, and that will put Saunders into good humour. I want to tell you about this murder,' he continued, dropping his voice, and speaking hoarse and low. 'She was an old woman, and he killed her, sitting reading her Bible by her own fireside!' He looked at Mr Davis with a strange searching gaze, as if trying to find some sympathy in the horror which the idea presented to him.

'Who do you mean, my dear sir? What is this murder you are so full of? No one has been murdered here.'

'No, you fool! I tell you it was in Bath!' said Mr Higgins, with sudden passion; and then calming himself to most velvet-smoothness of manner, he laid his hand on Mr Davis's knee, there, as they sat by the fire, and gently detaining him, began the narration of the crime he was so full of; but his voice and manner were constrained to a stony quietude: he never looked in Mr Davis's face; once or twice, as Mr Davis remembered afterwards, his grip tightened like a compressing vice.

'She lived in a small house in a quiet old-fashioned street, she and her maid. People said she was a good old woman; but for all that she hoarded and hoarded, and never gave to the poor. Mr Davis, it is wicked not to give to the poor – wicked – wicked, is it not? I always give to the poor, for once I read in the Bible that "Charity covereth a multitude of sins." The wicked old woman never gave, but hoarded her money, and saved. Some one heard of it; I say she threw a temptation in his way, and God will punish her for it. And this man – or it might be a woman, who knows? – and this person – heard also that she went to church in the mornings, and her maid in the afternoons; and so – while the maid was at church, and the street and the house quite still, and the darkness of a winter afternoon coming on – she was nodding over the Bible – and that, mark you! is a sin, and one that God will avenge sooner or later; and a step came in the dusk up the stair, and that person I told you of stood in the room. At first he – no! At first, it is supposed – for, you understand, all this is mere guess-work – it is supposed that he asked her civilly enough to give him her money, or to tell him where it was; but the old miser defied him, and would not ask for mercy and give up her keys, even when he threatened her, but looked him in the face as if he had been a baby – Oh, God! Mr Davis, I once dreamt when I was a little innocent boy that I should commit a crime like this, and I wakened up crying; and my mother comforted me – that is the reason I tremble so now – that and the cold, for it is very cold!'

'But did he murder the old lady?' asked Mr Davis. 'I beg your pardon, sir, but I am interested by your story.'

'Yes! he cut her throat; and there she lies yet in her quiet little parlour, with her face upturned and all ghastly white, in the middle of a pool of blood. Mr Davis, this wine is no better than water; I must have some brandy!'

Mr Davis was horror-struck by the story, which seemed to have fascinated him as much as it had done his companion.

'Have they got any clue to the murderer?' said he. Mr Higgins drank down half a tumbler of raw brandy before he answered.

'No! no clue whatever. They will never be able to discover him, and I should not wonder – Mr Davis – I should not wonder if he repented after all, and did bitter penance for his crime; and if so – will there be mercy for him at the last day?'

'God knows!' said Mr Davis, with solemnity. 'It is an awful story,' continued he, rousing himself; 'I hardly like to leave this warm light room and go out into the darkness after hearing it. But it must be done,' buttoning on his great-coat – 'I can only say I hope and trust they will find out the murderer and hang him. – If you'll take my advice, Mr Higgins, you'll have your bed warmed, and drink a treacle-posset just the last thing; and, if you'll allow me, I'll send you my answer to Philologus before it goes up to old Urban.'

The next morning Mr Davis went to call on Miss Pratt, who was not very well; and by way of being agreeable and entertaining, he related to her all he had heard the night before about the murder at Bath; and really he made a very pretty connected story out of it, and interested Miss Pratt very much in the fate of the old lady – partly because of a similarity in their situations; for she also privately hoarded money, and had but one servant, and stopped at home alone on Sunday afternoons to allow her servant to go to church.

'And when did all this happen?' she asked.

'I don't know if Mr Higgins named the day; and yet I think it must have been on this very last Sunday.'

'And today is Wednesday. Ill news travels fast.'

'Yes, Mr Higgins thought it might have been in the London news-paper.'

'That it could never be. Where did Mr Higgins learn all about it?'

'I don't know, I did not ask; I think he only came home yesterday; he had been south to collect his rents, somebody said.'

Miss Pratt grunted. She used to vent her dislike and suspicions of Mr Higgins in a grunt whenever his name was mentioned.

'Well, I shan't see you for some days. Godfrey Merton has asked me to go and stay with him and his sister; and I think it will do me good. Besides,' added she, 'these winter evenings – and these murderers at large in the country – I don't quite like living with only Peggy to call to in case of need.'

Miss Pratt went to stay with her cousin, Mr Merton. He was an active magistrate, and enjoyed his reputation as such. One day he came in, having just received his letters.

'Bad account of the morals of your little town here, Jessy!' said he, touching one of his letters. 'You've either a murderer among you, or some friend of a murderer. Here's a poor old lady at Bath had her throat cut last Sunday week; and I've a letter from the Home Office, asking to lend them "my very efficient aid," as they are pleased to call it, towards finding out the culprit. It seems he must have been thirsty, and of a comfortable jolly turn; for before going to his horrid work he tapped a barrel of ginger wine the old lady had set by to work; and he wrapped the spigot round with a piece of a letter taken out of his pocket, as may be supposed; and this piece of a letter was found afterwards; there are only these letters on the outside, "ns, Esq., -arford, -egworth," which someone has ingeniously made out to mean Barford, near Kegworth. On the other side there is some allusion to a racehorse, I conjecture, though the name is singular enough: "Church-and-King-and-down-with-the-Rump."'

Miss Pratt caught at this name immediately; it had hurt her feelings as a dissenter only a few months ago, and she remembered it well.

'Mr Nat Hearn has – or had (as I am speaking in the witness-box, as it were, I must take care of my tenses) – a horse with that ridiculous name.'

'Mr Nat Hearn,' repeated Mr Merton, making a note of the intelligence; then he recurred to his letter from the Home Office again.

'There is also a piece of a small key, broken in the futile attempt to open a desk – well, well. Nothing more of consequence. The letter is what we must rely upon.'

'Mr Davis said that Mr Higgins told him—' Miss Pratt began.

'Higgins!' exclaimed Mr Merton, 'ns. Is it Higgins, the blustering fellow that ran away with Nat Hearn's sister?'

'Yes!' said Miss Pratt. 'But though he has never been a favourite of mine—'

'ns,' repeated Mr Merton. 'It is too horrible to think of; a member of the hunt – kind old Squire Hearn's son-in-law! Who else have you in Barford with names that end in ns?'

'There's Jackson, and Higginson, and Blenkinsop, and Davis, and Jones. Cousin! One thing strikes me – how did Mr Higgins know all about it to tell Mr Davis on Tuesday what had happened on Sunday afternoon?'

There is no need to add much more. Those curious in lives of the highwaymen may find the name of Higgins as conspicuous among those annals as that of Claude Duval. Kate Hearn's husband collected his rents on the highway, like many another 'gentleman' of the day; but, having been unlucky in one or two of his adventures, and hearing exaggerated accounts of the hoarded wealth of the lady at Bath, he was led on from robbery to murder, and was hanged for his crime at Derby in 1775.

He had not been an unkind husband; and his poor wife took lodgings in Derby to be near him in his last moments – his awful last moments. Her old father went with her everywhere, but into her husband's cell; and wrung her heart by constantly accusing himself of having promoted her marriage with a man of whom he knew so little. He abdicated his squireship in favour of his son Nathaniel. Nat was prosperous, and the helpless silly father could be of no use to him; but to his widowed daughter the foolish old man was all in all; her knight, her protector, her companion – her most faithful loving companion. Only he never declined assuming the office of her counsellor – shaking his head sadly, and saying:

'Ah! Kate, Kate! if I had had more wisdom to have advised thee better, thou need'st not have been an exile here in Brussels, shrinking from the sight of every English person as if they knew thy story.'

I saw the White House not a month ago; it was to let perhaps for the twentieth time since Mr Higgins occupied it; but still the tradition goes in Barford that once upon a time a highwayman lived there, and amassed untold treasures; and that the ill-gotten wealth yet remains walled up in some unknown concealed chamber; but in what part of the house no one knows.

Earth to Earth

Robert Graves

Elsie and Roland Hedge – she a book illustrator, he an architect with suspect lungs – had been warned against Dr Eugen Steinpilz. 'He'll bring you no luck,' I told them. 'My little finger says so decisively.'

'You too?' asked Elsie indignantly. (This was at Brixham, South Devon, in March, 1940.) 'I suppose you think that because of his foreign accent and his beard he must be a spy?'

'No,' I said coldly, 'that point hadn't occurred to me. But I won't contradict you.' I was annoyed.

The very next day Elsie deliberately picked a friendship – I don't like that phrase, but that's what she did – with the Doctor, an Alsatian with an American passport, who described himself as a *Naturphilosoph*; and both she and Roland were soon immersed in Steinpilzeri up to the nostrils. It began when he invited them to lunch and gave them cold meat and two rival sets of vegetable dishes – potatoes (baked), carrots (creamed), bought from the local fruiterer; and potatoes (baked) and carrots (creamed), grown on compost in his own garden.

The superiority of the latter over the former in appearance, size, and especially flavour came as an eye-opener to Elsie and Roland; and so Dr Steinpilz soon converted the childless and devoted couple to the Steinpilz method of composting. It did not, as a matter of fact, vary greatly from the methods you read about in the *Gardening Notes* of your favourite national newspaper, except that it was far more violent. Dr Steinpilz had invented a formula for producing extremely fierce bacteria, capable (Roland claimed) of breaking down an old boot or the family Bible or a torn woollen vest into beautiful black humus almost as you watched.

The formula could not be bought, however, and might be communicated under oath of secrecy only to members of the Eugen Steinpilz Fellowship – which I refused to join. I won't pretend therefore to know the formula myself, but one night I overheard Elsie and Roland arguing as to whether the planetary influences were favourable; and they also mentioned a ram's horn in which, it seems, a complicated mixture of triturated animal and vegetable products – technically called 'the Mother' – was to be cooked up. I gather also that a bull's foot and a goat's pancreas were part of the works, because Mr Pook, the butcher, afterwards told me that he had been puzzled by Roland's request for these unusual cuts. Milkwort and pennyroyal and bee-orchid and vetch certainly figured among 'the Mother's' herbal ingredients; I recognized these one day in a gardening basket Elsie had left in the post office.

The Hedges soon had their first compost heap cooking away in the garden, which was about the size of a tennis court and consisted mostly of well-kept lawn. Dr Steinpilz, who supervised, now began to haunt the cottage like the smell of drains; I had to give up calling on them. Then, after the Fall of France, Brixham became a war zone whence everyone but we British and our Free French or Free Belgian allies was extruded. Consequently Dr Steinpilz had to leave; which he did with very bad grace, and was killed in a Liverpool air raid the day before he should have sailed back to New York.

I think Elsie must have been in love with the Doctor, and certainly Roland had a hero worship for him. They treasured a signed collection of all his esoteric books, each titled after a different semi-precious stone; and used to read them out loud to each other at meals, in turns. And to show that this was a practical philosophy, not just a random assembly of beautiful thoughts about Nature, they began composting in a deeper and even more religious way than before. The lawn had come up, of course; but they used the sods to sandwich layers of kitchen waste, which they mixed with the scrapings of an abandoned pigsty, two barrowfuls of sodden poplar leaves from the recreation ground, and a sack of rotten turnips. Once I caught the fanatic gleam in Elsie's eye as she turned the hungry bacteria loose on the heap, and could not repress a premonitory shudder.

So far, not too bad, perhaps. But when serious bombing started and food became so scarce that housewives were fined for not making over their swill to the national pigs, Elsie and Roland grew worried. Having already abandoned their ordinary sanitary system and built an earth-closet in the garden, they now tried to convince neighbours of their duty to do the same, even at the risk of catching cold and getting spiders down the neck. Elsie also sent Roland after the slow-moving Red Devon cows as they lurched home along the lane at dusk, to rescue the precious droppings with a kitchen shovel; while she visited the local ash dump with a packing case mounted on wheels, and collected whatever she found there of an organic nature – dead cats, old rags, withered flowers, cabbage stalks, and such household waste as even a national war-time pig would have coughed at. She also saved every drop of their bath water for sprinkling the heaps; because it contained, she said, valuable animal salts.

The test of a good compost heap, as every illuminate knows, is whether a certain revolting-looking, if beneficial fungus sprouts from it. Elsie's heaps were grey with this crop, and so hot inside they could be used for haybox cookery; which must have saved her a deal of fuel. I called them 'Elsie's heaps', because she now considered herself Dr Steinpilz's earthly delegate; and loyal Roland did not dispute this claim.

A critical stage in the story came during the Blitz. It will be remembered that trainloads of Londoners, who had been evacuated to South Devon when War broke out, thereafter de-evacuated and re-evacuated and re-de-evacuated themselves, from time to time, in a most disorganized fashion. Elsie and Roland, as it happened, escaped having evacuees billeted on them, because they had no spare bedroom; but one night an old naval pensioner came knocking at their door and demanded lodging for the night. Having been burned out of Plymouth, where everything was chaos, he had found himself walking away and blundering along in a daze until he fetched up here, hungry and dead-beat. They gave him a meal and bedded him on the sofa; but when Elsie came down in the morning to fork over the heaps, she found him dead of heart failure.

Roland broke a long silence by coming, in some embarrassment, to ask my advice. Elsie, he said, had decided that it would be wrong to trouble the police about the case; because the police were so busy these days, and the poor old fellow had claimed to possess neither kith nor kin. So they'd read the burial service over him and, after removing his belt buckle, trouser buttons, metal spectacle case, and a bunch of keys, which were irreducible, had laid him reverently in the new compost heap. Its other contents, Roland added, were a cartload of waste from the cider factory and salvaged cow dung.

'If you mean "Will I report you to Civil Authorities?" the answer is no,' I assured him. 'I wasn't looking at the relevant hour, and, after all, what you tell me is only hearsay.'

The War went on. Not only did the Hedges convert the whole garden into serried rows of Eugen Steinpilz memorial heaps, leaving no room for planting the potatoes or carrots to which the compost had been prospectively devoted, but they regularly scavenged offal from the fish-market. Every Spring, Elsie used to pick big bunches of primroses and put them straight on the compost, without even a last wistful sniff; virgin primroses were supposed to be particularly relished by the fierce bacteria.

Here the story becomes a little painful for readers of a family journal like this; I will soften it as much as possible. One morning a policeman called on the Hedges with a summons, and I happened to see Roland peep anxiously out of the bedroom window, but quickly pull his head in again.

The policeman rang and knocked and waited, then tried the back door; and presently went away. The summons was for a blackout offence, but apparently the Hedges did not know this.

Next morning the policeman called again, and when nobody answered, forced the lock of the back door. They were found dead in bed together, having taken an overdose of sleeping tablets. A note on the coverlet ran simply:

> Please lay our bodies on the heap nearest the pigsty. Flowers by request. Strew some on the bodies, mixed with a little kitchen waste, and then fork the earth lightly over.
>
> E.H., R.H.

George Irks, the new tenant, proposed to grow potatoes and dig for victory. He hired a cart and began throwing the compost into the River Dart, 'not liking the look of them toadstools.' The five beautifully clean human skeletons which George unearthed in the process were still awaiting identification when the War ended.

Mrs Manifold

Stephen Grendon

I don't know whether I would have gone into the Sailor's Rest if I had seen its proprietress before I saw the grimy card with its scrawled 'Clerk Wanted' in the window. But perhaps I would – a man with less than a shilling in his pocket, and little chance to add to that, can't hesitate too much. Still, there was something about Mrs Manifold, something you could feel but hardly put into words. I never saw anyone so fat; though she was a short woman, she weighed over three hundred pounds, and it was easy to understand why she preferred to keep to her own room on the fourth floor – a gable room.

'Ever been a clerk before, Mr Robinson?' she asked me.

Her voice was thin, high, almost piping: it was a small voice for so big a woman, and because it was so shrill and penetrating, the contrast was the more startling.

'No. But I can read and write; I can add figures, if it comes to that,' I said.

She gave me a sharp glance. 'It's plain to see you've had some schooling. Down on your luck, is it?'

I admitted that.

She sat looking at me, humming a queer little tune, which I came to recognize later when she sang it: a sea-chanty. In all that tremendous bulk, only her eyes seemed to move: small, black, with short-lashed eyelids: there was no evidence that she breathed, no tremor disturbed her flesh, clad in a dress of black satin, which, despite her great mass, was frilled and ruffled like a child's frock and looked almost obscene. Her eyes scrutinized me with a kind of bold furtiveness, her fat fingers resting on the arms of the chair which contained her strangely motionless body. There was something horrible, not in a bestial sense, but in a spiritual way, about her – not in any one facet, but in everything – something that suggested terror and cold grue.

'My clientele,' she said in a voice suddenly subdued, but with a crafty smile, 'might not always be a nice one, Mr Robinson. A rough lot, Mr

Robinson. You wouldn't expect anything else of Wapping, now, would you? Or of somebody like Mrs Ambrose Manifold?'

Then she tittered. A faint ripple disturbed that vast bulk, and the effect was wholly horrible.

'I can hold my own,' I said.

'Perhaps. Perhaps. We shall see, Mr Robinson. Your duties will be simple. You know what an innkeeper's clerk must do. Make them sign the register, Mr Robinson. Sometimes they have reason to avoid it. Once a week, you will bring the register up to me. I wish to examine it. The money will be deposited to my account at the Bridsley Bank whenever and as soon as it collects to fifty pounds. I am not at home to anyone. Begin now.'

Thereupon she rang a little bell, and the old man who had conducted me up the stairs led the way back down, having been instructed by Mrs Manifold that I was to begin my duties at once.

I lost no time acquainting myself with my surroundings. While the old man, whose name was Mr Claitor, removed the sign from the window and put it carefully away, with an air of doubtless needing it soon again, I took a look at the register. It was nothing but an old ledger, on the first page of which someone had written in a flowing hand, 'Sailors' Rest – Register'. There were two floors of rooms, which someone's fancy had numbered, to make seven in all – four on the second, three on the third; the first floor being given over to the kitchen, the small lobby, and three closet-like rooms for the staff. One of these was occupied by Mr Claitor, another by Mr and Mrs Jeffers, and the third by the clerk of Sailors' Rest. Six of the rooms were occupied at four shillings the night, six for day and night; evidently there were no rates by the week. The lobby had an appearance of genteel shabbiness; it was not exactly dirty, but it was certainly not clean, and it conveyed the impression of never having been quite clean within the memory of any living person. The glass in the window and the door facing the street was fly-specked and dust-streaked, and there was about the entire building a faint but unmistakable odour of the river. The Thames flowed not far away, and at night its musk, rising with the fog, enclosed and permeated the old building.

Mr Claitor, who was tall, thin, and grey, with the lugubrious expression of a very tired Great Dane, got around to instructing me, finally, that the lobby was to be closed promptly at nine o'clock every night, though, thereafter, I might expect to be summoned to open the door for one or more of our tenants come roistering home.

Probably there is nothing so tiring as the position as clerk in a shabby, hole-in-a-corner inn, which seems designed to attract only the dregs of mankind: the bitter, disillusioned old men of the sea – the hopeless wanderers haunting Limehouse and Whitechapel and Wapping – the hunted and the haunted and the lost. Yet, I suppose everyone in a position not especially to his liking is similarly convinced; the human being is essentially weak and insecure, no matter what his place in life, and if that place is not felicitous, that weakness makes itself manifest in dissatisfaction, out of which grows the conviction that anything at all is better than the present position. Work at the Sailors' Rest was monotonous, even when there were books to be read – which was not often, and it soon became a pattern.

But the weekly trip to Mrs Manifold's gable room was somehow never quite part of that pattern. There was something a little different every time, despite the fact that her position never seemed to have changed; for all her appearance, she need never have moved from one week to the next, and not at all since first I saw her. Every time she would take the register and examine the new entries.

'Roald Jensen,' she read out slowly. 'Now, what is he like? Is he a tall man or is he short?'

'Tall, thin, sandy-red hair, one wooden leg. He wears a moustache. Last sailed on the *Lofoten* out of Oslo.'

'Frederick Schwartz, then. What is he like?'

'Short, fat. Looks like a German burgomaster. Red cheeks, blue eyes. Very talkative. Heavy German accent. Last sailed on the *Stresemann* out of Hamburg.'

'Good gracious, Mr Robinson,' she said on occasion, 'you should have been a policeman. I admire the quality of observation.'

But, each time she said it, I caught the unmistakable impression that she was laughing at me behind her small, dark eyes; and each time she finished her examination of the register, I could not escape the conviction that she did so with relief, so that I wondered often why she insisted on taking this trouble at all if she concluded it always with such manifest satisfaction at being done with it.

Once, she was talkative. She said comparatively little, but I learned from her that she had had some kind of place in Singapore half a dozen years ago or thereabouts; she and her husband had run it. Then she had come to England.

'And where is Mr Manifold now?' I asked her.

'Ah, nobody knows, nobody knows. Nobody, Mr Robinson.'

Thereafter she had given the unmistakable sign of having finished with me – closing her eyes and leaning back, inert, save for a trembling of her thick lips, as she hummed the chanty she sometimes sang.

> *'Oh, the Captain's in the brig, Lads,*
> *The First Mate's brains are blown;*
> *We'll sail the Seven Seas, Lads,*
> *And make them all our own . . .'*

But there were diversions, though they were out of the ordinary.

Sometimes gentlemen from the CID at Scotland Yard came around to look for somebody – on the average, once a fortnight. Sometimes one of our registrants walked out and never came back, leaving all his baggage behind to be stored against his return – which might not happen. Things could happen in the fogs; things could take place no one ever found out – robbery and sudden death, suicide sometimes. I never felt any inclination to go outside on a foggy night; daytime was dreary enough, for the Sailors' Rest was not in a good neighbourhood – oh, good enough, for what it was, I suppose, but not good enough for what it might have been. And there was something about Mrs Manifold, too, that seemed to say she had known better days and a better business than this, even if in Singapore.

Singapore! Perhaps it had its holes like Sailors' Rest, its districts like Wapping, too – but, being far away, it was caught in a kind of magic aura, it took on colour and life and drama built up solely in imagination, as of all faraway places which are never, somehow, quite real, and always, always wonderfully exciting. Why had Mrs Manifold left Singapore to come to London? And why had she come down into Wapping, of all places? But here she was, and apparently content to be here, making no complaint, occasionally even making sly remarks about her reduced station in life. Yet she need not have been here, for her balance at the bank was always written in five figures – in ready funds alone, she was worth more than fifty thousand pounds.

But for all the signs of breeding which showed through, there was never anything which could dispel that feeling of terror she could induce. Did it arise out of her shocking obesity, or from some other, hidden source? All too often revulsion stimulates dislike and hatred; it is impossible sometimes to uncover the roots of fear or horror. Curiously, she had but one taboo, about which I heard from Mr Claitor, when he came to my room one night.

'Mrs Manifold says you are not to drink wine, Mr Robinson. No wine in the house, she says. It's the rule of Sailors' Rest.'

When I mentioned it to her, she confirmed it. 'Wine I cannot abide, Mr Robinson. Ale, yes. Whisky, yes. Gin, if you like. Vermouth, certainly. Whatever you wish – but no wine.'

She occupied her gable in lordly splendour. Splendour being relative, her self-denial did not diminish it. She ruled Sailors' Rest with an un-challenged and indomitable will. In a sense, she was Sailors' Rest, and Sailors' Rest was Mrs Manifold; sometimes at night, in that borderland between sleep and waking, I thought of the old building as somehow alive, squatting obscenely in its row of ancient buildings, with small black window-eyes, like Mrs Manifold's, and straight black hair, parted in the middle and drawn around back over invisible ears, and gold hoops for ear-rings; I thought of the wide, fly-specked, dust-streaked window in front expanding briefly, fleetingly into a sly-lipped smile, something akin to a leer. Like the fog and the musk of the Thames, Mrs Manifold's presence permeated the very walls, made itself felt in every nook and cranny, and lingered in the quiet air.

In the middle of my eleventh week, early one hot summer night, there came an old sailor just in on HMS *Malaya*, out of Singapore. A Yankee, by the look of him, with a brush of short beard reaching around his chin from one ear to another: a Quaker cut, I think they call it. He was in his sixties, I judged, and did not like the look of the place, saying so, and adding that there was no other.

'I'll stay the night,' he said.

'American?' I asked.

'Born there. Spent most of my life in Singapore.'

Perhaps it was natural that I should ask whether he had ever heard of Mrs Ambrose Manifold. There was nothing to show that he was within shouting distance of her.

'Mrs Manifold,' he said, and grinned. 'Mister, there was a woman. Big enough for half a dozen women. Never been as good a house in Singapore since she lit out for parts unknown.'

'Why did she leave?'

'Who knows? Women don't do things sensible, Mister. She was making money faster'n they could spend it. Then Amby run out on her, and she closed up her place, and off she went. Biggest thing I ever seen to drop out of sight like that!'

'What happened to him?' I asked.

'Nobody knows that, Mister. They didn't get along too well sometimes. Amby liked to drink – but he was a wine drinker – in Singapore! He could get sick stewed on wine faster'n you could say Jack Robinson. Your name ain't Jack, is it?'

'No,' I said. 'It doesn't matter.'

'Well, Amby run out on her. though how he did it, God knows. And he took along the biggest cask of wine they had in the cellar. The way she watched him and all, he was sly and fast to get out – and with that wine, too! Nobody ever saw him go – but the cask of wine he had hauled out bold as brass! He had his mind made up, Mister – and so would you, if you ever saw Mrs Manifold. What could a man do with a woman as fat as that, eh, Mister?'

He poked me in the ribs and said that he was tired.

In the morning he was gone, but he had paid in advance; so it was his privilege to go when he liked. It was necessary to get one-night pay-ment in advance to guard against this method of departure.

And that weekend, when Mrs Manifold came upon his name, her

eyes held to it, and she began to tremble – strange sight, like the shaking of a jelly, a shuddering and trembling that was unpleasant to behold.

'Joshua Bennington. Mr Robinson – a well-built man with a brown beard, was he? From Singapore. One night, too! In midweek. Ah, too bad, too bad! Why didn't you let me know?'

'I had no idea you would want to know before now. I have my instructions.'

'Yes, yes – that's true. Singapore! I would have liked to talk to him.'

She said no more, but there was a strange expression in her eyes. I could not fathom it. Triumph, amusement, regret – all these were there – or were they only reflections from my own imagination? It was difficult to tell with Mrs Manifold. But the trembling in her body continued for a long time, and I was anxious to get away, to get out of that gable room, to escape the burden of her eyes.

Three days after that, something changed in that old inn.

The change was in Mrs Manifold, too, and it happened after the empty seventh room was filled. He came in just before closing time, a small man with a limp, with his hat pulled down low, and his face all muffled up against the fog which was so thick it had got into the lobby and was yellow in the light at the desk. He was wet with it, wet with fog – and inside wet – with wine. For he reeked of it – stronger than the room reeked of the fog and the river's smell; the sickish smell of sweet wine hung about him like a cloud.

A strange man and a silent one.

'Good evening, sir,' I said.

No answer.

I turned the register towards him, holding out the pen. 'Number Seven left, sir,' I said. 'Will it be for the night or longer?'

What he said sounded like 'Longer', but his voice was so muffled I could not easily tell.

'A wet night, sir,' I said.

He signed the register in a crabbed hand, writing with difficulty, and without removing his tattered gloves.

'Third floor back, last door. It's standing open,' I said.

Without a word he left the lobby for the stairs, trailing that nauseating smell of wine.

I looked at the register.

The writing was difficult, but it could be read, after a fashion. Unless the fog and the addling sweetness of the wine smell and my imagination deceived me, I read there, '*Amb. Manifold, late of Singapore, out of Madeira.*'

I took the register and mounted to the fourth floor. The crack under the door showed a light, still. I knocked.

'It's Robinson, Mrs Manifold,' I said. 'You told me if we ever got anybody else from Singapore . . .'

'Come in.'

I went in. She was still sitting there in her black satin dress, like a queen in the middle of the room.

'Let me see,' she said eagerly.

I put the register before her.

And then she saw. Her dark-skinned face went pale, and if she had trembled before, she shook now – a great, obscene shaking animating that mass of flesh. She pushed the book away, and it fell to the floor. I bent and picked it up.

'Seems to be the same name as your own,' I said.

With some effort at control, she asked the familiar question. 'What is he like?'

'Short – a small man – with a limp.'

'Where is he?'

'In Number Seven – just under you.'

'I want to see him.'

'Now?'

'Now, Mr Robinson.'

I went down the stairs and knocked on the door of Number Seven. No answer. I knocked louder. Still no answer. A surly, unpleasant man, certainly. I knocked once more. Still no answer.

I tried the door. It was open.

I pushed it ajar and said softly into the darkness, 'Mr Manifold?'

No answer.

I opened the door all the way and turned up the light.

The room was empty. Empty, that is, of human occupation – it was alive with the rich headiness of wine, a sickening sweetness, cloying and repelling. There was no sign that the bed had been touched; yet the door of the room was closed, where it had been open before; so he had been there, since no one else had.

I went downstairs into the lobby, but no one was there, and the outer door was locked, as I had left it. Mr Manifold was nowhere to be seen.

I went back to the gable room where Mrs Manifold waited.

'Well?' she asked, seeing me alone.

'I can't find him,' I said. 'I tried his room, but he's gone.'

She was still shaking, but in the midst of her inner turmoil, she asked, 'Mr Robinson, have you been drinking wine?'

'No. That smell came in with him. He's been drinking, I suspect. Madeira, I think – or something equally heavy. A sweet port . . .'

But she was not listening. Or rather, she was not listening to me. Her little eyes had narrowed, and she was leaning a little to one side, with her massive head on her great shoulders cocked somewhat to the left and down, as if she were listening to something from below.

'Do you hear someone singing, Mr Robinson?' she asked in a harsh whisper.

'Can't say as I do,' I answered, after a moment of listening.

'It goes like this,' she said, and sang with horrible urgency the familiar lines of her own chanty—

> *'Oh, the Captain's in the brig, Lads,*
> *The First Mate's brains are blown;*
> *We'll sail the Seven Seas, Lads,*
> *And make them all our own . . .'*

'No,' I said.

She closed her eyes and leaned back. 'Let me know when you see him again, Mr Robinson.'

After that, Mrs Manifold's bell rang several times a day for me.

First it was, 'Get that smell of wine out of this house, Mr Robinson.'

But I couldn't. Open doors and windows as I would, I couldn't get that smell of wine out: there it was – rich, heady, nauseating; it had come in to stay, and there was nothing to do but live with it. I could imagine how it bothered her, what with her hatred for the stuff, but it was in her room, too, and she had to endure it as well as the rest of us.

Then, afterwards, it was about Mr Manifold. Had I seen him?

No, I had not. I never saw him again. He had gone without paying, but then, he never rightly used that room except to put the smell of wine into it, and there was no charge for that.

And did I hear that singing?

I never did.

But she did, and it bothered her. And it bothered her, too, to hear Mr Manifold the way she said she did. She knew his walk; there was a slight drag because of that limp. I never heard anything like that, and neither did anyone else, for she did ask Mr Claitor, who had not even seen Mr Manifold, as I had.

I used to ask myself, if it were indeed her husband, why had he come? And, having come, why had he gone without so much as saying hello or goodbye to his wife? It was strange – but Sailors' Rest was a place for strange things to happen even in the ordinary course of its monotonous existence.

Mrs Manifold was not the same.

If anything, she was more terrible. There was a greater furtiveness about her; there was less sly humour, almost nothing of humour at all; there was an unmistakable grimness, a kind of terrible bravado; and there was above everything else something about her that made her far more horrible than she had ever seemed to me – something that made me think of death and fear of death, of violence and unimaginable horror, something eldritch and ineffably terrible, something that throbbed in the core of Mrs Manifold as the red blood coursed through the heart keeping life in that bulging mound of flesh.

And being with her even for the little while I had to be there was infinitely unpleasant, for she was always listening, catching her breath and listening, and hearing things when there was nothing to hear. And she was always asking questions I couldn't answer to please her, and scolding at me to clear the air of that wine smell, which was impossible – but I needn't ever have told her for all the impression it made on her. And she went on, sometimes, about her husband.

'Always the wine and never tending to business, that was Ambrose,' she said. 'And the women, too. Never could leave them alone. I gave him wine – more than he could drink, damn his black soul!'

I heard that over and over. If I heard it once, I heard it a score of times. It was better than that terrible listening. You can't imagine what it is until you go through such a thing by yourself. Even today, long after my short tenure at Sailors' Rest, I can see that horrible, obese woman with her flesh lapping out over the sides of her chair, pushing out between the slats, leaning that vast bulk over to listen with her black-haired head and the golden hooped ear-rings glistening in the feeble yellow light that was in the room, to listen for the sound of singing and the dragging limp; I can still hear her shrill, piping voice complain about the stench of wine, the nauseating sweetness of that cloying odour brought into the Sailors' Rest on that fateful night of fog.

And then, one night, the end came.

I woke out of my sleep, and that wine smell was thick enough to choke me. I got up and opened the door of my room, and then I heard the singing – something like she said, only a little different, and it went like this –

> '*Oh, the Old Man's in the Deep, Lads,*
> *The Madam's packed and flown—*
> *I'll sail the Seven Seas, Lads,*
> *Until I find her home . . .*'

It was coming from somewhere upstairs; so I went back and put something on. I came out again and started up the stairs, and I thought I could hear that dragging walk Mrs Manifold always said she heard, but I could not be sure.

I got up to the third flight of stairs when I heard her scream. It was Mrs Manifold's voice, shrill and awful, and she was screaming at her husband.

'Go away, Ambrose! Go back!' she cried in that horrible, piping voice that came so unnaturally from her obese body. 'Don't touch me!'

And then there was just a terrible, unnatural scream, diminishing into a choking, gurgling sound.

I was struck motionless with fright until Claitor came up behind me, agitated and scared; then I pulled myself together and ran up to the fourth floor. Claitor was right behind me, which turned out to be the best thing for me, since he could testify later on, and there was nothing the people at Scotland Yard could do to me.

Because Mrs Manifold was dead – choked to death. She lay there on the floor, with her black satin dress ripped down one side, and her white flesh pushing out from the tear, and her eyes turned up. All over the room there was a smell of sweet wine so thick that it seemed there was no air left – only that sickening smell.

And there was something else – something that shouldn't have been, something nobody could explain.

There were bones scattered in the room, human bones, a man's bones – and sharp, deep marks in Mrs Manifold's neck where she had been choked, and pieces of cloth and a battered old hat I had seen once before on a night when the fog was yellow in the light at the desk of the Sailors' Rest ...

There was nothing Scotland Yard could say to explain all that.

But then, there was no reason why they should think of any connexion between what happened up there in that gable room where Mrs Manifold was hiding and what they found up the Thames from its mouth, far up, in Wapping. An old wine cask out of Singapore, a cask that had once held Madeira and now was stove in at one end, and held nothing but the bones of two toes and a finger – nothing to tell them that Mrs Manifold had killed her husband and put his body in that cask of wine and had it carried far out to sea, weighted perhaps, to sink until time and the tide carried it far from Singapore – just as whatever it was came into the Sailors' Rest that foggy night put it down in the register –

'*Amb. Manifold, late of Singapore, out of Madeira.*'

Or was it somebody's ghoulish sense of humour? Out of Madeira indeed! I cannot abide the smell of it to this day!

The Two Vaynes

L. P. Hartley

Those garden-statues! My host was pardonably proud of them. They crowned the balustrade of the terrace; they flanked its steps; they dominated the squares and oblongs – high, roofless chambers of clipped yew – which, seen from above, had somewhat the appearance of a chess-board. In fact, they peopled the whole vast garden; and as we went from one to another in the twilight of a late September evening, I gave up counting them. Some stood on low plinths on the closely-shaven grass; others, water-deities, rose out of goldfish-haunted pools. Each was supreme in its own domain and enveloped in mystery, secrecy and silence.

'What do you call these?' I asked my host, indicating the enclosures. 'They have such an extraordinary shut-in feeling.'

'Temene,' he said, carefully stressing the three syllables. 'Temenos is Greek for the precincts of a god.'

'The Greeks had a word for it,' I said, but he was not amused.

Some of the statues were of grey stone, on which lichen grew in golden patches; others were of lead, the sooty hue of which seemed sun-proof. These were already gathering to themselves the coming darkness: perhaps they had never really let it go.

It was the leaden figures that my host most resembled; in his sober country clothes of almost clerical cut – breeches, tight at the knee, sur-mounting thin legs cased in black stockings, with something recalling a Norfolk jacket on top – he looked so like one of his own duskier exhibits that, as the sinking sun plunged the temene in shadow, and he stood with outstretched arm pointing at a statue that was also pointing, he might have been mistaken for one.

'I have another to show you,' he said, 'and then I'll let you go and dress.'

Rather to my surprise, he took my arm and steered me to the opening, which, I now saw, was in the further corner. (Each temenos had an inlet and an outlet, to connect it with its neighbours.) As we passed through, he let go of my arm and bent down as though to tie up his

shoe-lace. I walked slowly on towards a figure which, even at this distance, seemed in some way to differ from the others.

They were all gods and goddesses, nymphs and satyrs, dryads and
oreads, divinities of the ancient world: but this was not. I quickened
my steps. It was the figure of a man in modern dress, and something
about it was familiar. But was it a statue? Involuntarily I stood still
and looked back. My host was not following me; he had disappeared.
Yet here he was, facing me, with his arm stretched out, almost as if
he were going to shake hands with me. But no; the bent forefinger showed
that he was beckoning.

Again I looked behind me to the opening now shrouded in shadow,
but there was no one. Stifling my repugnance, and to be frank, my fear,
and putting into my step all the defiance I could muster, I approached
the figure. It was smiling with the faint sweet smile of invitation that
one sees in some of Leonardo's pictures. So life-like was the smile, such
a close copy of the one I had seen on my host's face, that I stopped
again, wondering which to believe: my common sense or my senses.
While I was debating, a laugh rang out. I jumped – the figure might
have uttered it; it sounded so near. But the smiling features never
changed, and a second later I saw my host coming to me across the
grass.

He laughed again, less histrionically, and rather uncertainly I joined
in.

'Well,' he said, 'you must forgive my practical joke. But you'll understand how it amuses me to see what my guests will *do* when they see
that figure. I've had a hole made through the hedge to watch. Some
of them have been quite frightened. Some see through the trick at once
and laugh before I get the chance to – the joke is then on me. But
most of them do what you did – start and stop, and start and stop,
wondering if they can trust their eyes. It's fun watching people when
they don't know they are being watched. I can always tell which are
the ... the imaginative ones.'

I laughed a little wryly.

'Cheer up,' he said, though I would have rather he had not noticed
my loss of poise. 'You came through the ordeal very well. Not an absolute
materialist like the brazen ones, who know no difference between seeing
and believing. And not – certainly not – well, a funk, like some of them.
Mind you, I don't despise them for it. You stood your ground. A well-
balanced man, I should say, hard-headed but open-minded, cautious but
resolute. You said you were a writer?'

'In my spare time,' I mumbled.

'Then you are used to looking behind appearances.'

While he was speaking, I compared him to the figure, and though
the general resemblance was striking – the same bold nose, the same

retreating forehead – I wondered how I could have been taken in by it. The statue's texture was so different! Lead, I supposed. Having lost my superstitious horror, I came nearer. I detected a thin crack in the black stocking, and thoughtlessly put my finger-nail into it.

'Don't do that,' he warned me. 'The plaster flakes off so easily.'

I apologized. 'I didn't mean to pull your leg. But is it plaster? It's so dark, as dark as, well – your suit.'

'It was painted that colour,' my host said, 'to make the likeness closer.'

I looked again. The statue's face and hands were paler than its clothes, but only a pale shade of the same tone. And this, I saw, was true to life. A leaden tint underlay my host's natural swarthiness.

'But the other statues are of stone, aren't they?' I asked.

'Yes,' he said, 'they are. This one was an experiment.'

'An experiment?'

'My experiment,' he said. 'I made it.' He did not try to conceal his satisfaction.

'How clever of you!' I exclaimed, stepping back to examine the cast more critically. 'It's you to the life. It almost seems to move.'

'Move?' he repeated, his voice distant and discouraging.

'Yes, move,' I said, excited by my fantasy. 'Don't you see how flat the grass is round it? Wouldn't a statue let the grass grow under its feet?'

He answered still more coldly: 'My gardeners have orders to clip the grass with shears.'

Snubbed and anxious to retrieve myself, I said, 'Oh, but it's the living image!' I remembered the motto on his crested writing-paper. '*Vayne sed non vanus*. I adore puns. "Vayne but not vain." You but not you. How do you translate it?'

'We usually say, "Vayne but not empty".' My host's voice sounded mollified.

'How apt!' I prattled on. 'It's Vayne all right, but is it empty? Is it just a suit of clothes?'

He looked hard at me and said:

'Doesn't the apparel oft proclaim the man?'

'Of course,' I said, delighted by the quickness of his answer. But isn't this Vayne a bigger man than you are – in the physical sense, I mean?'

'I like things to be over-life size,' he replied. 'I have a passion for the grand scale.'

'And here you are able to indulge it,' I said, glancing towards the great house which made a rectangle of intense dark in the night sky.

'But service isn't what it was before the war,' he rather platitudinously remarked. 'The trouble I've had, looking for a footman! Still, I think you'll find your bath has been turned on for you.'

I took the hint and was moving away when suddenly he called me back.

'Look!' he said, 'don't let's change for dinner. I've got an idea. Fair-clough hasn't been before; it's his first visit, too. He hasn't seen the statues. After dinner we'll play a game of hide and seek. I'll hide, and you and he shall seek – here, among the statues. It may be a bit dull for you, because you'll be in the secret. But if you're bored, you can hunt for me, too – I don't think you'll find me. That's the advantage of knowing the terrain – perhaps rather an unfair one. We'll have a time-limit. If you haven't found me within twenty minutes, I'll make a bolt for home, whatever the circumstances.'

'Where will "home" be?'

'I'll tell you later. But don't say anything to Fairclough.'

I promised not to. 'But, forgive me,' I said, 'I don't quite see the point—'

'Don't you? What I want to happen is for Fairclough to mistake the statue for me. I want to see him ... well ... startled by it.'

'He might tackle it low and bring it crashing down.'

My host looked at me with narrowed eyes.

'If you think that, you don't know him. He's much too timid. He won't touch it – they never do until they know what it is.'

By 'they' I supposed him to mean his dupes, past, present and to come.

We talked a little more and parted.

I found the footman laying out my dress-suit on the bed. I told him about not changing and asked if Mr Fairclough had arrived yet.

'Yes, sir, he's in his room.'

'Could you take me to it?'

I followed along a passage inadequately lit by antique hanging lanterns, most of which were solid at the bottom.

Fairclough was changing. I told him we were to wear our ordinary clothes.

'What!' he exclaimed. 'But he always changes for dinner.'

'Not this evening.' I didn't altogether like my rôle of accomplice, but Fairclough had the weakness of being a know-all. Perhaps it would do him no harm to be surprised for once.

'I wonder if Postgate changed,' I said, broaching the topic which had been exercising my mind ever since I set foot in the house.

'He must have done,' said Fairclough. 'Didn't you know? His dress-clothes were never found.'

'I don't remember the story at all well,' I prompted him.

'There's very little to remember,' Fairclough said. 'He arrived, as we have; they separated to change for dinner, as we have; and he was never seen or heard of again.'

'There were other guests, weren't there?'

'Yes, the house was full of people.'

'When exactly did it happen?'

'Three years ago, two years after Vayne resigned the chairmanship.'

'Postgate had a hand in that, hadn't he?'

'Yes, don't you know?' said Fairclough. 'It was rather generous of Vayne to forgive him in the circumstances. It didn't make much difference to Vayne; he'd probably have resigned in any case, when he inherited this place from his uncle. It was meant to be a sort of reconciliation party, burying the hatchet, and all that.'

I agreed that it was magnanimous of Vayne to make it up with someone who had got him sacked. 'And he's still loyal to the old firm,' I added, 'or we shouldn't be here.'

'Yes, and we're such small fry,' Fairclough said. 'It's the company, not us, he's being kind to.'

I thought of the small ordeal ahead of Fairclough, but it hardly amounted to a breach of kindness.

'I suppose we mustn't mention Postgate to him?' I said.

'Why not? I believe he likes to talk about him. Much better for him than bottling it up.'

'Would you call him a vain man?' I asked.

'Certainly, Vayne by name and vain by nature.'

'He seemed rather pleased with himself as a sculptor,' I remarked.

'A sculptor?' echoed Fairclough.

I realized my indiscretion, but had gone too far to draw back. 'Yes, didn't you know?' I asked maliciously. 'He's done a statue. A sort of portrait. And he talks of doing some more. Portraits of his friends in plaster. He asked me if I'd be his model.'

'I wonder if he'd do one of me?' asked Fairclough, with instinctive egotism. 'I should make rather a good statue, I think.' Half-undressed, he surveyed himself in the mirror. Long and willowy, fair complexioned as his name, he had a bulging knobby forehead under a thin thatch of hair. 'Did you say yes?' he asked.

'I said I couldn't stand, but if he would make it a recumbent effigy, I would lie to him.'

We both laughed.

'Where's his studio?' asked Fairclough, almost humbly.

'Underground. He says he prefers to work by artificial light.'

We both thought about this, and some association of ideas made me ask:

'Is the house haunted?'

'Not that I ever heard of,' Fairclough said. 'But there's a legend about a bath.'

'A bath?'

'Yes, it's said to be on the site of an old lift-shaft, and to go up and down. Funny how such stories get about. And talking of baths,' Fairclough went on, 'I must be getting into mine. You may not know it, but he doesn't like one to be a minute late.'

'Just let me look at it,' I said. 'Mine's down a passage. You have one of your own, you lucky dog.'

We inspected the appointments, which were marble and luxurious, and very up to date, except for the bath itself, which was an immense, old-fashioned mahogany contraption with a lid.

'A lid!' I exclaimed. 'Don't you know the story of the Mistletoe Bough?' Fairclough clearly didn't, and with this parting shot I left him.

In spite of Fairclough's warning, I was a few minutes late for dinner. How that came about occupied my thoughts throughout the marvellous meal, though I could not bring myself to speak of it and would much rather not have thought about it. I'm afraid I was a dull guest, and Vayne himself was less animated than he had been before dinner. After dinner, however, he cheered up, and when he was giving us our orders for the evening, editing them somewhat for Fairclough's benefit, he had recovered all his old assurance. We were to divide, he said; I was to take the left-hand range of yew compartments, or temene, as he liked to call them, Fairclough the right. From the top of the terrace steps, a long steep flight, he indicated to us our spheres of action. 'And home will be here, where I'm standing,' he wound up. 'I'll call "coo-ee" when I'm ready.'

He strolled off in the direction of the house. Fairclough and I walked cautiously down the steps on to the great circle of grass from which the two blocks of temene diverged. Here we bowed ceremoniously and parted. Fairclough disappeared into the black wall of yew.

At last I was alone with my thoughts. Of course it was only another of Vayne's practical jokes; I realized that now. But at the moment when it happened, I was scared stiff. And I still couldn't help wondering what would have become of me if – well, if I had got into the bath. I just put my foot in, as I often do, to test the water. I didn't pull it out at once, for the water was rather cool. In fact I put my whole weight on it.

'Coo-ee!'

Now the hunt was up. Fairclough would be peering in the shadows. But mine was merely a spectator's rôle; I was Vayne's stooge. His stooge . . .

Directly I felt something give, I pulled my foot out, and the lid came down and the bath sank through the floor like a coffin at a cremation service. Goodness, how frightened I was! I heard the click as the bath touched bottom; but I couldn't see it down the shaft. Then I heard rumbling again, and saw the bath-lid coming up. But I did not risk getting in, not I.

'Coo-ee!'

I jumped. It sounded close beside me. I moved into another temenos, trying to pretend that I was looking for Vayne. Really it would serve him right if I gave him away to Fairclough. He had no business to frighten people like that.

'Coo-ee!'

Right over on Fairclough's side, now. But it sounded somehow different; was it an owl? It might not be very easy to find Fairclough; there must be half a hundred of these blasted temene, and the moon was hidden by clouds. he might go out through one opening just as I was entering by another, and so we might go on all night. Thank goodness the night was warm. But what a silly farce it was.

I could just see to read my watch. Another quarter of an hour to go. Fairclough must be getting jumpy. I'll go and find him, I thought, and put him wise about the figure. Vayne would never know. Or would he? One couldn't tell where he was, he might be in the next temenos, watching me through a hole.

A light mist was descending, which obscured the heads of such statues as I could see projecting above the high walls of the temene. If it grew thicker, I might not see Fairclough even if he were close to me, and we might wander about till Doomsday – at least, for another ten minutes, which seemed just as long to wait.

I looked down, and saw that my feet had left tracks, dark patches in the wet grass. They seemed to lead in all directions. But were they all mine? Had I really walked about as much as that? I tried to identify the footprints and see if they tallied.

'Coo-ee!'

That almost certainly was an owl; the sound seemed to come from above. But perhaps Vayne added ventriloquism to his other accomplishments. He was capable of anything. Not a man one could trust. Postgate hadn't trusted him – not, at least, as the chairman of the company.

It was my duty, I now felt, to warn Fairclough. And I should be quite glad to see him myself, quite glad. But where was he?

I found myself running from one temenos to another and getting back to the one I started from. I could tell by the figure: at least that didn't move. I started off again. Steady, steady. Here was a temenos with no footprints on it – a virgin temenos. I crossed it and found myself in the central circle. I crossed that too.

Now I was in Fairclough's preserves. Poor Fairclough! To judge by the footprints, he had been running round even more than I had. But were they all his? Here was the figure of Pan – the god of panic. Very appropriate.

'Fairclough! Fairclough!' I began to call as loudly as I dared, having nearly but not quite lost my head.

'Fairclough! Fairclough!' I couldn't bring myself to hug the walls; the shadows were too thick; I stuck to the middle of each space.

I suppose I was expecting to find him, and yet when I heard him answer 'Here!' I nearly jumped out of my skin. He was crouching against a hedge. He evidently had the opposite idea from mine; he felt the hedge was a protection; and I had some difficulty in persuading him to come out into the open.

'Listen!' I whispered. 'What you've got to do is —'

'But I've seen him,' Fairclough said. 'There's his footmark.'

I looked: the footmark was long and slurred, quite unlike his or mine.

'If you were sure it was him,' I said, 'why didn't you speak to him?'

'I did,' said Fairclough, 'but he didn't answer. he didn't even turn round.'

'Someone may have got into the garden,' I said, 'some third person. But we'll find out. I'll take you to the statue.'

'The statue?'

'I'll explain afterwards.'

I had regained my confidence, but could not remember in which direction Vayne's statue lay.

Suddenly I had an idea.

'We'll follow the footprints.'

'Which?' asked Fairclough.

'Well, the other person's.'

Easy to say; easy to distinguish them from ours; but which way were they pointing? That was the question.

'He walks on his heels,' I said. 'It's this way.'

We followed and reached the temenos where the statue had stood. No possibility of mistake. We saw the patches of dead grass where its feet had been; we saw the footprints leading away from them. But the statue was not there.

'Vayne!' I shouted. 'Vayne!'

'Coo-ee!' came a distant call.

'To the steps,' I cried. 'To the steps! Let's go together!'

Vayne was standing on the terrace steps: I saw him plainly; and I also saw the figure that was stalking him: the other Vayne. Two Vaynes. Vayne our host, the shorter of the two, stood lordly, confident, triumphing over the night. 'Coo-ee!' he hooted to his moonlit acres. 'Coo-ee!' But the other Vayne had crept up the grass slope and was crouching at his back.

For a moment the two figures stood one behind the other, motionless as cats. Then a scream rang out; there was a whirl of limbs, like the Manxman's wheel revolving; a savage snarl, a headlong fall, a crash. Both fell, both Vaynes. When the thuds of their descent were over, silence reigned.

They were lying in a heap together, a tangled heap of men and plaster. A ceiling might have fallen on them, yet it was not a ceiling; it was almost a third man, for the plaster fragments still bore a human shape. Both Vaynes were dead but one of them, we learned afterwards, had been dead for a long time. And this Vayne was not Vayne at all, but Postgate.

August Heat

W. F. Harvey

PENISTONE ROAD, CLAPHAM,
20th August, 190–.

I have had what I believe to be the most remarkable day in my life, and while the events are still in my mind, I wish to put them down on paper as clearly as possible.

Let me say at the outset that my name is James Clarence Withencroft. I am forty years old, in perfect health, never having known a day's illness. By profession I am an artist, not a very successful one, but I earn enough money by my black-and-white work to satisfy my necessary wants. My only near relative, a sister, died five years ago, so that I am independent.

I breakfasted this morning at nine, and after glancing through the morning paper I lighted my pipe and proceeded to let my mind wander in the hope that I might chance upon some subject for my pencil.

The room, though door and windows were open, was oppressively hot, and I had just made up my mind that the coolest and most comfortable place in the neighbourhood would be the deep end of the public swimming-bath, when the idea came.

I began to draw. So intent was I on my work that I left my lunch untouched, only stopping work when the clock of St Jude's stuck four.

The final result, for a hurried sketch, was, I felt sure, the best thing I had done. It showed a criminal in the dock immediately after the judge had pronounced sentence. The man was fat – enormously fat. The flesh hung in rolls about his chin; it creased his huge, stumpy neck. He was clean-shaven (perhaps I should say a few days before he must have been clean-shaven) and almost bald. He stood in the dock, his short, clumsy fingers clasping the rail, looking straight in front of him. The feeling that his expression conveyed was not so much one of horror as of utter, absolute collapse.

There seemed nothing in the man strong enough to sustain that mountain of flesh.

I rolled up the sketch, and without quite knowing why, placed it in my pocket. Then with the rare sense of happiness which the knowledge of a good thing well done gives, I left the house.

I believe that I set out with the idea of calling upon Trenton, for I remember walking along Lytton Street and turning to the right along Gilchrist Road at the bottom of the hill where the men were at work on the new tram lines.

From there onwards I have only the vaguest recollection of where I went. The one thing of which I was fully conscious was the awful heat, that came up from the dusty asphalt pavement as an almost palpable wave. I longed for the thunder promised by the great banks of copper-coloured cloud that hung low over the western sky.

I must have walked five or six miles, when a small boy roused me from my reverie by asking the time.

It was twenty minutes to seven.

When he left me I began to take stock of my bearings. I found myself standing before a gate that led into a yard bordered by a strip of thirsty earth, where there were flowers, purple stock and scarlet geranium. Above the entrance was a board with the inscription:

CHS. ATKINSON.   MONUMENTAL MASON.
WORKER IN ENGLISH AND ITALIAN MARBLES.

From the yard itself came a cheery whistle, the noise of hammer blows, and the cold sound of steel meeting stone.

A sudden impulse made me enter.

A man was sitting with his back towards me, busy at work on a slab of curiously veined marble. He turned round as he heard my steps and I stopped short.

It was the man I had been drawing, whose portrait lay in my pocket.

He sat there, huge and elephantine, the sweat pouring from his scalp, which he wiped with a red silk handkerchief. But though the face was the same, the expression was absolutely different.

He greeted me smiling, as if we were old friends, and shook my hand.

I apologized for my intrusion.

'Everything is hot and glary outside,' I said. 'This seems an oasis in the wilderness.'

'I don't know about the oasis,' he replied, 'but it certainly is hot, as hot as hell. Take a seat, sir!'

He pointed to the end of the gravestone on which he was at work, and I sat down.

'That's a beautiful piece of stone you've got hold of,' I said.

He shook his head. 'In a way it is,' he answered; 'the surface here is as fine as anything you could wish, but there's a big flaw at the back, though I don't expect you'd ever notice it. I could never make really a good job of a bit of marble like that. It would be all right in a summer like this; it wouldn't mind the blasted heat. But wait till the winter comes. There's nothing quite like frost to find out the weak points in stone.'

'Then what's it for?' I asked.

The man burst out laughing.

'You'd hardly believe me if I was to tell you it's for an exhibition, but it's the truth. Artists have exhibitions: so do grocers and butchers; we have them too. All the latest little things in headstones, you know.'

He went on to talk of marbles, which sort best withstood wind and rain, and which were easiest to work; then of his garden and a new sort of carnation he had bought. At the end of every other minute he would drop his tools, wipe his shining head, and curse the heat.

I said little, for I felt uneasy. There was something unnatural, uncanny, in meeting this man.

I tried at first to persuade myself that I had seen him before, that his face, unknown to me, had found a place in some out-of-the-way corner of my memory, but I knew that I was practising little more than a plausible piece of self-deception.

Mr Atkinson finished his work, spat on the ground, and got up with a sigh of relief.

'There! what do you think of that?' he said, with an air of evident pride.

The inscription which I read for the first time was this:

SACRED TO THE MEMORY
OF
JAMES CLARENCE WITHENCROFT.
BORN JAN. 18TH, 1860.
HE PASSED AWAY VERY SUDDENLY
ON AUGUST 20TH, 190–
'In the midst of life we are in death'

For some time I sat in silence. Then a cold shudder ran down my spine. I asked him where he had seen the name.

'Oh, I didn't see it anywhere,' replied Mr Atkinson. 'I wanted some name, and I put down the first that came into my head. Why do you want to know?'

'It's a strange coincidence, but it happens to be mine.'

He gave a long, low whistle. 'And the dates?'

'I can only answer for one of them, and that's correct.'

'It's a rum go!' he said.

But he knew less than I did. I told him of my morning's work. I took the sketch from my pocket and showed it to him. As he looked, the expression of his face altered until it became more and more like that of the man I had drawn.

'And it was only the day before yesterday,' he said, 'that I told Maria there were no such things as ghosts!'

Neither of us had seen a ghost, but I knew what he meant.

'You probably heard my name,' I said.

'And you must have seen me somewhere and have forgotten it! Were you at Clacton-on-Sea last July?'

I had never been to Clacton in my life. We were silent for some time. We were both looking at the same thing, the two dates on the gravestone, and one was right.

'Come inside and have some supper,' said Mr Atkinson.

His wife is a cheerful little woman, with the flaky red cheeks of the country-bred. Her husband introduced me as a friend of his who was an artist. The result was unfortunate, for after the sardines and watercress had been removed, she brought out a Doré Bible, and I had to sit and express my admiration for nearly half an hour.

I went outside, and found Atkinson sitting on the gravestone smoking. We resumed the conversation at the point we had left off.

'You must excuse my asking,' I said, 'but do you know of anything you've done for which you could be put on trial?'

He shook his head.

'I'm not a bankrupt, the business is prosperous enough. Three years ago I gave turkeys to some of the guardians at Christmas, but that's all I can think of. And they were small ones, too,' he added as an after-thought.

He got up, fetched a can from the porch, and began to water the flowers. 'Twice a day regular in the hot weather,' he said, 'and then the heat sometimes gets the better of the delicate ones. And ferns, good Lord! they could never stand it. Where do you live?'

I told him my address. It would take an hour's quick walk to get back home.

'It's like this,' he said. 'We'll look at the matter straight. If you go back home tonight, you take your chance of accidents. A cart may run over you, and there's always banana skins and orange peel, to say nothing of falling ladders.'

He spoke of the improbable with an intense seriousness that would have been laughable six hours before. But I did not laugh.

'The best thing we can do,' he continued, 'is for you to stay here till twelve o'clock. We'll go upstairs and smoke; it may be cooler inside.' To my surprise I agreed.

We are sitting now in a long, low room beneath the eaves. Atkinson has sent his wife to bed. He himself is busy sharpening some tools at a little oilstone, smoking one of my cigars the while.

The air seems charged with thunder. I am writing this at a shaky table before the open window. The leg is cracked, and Atkinson, who seems a handy man with his tools, is going to mend it as soon as he has finished putting an edge on his chisel.

It is after eleven now. I shall be gone in less than an hour.

But the heat is stifling.

It is enough to send a man mad.

Dark Journey

Francis Iles

Cayley was going to commit murder.

He had worked it all out very carefully. For weeks now his plan had been maturing. He had pondered over it, examined it, tested it in the light of every possibility; and he was satisfied that it was impregnable. Now he was going to put it into practice.

Cayley did not really want to kill Rose Fenton.

Indeed, the idea made him shudder, even when he had been drinking. But what else could he do? He was desperate. Rose would not leave him alone. She thought, too, now that she had a claim on him; and she was plainly determined to exercise it. And Cayley very much did not want to marry Rose Fenton.

He never had thought of marrying her. A solicitor's clerk, with a position to make in the world – a solicitor's clerk with every chance of an ultimate partnership in his firm – cannot afford to marry a girl like Rose Fenton. Respectability is the bread of a solicitor's life. Besides, now there was Miriam. Miriam Seale, the only daughter of old Seale himself, the senior partner in Cayley's own firm. . . .

Cayley knew now that he had been risking his whole future by taking up with Rose at all. It had not seemed like that at first. Other men have adventures, why not he? But adventures in any case are not safe for solicitors, and now Rose had decided not to be an adventure at all, but a job. As Cayley knew only too well, Rose was a determined girl. Rose knew nothing of Miriam.

It seemed curious to Cayley now to remember that once he had been quite fond of Rose. Now, of course, he detested her. He would sit for hours in his cottage over a bottle of whisky, thinking how much he hated Rose. Before Rose became impossible, Cayley had never drunk whisky alone. Now he was depending on it more and more, and one cannot go on like that. One must make an end somehow.

Rose had brought it on herself. She would not leave him alone. She would not see when an affair was – finished. Cayley did not at all want to kill Rose, but he gloated over the idea of Rose dead. And he would

never be his own man again till Rose was dead. He knew that. No;
Cayley did not at all want to kill Rose, but what else could he do?

And now he was waiting for Rose to come; waiting by the side of
the road, in the dark, with his stomach full of whisky and a revolver
in his pocket.

As he waited, Cayley felt as if he were made of lead. The night was
warm, but he felt neither warm nor cold, afraid nor brave, despairing
nor exultant. He felt nothing at all. Both body and mind seemed to
have gone inert, so that he just waited and hardly noticed whether the
time went fast or slowly.

The noise of the bus roused him from his torpor. He followed its progress along the main road: loud when the line between it and himself
was clear, with curious mufflings and dim silences when hedges or a
fold in the ground intervened. Rose was in the bus, but Cayley did not
feel any excitement at the thought. Everything had become in some
strange way inevitable.

Cayley was waiting a couple of hundred yards down a side turning.
It was a convenient little lane which Cayley had marked weeks and
weeks ago, when he first thought of killing Rose. He and Rose had
picnicked there one Sunday, on Rose's afternoon off. They had sat on
the wide grassy margin which bordered one side, and Cayley had thought
then how he would be able to wheel his motor-bicycle on to it and
put out the lights while he waited for Rose. In such a deserted spot,
in the dark, with his headlights out, it would be impossible that their
meeting could be seen.

Rose had not been able to understand at first why Cayley should
want to meet her in such an out-of-the-way place and so far from both
the cottage and from Merchester; but Cayley had been able to make
her see reason.

Both the plan in his heart and the plan on his lips depended on his
meeting with Rose remaining secret, and that had been very convenient for the former. That explained why Rose was coming to meet
him in the last bus from Stanford to Merchester, and not in that from
Merchester to Stanford, although it was in Merchester that Rose was
in service and Cayley worked.

Stanford and Merchester, both towns of some size, were eighteen miles
apart, and while it was unlikely that Rose, not indigenous to the
district, should be recognized leaving Merchester, it was almost impossible that she could be recognized leaving Stanford. Cayley had been
taking no chances at all.

The bus had grumbled to a halt just beyond the turning and roared
on again. Cayley heard footsteps coming towards him, scraping in the
dark on the gritty surface of the lane. He waited where he stood until
they were almost abreast of him, disregarding the calls of his name,

rather louder than he liked, which Rose sent out before her in waves of sound through the still night like a swimmer urging the water in front of her.

'Rose,' he said quietly.

Rose uttered a little scream. 'Coo! You didn't half make me jump. Why didn't you answer when I called?'

'Have you put your trunk and things in the cloakroom?' It was essential to Cayley's plan that Rose should have left her luggage that afternoon at Liverpool Street Station, in London.

'Course I have.... Well,' added Rose archly, 'aren't you going to give us a kiss?'

'What else do you think I've been waiting for?' Cayley's heart was beating a little faster as he kissed Rose for the last time. He thought of Judas. It made him feel uncomfortable, and he cut the kiss as short as he decently could.

Rose sniffed at him. 'Been drinking, haven't you?'

'Nothing, really,' Cayley returned easily, feeling for his bicycle in the darkness. 'Just a drop.'

'It's been too many drops with you lately, my lad. I'm going to put a stop to it. Not going to have a drunkard for a husband, I'm not.'

Cayley writhed. Rose's voice was full of possession; full of complacent assurance that in future he would have no life but what she chose to allow him. Had any qualms remained in him, that tone of Rose's would have dispelled them.

'Come on,' he said sharply. 'Let's get off.'

'All right, all right. In a great hurry, aren't you? Where's the bike? Coo, I never saw it. It's that dark.'

Cayley had wheeled the bicycle into the lane and switched on the headlight. He helped Rose into the side-car, and jumped into his saddle.

'All serene. So off we go, on our honeymoon,' giggled Rose. 'Fancy you and me on our honeymoon, Norm.'

'Yes,' said Cayley. It was odd that, though this was the last time they would ever be together, Rose's hideous shortening of his Christian name grated on him as much as ever.

He drove slowly down the lane. 'See anyone you know in Stanford?' he asked as casually as possible.

'So likely, isn't it? A fat lot of people I know.'

'But did you?'

'No, Mr Inquisitive, I did not. Any more questions?'

They turned into the main road, and Cayley increased his speed.

The whisky he had drunk did not affect his driving. His hands held the machine quite steady, though he was now pushing it along as fast as it would go, anxious to arrive and get the business finished. He did not glance at Rose in the side-car beside him. Although it was the last

time that Rose would ever ride in that side-car alive, yet her presence
exasperated him as much as ever, and the way she would cock her feet
up under her so that her knees stuck up in the air. In a dim way Cayley
recognized the fact, and was surprised by it. He had expected to feel
tolerant now towards Rose's irritating ways. It was a relief to find that,
in fact, he had not softened.

Nor had his resolution weakened.

Now that it had come to the point, Cayley was quite calm.

He knew that, normally, he was not always calm, and he had feared
lest he might lose his head and somehow bungle things: be queer in
his manner, tremble, let Rose see that something dreadful was afoot.
But there was no longer any danger of that. Rose could not guess what
was going to happen to her; and as for Cayley himself, he felt almost
indifferent, as if the matter had all been taken somehow out of his hands.
The whole affair was preordained; events were moving forward of their
own volition; nothing that he, or Rose, or anyone else, might do now
could alter them.

Cayley drove on in a fatalistic trance. He realized vaguely that Rose
was protesting against the speed, but disregarded her. It was no use
Rose protesting against anything now.

Cayley's lonely little cottage was not on the main road. It, too, was
down a side turning, and a good half-mile from the village. The village
itself, with its couple of dozen cottages and two little shops, was tiny
enough, but Cayley had always been glad that he was half a mile from
it. He liked solitude. Since he had determined to kill Rose, he had realized
how his liking for solitude had played into his hands. Even so small
a thing as that was going to help to destroy Rose.

As he turned off the main road his love of solitude rose up in him
in a passionate wave. Had Rose really imagined that he was going to
let her into that little corner of the world that he had made for himself
– Rose, with her inevitable vulgarity of speech and mind?

A tremor of hatred shook him as he saw her sturdy form trampling
about the house which, a fire-blackened ruin when he bought it out
of his small savings, he had rebuilt with his own hands; Rose, marching
like a grenadier through the garden he had created; Rose, so assured
in her ownership of it all that he would be made to feel an interloper
in his own tiny domain. Miriam would never be like that. Besides, Miriam
was . . .

Cayley thought fiercely how peaceful everything would be again once
Rose was dead: how peaceful, and how hopeful.

A hundred yards away from the cottage he shut off his engine. Late
though the time was, it was just possible that old Mrs Wace, who 'did'
for him, might not yet have gone. She liked to potter and potter in
the evenings, and Cayley had not been so foolish as to try to hustle

her off the premises early. And slightly deaf though she was, Cayley had already been careful to find out that she could hear his motor-cycle drive up to the little shed at the bottom of the garden where he kept it.

Rose, of course, expostulated when his engine stopped, but Cayley was ready for that.

'Run out of juice,' he explained glibly. 'Lucky we got nearly home. Give me a hand to push her, Rose.'

'Well, that's a nice thing to ask a girl, I must say,' objected Rose for form's sake.

Between them they pushed the bicycle past the cottage.

Before they reached the shed, Rose evidently considered it due to herself to protest further.

'Here, this is a bit too much like hard work for me. You didn't ought to ask me to do a thing like that, Norm, and that's a fact.'

'All right,' Cayley said mildly. 'I can manage alone now.' There were indeed only a few more yards to cover.

'Well, it's your own fault, isn't it?'

Cayley did not answer. The bicycle was heavy, and he needed all his breath. Rose walked behind him.

'Here, half a mo'. I'll get my suit-case out before you put the bike away, if you *don't* mind.'

'It doesn't matter,' Cayley threw back over his shoulder. 'I'll get it out in a minute.'

He brought the bicycle to a standstill outside the shed and opened the door.

Rose, a dim figure in the velvety August night, was peering up at the stars.

'Coo, it's black enough for you to-night, I should think. Never known it so dark, I haven't.'

'The moon doesn't rise till after midnight,' Cayley answered absently, busy turning the bicycle round in the lane. It was better to turn it now, then it would be ready.

'Proper night to elope, and no mistake,' Rose's voice came rallyingly. 'Is that why you chose it, eh? Getting quite sloppy in your old age, Norm, aren't you? Well, that'll be a nice change, I must say.'

Cayley straightened up from the bicycle and wiped the sweat from his forehead. 'Why?'

'Oh, nothing. I just thought you'd been a bit stand-offish lately.' There was a sentimental, almost a yearning note in Rose's voice.

'Nonsense, darling. Of course I haven't.'

'In fact, I don't mind telling you, I thought at one time you didn't mean to treat me right.'

'I'm going to treat you right, Rose,' said Cayley.

'Still love us, Norm?'

'Of course I do.'

'Where are you, then?'

Cayley's fingers closed round the small revolver in his pocket. 'Here.'

'Well, can't you come a bit closer?' Rose giggled.

Cayley took her arm. 'Come inside the shed for a minute, Rose.'

'What ever for?'

'I want you to.'

Rose giggled again. 'Coo, Norm, you are a one, aren't you?'

Cayley's mouth and throat were dry as he drew Rose across the threshold and closed the door. But he was not really afraid. The dream-like state was on him again. Things were not real. All this had happened somewhere before. Rose was dead already. The two of them were only enacting, like ghosts, a deed that had been performed ages and ages ago, in some other existence; every movement and word had been already laid down, and there could be neither deviation nor will to deviate.

Once more Rose uttered her silly, throaty giggle.

'What do you want to shut the door for? I should have thought it was dark enough already.'

Cayley had already proved, by repeated experiment, that with the door of the shed closed Mrs Wace, even if she were in the cottage, could not hear a revolver-shot; but of course, he could not tell Rose that.

He drew the revolver from his pocket. He was still quite calm.

Hot hands were clutching for him in the darkness and he held the revolver out of their reach.

'Honest, I'm ever so fond of you, Norm,' whispered Rose.

'So am I of you, Rose. Where are you?'

'Well, that's a nice question. Where do you think I am? Can't you feel me?'

'Yes.' Cayley found her shoulder and gripped it gently while he edged behind her. Methodically he felt for the back of her neck and placed the muzzle of the revolver against it.

'Here, mind my hat, *if* you please. Here ... what's the game, Morm?'

Cayley fired.

The shot sounded so deafeningly loud in the little shed that it seemed to Cayley as if anyone not only at the cottage but in the village, too, must have heard it. A spasm of terror shook him. How could anyone in the whole of England not have heard it? He stood rigid, listening for the alarm that must inevitably follow.

Everything was quiet.

Cayley pulled himself together. Of course, the shot had been no louder than his experiments in the daytime. There was no time now to give way to fantastic panic of that sort. He realized that he was still holding Rose's body in his arms. He had been so close to her when he fired that she had slumped down against him, and he had caught her methodically. He laid her now on the floor of the shed. Then he lighted a stub of candle which he had brought here days ago for just that purpose. There was no window in the shed, and the door was still closed.

Cayley could not believe that Rose was dead.

It had been too easy, too quick. She could not have died in that tiny instant. Not Rose. She was too vigorous, too vital, to have the life blown out of her like that in a tiny fraction of a second.

He looked at her lying there, in her best frock of saxe-blue silk, her black straw hat, brown shoes, and pink silk stockings. People bled, didn't they, when they were shot? But there was no blood. Rose was not bleeding at all.

Cayley's forehead broke out into a cold sweat. Rose was not really dead, after all! He had missed her, somehow, in the darkness. The gun had not been touching her head at all, it had been touching something else. Rose was only stunned. Perhaps not even stunned: just pretending to be stunned: shamming.

Cayley dropped on his knees beside her and felt frantically for her heart. He knew Rose was dead, but he could not believe it. Her heart gave no movement.

'Rose!' he said, in a shaky voice. 'Rose – can't you speak to me? Rose!' He could not believe Rose was dead.

Rose lay on her back staring up at the roof of the little shed, her eyelids just drooping over her eyes. Cayley did not know why he had spoken to her aloud. Of course Rose could not answer. She was dead.

The tears came into Cayley's own eyes. He understood now that it was too late, that there had never been any need to kill Rose at all. He could have managed everything by being firm. Just by being firm. Rose would have understood. Rose had always been sensible. And now, for the want of a little firmness, Rose was dead and he was a murderer.

'Oh, God,' he moaned, 'I wish I hadn't done it. Oh, God, I wish I hadn't done it.'

But he had done it, and Rose was dead. Cayley got up slowly from his knees.

It was dreadful to see Rose lying there, with her head on the floor. There was an old pillion cushion on the shelf. Cayley took it down and put it under Rose's head. Somehow that made her look better.

Besides – Rose might not be dead. If she came to it would be nicer for her to have a cushion under her head.

Cayley stiffened. Had that been a noise outside? He stood stock-still, hardly daring to breathe. Was someone prowling about? He listened desperately. It was not easy to listen very well, because the blood was pounding so in his ears. It made a kind of muffled drumming, like waves on a distant shingle beach. Beyond the drumming he could detect no sound.

Very slowly he lifted the latch of the door. It was stiff, and for all his caution rose with a final jerk. Cayley started violently. The latch had made only a tiny click, but in his ears it had sounded like the crack of doom.

He edged the door open, got outside, and closed it behind him. Then he stood still, listening again. There was no sound. He began to walk softly towards the cottage, fifty yards away.

He walked more and more slowly. A horrible feeling had suddenly taken possession of him: that someone was following, just as softly, in his tracks. The back of his head tingled and pricked as the hair lifted itself on his scalp; for something was telling him that the door of the shed had opened and Rose had come noiselessly out. Now she was following him.

He could feel her presence, just behind him. Cold beads chased each other down his back. He tried to turn his head to make sure that Rose was not really there, but could not. It was physically impossible for him to look back towards the door of the shed. All he could do was to stand still and listen, between the pounding of the waves in his ears. The flesh of his back quivered and crept. Every second he expected Rose to come up and touch him on it. He could almost feel her touch already. It was all he could do to stop himself from shrieking.

At last, with a little sob, he forced himself to turn round.

There was nothing but inky darkness behind him.

But somewhere in that inky darkness, between himself and the shed, Cayley could not get rid of the feeling that someone, or something, stood. He dragged the revolver out of his pocket again and levelled it at the shed. At any moment a shape might loom towards him out of the blackness, and he must be ready. He stood rigid, waiting, his tongue parched and his throat dry. Then, with a sudden effort, he walked rapidly back to the shed.

The door was still closed.

Cayley put the revolver back into his pocket and walked quickly over to the cottage.

Outside it he halted for a few moments, working his jaws to obtain some saliva in order to moisten his tongue and throat. The kitchen was at the back of the cottage. As he peered round the angle, Cayley could see the light streaming out of the window. Mrs Wace had not gone.

Cayley's knees shook together. Mrs Wace had not gone, and she must have heard the shot. It was impossible that she could not have heard it, deaf as she was. He had miscalculated in his experiments. They had been made in the day-time, and sound travels further in the silence of night. He had not allowed for that. Mrs Wace had heard the shot, and now she was waiting to find out what it meant. Cayley stood for a minute in the grip of a panic so violent that his limbs shook and his teeth chattered, and he could not control them. It was all he could do at last to drag himself round the corner of the house, and, unseen, stare through the uncurtained kitchen window.

Mrs Wace was doing something by the larder door. She had her hat and coat on. Cayley watched her take up three onions, look at them, drop one into a string-bag and put the other two back into the larder. He searched her face. There seemed to be nothing on it but pre-occupation with what she was doing. Was it possible that she had not heard the shot after all?

He walked quickly round to the front of the house and went into his living-room.

From a cupboard on the wall he took a whisky-bottle and a glass. Then, putting back the glass, he pulled the cork out of the bottle and put the mouth of it to his lips, gulping down the neat spirit in thirsty haste. Not until half its remaining contents had gone did he put the bottle back on the shelf.

Almost immediately the stuff did him good. He waited a moment while the heartening glow steadied his limbs. Then he walked firmly into the kitchen.

Mrs Wace was just going out through the back door. She stopped when she saw him, and it seemed to Cayley that she looked at him queerly.

Cayley's fingers tightened round the revolver in his pocket as he searched her face.

'Ah, back, are you?' said Mrs Wace comfortably.

Cayley breathed with relief. His fingers relaxed on the revolver. The next instant they tightened again.

'Back? I haven't been away. I've been sitting in the garden, smoking.'

'Well, there's no accounting for tastes,' observed Mrs Wace in-differently. 'Good night, Mr Cayley.'

'Good night, Mrs Wace.'

Cayley went back to his living-room, his knees weak with relief. If Mrs Wace had heard anything, or voiced any suspicion, he would have shot her dead. He knew he would. It would have been madness, but he would have done it. He took the whisky-bottle and tumbler from the shelf and poured himself out a stiff dose. He realized now that he was trembling.

Instantly the same feeling came to him as in the shed. Rose was not dead at all. She had only been stunned. She would come to if he gave her some whisky. He caught up the bottle and hurried with it down the garden through the dark.

Outside the door of the shed he stopped. He could not go in: he just could not go inside. Suppose after all that . . .

'Rose!' he called shakily. 'Rose!'

It took a full minute, and another swig at the bottle, before he could get a grip on himself again.

Rose was lying just as he had left her. She was quite dead.

Cayley took another, smaller mouthful of whisky and set the bottle down on the shelf with a hand that no longer shook. What a fool he had been! Everything had gone splendidly. All he had to do now was to proceed with his plan.

It was a good plan.

To her mistress in Merchester and to her only living relative, an elderly aunt, living in Streatham, Rose had written, on Cayley's instructions, that she was going out to Canada to be married. Canada somehow sounded more convincing than America. Rose really had believed that Cayley was going out to Canada, to open a branch there for his firm.

Over her luggage Cayley had been equally clever. Rose was to have left Merchester that afternoon for London, and deposited her trunk at Liverpool-street Station. In a busy place like Liverpool-street Rose would never be noticed or remembered. Equally unnoticed, Cayley would be able to claim the trunk later with the check that would be in Rose's handbag, and dispose of it at his leisure. There would be nothing at all to connect him with Rose's disappearance.

Rose had made objections, of course. When, in Merchester, she was only half-a-dozen miles from Cayley's cottage, why travel all the way up to London and come back to Stanford? But Cayley had been able to convince her. He was not leaving for Canada till the next day.

It was essential that Rose should not be seen coming to the cottage. If she were, her good name would be lost, even though they were getting married in London the next morning before sailing. The argument had gone home, for Rose was always very careful about 'what people would say.'

So though she had demurred at the expense, for she had a parsimonious mind, Rose had in the end consented. If she had not consented, Cayley would never have dared to kill her. Rose had agreed to her own death when she agreed to take her trunk up to Liverpool-street Station.

Cayley stood now, looking down at her.

He was no longer afraid of Rose's dead body. The whisky he had drunk was making him sentimental. Two tears oozed out of his eyes and ran absurdly down his cheeks. Poor old Rose. She had not been such a bad sort, really. It was a shame that he had had to kill her. A rotten shame. Cayley wished very much that he had not had to kill Rose.

In a flash, sentiment fled before a sudden jab of terror.

Suppose Rose had not brought the check for the trunk with her after all! Suppose she had left it somewhere, or given it to someone else to claim for her! Cayley saw now that he had left this weak spot in the armour of his plan.

He had taken no steps to ensure that Rose should have the check with her: he had simply taken it for granted that she would. And if she had not, and he were unable to claim the trunk, everything would miscarry. In that case the trunk would sooner or later be opened, and then it would be known that Rose had disappeared, and then . . .

Cayley shivered with fear.

In vain he tried to point out to himself that even if it did become known that Rose had disappeared, there would still be nothing to connect her disappearance with himself. In Merchester he had always kept very quiet about his relations with Rose. But his mind, numb with panic, refused to accept the reasoning. Everything hung for him on the vital question: had Rose brought the check with her?

Rose's handbag lay on the floor, half underneath her. Cayley pushed her body roughly aside to snatch it up. His fingers shook so much that he could hardly open it.

The next moment he uttered a sob of relief. The check was there. 'One trunk . . .' The words danced before his eyes. He was safe.

He took another pull at the whisky-bottle.

He was safe: and now he must proceed, quite calmly, with the rest of his plan.

Cayley would never have believed that Rose was so heavy.

It had seemed simple, in advance, to put her into the side-car, prop her there to look natural, and drive with her to the disused quarry, where her grave was already prepared, and the spade waiting to fill it in. But now that it had come to the point, it was dreadful to have to pick her up and stagger with her through the darkness, like a sack of potatoes in his arms. Cayley was gasping for breath by the time he reached the side-car.

But the physical effort had helped him. He was no longer nervous. He was exultant. It takes courage and brains to commit a successful murder. Cayley, doubtful at times before, knew now that he had both. And there were people who thought him – Cayley knew they did – a weakling, a little rat. Now he could smile at them. Rats can bite.

Before he set out for the quarry, Cayley went back to the shed. The candle had to be put out, and he wanted to have a good look round to make sure that no traces were left. The risk was infinitesimal, but Cayley was not taking even infinitesimal risks; and there are always tramps.

There were no traces. Only a few spots of blood on the leather of the cushion, which Cayley wiped off with a wisp of cotton-waste, burning the waste at once in the flame of the candle. No one could possibly tell that a newly-dead body had been lying in that shed.

Before he blew out the candle Cayley pulled the precious check for the trunk out of his trouser-pocket, where he had stuffed it, in order to stow it away more carefully in his wallet. It was funny how he had nearly lost his head just now over a little thing like that. He glanced through it gloatingly before tucking it away. The wording, which before had shimmered in a blurred way before his panic-stricken eyes, was now soberly legible.

The next instant his heart seemed to stop beating. Then it began to race faster than the engine of his own motor-cycle. For the check was not on Liverpool-street at all: not even on Stanford. It was on the station quite close to Cayley's cottage. Rose had not been up to London. She had kept the money Cayley had given her, and travelled only to the local station. Cayley had committed the fatal mistake of under-rating Rose's parsimony. And by her parsimony Rose had ensured that her last appearance alive should be inevitably connected with her lover.

With a sick horror Cayley sat down in the doorway of the shed and nursed his head in his hands. Then he moaned aloud. What was he to do now? What, in Heaven's name, could he do now?

Cayley never knew how long he had sat like that, in a lethargy of self-pity and despair, nor how long it was before coherent thought returned to him. The first shock, which galvanized his mind into activity once more, was the realization that all this time Rose was waiting for him – waiting, in the side-car. Cayley choked down the hysterical laugh which leapt in his throat. Rose never had liked waiting.

He jumped up.

Instantly, as if it had only needed the reflex action of his muscles to stimulate his brain, he saw that the position was not, after all, so desperate. The trunk would remain in the cloakroom for days, perhaps for weeks, before anything was done about it. By that time Cayley could, if the worst came to the worst, be in South America.

But perhaps the best thing to do would be to claim it boldly, in a day or two's time. It was quite unlikely that the porter-cum-clerk would remember who had left it. Rose was not known there. It was not as if suspicion would ever be roused. Suspicion is only roused when a person is reported missing. Rose never would be so reported. No, the position was not desperate at all. Cayley's spirits began to rise. The position was not even bad. Except for a small adjustment or two, his plan still held perfectly good.

He began to whistle as he wrapped a rug carefully over Rose, and drove her off. It was only a couple of miles to the quarry. In a quarter of an hour the whole business would be done.

Yes, the boldest course usually paid. He would claim the trunk him-self. And he could arrange some slight disguise, just in case of accidents. A disguise, yes. Why . . .

Cayley's thoughts broke off with a jerk. He cursed. His engine had stopped.

He came to a standstill by the side of the road. The trouble was simple: he had run out of petrol. Cayley felt terribly frightened. He had filled the tank before first setting out to meet Rose; how could it have emptied so soon? It almost looked as though Providence ...

It was not Providence, but a leaking feed-pipe. Feverishly Cayley screwed up the loose nut and delved into the side-car for the spare tin of petrol, pushing Rose to one side without a thought. He blessed his foresight in having put the tin there. Really, every possibility had been foreseen.

As he got back into the saddle once more, a sound struck his whole body into frozen immobility. Someone was approaching along the lonely country road. Someone with large, heavy feet. Someone who flashed a lamp. It was the millionth chance, and it had come off.

Cayley kicked in agony at his starter, but the carburetter had emptied. He kicked and kicked, but not even a splutter came from the engine. Then, as the footsteps drew abreast of him, he stopped kicking and waited, petrified.

'Hullo,' said the constable. 'Breakdown?'

Cayley's dry tongue rustled over his drier lips. 'No,' he managed to mutter. 'Just – just filling up ... petrol.'

'Oh, it's you Mr Cayley. Ah! Fine night.'

'Yes. Well, I must be getting on.' Cayley prayed that his voice did not sound such a croak as he feared. The light of the constable's lamp flickered over him, and he winced. Before he could stop himself, the words had jumped out, 'Switch that light of yours off, man.'

'Sorry, Mr Cayley, I'm sure.' The constable sounded hurt.

'It was blinding me,' Cayley muttered.

'Ah, new battery. Well, good night, Mr Cayley. Nothing I can do?'

'Nothing, thanks.' Cayley kicked at his starter. Nothing happened.

The constable lingered. 'Quite a treat to see someone on a lonely beat like this.'

'Yes, it must be.' Cayley was still kicking. He wanted to scream at the man to go. He would scream, in a minute. No, he must not scream. He must hold the edges of his nerves together like flesh over a wound, to keep the panic within from welling out. 'Good night,' he said clearly.

'Well, good night, Mr Cayley. Got a load, I see?'

'Yes.' Cayley's head was bent. He spoke through almost closed teeth. 'Some potatoes I ...'

'Potatoes?'

'Yes, a sack. Look here, man, I said switch that light out.'

'Now, now, Mr Cayley, I don't take orders from you. I know my duty, and it's my belief—'

'Leave that rug alone!' screamed Cayley.

The constable paused, startled. Then he spoke weightily, the corner of the rug in his great hand.

'Mr Cayley, I must ask you to show me what you've got in this here side-car. It don't look like potatoes to me, and that's a fact. Besides—'

'All right then, damn you!' Cayley's voice was pitched hysterically. 'All right!'

The sound of the shot mingled with the sudden roar of the engine. As he twisted to fire Cayley's foot had trodden on the starter. This time it worked. The bicycle leapt forward.

Cayley drove on, as fast as his machine would carry him. His face was stiff with terror. He knew he had not killed the policeman, for he had seen him jump aside as the bicycle plunged forward.

What had possessed him to fire like that? And what, ten times more fatal, had possessed him to fire and not to kill? Now he was done for. Cayley knew that his only chance was to go back and find the policeman: to hunt him down and kill him where he stood. That was his only chance now – and he could not do it. No, he could not. Too late Cayley realized that he was not the man for murder.

What was he going to do?

Already the constable would be giving the alarm. Policemen everywhere would be on the look-out for him soon. He must not stop. His only hope was to get as far away as possible, in the quickest time.

He sped on madly, not knowing where he was going, turning now right, now left, as the road forked, intent only on putting as long and as confused a trail as possible between himself and the constable.

He drove till his eyes were almost blind and his arms were numb with pain, and Rose drove with him.

Rose!

He could not dispossess himself of her, he dared not leave her anywhere. He dared not even stop. If he stopped, they might pounce on him. And then they would find her. And if he did not stop – just stop to bury her somewhere – then they would find her just the same in the end. But he dared not stop. His one hope was to keep flying along. So long as he was moving he was safe.

He drove on: insanely, anywhere, everywhere, so long as he was still driving. His eyes never shifted from the road ahead of him; but after a time his lips began to move. He was talking to Rose, in the side-car.

'I got it for you, Rose. You would have it, instead of riding pillion. Well, now you've got it. This is our last drive together, Rose, so I hope you're enjoying it.'

What was to happen when his petrol gave out he dared not think. He could not think. His brain was numb. All he knew was that he must keep on driving: away, away, from that policeman and the alarm he had given. Where he might be he had no idea or the names of the villages and little towns through which he tore.

It did not matter so long as he kept on. One word only fixed itself in his sliding mind: Scotland. For some reason he had the idea that if he could but reach Scotland he would have a chance.

At breakneck speed he thrust on, with Rose, to Scotland.

But Cayley was not to reach Scotland that night. Whether it is that, in panic, the human animal really does move in circles, whether it was that in his numbed brain there still glowed an unconscious spark of his great plan, the fact is left that, while Cayley still thought himself headed for Scotland, he instinctively took a rough track which presented itself on the right of the road when he came to it, and that track led to the top of the same quarry in which he had meant to bury Rose.

But Cayley never knew that, any more than he recognized the wooden rails bordering the edge when they seemed to leap towards him in the beam of his headlight. Then it was too late to recognize anything, in this world.

There were other things, too, which Cayley never knew. He never knew that the constable, a motor-cyclist himself, had seen his inadvertent treading on the self-starter. He did not know that the constable, highly amused, had thought that Cayley's motor-cycle had run away with him. Above all, he did not know that the constable never had the remotest idea that a shot was ever fired at him.

The Well

W. W. Jacobs

Two men stood in the billiard-room of an old country house, talking. Play, which had been of a half-hearted nature, was over, and they sat at the open window, looking out over the park stretching away beneath them, conversing idly.

'Your time's nearly up, Jem,' said one at length; 'this time six weeks you'll be yawning out your honeymoon and cursing the man – woman, I mean – who invented them.'

Jem Benson stretched his long limbs in the chair and grunted in dissent.

'I've never understood it,' continued Wilfred Carr, yawning. 'It's not in my line at all; I never had enough money for my own wants, let alone for two. Perhaps if I were as rich as you, or Crœsus, I might regard it differently.'

There was just sufficient meaning in the latter part of the remark for his cousin to forbear replying to it. He continued to gaze out of the window and to smoke slowly.

'Not being as rich as Crœsus – or you,' resumed Mr Carr, regarding him from beneath lowered lids, 'I paddle my own canoe down the stream of Time, and tying it to my friends' door-posts, go in to eat their dinners.'

'Quite Venetian,' said Jem Benson, still looking out of the window. 'It's not a bad thing for you, Wilfred, that you have the door-posts and dinners – and friends.'

Mr Carr grunted in his turn. 'Seriously though Jem,' he said slowly, 'you're a lucky fellow, a very lucky fellow. If there's a better girl above ground than Olive I should like to see her.'

'Yes,' said the other quietly.

'She's such an exceptional girl,' continued Carr, staring out of the window. 'She's so good and gentle. She thinks you are a bundle of all the virtues.'

He laughed frankly and joyously, but the other man did not join him.

'Strong sense of right and wrong though,' continued Carr, musingly. 'Do you know, I believe that if she found out that you were not—'

'Not what?' demanded Benson, turning upon him fiercely. 'Not what?'

'Everything that you are,' returned his cousin, with a grin that belied his words. 'I believe she'd drop you.'

'Talk about something else,' said Benson slowly; 'your pleasantries are not always in the best taste.'

Wilfred Carr rose, and taking a cue from the rack, bent over the board and practised one or two favourite shots. 'The only other subject I can talk about just at present is my own financial affairs,' he said slowly, as he walked round the table.

'Talk about something else,' said Benson again, bluntly.

'And the two things are connected,' said Carr, and dropping his cue, he half sat on the table and eyed his cousin.

There was a long silence. Benson pitched the end of his cigar out of the window, and leaning back, closed his eyes.

'Do you follow me?' said Carr at length.

Benson opened his eyes and nodded at the window. 'Do you want to follow my cigar?' he demanded.

'I should prefer to depart by the usual way for your sake,' returned the other, unabashed. 'If I left by the window all sorts of questions would be asked, and you know what a talkative chap I am.'

'So long as you don't talk about my affairs,' returned the other, restraining himself by an obvious effort, 'you can talk yourself hoarse.'

'I'm in a mess,' said Carr slowly, 'a devil of a mess. If I don't raise fifteen hundred pounds by this day fortnight, I may be getting my board and lodging free.'

'Would that be any change?' questioned Benson.

'The quality would,' retorted the other. 'The address also would not be good. Seriously, Jem, will you let me have the fifteen hundred?'

'No,' said the other simply.

Carr went white. 'It's to save me from ruin,' he said thickly.

'I've helped you till I'm tired,' said Benson, turning and regarding him, 'and it is all to no good. If you've got in a mess, get out of it. You should not be so fond of giving autographs away.'

'It's foolish, I admit,' said Carr deliberately. 'I won't do so any more. By the way, I've got some to sell. You needn't sneer. They're not my own.'

'Whose are they?' enquired the other.

'Yours.'

Benson got up from his chair and crossed over to him. 'What is this?' he asked quietly. 'Blackmail?'

'Call it what you like,' said Carr. 'I've got some letters for sale, price fifteen hundred pounds. And I know a man who wants to buy them at that price for the mere chance of getting Olive from you. I'll give you first offer.'

'If you've got any letters bearing my signature, you will be good enough to give them to me,' said Benson very slowly.

'They're mine,' said Carr lightly; 'given to me by the lady you wrote them to. I must say that they are not all in the best possible taste.'

His cousin reached forward suddenly, and catching him by the collar of his coat pinned him down on the table.

'Give me those letters,' he breathed, sticking his face close to his cousin's.

'They're not here,' said Carr, struggling. 'I'm not a fool. Let me go, or I'll raise the price.'

The other man raised him from the table in his powerful hands, apparently with the intention of dashing his head against it. Then suddenly his hold relaxed as an astonished-looking maid-servant entered the room with letters. Carr sat up hastily.

'That's how it was done,' said Benson, for the girl's benefit, as he took the letters.

'I don't wonder at the other man making him pay for it then,' said Carr blandly.

'You will give me those letters?' said Benson suggestively, as the girl left the room.

'At the price I mentioned, yes,' said Carr, 'but so sure as I'm a living man, if you lay your clumsy hands on me again, I'll double it. Now, I'll leave you for a time while you think it over.'

He took a cigar from the box and lighting it carefully quitted the room. His cousin waited until the door had closed behind him, and then turning to the window sat there in a fit of fury as silent as it was terrible.

The air was fresh and sweet from the park, heavy with the scent of new-mown grass. The fragrance of a cigar was now added to it, and glancing out he saw his cousin pacing slowly by. He rose and went to the door, and then, apparently altering his mind, returned to the window and watched the figure of his cousin as it moved slowly away into the moonlight. Then he rose again, and for a long time the room was empty.

It was empty when Mrs Benson came in some time later to say good-night to her son on her way to bed. She walked slowly round the table, and pausing at the window gazed from it in idle thought, until she saw the figure of her son advancing with rapid strides to the house. He looked up at the window.

'Good-night,' said she.

'Good-night,' said Benson, in a deep voice.

'Where is Wilfred?'

'Oh, he has gone,' said Benson.

'Gone?'

'We had a few words; he was wanting money again, and I gave him a piece of my mind. I don't think we shall see him again.'

'Poor Wilfred!' sighed Mrs Benson. 'He is always in trouble of some sort. I hope that you were not too hard upon him.'

'No more than he deserved,' said her son sternly. 'Good-night.'

II

The well, which had long ago fallen into disuse, was almost hidden by the thick tangle of undergrowth which ran riot at that corner of the old park. It was partly covered by the shrunken half of a lid, above which a rusty windlass creaked in company with the music of the pines when the wind blew strongly. The full light of the sun never reached it, and the ground surrounding it was moist and green when other parts of the park were gaping with the heat.

Two people, walking slowly round the park in the fragrant stillness of a summer evening, strayed in the direction of the well.

'No use going through this wilderness, Olive,' said Benson, pausing on the outskirts of the pines and eyeing with some disfavour the gloom beyond.

'Best part of the park,' said the girl briskly; 'you know it's my favourite spot.'

'I know you're very fond of sitting on the coping,' said the man slowly, 'and I wish you wouldn't. One day you will lean back too far and fall in.'

'And make the acquaintance of Truth,' said Olive lightly. 'Come along.'

She ran from him and was lost in the shadow of the pines, the bracken crackling beneath her feet as she ran. Her companion followed slowly, and emerging from the gloom saw her poised daintily on the edge of the well with her feet hidden in the rank grass and nettles which surrounded it. She motioned her companion to take a seat by her side, and smiled softly as she felt a strong arm passed about her waist.

'I like this place,' said she, breaking a long silence, 'It is so dismal – so uncanny. Do you know I wouldn't dare to sit here alone, Jem. I should imagine that all sorts of dreadful things were hidden behind the bushes and trees, waiting to spring out on me. Ugh!'

'You'd better let me take you in,' said her companion tenderly; 'the well isn't always wholesome, especially in the hot weather. Let's make a move.'

The girl gave an obstinate little shake, and settled herself more securely on her seat.

'Smoke your cigar in peace,' she said quietly. 'I am settled here for a quiet talk. Has anything been heard of Wilfred yet?'

'Nothing.'

'Quite a dramatic disappearance, isn't it?' she continued.

'Another scrape, I suppose, and another letter for you in the same old strain: "Dear Jem, help me out."'

Jem Benson blew a cloud of fragrant smoke into the air, and holding his cigar between his teeth, brushed away the ash from his coat sleeve.

'I wonder what he would have done without you,' said the girl, pressing his arm affectionately. 'Gone under long ago, I suppose. When we are married, Jem, I shall presume upon the relationship to lecture him. He is very wild, but he has his good points, poor fellow.'

'I never saw them,' said Benson, with startling bitterness. 'God knows, I never saw them.'

'He is nobody's enemy but his own,' said the girl, startled by this outburst.

'You don't know much about him,' said the other shortly. 'He was not above blackmail; not above ruining the life of a friend to do himself a benefit. A loafer, a cur and a liar!'

The girl looked up at him soberly but timidly, and took his arm without a word, and they both sat silent while evening deepened into night and the beams of the moon, filtering through the branches, surrounded them with a silver network. Her head sank upon his shoulder, till suddenly, with a sharp cry, she sprang to her feet.

'What was that?' she cried breathlessly.

'What was what?' demanded Benson, springing up and clutching her fast by the arm.

She caught her breath and tried to laugh. 'You're hurting me, Jem.'

His hold relaxed.

'What is the matter?' he asked gently. 'What was it startled you?'

'I was startled,' she said, slowly putting her hands on his shoulder. 'I suppose the words I used just now are ringing in my ears, but I fancied that somebody behind us whispered, "Jem, help me out."'

'Fancy,' repeated Benson, and his voice shook; 'but these fancies are not good for you. You – are frightened – at the dark and the gloom of these trees. Let me take you back to the house.'

'No, I'm not frightened,' said the girl re-seating herself. 'I should never be really frightened of anything when you were with me, Jem. I'm surprised at myself for being so silly.'

The man made no reply but stood, a strong, dark figure, a yard or two from the well, as though waiting for her to join him.

'Come and sit down, sir,' cried Olive, patting the brickwork with her small white hand, 'one would think that you did not like your company.'

He obeyed slowly and took a seat by her side, drawing so hard at his cigar that the light of it shone upon his face at every breath. He passed his arm, firm and rigid as steel, behind her, with his hand resting on the brickwork beyond.

'Are you warm enough?' he asked tenderly, as she made a little movement.

'Pretty fair,' she shivered; 'one oughtn't to be cold at this time of the year, but there's a cold damp air comes up from the well.'

As she spoke a faint splash sounded from the depths below, and for the second time that evening she sprang from the well with a little cry of dismay.

'What is it now?' he asked in a fearful voice. He stood by her side and gazed at the well, as though half expecting to see the cause of her alarm emerge from it.

'Oh, my bracelet,' she cried in distress, 'my poor mother's bracelet. I dropped it down the well.'

'Your bracelet!' repeated Benson dully. 'Your bracelet! The diamond one?'

'The one that was my mother's,' said Olive. 'Oh, we can get it back, surely. We must have the water drained off.'

'Your bracelet!' repeated Benson stupidly.

'Jem,' said the girl in terrified tones, 'dear Jem, what is the matter?'

For the man she loved was standing regarding her with horror. The moon which touched it was not responsible for all the whiteness of the distorted face, and she shrank back in fear to the edge of the well. He saw her fear, and by a mighty effort regained his composure and took her hand.

'Poor little girl,' he murmured, 'you frightened me. I was not looking when you cried, and I thought that you were slipping from my arms, down – down – '

His voice broke, and the girl, throwing herself into his arms, clung to him convulsively.

'There, there,' said Benson fondly, 'don't cry, don't cry.'

'To-morrow,' said Olive, half laughing, half crying. 'we will all come round the well with hook and line and fish for it. It will be quite a new sport.'

'No, we must try some other way,' said Benson. 'You shall have it back.'

'How?' asked the girl.

'You shall see,' said Benson. 'To-morrow morning at latest you shall have it back. Till then promise me that you will not mention your loss to anyone. Promise.'

'I promise,' said Olive wonderingly. 'But why not?'

'It is of great value for one thing, and – but there – there are many reasons. For one thing, it is my duty to get it for you.'

'Wouldn't you like to jump down for it?' she asked mischievously. 'Listen.'

She stooped for a stone and dropped it down.

'Fancy being where that is now,' she said, peering into the blackness: 'fancy going round and round like a mouse in a pail, clutching at the slimy sides, with the water filling your mouth, and looking up to the little patch of sky above.'

'You had better come in,' said Benson very quietly. 'You are developing a taste for the morbid and horrible.'

The girl turned, and taking his arm walked slowly in the direction of the house. Mrs Benson, who was sitting in the porch, rose to receive them.

'You shouldn't have kept her out so long,' she said chidingly; 'where have you been?'

'Sitting on the well,' said Olive, smiling, 'discussing our future.'

'I don't believe that place is healthy,' said Mrs Benson emphatically. 'I really think it might be filled in, Jem.'

'All right,' said her son slowly. 'Pity it wasn't filled in long ago.'

He took the chair vacated by his mother as she entered the house with Olive, and with his hands hanging limply over the sides sat in deep thought. After a time he rose, and going upstairs to a room which was set apart for sporting requisites selected a sea fishing line and some hooks and stole softly downstairs again. He walked swiftly across the park in the direction of the well, turning before he entered the shadow of the trees to look back at the lighted windows of the house. Then, having arranged his line, he sat on the edge of the well and cautiously lowered it.

He sat with his lips compressed, occasionally looking about him in a startled fashion, as though he half expected to see something peering at him from the belt of trees. Time after time he lowered his line until at length in pulling it up he heard a little metallic tinkle against the side of the well.

He held his breath then, and forgetting his fears drew the line in inch by inch, so as not to lose its precious burden. His pulse beat rapidly, and his eyes were bright. As the line came slowly in he saw the catch hanging to the hook, and with a steady hand drew the last few feet in. Then he saw that instead of the bracelet he had hooked a bunch of keys.

With a faint cry he shook them from the hook into the water below, and stood breathing heavily. Not a sound broke the stillness of the night. He walked up and down a bit and stretched his great muscles, then he came back to the well and resumed his task.

For an hour or more the line was lowered without result. In his eagerness he forgot his fears, and with eyes bent down the well fished slowly and carefully. Twice the hook became entangled in something, and was with difficulty released. It caught a third time, and all his efforts failed to free it. Then he dropped the line down the well, and with head bent walked towards the house.

He went first to the stables at the rear, and then retiring to his room for some time paced restlessly up and down. Then without removing his clothes he flung himself upon the bed and fell into a troubled sleep.

III

Long before anybody else was astir he arose and stole softly downstairs. The sunlight was stealing in at every crevice, and flashing in long streaks across the darkened rooms. The dining-room into which he looked struck chill and cheerless in the dark yellow light which came through the lowered blinds. He remembered that it had the same appearance when his father lay dead in the house; now, as then, everything seemed ghastly and unreal; the very chairs, standing as their occupants had left them the night before, seemed to be indulging in some dark communication of ideas.

Slowly and noiselessly he opened the hall door and passed into the fragrant air beyond. The sun was shining on the drenched grass and trees, and a slowly vanishing white mist rolled like smoke about the grounds. For a moment he stood, breathing deeply the sweet air of the morning, and then walked slowly in the direction of the stables.

The rusty creaking of a pump-handle and a spatter of water upon the red-tiled courtyard showed that somebody else was astir, and a few steps farther he beheld a brawny, sandy-haired man gasping wildly under severe self-infliction at the pump.

'Everything ready, George?' he asked quietly.

'Yes, sir,' said the man, straightening up suddenly and touching his forehead. 'Bob's just finishing the arrangements inside. It's a lovely morning for a dip. The water in that well must be just icy.'

'Be as quick as you can,' said Benson impatiently.

'Very good, sir,' said George, burnishing his face harshly with a very small towel which had been hanging over the top of the pump. 'Hurry up, Bob.'

In answer to his summons, a man appeared at the door of the stable with a coil of stout rope over his arm and a large metal candlestick in his hand.

'Just to try the air, sir,' said George, following his master's glance, 'a well gets rather foul sometimes, but if a candle can live down it a man can.'

His master nodded, and the man, hastily pulling up the neck of his shirt and thrusting his arms through his waistcoat, followed him as he led the way slowly to the well.

'Beg pardon, sir,' said George, drawing up to his side, 'but you are not looking over and above well this morning. If you'll let me go down I'd enjoy the bath.'

'No, no,' said Benson peremptorily.

'You ain't fit to go down, sir,' persisted his follower. 'I've never seen you look so before. Now, if—'

'Mind your business,' said his master curtly.

George became silent, and the three walked with swinging strides through the long, wet grass to the well. Bob flung the rope on the ground, and at a sign from his master handed him the candlestick.

'Here's the line for it, sir,' said Bob, fumbling in his pockets.

Benson took it from him and slowly tied it to the candlestick. Then he placed it on the edge of the well and, striking a match, lit the candle and began slowly to lower it.

'Hold hard, sir,' said George quickly, laying his hand on his arm. 'you must tilt it or the string'll burn through.'

Even as he spoke the string parted and the candlestick fell into the water below.

Benson swore quietly.

'I'll soon get another,' said George, starting up.

'Never mind, the well's all right,' said Benson.

'It won't take a moment, sir,' said the other, over his shoulder.

'Are you master here, or am I?' said Benson hoarsely.

George came back slowly, a glance at his master's face stopped the protest upon his tongue, and he stood by watching him sulkily as he sat on the well and removed his outer garments. Both men watched him curiously, as having completed his preparation he stood grim and silent with his hands by his side.

'I wish you'd let me go sir,' said George, plucking up courage to address him. 'You ain't fit to go, you've got a chill or something. I shouldn't wonder it's the typhoid. They've got it in the village bad.'

For a moment Benson looked at him angrily, then his gaze softened. 'Not this time, George,' he said quietly. He took the looped end of the rope and placed it under his arms, and sitting down, threw one leg over the side of the well.

'How are you going about it, sir?' queried George, laying hold of the rope and signing to Bob to do the same.

'I'll call out when I reach the water,' said Benson; 'then pay out three yards more quickly so that I can get to the bottom.

'Very good, sir,' answered both.

Their master threw the other leg over the coping and sat motionless. His back was turned towards the men as he sat with head bent, looking down the shaft. He sat for so long that George became uneasy.

'All right, sir?' he enquired.

'Yes,' said Benson slowly. 'If I tug at the rope, George, pull up at once. Lower away.'

The rope passed steadily through their hands until a hollow cry from the darkness below and a faint splashing warned them that he had reached the water. They gave him three yards more, and stood with relaxed grasp and strained ears, waiting. 'He's gone under,' said Bob in a low voice.

The other nodded, and moistening his huge palms took a firmer grip of the rope.

Fully a minute passed, and the men began to exchange uneasy glances. Then a sudden tremendous jerk followed by a series of feebler ones nearly tore the rope from their grasp.

'Pull!' shouted George, placing one foot on the side and hauling desperately. 'Pull! pull! He's stuck fast; he's not coming; P—U—LL!'

In response to their terrific exertions the rope came slowly in, inch by inch, until at length a violent splashing was heard, and at the same moment a scream of unutterable horror came echoing up the shaft.

'What a weight he is!' panted Bob. 'He's stuck fast or something. Keep still, sir; for heaven's sake, keep still.'

For the taut rope was being jerked violently by the struggles of the weight at the end of it.

Both men with grunts and sighs hauled it in foot by foot.

'All right, sir,' cried George cheerfully.

He had one foot against the well, and was pulling manfully; the burden was nearing the top. A long pull and a strong pull, and the face of a dead man with mud in the eyes and nostrils came peering over the edge. Behind it was the ghastly face of his master; but this he saw too late, for with a great cry George let go his hold of the rope and stepped back. The suddenness overthrew his assistant, and the rope tore through his hands. There was a frightful splash.

'You fool!' stammered Bob, and ran to the well helplessly.

'Run!' cried George. 'Run for another line.'

He bent over the coping and called eagerly down as his assistant sped back to the stables shouting wildly. His voice re-echoed down the shaft, but all else was silence.

Moment of Power

P. D. James

'We close at twelve on Saturday,' said the blonde in the estate office. 'So if you keep the key after then, please drop it back through the letter box. It's the only key we have, and there may be other people wanting to view on Monday. Sign here, please, sir.'

The 'sir' was grudging, an afterthought. Her tone was reproving. She didn't really think he would buy the flat, this seedy old man with his air of spurious gentility, with his harsh voice. In her job you soon got a nose for the genuine inquirer. Ernest Gabriel. An odd name, half-common, half-fancy.

But he took the key politely enough and thanked her for her trouble. No trouble, she thought. God knew there were few enough people interested in that sordid little dump, not at the price they were asking. He could keep the key a week, for all she cared.

She was right. Gabriel hadn't come to buy, only to view. It was the first time he had been back since it all happened sixteen years ago. He came neither as a pilgrim nor a penitent. He had returned under some compulsion which he hadn't even bothered to analyze. He had been on his way to visit his only living relative, an elderly aunt, who had recently been admitted to a geriatric ward. He hadn't even realized the bus would pass the flat.

But suddenly they were lurching through Camden Town, and the road became familiar, like a photograph springing into focus; and with a *frisson* of surprise he recognised the double-fronted shop and the flat above. There was an estate agent's notice in the window. Almost without thinking, he had got off at the next stop, gone back to verify the name, and walked the half-mile to the office. It had seemed as natural and inevitable as his daily bus journey to work.

Twenty minutes later he fitted the key into the lock of the front door and passed into the stuffy emptiness of the flat. The grimy walls still held the smell of cooking. There was a spatter of envelopes on the worn linoleum, dirtied and trampled by the feet of previous viewers. The light bulb swung naked in the hall, and the door into the sitting room stood open. To his right was the staircase, to his left the kitchen.

Gabriel paused for a moment, then went into the kitchen. From the windows, half-curtained with grubby gingham, he looked upward to the great black building at the rear of the flat, eyeless except for the one small square of window high on the fifth floor. It was from this window, sixteen years ago, that he had watched Denis Speller and Eileen Morrisey play out their commonplace little tragedy to its end.

He had no right to be watching them, no right to be in the building at all after six o'clock. That had been the nub of his awful dilemma. It had happened by chance. Mr Maurice Bootman had instructed him, as the firm's filing clerk, to go through the papers in the late Mr Bootman's upstairs den in case there were any which should be in the files. They weren't confidential or important papers – those had been dealt with by the family and the firm's solicitors months before. They were just a miscellaneous, yellowing collection of out-of-date memoranda, old accounts, receipts, and fading press clippings which had been bundled together into old Mr Bootman's desk. He had been a great hoarder of trivia.

But at the back of the left-hand bottom drawer Gabriel had found a key. It was by chance that he tried it in the lock of the corner cupboard. It fitted. And in the cupboard Gabriel found the late Mr Bootman's small but choice collection of pornography.

He knew that he had to read the books; not just to snatch surreptitious minutes with one ear listening for a footstep on the stairs or the whine of the approaching elevator, and fearful always that his absence from his filing room would be noticed. No, he had to read them in privacy and in peace. So he devised his plan.

It wasn't difficult. As a trusted member of the staff, he had one of the Yale keys to the side door at which goods were delivered. It was locked on the inside at night by the porter before he went off duty. It wasn't difficult for Gabriel, always among the last to leave, to find the opportunity of shooting back the bolts before leaving with the porter by the main door. He dared risk it only once a week, and the day he chose was Friday.

He would hurry home, eat his solitary meal beside the gas fire in his bed-sitting-room, then make his way back to the building and let himself in by the side door. All that was necessary was to make sure he was waiting for the office to open on Monday morning so that, among the first in, he could lock the side door before the porter made his ritual visit to unlock it for the day's deliveries.

These Friday nights became a desperate but shameful joy to Gabriel. Their pattern was always the same. He would sit crouched in old Mr Bootman's low leather chair in front of the fireplace, his shoulders hunched over the book in his lap, his eyes following the pool of light

from his torch as it moved over each page. He never dared to switch
on the room light, and even on the coldest night he never lit the gas
fire. He was fearful that its hiss might mask the sound of approaching
feet, that its glow might shine through the thick curtains at the window,
or that, somehow, the smell of gas would linger in the room next Monday
morning to betray him. He was morbidly afraid of discovery, yet even
this fear added to the excitement of his secret pleasure.

It was on the third Friday in January that he first saw them. It was
a mild evening, but heavy and starless. An early rain had slimed the
pavements and bled the scribbled headlines from the newspaper
placards. Gabriel wiped his feet carefully before climbing to the fifth
floor. The claustrophobic room smelled sour and dusty, the air struck
colder than the night outside. He wondered whether he dared open the
window and let in some of the sweetness of the rain-cleansed sky.

It was then that he saw the woman. Below him were the back entrances
of the two shops, each with a flat above. One flat had boarded windows,
but the other looked lived in. It was approached by a flight of iron
steps leading to an asphalt yard. He saw the woman in the glow of a
street lamp as she paused at the foot of the steps, fumbling in her
handbag. Then, as if gaining resolution, she came swiftly up the steps
and almost ran across the asphalt to the flat door.

He watched as she pressed herself into the shadow of the doorway,
then swiftly turned the key in the lock and slid out of his sight. He had
time only to notice that she was wearing a pale mackintosh buttoned
high under a mane of fairish hair and that she carried a string bag of
what looked like groceries. It seemed an oddly furtive and solitary
homecoming.

Gabriel waited. Almost immediately he saw the light go on in the
room to the left of the door. Perhaps she was in the kitchen. He could
see her faint shadow passing to and fro, bending and then lengthening.
He guessed that she was unpacking the groceries. Then the light in the
room went out.

For a few moments the flat was in darkness. Then the light in the
upstairs window went on, brighter this time, so that he could see the
woman more plainly. She could not know how plainly. The curtains
were drawn, but they were thin. Perhaps the owners, confident that
they were not overlooked, had grown careless. Although the woman's
silhouette was only a faint blur, Gabriel could see that she was carrying
a tray. Perhaps she was intending to eat her supper in bed. She was
undressing now.

He could see her lifting the garments over her head and twisting
down to release stockings and take off her shoes. Suddenly she came
very close to the window, and he saw the outline of her body plainly.
She seemed to be watching and listening. Gabriel found that he was

holding his breath. Then she moved away, and the light dimmed. He guessed that she had switched off the central bulb and was using the bedside lamp. The room was now lit with a softer, pinkish glow within which the woman moved, insubstantial as a dream.

Gabriel stood with his face pressed against the cold window, still watching. Shortly after eight o'clock the boy arrived. Gabriel always thought of him as 'the boy.' Even from that distance his youth, his vulnerability, were apparent. He approached the flat with more confidence than the woman, but still swiftly, pausing at the top of the steps as if to assess the width of the rain-washed yard.

She must have been waiting for his knock. She let him in at once, the door barely opening. Gabriel knew that she had come naked to let him in. And then there were two shadows in the upstairs room, shadows that met and parted and came together again before they moved, joined, to the bed and out of Gabriel's sight.

The next Friday he watched to see if they would come again. They did, and at the same times, the woman first, at twenty minutes past seven, the boy forty minutes later. Again Gabriel stood, rigidly intent at his watching post, as the light in the upstairs window sprang on and then was lowered. The two naked figures, seen dimly behind the curtains, moved to and fro, joined and parted, fused and swayed together in a ritualistic parody of a dance.

This Friday Gabriel waited until they left. The boy came out first, sidling quickly from the half open door and almost leaping down the steps, as if in exultant joy. The woman followed five minutes later, locking the door behind her and darting across the asphalt, her head bent.

After that he watched for them every Friday. They held a fascination for him even greater than Mr Bootman's books. Their routine hardly varied. Sometimes the boy arrived a little late, and Gabriel would see the woman watching motionless for him behind the bedroom curtains. He too would stand with held breath, sharing her agony of impatience, willing the boy to come. Usually the boy carried a bottle under his arm, but one week it was in a wine basket, and he bore it with great care. Perhaps it was an anniversary, a special evening for them. Always the woman had the bag of groceries. Always they ate together in the bedroom.

Friday after Friday Gabriel stood in the darkness, his eyes fixed on that upstairs window, straining to decipher the outlines of their naked bodies, picturing what they were doing to each other.

They had been meeting for seven weeks when it happened. Gabriel was late at the building that night. His usual bus did not run, and the first to arrive was full. By the time he reached his watching post, there was already a light in the bedroom. He pressed his face to the window, his hot breath smearing the pane. Hastily rubbing it clear with the cuff of his coat, he looked again. For a moment he thought that there were two figures in the bedroom. But that must surely be a freak of the light. The boy wasn't due for thirty minutes yet. But the woman, as always, was on time.

Twenty minutes later he went into the washroom on the floor below. He had become much more confident during the last few weeks and now moved about the building, silently, and using only his torch for light, but with almost as much assurance as during the day. He spent nearly ten minutes in the washroom. His watch showed that it was just after eight by the time he was back at the window, and, at first, he thought that he had missed the boy. But no, the slight figure was even now running up the steps and across the asphalt to the shelter of the doorway.

Gabriel watched as he knocked and waited for the door to open. But it didn't open. She didn't come. There was a light in the bedroom, but no shadow moved on the curtains. The boy knocked again. Gabriel could just detect the quivering of his knuckles against the door. Again he waited. Then the boy drew back and looked up at the lighted window. Perhaps he was risking a low-pitched call. Gabriel could hear nothing, but he could sense the tension in that waiting figure.

Again the boy knocked. Again there was no response. Gabriel watched and suffered with him until, at twenty past eight, the boy finally gave up and turned away. Then Gabriel too stretched his cramped limbs and made his way into the night. The wind was rising, and a young moon reeled through the torn clouds. It was getting colder. He wore no coat and missed its comfort. Hunching his shoulders against the bite of the wind, he knew that this was the last Friday he would come late to the building. For him, as for that desolate boy, it was the end of a chapter.

He first read about the murder in his morning paper on his way to work the following Monday. He recognized the picture of the flat at once, although it looked oddly unfamiliar with the bunch of plainclothes detectives conferring at the door and the stolid uniformed policeman at the top of the steps.

The story so far was slight. A Mrs Eileen Morrisey, aged thirty-four, had been stabbed to death in a flat in Camden Town late on Sunday night. The discovery was made by the tenants, Mr and Mrs Kealy, who had returned late on Sunday from a visit to Mr Kealy's parents. The dead woman, who was the mother of twin daughters aged twelve, was a friend of Mrs Kealy. Detective Chief-Inspector William Holbrook was in charge of the investigation. It was understood that the dead woman had been sexually assaulted.

Gabriel folded his paper with the same precise care as he did on any

ordinary day. Of course, he would have to tell the police what he had
seen. He couldn't let an innocent man suffer, no matter what the inconvenience to himself. The knowledge of his intention, of his public-
spirited devotion to justice, was warmly satisfying. For the rest of the
day he crept around his filing cabinets with the secret complacency of
a man dedicated to sacrifice.

But somehow his first plan of calling at a police station on his way
home from work came to nothing. There was no point in acting hastily.
If the boy were arrested, he would speak. But it would be ridiculous to
prejudice his reputation and endanger his job before he even knew
whether the boy was a suspect. The police might never learn of the
boy's existence. To speak up now might only focus suspicion on the
innocent. A prudent man would wait. Gabriel decided to be prudent.

The boy was arrested three days later. Again Gabriel read about it
in his morning paper. There was no picture this time, and few details.
The news had to compete with a society elopement and a major air
crash and did not make the first page. The inch of newsprint stated briefly:
'Denis John Speller, a butcher's assistant, aged nineteen, who gave an
address at Muswell Hill, was today charged with the murder of Mrs
Eileen Morrisey, the mother of twelve-year-old twins, who was stabbed
to death last Friday in a flat in Camden Town.'

So the police now knew more precisely the time of death. Perhaps it
was time for him to see them. But how could he be sure that this Denis
Speller was the young lover he had been watching these past Friday
nights? A woman like that – well, she might have had any number of
men. No photograph of the accused would be published in any paper
until after the trial. But more information would come out at the
preliminary hearing. He would wait for that. After all, the accused
might not even be committed for trial.

Besides, he had himself to consider. There had been time to think of
his own position. If young Speller's life were in danger, then, of course,
Gabriel would tell what he had seen. But it would mean the end of his
job with Bootman's. Worse, he would never get another. Mr Maurice
Bootman would see to that. He, Gabriel, would be branded as a dirty-
minded, sneaking little voyeur, a Peeping Tom who was willing to
jeopardize his livelihood for an hour or two with a naughty book and
a chance to pry into other people's happiness. Mr Maurice would be
too angry at the publicity to forgive the man who had caused it.

And the rest of the firm would laugh. It would be the best joke in
years, funny and pathetic and futile. The pedantic, respectable,
censorious Ernest Gabriel found out at last! And they wouldn't even
give him credit for speaking up. It simply wouldn't occur to them that
he could have kept silent.

If only he could think of a good reason for being in the building that night. But there was none. He could hardly say that he had stayed behind to work late, when he had taken such care to leave with the porter. And it wouldn't do to say that he had returned later to catch up with his filing. His filing was always up-to-date, as he was fond of pointing out. His very efficiency was against him.

Besides, he was a poor liar. The police wouldn't accept his story without probing. After they had spent so much time on the case, they would hardly welcome his tardy revelation of new evidence. He pictured the circle of grim, accusing faces, the official civility barely concealing their dislike and contempt. There was no sense in inviting such an ordeal before he was sure of the facts.

But after the preliminary hearing, at which Denis Speller was sent up for trial, the same arguments seemed equally valid. By now he knew that Speller was the lover he had seen. There had never really been much room for doubt. By now, too, the outlines of the case for the Crown were apparent. The Prosecution would seek to prove that this was a crime of passion, that the boy, tormented by her threat to leave him, had killed in jealousy or revenge. The accused would deny that he had entered the flat that night, would state again and again that he had knocked and gone away. Only Gabriel could support his story. But it would still be premature to speak.

He decided to attend the trial. In that way he would hear the strength of the Crown's case. If it appeared likely that the verdict would be 'Not Guilty,' he could remain silent. And if things went badly, there was an excitement, a fearful fascination, in the thought of rising to his feet in the silence of that crowded court and speaking out his evidence before all the world. The questioning, the criticism, the notoriety would have come later. But he would have had his moment of glory.

He was surprised and a little disappointed by the court. He had expected a more imposing, more dramatic setting for justice than this modern, clean-smelling, businesslike room. Everything was quiet and orderly. There was no crowd at the door jostling for seats. It wasn't even a popular trial.

Sliding into his seat at the back of the court, Gabriel looked round, at first apprehensively and then with more confidence. But he needn't have worried. There was no one there he knew. It was really a very dull collection of people, hardly worthy, he thought, of the drama that was to be played out before them. Some of them looked as if they might have worked with Speller or lived in the same street. All looked ill-at-ease, with the slightly furtive air of people who find themselves in unusual or intimidating surroundings. There was a thin woman in black crying softly into a handkerchief. No one took any notice of her; no one comforted her.

From time to time one of the doors at the back of the court would open silently, and a newcomer would sidle almost furtively into his seat. When this happened, the row of faces would turn momentarily to him without interest, without recognition, before turning their eyes again to the slight figure in the dock.

Gabriel stared too. At first he dared to cast only fleeting glances, averting his eyes suddenly, as if each glance were a desperate risk. It was unthinkable that the prisoner's eyes should meet his, should somehow know that here was the man who could save him and should signal a desperate appeal. But when he had risked two or three glances, he realized that there was nothing to fear. That solitary figure was seeing no one, caring about no one except himself. He was only a bewildered and terrified boy, his eyes turned inward to some private hell. He looked like a trapped animal, beyond hope and beyond fight.

The judge was rotund, red-faced, his chins sunk into the bands at his neck. He had small hands, which he rested on the desk before him except when he was making notes. Then counsel would stop talking for a moment before continuing more slowly, as if anxious not to hurry his Lordship, watching him like a worried father explaining with slow deliberation to a not very bright child.

But Gabriel knew where lay the power. The judge's chubby hands, folded on the desk like a parody of a child in prayer, held a man's life in their grasp. There was only one person in the court with more power than that scarlet-sashed figure high under the carved coat-of-arms. And that was he, Gabriel. The realization came to him in a spurt of exultation, at once intoxicating and satisfying. He hugged his knowledge to himself gloatingly. This was a new sensation, terrifyingly sweet.

He looked round at the solemn watching faces and wondered how they would change if he got suddenly to his feet and called out what he knew. He would say it firmly, confidently. They wouldn't be able to frighten him. He would say, 'My Lord. The accused is innocent. He did knock and go away. I, Gabriel, saw him.'

And then what would happen? It was impossible to guess. Would the judge stop the trial so that they could all adjourn to his chambers and hear his evidence in private? Or would Gabriel be called now to take his stand in the witness box? One thing was certain – there would be no fuss, no hysteria.

But suppose the judge merely ordered him out of the court. Suppose he was too surprised to take in what Gabriel had said. Gabriel could picture him leaning forward irritably, hand to his ear, while the police at the back of the court came silently forward to drag out the offender. Surely in this calm, aseptic atmosphere, where justice itself seemed an academic ritual, the voice of truth would be merely a vulgar intrusion. No one would believe him. No one would listen. They had set this elaborate scene to play out their drama to the end. They wouldn't thank him for spoiling it now. The time to speak had passed.

Even if they did believe him, he wouldn't get any credit now for coming forward. He would be blamed for leaving it so late, for letting an innocent man get so close to the gallows. If Speller were innocent, of course. And who could tell that? They would say that he might have knocked and gone away, only to return later and gain access to kill. He, Gabriel, hadn't waited at the window to see. So his sacrifice would have been for nothing.

And he could hear those taunting office voices: 'Trust old Gabriel to leave it to the last minute. Bloody coward. Read any naughty books lately, Archangel?' He would be sacked from Bootman's without even the consolation of standing well in the public eye.

Oh, he would make the headlines, all right. He could imagine them: *Outburst in Old Bailey. Man Upholds Accused's Alibi.* Only it wasn't an alibi. What did it really prove? He would be regarded as a public nuisance, the pathetic little voyeur who was too much of a coward to go to the police earlier. And Denis Speller would still hang.

Once the moment of temptation had passed and he knew with absolute certainty that he wasn't going to speak, Gabriel began almost to enjoy himself. After all, it wasn't every day that one could watch British justice at work. He listened, noted, appreciated. It was a formidable case which the prosecution unfolded. Gabriel approved of the prosecuting counsel. With his high forehead, beaked nose, and bony, intelligent face, he looked so much more distinguished than the judge. This was how a famous lawyer should look. He made his case without passion, almost without interest. But that, Gabriel knew, was how the law worked. It wasn't the duty of prosecuting counsel to work for a conviction. His job was to state with fairness and accuracy the case for the Crown.

He called his witnesses. Mrs Brenda Kealy, the wife of the tenant of the flat. A blonde, smartly dressed, common little slut if ever Gabriel saw one. Oh, he knew her type, all right. He could guess what his mother would have said about her. Anyone could see what she was interested in. And by the look of her, she was getting it regularly, too. Dressed up for a wedding. A tart if ever he saw one.

Sniveling into her handkerchief and answering counsel's questions in a voice so low that the judge had to ask her to speak up. Yes, she had agreed to lend Eileen the flat on Friday nights. She and her husband went every Friday to visit his parents at Southend. They always left as soon as he shut the shop. No, her husband didn't know of the arrangement. She had given Mrs Morrisey the spare key without consulting him. There wasn't any other spare key that she knew of. Why had she done it? She was sorry for Eileen. Eileen had pressed her. She didn't think the Morriseys had much of a life together.

Here the judge interposed gently that the witness should confine herself to answering counsel's questions. She turned to him. 'I was only trying to help Eileen, my Lord.'

Then there was the letter. It was passed to the sniveling woman in the box, and she confirmed that it had been written to her by Mrs Morrisey. Slowly it was collected by the clerk and borne majestically across to counsel, who proceeded to read it aloud:

Dear Brenda,

We shall be at the flat on Friday after all. I thought I'd better let you know in case you and Ted changed your plans. But it will definitely be for the last time. George is getting suspicious, and I must think of the children. I always knew it would have to end. Thank you for being such a pal.

Eileen

The measured, upper-class voice ceased. Looking across at the jury, counsel laid the letter slowly down. The judge bent his head and made another notation. There was a moment of silence in the court. Then the witness was dismissed.

And so it went on. There was the paper-seller at the end of Moulton Street who remembered Speller buying an *Evening Standard* just before eight o'clock. The accused was carrying a bottle under his arm and seemed very cheerful. He had no doubt his customer was the accused.

There was the publican's wife from the Rising Sun at the junction of Moulton Mews and High Street who testified that she served the prisoner with a whisky shortly before half-past eight. He hadn't stayed long. Just long enough to drink it down. He had seemed very upset. Yes, she was quite sure it was the accused. There was a motley collection of customers to confirm her evidence. Gabriel wondered why the prosecution had bothered to call them, until he realized that Speller had denied visiting the Rising Sun, had denied that he had needed a drink.

There was George Edward Morrisey, described as an estate agent's clerk, thin-faced, tight-lipped, standing rigidly in his best blue serge suit. He testified that his marriage had been happy, that he had known nothing, suspected nothing. His wife had told him that she spent Friday evenings learning to make pottery at L.C.C. evening classes. The court tittered. The judge frowned.

In reply to counsel's questions, Morrisey said that he had stayed at home to look after the children. They were still a little young to be left alone at night. Yes, he had been at home the night his wife was killed. Her death was a great grief to him. Her liaison with the accused had come as a terrible shock. He spoke the word 'liaison' with an angry contempt, as if it were bitter on his tongue. Never once did he look at the prisoner.

There was the medical evidence – sordid, specific, but mercifully clinical and brief. The deceased had been raped, then stabbed three times through the jugular vein. There was the evidence of the accused's employer, who contributed a vague and imperfectly substantiated story about a missing meat-skewer. There was the prisoner's landlady, who testified that he had arrived home on the night of the murder in a distressed state and that he had not got up to go to work next morning. Some of the threads were thin. Some, like the evidence of the butcher, obviously bore little weight even in the eyes of the prosecution. But together they were weaving a rope strong enough to hang a man.

The defending counsel did his best, but he had the desperate air of a man who knows that he is foredoomed to lose. He called witnesses to testify that Speller was a gentle, kindly boy, a generous friend, a good son and brother. The jury believed them. They also believed that he had killed his mistress. He called the accused. Speller was a poor witness, unconvincing, inarticulate. It would have helped, thought Gabriel, if the boy had shown some sign of pity for the dead woman. But he was too absorbed in his own danger to spare a thought for anyone else. Perfect fear casteth out love, thought Gabriel. The aphorism pleased him.

The judge summed up with scrupulous impartiality, treating the jury to an exposition on the nature and value of circumstantial evidence and an interpretation of the expression 'reasonable doubt.' The jury listened with respectful attention. It was impossible to guess what went on behind those twelve pairs of watchful, anonymous eyes. But they weren't out long.

Within forty minutes of the court rising, they were back, the prisoner reappeared in the dock, the judge asked the formal question. The foreman gave the expected answer, loud and clear. 'Guilty, my Lord.' No one seemed surprised.

The judge explained to the prisoner that he had been found guilty of the horrible and merciless killing of the woman who had loved him. The prisoner, his face taut and ashen, stared wild-eyed at the judge, as if only half hearing. The sentence was pronounced, sounding doubly horrible spoken in those soft judicial tones.

Gabriel looked with interest for the black cap and saw with surprise and some disappointment that it was merely a square of some black material perched incongruously atop the judge's wig. The jury was thanked. The judge collected his notes like a businessman clearing his desk at the end of a busy day. The court rose. The prisoner was taken below. It was over.

The trial caused little comment at the office. No one knew that Gabriel had attended. His day's leave 'for personal reasons' was accepted with as little interest as any previous absence. He was too solitary, too unpopular, to be included in office gossip. In his dusty and ill-lit office, insulated by tiers of filing cabinets, he was the object of vague dislike or, at best, of a pitying tolerance. The filing room had never been a centre of cosy office chat. But he did hear the opinion of one member of the firm.

On the day after the trial, Mr Bootman, newspaper in hand, came into the general office while Gabriel was distributing the morning mail. 'I see they've disposed of our little local trouble,' Mr Bootman said. 'Apparently the fellow is to hang. A good thing too. It seems to have been the usual sordid story of illicit passion and general stupidity. A very commonplace murder.'

No one replied. The office staff stood silent, then stirred into life. Perhaps they felt that there was nothing more to be said.

It was shortly after the trial that Gabriel began to dream. The dream, which occurred about three times a week, was always the same. He was struggling across a desert under a blood-red sun, trying to reach a distant fort. He could sometimes see the fort clearly, although it never got any closer. There was an inner courtyard crowded with people, a silent black-clad multitude whose faces were all turned towards a central platform. On the platform was a gallows. It was a curiously elegant gallows, with two sturdy posts at either side and a delicately curved crosspiece from which the noose dangled.

The people, like the gallows, were not of this age. It was a Victorian crowd, the women in shawls and bonnets, the men in tophats or narrow-brimmed bowlers. He could see his mother there, her thin face peaked under the widow's veil. Suddenly she began to cry, and as she cried, her face changed and became the face of the weeping woman at the trial. Gabriel longed desperately to reach her, to comfort her. But with every step he sank deeper into the sand.

There were people on the platform now. One, he knew, must be the prison governor, tophatted, frockcoated, bewhiskered, and grave. His clothes were those of a Victorian gentleman, but his face, under that luxuriant beard, was the face of Mr Bootman. Beside him stood the chaplain, in gown and bands, and, on either side, were two warders, their dark jackets buttoned high to their necks.

Under the noose stood the prisoner. He was wearing breeches and an open-necked shirt, and his neck was as white and delicate as a woman's. It might have been that other neck, so slender it looked. The prisoner was gazing across the desert towards Gabriel, not with desperate appeal but with great sadness in his eyes. And, this time, Gabriel knew that he had to save him, had to get there in time.

But the sand dragged at his aching ankles, and although he called that he was coming, coming, the wind, like a furnace blast, tore the words from his parched throat. His back, bent almost double, was blistered by the sun. He wasn't wearing a coat. Somehow, irrationally, he was worried that his coat was missing, that something had happened to it that he ought to remember.

As he lurched forward, floundering through the gritty morass, he could see the fort shimmering in the heat haze. Then it began to recede, getting fainter and farther, until at last it was only a blur among the distant sandhills. He heard a high, despairing scream from the courtyard – then awoke to know that it was his voice and that the damp heat on his brow was sweat, not blood.

In the comparative sanity of the morning, he analyzed the dream and realized that the scene was one pictured in a Victorian newssheet which he had once seen in the window of an antiquarian bookshop. As he remembered, it showed the execution of William Corder for the murder of Maria Marten in the red barn. The remembrance comforted him. At least he was still in touch with the tangible and sane world.

But the strain was obviously getting him down. It was time to put his mind to his problem. He had always had a good mind, too good for his job. That, of course, was why the other staff resented him. Now was the time to use it. What, exactly, was he worrying about? A woman had been murdered. Whose fault had it been? Weren't there a number of people who shared the responsibility?

That blonde tart, for one, who had lent them the flat. The husband, who had been so easily fooled. The boy, who had enticed her away from her duty to husband and children. The victim herself – particularly the victim. The wages of sin are death. Well, she had taken her wages now. One man hadn't been enough for her.

Gabriel pictured again that dim shadow against the bedroom curtains, the raised arms as she drew Speller's head down to her breast. Filthy. Disgusting. Dirty. The adjectives smeared his mind. Well, she and her lover had taken their fun. It was right that both of them should pay for it. He, Ernest Gabriel, wasn't concerned. It had only been by the merest chance that he had seen them from that upper window, only by chance that he had seen Speller knock and go away again.

Justice was being served. He had sensed its majesty, the beauty of its essential rightness, at Speller's trial. And he, Gabriel, was a part of it. If he spoke now, an adulterer might even go free. His duty was clear. The temptation to speak had gone forever.

It was in this mood that he stood with the small silent crowd outside the prison on the morning of Speller's execution. At the first stroke of eight, he, like the other men present, took off his hat. Staring up at the sky high above the prison walls, he felt again the warm exultation of his authority and power. It was on his behalf, it was at his, Gabriel's, bidding that the nameless hangman inside was exercising his dreadful craft. . . .

But that was sixteen years ago. Four months after the trial the firm, expanding and conscious of the need for a better address, had moved from Camden Town to north London. Gabriel had moved with it. He was one of the few people on the staff who remembered the old building. Clerks came and went so quickly nowadays; there was no sense of loyalty to the job.

When Gabriel retired at the end of the year, only Mr Bootman and the porter would remain from the old Camden Town days. Sixteen years. Sixteen years of the same job, the same bed-sitting-room, the same half-tolerant dislike on the part of the staff. But he had had his moment of power. He recalled it now, looking round the small sordid sitting room with its peeling wallpaper, its stained boards. It had looked different sixteen years ago.

He remembered where the sofa had stood, the very spot where she had died. He remembered other things – the pounding of his heart as he made his way across the asphalt; the quick knock; the sidling through the half-opened door before she could realize it wasn't her lover; the naked body cowering back into the sitting room; the taut white throat; the thrust with his filing bodkin that was as smooth as puncturing soft rubber. The steel had gone in so easily, so sweetly.

And there was something else which he had done to her. But that was something it was better not to remember. And afterward he had taken the bodkin back to the office, holding it under the tap in the washroom until no spot of blood could have remained. Then he had replaced it in his desk drawer with half a dozen identical others. There had been nothing to distinguish it anymore, even to his eyes.

It had all been so easy. The only blood had been a gush on his right cuff as he withdrew the bodkin. And he had burned the coat in the office furnace. He still recalled the blast on his face as he thrust it in, and the spilled cinders like sand under his feet.

There had been nothing left to him but the key of the flat. He had seen it on the sitting-room table and had taken it away with him. He drew it now from his pocket and compared it with the key from the estate agent, laying them side by side on his outstretched palm. Yes, they were identical. They had had another one cut, but no one had bothered to change the lock.

He stared at the key, trying to recall the excitement of those weeks when he had been both judge and executioner. But he could feel nothing. It was all so long ago. He had been fifty then; now he was sixty-six. It was too old for feeling. And then he recalled the words of Mr Bootman. It was, after all, a very commonplace murder.

On Monday morning the girl in the estate office, clearing the mail from the letter box, called to the manager.

'That's funny! The old chap who took the key to the Camden Town flat has returned the wrong one. This hasn't got our label on it. Unless he pulled it off. Cheek! But why would he do that?'

She took the key over to the manager's desk, dumping his pile of letters in front of him. He glanced at it casually.

'That's the right key, anyway – it's the only one of that type we still have. Probably the label worked loose and fell off. You should put them on more carefully.'

'But I did!' Outraged, the girl wailed her protest. The manager winced.

'Then label it again, put it back on the board, and for God's sake don't fuss, that's a good girl.'

She glanced at him again, ready to argue. Then she shrugged. Come to think of it, he had always been a bit odd about that Camden Town flat.

'Okay, Mr Morrisey,' she said.

Another Shot in the Locker

Michael Kent

It was beyond dispute a very pretty plan, a perfect plan. Once the details were completed, it only required nerve, and Martin Culpepper was certain of his nerve. Contemplating it, he took quite an artist's delight in it over and above the fact that it had to be done for his own safety. You cannot say that of every murder.

It was his secretary's words as he went into his office that told him that the final arrangement had passed its preliminary trials with satisfaction.

'Sir Gerald rang you up about twenty minutes ago, sir. He wanted to know if you were in and he would like to see you when you were at liberty. Any time after half past six.'

'Sir Gerald?' Martin had said. 'Why didn't he send down?'

'He didn't ring up from the building, sir,' said the girl.

'Did he say where he was ringing from?' The matter appeared to puzzle Martin.

'No, sir. I supposed that he had rung up from some place where he was having lunch.'

'You are sure it was Sir Gerald?' queried the manager doubtfully. 'I am expecting an appointment with a friend. Did he give his name, Miss Burton?'

'As a matter of fact, he didn't,' said the girl. 'He asked if we were Ransomes, and without thinking I just replied, "General Manager's office, Sir Gerald." Sir Gerald's voice is quite unmistakable.'

'Of course it is.' Martin passed into his own office and closed the door.

The test had been entirely satisfactory. There was no bar now to carrying the affair through on the lines indicated. All the rest was a mere matter of detail. He had established the fact that, without giving a name or making any suggestion as to identity, he could imitate the voice of Sir Gerald over the 'phone in such a way as to deceive someone who had worked for a long time intimately with the governor. That was the main step towards the solution of all his difficulties. After that it was only a matter of confidence and nerve.

Mentally he ticked the programme off and examined it in all its aspects for the hundredth time for flaws. First there was the approach to Sir Gerald's office, since no one must either see him come or go. That was the simplest thing. A long corridor in the trough of the works' roof connected the owner's office with the general manager's. Martin had tried it out. It took fifteen seconds to get from one to the other at a normal rate. It was a matter of twenty or thirty paces. What did that remind him of? Something that turned up familiarly in the papers. Brrh! A gruesome thing to think about just then!

'From the condemned cell to the scaffold was not more than thirty paces.' They always put in something like that. Idiotic thing to think of now. It couldn't affect him – a careful, clever, businesslike man. The approach to the office was fixed, then. Miss Burton? He would have to be away not more than four and a half minutes. He had timed that on a dozen occasions by going to Sir Gerald's office when he knew the governor to be out. He would send Miss Burton to the gate for the clocking-on records. He generally had a look at them once a week. No one could find anything abnormal in that.

Miss Burton would be away a full four and a half minutes. She goes from the general manager's outer office then and puts up the 'engaged' notice as usual. No one would penetrate to his room. Fifteen seconds from the word 'Go' he would be outside the governor's door. In the normal course no one would be there. Still, one must always be ready for eventualities, never be found trapped in a dead end.

Always be sure of another shot in the locker.

If anyone was about he would go in and show Sir Gerald the week's production figures. They were a bit up. Sir Gerald would be pleased and for that day the scheme would be washed out. It was no good hurrying things and making blunders. This was the sort of case where blunders were never forgiven.

One always had to have another shot in the locker. Plan everything. Foresee everything. The rest was simple.

Presuming all was clear, in he'd go.

'Be careful to close the door after you. See to every little thing.'

Then the cue was:

'I would like you to see the week's figures, Sir Gerald.'

Chances? Reckon all the chances. It was a thousand to one against the boss not looking at them at once, but if he did delay for a minute or two, wash it all out! Begin again another day. He had only four and a half minutes to work in for certain. Take no risks. Better have another shot another day.

Good so far. Presuming everything went straight, Sir Gerald would almost immediately turn to the right-hand top-drawer of the desk to compare the earlier records. He took a childish pride in them. There would be the boss in his chair bending over the right-hand drawer to peer in and himself standing at his right shoulder. The loaded revolver lay underneath the records in that drawer. The governor had kept it there since the coal strike. Oh, wait a second!

Suppose Sir Gerald asked about his gloved right hand? Must have a glove. Can't risk finger-prints. Then a crushed finger was the excuse. These finger-stall things were unsightly and a glove kept in place better.

If anything occurred to wash out the – the programme after that, well then he'd have to fake some sort of accident to justify wearing the glove for the next time. Anyway, there were still three weeks to the audit, and as long as matters were – adjusted – before the audit, nothing mattered. Foresee everything. Provide for the minutest and longest chances. That was the only way to ensure success.

Now about the 'phone message. There would not be a second lost in that. The governor's calls were always answered at once. What would the girl at the works' exchange do when she heard? Faint, perhaps. So much the better. If she had hysterics it would be better still. But take the most unfavourable case and suppose she acted as a modern, sensible, businesslike girl. She would call the nearest ledger clerk and he would come to the 'phone to confirm the rumour perhaps.

In any case Martin had tried the distance between the exchange and the office, and it would take seventy-two seconds at a run. If you took the telephone message as the start of a race then he had a margin of safety of fifty-seven seconds, for he would be back in his own room in fifteen. There was a margin of safety of fifty-seven seconds. No need to flurry or hurry or doubt.

Anything else? Tracks along the roof path? A button, or a chance paper of his dropped in the governor's office? Those things didn't matter at all. He was along that path and in and out of that office three or four times a day.

Now what did he do when he got back, before the terrible news was announced? There was the Metropole tender to check. The papers were on his desk. He would be immersed in them. Miss Burton would not have got back. Someone would come rushing into the other office and make for his private door, would barge it open, shouting his name.

He would look up from the papers on his desk irritably.

'What in thunder is the matter? Is the place on fire?'

After that the needs of the case could be met as they arose. The difficult part would be over. Naturally, when the audit came off everything would be quite clear. There would be no further mystery at all.

Martin smiled to himself, and for a moment allowed his mind to dwell on the thought of a bank account at Salford which recorded a balance of eight thousand pounds in favour of Richard Heath. When

Richard Heath, who was only known to the bank by a signature, closed that account by a cheque in favour of Martin Culpepper, say in six or eight months' time, the entire incident was at an end.

Brains, care, foresight, attention to detail – those were the essentials of success!

Well, well! Everything was fixed. Nothing could possibly side-slip.

Martin scrutinized himself carefully in the mirror over his mantelpiece. He looked perfectly normal. Why shouldn't he? When one undertakes a perfectly simple task and has drilled oneself carefully in every step of it, why worry? He gave a little jerk to his tie, pulled the lapels of his coat and pressed the buzzer for Miss Burton.

Zero hour.

'You rang, sir?'

He had the tender papers before him, and when she came in hardly looked up.

'I'd like to have a look at the clocking-on slips, Miss Burton. As you come back will you bring me a range of the samples furnished in the Metropole tender, please – a complete range?'

A nice bit of embroidery on the main scheme that!

Miss Burton would be ten minutes before she came back now. Besides, she would know that he was working on the tender, as they would find him when they came.

Simplicity is the great note of good organization. Get a thing simple and you can control it so that nothing can go wrong.

Half a minute while he put the glove on his right hand and waited to be sure that Miss Burton would not have any after-thought and come back, and Martin straightened his coat and stepped into the roof corridor.

Thirty paces to— No, don't think of that! – envisage the programme. Here we are at the governor's door. Knock. Enter.

'I would like you to see the week's figures, Sir Gerald.'

Everything was O.K. There was nothing to show cause why the scheme should not go through. Let it rip.

'Culpepper?' Sir Gerald looked up with his usual benign interest. He wasn't really benign, thought Martin. He would never look benign at a ten-thousand pounds deficit. 'A good week, eh?'

'I hope you'll think so, sir.' Martin set the papers on the desk and stood at the governor's right shoulder. 'If I recollect, they are better than the week before last, which was exceptional, sir.'

'Capital!' Sir Gerald beamed. 'Top-hole! From management to machine-minder, Culpepper, I've a fine staff, devoted and loyal. We must look at last week's.'

He opened the drawer and took out the sheaf of papers. Under them was the file of records, and under that Martin saw the thing glint.

The old man bent to his scrutiny. It was less than a second's work to snatch the weapon. Now!

The report could not be heard above the racket of the shops below. It's surprisingly simple killing a man, thought Martin.

The old man had hardly moved, hardly raised an arm in protest, and there he was sagging in the revolving chair with his right arm hanging limp and already a little pool lazily forming on the carpet.

Close the right hand over the pistol on the desk, forefinger round the trigger. That was all right. There was no need to hurry. Work slowly, methodically.

Blood! Mind the blood.

Letters on the desk? What had he been writing? All clear.

Now for the great stunt. The thing that fixed everything finally, irrevocably.

Martin coughed twice to get just the right tone of huskiness and the timbre of the old man's voice. 'Good morning, Culpepper,' said he aloud, and knew that he had got the exact intonation. Then he took the receiver from its hook and waited.

'House exchange, Sir Gerald.'

'House exchange good,' he returned in his imitation of the old man's voice. 'Now I want you to listen carefully to this message. Don't interrupt me. For two years I've been robbing the shareholders right and left. The auditors will know all about it in a week or two. It won't matter, I shan't be here. My last chance of escape failed today and I'm finished. I am standing at the 'phone with a pistol in my hand now, and if you wait five seconds longer—'

Martin grinned. He knew that was a safe card. No girl at the other end of the 'phone would wait and listen for the shot.

Now things would move. He'd got his fifty-seven seconds to cross to his own room and get really busy with the tender.

He gave a last look round.

Everything was quite still, quite innocent, except for that – that— Whatever was in the chair could never harm him now. A very thorough piece of work. Foresight. Being prepared for every chance. That ensures success.

He walked to the door and pulled at the handle. It came off in his hand. For a second he stared while the pin, fastened to the heavier handle outside, joggled in the socket.

Even as he watched, with each joggle, it slid farther and farther through. In a sudden, frightful panic he grabbed at it maladroitly and pushed it through. Handle and pin dropped in the passage outside.

To force a bolt – to force a bolt quickly – something to force the latch! No fire-irons in the room, curse it. No time – no time to think or anything. Fifty-seven seconds, was it? Barely forty now. The windows! Waste of time to think of them. A cat couldn't escape from these windows without breaking its neck. Neck! Brrh!

He pulled at the lock of the door frantically. Fool, that's no good! Thought, not violence, was wanted. Cold, calm thought. Violence wastes time. There were barely thirty seconds now – thirty, what had he thought about barely thirty just now? From the condemned cell to the scaffold— Curse it! This was not the time to think of that. Force the latch back with a – with a – with a paper-knife. The thing split. It would.

Calm. Calm now! There must be a way – there must be some way. Everything had been so perfectly planned.

Suddenly, in the thousandth of a second, he saw it perfectly clear, perfectly obvious and safe as houses.

Blast those fools! Someone tearing up the stairs had disturbed him. Jolted the idea out of his head. Perhaps it hadn't existed. Perhaps it was only a fancy of his racing mind. Yet it had seemed so – it hadn't even seemed to matter if they had come and found him there. Mirage! There was no way out. No way out at all. Or had it been real, that momentary idea which he could not recapture? Think now, think, think!

They were hammering at the door. In view of that 'phone message they would break it down at once. That would be Eckridge barging against the panel, the brute. They had no feeling, no respect for the dead. They knew perfectly well that the governor lay there with a revolver in his fist, and there was Eckridge outside shouting orders.

'Someone go and find Culpepper. Don't stand gaping there.'

And the governor lying dead with the revolver in – a revolver? Was that the bright idea that had come to him, the safe way out? It might have been. He was so mixed – the panel had split – so mixed that he could not think. They did not give a fellow a chance. Anyhow, it was the only way now. Brrh! The governor was not cold. Unnatural that, not cold. Anyway the revolver was unclasped easily from his hand, and there were five more chambers. One could make a good job of it with five.

Another shot in the locker!

For a second those working frantically outside fell back at the sound, then Eckridge, the chief cashier, said brokenly: 'God forgive us, we might have been in time,' as the door gave way.

Inside, Culpepper slid to the floor with Sir Gerald's revolver still pressed to his ribs. He was conscious, but something told him that he could not last many minutes.

At that moment it came back to him, the idea which had flashed so clearly before his mind and been eclipsed. It was only necessary to say: 'As I came in at the door to see the governor the shot rang out. I was just too late.'

That would have been the cue. So simple.

Eckridge came over to him.

'My God, Culpepper,' he cried, 'what's the matter with you?'

The general manager looked up at him wisely, his head wobbled.

'Take my tip, Eckridge,' said he, 'and always remember the obvious thing.'

His head fell back on the floor with a thud.

The Return of Imray

Rudyard Kipling

Imray achieved the impossible. Without warning, for no conceivable motive, in his youth, at the threshold of his career he chose to disappear from the world – which is to say, the little Indian station where he lived.

Upon a day he was alive, well, happy, and in great evidence among the billiard-tables at his Club. Upon a morning, he was not, and no manner of search could make sure where he might be. He had stepped out of his place; he had not appeared at his office at the proper time, and his dog-cart was not upon the public roads. For these reasons, and because he was hampering, in a microscopical degree, the administration of the Indian Empire, that Empire paused for one microscopical moment to make inquiry into the fate of Imray.

Ponds were dragged, wells were plumbed, telegrams were despatched down the lines of railways and to the nearest seaport town – 1200 miles away; but Imray was not at the end of the drag-ropes nor the telegraph wires. He was gone, and his place knew him no more. Then the work of the great Indian Empire swept forward, because it could not be delayed, and Imray from being a man became a mystery – such a thing as men talk over at their tables in the Club for a month, and then forget utterly. His guns, horses, and carts were sold to the highest bidder. His superior officer wrote an altogether absurd letter to his mother, saying that Imray had unaccountably disappeared, and his bungalow stood empty.

After three or four months of the scorching hot weather had gone by, my friend Strickland, of the Police, saw fit to rent the bungalow from the native landlord. This was before he was engaged to Miss Youghal – an affair which has been described in another place – and while he was pursuing his investigations into native life. His own life was sufficiently peculiar, and men complained of his manners and customs. There was always food in his house, but there were no regular times for meals. He ate, standing up and walking about, whatever he might find at the sideboard, and this is not good for human beings. His domestic equipment was limited to six rifles, three shotguns, five saddles, and a collection of stiff-jointed mahseer-rods, bigger and stronger than the largest salmon-rods. These occupied one-half of his bungalow, and the other half was given up to Strickland and his dog Tietjens – an enormous Rampur slut who devoured daily the rations of two men. She spoke to Strickland in a language of her own; and whenever, walking abroad, she saw things calculated to destroy the peace of Her Majesty the Queen-Empress, she returned to her master and laid information.

Strickland would take steps at once, and the end of his labours was trouble and fine and imprisonment for other people. The natives believed that Tietjens was a familiar spirit, and treated her with the great reverence that is born of hate and fear. One room in the bungalow was set apart for her special use. She owned a bedstead, a blanket, and a drinking-trough, and if anyone came into Strickland's room at night her custom was to knock down the invader and give tongue till someone came with a light. Strickland owed his life to her, when he was on the Frontier, in search of a local murderer, who came in the grey dawn to send Strickland much farther than the Andaman Islands. Tietjens caught the man as he was crawling into Strickland's tent with a dagger between his teeth; and after his record of iniquity was established in the eyes of the law he was hanged. From that date Tietjens wore a collar of rough silver, and employed a monogram on her night-blanket; and the blanket was of double woven Kashmir cloth, for she was a delicate dog.

Under no circumstances would she be separated from Strickland; and once, when he was ill with fever, made great trouble for the doctors, because she did not know how to help her master and would not allow another creature to attempt aid. Macarnaght, of the Indian Medical Service, beat her over her head with a gun-butt before she could understand that she must give room for those who could give quinine.

A short time after Strickland had taken Imray's bungalow, my business took me through that Station, and naturally, the Club quarters being full, I quartered myself upon Strickland. It was a desirable bungalow, eight-roomed and heavily thatched against any chance of leakage from rain. Under the pitch of the roof ran a ceiling-cloth which looked just as neat as a whitewashed ceiling. The landlord had repainted it when Strickland took the bungalow. Unless you knew how Indian bungalows were built you would never have suspected that above the cloth lay the dark three-cornered cavern of the roof, where the beams and the underside of the thatch harboured all manner of rats, bats, ants, and foul things.

Tietjens met me in the verandah with a bay like the boom of the bell of St Paul's, putting her paws on my shoulder to show she was glad to see me. Strickland had contrived to claw together a sort of meal which he called lunch, and immediately after it was finished went out about his business. I was left alone with Tietjens and my own affairs. The heat of the summer had broken up and turned to the warm damp of the rains. There was no motion in the heated air, but the rain fell like ramrods on the earth, and flung up a blue mist when it splashed back. The bamboos, and the custard-apples, the poinsettias, and the mango-trees in the garden stood still while the warm water lashed through them, and the frogs began to sing among the aloe hedges.

A little before the light failed, and when the rain was at its worst, I sat in the back verandah and heard the water roar from the eaves, and scratched myself because I was covered with the thing called prickly-heat. Tietjens came out with me and put her head in my lap and was very sorrowful; so I gave her biscuits when tea was ready, and I took tea in the back verandah on account of the little coolness found there. The rooms of the house were dark behind me. I could smell Strickland's saddlery and the oil on his guns, and I had no desire to sit among these things. My own servant came to me in the twilight, the muslin of his clothes clinging tightly to his drenched body, and told me that a gentleman had called and wished to see someone.

Very much against my will, but only because of the darkness of the rooms, I went into the naked drawing-room, telling my man to bring the lights. There might or might not have been a caller waiting – it seemed to me that I saw a figure by one of the windows – but when the lights came, there was nothing save the spikes of the rain without, and the smell of the drinking earth in my nostrils. I explained to my servant that he was no wiser than he ought to be, and went back to the verandah to talk to Tietjens. She had gone out into the wet, and I could hardly coax her back to me; even with biscuits with sugar tops.

Strickland came home, dripping wet, just before dinner, and the first thing he said was: 'Has anyone called?'

I explained, with apologies, that my servant had summoned me into the drawing-room on a false alarm; or that some loafer had tried to call on Strickland, and thinking better of it had fled after giving his name. Strickland ordered dinner, without comment, and since it was a real dinner with a white tablecloth attached, we sat down.

At nine o'clock Strickland wanted to go to bed, and I was tired too. Tietjens, who had been lying underneath the table, rose up, and swung into the least exposed verandah as soon as her master moved to his own room, which was next to the stately chamber set apart for Tietjens. If a mere wife had wished to sleep out of doors in that pelting rain it would not have mattered; but Tietjens was a dog, and therefore the better animal.

I looked at Strickland, expecting to see him flay her with a whip. He smiled queerly, as a man would smile after telling some unpleasant domestic tragedy. 'She has done this ever since I moved in here,' said he. 'Let her go.'

The dog was Strickland's dog, so I said nothing, but I felt all that Strickland felt in being thus made light of. Tietjens encamped outside my bedroom window, and storm after storm came up, thundered on the thatch, and died away. The lightning spattered the sky as a thrown egg spatters a barn-door, but the light was pale blue, not yellow; and, looking through my split bamboo blinds, I could see the great dog standing, not sleeping, in the verandah, the hackles alift on her back and her feet anchored as tensely as the drawn wire-rope of a suspension bridge.

In the very short pauses of the thunder I tried to sleep, but it seemed that someone wanted me very urgently. He, whoever he was, was trying to call me by name, but his voice was no more than a husky whisper. The thunder ceased, and Tietjens went into the garden and howled at the low moon. Somebody tried to open my door, walked about and about through the house and stood breathing heavily in the verandah, and just when I was falling asleep I fancied that I heard a wild hammering and clamouring above my head or on the door.

I ran into Strickland's room and asked him whether he was ill, and had been calling for me. He was lying on his bed half dressed, a pipe in his mouth. 'I thought you'd come,' he said. 'Have I been walking round the house recently?'

I explained that he had been tramping in the dining-room and the smoking-room and two or three other places, and he laughed and told me to go back to bed. I went back to bed and slept till the morning, but through all my mixed dreams I was sure I was doing someone an injustice in not attending to his wants. What those wants were I could not tell; but a fluttering, whispering, bolt-fumbling, lurking, loitering Someone was reproaching me for my slackness, and, half awake, I heard the howling of Tietjens in the garden and the threshing of the rain.

I lived in that house for two days. Strickland went to his office daily, leaving me alone for eight or ten hours with Tietjens for my only companion. As long as the full light lasted I was comfortable, and so was Tietjens; but in the twilight she and I moved into the back verandah and cuddled each other for company. We were alone in the house, but nonetheless it was much too fully occupied by a tenant with whom I did not wish to interfere. I never saw him, but I could see the curtains between the rooms quivering where he had just passed through; I could hear the chairs creaking as the bamboos sprung under a weight that had just quitted them; and I could feel when I went to get a book from the dining-room that somebody was waiting in the shadows of the front verandah till I should have gone away.

Tietjens made the twilight more interesting by glaring into the darkened rooms with every hair erect, and following the motions of something that I could not see. She never entered the rooms, but her eyes moved interestedly: that was quite sufficient. Only when my servant came to trim the lamps and make all light and habitable she would come in with me and spend her time sitting on her haunches, watching an invisible extra man as he moved about behind my shoulder. Dogs are cheerful companions.

I explained to Strickland, gently as might be, that I would go over to the Club and find for myself quarters there. I admired his hospitality, was pleased with his guns and rods, but I did not much care for his house and its atmosphere. He heard me out to the end, and then smiled very wearily, but without contempt, for he is a man who understands things.

'Stay on,' he said, 'and see what this thing means. All you have talked about I have known since I took the bungalow. Stay on and wait. Tietjens has left me. Are you going too?'

I had seen him through one little affair, connected with a heathen idol, that had brought me to the doors of a lunatic asylum, and I had no desire to help him through further experiences. He was a man to whom unpleasantnesses arrived as do dinners to ordinary people.

Therefore I explained more clearly than ever that I liked him immensely, and would be happy to see him in the daytime; but that I did not care to sleep under his roof. This was after dinner, when Tietjens had gone out to lie in the verandah.

''Pon my soul, I don't wonder,' said Strickland, with his eyes on the ceiling-cloth. 'Look at that!'

The tails of two brown snakes were hanging between the cloth and the cornice of the wall. They threw long shadows in the lamplight.

'If you are afraid of snakes, of course—' said Strickland.

I hate and fear snakes, because if you look into the eyes of any snake you will see that it knows all and more of the mystery of man's fall, and that it feels all the contempt that the Devil felt when Adam was evicted from Eden. Besides which its bite is generally fatal, and it twists up trouser legs.

'You ought to get your thatch overhauled,' I said. 'Give me a mahseer-rod, and we'll poke 'em down.'

'They'll hide among the roof-beams,' said Strickland. 'I can't stand snakes overhead. I'm going up into the roof. If I shake 'em down, stand by with a cleaning-rod and break their backs.'

I was not anxious to assist Strickland in his work, but I took the cleaning-rod and waited in the dining-room while Strickland brought a gardener's ladder from the verandah, and set it against the side of the room. The snake-tails drew themselves up and disappeared. We could hear the dry rushing scuttle of long bodies running over the baggy ceiling-cloth. Strickland took a lamp with him, while I tried to make clear to him the danger of hunting roof-snakes between a ceiling-cloth and a thatch, apart from the deterioration of property caused by ripping out ceiling-cloths.

'Nonsense!' said Strickland. 'They're sure to hide near the walls by the cloth. The bricks are too cold for 'em, and the heat of the room is just what they like.' He put his hand to the corner of the stuff and ripped it from the cornice. It gave with a great sound of tearing, and Strickland put his head through the opening into the dark of the angle of the roof-beams. I set my teeth and lifted the cleaning-rod.

'H'm!' said Strickland, and his voice rolled and rumbled in the roof. 'There's room for another set of rooms up here, and, by Jove, someone is occupying 'em!'

'Snakes?' I said from below.

'No. It's a buffalo. Hand me up the two last joints of a mahseer-rod, and I'll prod it. It's lying on the main roof-beam.'

I handed up the rod.

'What a nest for owls and serpents! No wonder the snakes live here,' said Strickland, climbing farther into the roof. I could see his elbow thrusting with the rod. 'Come out of that, whatever you are! Heads below there! It's falling.'

I saw the ceiling-cloth nearly in the centre of the room bag with a shape that was pressing it downwards and downwards towards the lighted lamp on the table. I snatched the lamp out of danger and stood back. Then the cloth ripped out from the walls, tore, split, swayed, and shot down upon the table something that I dared not look at, till Strickland had slid down the ladder and was standing by my side.

He did not say much, being a man of few words; but he picked up the loose end of the tablecloth and threw it over the remnants on the table.

'It strikes me,' said he, putting down the lamp, 'our friend Imray has come back. Oh, you would, would you?'

There was a movement under the cloth, and a little snake wriggled out, to be back-broken by the butt of the mahseer-rod. I was sufficiently sick to make no remarks worth recording.

Strickland meditated, and helped himself to drinks. The arrangement under the cloth made no more signs of life.

'Is it Imray?' I said.

Strickland turned back the cloth for a moment, and looked.

'It is Imray,' he said; 'and his throat is cut from ear to ear.'

Then we spoke, both together and to ourselves: 'That's why he whispered about the house.'

Tietjens, in the garden, began to bay furiously. A little later her great nose heaved open the dining-room door.

She sniffed and was still. The tattered ceiling-cloth hung down almost to the level of the table, and there was hardly room to move away from the discovery.

Tietjens came in and sat down; her teeth bared under her lip and her forepaws planted. She looked at Strickland.

'It's a bad business, old lady,' said he. 'Men don't climb up into the roofs of their bungalows to die, and they don't fasten up the ceiling-cloth behind 'em. Let's think it out.'

'Let's think it out somewhere else,' I said.

'Excellent idea! Turn the lamps out. We'll get into my room.'

I did not turn the lamps out. I went into Strickland's room first, and allowed him to make the darkness. Then he followed me, and we lit tobacco and thought. Strickland thought. I smoked furiously, because I was afraid.

'Imray is back,' said Strickland. 'The question is – who killed Imray? Don't talk, I've a notion of my own. When I took this bungalow I took over most of Imray's servants. Imray was guileless and inoffensive, wasn't he?'

I agreed; though the heap under the cloth had looked neither one thing nor the other.

'If I call in all the servants they will stand fast in a crowd and lie like Aryans. What do you suggest?'

'Call 'em in one by one,' I said.

'They'll run away and give the news to all their fellows,' said Strickland. 'We must segregate 'em. Do you suppose your servant knows anything about it?'

'He may, for aught I know; but I don't think it's likely. He has only been here two or three days,' I answered. 'What's your notion?'

'I can't quite tell. How the dickens did the man get the wrong side of the ceiling-cloth?'

There was a heavy coughing outside Strickland's bedroom door. This showed that Bahadur Khan, his body-servant, had waked from sleep and wished to put Strickland to bed.

'Come in,' said Strickland. 'It's a very warm night, isn't it?'

Bahadur Khan, a great, green-turbaned, six-foot Mahomedan, said that it was a very warm night; but that there was more rain pending, which, by his Honour's favour, would bring relief to the country.

'It will be so, if God pleases,' said Strickland, tugging off his boots. 'It is in my mind, Bahadur Khan, that I have worked thee remorselessly for many days – ever since that time when thou first camest into my service. What time was that?'

'Has the Heaven-born forgotten? It was when Imray Sahib went secretly to Europe without warning given; and I – even I – came into the honoured service of the protector of the poor.'

'And Imray Sahib went to Europe?'

'It is so said among those who were his servants.'

'And thou wilt take service with him when he returns?'

'Assuredly, Sahib. He was a good master, and cherished his dependents.'

'That is true. I am very tired, but I go buck-shooting tomorrow. Give me the little sharp rifle that I use for black-buck; it is in the case yonder.'

The man stooped over the case; handed barrels, stock, and fore-end to Strickland, who fitted all together, yawning dolefully. Then he reached down to the gun-case, took a solid-drawn cartridge, and slipped it into the breech of the .360 Express.

'And Imray Sahib has gone to Europe secretly! That is very strange, Bahadur Khan, is it not?'

'What do I know of the ways of the white man, Heaven-born?'

'Very little, truly. But thou shalt know more anon. It has reached me that Imray Sahib has returned from his so long journeys, and that even now he lies in the next room, waiting his servant.'

'Sahib!'

The lamplight slid along the barrels of the rifle as they levelled themselves at Bahadur Khan's broad breast.

'Go and look!' said Strickland. 'Take a lamp. Thy master is tired, and he waits thee. Go!'

The man picked up a lamp, and went into the dining-room, Strickland following, and almost pushing him with the muzzle of the rifle. He looked for a moment at the black depths behind the ceiling-cloth; at the writhing snake underfoot; and last, a grey glaze settling on his face, at the thing under the tablecloth.

'Hast thou seen?' said Strickland after a pause.

'I have seen. I am clay in the white man's hands. What does the Presence do?'

'Hang thee within the month. What else?'

'For killing him? Nay, Sahib, consider. Walking among us, his servants, he cast his eyes upon my child, who was four years old. Him he bewitched, and in ten days he died of the fever – my child!'

'What said Imray Sahib?'

'He said he was a handsome child, and patted him on the head; wherefore my child died. Wherefore I killed Imray Sahib in the twilight, when he had come back from office, and was sleeping. Wherefore I dragged him up into the roof-beams and made all fast behind him. The Heaven-born knows all things. I am the servant of the Heaven-born.'

Strickland looked at me above the rifle, and said, in the vernacular, 'Thou art witness to this saying? He has killed.'

Bahadur Khan stood ashen grey in the light of the one lamp. The need for justification came upon him very swiftly. 'I am trapped,' he said, 'but the offence was that man's. He cast an evil eye upon my child, and I killed and hid him. Only such as are served by devils,' he glared at Tietjens, crouched stolidly before him, 'only such could know what I did.'

'It was clever. But thou shouldst have lashed him to the beam with a rope. Now, thou thyself wilt hang by a rope. Orderly!'

A drowsy policeman answered Strickland's call. He was followed by another, and Tietjens sat wondrous still.

'Take him to the police-station,' said Strickland. 'There is a case toward.'

'Do I hang, then?' said Bahadur Khan, making no attempt to escape, and keeping his eyes on the ground.

'If the sun shines or the water runs – yes!' said Strickland.

Bahadur Khan stepped back one long pace, quivered, and stood still. The two policemen waited further orders.

'Go!' said Strickland.

'Nay; but I go very swiftly,' said Bahadur Khan. 'Look! I am even now a dead man.'

He lifted his foot, and to the little toe there clung the head of the half-killed snake, firm fixed in the agony of death.

'I come of land-holding stock,' said Bahadur Khan, rocking where he stood. 'It were a disgrace to me to go to the public scaffold: therefore I take this way. Be it remembered that the Sahib's shirts are correctly enumerated, and that there is an extra piece of soap in his washbasin. My child was bewitched, and I slew the wizard. Why should you seek to slay me with the rope? My honour is saved, and – and – I die.'

At the end of an hour he died, as they die who are bitten by the little brown *karait*, and the policemen bore him and the thing under the tablecloth to their appointed places.

'This,' said Strickland, very calmly, as he climbed into bed, 'is called the Nineteenth Century. Did you hear what that man said?'

'I heard,' I answered. 'Imray made a mistake.'

'Simply and solely through not knowing the nature of the Oriental, and the coincidence of a little seasonal fever. Bahadur Khan had been with him for four years.'

I shuddered. My own servant had been with me for exactly that length of time. When I went over to my own room I found my man waiting, impassive as the copper head on a penny, to pull off my boots.

'What has befallen Bahadur Khan?' said I.

'He was bitten by a snake and died. The rest the Sahib knows,' was the answer.

'And how much of this matter hast thou known?'

'As much as might be gathered from One coming in in the twilight to seek satisfaction. Gently, Sahib. Let me pull off those boots.'

I had just settled to the sleep of exhaustion when I heard Strickland shouting from his side of the house—

'Tietjens has come back to her place!'

And so she had. The great deerhound was couched statelily on her own bedstead on her own blanket, while, in the next room, the idle, empty, ceiling-cloth waggled as it trailed on the table.

The Lady with the Hatchet

Maurice Leblanc

One of the most incomprehensible incidents that preceded the great war was certainly the one which was known as the episode of the lady with the hatchet. The solution of the mystery was unknown and would never have been known, had not circumstances in the cruellest fashion obliged Prince Rénine – or should I say, Arsène Lupin? – to take up the matter and had I not been able today to tell the true story from details supplied by him.

Let me recite the facts. In a space of eighteen months, five women disappeared, five women of different stations in life, all between twenty and thirty years of age and living in Paris or the Paris district.

I will give their names: Madame Ladoue, the wife of a doctor; Mlle Ardant, the daughter of a banker; Mlle Covereau, a washer-woman of Courbevoie; Mlle Honorine Vernisset, a dressmaker; and Madame Grollinger, an artist. These five women disappeared without the possibility of discovering a single particular to explain why they had left their homes, why they did not return to them, who had enticed them away, and where and how they were detained.

Each of these women, a week after her departure, was found some-where or other in the western outskirts of Paris; and each time it was a dead body that was found, the dead body of a woman who had been killed by a blow on the head from a hatchet. And each time, not far from the woman, who was firmly bound, her face covered with blood and her body emaciated by lack of food, the marks of carriage wheels proved that the corpse had been driven to the spot.

The five murders were so much alike that there was only a single investigation, embracing all the five enquiries and, for that matter, leading to no result. A woman disappeared; a week later, to a day, her body was discovered; and that was all. The bonds that fastened her were similar in each case; so were the tracks left by the wheels; so were the blows of the hatchet, all of which were struck vertically at the top and right in the middle of the forehead.

The motive of the crime? The five women had been completely

stripped of their jewels, purses and other objects of value. But the robberies might well have been attributed to marauders or any passers-by, since the bodies were lying in deserted spots. Were the authorities to believe in the execution of a plan of revenge or of a plan intended to do away with the series of persons mutually connected, persons, for instance, likely to benefit by a future inheritance? Here again the same obscurity prevailed. Theories were built up, only to be demolished forthwith by an examination of the facts. Trails were followed and at once abandoned.

And suddenly there was a sensation. A woman engaged in sweeping the roads picked up on the pavement a little notebook which she brought to the local police station. The leaves of this notebook were all blank, excepting one, on which was written a list of the murdered women, with their names set down in order of date and accompanied by three figures: Ladoue, 132; Vernisset, 118; and so on.

Certainly no importance would have been attached to these entries, which anybody might have written, since everyone was acquainted with the sinister list. But, instead of five names, it included six! Yes, below the words 'Grollinger, 128,' there appeared 'Williamson, 114.' Did this indicate a sixth murder?

The obviously English origin of the name limited the field of the investigations, which did not in fact take long. It was ascertained that, a fortnight ago, a Miss Hermione Williamson, a governess in a family at Auteuil, had left her place to go back to England and that, since then, her sisters, though she had written to tell them that she was coming over, had heard no more of her.

A fresh enquiry was instituted. A postman found the body in the Meudon woods. Miss Williamson's skull was split down the middle.

I need not describe the public excitement at this stage nor the shudder of horror which passed through the crowd when it read this list, written without a doubt in the murderer's own hand. What could be more frightful than such a record, kept up to date like a careful tradesman's ledger:

'On such a day, I killed so-and-so; on such a day so-and-so!'

And the sum total was six dead bodies.

Against all expectation, the experts in handwriting had no difficulty in agreeing and unanimously declared that the writing was 'that of a woman, an educated woman, possessing artistic tastes, imagination and an extremely sensitive nature.' The 'lady with the hatchet,' as the journalists christened her, was decidedly no ordinary person; and scores of newspaper articles made a special study of her case, exposing her mental condition and losing themselves in far-fetched explanations.

Nevertheless it was the writer of one of these articles, a young journalist whose chance discovery made him the centre of public attention, who supplied the one element of truth and shed upon the darkness the only ray of light that was to penetrate it. In casting about for the meaning of the figures which followed the six names, he had come to ask himself whether those figures did not simply represent the number of the days separating one crime from the next. All that he had to do was to check the dates. He at once found that his theory was correct. Mlle Vernisset had been carried off one hundred and thirty-two days after Madame Ladoue; Mlle Covereau, one hundred and eighteen days after Honorine Vernisset; and so on.

There was therefore no room for doubt; and the police had no choice but to accept a solution which so precisely fitted the circumstances: the figures corresponded with the intervals. There was no mistake in the records of the lady with the hatchet.

But then one deduction became inevitable. Miss Williamson, the latest victim, had been carried off on the 26th day of June last, and her name was followed by the figures 114: was it not to be presumed that a fresh crime would be committed a hundred and fourteen days later, that is to say, on the 18th of October? Was it not probable that the horrible business would be repeated in accordance with the murderer's secret intentions? Were they not bound to pursue to its logical conclusion the argument which ascribed to the figures – to all the figures, to the last as well as to the others – their value as eventual dates?

Now precisely this deduction which was drawn and was being weighed and discussed during the few days that preceded the 18th of October, when logic demanded the performance of yet another act of the abominable tragedy. And it was only natural that, on the morning of that day, Prince Rénine and Hortense, when making an appointment by telephone for the evening, should allude to the newspaper articles which they had both been reading:

'Look out!' said Rénine, laughing. 'If you meet the lady with the hatchet, take the other side of the road!'

'And, if the good lady carries me off, what am I to do?'

'Strew your path with little white pebbles and say, until the very moment when the hatchet flashes in the air, "I have nothing to fear; he will save me." *He* is myself . . . and I kiss your hands. Till this evening, my dear.'

That afternoon, Rénine had an appointment with Rose Andrée and Dalbrèque to arrange for their departure for the States. Between four and seven o'clock, he bought the different editions of the evening papers. None of them reported any abduction.

At nine o'clock he went to the Gymnase, where he had taken a private box.

At half-past nine, as Hortense had not arrived, he rang her up, though without thought of anxiety. The maid replied that Madame Daniel had not come in yet.

Seized with a sudden fear, Rénine hurried to the furnished flat which Hortense was occupying for the time being, near the Parc Monceau, and questioned the maid, whom he had engaged for her and who was completely devoted to him. The woman said that her mistress had gone out at two o'clock, with a stamped letter in her hand, saying that she was going to the post and that she would come back to dress. This was the last that had been seen of her.

'To whom was the letter addressed?'

'To you, sir. I saw the writing on the envelope: Prince Serge Rénine.'

He waited until midnight, but in vain. Hortense did not return; nor did she return next day.

'Not a word to anyone,' said Rénine to the maid. 'Say that your mistress is in the country and that you are going to join her.'

For his own part, he had not a doubt: Hortense's disappearance was explained by the very fact of the date, the 18th of October. She was the seventh victim of the lady with the hatchet.

'The abduction,' said Rénine to himself, 'precedes the blow of the hatchet by a week. I have, therefore, at the present moment, seven full days before me. Let us say six, to avoid any surprise. This is Saturday: Hortense must be set free by midday on Friday; and, to make sure of this, I must know her hiding place by nine o'clock on Thursday evening at latest.'

Rénine wrote, 'THURSDAY EVENING, NINE O'CLOCK,' in big letters, on a card which he nailed above the mantelpiece in his study. Then at midday on Saturday, the day after the disappearance, he locked himself into the study, after telling his man not to disturb him except for meals and letters.

He spent four days there, almost without moving. He had immediately sent for a set of all the leading newspapers which had spoken in detail of the first six crimes. When he had read and reread them, he closed the shutters, drew the curtains and lay down on the sofa in the dark, with the door bolted, thinking.

By Tuesday evening he was no further advanced than on the Saturday. The darkness was as dense as ever. He had not discovered the smallest clue for his guidance, nor could he see the slightest reason to hope.

At times, notwithstanding his immense power of self-control and his unlimited confidence in the resources at his disposal, at times he would quake with anguish. Would he arrive in time? There was no reason why he should see more clearly during the last few days than during those which had already elapsed. And this meant that Hortense Daniel would inevitably be murdered.

The thought tortured him. He was attached to Hortense by a much stronger and deeper feeling than the appearance of the relations between them would have led an onlooker to believe. The curiosity at the beginning, the first desire, the impulse to protect Hortense, to distract her, to inspire her with a relish for existence: all this had simply turned to love. Neither of them was aware of it, because they barely saw each other save at critical times when they were occupied with the adventures of others and not with their own. But, at the first onslaught of danger, Rénine realized the place which Hortense had taken in his life and he was in despair at knowing her to be a prisoner and a martyr and at being unable to save her.

He spent a feverish, agitated night, turning the case over and over from every point of view. The Wednesday morning was also a terrible time for him. He was losing ground. Giving up his hermit-like seclusion, he threw open the windows and paced to and fro through his rooms, ran out into the street and came in again, as though fleeing before the thought that obsessed him:

'Hortense is suffering. . . . Hortense is in the depths. . . . She sees the hatchet. . . . She is calling to me. . . . She is entreating me. . . . And I can do nothing. . . .'

It was at five o'clock in the afternoon that, on examining the list of the six names, he received that little inward shock which is a sort of signal of the truth that is being sought for. A light shot through his mind. It was not, to be sure, that brilliant light in which every detail is made plain, but it was enough to tell him in which direction to move.

His plan of campaign was formed at once. He sent Adolphe, his chauffeur, to the principal newspapers, with a few lines which were to appear in large type among the next morning's advertisements. Adolphe was also told to go to the laundry at Courbevoie, where Mlle Covereau, the second of the six victims, had been employed.

On the Thursday, Rénine did not stir out of doors. In the afternoon, he received several letters in reply to his advertisement. Then two telegrams arrived. Lastly, at three o'clock, there came a pneumatic letter, bearing the Trocadéro postmark, which seemed to be what he was expecting.

He turned up a directory, noted an address – 'M. de Lourtier-Vanuea, retired colonial governor, 47 *bis*, Avenue Kléber' – and ran down to his car:

'Adolphe, 47 *bis*, Avenue Kléber.'

He was shown into a large study furnished with magnificent bookcases containing old volumes in costly bindings. M. de Lourtier-Vaneau was a man still in the prime of life, wearing a slightly grizzled beard and, by his affable manners and genuine distinction, commanding confidence and liking.

'M. de Lourtier,' said Rénine, 'I have ventured to call on your excellency because I read in last year's newspapers that you used to know one of the victims of the lady with the hatchet, Honorine Vernisset.'

'Why, of course we knew her!' cried M. de Lourtier. 'My wife used to employ her as a dressmaker by the day. Poor girl!'

'M. de Lourtier, a lady of my acquaintance has disappeared as the other six victims disappeared.'

'What!' exclaimed M. de Lourtier, with a start. 'But I have followed the newspapers carefully. There was nothing on the 18th of October.'

'Yes, a woman of whom I am very fond, Madame Hortense Daniel, was abducted on the 17th of October.'

'And this is the 22nd!'

'Yes; and the murder will be committed on the 24th.'

'Horrible! Horrible! It must be prevented at all costs. . . .'

'And I shall perhaps succeed in preventing it, with your excellency's assistance.'

'But have you been to the police?'

'No. We are faced by mysteries which are, so to speak, absolute and compact, which offer no gap through which the keenest eyes can see and which it is useless to hope to clear up by ordinary methods, such as inspection of the scenes of the crimes, police enquiries, searching for fingerprints and so on. As none of those proceedings served any good purpose in the previous cases, it would be waste of time to resort to them in a seventh, similar case. An enemy who displays such skill and subtlety would not leave behind her any of those clumsy traces which are the first things that a professional detective seizes upon.'

'Then what have you done?'

'Before taking any action, I have reflected. I gave four days to thinking the matter over.'

M. de Lourtier-Vaneau examined his visitor closely and, with a touch of irony, asked:

'And the result of your meditations . . . ?'

'To begin with,' said Rénine, refusing to be put out of countenance, 'I have submitted all these cases to a comprehensive survey, which hitherto no one else had done. This enabled me to discover their general meaning, to put aside all the tangle of embarrassing theories and, since no one was able to agree as to the motives of all this filthy business, to attribute it to the only class of persons capable of it.'

'That is to say?'

'Lunatics, your excellency.'

M. de Lourtier-Vaneau started:

'Lunatics? What an idea!'

'M. de Lourtier, the woman known as the lady with the hatchet is a madwoman.'

'But she would be locked up!'

'We don't know that she's not. We don't know that she is not one of those half-mad people, apparently harmless, who are watched so slightly that they have full scope to indulge their little manias, their wild-beast instincts. Nothing could be more crafty, more patient, more persistent, more dangerous and at the same time more absurd and more logical, more slovenly and more methodical. All these epithets, M. de Lourtier, may be applied to the doings of the lady with the hatchet. The obsession of an idea and the continual repetition of an act are characteristics of the maniac. I do not yet know the idea by which the lady with the hatchet is obsessed but I do know the act that results from it; and it is always the same. The victim is bound with precisely similar rope. She is killed after the same number of days. She is struck by an identical blow, with the same instrument, in the same place, the middle of the forehead, producing an absolutely vertical wound. An ordinary murderer displays some variety. His trembling hand swerves aside and strikes awry. The lady with the hatchet does not tremble. It is as though she had taken measurements; and the edge of her weapon does not swerve by a hair's breadth. Need I give you any further proofs or examine all the other details with you? Surely not. You now possess the key to the riddle; and you know as I do that only a lunatic can behave in this way, stupidly, savagely, mechanically, like a striking clock or the blade of the guillotine. . . .'

M. de Lourtier-Vaneau nodded his head:

'Yes, that is so. One can see the whole affair from that angle . . . and I am beginning to believe that this is how one ought to see it. But, if we admit that this madwoman has the sort of mathematical logic which governed the murders of the six victims, I see no connection between the victims themselves. She struck at random. Why this victim rather than that?'

'Ah,' said Rénine. 'Your excellency is asking me a question which I asked myself from the first moment, the question which sums up the whole problem and which cost me so much trouble to solve! Why Hortense Daniel rather than another? Among two millions of women who might have been selected, why Hortense? Why little Vernisset? Why Miss Williamson? If the affair is such as I conceived it, as a whole, that is to say, based upon the blind and fantastic logic of a madwoman, a choice was inevitably exercised. Now in what did that choice consist? What was the quality, or the defect, or the sign needed to induce the lady with the hatchet to strike? In a word, if she chose – and she must have chosen – what directed her choice?'

'Have you found the answer?'

Rénine paused and replied:

'Yes, your excellency, I have. And I could have found it at the very outset, since all that I had to do was to make a careful examination of the list of victims. But these flashes of truth are never kindled save in a brain overstimulated by effort and reflection. I stared at the list twenty times over, before that little detail took a definite shape.'

'I don't follow you,' said M. de Lourtier-Vaneau.

'M. de Lourtier, it may be noted that, if a number of persons are brought together in any transaction, or crime, or public scandal or what not, they are almost invariably described in the same way. On this occasion, the newspapers never mentioned anything more than their surnames in speaking of Madame Ladoue, Mlle Ardant or Mlle Covereau. On the other hand, Mlle Vernisset and Miss Williamson were always described by their Christian names as well: Honorine and Hermione. If the same thing had been done in the case of all the six victims, there would have been no mystery.'

'Why not?'

'Because we should at once have realized the relation existing between the six unfortunate women, as I myself suddenly realized it on comparing those two Christian names with that of Hortense Daniel. You understand now don't you? You see the three Christian names before your eyes. . . .'

M. de Lourtier-Vaneau seemed to be perturbed. Turning a little pale, he said:

'What do you mean? What do you mean?'

'I mean,' continued Rénine in a clear voice, sounding each syllable separately, 'I mean that you see before your eyes three Christian names which all three begin with the same initial and which all three, by a remarkable coincidence, consist of the same number of letters, as you may prove. If you inquire at the Courbevoie laundry, where Mlle Covereau used to work, you will find that her name was Hilairie. Here again we have the same initial and the same number of letters. There is no need to seek any farther. We are sure, are we not, that the Christian names of all the victims offer the same peculiarities? And this gives us, with absolute certainty, the key to the problem which was set us. It explains the madwoman's choice. We now know the connection between the unfortunate victims. There can be no mistake about it. It's that and nothing else. And how this method of choosing confirms my theory! What proof of madness! Why kill these women rather than any others? Because their names begin with an H and consist of eight letters! You understand me, M. de Lourtier, do you not? The number of letters is eight. The initial letter is the eighth letter of the alphabet; and the word *huit*, eight, begins with an H. Always the letter H. *And the implement used to commit the crime was a hatchet.* Is your excellency prepared to tell me that the lady with the hatchet is not a madwoman?'

Rénine interrupted himself and went up to M. de Lourtier-Vaneau:

'What's the matter, your excellency? Are you unwell?'

'No, no,' said M. de Lourtier, with the perspiration streaming down

his forehead. 'No ... but all this story is so upsetting! Only think, I
knew one of the victims! And then ...'

Rénine took a water-bottle and tumbler from a small table, filled
the glass and handed it to M. de Lourtier, who sipped a few mouthfuls
from it and then, pulling himself together, continued, in a voice which
he strove to make firmer than it had been:

'Very well. We'll admit your supposition. Even so, it is necessary that
it should lead to tangible results. What have you done?'

'This morning I published in all the newspapers an advertisement
worded as follows: "Excellent cook seeks situation. Write before 5 P.M.
to Herminie, Boulevard Haussmann, etc." You continue to follow me,
don't you, M. de Lourtier? Christian names beginning with an H and
consisting of eight letters are extremely rare and are all rather out of
date: Herminie, Hilairie, Hermione. Well, these Christian names, for
reasons which I do not understand, are essential to the madwoman.
She cannot do without them. To find women bearing one of these
Christian names and for this purpose only she summons up all her remaining powers of reason, discernment, reflection and intelligence. She hunts
about. She asks questions. She lies in wait. She reads newspapers which
she hardly understands, but in which certain details, certain capital
letters catch her eye. And consequently I did not doubt for a second
that this name of Herminie, printed in large type, would attract her
attention and that she would be caught today in the trap of my
advertisement.'

'Did she write?' asked M. de Lourtier-Vaneau, anxiously.

'Several ladies,' Rénine continued, 'wrote the letters which are usual
in such cases, to offer a home to the so-called Herminie. But I received
an express letter which struck me as interesting.'

'From whom?'

'Read it, M. de Lourtier.'

M. de Lourtier-Vaneau snatched the sheet from Rénine's hands and
cast a glance at the signature. His first movement was one of surprise,
as though he had expected something different. Then he gave a long,
loud laugh of something like joy and relief.

'Why do you laugh, M. de Lourtier? You seem pleased.'

'Pleased, no. But this letter is signed by my wife.'

'And you were afraid of finding something else?'

'Oh, no! But since it's my wife ...'

He did not finish his sentence and said to Rénine:

'Come this way.'

He led him through a passage to a little drawing-room where a fair-
haired lady, with a happy and tender expression on her comely face,
was sitting in the midst of three children and helping them with their
lessons.

She rose. M. de Lourtier briefly presented his visitor and asked his wife:

'Suzanne, is this express message from you?'

'To Mlle Herminie, Boulevard Haussmann? Yes,' she said, 'I sent it. As you know, our parlourmaid's leaving and I'm looking out for a new one.'

Rénine interrupted her:

'Excuse me, madame. Just one question: where did you get the woman's address?'

She flushed. Her husband insisted:

'Tell us, Suzanne. Who gave you the address?'

'I was rung up.'

'By whom?'

She hesitated and then said:

'Your old nurse.'

'Félicienne?'

'Yes.'

M. de Lourtier cut short the conversation and, without permitting Rénine to ask any more questions, took him back to the study:

'You see, monsieur, that pneumatic letter came from a quite natural source. Félicienne, my old nurse, who lives not far from Pairs on an allowance which I make her, read your advertisement and told Madame de Lourtier of it. For, after all,' he added laughing, 'I don't suppose that you suspect my wife of being the lady with the hatchet.'

'No.'

'Then the incident is closed ... at least on my side. I have done what I could, I have listened to your arguments and I am very sorry that I can be of no more use to you. ...'

He drank another glass of water and sat down. His face was distorted.

Rénine looked at him for a few seconds, as a man will look at a failing adversary who has only to receive the knock-out blow, and, sitting down beside him, suddenly gripped his arm:

'Your excellency, if you do not speak, Hortense Daniel will be the seventh victim.'

'I have nothing to say, monsieur! What do you think I know?'

'The truth! My explanations have made it plain to you. Your distress, your terror are positive proofs.'

'But after all, monsieur, if I knew, why should I be silent?'

'For fear of scandal. There is in your life, so a profound intuition assures me, something that you are constrained to hide. The truth about this monstrous tragedy, which suddenly flashed upon you, this truth, if it were known, would spell dishonour to you, disgrace ... and you are shrinking from your duty.'

M. de Lourtier did not reply. Rénine leaned over him and, looking him in the eyes, whispered.

'There will be no scandal. I shall be the only person in the world to know what has happened. And I am as much interested as yourself in not attracting attention, because I love Hortense Daniel and do not wish her name to be mixed up in your horrible story.'

They remained face to face during a long interval. Rénine's expression was harsh and unyielding. M. de Lourtier felt that nothing would bend him if the necessary words remained unspoken; but he could not bring himself to utter them.

'You are mistaken,' he said. 'You think you have seen things that don't exist.'

Rénine received a sudden and terrifying conviction that, if this man took refuge in a stolid silence, there was no hope for Hortense Daniel; and he was so much infuriated by the thought that the key to the riddle lay there, within reach of his hand, that he clutched M. de Lourtier by the throat and forced him backwards:

'I'll have no more lies! A woman's life is at stake! Speak . . . and speak at once! If not . . . !'

M. de Lourtier had no strength left in him. All resistance was impossible. It was not that Rénine's attack alarmed him, or that he was yielding to this act of violence, but he felt crushed by that indomitable will, which seemed to admit no obstacle, and he stammered:

'You are right. It is my duty to tell everything, whatever comes of it.'

'Nothing will come of it, I pledge my word, on condition that you save Hortense Daniel. A moment's hesitation may undo us all. Speak. No details, but the actual facts.'

'Madame de Lourtier is not my wife. The only woman who has the right to bear my name is one whom I married when I was a young colonial official. She was a rather eccentric woman, of feeble mentality and incredibly subject to impulses that amounted to monomania. We had two children, twins, whom she worshipped and in whose company she would no doubt have recovered her mental balance and moral health, when, by a stupid accident – a passing carriage – they were killed before her eyes. The poor thing went mad . . . with the silent, secretive madness which you imagined. Some time afterwards, when I was appointed to an Algerian station, I brought her to France and put her in the charge of a worthy creature who had nursed me and brought me up. Two years later, I made the acquaintance of the woman who was to become the joy of my life. You saw her just now. She is the mother of my children and she passes as my wife. Are we to sacrifice her? Is our whole existence to be shipwrecked in horror and must our name be coupled with this tragedy of madness and blood?'

Rénine thought for a moment and asked:

'What is the other one's name?'

'Hermance.'

'Hermance! Still that initial . . . still those eight letters!'

'That was what made me realize everything just now,' said M. de Lourtier. 'When you compared the different names, I at once reflected that my unhappy wife was called Hermance and that she was mad . . . and all the proofs leapt to my mind.'

'But, though we understand the selection of the victims, how are we to explain the murders? What are the symptoms of her madness? Does she suffer at all?'

'She does not suffer very much at present. But she has suffered in the past, the most terrible suffering that you can imagine since the moment when her two children were run over before her eyes, night and day she had the horrible spectacle of their death before her eyes, without a moment's interruption, for she never slept for a single second. Think of the torture of it! To see her children dying through all the hours of the long day and all the hours of the interminable night!'

'Nevertheless,' Rénine objected, 'it is not to drive away that picture that she commits murder?'

'Yes, possibly,' said M. de Lourtier, thoughtfully, 'to drive it away by sleep.'

'I don't understand.'

'You don't understand, because we are talking of a madwoman . . . and because all that happens in that disordered brain is necessarily incoherent and abnormal?'

'Obviously. But, all the same, is your supposition based on facts that justify it?'

'Yes, on facts which I had, in a way, overlooked but which today assume their true significance. The first of these facts dates a few years back, to a morning when my old nurse for the first time found Hermance fast asleep. Now she was holding her hands clutched around a puppy which she had strangled. And the same thing was repeated on three other occasions.'

'And she slept?'

'Yes, each time she slept a sleep which lasted for several nights.'

'And what conclusion did you draw?'

'I concluded that the relaxation of the nerves provoked by taking life exhausted her and predisposed her for sleep.'

Rénine shuddered:

'That's it! There's not a doubt of it! The taking of life, the effort of killing makes her sleep. And she began with women what had served her so well with animals. All her madness has become concentrated on that one point: she kills them to rob them of their sleep! She wanted sleep; and she steals the sleep of others! That's it, isn't it? For the past two years, she has been sleeping?'

'For the past two years, she has been sleeping,' stammered M. de Lourtier.

Rénine gripped him by the shoulder:

'And it never occurred to you that her madness might go farther, that she would stop at nothing to win the blessing of sleep! Let us make haste, monsieur! All this is horrible!'

They were both making for the door, when M. de Lourtier hesitated. The telephone bell was ringing.

'It's from there,' he said.

'From there?'

'Yes, my old nurse gives me the news at the same time every day.' He unhooked the receivers and handed one to Rénine, who whispered in his ear the questions which he was to put.

'Is that you, Félicienne? How is she?'

'Not so bad, sir.'

'Is she sleeping well?'

'Not very well, lately. Last night, indeed, she never closed her eyes. So she's very gloomy just now.'

'What is she doing at the moment?'

'She is in her room.'

'Go to her, Félicienne, and don't leave her.'

'I can't. She locked herself in.'

'You must, Félicienne. Break open the door. I'm coming straight on ... Hullo! Hullo! ... Oh, damnation, they've cut us off!'

Without a word, the two men left the flat and ran down to the avenue. Rénine hustled M. de Lourtier into the car:

'What address?'

'Ville d'Avray.'

'Of course! In the very centre of her operations ... like a spider in the middle of her web! Oh, the shame of it!'

He was profoundly agitated. He saw the whole adventure in its monstrous reality.

'Yes, she kills them to steal their sleep, as she used to kill the animals. It is the same obsession, but complicated by a whole array of utterly incomprehensible practices and superstitions. She evidently fancies that the similarity of the Christian names to her own is indispensable and that she will not sleep unless her victim is an Hortense or an Honorine. It's a madwoman's argument; its logic escapes us and we know nothing of its origin; but we can't get away from it. She has to hunt and has to find. And she finds and carries off her prey beforehand and watches over it for the appointed number of days, until the moment when, crazily, through the hole which she digs with a hatchet in the middle of the skull, she absorbs the sleep which stupefies her and grants her oblivion for a given period. And here again we see absurdity and madness. Why does she fix that period at so many days? Why should one victim ensure her a hundred and twenty days of sleep and another a hundred and twenty-five? What insanity! The calculation is mysterious and of course mad; but the fact remains that, at the end of a hundred or a hundred and twenty-five days, as the case may be, a fresh victim is sacrificed; and there have been six already and the seventh is awaiting her turn. Ah, monsieur, what a terrible responsibility for you! Such a monster as that! She should never have been allowed out of sight!'

M. de Lourtier-Vaneau made no protest. His air of dejection, his pallor, his trembling hands, all proved his remorse and his despair.

'She deceived me,' he murmured. 'She was outwardly so quiet, so docile! And, after all, she's in a lunatic asylum.'

'Then how can she . . . ?'

'The asylum,' explained M. de Lourtier, 'is made up of a number of separate buildings scattered over extensive grounds. The sort of cottage in which Hermance lives stands quite apart. There is first a room occupied by Félicienne, then Hermance's bedroom and two separate rooms, one of which has its windows overlooking the open country. I suppose it is there that she locks up her victims.'

'But the carriage that conveys the dead bodies?'

'The stables of the asylum are quite close to the cottage. There's a horse and carriage there for station work. Hermance no doubt gets up at night, harnesses the horse and slips the body through the window.'

'And the nurse who watches her?'

'Félicienne is very old and rather deaf.'

'But by day she sees her mistress moving to and fro, doing this and that. Must we not admit a certain complicity?'

'Never! Félicienne herself has been deceived by Hermance's hypocrisy.'

'All the same, it was she who telephoned to Madame de Lourtier first, about that advertisement. . . .'

'Very naturally. Hermance, who talks now and then, who argues, who buries herself in the newspapers, which she does not understand, as you were saying just now, but reads through them attentively, must have seen the advertisement and, having heard that we were looking for a servant, must have asked Félicienne to ring me up.'

'Yes . . . yes . . . that is what I felt,' said Rénine, slowly. 'She marks down her victims. . . . With Hortense dead, she would have known, once she had used up her allowance of sleep, where to find an eighth victim . . . But how did she entice the unfortunate women?'

The car was rushing along, but not fast enough to please Rénine, who rated the chauffeur.

'Push her along, Adolphe, can't you? . . . We're losing time, my man.'

Suddenly the fear of arriving too late began to torture him. The logic of the insane is subject to sudden changes of mood, to any perilous idea that may enter the mind. The madwoman might easily mistake the date and hasten the catastrophe, like a clock out of order which strikes an hour too soon.

On the other hand, as her sleep was once more disturbed, might she not be tempted to take action without waiting for the appointed moment? Was this not the reason why she had locked herself into her room? Heavens, what agonies her prisoner must be suffering! What shudders of terror at the executioner's least movement!

'Faster, Adolphe, or I'll take the wheel myself! Faster, hang it.'

At last they reached Ville d'Avray. There was a steep, sloping road on the right and walls interrupted by a long railing.

'Drive round the grounds, Adolphe. We mustn't give warning of our presence, must we, M. de Lourtier? Where is the cottage?'

'Just opposite,' said M. de Lourtier-Vaneau.

They got out a little farther on. Rénine began to run along a bank at the side of an ill-kept sunken road. It was almost dark. M. de Lourtier said:

'Here, this building standing a little way back. . . . Look at that window on the ground floor. It belongs to one of the separate rooms . . . and that is obviously how she slips out.'

'But the window seems to be barred.'

'Yes; and that is why no one suspected anything. But she must have found some way to get through.'

The ground floor was built over deep cellars. Rénine quickly clambered up, finding a foothold on a projecting ledge of stone.

Sure enough, one of the bars was missing.

He pressed his face to the windowpane and looked in.

The room was dark inside. Nevertheless he was able to distinguish at the back a woman seated beside another woman, who was lying on a mattress. The woman seated was holding her forehead in her hands and gazing at the woman who was lying down.

'It's she,' whispered M. de Lourtier, who had also climbed the wall. 'The other one is bound.'

Rénine took from his pocket a glazier's diamond and cut out one of the panes without making enough noise to arouse the madwoman's attention. He next slid his hand to the window-fastening and turned it softly, while with his left hand he levelled a revolver.

'You're not going to fire, surely!' M. de Lourtier-Vaneau entreated.

'If I must, I shall.'

Rénine pushed open the window gently. But there was an obstacle of which he was not aware, a chair which toppled over and fell.

He leapt into the room and threw away his revolver in order to seize the madwoman. But she did not wait for him. She rushed to the door, opened it and fled, with a hoarse cry.

M. de Lourtier made as though to run after her.

'What's the use?' said Rénine, kneeling down. 'Let's save the victim first.'

He was instantly reassured: Hortense was alive.

The first thing that he did was to cut the cords and remove the gag that was stifling her. Attracted by the noise, the old nurse had hastened in with a lamp, which Rénine took from her, casting its light on Hortense.

He was astounded: though livid and exhausted, with emaciated features and eyes blazing with fever, Hortense was trying to smile. She whispered:

'I was expecting you.... I did not despair for a moment.... I was sure of you....'

She fainted.

An hour later, after useless searching around the cottage, they found the madwoman locked into a large cupboard in the loft. She had hanged herself.

Hortense refused to stay another night. Besides, it was better that the cottage should be empty when the old nurse announced the madwoman's suicide. Rénine gave Félicienne minute directions as to what she should do and say; and then, assisted by the chauffeur and M. de Lourtier, carried Hortense to the car and brought her home.

She was soon convalescent. Two days later, Rénine carefully questioned her and asked her how she had come to know the madwoman.

'It was very simple,' she said. 'My husband, who is not quite sane, as I have told you, is being looked after at Ville d'Avray; and I sometimes go to see him, without telling anybody, I admit. That was how I came to speak to that poor madwoman and how, the other day, she made signs that she wanted me to visit her. We were alone. I went into the cottage. She threw herself upon me and overpowered me before I had time to cry for help. I thought it was a jest; and so it was, wasn't it: a madwoman's jest? She was quite gentle with me.... All the same, she let me starve. But I was so sure of you!'

'And weren't you frightened?'

'Of starving? No. Besides, she gave me some food, now and then, when the fancy took her.... And then I was sure of you!'

'Yes, but there was something else: that other peril ...'

'What other peril?' she asked, ingenuously.

Rénine gave a start. He suddenly understood – it seemed strange at first, though it was quite natural – that Hortense had not for a moment suspected and did not yet suspect the terrible danger which she had run. Her mind had not connected with her own adventure the murders committed by the lady with the hatchet.

He thought that it would always be time enough to tell her the truth. For that matter, a few days later her husband, who had been locked up for years, died in the asylum at Ville d'Avray, and Hortense, who had been recommended by her doctor a short period of rest and solitude, went to stay with a relation living near the village of Bassicourt, in the centre of France.

A Thousand Deaths

Jack London

I had been in the water about an hour, and cold, exhausted, with a terrible cramp in my right calf, it seemed as though my hour had come. Fruitlessly struggling against the strong ebb tide, I had beheld the maddening procession of the water-front lights slip by; but now I gave up attempting to breast the stream and contented myself with the bitter thoughts of a wasted career, now drawing to a close.

It had been my luck to come of good, English stock, but of parents whose account with the bankers far exceeded their knowledge of child-nature and the rearing of children. While born with a silver spoon in my mouth, the blessed atmosphere of the home circle was to me unknown. My father, a very learned man and a celebrated antiquarian, gave no thought to his family, being constantly lost in the abstractions of his study; while my mother, noted far more for her good looks than her good sense, sated herself with the adulation of the society in which she was perpetually plunged. I went through the regular school and college routine of a boy of the English bourgeois, and as the years brought me increasing strength and passions, my parents suddenly became aware that I was possessed of an immortal soul, and endeavoured to draw the curb. But it was too late; I perpetrated the wildest and most audacious folly, and was disowned by my people, ostracized by the society I had so long outraged, and with the thousand pounds my father gave me, with the declaration that he would neither see me again nor give me more, I took a first-class passage to Australia.

Since then my life had been one long peregrination – from the Orient to the Occident, from the Arctic to the Antarctic – to find myself at last, an able seaman at thirty, in the full vigour of my manhood, drowning in San Francisco Bay because of a disastrously successful attempt to desert my ship.

My right leg was drawn up by the cramp, and I was suffering the keenest agony. A slight breeze stirred up a choppy sea, which washed into my mouth and down my throat, nor could I prevent it. Though I still contrived to keep afloat, it was merely mechanical, for I was rapidly

becoming unconscious. I have a dim recollection of drifting past the
sea-wall, and of catching a glimpse of an up-river steamer's starboard
light; then everything became a blank.

I heard the low hum of insect life, and felt the balmy air of a spring
morning fanning my cheek. Gradually it assumed a rhythmic flow, to
whose soft pulsations my body seemed to respond. I floated on the gentle
bosom of a summer's sea, rising and falling with dreamy pleasure on
each crooning wave. But the pulsations grew stronger; the humming
louder; the waves, larger, fiercer – I was dashed about on a stormy sea.
A great agony fastened upon me. Brilliant, intermittent sparks of light
flashed athwart my inner consciousness; in my ears there was the sound
of many waters; then a sudden snapping of an intangible something,
and I awoke.

The scene, of which I was protagonist, was a curious one. A glance
sufficed to inform me that I lay on the cabin floor of some gentleman's
yacht, in a most uncomfortable posture. On either side, grasping my
arms and working them up and down like pump handles, were two
peculiarly clad, dark-skinned creatures. Though conversant with most
aboriginal types, I could not conjecture their nationality. Some attach-
ment had been fastened about my head, which connected my respiratory
organs with the machine I shall next describe. My nostrils, however,
had been closed, forcing me to breathe through the mouth. Fore-
shortened by the obliquity of my line of vision, I beheld two tubes, similar
to small hosing but of different composition, which emerged from my
mouth and went off at an acute angle from each other. The first came
to an abrupt termination and lay on the floor beside me; the second
traversed the floor in numerous coils, connecting with the apparatus
I have promised to describe.

In the days before my life had become tangential, I had dabbled
not a little in science, and conversant with the appurtenances and general
paraphernalia of the laboratory, I appreciated the machine I now
beheld. It was composed chiefly of glass, the construction being of that
crude sort which is employed for experimentative purposes. A vessel
of water was surrounded by an air chamber, to which was fixed a vertical
tube, surmounted by a globe. In the centre of this was a vacuum gauge.
The water in the tube moved upward and downward, creating alternate
inhalations and exhalations, which were in turn communicated to me
through the hose. With this, and the aid of the men who pumped my
arms so vigorously, had the process of breathing been artificially carried
on, my chest rising and falling and my lungs expanding and contracting,
till nature could be persuaded to again take up her wonted labour.

As I opened my eyes the appliance about my head, nostrils and mouth
was removed. Draining a stiff three fingers of brandy, I staggered to

my feet to thank my preserver, and confronted – my father. But long years of fellowship with danger had taught me self-control, and I waited to see if he would recognize me. Not so; he saw in me no more than a runaway sailor and treated me accordingly.

Leaving me to the care of the blacks, he fell to revising the notes he had made on my resuscitation. As I ate of the handsome fare served up to me, confusion began on deck, and from the chanteys of the sailors and the rattling of blocks and tackles I surmised that we were getting under way. What a lark! Off on a cruise with my recluse father into the wide Pacific! Little did I realize, as I laughed to myself, which side the joke was to be on. Aye, had I known, I would have plunged overboard and welcomed the dirty fo'c'sle from which I had just escaped.

I was not allowed on deck till we had sunk the Farallones and the last pilot boat. I appreciated this forethought on the part of my father and made it a point to thank him heartily, in my bluff seaman's manner. I could not suspect that he had his own ends in view, in thus keeping my presence secret to all save the crew. He told me briefly of my rescue by his sailors, assuring me that the obligation was on his side, as my appearance had been most opportune. He had constructed the apparatus for the vindication of a theory concerning certain biological phenomena, and had been waiting for an opportunity to use it.

'You have proved it beyond all doubt,' he said; then added with a sigh, 'But only in the small matter of drowning.'

But, to take a reef in my yarn – he offered me an advance of two pounds on my previous wages to sail with him and this I considered handsome, for he really did not need me. Contrary to my expectations, I did not join the sailors' mess, for'ard, being assigned to a comfortable stateroom and eating at the captain's table. He had perceived that I was no common sailor, and I resolved to take this chance for reinstating myself in his good graces. I wove a fictitious past to account for my education and present position, and did my best to come in touch with him. I was not long in disclosing a predilection for scientific pursuits, nor he in appreciating my aptitude. I became his assistant, with a corresponding increase in wages, and before long, as he grew confidential and expounded his theories, I was as enthusiastic as himself.

The days flew quickly by, for I was deeply interested in my new studies, passing my waking hours in his well-stocked library, or listening to his plans and aiding him in his laboratory work. But we were forced to forgo many enticing experiments, a rolling ship not being exactly the proper place for delicate or intricate work. He promised me, however, many delightful hours in the magnificent laboratory for which we were bound. He had taken possession of an uncharted South Sea island, as he said, and turned it into a scientific paradise.

We had not been on the island long, before I discovered the horrible mare's nest I had fallen into. But before I describe the strange things which came to pass, I must briefly outline the causes which culminated in as startling an experience as ever fell to the lot of man.

Late in life, my father had abandoned the musty charms of antiquity and succumbed to the more fascinating ones embraced under the general head of biology. Having been thoroughly grounded during his youth in the fundamentals, he rapidly explored all the higher branches as far as the scientific world had gone, and found himself on the no man's land of the unknowable. It was his intention to pre-empt some of this unclaimed territory, and it was at this stage of his investigations that we had been thrown together. Having a good brain, though I say it myself, I had mastered his speculations and methods of reasoning, becoming almost as mad as himself. But I should not say this. The marvellous results we afterward obtained can only go to prove his sanity. I can but say that he was the most abnormal specimen of cold-blooded cruelty I have ever seen.

After having penetrated the dual mysteries of physiology and psychology, his thought had led him to the verge of a great field, for which, the better to explore, he began studies in higher organic chemistry, pathology, toxicology and other sciences and sub-sciences rendered kindred as accessories to his speculative hypotheses. Starting from the proposition that the direct cause of the temporary and permanent arrest of vitality was due to the coagulation of certain elements and compounds in the protoplasm, he had isolated and subjected these various substances to innumerable experiments. Since the temporary arrest of vitality in an organism brought coma, and a permanent arrest death, he held that by artificial means this coagulation of the protoplasm could be retarded, prevented, and even overcome in the extreme states of solidification. Or, to do away with the technical nomenclature, he argued that death, when not violent and in which none of the organs had suffered injury, was merely suspended vitality; and that, in such instances, life could be induced to resume its functions by the use of proper methods. This, then, was his idea: To discover the method – and by practical experimentation prove the possibility – of renewing vitality in a structure from which life had seemingly fled. Of course, he recognized the futility of such endeavour after decomposition had set in; he must have organisms which but the moment, the hour, or the day before, had been quick with life. With me, in a crude way, he had proved this theory. I was really drowned, really dead, when picked from the water of San Francisco Bay – but the vital spark had been renewed by means of his aerotherapeutical apparatus, as he called it.

Now to his dark purpose concerning me. He first showed me how completely I was in his power. He had sent the yacht away for a year, retaining only his two blacks, who were utterly devoted to him. He then made an exhaustive review of his theory and outlined the method of proof he had adopted, concluding with the startling announcement that I was to be his subject.

I had faced death and weighed my chances in many a desperate venture, but never in one of this nature. I can swear I am no coward, yet this proposition of journeying back and forth across the borderland of death put the yellow fear upon me. I asked for time, which he granted, at the same time assuring me that but the one course was open – I must submit. Escape from the island was out of the question; escape by suicide was not to be entertained, though really preferable to what it seemed I must undergo; my only hope was to destroy my captors. But this latter was frustrated through the precautions taken by my father. I was subjected to a constant surveillance, even in my sleep being guarded by one or the other of the blacks.

Having pleaded in vain, I announced and proved that I was his son. It was my last card, and I had placed all my hopes upon it. But he was inexorable; he was not a father but a scientific machine. I wonder yet how it ever came to pass that he married my mother or begat me, for there was not the slightest grain of emotion in his make-up. Reason was all in all to him, nor could he understand such things as love or sympathy in others, except as petty weaknesses which should be overcome. So he informed me that in the beginning he had given me life, and who had better right to take it away than he? Such, he said, was not his desire, however; he merely wished to borrow it occasionally, promising to return it punctually at the appointed time. Of course, there was a liability of mishaps, but I could do no more than take the chances, since the affairs of men were full of such.

The better to insure success, he wished me to be in the best possible condition, so I was dieted and trained like a great athlete before a decisive contest. What could I do? If I had to undergo the peril, it were best to be in good shape. In my intervals of relaxation he allowed me to assist in the arranging of the apparatus and in the various subsidiary experiments. The interest I took in all such operations can be imagined. I mastered the work as thoroughly as he, and often had the pleasure of seeing some of my suggestions or alterations put into effect. After such events I would smile grimly, conscious of officiating at my own funeral.

He began by inaugurating a series of experiments in toxicology. When all was ready, I was killed by a stiff dose of strychnine and allowed to lie dead for some twenty hours. During that period my body was dead, absolutely dead. All respiration and circulation ceased; but the frightful part of it was, that while the protoplasmic coagulation proceeded, I retained consciousness and was enabled to study it in all its ghastly details.

The apparatus to bring me back to life was an air-tight chamber, fitted to receive my body. The mechanism was simple – a few valves, a rotary shaft and crank, and an electric motor. When in operation, the interior atmosphere was alternately condensed and rarefied, thus communicating to my lungs an artificial respiration without the agency of the hosing previously used. Though my body was inert, and, for all I know, in the first stages of decomposition, I was cognisant of everything that transpired. I knew when they placed me in the chamber, and though all my senses were quiescent, I was aware of the hypodermic injections of a compound to react upon the coagulatory process. Then the chamber was closed and the machinery started. My anxiety was terrible; but the circulation became gradually restored, the different organs began to carry on their respective functions, and in an hour's time I was eating a hearty dinner.

It cannot be said that I participated in this series, nor in the subsequent ones, with much verve; but after two ineffectual attempts at escape, I began to take quite an interest. Besides, I was becoming accustomed. My father was beside himself at his success, and as the months rolled by his speculations took wilder and yet wilder flights. We ranged through the three great classes of poisons, the neurotics, the gaseous and the irritants, but carefully avoided some of the mineral irritants and passed the whole group of corrosives. During the poison regime I became quite accustomed to dying, and had but one mishap to shake my growing confidence. Scarifying a number of lesser blood vessels in my arm, he introduced a minute quantity of that most frightful of poisons, the arrow poison, or curare. I lost consciousness at the start, quickly followed by the cessation of respiration and circulation, and so far had the solidification of the protoplasm advanced, that he gave up all hope. But at the last moment he applied a discovery he had been working upon, receiving such encouragement as to redouble his efforts.

In a glass vacuum, similar but not exactly like a Crookes' tube, was placed a magnetic field. When penetrated by polarized light, it gave no phenomena of phosphorescence nor of rectilinear projection of atoms, but emitted non-luminous rays, similar to the X ray. While the X ray could reveal opaque objects hidden in dense mediums, this was possessed of far subtler penetration. By this he photographed my body, and found on the negative an infinite number of blurred shadows, due to the chemical and electric motions still going on. This was an infallible proof that the rigor mortis in which I lay was not genuine; that is, those mysterious forces, those delicate bonds which held my soul to my body, were still in action. The resultants of all other poisons were unapparent, save those of mercurial compounds, which usually left me languid for several days.

Another series of delightful experiments was with electricity. We verified Tesla's assertion that high currents were utterly harmless by passing 100,000 volts through my body. As this did not affect me, the current was reduced to 2,500, and I was quickly electrocuted. This time he ventured so far as to allow me to remain dead, or in a state of suspended vitality, for three days. It took four hours to bring me back.

Once, he superinduced lockjaw, but the agony of dying was so great that I positively refused to undergo similar experiments. The easiest deaths were by asphyxiation, such as drowning, strangling, and suffoca-- tion by gas; while those by morphine, opium, cocaine and chloroform, were not at all hard.

Another time, after being suffocated, he kept me in cold storage for three months, not permitting me to freeze or decay. This was without my knowledge, and I was in a great fright on discovering the lapse of time. I became afraid of what he might do with me when I lay dead, my alarm being increased by the predilection he was beginning to betray toward vivisection. The last time I was resurrected, I discovered that he had been tampering with my breast. Though he had carefully dressed and sewed the incisions up, they were so severe that I had to take to my bed for some time. It was during this convalescence that I evolved the plan by which I ultimately escaped.

While feigning unbounded enthusiasm in the work, I asked and received a vacation from my moribund occupation. During this period I devoted myself to laboratory work, while he was too deep in the vivisection of the many animals captured by the blacks to take notice of my work.

It was on these two propositions that I constructed my theory: First, electrolysis, or the decomposition of water into its constituent gases by means of electricity; and, second, by the hypothetical existence of a force, the converse of gravitation, which Astor has named 'apergy.' Terrestrial attraction, for instance, merely draws objects together but does not combine them; hence, apergy is merely repulsion. Now, atomic or molecular attraction not only draws objects together but integrates them; and it was the converse of this, or a disintegrative force, which I wished to not only discover and produce, but to direct at will. Thus the molecules of hydrogen and oxygen reacting on each other, separate and create new molecules, containing both elements and forming water. Electrolysis causes these molecules to split up and resume their original condition, producing the two gases separately. The force I wished to find must not only do this with two, but with all elements, no matter in what compounds they exist. If I could then entice my father within its radius, he would be instantly disintegrated and sent flying to the four quarters, a mass of isolated elements.

It must not be understood that this force, which I finally came to control, annihilated matter, it merely annihilated form. Nor, as I soon discovered, had it any effect on inorganic structure; but to all organic form it was absolutely fatal. This partiality puzzled me at first, though had I stopped to think deeper I would have seen through it. Since the number of atoms in organic molecules is far greater than in the most complex mineral molecules, organic compounds are characterized by their instability and the ease with which they are split up by physical forces and chemical reagents.

By two powerful batteries, connected with magnets constructed specially for this purpose, two tremendous forces were projected. Considered apart from each other, they were perfectly harmless; but they accomplished their purpose by focusing at an invisible point in mid-air. After practically demonstrating its success, besides narrowly escaping being blown into nothingness, I laid my trap. Concealing the magnets, so that their force made the whole space of my chamber doorway a field of death, and placing by my couch a button by which I could throw on the current from the storage batteries, I climbed into bed.

The blacks still guarded my sleeping quarters, one relieving the other at midnight. I turned on the current as soon as the first man arrived. Hardly had I begun to doze, when I was aroused by a sharp, metallic tinkle. There, on the mid-threshold, lay the collar of Dan, my father's St Bernard. My keeper ran to pick it up. He disappeared like a gust of wind, his clothes falling to the floor in a heap. There was a slight whiff of ozone in the air, but since the principal gaseous components of his body were hydrogen, oxygen and nitrogen, which are equally colourless and odourless, there was no other manifestation of his departure. Yet when I shut off the current and removed the garments, I found a deposit of carbon in the form of animal charcoal; also other powders, the isolated, solid elements of his organism, such as sulphur, potassium and iron. Resetting the trap, I crawled back to bed. At midnight I got up and removed the remains of the second black, and then slept peacefully till morning.

I was awakened by the strident voice of my father, who was calling to me from across the laboratory. I laughed to myself. There had been no one to call him and he had overslept. I could hear him as he approached my room with the intention of rousing me, and so I sat up in bed, the better to observe his translation – perhaps apotheosis were a better term. He paused a moment at the threshold, then took the fatal step. Puff! It was like the wind sighing among the pines. He was gone. His clothes fell in a fantastic heap on the floor. Besides ozone, I noticed the faint, garlic-like odour of phosphorus. A little pile of elementary solids lay among his garments. That was all. The wide world lay before me. My captors were not.

Homicidal Hiccup

John D. MacDonald

You say you've been reading the series of articles in the Baker City *Journal* about how Mayor Willison cleaned up the city?

Brother, those articles are written for the sucker trade – meaning no offence, you understand.

Oh, I'll admit that the city is clean now – but not because of Willison. Willison is a cloth-head. He doesn't even know how Baker City got cleaned up. Being a politician, he's glad to jump in and take credit, naturally.

That's right. I know exactly how it happened, and it isn't going to be printed in any newspapers, even if I am a reporter. You spring for a few rounds of bourbon and I'll give it to you – just the way it happened.

You know about Johnny Howard. I don't pretend to understand him, or the guys like him. Maybe something happens when they're little kids, and by the time they get grown up, they have to run everything.

Nice-looking guy, in a way. Lean and dark and tall. But those grey eyes of his could look right through you and come out the other side. He came into town five, six years ago. Just discharged after three months in the Army. Heart or something. Twenty-six, he was then. Nice dresser. Sam Jorio and Buddy Winski were running the town between them. Anyway, Johnny Howard went to work for Sam Jorio. Two months later I hear talk that they're having some kind of trouble and that is ten days before Sam Jorio, all alone in his car, goes off that cliff just south of town. Burned to nothing. Nobody can prove it isn't an accident, but there's lots of guessing.

With the boss gone, Buddy Winski tried to move in and take over Sam's boys. But he didn't figure on Johnny. He met Johnny at the bar of the Kit Club on Greentree Road and Johnny busted his beer bottle on the edge of the bar and turned Buddy Winski's face into hamburg. When Buddy got out of the hospital, he left town. There wasn't anything else to do. All his boys had teamed up with Johnny Howard.

Inside of a year Johnny not only had everything working smooth as glass in town, but he had things organized that Sam Jorio and Buddy

Winski hadn't even thought of. Take a little thing like treasury pools. Syndicates are always trying to move in on a town this size. Buddy and Sam used to each have their own. Not Johnny. He folded up Sam's pool and Buddy's pool and let the syndicate come in. He gave them protection in return for two cents on every two-bit ticket. He made more out of it than Winski and Jorio ever thought of.

Another thing. No flashy cars for Johnny. No, sir. A little old black sedan with special plates in the body and special glass in the windows. That was Johnny. No going into clubs, even the two that belonged to him, with a big gang and a batch of fancy women. Johnny had all his parties in the suite on the top floor of the Baker Hotel. All kinds of wine. Good musicians.

And, of course, Bonny was always with him. Always the same girl. Bonny Gerlacher is the right name. Bonny Powers, she called herself.

Five-foot-two on tiptoe with ocean-colour eyes, dark red hair, and a build you wanted to tack on the wall over your bed.

Twenty-three or so, and looked sixteen.

Nobody messed with Bonny. And kept on living. Not with Johnny Howard around.

Well, things went along for a few years, and I guess Johnny was filling up safe-deposit boxes all over this part of the country with that green stuff. Johnny and Bonny. He was smart. Nobody could touch him. Estimates on his personal take went as high as a million and a half a year. He paid taxes on the net from the two clubs. Nothing else. The Feds smelled around for a long time, but they couldn't find anything.

The way he kept on top was by cracking down on anybody who stepped out of line so hard and so fast that it gave you the shivers.

Then Satch Connel got sick and the doc told him to retire and go to Florida if he wanted to live more than another half-hour.

Satch Connel ran a store next to the big high school. And he gave his regular payoff to Johnny Howard. Howard's boys kept Satch supplied with slot machines for the back room, reefers for the kids, dirty pictures and books. Stuff like that. I don't think Johnny Howard's end of the high school trade ran to more than three hundred a week. Peanuts to a guy like Johnny Howard.

So Satch sold out and a fellow named Walter Maybree bought it. This Maybree is from out of town and he has the cash in his pants and he buys it.

The same week he takes over, he tosses out the pinball machines and the punch boards and the other special items for the high school kids. You see, this Maybree has two kids in the high school. It gave him a different point of view from what Satch had. With Satch, nothing counted.

This Maybree paints the place inside and out and puts in a juke box and a lot of special sticky items at the soda bar and pretty soon it is like a recreation room you can maybe find run by a church.

Johnny Howard sends a few boys over to this Maybree, but Walt Maybree, being fairly husky, tosses them out onto the sidewalk. If that was all he did, maybe Johnny would have let the whole thing drop. But, no. Maybree writes a letter to the paper, and the stupid paper lets it get printed, and it says some pretty harsh things about a certain racketeer who wants him to cheat the school kids and sell them dope and filth.

Some of the wise boys around town talk to Johnny Howard and Johnny says, in that easy way of his. 'Maybree'll either play along or stop breathing.'

You got to understand about a statement like that. Once Johnny makes it, he has to follow through. If he doesn't, every small fry in town will figure Johnny is losing his grip and they'll try to wriggle out from under and maybe the organization will go to hell.

So, being in the line of business he's in, once Johnny Howard makes a statement like that, he has to do exactly like he says.

It would have been like pie, a shot from a car or even a ride into the country, except that a number of citizens are tired of Johnny Howard, and they get to Maybree and convince him that he is in trouble. The next thing, Maybree's wife and kids leave town with no forwarding address and the talk is that when the heat's off they'll come back and not before.

Walter Maybree moves a bunk into the back of the store, so there is no chance of catching him on the street. A whole bunch of square citizens get gun licences before Johnny can get to the cops to stop the issuing of them, and they all do guard duty with Walt Maybree.

Business goes on as usual, and Maybree has a tight look around his mouth and eyes, and without it being in the paper all of Baker City knows what's going on and are pulling for Maybree. That's the trouble with ordinary citizens. They sit on the sidelines and cheer, but only once in a blue moon is one of them, like Maybree, out there in front with his guard up.

The bomb that was tossed out of a moving car didn't go over so good. The boys in the car were in a hurry, so the bomb bounced off the door frame instead of going through the plate-glass window. It busted the windows when it went off, but it didn't do any other damage. At the corner, the sedan took a slug in the tyre and slewed into a lamppost and killed the driver. The other guy tried to fight his way clear and took a slug between the eyes.

The next day Johnny Howard was really in trouble. His organization began to fall apart right in front of his face, and everybody in the know was laughing at him because a punk running a soda shop was bluffing him to a standstill.

I can't tell you how I found out about this next part, but Johnny spends two days thinking, and then he gets hold of Madge Spain, who keeps the houses in line, and gives her some orders, and she shows up at the Baker Hotel with three of her youngest gals.

Johnny looks them over carefully, but they won't do because they look too hard and no amount of frosting on the cake is going to make any one of them look like a high school kid. Their high school days are too far behind them.

But he knows the idea is good and he is doing a lot of brooding about it and he has the dope he wants from Doc Harrington, one of his boys, who is sort of an amateur physician. He has the method all worked out, but nobody who can do it.

Bonny is worried about him, and finally she gets him talking and he tells her all about his plan, and she says that the whole thing is simple. *She'll* do it.

You've got to understand that in their own funny way they love each other. It just about makes Johnny sick to think of his Bonny killing anybody, because that is not woman's work. And maybe Bonny wouldn't normally knock anybody off, but because it is her Johnny who is in this mess, she will wiggle naked over hot coals to get him out of it.

The plan isn't bad. As soon as Maybree dies, all this trouble Johnny is having dies with him. It doesn't much matter how Maybree gets it, as long as he does.

This Doc Harrington has got hold of some curare. It is a South American poison and they use it in this country in small doses to make convulsions ease up when they give people shock therapy. It paralyses muscles. Jam a little bit in the bloodstream and it will paralyse the heart action. *Poof!* Like that. Quick as a bullet.

The bodyguards that are protecting Walt Maybree during business hours are on the lookout for hard characters who look like they might rub Maybree out in a direct way. Johnny Howard figures they will not be on the lookout for high school gals.

For the next two days he has Bonny practising with a soda straw and these little wooden darts he has fixed up. They just fit in a soda straw. A needle on one end and paper things on the other to make them fly right.

Walt Maybree works behind his own soda fountain.

The idea is that Bonny goes in there as a high school girl and she has the little dart with the curare on the end in her hand. She sits at the fountain and tucks the dart in the end of the soda straw, puts it up to her lips, and puffs, sticking the little dart into the back of Maybree's hand, or, better yet, his throat.

When he keels over, she goes out with the crowd.

Probably Bonny laughed and kidded a lot when she was up in the suite practising on the cork target with the little darts. Probably Johnny Howard kidded back, but neither of them must have thought it was very funny. To Johnny Howard it was okay to rub out the competition with hot lead, but sending your gal out to kill somebody with a blowgun is something else indeed.

Anyway, the pressure on Johnny was getting worse every day, and his boys were mumbling and it was only a question of time until somebody turned hero and blasted Johnny.

On the day that was set, Bonny went in her black dress and her high heels and her dark red hair piled high on her head and unlocked the door to the room she had rented near the high school. The little dart with the sticky stuff on the needle end was wrapped in tissue paper and was in a little box in her purse. She had a suitcase with her.

The black dress fitted snugly on Bonny's curves. She took off the dress and the nylons and the high-heeled shoes and put on scuffed, flat moccasins and a shortish tweed skirt and a sloppy sweater. She let that wonderful red hair fall around her shoulders, and she tied a scarf thing around her shining head.

She had schoolbooks with her. She took them out of the suitcase, held them in her arm, and looked in the chipped mirror over the oak bureau. Carefully she smiled. Bonny the high school lass. But with too much makeup. She swabbed all the makeup off and put back just a little. It looked better.

Her knees were shaking and her lips felt numb. Her heart was fluttering. No woman can go out to commit murder without something taking place inside her.

One little thing had to be added. She took the big purse she was leaving behind, took out the half-pint flask that Johnny Howard had given her two years before, and tilted it up to her lips. The raw liquor burned like fire, but it steadied her down. That was what she wanted.

It had all been timed just right. She left the room, carrying the books, and walked to the high school. She went in the door, and, when she got halfway down the hall, the noon whistle went off and the doors opened and the hall filled with kids.

Bonny felt funny until she saw that she wasn't being noticed. She went right through the building and out the other door and became part of the crew that stormed the gates of Walt Maybree's Drugstore.

Between the thumb and first finger of her right hand she tightly held the little messenger of death.

The liquor was warm in her stomach, and she made an effort not to breathe in anybody's face. She was a little late to get a seat at the counter, and so she waited, quietly and patiently, and while she waited she thought of Johnny Howard. It was only by thinking of Johnny that she could go through with the whole thing.

When there was a vacant stool she edged in, piled her books on the counter, made her voice higher, her eyes wider, and ordered what she had heard one of the other kids order – 'A special milkshake.'

She selected a straw out of the metal container near her, peeled the paper off it, and waited. Maybree was down at the other end of the counter, and a boy with a pimply face made her milkshake and put it in front of her. It was 'special.' It contained two kinds of ice cream, a handful of malt, and an egg.

Bonny dipped her straw into it and sucked up the sweet, heavy mixture. She kept her eye on Maybree. He began to move up towards her. She pinched her straw so that it was useless, selected a fresh one, and stripped the paper off it. With a deft, practised gesture, she slipped the little dart, point first, into the end of it.

She lifted it to her lips.

Maybree strolled down near her and stood still, his hand braced on the inside edge of the counter.

It was thus that he glanced at the very good-looking high school girl with the sea-coloured eyes. He heard an odd sound, saw those sea-coloured eyes glaze, and he gasped as she went over backwards, her pretty head striking the asphalt tile of the floor with a heavy thud, her dark red hair spilling out of the bandanna when the knot loosened. She was dead even as she hit the floor.

That's why I get a bang out of the mayor claiming to have cleaned up this town. Hell, he couldn't have cleaned it up if Johnny Howard had been running things. When the mayor started his cleanup, Johnny Howard was gone, and weak sisters were trying to climb into the vacated saddle.

Yeah, Johnny Howard disappeared that same day that Bonny died. They didn't locate him for five days. They found him in that furnished room that still held Bonny's usual clothes. The landlady had been hearing a funny noise. They found Johnny Howard on his hands and knees, going around and around the room, butting his head into the wall now and then. He told them he was looking for Bonny. They've got him out in the state sanitarium now, giving him shock treatments, but they say it'll never work with him.

That's right. Bonny made a mistake. Just one mistake. You see, she didn't realize that by taking that huge slug of bourbon and then drinking half of that sticky milkshake she'd signed her own death warrant. They found the little dart embedded in the inside of her lower lip.

You can't mix bourbon and milkshake without getting a terrible case of hiccups.

The Sound of Murder

William P. McGivern

The Orient Express stops for an hour or more at the Yugoslav-Trieste border. Customs are a formality as a rule, but the changing of foreign currencies into dinars takes quite a bit of time.

Knowing this, Adam James yawned slightly as the train pulled into Sesana. He wasn't really bored; he merely wished he were in Belgrade, at work, instead of here at the frontier. He rubbed the windows of his compartment with the palm of his hand. There was little to see outside – uniformed customs officials waiting to board the train, an oiler walking down the opposite track, and beyond the wooden station, white foothills under a dark sky. It was a cheerless prospect; the hills were huddled together, as if the earth had hunched its shoulders against the bitter weather.

The customs official knocked and entered, bringing in a touch of coldness on his clothes and breath. He was cordial and efficient, and bowed himself out with a smile a few minutes later. The money-control officer was equally cordial, but his work took more time. Finally he too went away, and Adam sat down with his book, a dull but important one on Yugoslavian politics, and lit his pipe.

However, his moment of peace was brief. The argument between the couple in the adjoining compartment flared up again, and he closed his book with a sigh. They had been at it, off and on, since the Express had left Trieste an hour or so ago, and the partition between the compartments was so thin that Adam could hardly ignore the noise. They spoke Croatian or Serbian, neither of which he understood, but the anger in their voices was unmistakable – no matter what the language.

He had noticed them in Trieste where thay had boarded the train. The woman was very attractive, with light blonde hair, clear fresh skin, and the slender, gracefully muscled legs of a dancer. She was in her early thirties, Adam had guessed, and wore a plum-coloured tweed suit under a good fur coat. The man was stout and florid with small alert eyes and a manner of petulant importance. He was fastidiously turned out in a black overcoat with a fur-trimmed collar, a black Homburg, and, rather inevitably Adam had thought, carried a cane. His grey flannel trousers were sharply creased, and his spats gleamed whitely against his glossy black shoes.

There was something about them, some constraint in their manner, that had caught Adam's attention. They said little to each other as they waited to board the train, but there was a quality in the set of their shoulders which indicated they had plenty to say and were only waiting for the chance to say it.

Unfortunately for himself, Adam thought, they got their chance when they were finally alone in their compartment. At first he'd been mildly interested in their bickering; but as they became angrier and louder, he had become bored and irritated.

There was a knock on the door, and the conductor entered. He was a small, neatly built man with quick intelligent eyes, and had a tiny black moustache above a generous but cautious mouth.

'Your passport, sir,' he said, handing Adam the slim green gold-lettered booklet. 'Everything is in order. You will not be disturbed again until we arrive in Belgrade.'

'Thanks, but I haven't been disturbed,' Adam said.

The conductor raised his eyebrows. 'That's an unusual reaction for an American. Most of you are – well, impulsive. You have no patience.'

'Oh, there are all types of Americans,' Adam said with a smile. 'Also, there are all types of French, British, and even Yugoslavians, I imagine.'

'No, you are wrong. Here in Yugoslavia we grow up with the land, and become like it, slow and patient. You Americans are different. Excitable, I mean. You leap at things. That is desirable in some matters, but it can also cause trouble.'

'Well, that may be,' Adam said. He had spent fifteen years of his life as a foreign correspondent, and his job, reduced to an over-simplification, was to find out what people thought, and why they thought it. He was interested in the conductor's opinions, and he wanted to put the man at ease. He raised a hand as the argument in the next compartment broke out again. 'Are they Americans?' he asked innocently.

'No, of course not.'

'Well, *they* seem pretty excitable.'

The conductor looked blank. Then he smiled good-humouredly. 'I asked for that, as you say. No, they are Yugoslavians. The Duvecs – she is a dancer, and he is an actor.' The conductor listened to the argument with a little smile. 'The artistic temperament,' he said. 'Well, I must go on with my work. I have not offended you with my direct-ness, eh?'

'Certainly not. Stop by when you get a minute and we'll finish our talk.'

'Thank you, I shall try.'

The conductor went away and Adam returned to his book. He was grateful, a chapter later, when the train began to move. Sesana was behind them now. They would pass Zagreb sometime after dinner and be in Belgrade the following morning. He would have been almost cheerful if it weren't for the argument in the next compartment.

The couple had reached a new and higher pitch after a few moments of blessed silence. The woman's voice was shrill now, where before it had been somewhat controlled. The man shouted at her whenever she ceased speaking. This continued for a few moments, and then Adam heard the door of the compartment jerked open energetically. The man shouted a last sentence or two; then the door was banged shut with angry finality. Adam heard the man's heavy footsteps pass his door and fade away in the direction of the dining-car.

'Well, well,' he thought, 'peace at last!' There was nothing quite like a door-slamming exit to put an end to an argument. Perversely, however, now that everything was quiet, he lost interest in his book. He decided to have dinner and finish his reading later – though probably by then the argument would be on again, he thought wryly, and he'd berate himself for missing the present opportunity.

He washed his face, combed his hair, and walked through the lurching train to the dining-car. There were two third-class coaches connected to the *wagon-lit*, filled with stolid, impassive soldiers who endured the unheated compartments with the stoic acceptance of domestic animals.

There was no menu on the Express, just the one *préfixe* dinner: soup, roast veal and vegetables served with a theoretically white but in fact orange-looking Dalmatian wine. This was followed by stewed prunes and thick sweet Turkish coffee.

The man in the fur-trimmed overcoat, Duvec, was seated at the far end of the diner, hungrily and belligerently attacking a bowl of soup. He wore an angrily righteous look, Adam thought, and was probably reviewing the argument with his wife in the most favourable possible light. Duvec wore his overcoat buttoned up to his throat, and occasionally put down his spoon and rubbed his plump hands together to warm them, though the diner wasn't cold; Adam was comfortable enough in his suit-coat.

The sleeping-car conductor entered the diner a few moments later, looking pale and agitated. He glanced about quickly; then, striding to Duvec's table, he bent and whispered a few words. Their effect was electric. Duvec sprang to his feet, almost overturning his table, and his mouth opened and closed soundlessly.

'Please come with me,' the conductor said in a firm voice.

The two men hurried from the car, the other diners staring after them curiously. Adam frowned at the tablecloth for a moment or so, oddly disturbed. Finally, obeying a compulsion he didn't quite understand, he rose and started back through the train for the sleeping-car. But at the vestibule he was stopped by a blue-uniformed mail-car guard. The man put a hand against Adam's chest.

'You must not enter,' he said in slow, laborious English.

'But this is my car,' Adam said.

'You must not come in.'

'Has something happened?'

The guard merely shook his round head stubbornly.

At this point the sleeping-car conductor appeared in the opposite vestibule. He opened the door and spoke a few words to the mail-car guard, and the man took his hand from Adam's chest.

'You may come in,' the conductor said.

'What has happened?' Adam asked.

'A great tragedy, a great tragedy,' the conductor said, rubbing his moustache nervously. Adam became aware that the train was slowing down.

'We're stopping?' he asked.

'Yes, yes. Please come inside.'

Adam followed him into the sleeping-car and turned the corner into the aisle. Duvec stood before the open door of his compartment, sobbing terribly. Beyond him, held by two mail-car guards, was a stocky Yugo-slavian soldier in a patched and dirty uniform. Duvec turned away from his compartment and sagged weakly against the wall. He beat a fist slowly against his forehead, and his lips opened and closed as if he were praying.

Adam stepped forward and glanced into Duvec's compartment. He knew what he would see. Somehow he had anticipated this; but it was still a jarring, shocking sight. Mrs Duvec lay on the floor in the careless, undignified sprawl of death. One slender leg was doubled under her body, and a lock of blonde hair lay across her pale throat. The bronze handle of a letter-opener – or a knife – protruded from between her breasts.

The train had come to a full stop. There was no sound as Adam stepped back from the compartment except Duvec's hoarse, strangled sobs.

The conductor touched Adam's arm. 'You will be good enough to remain in your compartment, please. I have sent a messenger back to the police in Sesana. We will wait until they arrive.'

'Naturally,' Adam rejoined. 'But what happened?'

'It was the soldier. He thought all the passengers were in the dining-car. He come in to pilfer what he could, I imagine. He was surprised when he found the woman here; he lost his head—' The conductor shrugged eloquently. 'It is a great tragedy.'

The soldier seemed to understand what was being said. His eyes were wild and frightened. He suddenly shouted, '*Nil! Nil!*' and chattered out a stream of words which Adam didn't understand.

'He protests his innocence,' the conductor said matter-of-factly. 'That is to be expected.'

'He lies, he lies!' Duvec said in a ragged voice. 'He killed my wife, and he must die for it.'

'There is no doubt he is guilty,' the conductor agreed. 'We can establish that easily. Your wife was alive when you left her?'

'Yes, yes! My God, yes!' Duvec cried. He began to sob again, hopelessly, piteously. 'We had a quarrel, a silly, stupid quarrel, and I left in anger. But she was alive, alive as we are now.' He glanced at Adam, as if noticing him for the first time. 'But *you* must have heard our quarrel.'

'Yes, I heard it,' Adam said.

'Then you heard our voices until the moment I left.'

Adam nodded. 'Yes, I heard you.'

The conductor shrugged. 'Then there is proof that she was alive when her husband left. The soldier admits going into her compartment – but at that point he loses his love for the truth.'

'What's his story?' Adam asked.

'He says that Mrs Duvec was already dead. This is why he attempted to flee, he tells us.'

'Who caught him?'

'I had appointed a guard for this car while I worked out space plans with the attendant in the next car,' the conductor said. 'We get a crowd at Zagreb, and it is necessary to prepare for them in advance, you see. I appointed a guard because the sleeping-car is empty during the dinner hour, and the soldiers – well, you understand how it is with soldiers. The guard, a man from the mail-car, was at the opposite vestibule – that is, he was at the other end of the car from where we now stand. Something caused him to turn and glance down the aisle. He saw the soldier backing out of the Duvecs' compartment. He shouted, and the soldier attempted to run back to his own car. But the guard caught him, fortunately.'

'What caused the guard to look down the aisle?'

The conductor raised his eyebrows. 'Who can tell? The good Lord, perhaps; it was an impulse – and it apprehended a murderer. The guard will be officially congratulated.'

'Yes, yes, of course,' Adam muttered. 'Catching murderers is always a cause for congratulations. Whose knife did the soldier use, by the way?'

The conductor looked blank. He turned to Duvec, who said, 'It was my wife's letter-opener. Perhaps she was using it when the soldier burst in on her.'

'That is logical,' the conductor said, nodding. 'We will get the truth from him, all of it; you will see.'

Suddenly the soldier shouted wildly and broke away from his two guards. He ran down the narrow aisle, jerked open the door at the end of the car, and disappeared. The guards lumbered after him, and Duvec screamed, 'Get him, get him, the murderer!'

The conductor remained calm. 'He cannot leave the train,' he said. 'The vestibule doors are secured from the outside. That was my first order. He will be caught, never fear.'

Adam glanced at Duvec and the conductor, frowning. Finally he said, 'Excuse me, please,' and entered his own compartment. He sat down and lit his pipe.

Something was wrong about all this, wrong as the very devil, and he could feel it in his bones. But how could he prove it? He stretched his long legs out in front of him and rested his head against the back of the seat. Proof ... where was it? He puffed on his pipe, trying to recall everything that had happened since the Express left Trieste. He sorted out all the details he could remember, and juggled them into different relationships, turned them upside down and inside out, trying desperately to justify his conviction.

The conductor appeared in his doorway ten minutes later, wearing a small pleased smile. 'It is finished,' he said. 'We have caught him. He sought to hide in the coal-car, but was found.'

Adam stood up and began knocking the dottle from his pipe. 'That's fine,' he said. 'The only thing is, you've got the wrong man.'

'The wrong man? Impossible! His guilt is proven by his attempt to escape.'

'Nonsense. He's simply scared out of his wits. Bring everyone here, and I'll show you the murderer,' Adam said, marvelling slightly at the ring of confidence in his voice.

The conductor squared his shoulders stubbornly. 'This is a police matter, I must remind you.'

'Yes, but it won't redound to your credit to present them with an innocent suspect when they arrive.'

The conductor rubbed his thin black moustache. 'Very well,' he said at last. 'I am not afraid to test your opinion against mine. I have reached my conclusions logically. I am not in error.'

'We'll see,' Adam said.

The soldier was brought back down the aisle, securely held by two mail-car guards. He was not more than eighteen, Adam saw, a strongly built youth with a dull face and blank hopeless eyes; obviously he had resigned himself to his fate. Duvec, who still wore his fur-trimmed over-coat, stood at the end of the aisle, occasionally rubbing a hand despairingly over his broad forehead.

Adam was in the doorway of his compartment. The soldier and his guards were at his left, Duvec and the conductor on his right. They all watched him expectantly.

'This soldier did not kill Mrs Duvec,' Adam said quietly.

'What do you know about it?' Duvec shouted.

'If you listen, you will find out.'

'I will not listen. You have no authority here.'

'Silence!' the conductor said in a sharp voice. 'I am in charge until the police arrive. I have given the American permission to speak.'

'Thank you,' said Adam. 'I'll continue. As I have said, the soldier did not kill Mrs Duvec. I think I can prove that to everyone's satisfaction. First of all, has it not struck you as odd that the guard in this car did not hear Mrs Duvec scream?'

For an instant there was silence. Then the conductor said, 'She was struck down before she could cry out.' However, Adam's question brought a tiny frown to his face.

'I think that's an unlikely explanation,' Adam said. 'Let's reconstruct what must have happened if the soldier is the murderer. First, he opened the door of the compartment. Mrs Duvec looked up at him, startled and probably frightened. What would one expect her to do? Scream, of course.'

'My wife was no silly maiden,' Duvec snapped. 'She would not scream at the sight of a man; she would have ordered him from the compartment. That is unquestionably what happened. She asked him to leave, ordered him to leave. He took advantage of that moment to seize the letter-opener from her and plunge it into her heart. Yes, he silenced her before she could scream.'

The conductor nodded, looking somewhat relieved. 'Yes, certainly that is it,' he said.

'No, that isn't it,' Adam said. 'Why would a strong, agile young man use a knife on a woman? If he wanted to silence her, he would use his hands. In the time it would take him to grasp the knife away from her, and strike her down with it, she might have screamed half a dozen times. And yet, I repeat, the guard in this car heard no sound at all from Mrs Duvec.'

The conductor shook his head impatiently. 'You are making up theories. We are dealing with facts. According to your own testimony, Mrs Duvec was alive when her husband left the compartment. She was dead when the soldier left the compartment. Those are the facts. No one but the soldier could have killed her.'

'You're wrong, but it's partly my fault,' Adam said. 'I've misled you. However, I'll clear things up now. There's the murderer,' he said – and he pointed at Duvec.

'Monstrous!' Duvec shouted. 'I will not stand for these slanders.'

'Let me ask you this,' Adam said. 'Why are you wearing a heavy overcoat in a comfortably heated train? What is under it, Duvec? Or, more to the point, what *isn't* under it?'

'I don't know what you're talking about,' Duvec snapped.

'I'll tell you, then,' Adam said. 'What *isn't* under that overcoat is your suit-coat – the suit-coat which was bloodied when you murdered your wife. When I saw you in the diner I knew something was odd. You wouldn't have worn an overcoat all the way from Trieste, so you must have put it on before leaving your compartment. However, the emotional fireworks accompanying your departure made it seem unlikely that you would have stopped to put on an overcoat. That routine bit of business would have shattered the effect of your exit. But why wear the coat at all? The train isn't cold. Therefore, I decided, it was worn not for comfort but for camouflage. And what was it you were so eager to camouflage?'

'You are talking like a madman,' Duvec said. 'My wife was alive when I left her. You know that is true. You said you heard us.'

'I said I heard *you*,' Adam corrected him. 'Duvec, you killed your wife in a moment of rage. This puts you in a tough predicament. There was a witness of sorts to the crime – an auditory witness, in the next compartment – myself, of course. But I could be used to your advantage. You could create the illusion that your wife was alive when you left her by taking both parts of the dialogue for a moment or so before banging out of the compartment. This was no trick for an actor. Meanwhile, as you imitated your wife's voice, you removed your bloodstained suit-coat and got into your overcoat. Then you left the compartment with a final artistic bellow at your wife. The suit-coat, I'll bet, you either hid in your compartment or threw off the train on the way to the diner. In either event, a search will produce it.'

'Talk, talk, talk!' Duvec cried.

'Take off your overcoat,' said Adam.

'This is childish nonsense,' Duvec said angrily. He unbuttoned his overcoat and flung it open. He wore a grey tweed jacket above grey flannel trousers. There was a little silence in which Adam felt his stomach contract unpleasantly. 'Are you satisfied now?' Duvec said contemptuously.

The conductor had unconsciously placed a hand on Duvec's arm as Adam had talked. Now he removed it hastily. 'Forgive me,' he said.

'Wait a minute,' Adam said, frowning. He had noticed that Duvec wore ruby cuff-links. What was wrong with that?

'No – enough,' the conductor said angrily. 'There will be no more of these wild accusations.'

'No, I'm right,' Adam snapped. 'He wouldn't wear cuff-links with a tweed jacket, any more than he'd wear black shoes with a brown suit. Of course! He changed into the tweed jacket and hid the blood-stained suit-coat underneath the overcoat. He threw the suit-coat out one of the vestibule doors. He was fairly safe then; at least he had an alibi. But luck joined forces with him and provided the crime with a reasonable suspect. The soldier blundered onto the scene and put Duvec completely into the clear. But it didn't work. I'll bet one hundred dollars to a dinar that the police will find a bloodstained flannel jacket within ten miles of this spot.'

Duvec began to weep. 'I can stand no more!' he cried. 'My wife is dead, and I hear myself called her murderer!' He turned aside, still sobbing, and put a hand to the vestibule door for support. The gesture was so natural that no one noticed him reach for the doorknob. He jerked open the door and was into the vestibule before anyone could move. The conductor shouted at the mail-car guards who still held the soldier. They plunged out of the car after Duvec, with the conductor on their heels.

They caught him in the next coach and dragged him back to the sleeping-car. Duvec offered no resistance. He stared straight ahead with shoulders slumped, and there was an expression of terrible anguish on his face. Adam realized that for the first time since the murder of his wife Duvec had ceased to act.

In a low, trembling voice he said, 'She was going to leave me, you see. I – couldn't stand that. I – couldn't.'

Half an hour later the conductor came to Adam's compartment. 'You must excuse me,' he said rather sheepishly. 'I think of what I said about the excitable Americans, and my face becomes hot with shame. I must apologize.'

'Please don't worry about that,' Adam said.

'But I do not understand completely. Your proof was not over-whelming, I do not think. And yet you seemed so *sure*.'

'I was sure,' Adam said. 'You see, in the classic tradition, Duvec made one mistake which I didn't bother to mention. When he acted out the scene with his dead wife, he engineered the dialogue badly. He shouted a few last words at her, you will remember, and then banged the door.'

The conductor looked blank. Finally he rubbed his moustache and smiled slowly.

'You understand, of course,' Adam said. 'In Yugoslavia or America, anywhere for that matter, arguments between husbands and wives very seldom end that way. When I realized that, I knew Duvec was guilty. Mrs Duvec wouldn't have let him get away with the last word – if she were alive, that is.'

'But of course,' the conductor agreed, nodding gravely.

An Official Position

W. Somerset Maugham

He was a sturdy broad-shouldered fellow, of the middle height; though his bones were well covered as became his age, which was fifty, he was not fat; he had a ruddy complexion which neither the heat of the sun nor the unwholesomeness of the climate had affected. It was good rich blood that ran through his veins. His hair was brown and thick, and only at the temples touched with grey; he was very proud of his fair, handsome moustache and he kept it carefully brushed. There was a pleasant twinkle in his blue eyes. You would have said that this was a man whom life had treated well. There was in his appearance an air of good nature and in his vigour a glow of health that gave you confidence. He reminded you of one of those well-fed, rubicund burghers in an old Dutch picture, with their pink-cheeked wives, who made money and enjoyed the good things with which their industry provided them. He was, however, a widower. His name was Louis Remire, and his number 68763. He was serving a twelve-year sentence at St Laurent de Maroni, the great penal settlement of French Guiana, for killing his wife, but partly because he had served in the police force at Lyons, his native town, and partly on account of his good character, he had been given an official position. He had been chosen among nearly two hundred applicants to be the public executioner.

That was why he was allowed to sport the handsome moustache of which he took so much care. He was the only convict who wore one. It was in a manner of speaking his badge of office. That also was why he was allowed to wear his own clothes. The convicts wear pyjamas in pink and white stripes, round straw hats, and clumsy boots with wooden soles and leather tops. Louis Remire wore espadrilles on his bare feet, blue cotton trousers, and a khaki shirt the open neck of which exposed to view his hairy and virile chest. When you saw him strolling about the public garden, with a kindly eye looking at the children, black or half-caste, who played there, you would have taken him for a respectable shopkeeper who was enjoying an hour's leisure. He had his own house. That was not only one of the perquisites of his office, but it was a necessity, since if he had lodged in the prison camp the convicts would have made short work of him. One morning he would have been found with his belly ripped open. It was true that the house was small, it was just a wooden shack of one room, with a lean-to that served as a kitchen; but it was surrounded by a tiny garden, within a palisade, and in the garden grew bananas, papaias, and such vegetables as the climate allowed him to raise. The garden faced the sea and was surrounded by a coconut grove. The situation was charming. It was only a quarter of a mile from the prison, which was convenient for his rations. They were fetched by his assistant, who lived with him. The assistant, a tall, gawky, ungainly fellow, with deep-set, staring eyes and cavernous jaws, was serving a life sentence for rape and murder; he was not very intelligent, but in civil life he had been a cook and it was wonderful what, with the help of the vegetables they grew and such condiments as Louis Remire could afford to buy at the Chinese grocer's, he managed to do with the soup, potatoes and cabbage, and eternal beef, beef for three hundred and sixty-five days of the year, which the prison kitchens provided. It was on this account that Louis Remire had pressed his claim on the commandant when it had been found necessary to get a new assistant. The last one's nerves had given way and, absurdly enough, thought Louis Remire with a good-natured laugh, he had developed scruples about capital punishment; now, suffering from neurasthenia, he was on the Ile St Joseph, where the insane were confined.

His present assistant happened to be ill. He had high fever, and looked very much as if he were going to die. It had been necessary to send him to hospital. Louis Remire was sorry; he would not easily find so good a cook again. It was bad luck that this should have happened just now, for next day there was a job of work to be done. Six men were to be executed. Two were Algerians, one was a Pole, another a Spaniard from the mainland, and only two were French. They had escaped from prison in a band and gone up the river. For nearly twelve months, stealing, raping, and killing they had spread terror through the colony. People scarcely dared move from their homesteads. Recaptured at last, they had all been sentenced to death, but the sentence had to be confirmed by the Minister of the Colonies, and the confirmation had only just arrived. Louis Remire could not manage without help, and besides there was a lot to arrange beforehand; it was particularly unfortunate that on this occasion of all others he should have to depend on an inexperienced man. The commandant had assigned to him one of the turnkeys. The turnkeys are convicts like the others, but they have been given their places for good behaviour and they live in separate quarters. They are on the side of the authorities and so are disliked by the other prisoners. Louis Remire was a conscientious fellow, and he was anxious that everything next day should go without a hitch. He arranged that his temporary assistant should come that afternoon to the place where the guillotine was kept so that he might explain to him thoroughly how it worked and show him exactly what he would have to do.

The guillotine, when not in use, stood in a small room which was part of the prison building, but which was entered by a separate door from the outside. When he sauntered along there at the appointed hour he found the man already waiting. He was a large-limbed, coarse-faced fellow. He was dressed in the pink and white stripes of the prison garb, but as turnkey he wore a felt hat instead of the straw of common convicts.

'What are you here for?'

The man shrugged his shoulders.

'I killed a farmer and his wife.'

'H'm. How long have you got?'

'Life.'

He looked a brute, but you could never be sure of people. He had himself seen a warder, a big, powerful man, faint dead away at an execution. He did not want his assistant to have an attack of nerves at the wrong moment. He gave him a friendly smile, and with his thumb pointed to the closed door behind which stood the guillotine.

'This is another sort of job,' he said. 'There are six of them, you know. They're a bad lot. The sooner they're out of the way the better.'

'Oh, that's all right. After what I've seen in this place I'm scared of nothing. It means no more to me than cutting the head off a chicken.'

Louis Remire unlocked the door and walked in. His assistant followed him. The guillotine in that small room, hardly larger than a cell, seemed to take up a great deal of space. It stood grim and sinister. Louis Remire heard a slight gasp and turning round saw that the turnkey was staring at the instrument with terrified eyes. His face was sallow and drawn from the fever and the hookworm from which all the convicts inter-mittently suffered, but now its pallor was ghastly. The executioner smiled good-naturedly.

'Gives you a turn, does it? Have you never seen it before?'

'Never.'

Louis Remire gave a little throaty chuckle.

'If you had, I suppose you wouldn't have survived to tell the tale. How did you escape it?'

'I was starving when I did my job. I'd asked for something to eat and they set the dogs on me. I was condemned to death. My lawyer went to Paris and he got the President to reprieve me.'

'It's better to be alive than dead, there's no denying that,' said Louis Remire, with that agreeable twinkle in his eyes.

He always kept his guillotine in perfect order. The wood, a dark hard native wood somewhat like mahogany, was highly polished; but there was a certain amount of brass, and it was Louis Remire's pride that this should be as bright and clean as the brass-work on a yacht. The knife shone as though it had just come out of the workshop. It was necessary not only to see that everything functioned properly, but to show his assistant how it functioned. It was part of the assistant's duty to refix the rope when the knife had dropped, and to do this he had to climb a short ladder.

It was with the satisfaction of a competent workman who knows his job from A to Z that Remire entered upon the necessary explanations. It gave him a certain quiet pleasure to point out the ingenuity of the apparatus. The condemned man was strapped to the bascule, a sort of shelf, and this by a simple mechanism was precipitated down and forwards so that the man's neck was conveniently under the knife. The conscientious fellow had brought with him a banana stem, about five feet long, and the turnkey wondered why. He was now to learn. The stem was of about the same circumference and consistency as the human neck, so that it afforded a very good way, not only of showing a novice how the apparatus worked, but of making sure beforehand that it was in perfect order. Louis Remire placed the banana stem in position. He released the knife. It fell with increadible speed and with a great bang. From the time the man was attached to the bascule to the time his head was off only thirty seconds elapsed. The head fell in the basket. The executioner took it up by the ears and exhibited it to those whose duty it was to watch the execution. He uttered the solemn words:

'*Au nom du peuple français justice est faite.* In the name of the French people justice is done.'

Then he dropped the head into the basket. Tomorrow, with six to be dispatched, the trunk would have to be unstrapped from the bascule and placed with the head on a stretcher, and the next man brought forward. They were taken in order of their guilt. The least guilty, executed first, were spared the horror of seeing the death of their mates.

'We shall have to be careful that the right head goes with the right body,' said Louis Remire, in that rather jovial manner of his, 'or there may be no end of confusion at the Resurrection.'

He let down the knife two or three times in order to make quite sure that the assistant understood how to fix it, and then getting his cleaning-materials from the shelf on which he kept them set him to work on the brass. Though it was spotless he thought that a final polish would do no harm. He leaned against the wall and idly smoked cigarettes.

Finally everything was in order and Louis Remire dismissed the assistant till midnight. At midnight they were moving the guillotine from the room in which it stood to the prison yard. It was always a bit of a job to set it up again, but it had to be in place an hour before dawn, at which time the execution took place. Louis Remire strolled slowly home to his shack. The afternoon was drawing to its close, and as he walked along he passed a working party who were returning to the prison. They spoke to one another in undertones and he guessed that they spoke of him; some looked down, two or three threw him a glance of hatred, and one spat on the ground. Louis Remire, the end of a cigarette sticking to his lip, looked at them with irony. He was indifferent to the loathing, mingled with fear, with which they regarded him. It did not matter to him that not one of them would speak to him, and it only amused him to think that there was hardly one who would not gladly have thrust a knife into his guts. He had a supreme contempt for them all. He could take care of himself. He could use a knife as well as any of them, and he had confidence in his strength. The convicts knew that men were to be executed next day, and as always before an execution they were depressed and nervous. They went about their work in sullen silence, and the warders had to be more than usually on the alert.

'They'll settle down when it's all over,' said Louis Remire as he let himself into his little compound.

The dogs barked as he came along, and brave though he was, he listened to their uproar with satisfaction. With his own assistant ill, so that he was alone in the house, he was not sorry that he had the protection of those two savage mongrels. They prowled about the coconut grove outside his compound all night and they would give him good warning if anyone lurked there. They could be relied on to spring at the throat of any stranger who ventured too near. If his predecessor had had these dogs he wouldn't have come to his end.

The man who had been executioner before Louis Remire had only held the job a couple of years when one day he disappeared. The authorities thought he had run away; he was known to have a bit of money, and it was very probable that he had managed to make arrangements with the captain of a schooner to take him to Brazil. His nerves had given way. He had gone two or three times to the governor of the prison and told him that he feared for his life. He was convinced that the convicts were out to kill him. The governor felt pretty sure that his fears were groundless and paid no attention, but when the man was nowhere to be found he concluded that his terror had got the better of him and he had preferred to run the danger of escape, and the danger of being recaptured and put back into prison, rather than face the risk of an avenging convict's knife. About three weeks later the warder in charge of a working party in the jungle noticed a great flock of vultures clustered round a tree. These vultures, called urubus, are large black birds, of a horrible aspect, and they fly about the market-place of St

Laurent, picking up the offal that is left there by the starving liberated convicts, and flit heavily from tree to tree in the neat, well-kept streets of the town. They fly in the prison yard to remind the convicts that if they attempt an escape into the jungle their end, ten to one, will be to have their bones picked clean by these loathsome creatures. They were fighting and screaming in such a mass round the tree that the warder thought there was something strange there. He reported it and the commandant sent a party to see. They found a man hanging by the neck from one of the branches, and when they cut him down discovered that he was the executioner. It was given out that he had committed suicide, but there was a knife-thrust in his back, and the convicts knew that he had been stabbed and then, still alive, taken to the jungle and hanged.

Louis Remire had no fear that anything of that sort would happen to him. He knew how his predecessor had been caught. The job had not been done by the convicts. By the French law when a man is sentenced to hard labour for a certain number of years he has at the expiration of his sentence to remain in the colony for the same number of years. He is free, but he may not stir from the spot that is assigned to him as a residence. In certain circumstances he can get a concession and if he works hard he manages to scrape a bare living from it, but after a long term of penal servitude, during which he has lost all power of initiative, what with the debilitating effect of fever, hookworm, and so on, he is unfit for heavy and continuous labour, and so most of the liberated men subsist on begging, larceny, smuggling tobacco or money to the prisoners, and loading and unloading cargoes when two or three times a month a steamer comes into the harbour. It was the wife of one of these freed men that had been the means of the undoing of Louis Remire's predecessor. She was a coloured woman, young and pretty, with a neat little figure and mischievous eyes. The plot was well-considered. The executioner was a burly, sanguine man, of ardent passions. She had thrown herself in his way, and when she caught his approving glance, had cast him a saucy look. He saw her a day or two later in the public garden. He did not venture to speak to her (no one, man, woman, or child, would be seen speaking to him), but when he winked at her she smiled. One evening he met her walking through the coconut grove that surrounded his compound. No one was about. He got into conversation with her. They only exchanged a few words, for she was evidently terrified of being seen with him. But she came again to the coconut grove. She played him carefully till his suspicions were allayed; she teased his desires; she made him give her little presents, and at last on the promise of what was for both of them quite a sum of money she agreed to come one dark night to the compound. A ship had just come in and her husband would be working till dawn. It was when he opened the door for her and she hesitated to come in as though at the last moment she could not make up her mind, that he stepped outside to draw her in, and fell to the ground with the violence of the knife-thrust in his back.

'The fool,' muttered Louis Remire. 'He only got what he deserved. He should have smelt a rat. The eternal vanity of man.'

For his part he was through with women. It was on account of women that he found himself in the situation he was in now, at least on account of one woman; and besides, at his time of life, his passions were assuaged. There were other things in life and after a certain age a man, if he was sensible, turned his attention to them. He had always been a great fisherman. In the old days, at home in France before he had had his misfortune, as soon as he came off duty, he took his rod and line and went down to the Rhône. He got a lot of fishing now. Every morning, till the sun grew hot, he sat on his favourite rock and generally managed to get enough for the prison governor's table. The governor's wife knew the value of things and beat him down on the price he asked, but he did not blame her for that; she knew that he had to take what she was prepared to give and it would have been stupid of her to pay a penny more than she had to. In any case it brought in a little money useful for tobacco and rum and other odds and ends. But this evening he was going to fish for himself. He got his bait from the lean-to, and his rod, and settled down on his rock. No fish were so good as the fish you caught yourself, and by now he knew which were those that were good to eat and which were so tough and flavourless that you could only throw them back into the sea. There was one sort that, fried in real olive oil, was as good as mullet. He had not been sitting there five minutes when his float gave a sudden jerk, and when he pulled up his line, there, like an answer to prayer, was one of those very fish wriggling on the hook. He took it off, banged its head on the rock, and putting it down, replaced his bait. Four of them would make a good supper, the best a man could have, and with a night's hard work before him he needed a hearty meal. He would not have time to fish tomorrow morning. First of all the scaffold would have to be taken down and the pieces brought back to the room in which it was kept, and there would be a lot of cleaning to do. It was a bloody business; last time he had had his pants so soaked that he had been able to do nothing with them and had had to throw them away. The brass would have to be polished, the knife would have to be honed. He was not a man to leave a job half finished, and by the time it was through he would be pretty peckish. It would be worth while to catch a few more fish and put them in a cool place so that he could have a substantial breakfast. A cup of coffee, a couple of eggs, and a bit of fried fish, he could do with that. Then he would have a good sleep; after a night on his feet, the anxiety of an inexperienced assistant, and the clearing away of all the mess, God knew he would deserve it.

In front of him was spread the bay in a noble sweep, and in the distance was a little island green with trees. The afternoon was exquisitely still. Peace descended on the fisherman's soul. He watched his float idly. When he came to think of it, he reflected, he might be a great deal worse off; some of them, the convicts/ he meant, the convicts who swarmed in the prison a few hundred yards away from him, some of them had such a nostalgia for France that they went mad with melancholy; but he was a bit of a philosopher, so long as he could fish he was content; and did it really matter if he watched his float on the southern sea or in the Rhône? His thoughts wandered back to the past. His wife was an intolerable woman and he did not regret that he had killed her. He had never meant to marry her. She was a dressmaker, and he had taken a fancy to her because she was always neatly and smartly dressed. She seemed respectable and ladylike. He would not have been surprised if she had looked upon herself as a cut above a policeman. But he had a way with him. She soon gave him to understand that she was no snob, and when he made the customary advances he discovered to his relief, for he was not a man who considered that resistance added a flavour to conquest, that she was no prude. He liked to be seen with her when he took her out to dinner. She talked intelligently, and she was economical. She knew where they could dine well at the cheapest price. His situation was enviable. It added to his satisfaction that he could gratify the sexual desires natural to his healthy temperament at so moderate an expense. When she came to him and said she was going to have a baby it seemed natural enough that they should get married. He was earning good wages, and it was time that he should settle down. He often grew tired of eating, *en pension*, at a restaurant, and he looked forward to having his own home and home cooking. Well, it turned out that it had been a mistake about the baby, but Louis Remire was a good-natured fellow, and he didn't hold it up against Adèle. But he found, as many men have found before, that the wife was a very different woman from the mistress. She was jealous and possessive. She seemed to think that on a Sunday afternoon he ought to take her for a walk instead of going fishing, and she made it a grievance that, on coming off duty, he would go to the café. There was one café he frequented where other fishermen went and where he met men with whom he had a lot in common. He found it much pleasanter to spend his free evenings there over a glass or two of beer, whiling away the time with a game of cards, than to sit at home with his wife. She began to make scenes. Though sociable and jovial by nature he had a quick temper. There was a rough crowd at Lyons, and sometimes you could not manage them unless you were prepared to show a certain amount of firmness.

When his wife began to make a nuisance of herself it never occurred to him that there was any other way of dealing with her than that he adopted. He let her know the strength of his hand. If she had been a sensible woman she would have learnt her lesson, but she was not a sensible woman. He found occasion more and more often to apply a necessary correction; she revenged herself by screaming the place down and by telling the neighbours – they lived in a two-roomed apartment on the fifth floor of a big house – what a brute he was. She told them that she was sure he would kill her one day. And yet never was there a more good-natured man than Louis Remire; she blamed him for the money he spent at the café, she accused him of wasting it on other women; well, in his position he had opportunities now and then, and as any man would he took them, and he was easy with his money, he never minded paying a round of drinks for his friends, and when a girl who had been nice to him wanted a new hat or a pair of silk stockings he wasn't the man to say no. His wife looked upon money that he did not spend on her as money stolen from her; she tried to make him account for every penny he spent, and when in his jovial way he told her he had thrown it out of the window, she was infuriated. Her tongue grew bitter and her voice was rasping. She was in a sullen rage with him all the time. She could not speak without saying something disagreeable. They led a cat-and-dog life. Louis Remire used to tell his friends what a harridan she was, he used to tell them that he wished ten times a day that he had never married her, and sometimes he would add that if an epidemic of influenza did not carry her off he would really have to kill her.

It was these remarks, made merely in jest, and the fact that she had so often told the neighbours that she knew he would murder her, that had sent him to St Laurent de Maroni with a twelve-year sentence. Otherwise he might very well have got off with three or four years in a French prison. The end had come one hot summer's day. He was, which was rare for him, in a bad temper. There was a strike in progress and the strikers had been violent. The police had had to make a good many arrests and the men had not submitted to this peaceably. Louis Remire had got a nasty blow on the jaw and he had had to make free use of his truncheon. To get the arrested men to the station had been a hot and tiring job. On coming off duty he had gone home to get out of his uniform and was intending to go to the café and have a glass of beer and a pleasant game of cards. His jaw was hurting him. His wife chose that moment to ask him for money and when he told her that he had none to give her she made a scene. He had plenty of money to go to the café, but none for her to buy a scrap of food with, she could starve for all he cared. He told her to shut up, and then the row began. She got in front of the door and swore that he should not pass till he gave her money. He told her to get out of the way, and took a step towards her. She whipped out his service revolver which he had taken off when he removed his uniform and threatened that she would shoot him if he moved a step. He was used to dealing with dangerous criminals, and the words were hardly out of her mouth before he had sprung upon her and snatched the revolver out of her hand. She screamed and hit him in the face. She hit him exactly where his jaw most hurt him. Blind with rage and mad with pain, he fired, he fired twice and she fell to the floor. For a moment he stood and stared at her. He was dazed. She looked as if she were dead. His first feeling was one of indescribable relief. He listened. No one seemed to have heard the sound of the shot. The neighbours must be out. That was a bit of luck, for it gave him time to do what he had to do in his own way. He changed back into his uniform, went out, locking the door behind him and putting the key in his pocket; he stopped for five minutes at his familiar café to have a glass of beer and then returned to the police-station he had lately left. On account of the day's disturbances the chief inspector was still there. Louis Remire went to his room and told him what had happened. He spent the night in a cell adjoining those of the strikers he had so recently himself arrested. Even at that tragic moment he was struck by the irony of the situation.

Louis Remire had on frequent occasions appeared as a police witness in criminal cases and he knew how eager are a man's companions to give any information that may damage him when he gets into trouble. It had caused him a certain grim amusement to realize how often it happened that a conviction was obtained only by the testimony of a prisoner's best friends. But notwithstanding his experience he was amazed, when his own case came up for trial, to listen to the evidence given by the proprietor of the little café he had so much frequented, and to that of the men who for years had fished with him, played cards with him, and drunk with him. They seemed to have treasured every careless word he had ever uttered, the complaints he had made about his wife and the joking threats he had from time to time made that he would get even with her. He knew that at the time they had taken them no more seriously than he meant them. If he was able to do them a small service, and a man in the force often has it in his power to do one, he never hesitated. He had never been ungenerous with his money. You would have thought as you listened to them in the witness-box that it gave them the most intense satisfaction to disclose every trivial detail that could damage him.

From what appeared at the trial you would have thought that he was a bad man, dissolute, of violent temper, extravagant, idle, and corrupt. He knew that he was nothing of the kind. He was just an ordinary, good-natured, easy-going fellow, who was willing to let you go your way if you would let him go his. It was true that he liked his game of cards and his glass of beer, it was true that he liked a pretty girl, but what of it? When he looked at the jury he wondered how many of them would come out of it any better than he if all their errors, all their rash words, all their follies were thus laid bare. He did not resent the long term of penal servitude to which he was sentenced. He was an officer of the law; he had committed a crime and it was right that he should be punished. But he was not a criminal; he was the victim of an unfortunate accident.

At St Laurent de Maroni, in the prison camp, wearing the pink and white stripe of the prison garb and the ugly straw hat, he remembered still that he had been a policeman and that the convicts with whom he must now consort had always been his natural enemies. He despised and disliked them. He had as little to do with them as he could. And he was not frightened of them. He knew them too well. Like all the rest he had a knife and he showed that he was prepared to use it. He did not want to interfere with anybody, but he was not going to allow anyone to interfere with him.

The chief of the Lyons police had liked him, his character while in the force had been exemplary, and the *fiche* which accompanied every prisoner spoke well of him. He knew that what officials like is a prisoner who gives no trouble, who accepts his position with cheerfulness, and who is willing. He got a soft job; very soon he got a cell of his own and so escaped the horrible promiscuity of the dormitories; he got on well with the warders, they were decent chaps, most of them, and knowing that he had formerly been in the police they treated him more as a comrade than as a convict. The commandant of the prison trusted him. Presently he got the job of servant to one of the prison officials. He slept in the prison, but otherwise enjoyed complete freedom. He took the children of his master to school every day and fetched them at the end of their school hours. He made toys for them. He accompanied his mistress to market and carried back the provisions she bought. He spent long hours gossiping with her. The family liked him. They liked his chaffing manner and his good-natured smile. He was industrious and trustworthy. Life once more was tolerable.

But after three years his master was transferred to Cayenne. It was a blow. But it happened just then that the post of executioner fell free and he obtained it. Now once more he was in the service of the state. He was an official. However humble his residence it was his own. He need no longer wear the prison uniform. He could grow his hair and his moustache. He cared little if the convicts looked upon him with horror and contempt. That was how he looked upon them. Scum. When he took the bleeding head of an executed man from the basket and holding it by the ears pronounced those solemn words: *Au nom du peuple français justice est faite,* he felt that he did represent the Republic. He stood for law and order. He was the protector of society against that vast horde of ruthless criminals.

He got a hundred francs for each execution. That and what the governor's wife paid him for his fish provided him with many a pleasant comfort and not a few luxuries. And now as he sat on his rock in the peace of eventide he considered what he would do with the money he would earn next day. Occasionally he got a bite, now and then a fish; he drew it out of the water, took it off the hook, and put on fresh bait; but he did this mechanically, and it did not disturb the current of his thoughts. Six hundred francs. It was a respectable sum. He scarcely knew what to do with it. He had everything he wanted in his little house, he had a good store of groceries, and plenty of rum for one who was as little of a drinker as he was; he needed no fishing tackle; his clothes were good enough. The only thing was to put it aside. He already had a tidy little sum hidden in the ground at the root of a papaia tree. He chuckled when he thought how Adèle would have stared had she known that he was actually saving. It would have been balm to her avaricious soul. He was saving up gradually for when he was released. That was the difficult moment for the convicts. So long as they were in prison they had a roof over their heads and food to eat, but when they were released, with the obligation of staying for so many years more in the colony, they had to shift for themselves. They all said the same thing: it was at the expiration of their term that their real punishment began. They could not get work. Employers mistrusted them. Contractors would not engage them because the prison authorities hired out convict labour at a price that defied competition. They slept in the open, in the market-place, and for food were often glad to go to the Salvation Army. But the Salvation Army made them work hard for what they gave and besides forced them to listen to their services. Sometimes they committed a violent crime merely to get back to the safety of prison. Louis Remire was not going to take any risks. He meant to amass a sufficient capital to start in business. He ought to be able to get permission to settle in Cayenne, and there he might open a bar. People might hesitate to come at first because he had been the executioner, but if he provided good liquor they would get over their prejudice, and with his jovial manner, with his experience in keeping order, he ought to be able to make a go of it. Visitors came to Cayenne now and then and they would come out of curiosity. It would be something interesting to tell their friends when they got home that the best rum punch they had had in Cayenne was at the executioner's. But he had a good many years to go yet, and if there really was something he needed there was no reason why he shouldn't get it. He racked his brains. No, there wasn't a thing in the world he wanted. He was surprised. He allowed his eyes to wander from his float. The sea was wonderfully calm and now it was rich with all the colour of the setting sun. In the sky already a solitary star twinkled. A thought came to him that filled him with an extraordinary sensation.

'But if there's nothing in the world you want, surely that's happiness.' He stroked his handsome moustache and his blue eyes shone softly. 'There are no two ways about it, I'm a happy man and till this moment I never knew it.'

The notion was so unexpected that he did not know what to make of it. It was certainly a very odd one. But there it was, as obvious to anyone with a logical mind as a proposition of Euclid.

'Happy, that's what I am. How many men can say the same? In St Laurent de Maroni of all places, and for the first time in my life.'

The sun was setting. He had caught enough fish for his supper and enough for his breakfast. He drew in his line, gathered up his fish, and went back to his house. It stood but a few yards from the sea. It did not take him long to light his fire and in a little while he had four little fish cheerfully frizzling in a pan. He was always very particular about the oil he used. The best olive oil was expensive, but it was worth the money. The prison bread was good, and after he had fried his fish, he fried a couple of pieces of bread in the rest of the oil. He sniffed the savoury smell with satisfaction. He lit a lamp, washed a lettuce grown in his own garden, and mixed himself a salad. He had a notion that no one in the world could mix a salad better than he. He drank a glass of rum and ate his supper with appetite. He gave a few odds and ends to the two mongrel dogs who were lying at his feet, and then, having washed up, for he was by nature a tidy man and when he came in to breakfast next morning did not want to find things in a mess, let the dogs out of the compound to wander about the coconut grove. He took the lamp into the house, made himself comfortable in his deck-chair, and smoking a cigar smuggled in from the neighbouring Dutch Colony settled down to read one of the French papers that had arrived by the last mail. Replete, his mind at ease, he could not but feel that life, with all its disadvantages, was good to live. He was still affected by the amused surprise that had overcome him when it suddenly occurred to him that he was a happy man. When you considered that men spent their lives seeking for happiness, it seemed hardly believable that he had found it. Yet the fact stared him in the face. A man who has everything he wants is happy, he had everything he wanted; therefore he was happy. He chuckled as a new thought crossed his mind.

'There's no denying it, I owe it to Adèle.'

Old Adèle. What a foul woman!

Presently he decided that he had better have a nap; he set his alarm clock for a quarter to twelve and lying down on his bed in a few minutes was fast asleep. He slept soundly and no dreams troubled him. He woke

with a start when the alarm sounded, but in a moment remembered
why he had set it. He yawned and stretched himself lazily.

'Ah, well, I suppose I must get to work. Every job has its incon-
veniences.'

He slipped from under his mosquito-net and relit his lamp. To freshen
himself he washed his hands and face, and then as a protection against
the night air drank a glass of rum. He thought for a moment of his
inexperienced assistant and wondered whether it would be wise to take
some rum in a flask with him.

'It would be a pretty business if his nerves went back on him.'

It was unfortunate that so many as six men had to be executed. If
there had been only one, it wouldn't have mattered so much his assistant
being new to the game; but with five others waiting there, it would
be awkward if there were a hitch. He shrugged his shoulders. They would
just have to do the best they could. He passed a comb through his tousled
hair and carefully brushed his handsome moustache. He lit a cigarette.
He walked through his compound, unlocked the door in the stout
palisade that surrounded it, and locked it again behind him. There was
no moon. He whistled for his dogs. He was surprised that they did not
come. He whistled again. The brutes. They'd probably caught a rat
and were fighting over it. He'd give them a good hiding for that; he'd
teach them not to come when he whistled. He set out to walk in the
direction of the prison. It was dark under the coconut trees and he would
just as soon have had the dogs with him. Still there were only fifty yards
to go and then he would be out in the open. There were lights in the
governor's house, and it gave him confidence to see them. He smiled,
for he guessed what those lights at that late hour meant: the governor,
with the execution before him at dawn, was finding it hard to sleep.
The anxiety, the malaise, that affected convicts and ex-convicts alike
on the eve of an execution, had got on his nerves. It was true that there
was always the chance of an outbreak then, and the warders went around
with their eyes skinned and their hands ready to draw their guns at
a suspicious movement.

Louis Remire whistled for his dogs once more, but they did not come.
He could not understand it. It was a trifle disquieting. He was a man
who habitually walked slowly, strolling along with a sort of roll, but
now he hastened his pace. He spat the cigarette out of his mouth. It
had struck him that it was prudent not to betray his whereabouts by
the light it gave. Suddenly he stumbled against something. He stopped
dead. He was a brave man, with nerves of steel, but on a sudden he
felt sick with terror. It was something soft and rather large that he had
stumbled against, and he was pretty sure what it was. He wore
espadrilles, and with one foot he cautiously felt the object on the ground
before him. Yes, he was right. It was one of his dogs. It was dead. He

took a step backwards and drew his knife. He knew it was no good to shout. The only house in the neighbourhood was the prison governor's, it faced the clearing just beyond the coconut grove; but they would not hear him, or if they did would not stir. St Laurent de Maroni was not a place where you went out in the dead of night when you heard a man calling for help. If next day one of the freed convicts was found lying dead, well, it was no great loss. Louis Remire saw in a flash what had happened.

He thought rapidly. They had killed his dogs while he was sleeping. They must have got them when he had put them out of his compound after supper. They must have thrown them some poisoned meat and the brutes had snatched at it. If the one he had stumbled over was near his house it was because it tried to crawl home to die. Louis Remire strained his eyes. He could see nothing. The night was pitch black. He could hardly see the trunks of the coconut trees a yard away from him. His first thought was to make a rush for his shack. If he got back to the safety of that he could wait till the prison people, wondering why he did not come, sent to fetch him. But he knew he could never get back. He knew they were there in the darkness, the men who had killed his dogs; he would have to fumble with the key to find the lock and before he found it he would have a knife plunged in his back. He listened intently. There was not a sound. And yet he felt that there were men there, lurking behind the trees, and they were there to kill him. They would kill him as they had killed his dogs. And he would die like a dog. There was more than one certainly. He knew them, there were three or four of them at least, there might be more, convicts in service in private houses who were not obliged to get back to the camp till a late hour, or desperate and starving freed men who had nothing to lose. For a moment he hesitated what to do. He dared not make a run for it, they might easily have put a rope across the pathway that led from his house to the open, and if he tripped he was done for. The coconut trees were loosely planted and among them his enemies would see him as little as he saw them. He stepped over the dead dog and plunged into the grove. He stood with his back to a tree to decide how he should proceed. The silence was terrifying. Suddenly he heard a whisper and the horror of it was frightful. Again a dead silence. He felt he must move on, but his feet seemed rooted to the ground. He felt that they were peering at him out of the darkness and it seemed to him that he was as visible to them as though he stood in the broad light of day. Then from the other side was a little cough. It came as such a shock that Louis Remire nearly screamed. He was conscious now that they were all round him. He could expect no mercy from those robbers and murderers. He remembered the other executioner, his predecessor, whom they had carried still alive into the jungle, whose eyes they had gouged out, and whom they had left hanging for the vultures to devour. His knees began to tremble. What a fool he had been to take on the job! There were soft jobs he could have found in which you ran no risk. It was too late to think of that. He pulled himself together. He had no chance of getting out of the coconut grove alive, he knew that; he wanted to be sure that he would be dead. He tightened his grip on his knife. The awful part was that he could hear no one, he could see no one, and yet he knew that they were lurking there waiting to strike. For one moment he had a mad idea, he would throw his knife away and shout out to them that he was unarmed and they could come and kill him in safety. But he knew them; they would never be satisfied merely to kill him. Rage seized him. He was not the man to surrender tamely to a pack of criminals. He was an honest man and an official of the state; it was his duty to defend himself. He could not stay there all night. It was better to get it over quickly. Yet that tree at his back seemed to offer a sort of security, he could not bring himself to move. He stared at the trunk of a tree in front of him and suddenly it moved and he realized with horror that it was a man. That made up his mind for him and with a huge effort he stepped forwards. He advanced slowly and cautiously. He could hear nothing, he could see nothing. But he knew that as he advanced they advanced too. It was as though he was accompanied by an invisible bodyguard. He thought he could hear the sound of their naked feet on the ground. His fear had left him. He walked on, keeping as close to the trees as he could, so that they should have less chance of attacking him from behind; a wild hope sprang up in his breast that they would be afraid to strike, they knew him, they all knew him, and whoever struck the first blow would be lucky if he escaped a knife in his own guts; he had only another thirty yards to go, and once in the open, able to see, he could make a fight for it. A few yards more and then he would run for his life. Suddenly something happened that made him start out of his skin, and he stopped dead. A light was flashed and in that heavy darkness the sudden glare was terrifying. It was an electric torch. Instinctively he sprang to a tree and stood with his back to it. He could not see who held the light. He was blinded by it. He did not speak. He held his knife low, he knew that when they struck it was in the belly, and if someone flung himself at him he was prepared to strike back. He was going to sell his life dearly. For half a minute perhaps the light shone on his face, but it seemed to him an eternity. He thought now that he discerned dimly the faces of men. Then a word broke the horrible silence.

'Throw.'

At the same instant a knife came flying through the air and struck him on the breast-bone. He threw up his hands and as he did so someone sprang at him and with a great sweep of the knife ripped up his belly. The light was switched off. Louis Remire sank to the ground with a groan, a terrible groan of pain. Five, six men gathered out of the gloom and stood over him. With his fall the knife that had stuck in his breast-bone was dislodged. It lay on the ground. A quick flash of the torch showed where it was. One of the men took it and with a single, swift motion cut Remire's throat from ear to ear.

'*Au nom du peuple français justice est faite,*' he said.

They vanished into the darkness and in the coconut grove was the immense silence of death.

Vendetta

Guy de Maupassant

Palo Saverini's widow dwelt alone with her son in a small, mean house on the ramparts of Bonifacio. Built on a spur of the mountain and in places actually overhanging the sea, the town looks across the rock-strewn Straits to the low-lying coast of Sardinia. On the other side, girdling it almost completely, there is a fissure in the cliff, like an immense corridor, which serves as a port, and down this long channel, as far as the first houses, sail the small Italian and Sardinian fishing-boats, and once a fortnight the broken-winded old steamer from Ajaccio. Clustered together on the white hillside, the houses form a patch of even more dazzling whiteness. Clinging to the rock, gazing down upon those deadly Straits where scarcely a ship ventures, they look like the nests of birds of prey. The sea and the barren coast, stripped of all but a scanty covering of grass, are forever harassed by a restless wind, which sweeps along the narrow funnel, ravaging the banks on either side. In all directions the black points of innumerable rocks jut out from the water, with trails of white foam streaming from them, like torn shreds of cloth, floating and quivering on the surface of the waves.

The widow Saverini's house was planted on the very edge of the cliff, and its three windows opened upon this wild and dreary prospect. She lived there with her son Antoine and their dog Sémillante, a great gaunt brute of the sheep-dog variety, with a long, rough coat, whom the young man took with him when he went out shooting.

One evening, Antoine Saverini was treacherously stabbed in a quarrel by Nicolas Ravolati, who escaped that same night to Sardinia.

At the sight of the body, which was brought home by passers-by, the old mother shed no tears, but she gazed long and silently at her dead son. Then, laying her wrinkled hand upon the corpse, she promised him the Vendetta. She would not allow anyone to remain with her, and shut herself up with the dead body. The dog Sémillante, who remained with her, stood at the foot of the bed and howled, with her head turned towards her master and her tail between her legs. Neither of them stirred, neither the dog nor the old mother, who was now leaning over the body, gazing at it fixedly, and silently shedding great tears. Still wearing his rough jacket, which was pierced and torn at the breast, the boy lay on his back as if asleep, but there was blood all about him, on his shirt, which had been stripped off in order to expose the wound, on his waistcoat, trousers, face and hands. His beard and hair were matted with clots of blood.

The old mother began to talk to him, and at the sound of her voice the dog stopped howling.

'Never fear, never fear, you shall be avenged, my son, my little son, my poor child. You may sleep in peace. You shall be avenged, I tell you. You have your mother's word, and you know she never breaks it.'

Slowly she bent down and pressed her cold lips to the dead lips of her son.

Sémillante resumed her howling, uttering a monotonous, long-drawn wail, heart-rending and terrible. And thus the two remained, the woman and the dog, till morning.

The next day Antoine Saverini was buried, and soon his name ceased to be mentioned in Bonifacio.

He had no brother, nor any near male relation. There was no man in the family who could take up the vendetta. Only his mother, his old mother, brooded over it.

From morning till night she could see, just across the Straits, a white speck upon the coast. This was the little Sardinian village of Longosardo, where the Corsican bandits took refuge whenever the hunt for them grew too hot. They formed almost the entire population of the hamlet. In full view of their native shores they waited for a chance to return home and regain the bush. She knew that Nicolas Ravolati had sought shelter in that village.

All day long she sat alone at her window gazing at the opposite coast and thinking of her revenge, but what was she to do with no one to help her, and she herself so feeble and near her end? But she had promised, she had sworn by the dead body of her son, she could not forget, and she dared not delay. What was she to do? She could not sleep at night, she knew not a moment of rest or peace, but racked her brains unceasingly. Sémillante, asleep at her feet, would now and then raise her head and emit a piercing howl. Since her master had disappeared, this had become a habit, it was as if she were calling him, as if she, too, were inconsolable and preserved in her canine soul an ineffaceable memory of the dead.

One night, when Sémillante began to whine, the old mother had an inspiration of savage, vindictive ferocity. She thought about it till morning. At daybreak she rose and betook herself to church. Prostrate on the stone floor, humbling herself before God, she besought Him to aid and support her, to lend to her poor, worn-out body the strength she needed to avenge her son.

Then she returned home. In the yard stood an old barrel with one end knocked in, in which was caught the rain-water from the eaves. She turned it over, emptied it, and fixed it to the ground with stakes and stones. Then she chained up Sémillante to this kennel and went into the house.

With her eyes fixed on the Sardinian coast, she walked restlessly up and down her room. He was over there, the murderer.

The dog howled all day and all night. The next morning the old woman brought her a bowl of water, but no food, neither soup nor bread. Another day passed. Sémillante was worn out and slept. The next morning her eyes were gleaming, and her coat staring, and she tugged frantically at her chain. And again the old woman gave her nothing to eat. Maddened with hunger Sémillante barked hoarsely. Another night went by.

At daybreak, the widow went to a neighbour and begged for two trusses of straw. She took some old clothes that had belonged to her husband, stuffed them with straw to represent a human figure, and made a head out of a bundle of old rags. Then, in front of Sémillante's kennel, she fixed a stake in the ground and fastened the dummy to it in an upright position.

The dog looked at the straw figure in surprise and, although she was famished, stopped howling.

The old woman went to the pork butcher and bought a long piece of black pudding. When she came home she lighted a wood fire in the yard, close to the kennel, and fried the black pudding. Sémillante bounded up and down in a frenzy, foaming at the mouth, her eyes fixed on the gridiron with its maddening smell of meat.

Her mistress took the steaming pudding and wound it like a tie round the dummy's neck. She fastened it on tightly with string as if to force it inwards. When she had finished she unchained the dog.

With one ferocious leap, Sémillante flew at the dummy's throat and with her paws on its shoulders began to tear it. She fell back with a portion of her prey between her jaws, sprang at it again, slashing at the string with her fangs, tore away some scraps of food, dropped for a moment, and hurled herself at it in renewed fury. She tore away the whole face with savage rendings and reduced the neck to shreds.

Motionless and silent, with burning eyes, the old woman looked on. Presently she chained the dog up again. She starved her another two days, and then put her through the same strange performance. For three months she accustomed her to this method of attack, and to tear her meals away with her fangs. She was no longer kept on the chain.

At a sign from her mistress, the dog would fly at the dummy's throat.

She learned to tear it to pieces even when no food was concealed about its throat. Afterwards as a reward she was always given the black pudding her mistress had cooked for her.

As soon as she caught sight of the dummy, Sémillante quivered with excitement and looked at her mistress, who would raise her finger and cry in a shrill voice, 'Tear him.'

One Sunday morning when she thought the time had come, the widow Saverini went to Confession and Communion, in an ecstasy of devotion. Then she disguised herself like a tattered old beggar man, and struck a bargain with a Sardinian fisherman, who took her and her dog across to the opposite shore.

She carried a large piece of black pudding wrapped in a cloth bag. Sémillante had been starved for two days and her mistress kept exciting her by letting her smell the savoury food.

The pair entered the village of Longosardo. The old woman hobbled along to a baker and asked for the house of Nicolas Ravolati. He had resumed his former occupation, which was that of a joiner, and he was working alone in the back of his shop.

The old woman threw open the door and called:

'Nicolas! Nicolas!'

He turned round. Slipping the dog's lead, she cried:

'Tear him! Tear him!'

The maddened dog flew at his throat. The man flung out his arms, grappled with the brute and they rolled on the ground together. For some moments he struggled, kicking the floor with his feet. Then he lay still, while Sémillante tore his throat to shreds.

Two neighbours, seated at their doors, remembered to have seen an old beggar man emerge from the house and, at his heels, a lean black dog, which was eating as it went along some brown substance that its master was giving it.

By the evening the old woman had reached home again.

That night she slept well.

Such a Good Idea

Andrea Newman

He hasn't noticed yet. It really is extraordinary, but he just hasn't noticed. He's been locked in that room for an hour and a half but he doesn't know.

I didn't mean to do it. That's what they all say, of course, oh, about serious things, in court, things like that, but I didn't. Until I did it, I had no idea I was going to. The key looked so tempting. Silly to have a key anyway, so unnecessary in a place like this, as if any burglar would ever come out here and what in hell would he find to burgle? But there it was in the lock, I'd put down the tray and as usual he didn't even notice let alone say thank you, just went on writing, while I picked up the other tray, hardly touched though I'd tried so hard to make it look nice. And then when I came out and shut the door it was as if I'd seen the key in the lock for the first time, suddenly realized what it was for. So I turned it.

I've had a wonderful hour and a half. It's been such fun; just knowing that for once I've got the upper hand has made everything such fun. I haven't done anything special, but I've felt so light-hearted. It's like being young again. It can't last, though; he's bound to notice eventually. I won't think about that. I won't let it spoil my fun. Right now, at this minute, I'm boss. He's in that room and he has to stay there till I let him out, because I turned his stupid key.

Oh God, it's started. He's turning the handle and it won't open. He's rattling it. What an awful noise he's making. I should run and open it really while he's making all that noise and then he'd never know. He's going to be so angry. He'll want to know why I did it and I don't know.

'Sarah. Sarah.'

Now he's calling me. I can't move. My feet just won't move. It's like forgetting how to walk downstairs; you can fall and break your neck all because you're thinking too hard about something that should happen naturally. Like a door opening when you turn the handle. Unless it's locked, of course. Then it's natural for it not to open. That's funny, really. I mustn't laugh. He mustn't hear me laughing when I've done something awful. It isn't funny; it's stupid. I've been naughty. A naughty girl.

'Sarah, what's the matter with this door?'

You're on the wrong side of it, that's what I want to say. There's nothing wrong with the door. I think that's funny. Oh dear, I mustn't laugh. I've got to answer him.

'Sarah, what the hell's going on?'

He sounds so angry; I knew he would be. I'll have to go. I wish my legs would work. It's no good just sitting here looking at my feet; I should be using them. Perhaps if I try very hard. Looking at my feet makes me feel they have a life of their own. They look so powerful, so purposeful. Maybe they don't want to move and they never will again. He's still shouting. I wish he wouldn't.

'I'm coming.' I actually managed to answer him, well, a sort of croak it sounds like, but it's better than nothing and my feet are actually moving, out of sheer surprise I dare say.

'What the hell have you done to this door?'

What does he think I've done? I must answer. 'I've locked it.'

A shocked pause. I suppose it's a shocking thing to be told that your wife's locked you in your study though if it takes you an hour and a half to notice I can't see that it's quite so terrible.

'Then you'd better open it, hadn't you?'

His cold voice. He's not shouting any more. I wanted him to stop but now he has it's much worse. I'm shaking all over and it's really quite a warm day.

'Sarah, do you hear me? I said you'd better open it.'

That terrible voice. But I don't know. I mean, had I better open it? What will he do? It's bad enough when he's just shouting. If I open the door he may hit me. I've never made him so angry before.

'What the bloody hell d'you think you're playing at?'

That's just it. I don't know. I *was* playing at first, I mean it was a game, just to see when he'd notice, just to get the upper hand, just – I don't know. I must have had a reason. No. It just seemed the obvious thing to do, quite suddenly, like seeing the solution to a problem all in a flash. But it's not a game any more. I'm scared.

'Sarah, open this door before I break it down.'

But he can't. It's too thick, and the times he's boasted about that. Good solid craftsmanship. He knows he can't break it down. He's only saying that, and he's stopped swearing too. He must be thinking. Getting his great brain to work; he's sure to find a solution. After all, he's clever, isn't he, not like me. But I've got the key.

*

Tuesday

He didn't break it down; of course he didn't. He couldn't, and he knew it all the time. But he didn't call out or swear any more either. At least if he did I never heard him. I went away to the other end of the house because the silence was beginning to frighten me more than anything and I played some records and opened a tin of pilchards for my supper. He hates the smell so I never have them. They tasted wonderful. I had milk and chocolate biscuits on a tray in bed and no one to go on about the crumbs: I was even careless on purpose when I bit into the biscuits so as to make lots of crumbs. I've never done that before though he always said I did. You don't quite realize what a lot you are giving up till you get it back. I listened to the play on the wireless and I didn't have to agree it was rubbish and he could do much better. I thought I wouldn't sleep but I did. I wasn't even worried; I felt sure I'd wake up with the answer. Well, I mean wake up brave enough to unlock the door and face him and have it out. . . .

I went down to the beach this morning. Just for a walk to think things out. I didn't wake up brave after all. I felt funny instead. Sort of . . . distant, as if he'd gone away or I wasn't really married to him. I stood and looked at the sea for a long time. It's so restful; I'm sure it's good for people. Doctors ought to prescribe it instead of those silly pills and things. But I didn't really do any thinking after all. I just walked about and felt peaceful and . . . rather clever, like a scientist making an important discovery.

All day I worked myself up to walking past the room but when I did I wasn't sure he was in there. It could have been anyone; or no-one. Of course I *knew* he was – he couldn't open the door and the ventilation grills would hardly let a sparrow through. He's done it himself really; I mean, no normal person finds a window spoils his concentration. I bet he's sorry about that now, though even so it's a nasty drop. But he didn't speak. Maybe he didn't hear me. Asleep perhaps. I had the key in my pocket; I felt I ought to take it though I didn't really intend to use it then. Cold metal. I touched it with my fingers and frightened me.

Wednesday

We had a conversation today. I walked past the room early; I think I felt curious, and he called out, 'Sarah, is that you?' Silly, really, like on the telephone. If we'd had a telephone. Then he started, in this reasonable, gentle voice: 'I know I haven't been an easy husband, too wrapped up in my work. You've made me stop and think. It may be a good thing. Unlock the door, there's a good girl, and we'll talk it over. I'm not cross any more. Really.'

Then I don't know what happened to me. I started saying things I hadn't planned at all. Usually I pick my words so carefully to talk to him, not to say something stupid, I mean, or tactless, but this time I didn't even know what I was going to say till I said it. I said, 'It's too late.'

He said, Whatever do you mean?'

I said, 'I'm too old to have a baby now,' and I started crying. I hadn't cried for years, not since – oh, not for years. Then I found I was sitting on the floor outside the door. I said, 'I'm too old. I'm not even pretty any more,' and went on crying. I was very noisy. Presently he said in a terribly soothing voice, 'Just unlock the door and we'll talk about it. You can tell me all about it.' He'd never been so gentle; the door made us equal. The door was my friend. I stroked it. I said, 'You never wanted me; you just wanted someone to admire you.'

'That's not true,' he said.

'Yes, it is.' I'd never contradicted him before.

'All right.' I couldn't believe it; he was actually agreeing with me. 'Perhaps you're right. But it's not too late. You unlock the door and we'll have a long talk.'

'I'm too old,' I said. 'I'm ugly.' I went on crying.

He said, 'Sarah, listen to me. Open this door and we'll talk about it.'

I said, 'I haven't got the key.' I was still crying.

He said very patiently, carefully, 'You're overwrought. Take one of your pills and get the key. Then we'll have a nice long talk.'

I didn't answer.

'It's the only sensible thing to do,' he said.

Presently, when I had stopped crying and he had stopped saying things to me, I got up and went away. But I didn't take a pill and I didn't fetch the key. I just didn't go back at all. I had a very hot bath and looked at my body and thought how wrinkled and yellow it was. But it didn't really matter. Then I went to bed.

Thursday

I wish he wouldn't make all that noise. It makes my head ache. Yesterday he was all reasonable and talking to me but today he's like a madman, and he always said *I* was unstable.

It started in the night. Banging and crashing, really an awful row. It would have brought all the neighbours round, if we'd had any. I'd have had to apologize to them; it would have been most embarrassing. So I've hardly slept at all. He knows I need my sleep but he was always selfish.

Even now I feel funny admitting that. I've believed for years I didn't understand him, he was too clever for me, all that. *I've been such a fool.*

But I don't like this noise. He's always been so dignified. Remote, you might say. I don't like him like this. I despise him. A key's not a very big thing but it makes quite a difference. He's been shouting for hours, things about food and water, in a very hoarse voice. He sounds frightened. No one's ever been frightened of me before, least of all him. It's rather odd. He's only been in there four days and he did have that last tray. I bet he wishes he hadn't turned up his nose at the other one now. I wonder if he's really in such a bad way as he says. He insists he needs a doctor and I must realize, etc., etc. He keeps going on about common humanity. Will I really have to get him a doctor and nurse him and get him well just so that we can go on as before?

I wonder if he looks any different. I wonder what four days like that do to a person. Is he a lot thinner? Swollen lips, cracked and black? No, that's the desert, in films anyway, not very likely here. But I don't want to know. It's horrible. I'd rather not think about it. The doctor said I shouldn't think about things that upset me. Not that I've had much choice, until lately.

Life doesn't turn out a bit the way you expect. Being ignored and taken for granted and looked down upon, well, nobody would get married if they knew all that was going to happen. It wasn't like that at first. Not when I was pretty. But there wasn't any reason to make a fuss, nothing people would take seriously, I mean. I didn't even think about it. I thought I loved him, I really thought, right up to the moment I turned the key. It's only now I can get it clear. I can't love him. I can't even like him, can I, or I'd have let him out days ago. Or never have locked him in there in the first place. I don't know. It seemed such a good idea at the time, still is really, and now he's stopped shouting I can think; it's really peaceful. But I didn't mean to leave him in so long. I didn't mean anything, just to do something positive for the first time in thirty years.

He doesn't seem real any more. It's not my husband – no, himself, now I see why the Irish have that expression – it's not himself in there. It's some horrible stranger who looks different and shouts all these awful things to frighten me. He's somewhere else. I don't know where; I don't want to know. Would Doctor Anderson think I'm making progress now I've done something positive? Or would he be cross? I won't tell him. I won't tell him. I don't like people being cross with me.

I never meant to leave him, really I didn't. What would I have done? But it wasn't just that. I mean I couldn't have left him. I couldn't have done anything so positive. I still can't. But now it's as if he's left me. He's gone into that room as usual one day and never come back. It's better that way. It's the only way. I wonder why I never thought of it before.

Friday

Doctor Anderson said I should have reasons for what I do, to stop me drifting. I see that now. And really the truth is there's no *reason* to go upstairs and unlock the door. So I must be doing the right thing; I must be. That makes me feel better. I've always tried to do the right thing, only I haven't been very successful.

*

A quiet night. I'm sleeping in another room now so I can't hear anything, if there's anything to hear. But I'm frightened of that key. I'm sure it's dangerous. I keep looking at it, touching it – well, it's absurd that such a small thing can be so powerful.

I ought to do something about it. But it's so hard to do anything.

Saturday
I went for a walk this morning, just along the beach. The sea was wonderful. There's always the sea, no matter what happens. I had the key in my pocket. The water was all blue and grey and marvellous. It made me feel better just to look at it. Sometimes it's quite hard, when I get outside or on the beach, to remember what's been happening lately. I used to have very confused bad dreams like that, with a problem to solve and lots of darkness. It's been like that. But it isn't any more. I threw the key in the water. The tide was going out and I made my arm as strong as I could. The key went out with the tide.

I know I've done the right thing. The key was dangerous. I might have done something with it for no reason.

I feel very peaceful now. I don't know what I'm going to do. I might stay here or I might go away. I don't know yet. But I shan't go up to that room again; I know that. There's no point.

The Regent's Park Murder

Baroness Orczy

Miss Polly Burton had become quite accustomed to her extraordinary *vis-à-vis* in the corner.

He was always there, when she arrived, in the selfsame corner, dressed in one of his remarkable check tweed suits; he seldom said good morning, and invariably when she appeared he began to fidget with increased nervousness, with some tattered and knotty piece of string.

'Were you ever interested in the Regent's Park murder?' he asked her one day.

Polly replied that she had forgotten most of the particulars connected with that curious murder, but that she fully remembered the stir and flutter it had caused in a certain section of London Society.

'The racing and gambling set, particularly, you mean,' he said. 'All the persons implicated in the murder, directly or indirectly, were of the type commonly called "Society men", or "men about town", whilst the Harewood Club in Hanover Square, round which centred all the scandal in connection with the murder, was one of the smartest clubs in London.

'Probably the doings of the Harewood Club, which was essentially a gambling club, would for ever have remained "officially" absent from the knowledge of the police authorities but for the murder in the Regent's Park and the revelations which came to light in connection with it.

'I dare say you know the quiet square which lies between Portland Place and the Regent's Park and is called Park Crescent at its south end, and subsequently Park Square East and West. The Marylebone Road, with all its heavy traffic, cuts straight across the large square and its pretty gardens, but the latter are connected together by a tunnel under the road; and of course you must remember that the new tube station in the south portion of the Square had not yet been planned.

'February 6th, 1907, was a very foggy night, nevertheless Mr Aaron Cohen, of 30, Park Square West, at two o'clock in the morning, having finally pocketed the heavy winnings which he had just swept off the green table of the Harewood Club, started to walk home alone. An hour later most of the inhabitants of Park Square West were aroused from their peaceful slumbers by the sounds of a violent altercation in the road. A man's angry voice was heard shouting violently for a minute or two, and was followed immediately by frantic screams of "Police" and "Murder." Then there was the double sharp report of firearms, and nothing more.

'The fog was very dense, and, as you no doubt have experienced yourself, it is very difficult to locate sound in a fog. Nevertheless, not more than a minute or two had elapsed before Constable F 18, the point policeman at the corner of Marylebone Road, arrived on the scene, and, having first of all whistled for any of his comrades on the beat, began to grope his way about in the fog, more confused than effectually assisted by contradictory directions from the inhabitants of the houses close by, who were nearly falling out of the upper windows as they shouted out to the constable.

' "By the railings, policeman."

' "Higher up the road."

' 'No, lower down."

' 'It was on this side of the pavement I am sure."

' "No, the other."

'At last it was another policeman, F 22, who, turning into Park Square West from the north side, almost stumbled upon the body of a man lying on the pavement with his head against the railings of the Square. By this time quite a little crowd of people from the different houses in the road had come down, curious to know what had actually happened.

'The policeman turned the strong light of his bull's-eye lantern on the unfortunate man's face.

' "It looks as if he had been strangled, don't it?" he murmured to his comrade.

'And he pointed to the swollen tongue, the eyes half out of their sockets, bloodshot, and congested, the purple, almost black, hue of the face.

'At this point one of the spectators, more callous to horrors, peered curiously into the dead man's face. He uttered an exclamation of astonishment.

' "Why, surely, it's Mr Cohen from No. 30!"

'The mention of a name familiar down the length of the street had caused two or three other men to come forward and to look more closely into the horribly distorted mask of the murdered man.

' "Our next-door neighbour, undoubtedly," asserted Mr Ellison, a young barrister, residing at No. 31.

' "What in the world was he doing this foggy night all alone, and on foot?" asked somebody else.

' "He usually came home very late. I fancy he belonged to some gambling club in town. I dare say he couldn't get a cab to bring him out here, Mind you, I don't know much about him. We only knew him to nod to."

' "Poor beggar! it looks almost like an old-fashioned case of garrotting."

' "Anyway, the blackguardly murderer, whoever he was, wanted to make sure he had killed his man!" added Constable F 18, as he picked up an object from the pavement. "Here's the revolver, with two cartridges missing. You gentlemen heard the report just now?"

' "He don't seem to have hit him though. The poor bloke was strangled, no doubt."

' "And tried to shoot at his assailant, obviously," asserted the young barrister with authority.

' "If he succeeded in hitting the brute, there might be a chance of tracing the way he went."

' "But not in the fog."

'Soon, however, the appearance of the inspector, detective, and medical officer, who had quickly been informed of the tragedy, put an end to further discussion.

'The bell at No. 30 was rung, and the servants – all four of them women – were asked to look at the body.

'Amidst tears of horror and screams of fright, they all recognized in the murdered man their master, Mr Aaron Cohen. He was therefore conveyed to his own room pending the coroner's inquest.

'The police had a pretty difficult task, you will admit; there were so very few indications to go by, and at first literally no clue.

'The inquest revealed practically nothing. Very little was known in the neighbourhood about Mr Aaron Cohen and his affairs. His female servants did not even know the name or whereabout of the various clubs he frequented.

'He had an office in Throgmorton Street and went to business every day. He dined at home, and sometimes had friends to dinner. When he he was alone he invariably went to the club, where he stayed until the small hours of the morning.

'The night of the murder he had gone out at about nine o'clock. That was the last his servants had seen of him. With regard to the revolver, all four servants swore positively that they had never seen it before, and that, unless Mr Cohen had bought it that very day, it did not belong to their master.

'Beyond that, no trace whatever of the murderer had been found, but on the morning after the crime a couple of keys linked together by a short metal chain were found close to a gate at the opposite end of the Square, that which immediately faced Portland Place. These were proved to be, firstly, Mr Cohen's latch-key, and secondly, his gate-key of the Square.

'It was therefore presumed that the murderer, having accomplished his fell design and ransacked his victim's pockets, had found the keys and made good his escape by slipping into the Square, cutting under the tunnel, and out again by the further gate. He then took the precaution not to carry the keys with him any further, but threw them away and disappeared in the fog.

'The jury returned a verdict of wilful murder against some person or persons unknown, and the police were put on their mettle to discover the unknown and daring murderer. The result of their investigations, conducted with marvellous skill by Mr William Fisher, led, about a week after the crime, to the sensational arrest of one of London's smartest young bucks.

'The case Mr Fisher had got up against the accused briefly amounted to this:

'On the night of February 6th, soon after midnight, play began to run very high at the Harewood Club, in Hanover Square. Mr Aaron Cohen held the bank at roulette against some twenty or thirty friends, mostly young fellows with no wits and plenty of money. "The Bank" was winning heavily, and it appears that this was the third consecutive night on which Mr Aaron Cohen had gone home richer by several hundreds than he had been at the start of play.

'Young John Ashley, who is the son of a very worthy county gentleman who is M.F.H. somewhere in the Midlands, was losing heavily, and in his case also it appears that it was the third consecutive night that Fortune had turned her face against him.

'Remember,' continued the man in the corner, 'that when I tell you all these details and facts, I am giving you the combined evidence of several witnesses, which it took many days to collect and to classify.

'It appears that young Mr Ashley, though very popular in society, was generally believed to be in what is vulgarly termed "low water"; up to his eyes in debt, and mortally afraid of his dad, whose younger son he was, and who had on one occasion threatened to ship him off to Australia with a £5 note in his pocket if he made any further extravagant calls upon his paternal indulgence.

'It was also evident to all John Ashley's many companions that the worthy M.F.H. held the purse-strings in a very tight grip. The young man, bitten with the desire to cut a smart figure in the circles in which he moved, had often recourse to the varying fortunes which now and again smiled upon him across the green tables in the Harewood Club.

'Be that as it may, the general consensus of opinion at the Club was that young Ashley had changed his last "pony" before he sat down to a turn of roulette with Aaron Cohen on that particular night of February 6th.

'It appears that all his friends, conspicuous among whom was Mr

Walter Hatherell, tried their very best to dissuade him from pitting his
luck against that of Cohen, who had been having a most unprecedented
run of good fortune. But young Ashley, heated with wine, exasperated
at his own bad luck, would listen to no one; he tossed one £5 note after
another on the board, he borrowed from those who would lend, then
played on parole for a while. Finally, at half-past one in the morning,
after a run of nineteen on the red, the young man found himself without
a penny in his pockets, and owing a debt – a gambling debt – a debt of
honour of £1,500 to Mr Aaron Cohen.

'Now we must render this much maligned gentleman that justice
which was persistently denied to him by press and public alike; it was
positively asserted by those present that Mr Cohen himself repeatedly
tried to induce young Mr Ashley to give up playing. He himself was in a
delicate position in the matter, as he was the winner, and once or twice
the taunt had risen to the young man's lips, accusing the holder of the
bank of the wish to retire on a competence before the break in his luck.

'Mr Aaron Cohen, smoking the best of Havanas, had finally shrugged
his shoulders and said: "As you please!"

'But at half-past one he had had enough of the player who always lost
and never paid – never could pay, so Mr Cohen probably believed. He
therefore at that hour refused to accept Mr John Ashley's "promissory"
stakes any longer. A very few heated words ensued, quickly checked by
the management, who are ever on the alert to avoid the least suspicion of
scandal.

'In the meanwhile Mr Hatherell, with great good sense, persuaded
young Ashley to leave the Club and all its temptations and go home; if
possible to bed.

'The friendship of the two young men, which was very well known in
society, consisted chiefly, it appears, in Walter Hatherell being the willing companion and helpmeet of John Ashley in his mad and extravagant
pranks. But tonight the latter, apparently tardily sobered by his terrible
and heavy losses, allowed himself to be led away by his friend from the
scene of his disasters. It was then about twenty minutes to two.

'Here the situation becomes interesting,' continued the man in the
corner in his nervous way. 'No wonder that the police interrogated at
least a dozen witnesses before they were quite satisfied that every statement was conclusively proved.

'Walter Hatherell, after about ten minutes' absence, that is to say
at ten minutes to two, returned to the club room. In reply to several
inquiries, he said that he had parted with his friend at the corner of New
Bond Street, since he seemed anxious to be alone, and that Ashley said
he would take a turn down Piccadilly before going home – he thought
a walk would do him good.

'   'At two o'clock or thereabouts Mr Aaron Cohen, satisfied with his evening's work, gave up his position at the bank and, pocketing his heavy winnings, started on his homeward walk, while Mr Walter Hatherell left the club half an hour later.

'At three o'clock precisely the cries of "Murder" and the report of fire-arms were heard in Park Square West, and Mr Aaron Cohen was found strangled outside the garden railings.'

'Now at first sight the murder in the Regent's Park appeared both to police and public as one of those silly, clumsy crimes, obviously the work of a novice, and absolutely purposeless, seeing that it could but inevitably lead its perpetrators, without any difficulty, to the gallows.

'You see, a motive had been established. "Seek him whom the crime benefits," say our French *confrères*. But there was something more than that.

'Constable James Funnell, on his beat, turned from Portland Place into Park Crescent a few minutes after he had heard the clock at Holy Trinity Church, Marylebone, strike half-past two. The fog at that moment was perhaps not quite so dense as it was later on in the morning, and the policeman saw two gentlemen in overcoats and top-hats leaning arm in arm against the railings of the Square, close to the gate. He could not, of course, distinguish their faces because of the fog, but he heard one of them saying to the other:

' "It is but a question of time, Mr Cohen. I know my father will pay the money for me, and you will lose nothing by waiting."

'To this the other apparently made no reply, and the constable passed on; when he returned to the same spot, after having walked over his beat, the two gentlemen had gone, but later on it was near this very gate that the two keys referred to at the inquest had been found.

'Another interesting fact,' added the man in the corner, with one of those sarcastic smiles of his which Polly could not quite explain, 'was the finding of the revolver upon the scene of the crime. That revolver, shown to Mr Ashley's valet, was sworn to by him as being the property of his master.

'All these facts made, of course, a very remarkable, so far quite unbroken, chain of circumstantial evidence against Mr John Ashley. No wonder, therefore, that the police, thoroughly satisfied with Mr Fisher's work and their own, applied for a warrant against the young man, and arrested him in his rooms in Clarges Street exactly a week after the committal of the crime.

'As a matter of fact, you know, experience has invariably taught me that when a murderer seems particularly foolish and clumsy, and proofs against him seem particularly damning, that is the time when the police should be most guarded against pitfalls.

'Now in this case, if John Ashley had indeed committed the murder in Regent's Park in the manner suggested by the police, he would have been a criminal in more senses than one, for idiocy of that kind is to my mind worse than many crimes.

'The prosecution brought its witnesses up in triumphal array one after another. There were the members of the Harewood Club – who had seen the prisoner's excited condition after his heavy gambling losses to Mr Aaron Cohen; there was Mr Hatherell, who, in spite of his friendship for Ashley, was bound to admit that he had parted from him at the corner of Bond Street at twenty minutes to two, and had not seen him again till his return home at five a.m.

'Then came the evidence of Arthur Chipps, John Ashley's valet. It proved of a very sensational character.

'He deposed that on the night in question his master came home at about ten minutes to two. Chipps had then not yet gone to bed. Five minutes later Mr Ashley went out again, telling his valet not to sit up for him. Chipps could not say at what time either of the young gentlemen had come home.

'That short visit home – presumably to fetch the revolver – was thought to be very important, and Mr John Ashley's friends felt that his case was practically hopeless.

'The valet's evidence and that of James Funnell, the constable, who had overheard the conversation near the park railings, were certainly the two most damning proofs against the accused. I assure you I was having a rare old time that day. There were two faces in court to watch which was the greatest treat I had had for many a day. One of these was Mr John Ashley's.

'Here's his photo – short, dark, dapper, a little "racy" in style, but otherwise he looks a son of a well-to-do farmer. He was very quiet and placid in court, and addressed a few words now and again to his solicitor. He listened gravely, and with an occasional shrug of the shoulders, to the recital of the crime, such as the police had reconstructed it, before an excited and horrified audience.

'Mr John Ashley, driven to madness and frenzy by terrible financial difficulties, had first of all gone home in search of a weapon, then waylaid Mr Aaron Cohen somewhere on that gentleman's way home. The young man had begged for delay. Mr Cohen perhaps was obdurate; but Ashley followed him with his importunities almost to his door.

'There, seeing his creditor determined at last to cut short the painful interview, he had seized the unfortunate man at an unguarded moment from behind, and strangled him; then, fearing that his dastardly work was not fully accomplished, he had shot twice at the already dead body, missing it both times from sheer nervous excitement. The murderer then must have emptied his victim's pockets, and, finding the key of the garden, thought that it would be a safe way of evading capture by cutting across the squares, under the tunnel, and so through the more distant gate which faced Portland Place.

'The loss of the revolver was one of those unforeseen accidents which a retributive Providence places in the path of the miscreant, delivering him by his own act of folly into the hands of human justice.

'Mr John Ashley, however, did not appear the least bit impressed by the recital of his crime. He had not engaged the services of one of the most eminent lawyers, expert at extracting contradictions from witnesses by skilful cross-examinations – oh, dear me, no! he had been contented with those of a dull, prosy, very second-rate limb of the law, who, as he called his witnesses, was completely innocent of any desire to create a sensation.

'He rose quietly from his seat, and, amidst breathless silence, called the first of three witnesses on behalf of his client. He called three – but he could have produced twelve – gentlemen, members of the Ashton Club in Great Portland Street, all of whom swore that at three o'clock on the morning of February 6th, that is to say, at the very moment when the cries of "Murder" roused the inhabitants of Park Square West, and the crime was being committed, Mr John Ashley was sitting quietly in the club-rooms of the Ashton playing bridge with the three witnesses. He had come in a few minutes before three – as the hall porter of the Club testified – and stayed for about an hour and a half.

'I need not tell you that this undoubted, this fully proved, *alibi* was a positive bomb-shell in the stronghold of the prosecution. The most accomplished criminal could not possibly be in two places at once, and though the Ashton Club transgresses in many ways against the gambling laws of our very moral country, yet its members belong to the best, most unimpeachable classes of society. Mr Ashley had been seen and spoken to at the very moment of the crime by at least a dozen gentlemen whose testimony was absolutely above suspicion.

'Mr John Ashley's conduct throughout this astonishing phase of the inquiry remained perfectly calm and correct. It was no doubt the consciousness of being able to prove his innocence with such absolute conclusion that had steadied his nerves throughout the proceedings.

'His answers to the magistrate were clear and simple, even on the ticklish subject of the revolver.

' "I left the club, sir," he explained, "fully determined to speak with Mr Cohen alone in order to ask him for a delay in the settlement of my debt to him. You will understand that I should not care to do this in the presence of other gentlemen. I went home for a minute or two – not in order to fetch a revolver, as the police assert, for I always carry a revolver about with me in foggy weather – but in order to see if a very important business letter had come for me in my absence.

' " Then I went out again, and met Mr Aaron Cohen not far from the Harewood Club. I walked the greater part of the way with him, and our conversation was of the most amicable character. We parted at the top of Portland Place, near the gate of the Square, where the policeman saw us. Mr Cohen then had the intention of cutting across the Square, as being a shorter way to his own house. I thought the Square looked dark and dangerous in the fog, especially as Mr Cohen was carrying a large sum of money.

' "We had a short discussion on the subject, and finally I persuaded him to take my revolver, as I was going home only through very frequented streets, and moreover carried nothing that was worth stealing. After a little demur Mr Cohen accepted the loan of my revolver, and that is how it came to be found on the actual scene of the crime; finally I parted from Mr Cohen a very few minutes after I had heard the church clock striking a quarter before three. I was at the Oxford Street end of Great Portland Street at five minutes to three, and it takes at least ten minutes to walk from where I was to the Ashton Club."

'This explanation was all the more credible, mind you, because the question of the revolver had never been very satisfactorily explained by the prosecution. A man who has effectually strangled his victim would not discharge two shots of his revolver for, apparently, no other purpose than that of rousing the attention of the nearest passer-by. It was far more likely that it was Mr Cohen who shot – perhaps wildly into the air, when suddenly attacked from behind. Mr Ashley's explanation therefore was not only plausible, it was the only possible one.

'You will understand therefore how it was that, after nearly half an hour's examination, the magistrate, the police, and the public were alike pleased to proclaim that the accused left the court without a stain upon his character.'

'Yes,' interrupted Polly eagerly, since, for once, her acumen had been at least as sharp as his, 'but suspicion of that horrible crime only shifted its taint from one friend to another, and, of course, I know—'

'But that's just it,' he quietly interrupted, 'you don't know – Mr Walter Hatherell, of course, you mean. So did every one else at once. The friend, weak and willing, committing a crime on behalf of his cowardly, yet more assertive friend who had tempted him to evil. It was a good theory; and was held pretty generally, I fancy, even by the police.

'I say "even" because they worked really hard in order to build up a case against young Hatherell, but the great difficulty was that of time. At the hour when the policeman had seen the two men outside Park Square together, Walter Hatherell was still sitting in the Harewood Club, which he never left until twenty minutes to two. Had he wished to waylay and rob Aaron Cohen he would not have waited surely till the time when presumably the latter would already have reached home.

'Moreover, twenty minutes was an incredibly short time in which to walk from Hanover Square to Regent's Park without the chance of cutting across the squares, to look for a man, whose whereabouts you could not determine to within twenty yards or so, to have an argument with him, murder him, and ransack his pockets. And then there was the total absence of motive.'

'But—' said Polly meditatively, for she remembered now that the Regent's Park murder, as it had been popularly called, was one of those which had remained as impenetrable a mystery as any other crime had ever been in the annals of the police.

The man in the corner cocked his funny bird-like head well on one side and looked at her, highly amused evidently at her perplexity.

'You do not see how that murder was committed?' he asked with a grin.

Polly was bound to admit that she did not.

'If you had happened to have been in Mr John Ashley's predicament,' he persisted, 'you do not see how you could conveniently have done away with Mr Aaron Cohen, pocketed his winnings, and then led the police of your country by the nose, by proving an indisputable *alibi*?'

'I could not arrange conveniently,' she retorted, 'to be in two different places half a mile apart at one and the same time.'

'No! I quite admit that you could not do this unless you also had a friend—'·

'A friend? But you say—'

'I say that I admired Mr John Ashley, for his was the head which planned the whole thing, but he could not have accomplished the fascinating and terrible drama without the help of willing and able hands.'

'Even then—' she protested.

'Point number one,' he began excitedly, fidgeting with his inevitable piece of string. 'John Ashley and his friend Walter Hatherell leave the club together, and together decide on the plan of campaign. Hatherell returns to the club, and Ashley goes to fetch the revolver – the revolver which played such an important part in the drama, but not the part assigned to it by the police. Now try to follow Ashley closely, as he dogs Aaron Cohen's footsteps. Do you believe that he entered into conversation with him? That he walked by his side? That he asked for delay? No! He sneaked behind him and caught him by the throat, as the garrotters used to do in the fog. Cohen was apoplectic, and Ashley is young and powerful. Moreover, he meant to kill—'

'But the two men talked together outside the Square gates,' protested Polly, 'one of whom was Cohen, and the other Ashley.'

'Pardon me,' he said, jumping up in his seat like a monkey on a stick, 'there were not two men talking outside the Square gates. According to the testimony of James Funnell, the constable, two men were leaning arm in arm against the railings and *one* man was talking.'

'Then you think that—'

'At the hour when James Funnell heard Holy Trinity clock striking half-past two Aaron Cohen was already dead. Look how simple the whole thing is,' he added eagerly, 'and how easy after that – easy, but oh, dear me! how wonderfully, how stupendously clever. As soon as James Funnell has passed on, John Ashley, having opened the gate, lifts the body of Aaron Cohen in his arms and carries him across the Square. The Square is deserted, of course, but the way is easy enough, and we must presume that Ashley had been in it before. Anyway, there was no fear of meeting any one.

'In the meantime Hatherell has left the club: as fast as his athletic legs can carry him he rushes along Oxford Street and Portland Place. It had been arranged between the two miscreants that the Square gate should be left on the latch.

'Close on Ashley's heels now, Hatherell too cuts across the Square, and reaches the further gate in good time to give his confederate a hand in disposing the body against the railings. Then, without another instant's delay, Ashley runs back across the gardens, straight to the Ashton Club, throwing away the keys of the dead man, on the very spot where he had made it a point of being seen and heard by a passer-by.

'Hatherell gives his friend six or seven minutes' start, then he begins the altercation which lasts two or three minutes, and finally rouses the neighbourhood with cries of "Murder" and report of pistol in order to establish that the crime was committed at the hour when its perpetrator has already made out an indisputable *alibi*.

'I don't know what you think of it all, of course,' added the funny creature as he fumbled for his coat and his gloves, 'but I call the planning of that murder – on the part of novices, mind you – one of the cleverest pieces of strategy I have ever come across. It is one of those cases where there is no possibility whatever now of bringing the crime home to its perpetrator or his abettor. They have not left a single proof behind them; they foresaw everything, and each acted his part with a coolness and courage which, applied to a great and good cause, would have made fine statesmen of them both.

'As it is, I fear, they are just a pair of young blackguards, who have escaped human justice, and have only deserved the full and un-grudging admiration of yours very sincerely.'

He had gone. Polly wanted to call him back, but his meagre person was no longer visible through the glass door. There were many things she would have wished to ask him – what were his proofs, his facts? His were theories, after all, and yet, somehow, she felt that he had solved once again one of the darkest mysteries of great criminal London.

The Blind Spot

Barry Perowne

Annixter loved the little man like a brother. He put an arm around the little man's shoulders, partly from affection and partly to prevent himself from falling.

He had been drinking earnestly since seven o'clock the previous evening. It was now nudging midnight, and things were a bit hazy. The lobby was full of the thump of hot music; down two steps, there were a lot of tables, a lot of people, a lot of noise. Annixter had no idea what this place was called, or how he had got here, or when. He had been in so many places since seven o'clock the previous evening.

'In a nutshell,' confided Annixter, leaning heavily on the little man, 'a woman fetches you a kick in the face, or fate fetches you a kick in the face. Same thing, really – a woman and fate. So what? So you think it's the finish, an' you go out and get plastered. You get good an' plastered,' said Annixter, 'an' you brood.

'You sit there an' you drink an' you brood – an' in the end you find you've brooded up just about the best idea you ever had in your life! 'At's the way it goes,' said Annixter, 'an' 'at's my philosophy – the harder you kick a playwright, the better he works!'

He gestured with such vehemence that he would have collapsed if the little man hadn't steadied him. The little man was poker-backed, his grip was firm. His mouth was firm, too – a straight line, almost colourless. He wore hexagonal rimless spectacles, a black hard-felt hat, a neat pepper-and-salt suit. He looked pale and prim beside the flushed, rumpled Annixter.

From her counter, the hat-check girl watched them indifferently.

'Don't you think,' the little man said to Annixter, 'you ought to go home now? I've been honoured you should tell me the scenario of your play, but—'

'I had to tell someone,' said Annixter, 'or blow my top! Oh, boy, what a play, what a play! What a murder, eh? That climax—'

The full, dazzling perfection of it struck him again. He stood frowning, considering, swaying a little – then nodded abruptly, groped for the little man's hand, warmly pumphandled it.

'Sorry I can't stick around,' said Annixter. 'I got work to do.'

He crammed his hat on shapelessly, headed on a slightly elliptical course across the lobby, thrust the double doors open with both hands, lurched out into the night.

It was, to his inflamed imagination, full of lights, winking and tilting across the dark. *Sealed Room* by James Annixter. No. *Room Reserved* by James— No, no. *Blue Room. Room Blue. Room Blue* by James Annixter—

He stepped, oblivious, off the kerb, and a taxi, swinging in towards the place he had just left, skidded with suddenly locked, squealing wheels on the wet road.

Something hit Annixter violently in the chest, and all the lights he had been seeing exploded in his face.

Then there weren't any lights.

Mr James Annixter, the playwright, was knocked down by a taxi late last night when leaving the Casa Havana. After hospital treatment for shock and superficial injuries, he returned to his home.

The lobby of the Casa Havana was full of the thump of music; down two steps there were a lot of tables, a lot of people, a lot of noise. The hat-check girl looked wonderingly at Annixter – at the plaster on his forehead, the black sling which supported his left arm.

'My,' said the hat-check girl, 'I certainly didn't expect to see *you* again so soon!'

'You remember me, then?' said Annixter, smiling.

'I ought to,' said the hat-check girl. 'You cost me a night's sleep! I heard those brakes squeal right after you went out the door that night – and there was a sort of a thud!' She shuddered. 'I kept hearing it all night long. I can still hear it now – a week after! Horrible!'

'You're sensitive,' said Annixter.

'I got too much imagination,' the hat-check girl admitted. 'F'rinstance, I just *knew* it was you even before I run to the door and see you lying there. That man you was with was standing just outside. "My heavens," I says to him, "it's your friend!"'

'What did he say?' Annixter asked.

'He says, "He's not my friend. He's just someone I met." Funny, eh?'

Annixter moistened his lips.

'How d'you mean,' he said carefully, 'funny? I *was* just someone he'd met.'

'Yes, but – man you been drinking with,' said the hat-check girl, 'killed before your eyes. Because he must have seen it; he went out right after you. You'd think he'd 'a' been interested, at least. But when the taxi driver starts shouting for witnesses it wasn't his fault, I looks around for that man – an' he's gone!'

Annixter exchanged a glance with Ransome, his producer, who was with him. It was a slightly puzzled, slightly anxious glance. But he smiled, then, at the hat-check girl.

'Not quite "killed before his eyes,"' said Annixter. 'Just shaken up a bit, that's all.'

There was no need to explain to her how curious, how eccentric, had been the effect of that 'shaking up' upon his mind.

'If you could 'a' seen yourself lying there with the taxi's lights shining on you—'

'Ah, there's that imagination of yours!' said Annixter.

He hesitated for just an instant, then asked the question he had come to ask – the question which had assumed so profound an importance for him.

He asked, 'That man I was with – who was he?'

The hat-check girl looked from one to the other. She shook her head.

'I never saw him before,' she said, 'and I haven't seen him since.'

Annixter felt as though she had struck him in the face. He had hoped, hoped desperately, for a different answer; he had counted on it.

Ransome put a hand on his arm, restrainingly.

'Anyway,' said Ransome, 'as we're here, let's have a drink.'

They went down the two steps into the room where the band thumped. A waiter led them to a table, and Ransome gave him an order.

'There was no point in pressing that girl,' Ransome said to Annixter. 'She doesn't know the man, and that's that. My advice to you, James, is: Don't worry. Get your mind on to something else. Give yourself a chance. After all, it's barely a week since—'

'A week!' Annixter said. 'Hell, look what I've done in that week! The whole of the first two acts, and the third act right up to that crucial point – the climax of the whole thing: the solution: the scene that the play stands or falls on! It would have been done, Bill – the whole play, the best thing I ever did in my life – it would have been finished two days ago if it hadn't been for this—' he knuckled his forehead – 'this extraordinary blind spot, this damnable little trick of memory!'

'You had a very rough shaking-up—'

'That?' Annixter said contemptuously. He glanced down at the sling on his arm. 'I never even felt it; it didn't bother me. I woke up in the ambulance with my play as vivid in my mind as the moment the taxi hit me – more so, maybe, because I was stone cold sober then, and knew what I had. A winner – a thing that just couldn't miss!'

'If you'd rested,' Ransome said, 'as the doc told you, instead of sitting up in bed there scribbling night and day—'

'I had to get it on paper. Rest?' said Annixter, and laughed harshly.

'You don't rest when you've got a thing like that. That's what you live
for – if you're a playwright. That *is* living! I've lived eight whole lifetimes,
in those eight characters, during the past five days, I've lived so utterly
in them, Bill, that it wasn't till I actually came to write that last scene
that I realized what I'd lost! Only my whole play, that's all! How was
Cynthia stabbed in that windowless room into which she had locked
and bolted herself? How did the killer get to her? *How was it done?*

'Hell,' Annixter said, 'scores of writers, better men than I am, have
tried to put that sealed room murder over – and never quite done it
convincingly: never quite got away with it: been over-elaborate, phony!
I had it – heaven help me, *I* had it! Simple, perfect, glaringly obvious
when you've once seen it! And it's my whole play – the curtain rises
on that sealed room and falls on it! That was my revelation – *how it
was done!* That was what I got, by way of playwright's compensation,
because a woman I thought I loved kicked me in the face – I brooded
up the answer to the sealed room! And a taxi knocked it out of my
head!'

He drew a long breath.

'I've spent two days and two nights, Bill, trying to get that idea back
– *how it was done!* It won't come. I'm a competent playwright; I know
my job; I could finish my play, but it'd be like all those others – not
quite right, phony! It wouldn't be *my play!* But there's a little man walking
around this city somewhere – a little man with hexagonal glasses – who's
got my idea in his head! He's got it because I told it to him. I'm going
to find that little man, and get back what belongs to me! I've got to!
Don't you see that, Bill? I've *got* to!'

>   *If the gentleman who, at the Casa Havana on the night of January 27th,
>   so patiently listened to a playwright's outlining of an idea for a drama will
>   communicate with the Box No. below, he will hear of something to his
>   advantage.*

A little man who had said, 'He's not my friend. He's just someone
I met—'

A little man who'd seen an accident but hadn't waited to give
evidence—

The hat-check girl had been right. There *was* something a little queer
about that.

A little queer?

During the next few days, when the advertisements he'd inserted failed
to bring any reply, it began to seem to Annixter very queer indeed.

His arm was out of its sling now, but he couldn't work. Time and
again he sat down before his almost completed manuscript, read it
through with close, grim attention, thinking, 'It's *bound* to come back

this time!' – only to find himself up against that blind spot again, that blank wall, that maddening hiatus in his memory.

He left his work and prowled the streets; he haunted bars and saloons; he rode for miles on buses and subway, especially at the rush hours. He saw a million faces, but the face of the little man with hexagonal glasses he did not see.

The thought of him obsessed Annixter. It was infuriating, it was unjust, it was torture to think that a little, ordinary, chance-met citizen was walking blandly around somewhere with the last link of his, the celebrated James Annixter's play – the best thing he'd ever done – locked away in his head. And with no idea of what he had: without the imagination, probably, to appreciate what he had! And certainly with no idea of what it meant to Annixter!

Or *had* he some idea? Was he, perhaps, not quite so ordinary as he'd seemed? Had he seen those advertisements, drawn from them tortuous inferences of his own? Was he holding back with some scheme for shaking Annixter down for a packet?

The more Annixter thought about it, the more he felt that the hat-check girl had been right, that there was something very queer indeed about the way the little man had behaved after the accident.

Annixter's imagination played around the man he was seeking, tried to probe into his mind, conceived reasons for his fading away after the accident, for his failure to reply to the advertisements.

Annixter's was an active and dramatic imagination. The little man who had seemed so ordinary began to take on a sinister shape in Annixter's mind—

But the moment he actually saw the little man again, he realized how absurd that was. It was so absurd that it was laughable. The little man was so respectable; his shoulders were so straight; his pepper-and-salt suit was so neat; his black hard-felt hat was set so squarely on his head—

The doors of the subway train were just closing when Annixter saw him, standing on the platform with a brief case in one hand, a folded evening paper under his other arm. Light from the train shone on his prim, pale face; his hexagonal spectacles flashed. He turned towards the exit as Annixter lunged for the closing doors of the train, squeezed between them onto the platform.

Craning his head to see above the crowd, Annixter elbowed his way through, ran up the stairs two at a time, put a hand on the little man's shoulder.

'Just a minute,' Annixter said. 'I've been looking for you.'

The little man checked instantly, at the touch of Annixter's hand. Then he turned his head and looked at Annixter. His eyes were pale behind the hexagonal, rimless glasses – a pale grey. His mouth was a straight line, almost colourless.

Annixter loved the little man like a brother. Merely finding the little man was a relief so great that it was like the lifting of a black cloud from his spirits. He patted the little man's shoulder affectionately.

'I've got to talk to you,' said Annixter. 'It won't take a minute. Let's go somewhere.'

The little man said, 'I can't imagine what you want to talk to me about.'

He moved slightly to one side, to let a woman pass. The crowd from the train had thinned, but there were still people going up and down the stairs. The little man looked, politely inquiring, at Annixter.

Annixter said, 'Of course you can't, it's so damned silly! But it's about that play—'

'Play?'

Annixter felt a faint anxiety.

'Look,' he said, 'I was drunk that night – I was very, very drunk! But looking back, my impression is that you were dead sober. You were, weren't you?'

'I've never been drunk in my life.'

'Thank heaven for that!' said Annixter. 'Then you won't have any difficulty in remembering the little point I want you to remember.' He grinned, shook his head. 'You had me going there, for a minute. I thought—'

'I don't know what you thought,' the little man said. 'But I'm quite sure you're mistaking me for somebody else. I haven't any idea what you're talking about. I never saw you before in my life. I'm sorry. Good night.'

He turned and started up the stairs. Annixter stared after him. He couldn't believe his ears. He stared blankly after the little man for an instant, then a rush of anger and suspicion swept away his bewilderment. He raced up the stairs, caught the little man by the arm.

'Just a minute,' said Annixter. 'I may have been drunk, but—'

'That,' the little man said, 'seems evident. Do you mind taking your hand off me?'

Annixter controlled himself. 'I'm sorry,' he said. 'Let me get this right, though. You say you've never seen me before. Then you weren't at the Casa Havana on the 27th – somewhere between ten o'clock and midnight? You didn't have a drink or two with me, and listen to an idea for a play that had just come into my mind?'

The little man looked steadily at Annixter.

'I've told you,' the little man said. 'I've never set eyes on you before.'

'You didn't see me get hit by a taxi?' Annixter pursued, tensely. 'You didn't say to the hat-check girl, "He's not my friend. He's just someone I met"?'

'I don't know what you're talking about,' the little man said sharply.

He made to turn away, but Annixter gripped his arm again.

'I don't know,' Annixter said, between his teeth, 'anything about your private affairs, and I don't want to. You may have had some good reason for wanting to duck giving evidence as a witness of that taxi accident. You may have some good reason for this act you're pulling on me, now. I don't know and I don't care. But it is an act! You *are* the man I told my play to!

'I want you to tell that story back to me as I told it to you; I have my reasons – personal reasons, of concern to me and me only. I want you to tell the story back to me – that's all I want! I don't want to know who you are, or anything about you. *I just want you to tell me that story!*'

'You ask,' the little man said, 'an impossibility, since I never heard it.'

Annixter kept an iron hold on himself.

He said, 'Is it money? Is this some sort of a hold-up? Tell me what you want; I'll give it to you. Lord help me, I'd go so far as to give you a share in the play! That'll mean real money. I know, because I know my business. And maybe – maybe,' said Annixter, struck by a sudden thought, '*you* know it, too! Eh?'

'You're insane or drunk!' the little man said.

With a sudden movement, he jerked his arm free, raced up the stairs. A train was rumbling in, below. People were hurrying down. He weaved and dodged among them with extraordinary celerity.

He was a small man, light, and Annixter was heavy. By the time he reached the street, there was no sign of the little man. He was gone.

Was the idea, Annixter wondered, to steal his play? By some wild chance did the little man nurture a fantastic ambition to be a dramatist? He had, perhaps, peddled his precious manuscripts in vain, for years, around the managements? Had Annixter's play appeared to him as a blinding flash of hope in the gathering darkness of frustration and failure: something he had imagined he could safely steal because it had seemed to him the random inspiration of a drunkard who by morning would have forgotten he had ever given birth to anything but a hangover?

That, Annixter thought, would be a laugh! That would be irony—

He took another drink. It was his fifteenth since the little man with the hexagonal glasses had given him the slip, and Annixter was beginning to reach the stage where he lost count of how many places he had had drinks in tonight. It was also the stage, though, where he was beginning to feel better, where his mind was beginning to work.

He could imagine just how the little man must have felt as the quality of the play he was being told, with hiccups, gradually had dawned upon him.

'This is mine!' the little man would have thought. 'I've got to have this. He's drunk, he's soused, he's bottled – he'll have forgotten every word of it by the morning! Go on! go on, mister! Keep talking!'

That was a laugh, too – the idea that Annixter would have forgotten his play by the morning. Other things Annixter forgot, unimportant things; but never in his life had he forgotten the minutest detail that was to his purpose as a playwright. Never!

Except once, because a taxi had knocked him down.

Annixter took another drink. He needed it. He was on his own now. There wasn't any little man with hexagonal glasses to fill in that blind spot for him. The little man was gone. He was gone as though he'd never been. To hell with him! Annixter had to fill in that blind spot himself. He *had* to do it – somehow!

He had another drink. He had quite a lot more drinks. The bar was crowded and noisy, but he didn't notice the noise – till someone came up and slapped him on the shoulder. It was Ransome.

Annixter stood up, leaning with his knuckles on the table.

'Look, Bill,' Annixter said, 'how about this? Man forgets an idea, see? He wants to get it back – gotta get it back! Idea comes from inside, works outwards – right? So he starts on the outside, works back inward. How's that?'

He swayed, peering at Ransome.

'Better have a little drink,' said Ransome. 'I'd need to think that out.'

'I,' said Annixter, '*have* thought it out!' He crammed his hat shapelessly on to his head. 'Be seeing you, Bill. I got work to do!'

He started, on a slightly tacking course, for the door – and his apartment.

It was Joseph, his 'man,' who opened the door of his apartment to him, some twenty minutes later. Joseph opened the door while Annixter's latchkey was still describing vexed circles around the lock.

'Good evening, sir,' said Joseph.

Annixter stared at him. 'I didn't tell you to stay in tonight.'

'I hadn't any real reason for going out, sir,' Joseph explained. He helped Annixter off with his coat. 'I rather enjoy a quiet evening in, once in a while.'

'You got to get out of here,' said Annixter.

'Thank you, sir,' said Joseph. 'I'll go and throw a few things into a bag.'

Annixter went into his big living-room-study, poured himself a drink.

The manuscript of his play lay on the desk. Annixter, swaying a little, glass in hand, stood frowning down at the untidy stack of yellow paper, but he didn't begin to read. He waited until he heard the outer door click shut behind Joseph, then he gathered up his manuscript, the decanter and a glass, and the cigarette box. Thus laden, he went into the hall, walked across it to the door of Joseph's room.

There was a bolt on the inside of this door, and the room was the only one in the apartment which had no window – both facts which made the room the only one suitable to Annixter's purpose.

With his free hand, he switched on the light.

It was a plain little room, but Annixter noticed, with a faint grin, that the bedspread and the cushion in the worn basket chair were both blue. Appropriate, he thought – a good omen. *Room Blue* by James Annixter—

Joseph had evidently been lying on the bed, reading the evening paper; the paper lay on the rumpled quilt, and the pillow was dented. Beside the head of the bed, opposite the door, was a small table littered with shoebrushes and dusters.

Annixter swept this paraphernalia onto the floor. He put his stack of manuscript, the decanter and glass and cigarette box on the table, and went across and bolted the door. He pulled the basket chair up to the table, sat down, lighted a cigarette.

He leaned back in the chair, smoking, letting his mind ease into the atmosphere he wanted – the mental atmosphere of Cynthia, the woman in his play, the woman who was afraid, so afraid that she had locked and bolted herself into a windowless room, a sealed room.

'This is how she sat,' Annixter told himself, 'just as I'm sitting now: in a room with no windows, the door locked and bolted. Yet he got at her. He got at her with a knife – in a room with no windows, the door remaining locked and bolted on the inside. *How was it done?*'

There was a way in which it could be done. He, Annixter, had thought of that way; he had conceived it, invented it – and forgotten it. His idea had produced the circumstances. Now, deliberately, he had reproduced the circumstances, that he might think back to the idea. He had put his person in the position of the victim, that his mind might grapple with the problem of the murderer.

It was very quiet: not a sound in the room, the whole apartment. For a long time, Annixter sat unmoving. He sat unmoving until the intensity of his concentration began to waver. Then he relaxed. He pressed the palms of his hands to his forehead for a moment, then reached for the decanter. He splashed himself a strong drink. He had almost recovered what he sought; he had felt it close, had been on the very verge of it.

'Easy,' he warned himself, 'take it easy. Rest. Relax. Try again in a minute.'

He looked around for something to divert his mind, picked up the paper from Joseph's bed.

At the first words that caught his eye, his heart stopped.

*

The woman, in whose body were found three knife wounds, any of which might have been fatal, was in a windowless room, the only door to which was locked and bolted on the inside. These elaborate precautions appear to have been habitual with her, and no doubt she went in continual fear of her life, as the police know her to have been a persistent and pitiless blackmailer.

Apart from the unique problem set by the circumstance of the sealed room is the problem of how the crime could have gone undiscovered for so long a period, the doctor's estimate from the condition of the body at some twelve to fourteen days.

Twelve to fourteen days—

Annixter read back over the remainder of the story; then let the paper fall to the floor. The pulse was heavy in his head. His face was grey. Twelve to fourteen days? he could put it closer than that. *It was exactly thirteen nights ago that he had sat in the Casa Havana and told a little man with hexagonal glasses how to kill a woman in a sealed room!*

Annixter sat very still for a minute. Then he poured himself a drink. It was a big one, and he needed it. He felt a strange sense of wonder, of awe.

They had been in the same boat, he and the little man – thirteen nights ago. They had both been kicked in the face by a woman. One, as a result, had conceived a murder play. The other had made the play reality!

'And I actually, tonight, offered him a share!' Annixter thought. 'I talked about "real" money!'

That was a laugh. All the money in the universe wouldn't have made that little man admit that he had seen Annixter before – that Annixter had told him the plot of a play about how to kill a woman in a sealed room! Why, he, Annixter, was the one person in the world who could denounce that little man! Even if he couldn't tell them, because he had forgotten, just *how* he had told the little man the murder was to be committed, he could still put the police on the little man's track. He could describe him, so that they could trace him. And once on his track, the police would ferret out links, almost inevitably, with the dead woman.

A queer thought – that he, Annixter, was probably the only menace, the only danger, to the little prim, pale man with the hexagonal spectacles. The only menace – as, of course, the little man must know very well.

He must have been very frightened when he had read that the play-wright who had been knocked down outside the Casa Havana had only received 'superficial injuries.' He must have been still more frightened when Annixter's advertisements had begun to appear. *What must he have felt tonight, when Annixter's hand had fallen on his shoulder?*

A curious idea occurred, now, to Annixter. It was from tonight, precisely from tonight, that he was a danger to that little man. He was, because of the inferences the little man must infallibly draw, a deadly danger as from the moment the discovery of the murder in the sealed room was published. That discovery had been published tonight and the little man had had a paper under his arm—

Annixter's was a lively and resourceful imagination.

It was, of course, just in the cards that, when he'd lost the little man's trail at the subway station, the little man might have turned back, picked up *his*, Annixter's trail.

And Annixter had sent Joseph out. He was, it dawned slowly upon Annixter, alone in the apartment – alone in a windowless room, with the door locked and bolted on the inside, at his back.

Annixter felt a sudden, icy and wild panic.

He half rose, but it was too late.

It was too late, because at that moment the knife slid, thin and keen and delicate, into his back, fatally, between the ribs.

Annixter's head bowed slowly forward until his cheek rested on the manuscript of his play. He made only one sound – a queer sound, indistinct, yet identifiable as a kind of laughter.

The fact was, Annixter had just remembered.

The Cask of Amontillado

Edgar Allan Poe

The thousand injuries of Fortunato I had borne as I best could, but when he ventured upon insult, I vowed revenge. You, who so well know the nature of my soul, will not suppose, however, that I gave utterance to a threat. *At length* I would be avenged; this was a point definitively settled – but the very definitiveness with which it was resolved precluded the idea of risk. I must not only punish, but punish with impunity. A wrong is unredressed when retribution overtakes its redresser. It is equally unredressed when the avenger fails to make himself felt as such to him who has done the wrong.

It must be understood that neither by word nor deed had I given Fortunato cause to doubt my good will. I continued, as was my wont, to smile in his face, and he did not perceive that my smile *now* was at the thought of his immolation.

He had a weak point – this Fortunato – although in other regards he was a man to be respected and even feared. He prided himself on his connoisseurship in wine. Few Italians have the true virtuoso spirit. For the most part their enthusiasm is adopted to suit the time and opportunity to practise imposture upon the British and Australian *millionaires*. In painting and gemmary Fortunato, like his countrymen, was a quack, but in the matter of old wines he was sincere. In this respect I did not differ from him materially; I was skilful in the Italian vintages myself, and bought largely whenever I could.

It was about dusk, one evening during the supreme madness of the carnival season, that I encountered my friend. He accosted me with excessive warmth, for he had been drinking much. The man wore motley. He had on a tight-fitting parti-striped dress, and his head was surmounted by the conical cap and bells. I was so pleased to see him, that I thought I should never have done wringing his hand.

I said to him – 'My dear Fortunato, you are luckily met. How remarkably well you are looking today! But I have received a pipe of what passes for Amontillado, and I have my doubts.'

'How?' said he, 'Amontillado? A pipe? Impossible? And in the middle of the carnival?'

'I have my doubts,' I replied; 'and I was silly enough to pay the full Amontillado price without consulting you in the matter. You were not to be found, and I was fearful of losing a bargain.'

'Amontillado!'

'I have my doubts.'

'Amontillado!'

'And I must satisfy them.'

'Amontillado!'

'As you are engaged, I am on my way to Luchesi. If any one has a critical turn, it is he. He will tell me —'

'Luchesi cannot tell Amontillado from Sherry.'

'And yet some fools will have it that his taste is a match of your own.'

'Come let us go.'

'Whither?'

'To your vaults.'

'My friend, no; I will not impose upon your good nature. I perceive you have an engagement. Luchesi—'

'I have no engagement; come.'

'My friend, no. It is not the engagement, but the severe cold with which I perceive you are afflicted. The vaults are insufferably damp. They are encrusted with nitre.'

'Let us go, nevertheless. The cold is merely nothing. Amontillado! You have been imposed upon; and as for Luchesi, he cannot distinguish Sherry from Amontillado.'

Thus speaking, Fortunato possessed himself of my arm. Putting on a mask of black silk and drawing *a roquelaure* closely about my person, I suffered him to hurry me to my palazzo.

There were no attendants at home; they had absconded to make merry in honour of the time. I had told them that I should not return until the morning, and had given them explicit orders not to stir from the house. These orders were sufficient, I well knew, to insure their immediate disappearance, one and all, as soon as my back was turned.

I took from their sconces two flambeaux, and giving one to Fortunato, bowed him through several suites of rooms to the archway that led into the vaults. I passed down a long and winding staircase, requesting him to be cautious as he followed. We came at length to the foot of the descent, and stood together on the damp ground of the catacombs of the Montresors.

The gait of my friend was unsteady, and the bells upon his cap jingled as he strode.

'The pipe,' said he.

'It is farther on,' said I; 'but observe the white webwork which gleams from the these cavern walls.'

He turned towards me, and looked into my eyes with two filmy orbs that distilled the rheum of intoxication.

'Nitre?' he asked, at length.

'Nitre,' I replied. 'How long have you had that cough!'

'Ugh! ugh! ugh! – ugh! ugh! ugh! – ugh! ugh! ugh! – ugh! ugh! ugh! – ugh! ugh! ugh!'

My poor friend found it impossible to reply for many minutes.

'It is nothing,' he said, at last.

'Come,' I said, with decision, 'we will go back; your health is precious. You are rich, respected, admired, beloved; you are happy, as once I was. You are a man to be missed. For me it is no matter. We will go back; you will be ill, and I cannot be responsible. Besides, there is Luchesi—'

'Enough,' he said; 'the cough is a mere nothing; it will not kill me. I shall not die of a cough.'

'True – true,' I replied; 'and, indeed, I had no intention of alarming you unnecessarily – but you should use all proper caution. A draught of this Medoc will defend us from the damps.'

Here I knocked off the neck of a bottle which I drew from a long row of its fellows that lay upon the mould.

'Drink,' I said, presenting him the wine.

He raised it to his lips with a leer. He paused and nodded to me familiarly, while his bells jingled.

'I drink,' he said, 'to the buried that repose around us.'

'And I to your long life.'

He again took my arm, and we proceeded.

'These vaults,' he said, 'are extensive.'

'The Montresors,' I replied, 'were a great and numerous family.'

'I forget your arms.'

'A huge human foot d'or, in a field azure; the foot crushes a serpent rampant whose fangs are imbedded in the heel.'

'And the motto?'

'*Nemo me impune lacessit.*'

'Good!' he said.

The wine sparkled in his eyes and the bells jingled. My own fancy grew warm with the Medoc. We had passed through walls of piled bones, with casks and puncheons intermingling, into the inmost recesses of the catacombs. I paused again, and this time I made bold to seize Fortunato by an arm above the elbow.

'The nitre!' I said: 'see, it increases. It hangs like moss upon the vaults. We are below the river's bed. The drops of moisture trickle among the bones. Come, we will go back ere it is too late. Your cough—'

'It is nothing,' he said; 'let us go on. But first, another draught of the Medoc.'

I broke and reached him a flacon of De Grave. He emptied it at a breath. His eyes flashed with a fierce light. He laughed and threw the bottle upwards with a gesticulation I did not understand.

I looked at him in surprise. He repeated the movement – a grotesque one.

'You do not comprehend?' he said.

'Not I,' I replied.

'Then you are not of the brotherhood.'

'How?'

'You are not of the masons.'

'Yes, yes,' I said, 'yes, yes.'

'You? Impossible! A mason?'

'A mason,' I replied.

'A sign,' he said.

'It is this,' I answered, producing a trowel from beneath the folds of my *roquelaure*.

'You jest,' he exclaimed, recoiling a few paces. 'But let us proceed to the Amontillado.'

'Be it so,' I said, replacing the tool beneath the cloak, and again offering him my arm. He leaned upon it heavily. We continued our route in search of the Amontillado. We passed through a range of low arches, descended, passed on, and descending again, arrived at a deep crypt, in which the foulness of the air caused our flambeaux rather to glow than flame.

At the most remote end of the crypt there appeared another less spacious. Its walls had been lined with human remains piled to the vault overhead, in the fashion of the great catacombs of Paris. Three sides of this interior crypt were still ornamented in this manner. From the fourth the bones had been thrown down, and lay promiscuously upon the earth, forming at one point a mound of some size. Within the wall thus exposed by the displacing of the bones, we perceived a still interior recess, in depth about four feet, in width three, in height six or seven. It seemed to have been constructed for no especial use within itself, but formed merely the interval between two of the colossal supports of the roof of the catacombs, and was backed by one of their circumscribing walls of solid granite.

It was in vain that Fortunato, uplifting his dull torch, endeavoured to pry into the depths of the recess. Its termination the feeble light did not enable us to see.

'Proceed,' I said; 'herein is the Amontillado. As for Luchesi—'

'He is an ignoramus,' interrupted my friend, as he stepped unsteadily forward, while I followed immediately at his heels. In an instant he had reached the extremity of the niche, and finding his progress arrested by the rock, stood stupidly bewildered. A moment more and I had fettered him to the granite. In its surface were two iron staples, distant from each other about two feet, horizontally. From one of these depended a short chain, from the other a padlock. Throwing the links about his waist, it was but the work of a few seconds to secure it. He was too much astounded to resist. Withdrawing the key I stepped back from the recess.

'Pass your hand,' I said, 'over the wall; you cannot help feeling the nitre. Indeed it is *very* damp. Once more let me implore you to return. No? Then I must positively leave you. But I must first render you all the little attention in my power.'

'The Amontillado!' ejaculated my friend, not yet recovered from his astonishment.

'True,' I replied; 'the Amontillado.'

As I said these words I busied myself among the pile of bones of which I have before spoken. Throwing them aside, I soon uncovered a quantity of building stone and mortar. With these materials and with the aid of my trowel, I began vigorously to wall up the entrance of the niche.

I had scarcely laid the first tier of the masonry when I discovered that the intoxication of Fortunato had in a great measure worn off. The earliest indication I had of this was a low moaning cry from the depth of the recess. It was *not* the cry of a drunken man. There was then a long and obstinate silence. I laid the second tier, and the third, and the fourth; and then I heard the furious vibrations of the chain. The noise lasted for several minutes, during which, that I might hearken to it with the more satisfaction, I ceased my labours and sat down upon the bones. When at last the clanking subsided, I resumed the trowel, and finished without interruption the fifth, the sixth, and the seventh tier. The wall was now nearly upon a level with my breast. I again paused, and holding the flambeaux over the mason-work, threw a few feeble rays upon the figure within.

A succession of loud and shrill screams, bursting suddenly from the throat of the chained form, seemed to thrust me violently back. For a brief moment I hesitated – I trembled. Unsheathing my rapier, I began to grope with it about the recess; but the thought of an instant reassured me. I placed my hand upon the solid fabric of the catacombs, and felt satisfied. I reapproached the wall. I replied to the yells of him who clamoured. I re-echoed – I aided – I surpassed them in volume and in strength. I did this, and the clamourer grew still.

It was now midnight, and my task was drawing to a close. I had completed the eighth, the ninth, and the tenth tier. I had finished a portion of the last and the eleventh; there remained but a single stone to be fitted and plastered in. I struggled with its weight; I placed it partially in its destined position. But now there came from out of the niche a low laugh that erected the hairs upon my head. It was succeeded by a sad voice, which I had difficulty in recognizing as that of the noble Fortunato. The voice said—

'Ha! ha! ha! – he! he! a very good joke indeed – an excellent jest. We will have many a rich laugh about it at the palazzo – he! he! he! – over our wine – he! he! he!'

'The Amontillado!' I said.

'He! he! he! – he! he! he – yes, the Amontillado. But is it not getting late? Will not they be awaiting us at the palazzo, the Lady Fortunato and the rest? Let us be gone.'

'Yes,' I said, 'let us be gone.'

'*For the love of God, Montresor!*'

'Yes,' I said, 'for the love of God!'

But to these words I hearkened in vain for a reply. I grew impatient. I called aloud –

'Fortunato!'

No answer. I called again—

'Fortunato!'

No answer still. I thrust a torch through the remaining aperture and let it fall within. There came forth in return only a jingling of the bells. My heart grew sick – on account of the dampness of the catacombs. I hastened to make an end of my labour. I forced the last stone into its position; I plastered it up. Against the new masonry I re-erected the old rampart of bones. For the half of a century no mortal has disturbed them. *In pace requiescat!*

The House by the Headland

Sapper

'You'll no get there, zurr. There'll be a rare storm this night. Best bide here, and be going tomorrow morning after 'tis over.'

The warning of my late host, weather-wise through years of experience, rang through my brain as I reached the top of the headland, and, too late, I cursed myself for not having heeded his words. With a gasp I flung my pack down on the ground, and loosened my collar. Seven miles behind me lay the comfortable inn where I had lunched; eight miles in front the one where I proposed to dine. And midway between them was I, dripping with perspiration and panting for breath.

Not a breath of air was stirring; not a sound broke the death-like stillness, save the sullen lazy beat of the sea against the rocks below. Across the horizon, as far as the eye could see, stretched a mighty bank of black cloud, which was spreading slowly and relentlessly over the whole heaven. Already its edge was almost overhead, and as I felt the first big drop of rain on my forehead, I cursed myself freely once again. If only I had listened to mine host: if only I was still in his comfortable oak-beamed coffee-room, drinking his most excellent ale ... I felt convinced he was the type of man who would treat such trifles as regulation hours with the contempt they deserved. And, even as I tasted in imagination the bite of the grandest of all drinks on my parched tongue, and looked through the glass bottom of the tankard at the sanded floor, the second great drop of rain splashed on my face.

For a moment or two I wavered. Should I go back that seven miles, and confess myself a fool, or should I go on the further eight and hope that the next cellar would be as good as the last? In either case I was bound to get drenched to the skin, and at length I made up my mind. I would not turn back for any storm, and the matter of the quality of the ale must remain in the lap of the gods. And at that moment, like a solid wall of water, the rain came.

I have travelled into most corners of the world, in the course of forty years' wandering; I have been through the monsoon going south to Singapore from Japan, I have been caught on the edge of a water-spout

in the South Sea Islands; but I have never known anything like the
rain which came down that June evening on the south-west coast of
England. In half a minute every garment I wore was soaked; the hills
and the sea were blotted out, and I stumbled forward blindly, unable
to see more than a yard in front of me. Then, almost as abruptly as
it had started, the rain ceased. I could feel the water squelching in
my boots, and trickling down my back, as I kept steadily descending
into the valley beyond the headland.

There was nothing for it now but to go through with it. I couldn't
get any wetter than I was; so that, when I suddenly rounded a little
knoll and saw in front a low-lying, rambling house, the idea of
sheltering there did not at once occur to me. I glanced at it casually
in the semi-darkness, and was trudging past the gate, my mind busy
with other things, when a voice close behind me made me stop with
a sudden start. A man was speaking, and a second before I could have
sworn I was alone.

'A bad night, sir,' he remarked, in a curiously deep voice, 'and it
will be worse soon. The thunder and lightning is nearly over. Will you
not come in and shelter? I can supply you with a change of clothes
if you are wet?'

'You are very good, sir,' I answered slowly, peering at the tall,
gaunt figure beside me. 'But I think I will be getting on, thank you
all the same.'

'As you like,' he answered indifferently, and even as he spoke a vivid
flash of lightning quivered and died in the thick blackness of the sky,
and almost instantaneously a deafening crash of thunder seemed to come
from just over our heads. 'As you like,' he repeated, 'but I shall be glad
of your company if you cared to stay the night.'

It was a kind offer, though in a way the least one would expect in
similar circumstances, and I hesitated. Undoubtedly there was little
pleasure to be anticipated in an eight-mile tramp under such conditions,
and yet there was something – something indefinable, incoherent – which
said to me insistently: 'Go on; don't stop. Go on.'

I shook myself in annoyance, and my wet clothes clung to me
clammily. Was I, at my time of life, nervous, because a man had spoken
to me unexpectedly?

'I think if I may,' I said, 'I will change my mind and avail myself
of your kind offer. It is no evening for walking for pleasure.'

Without a word he led the way into the house, and I followed.
Even in the poor light I could see that the garden was badly kept, and
that the path leading to the front door was covered with weeds. Bushes,
wet with the rain, hung in front of our faces, dripping dismally on to
steps leading up to the door, giving the impression almost of a mosaic.

Inside the hall was in darkness, and I waited while he opened the door into one of the rooms. I heard him fumbling for a match, and at that moment another blinding flash lit up the house as if it had been day. I had a fleeting vision of the stairs – a short, broad flight – with a window at the top; of the two doors, one apparently leading to the servants' quarters, the other opposite the one my host had already opened. But most vivid of all in that quick photograph was the condition of the hall itself. Three or four feet above my head a lamp hung from the ceiling, and from it, in every direction, there seemed to be spiders' webs coated with dust and filth. They stretched to every picture; they stretched to the top of all the doors. One long festoon was almost brushing against my face, and for a moment a wave of unreasoning panic filled me.

Almost did I turn and run, so powerful was it; then, with an effort, I pulled myself together. For a grown man to become nervous of a spider's web is rather too much of a good thing, and after all it was none of my business. In all probability the man was a recluse, who was absorbed in more important matters than the cleanliness of his house. Though how he could stand the smell – dank and rotten – defeated me. It came to my nostrils as I stood there, waiting for him to strike a match, and the scent of my own wet Harris tweed failed to conceal it. It was the smell of an unlived-in house, grown damp and mildewed with years of neglect, and once again I shuddered. Confound the fellow! Would he never get the lamp lit? I didn't mind his spiders' webs and the general filth of his hall, provided I could get some dry clothes on.

'Come in.' I looked up to see him standing in the door. 'I regret that there seems to be no oil in the lamp, but there are candles on the mantelpiece, should you care to light them.'

Somewhat surprised I stepped into the room, and then his next remark made me halt in amazement.

'When my wife comes down, I must ask her about the oil. Strange of her to have forgotten.'

Wife! What manner of woman could this be who allowed her house to get into such a condition of dirt and neglect? And were there no servants? However, again, it was none of my business, and I felt in my pockets for matches. Luckily they were in a watertight box, and with a laugh I struck one and lit the candles.

'It's so infernally dark,' I remarked, 'that the stranger within the gates requires a little light, to get his bearings.'

In some curiosity I glanced at my host's face in the flickering light. As yet I had had no opportunity of observing him properly, but now as unostentatiously as possible I commenced to study it. Cadaverous almost to the point of emaciation, he had a ragged, bristly moustache, while his hair, plentifully flecked with grey, was brushed untidily back from his forehead. But dominating everything were his eyes, which glowed and smouldered from under his bushy eyebrows, till they seemed to burn into me.

More and more I found myself regretting the fact that I had accepted his offer. His whole manner was so strange that for the first time doubts as to his sanity began to creep into my mind. And to be alone with a madman in a deserted house, miles from any other habitation, with a terrific thunderstorm raging, was not a prospect which appealed to me greatly. Then I remembered his reference to his wife, and felt more reassured . . .

'You and your wife must find it lonely here,' I hazarded, when the silence had lasted some time.

'Why should my wife feel the loneliness?' he answered, harshly. 'She has me – her husband . . . What more does a woman require?'

'Oh! Nothing, nothing,' I replied hastily, deeming discretion the better part of veracity. 'Wonderful air; beautiful view. I wonder if I could have a dry coat as you so kindly suggested?'

I took off my own wet one as I spoke, and threw it over the back of a chair. Then, receiving no answer to my request, I looked at my host. His back was half towards me, and he was staring into the hall outside. He stood quite motionless, and as apparently he had failed to hear me, I was on the point of repeating my remark when he turned and spoke to me again.

'A pleasant surprise for my wife, sir, don't you think? She was not expecting me home until tomorrow morning.'

'Very,' I assented . . .

'Eight miles I have walked, in order to prevent her being alone. That should answer your remark about her feeling the loneliness.'

He peered at me fixedly, and I again assented.

'Most considerate of you,' I murmured, 'most considerate.'

But the man only chuckled by way of answer, and swinging round, continued to stare into the gloomy, filthy hall.

Outside the storm was increasing in fury. Flash followed flash with such rapidity that the whole sky westwards formed into a dancing sheet of flame, while the roll of the thunder seemed like the continuous roar of a bombardment with heavy guns. But I was aware of it only subconsciously; my attention was concentrated on the gaunt man standing so motionless in the centre of the room.

So occupied was I with him that I never heard his wife's approach until suddenly, looking up, I saw that by the door there stood a woman – a woman who paid no attention to me, but only stared fearfully at her husband, with a look of dreadful terror in her eyes. She was young, far younger than the man – and pretty in a homely, countrified way. And as she stared at the gaunt, cadaverous husband she seemed to be trying to speak, while ceaselessly she twisted a wisp of a pocket handkerchief in her hands.

'I didn't expect you home so soon, Rupert,' she stammered at length. 'Have you had a good day?'

'Excellent,' he answered, and his eyes seemed to glow more fiendishly than ever. 'And now I have come home to my little wife, and her loving welcome.'

She laughed a forced, unnatural laugh, and came a few steps into the room.

'There is no oil in the lamp, my dear,' he continued, suavely. 'Have you been too busy to remember to fill it?'

'I will go and get some,' she said, quickly turning towards the door. But the man's hand shot out and caught her arm, and at his touch she shrank away, cowering.

'I think not,' he cried, harshly. 'We will sit in the darkness, my dear, and – wait.'

'How mysterious you are, Rupert!' She forced herself to speak lightly. 'What are we going to wait for?'

But the man only laughed – a low, mocking chuckle – and pulled the girl nearer to him.

'Aren't you going to kiss me, Mary? It's such a long time since you kissed me – a whole twelve hours.'

The girl's free hand clenched tight, but she made no other protest as her husband took her in his arms and kissed her. Only it seemed to me that her whole body was strained and rigid, as if to brace herself to meet a caress she loathed . . . In fact the whole situation was becoming distinctly embarrassing. The man seemed to have completely forgotten my existence, and the girl so far had not even looked at me. Undoubtedly a peculiar couple, and a peculiar house. Those cobwebs: I couldn't get them out of my mind.

'Hadn't I better go and fill the lamp now?' she asked after a time. 'Those candles give a very poor light, don't they?'

'Quite enough for my purpose, my dear wife,' replied the man. 'Come and sit down and talk to me.'

With his hand still holding her arm he drew her to a sofa, and side by side they sat down. I noticed that all the time he was watching her covertly out of the corner of his eye, while she stared straight in front of her as if she was waiting for something to happen . . . And at that moment a door banged, upstairs.

'What's that?' the girl half rose, but the man pulled her back.

'The wind, my dear,' he chuckled. 'What else could it be? The house is empty save for us.'

'Hadn't I better go up and see that all the windows are shut?' she said, nervously. 'The storm makes me feel frightened.'

'That's why I hurried back to you, my love. I couldn't bear to think of you spending tonight alone.' Again he chuckled horribly, and peered at the girl beside him. 'I said to myself, "She doesn't expect me back till tomorrow morning. I will surprise my darling wife, and go back home tonight." Wasn't it kind of me, Mary?'

'Of course it was, Rupert,' she stammered. 'Very kind of you. I think I'll just go up and put on a jersey. I'm feeling a little cold.'

She tried to rise, but her husband still held her; and then suddenly there came on her face such a look of pitiable terror that involuntarily I took a step forward. She was staring at the door, and her lips were parted as if to cry out, when the man covered her mouth with his free hand and dragged her brutally to her feet.

'Alone, my wife – all alone,' he snarled. 'My dutiful, loving wife all alone. What a good thing I returned to keep her company!'

For a moment or two she struggled feebly; then he half carried, half forced her close by me to a position behind the open door. I could have touched them as they passed; but I seemed powerless to move. Instinctively I knew what was going to happen; but I could do nothing save stand and stare at the door, while the girl, half fainting, crouched against the wall, and her husband stood over her motionless and terrible. And thus we waited, while the candles guttered in their sockets, listening to the footsteps which were coming down the stairs . . .

Twice I strove to call out; twice the sound died away in my throat. I felt as one does in some awful nightmare, when a man cries aloud and no sound comes, or runs his fastest and yet does not move. In it, I was yet not of it; it was as if I was the spectator of some inexorable tragedy with no power to intervene.

The steps came nearer. They were crossing the hall now – the cobwebby hall – and the next moment I saw a young man standing in the open door.

'Mary, where are you, my darling?' He came into the room and glanced around. And, as he stood there, one hand in his pocket, smiling cheerily, the man behind the door put out his arm and gripped him by the shoulder. In an instant the smile vanished and the youngster spun round, his face set and hard.

'Here is your darling, John Trelawnay,' said the husband quietly. 'What do you want with her?'

'Ah!' The youngster's breath came a little faster, as he stared at the older man. 'You've come back unexpectedly, have you? It's the sort of damned dirty trick you would play.'

I smiled involuntarily: this was carrying the war into the enemy's camp with a vengeance.

'What are you doing in this house alone with my wife, John Trelawnay?' Into the quiet voice had crept a note of menace, and, as I glanced at the speaker and noticed the close clenching and unclenching of his powerful hands, I realized that there was going to be trouble.

The old, old story again, but, rightly or wrongly, with every sympathy of mine on the side of the sinners.

'Your wife by a trick only, Rupert Carlingham,' returned the other hotly. 'You know she's never loved you; you know she has always loved me.'

'Nevertheless – my wife. But I ask you again, what are you doing in this house while I am away?'

'Did you expect us to stand outside in the storm?' muttered the other.

For a moment the elder man's eyes blazed, and I thought he was going to strike the youngster. Then, with an effort, he controlled himself, and his voice was ominously quiet as he spoke again.

'You lie, John Trelawnay.' His brooding eyes never left the other's face. 'It was no storm that drove you here today; no thunder that made you call my wife your darling. You came because you knew I was away; because you thought – you and your mistress – that I should not return till tomorrow.'

For a while he was silent, while the girl still crouched against the wall staring at him fearfully, and the youngster, realizing the hopelessness of further denial, faced him with folded arms. In silence I watched them from the shadow beyond the fireplace, wondering what I ought to do. There is no place for any outsider in such a situation, much less a complete stranger; and had I consulted my own inclinations I would have left the house there and then and chanced the storm still raging outside. I got as far as putting on my coat again, and making a movement towards the door, when the girl looked at me with such an agony of entreaty in her eyes that I paused. Perhaps it was better that I should stop; perhaps if things got to a head, and the men started fighting, I might be of some use.

And at that moment Rupert Carlingham threw back his head and laughed. It echoed and re-echoed through the room, peal after peal of maniacal laughter, while the girl covered her face with her hands and shrank away, and the youngster, for all his pluck, retreated a few steps. The man was mad, there was no doubt about it: and the laughter of a mad man is perhaps the most awful thing a human being may hear.

Quickly I stepped forward; it seemed to me that if I was to do anything at all the time had now come.

'I think, Mr Carlingham,' I said, firmly, 'that a little quiet discussion would be of advantage to everyone.'

He ceased laughing, and stared at me in silence. Then his eyes left my face and fixed themselves again on the youngster. It was useless; he was blind to everything except his own insensate rage. And, before I could realize his intention, he sprang.

'You'd like me to divorce her, wouldn't you?' he snarled, as his hand sought John Trelawnay's throat. 'So that you could marry her.... But I'm not going to – no. I know a better thing than divorce.'

The words were choked on his lips by the youngster's fist, which crashed again and again into his face; but the man seemed insensible to pain. They swayed backwards and forwards, while the lightning, growing fainter and fainter in the distance, quivered through the room from time to time, and the two candles supplied the rest of the illumination. Never for an instant did the mad man relax his grip on the youngster's throat: never for an instant did the boy cease his sledge-hammer blows on the other's face. But he was tiring, it was obvious; no normal flesh and blood could stand the frenzied strength against him. And, suddenly, it struck me that murder was being done, in front of my eyes.

With a shout I started forward – somehow they must be separated. And then I stopped motionless again: the girl had slipped past me with her face set and hard. With a strength for which I would not have given her credit she seized both her husband's legs about the knees, and lifted his feet off the ground, so that his only support was the grip of his left hand on the youngster's throat and the girl's arms about his knees. He threw her backwards and forwards as if she had been a child, but still she clung on, and then, in an instant, it was all over. His free right hand had been forgotten ...

I saw the boy sway nearer in his weakness, and the sudden flash of a knife. There was a little choking gurgle, and they all crashed down together, with the youngster underneath. And when the madman rose the boy lay still, with the shaft of the knife sticking out from his coat above his heart.

It was then that Rupert Carlingham laughed again, while his wife, mad with grief, knelt beside the dead boy, pillowing his head on her lap. For what seemed an eternity I stood watching, unable to move or speak; then the murderer bent down and swung his wife over his shoulder. And, before I realized what he was going to do, he had left the room, and I saw him passing the window outside.

The sight galvanized me into action; there was just a possibility I might avert a double tragedy. With a loud shout I dashed out of the front door, and down the ill-kept drive; but when I got to the open ground he seemed to have covered an incredible distance, considering his burden. I could see him shambling over the turf, up the side of the valley which led to the headland where the rain had caught me, and, as fast as I could, I followed him, shouting as I ran. But it was no use – gain on him I could not. Steadily, with apparent ease, he carried the girl up the hill, taking no more notice of my cries than he had of my presence earlier in the evening. And, with the water squelching from my boots, I ran after him – no longer wasting my breath on shouting, but saving it all in my frenzied endeavour to catch him before it was too late. For once again I knew what was going to happen, even as I had known when I heard the footsteps coming down the stairs.

I was still fifty yards from him when he reached the top of the cliff; and for a while he paused there silhouetted against the angry sky. He seemed to be staring out to sea, and the light from the flaming red sunset, under the black of the storm, shone on his great, gaunt figure, bathing it in a wonderful splendour. The next moment he was gone ... I heard him give one loud cry; then he sprang into space with the girl still clasped in his arms.

And when I reached the spot and peered over, only the low booming of the sullen Atlantic three hundred feet below came to my ears ... That, and the mocking shrieks of a thousand gulls. Of the mad man and his wife there was no sign.

At last I got up and started to walk away mechanically. I felt that somehow I was to blame for the tragedy, that I should have done something, taken a hand in that grim fight. And yet I knew that if I was called upon to witness it again, I should act in the same way. I should feel as powerless to move as I had felt in that ill-omened house, with the candles guttering on the mantelpiece, and the lightning flashing through the dirty window. Even now I seemed to be moving in a dream, and after a while I stopped and made a determined effort to pull myself together.

'You will go back,' I said out loud, 'to that house. And you will make sure that that boy is dead. You are a grown man, and not an hysterical woman. You will go back.'

And as if in answer a seagull screamed discordantly above my head. Not for five thousand pounds would I have gone back to that house alone, and when I argued with myself and said, 'You are a fool, and a coward,' the gull shrieked mockingly again.

'What is there to be afraid of?' I cried. 'A dead body: and you have seen many hundreds.'

It was as I asked the question out loud that I came to a road and sat down beside it. It was little more than a track, but it seemed to speak of other human beings, and I wanted human companionship at that moment – wanted it more than I had ever wanted anything in my life. At any other time I would have resented sharing with strangers the glorious beauty of the moors as they stretched back to a rugged tor a mile or two away, with their wonderful colouring of violet and black, and the scent of the wet earth rising all around. But now ...

With a shudder I rose, conscious for the first time that I was feeling chilled. I must get somewhere – talk to someone; and, as if in answer to my thoughts, a car came suddenly in sight, bumping over the track.

There was an elderly man inside, and two girls, and he pulled up at once on seeing me.

'By Jove!' he cried, cheerily, 'you're very wet. Can I give you a lift anywhere?'

'It is very good of you,' I said. 'I want to get to the police as quickly as possible.'

'The police?' He stared at me surprised. 'What's wrong?'

'There's been a most ghastly tragedy,' I said. 'A man has been murdered and the murderer has jumped over that headland, with his wife in his arms. The murderer's name was Rupert Carlingham.'

I was prepared for my announcement startling them; I was not prepared for the extraordinary effect it produced. With a shriek of terror the two girls clung together, and the man's ruddy face went white.

'What name did you say?' he said at length, in a shaking voice.

'Rupert Carlingham,' I answered, curtly. 'And the boy he murdered was called John Trelawnay. Incidentally I want to get a doctor to look at the youngster. It's possible the knife might have just missed his heart.'

'Oh, Daddy, drive on, drive on quick!' implored the girls, and I glanced at them in slight surprise. After all, a murder is a very terrible thing, but it struck me they were becoming hysterical over it.

'It was just such an evening,' said the man, slowly; 'just such a storm as we've had this afternoon, that it happened.'

'That what happened?' I cried a trifle irritably; but he made no answer, and only stared at me curiously.

'Do you know these parts, sir?' he said at length.

'It's the first time I've ever been here,' I answered. 'I'm on a walking tour.'

'Ah! A walking tour. Well, I'm a doctor myself, and unless you get your clothes changed pretty quickly, I predict that your walking tour will come to an abrupt conclusion – even if it's only a temporary one. Now, put on this coat, and we'll get off to a good inn.'

But, anxious as I was to fall in with his suggestion myself, I felt that that was more than I could do.

'It's very good of you, doctor,' I said; 'but, seeing that you are a medical man, I really must ask you to come and look at this youngster first. I'd never forgive myself if by any chance he wasn't dead. As a matter of fact, I've seen death too often not to recognize it, and the boy was stabbed clean through the heart right in front of my eyes – but ...'

I broke off, as one of the girls leaned forward and whispered to her father. But he only shook his head, and stared at me curiously.

'Did you make no effort to stop the murder?' he asked at length.

It was the question I had been dreading, the question I knew must come sooner or later. But, now that I was actually confronted with it,

I had no answer ready. I could only shake my head and stammer out confusedly:

'It seems incredible for a man of my age and experience to confess it, doctor – but I didn't. I couldn't . . . I was just going to try and separate them, when the girl rushed in . . . and . . .'

'What did she do?' It was one of the daughters who fired the question at me so suddenly that I looked at her in amazement. 'What did Mary do?'

'She got her husband by the knees,' I said, 'and hung on like a bulldog. But he'd got a grip on the boy's throat and then – suddenly – it was all over. They came crashing down as he stabbed young Trelawnay.' Once again the girls clung together shuddering, and I turned to the doctor. 'I wish you'd come, doctor: it's only just a step. I can show you the house.'

'I know the house, sir, very well,' he answered, gravely. Then he put his arms on the steering-wheel and for a long time fidgeted restlessly, and the girls whispered together. What on earth was the man waiting for? I wondered: after all, it wasn't a very big thing to ask of a doctor . . . At last he got down from the car and stood beside me on the grass.

'You've never been here before, sir?' he asked again, looking at me fixedly.

'Never,' I answered, a shade brusquely. 'And I'm not altogether bursting with a desire to return.'

'Strange,' he muttered. 'Very, very strange. I will come with you.'

For a moment he spoke to his daughters as if to reassure them; then, together, we walked over the springy turf towards the house by the headland. He seemed in no mood for conversation, and my own mind was far too busy with the tragedy for idle talk.

But he asked me one question when we were about fifty yards from the house.

'Rupert Carlingham carried his wife up to the headland, you say?'

'Slung over his shoulder,' I answered, 'and then . . .'

But the doctor had stopped short, and was staring at the house, while, once again, every vestige of colour had left his face.

'My God!' he muttered, 'there's a light in the room . . . A light, man; don't you see it?'

'I left the candles burning,' I said, impatiently. 'Really, doctor, I suppose murder doesn't often come your way, but . . .'

I walked on quickly and he followed. Really the fuss was getting on my nerves, already distinctly ragged. The front door was open as I had left it, and I paused for a moment in the cobwebby hall. Then, pulling myself together, I stepped into the room where the body lay, to halt and stare open-mouthed at the floor . . .

The candles still flickered on the mantelpiece; the furniture was as

I had left it; but of the body of John Trelawnay there was not a trace. It had vanished utterly and completely.

'I don't understand, doctor,' I muttered foolishly. 'I left the body lying there.'

The doctor stood at the door beside me, and suddenly I realized that his eyes were fixed on me.

'I know,' he said, and his voice was grave and solemn. 'With the head near that chair.'

'Why, how do you know?' I cried, amazed. 'Have you taken the body away?'

But he answered my question by another.

'Do you notice anything strange in this room, sir?' he asked. 'On the floor?'

'Only a lot of dust,' I remarked.

'Precisely,' he said. 'And one would expect footprints in dust. I see yours going to the mantelpiece; I see no others.'

I clutched his arm, as his meaning came to me.

'My God!' I whispered. 'What do you mean?'

'I mean,' he said, 'that Rupert Carlingham murdered John Trelawnay, and then killed himself and his wife, five years ago . . . during just such another storm as we have had this evening.'

Suspicion

Dorothy L. Sayers

As the atmosphere of the railway carriage thickened with tobacco smoke, Mr Mummery became increasingly aware that his breakfast had not agreed with him.

There could have been nothing wrong with the breakfast itself. Brown bread, rich in vitamin content, as advised by the *Morning Star*'s health expert; bacon fried to a delicious crispness; eggs just nicely set; coffee made as only Mrs Sutton knew how to make it. Mrs Sutton had been a real find, and that was something to be thankful for. For Ethel, since her nervous breakdown in the summer, had really not been fit to wrestle with the untrained girls who had come and gone in tempestuous succession. It took very little to upset Ethel nowadays, poor child. Mr Mummery, trying hard to ignore his growing internal discomfort, hoped he was not in for an illness. Apart from the trouble it would cause at the office, it would worry Ethel terribly, and Mr Mummery would cheerfully have laid down his rather uninteresting little life to spare Ethel a moment's uneasiness.

He slipped a digestive tablet into his mouth – he had taken lately to carrying a few tablets about with him – and opened his paper. There did not seem to be very much news. A question had been asked in the House about government typewriters. The Prince of Wales had smilingly opened an all-British exhibition of footwear. A further split had occurred in the Liberal Party. The police were still looking for the woman who was supposed to have poisoned a family in Lincoln. Two girls had been trapped in a burning factory. A film star had obtained her fourth decree nisi.

At Paragon Station, Mr Mummery descended and took a tram. The internal discomfort was taking the form of a definite nausea. Happily he contrived to reach his office before the worst occurred. He was seated at his desk, pale but in control of himself, when his partner came breezing in. ''Morning, Mummery,' said Mr Brookes in his loud tones, adding inevitably, 'Cold enough for you?'

'Quite,' replied Mr Mummery. 'Unpleasantly raw, in fact.'

'Beastly, beastly,' said Mr Brookes. 'Your bulbs all in?'

'Not quite all,' confessed Mr Mummery. 'As a matter of fact I haven't been feeling—'

'Pity,' interrupted his partner. 'Great pity. Ought to get 'em in early. Mine were in last week. My little place will be a picture in the spring. For a town garden, that is. You're lucky, living in the country. Find it better than Hull, I expect, eh? Though we get plenty of fresh air up in the avenues. How's the missus?'

'Thank you, she's very much better.'

'Glad to hear that, very glad. Hope we shall have her about again this winter as usual. Can't do without her in the Drama Society, you know. By Jove! I shan't forget her acting last year in *Romance*. She and young Welbeck positively brought the house down, didn't they? The Welbecks were asking after her only yesterday.'

'Thank you, yes. I hope she will soon be able to take up her social activities again. But the doctor says she mustn't overdo it. No worry, he says – that's the important thing. She is to go easy and not rush about or undertake too much.'

'Quite right, quite right. Worry's the devil and all. I cut out worrying years ago and look at me! Fit as a fiddle, for all I shan't see fifty again. *You're* not looking altogether the thing, by the way.'

'A touch of dyspepsia,' said Mr Mummery. 'Nothing much. Chill on the liver, that's what I put it down to.'

'That's what it is,' said Mr Brookes, seizing his opportunity. 'Is life worth living? It depends upon the liver. Ha, ha! Well now, well now – we must do a spot of work, I suppose. Where's that lease of Ferraby's?'

Mr Mummery, who did not feel at his conversational best that morning, rather welcomed this suggestion, and for half an hour was allowed to proceed in peace with the duties of an estate agent. Presently, however, Mr Brookes burst into speech again.

'By the way,' he said abruptly, 'I suppose your wife doesn't know of a good cook, does she?'

'Well, no,' replied Mr Mummery. 'They aren't so easy to find nowadays. In fact, we've only just got suited ourselves. But why? Surely your old Cookie isn't leaving you?'

'Good lord, no!' Mr Brookes laughed heartily. 'It would take an earthquake to shake off old Cookie. No. It's for the Philipsons. Their girl's getting married. That's the worst of girls. I said to Philipson, "You mind what you're doing," I said. "Get somebody you know something about, or you may find yourself landed with this poisoning woman – what's her name – Andrews. Don't want to be sending wreaths to your funeral yet awhile," I said. He laughed, but it's no laughing matter and so I told him. What we pay the police for I simply don't know. Nearly a month now, and they can't seem to lay hands on the woman. All they say is, they think she's hanging about the neighbourhood and "may seek a situation as cook". As cook! Now I ask you!'

'You don't think she committed suicide, then?' suggested Mr Mummery.

'Suicide my foot!' retorted Mr Brookes coarsely. 'Don't you believe it, my boy. That coat found in the river was all eyewash. *They* don't commit suicide, that sort don't.'

'What sort?'

'Those arsenic maniacs. They're too damned careful of their own skins. Cunning as weasels, that's what they are. It's only to be hoped they'll manage to catch her before she tries her hand on anybody else. As I told Philipson—'

'You think Mrs Andrews did it, then?'

'Did it? Of course she did it. It's plain as the nose on your face. Looked after her old father, and he died suddenly – left her a bit of money, too. Then she keeps house for an elderly gentleman, and *he* dies suddenly. Now there's this husband and wife – man dies and woman taken very ill, of arsenic poisoning. Cook runs away, and you ask, did she do it? I don't mind betting that when they dig up the father and the other old bird they'll find *them* bung-full of arsenic, too. Once that sort gets started, they don't stop. Grows on 'em, as you might say.'

'I suppose it does,' said Mr Mummery. He picked up his paper again and studied the photograph of the missing woman. 'She looks harmless enough,' he remarked. 'Rather a nice, motherly-looking kind of woman.'

'She's got a bad mouth,' pronounced Mr Brookes. He had a theory that character showed in the mouth. 'I wouldn't trust that woman an inch.'

As the day went on, Mr Mummery felt better. He was rather nervous about his lunch, choosing carefully a little boiled fish and custard pudding and being particular not to rush about immediately after the meal. To his great relief, the fish and custard remained where they were put, and he was not visited by that tiresome pain which had become almost habitual in the last fortnight. By the end of the day he became quite lighthearted. The bogey of illness and doctor's bills ceased to haunt him. He bought a bunch of bronze chrysanthemums to carry home to Ethel, and it was with a feeling of pleasant anticipation that he left the train and walked up the garden path of Mon Abri.

He was a little dashed by not finding his wife in the sitting room. Still clutching the bunch of chrysanthemums he pattered down the passage and pushed open the kitchen door.

Nobody was there but the cook. She was sitting at the table with her back to him, and started up almost guiltily as he approached.

'Lor', sir,' she said, 'you give me quite a start. I didn't hear the front door go.'

'Where is Mrs Mummery? Not feeling bad again, is she?'

'Well, sir, she's got a bit of a headache, poor lamb. I made her lay down and took her up a nice cup o' tea at half past four. I think she's dozing nicely now.'

'Dear, dear,' said Mr Mummery.

'It was turning out the dining room done it, if you ask me,' said Mrs Sutton. ' "Now, don't you overdo yourself, ma'am," I says to her, but you know how she is, sir. She gets that restless, she can't abear to be doing nothing.'

'I know,' said Mr Mummery. 'It's not your fault, Mrs Sutton. I'm sure you look after us both admirably. I'll just run up and have a peep at her. I won't disturb her is she's asleep. By the way, what are we having for dinner?'

'Well, I *had* made a nice steak-and-kidney pie,' said Mrs Sutton, in accents suggesting that she would readily turn it into a pumpkin or a coach-and-four if it was not approved of.

'Oh!' said Mr Mummery. 'Pastry? Well, I—'

'You'll find it beautiful and light,' protested the cook, whisking open the oven door for Mr Mummery to see. 'And it's made with butter, sir, you having said that you found lard indigestible.'

'Thank you, thank you,' said Mr Mummery. 'I'm sure it will be most excellent. I haven't been feeling altogether the thing just lately, and lard does not seem to suit me nowadays.'

'Well, it don't suit some people, and that's a fact,' agreed Mrs Sutton. 'I shouldn't wonder if you've got a bit of a chill on the liver. I'm sure this weather is enough to upset anybody.' She bustled to the table and cleared away the picture paper which she had been reading.

'Perhaps the mistress would like her dinner sent up to her?' she suggested.

Mr Mummery said he would go and see, and tiptoed his way upstairs.

Ethel was lying snuggled under the eiderdown and looked very small and fragile in the big double bed. She stirred as he came in and smiled up at him. 'Hullo, darling!' said Mr Mummery.

'Hullo! You back? I must have been asleep. I got tired and headachy, and Mrs Sutton packed me off upstairs.'

'You've been doing too much, sweetheart,' said her husband, taking her hand in his and sitting down on the edge of the bed.

'Yes – it was naughty of me. What lovely flowers, Harold. All for me?'

'All for you, Tiddleywinks,' said Mr Mummery tenderly. 'Don't I deserve something for that?' Mrs Mummery smiled, and Mr Mummery took his reward several times over.

'That's quite enough, you sentimental old thing,' said Mrs Mummery. 'Run away, now, I'm going to get up.'

'Much better go to bed, my precious, and let Mrs Sutton send your dinner up,' said her husband.

Ethel protested, but he was firm with her. If she didn't take care of herself, she wouldn't be allowed to go to the Drama Society meetings. And everybody was so anxious to have her back. The Welbecks had been asking after her and saying that they really couldn't get on without her.

'Did they?' said Ethel with some animation. 'It's very sweet of them to want me. Well, perhaps I'll go to bed after all. And how has my old hubby been all day?'

'Not too bad, not too bad.'

'No more tummyaches?'

'Well, just a *little* tummyache. But it's quite gone now. Nothing for Tiddleywinks to worry about.'

Mr Mummery experienced no more distressing symptoms the next day or the next. Following the advice of the newspaper expert, he took to drinking orange juice, and was delighted with the results of the treatment. On Thursday, however, he was taken so ill in the night that Ethel was alarmed and insisted on sending for the doctor. The doctor felt his pulse and looked at his tongue and appeared to take the matter lightly. An inquiry into what he had been eating elicited the fact that dinner had consisted of pigs' trotters, followed by a milk pudding, and that, before retiring, Mr Mummery had consumed a large glass of orange juice, according to his new regime.

'There's your trouble,' said Dr Griffiths cheerfully. 'Orange juice is an excellent thing, and so are trotters, but not in combination. Pig and oranges together are extraordinarily bad for the liver. I don't know why they should be, but there's no doubt that they are. Now I'll send you round a little prescription and you stick to slops for a day or two and keep off pork. And don't you worry about him, Mrs Mummery, he's as sound as a trout. *You're* the one we've got to look after. I don't want to see those black rings under the eyes, you know. Disturbed night, of course – yes. Taking your tonic regularly? That's right. Well, don't be alarmed about your hubby. We'll soon have him out and about again.'

The prophecy was fulfilled, but not immediately. Mr Mummery, though confining his diet to baby food, bread and milk, and beef tea skilfully prepared by Mrs Sutton and brought to his bedside by Ethel, remained very seedy all through Friday, and was only able to stagger rather shakily downstairs on Saturday afternoon. He had evidently suffered a 'thorough upset'. However, he was able to attend to a few papers which Brookes had sent down from the office for his signature, and to deal with the household books. Ethel was not a businesswoman, and Mr Mummery always ran over the accounts with her. Having settled up with the butcher, the baker, the dairy and the coal merchant, Mr Mummery looked up inquiringly. 'Anything more, darling?'

'Well, there's Mrs Sutton. This is the end of her month, you know.'

'So it is. Well, you're quite satisfied with her, aren't you, darling?'

'Yes, rather – aren't you? She's a good cook, and a sweet, motherly old thing, too. Don't you think it was a real brainwave of mine, engaging her like that, on the spot?'

'I do, indeed,' said Mr Mummery.

'It was a perfect providence, her turning up like that, just after that wretched Janet had gone off without even giving notice. I was in absolute *despair*. It was a little bit of a gamble, of course, taking her without any references, but naturally, if she'd been looking after a widowed mother, you couldn't expect her to give references.'

'N-no,' said Mr Mummery. At the time he had felt uneasy about the matter, though he had not liked to say much because, of course, they simply had to have somebody. And the experiment had justified itself so triumphantly in practice that one couldn't say much about it now. He had once rather tentatively suggested writing to the clergyman of Mrs Sutton's parish but, as Ethel had said, the clergyman wouldn't have been able to tell them anything about cooking, and cooking, after all, was the chief point.

Mr Mummery counted out the month's money.

'And by the way, my dear,' he said, 'you might just mention to Mrs Sutton that if she *must* read the morning paper before I come down, I should be obliged if she would fold it neatly afterwards.'

'What an old fussbox you are, darling,' said his wife.

Mr Mummery sighed. He could not explain that it was somehow important that the morning paper should come to him fresh and prim, like a virgin. Women did not feel these things.

On Sunday, Mr Mummery felt very much better – quite his old self, in fact. He enjoyed the *News of the World* over breakfast in bed, reading the murders rather carefully. Mr Mummery got quite a lot of pleasure out of murders – they gave him an agreeable thrill of vicarious adventure, for, naturally, they were matters quite remote from daily life in the outskirts of Hull. He noticed that Brookes had been perfectly right. Mrs Andrews' father and former employer had been 'dug up' and had, indeed, proved to be 'bung-full' of arsenic.

He came downstairs for dinner – roast sirloin, with the potatoes done under the meat and Yorkshire pudding of delicious lightness, and an apple tart to follow. After three days of invalid diet, it was delightful to savour the crisp fat and underdone lean. He ate moderately, but with a sensuous enjoyment. Ethel, on the other hand, seemed a little lacking in appetite, but then, she had never been a great meat eater. She was fastidious and, besides, she was (quite unnecessarily) afraid of getting fat.

It was a fine afternoon, and at three o'clock, when he was quite certain that the roast beef was 'settling' properly, it occurred to Mr Mummery that it would be a good thing to put the rest of those bulbs in. He slipped on his old gardening coat and wandered out to the potting shed. Here he picked up a bag of tulips and a trowel, and then, remembering that he was wearing his good trousers, decided that it would be wise to take a mat to kneel on. When had he had the mat last? He could not recollect, but he rather fancied he had put it away in the corner under the potting shelf. Stooping down, he felt about in the dark among the flowerpots. Yes, there it was, but there was a tin of something in the way. He lifted the tin carefully out. Of course, yes – the remains of the weed killer.

Mr Mummery glanced at the pink label, printed in staring letters with the legend: ARSENICAL WEED KILLER. *POISON*, and observed, with a mild feeling of excitement, that it was the same brand of stuff that had been associated with Mrs Andrews' latest victim. He was rather pleased about it. It gave him a sensation of being remotely but definitely in touch with important events. Then he noticed, with surprise and a little annoyance, that the stopper had been put in quite loosely.

'However'd I come to leave it like that?' he grunted. 'Shouldn't wonder if all the goodness has gone off.' He removed the stopper and squinted into the can, which appeared to be half full. Then he rammed the thing home again, giving it a sharp thump with the handle of the trowel for better security. After that he washed his hands carefully at the scullery tap, for he did not believe in taking risks.

He was a trifle disconcerted, when he came in after planting the tulips, to find visitors in the sitting room. He was always pleased to see Mrs Welbeck and her son, but he would rather have had warning, so that he could have scrubbed the garden mould out of his nails more thoroughly. Not that Mrs Welbeck appeared to notice. She was a talkative woman and paid little attention to anything but her own conversation. Much to Mr Mummery's annoyance, she chose to prattle about the Lincoln poisoning case. A most unsuitable subject for the tea table, thought Mr Mummery, at the best of times. His own 'upset' was vivid enough in his memory to make him queasy over the discussion of medical symptoms, and besides, this kind of talk was not good enough for Ethel. After all, the poisoner was still supposed to be in the neighbourhood. It was enough to make even a strong-nerved woman uneasy. A glance at Ethel showed him that she was looking quite white and tremulous. He must stop Mrs Welbeck somehow, or there would be a repetition of one of the old dreadful, hysterical scenes. He broke into the conversation with violent abruptness. 'Those forsythia cuttings, Mrs Welbeck,' he said. 'Now is just about the time to take them. If you care to come down the garden I will get them for you.'

He saw a relieved glance pass between Ethel and young Welbeck.

Evidently the boy understood the situation and was chafing at his mother's tactlessness. Mrs Welbeck, brought up all standing, gasped slightly and then veered off with obliging readiness on the new tack. She accompanied her host down the garden and chattered cheerfully about horticulture while he selected and trimmed the cuttings. She complimented Mr Mummery on the immaculacy of his gravel paths. 'I simply *cannot* keep the weeds down.' she said.

Mr Mummery mentioned the weed killer and praised its efficacy.

'That stuff!' Mrs Welbeck stared at him. Then she shuddered. 'I wouldn't have it in my place for a thousand pounds,' she said, with emphasis.

Mr Mummery smiled. 'Oh, we keep it well away from the house,' he said. 'Even if I were a careless sort of person—'

He broke off. The recollection of the loosened stopper had come to him suddenly, and it was as though, deep down in his mind, some obscure assembling of ideas had taken place. He left it at that, and went into the kitchen to fetch a newspaper to wrap up the cuttings.

Their approach to the house had evidently been seen from the sitting-room window, for when they entered, young Welbeck was already on his feet and holding Ethel's hand in the act of saying good-bye. He manoeuvred his mother out of the house with tactful promptness and Mr Mummery returned to the kitchen to clear up the newspapers he had fished out of the drawer. To clear them up and to examine them more closely. Something had struck him about them, which he wanted to verify. He turned them over very carefully, sheet by sheet. Yes – he had been right. Every portrait of Mrs Andrews, every paragraph and line about the Lincoln poisoning case, had been carefully cut out.

Mr Mummery sat down by the kitchen fire. He felt as though he needed warmth. There seemed to be a curious cold lump of something at the pit of his stomach – something that he was chary of investigating.

He tried to recall the appearance of Mrs Andrews as shown in the newspaper photographs, but he had not a good visual memory. He remembered having remarked to Brookes that it was a 'motherly' face. They he tried counting up the time since the disappearance. Nearly a month, Brookes had said – and that was a week ago. Must be over a month now. A month. He had just paid Mrs Sutton her month's money.

Ethel! was the thought that hammered at the door of his brain. At all costs, he must cope with this monstrous suspicion on his own. He must spare her any shock or anxiety. And he must be sure of his ground. To dismiss the only decent cook they had ever had out of sheer, unfounded panic, would be wanton cruelty to both women. If he did it at all, it would have to be done arbitrarily, preposterously – he could not suggest horrors to Ethel. However it was done, there would be trouble. Ethel would not understand and he dared not tell her.

But if by any chance there was anything in this ghastly doubt – how could he expose Ethel to the appalling danger of having the woman in the house a moment longer? He thought of the family at Lincoln – the husband dead, the wife escaped by a miracle with her life. Was not any shock, any risk, better than that?

Mr Mummery felt suddenly very lonely and tired. His illness had taken it out of him. Those illnesses – they had begun, when? Three weeks ago he had had the first attack. Yes, but then he had always been rather subject to gastric troubles. Bilious attacks. Not so violent, perhaps, as these last, but undoubted bilious attacks.

He pulled himself together and went, rather heavily, into the sitting room. Ethel was tucked up in a corner of the chesterfield.

'Tired, darling?'

'Yes, a little.'

'That woman has worn you out with talking. She oughtn't to talk so much.'

'No.' Her head shifted wearily in the cushions. 'All about that horrible case. I don't like hearing about such things.'

'Of course not. Still, when a thing like that happens in the neighbourhood, people will gossip and talk. It would be a relief if they caught the woman. One doesn't like to think –'

'I don't want to think of anything so hateful. She must be a horrible creature.'

'Horrible. Brookes was saying the other day—'

'I don't want to hear what he said. I don't want to hear about it at all. I want to be quiet. I want to be quiet!'

He recognized the note of rising hysteria. 'Tiddleywinks shall be quiet. Don't worry, darling. We won't talk about horrors.'

No. It would not do to talk about them.

Ethel went to bed early. It was understood that on Sundays Mr Mummery should sit up till Mrs Sutton came in. Ethel was a little anxious about this, but he assured her that he felt quite strong enough. In body, indeed, he did; it was his mind that felt weak and confused. He had decided to make a casual remark about the mutilated newspapers – just to see what Mrs Sutton would say.

He allowed himself the usual indulgence of a whisky and soda as he sat waiting. At a quarter to ten he heard the familiar click of the garden gate. Footsteps passed up the gravel – squeak, squeak, to the back door. Then the sound of the latch, the shutting of the door, the rattle of the bolts being shot home. Then a pause. Mrs Sutton would be taking off her hat. The moment was coming. The step sounded in the passage. The door opened. Mrs Sutton in her neat black dress stood on the threshold. He was aware of a reluctance to face her. Then he looked up. A plump-faced woman, her eyes obscured by thick horn-rimmed spectacles. Was there, perhaps, something hard about the mouth? Or was it just that she had lost most of her front teeth?

'Would you be requiring anything tonight, sir, before I go up?'

'No, thank you, Mrs Sutton.'

'I hope you are feeling better, sir.' Her eager interest in his health seemed to him almost sinister, but the eyes, behind the thick glasses, were inscrutable.

'Quite better, thank you, Mrs Sutton.'

'Mrs Mummery is not indisposed, is she, sir? Should I take her up a glass of hot milk or anything?'

'No, thank you, no.' He spoke hurriedly, and fancied that she looked disappointed.

'Very well, sir. Good night, sir.'

'Good night. Oh! by the way, Mrs Sutton—'

'Yes, sir?'

'Oh, nothing,' said Mr Mummery, 'nothing.'

Next morning Mr Mummery opened his paper eagerly. He would have been glad to learn that an arrest had been made over the weekend. But there was no news for him. The chairman of a trust company had blown out his brains, and the headlines were all occupied with tales about lost millions and ruined shareholders. Both in his own paper and in those he purchased on the way to the office, the Lincoln poisoning tragedy had been relegated to an obscure paragraph on a back page, which informed him that the police were still baffled.

The next few days were the most uncomfortable that Mr Mummery had ever spent. He developed a habit of coming down early in the morning and prowling about the kitchen. This made Ethel nervous, but Mrs Sutton offered no remark. She watched him tolerantly, even, he thought, with something like amusement. After all, it was ridiculous. What was the use of supervising the breakfast, when he had to be out of the house every day between half past nine and six?

At the office, Brookes rallied him on the frequency with which he rang up Ethel. Mr Mummery paid no attention. It was reassuring to hear her voice and to know that she was safe and well.

Nothing happened, and by the following Thursday he began to think that he had been a fool. He came home late that night. Brookes had persuaded him to go with him to a little bachelor dinner for a friend who was about to get married. He left the others at eleven o'clock, however, refusing to make a night of it. The household was in bed when he got back but a note from Mrs Sutton lay on the table, informing

him that there was cocoa for him in the kitchen, ready for hotting up.
He hotted it up accordingly in the little saucepan where it stood. There
was just one good cupful.

He sipped it thoughtfully, standing by the kitchen stove. After the
first sip, he put the cup down. Was it his fancy, or was there something
queer about the taste? He sipped it again, rolling it upon his tongue.
It seemed to him to have a faint tang, metallic and unpleasant. In a
sudden dread he ran out to the scullery and spat the mouthful into the
sink.

After this, he stood quite still for a moment or two. Then, with a
curious deliberation, as though his movements had been dictated to him,
he fetched an empty medicine bottle from the pantry shelf, rinsed it
under the tap and tipped the contents of the cup carefully into it. He
slipped the bottle into his coat pocket and moved on tiptoe to the back
door. The bolts were difficult to draw without noise, but he managed
it at last. Still on tiptoe, he stole across the garden to the potting shed.
Stooping down, he struck a match. He knew exactly where he had left
the tin of weed killer, under the shelf behind the pots at the back.
Cautiously he lifted it out. The match flared up and burnt his fingers,
but before he could light another his sense of touch had told him what
he wanted to know. The stopper was loose again.

Panic seized Mr Mummery, standing there in the earthy-smelling
shed, in his dress suit and overcoat, holding the tin in one hand and
the matchbox in the other. He wanted very badly to run and tell somebody what he had discovered.

Instead, he replaced the tin exactly where he had found it and went
back to the house. As he crossed the garden again, he noticed a light
in Mrs Sutton's bedroom. This terrified him more than anything which
had gone before. Was she watching him? Ethel's window was dark. If
she had drunk anything deadly there would be lights everywhere, movements, calls for the doctor, just as when he himself had been attacked.
Attacked – that was the right word.

Still with the same odd presence of mind and precision, he went in,
washed out the utensils and made a second brew of cocoa, which he
left standing in the saucepan. He crept quietly to his bedroom.
Ethel's voice greeted him on the threshold.

'How late you are, Harold. Naughty old boy! Have a good time?'

'Not bad. You all right, darling?'

'Quite all right. Did Mrs Sutton leave something hot for you? She
said she would.'

'Yes, but I wasn't thirsty.'

Ethel laughed. 'Oh! it was *that* sort of party, was it?'

Mr Mummery did not attempt any denials. He undressed and got
into bed and clutched his wife to him as though defying death and hell

to take her from him. Next morning he would act. He thanked God that he was not too late.

Mr Dimthorpe, the chemist, was a great friend of Mr Mummery's. They had often sat together in the untidy little shop of Spring Bank and exchanged views on greenfly and clubroot. Mr Mummery told his story frankly to Mr Dimthorpe and handed over the bottle of cocoa. Mr Dimthorpe congratulated him on his prudence and intelligence. 'I will have it ready for you by this evening,' he said, 'and if it's what you think it is, then we shall have a clear case on which to take action.'

Mr Mummery thanked him, and was extremely vague and inattentive at business all day. But that hardly mattered, for Mr Brookes, who had seen the party through to a riotous end in the small hours, was in no very observant mood. At half past four, Mr Mummery shut up his desk decisively and announced that he was off early, he had a call to make. Mr Dimthorpe was ready for him.

'No doubt about it,' he said. 'I used the Marsh test. It's a heavy dose – no wonder you tasted it. There must be four or five grains of pure arsenic in that bottle. Look, here's the test tube. You can see the mirror for yourself.'

Mr Mummery gazed at the little glass tube with its ominous purple-black stain.

'Will you ring up the police from here?' asked the chemist.

'No,' said Mr Mummery. 'No – I want to get home. God knows what's happening there. And I've only just time to catch my train.'

'All right,' said Mr Dimthorpe. 'Leave it to me. I'll ring them up for you.'

The local train was not fast enough for Mr Mummery. Ethel – poisoned – dying – dead – Ethel – poisoned – dying – dead — the wheels drummed in his ears. He almost ran out of the station and along the road. A car was standing at his door. He saw it from the end of the street and broke into a gallop. It had happened already. The doctor was there. Fool, murderer that he was, to have left things so late.

Then, while he was still a hundred and fifty yards off, he saw the front door open. A man came out followed by Ethel herself. The visitor got into his car and was driven away. Ethel went in again. She was safe – safe! He could hardly control himself to hang up his hat and coat and go in looking reasonably calm. His wife had returned to the armchair by the fire and greeted him in some surprise. There were tea things on the table.

'Back early, aren't you?'

'Yes – business was slack. Somebody been to tea?'

'Yes, young Welbeck. About the arrangements for the Drama Society.' She spoke briefly but with an undertone of excitement.

A qualm came over Mr Mummery. Would a guest be any protection? His face must have shown his feelings, for Ethel stared at him in amazement.

'What's the matter, Harold, you look so queer?'

'Darling,' said Mr Mummery, 'there's something I want to tell you about.' He sat down and took her hand in his. 'Something a little unpleasant, I'm afraid—'

'Oh, ma'am!' The cook was in the doorway.

'I beg your pardon, sir – I didn't know you was in. Will you be taking tea or can I clear away? And oh, ma'am, there was a young man at the fishmonger's and he's just come from Grimsby and they've caught that dreadful woman – that Mrs Andrews. Isn't it a good thing? It's worritted me dreadful to think she was going about like that, but they've caught her. Taken a job as housekeeper she had to two elderly ladies and they found the wicked poison on her. Girl as spotted her will get a reward. I been keeping my eyes open for her, but it's at Grimsby she was all the time.'

Mr Mummery clutched at the arm of his chair. It had all been a mad mistake then. He wanted to shout or cry. He wanted to apologize to this foolish, pleasant, excited woman. All a mistake.

But there had been the cocoa. Mr Dimthorpe. The Marsh test. Five grains of arsenic. Who, then—?

He glanced around at his wife, and in her eyes he saw something that he had never seen before . . .

The Second Step

Margery Sharp

As the car hummed smoothly round the last bend, and as the walls of the villa began to appear through the trees, young Druten put on the brake and dropped to twenty. It was a moment, he felt, to be taken slowly; and from the tail of his eye he could see his wife's small distinguished head lifting eagerly beside him. Slowing down still more, Druten glanced back into the car, where a Chinese manservant and two little boys were wedged among the baggage. One small boy was Chinese, son of the servant, the other American, and son of the master.

'Is this it, Fu Lin?' asked Druten over his shoulder.

Fu Lin nodded. He was quite young, about the same age as his master, but with emotion so wrinkling his face he might have been anything up to a hundred. *Looks just like his father!* thought young Druten suddenly; and for an instant felt himself a child again, borne on a blue-clad shoulder and holding by a ropy tail of hair. . . .

The car turned in under palm trees and followed a wide sandy drive. After the fashion of that coast, the Villa Caterina stood sheerly against the sea, all its gardens in front and at the back only a broad stone terrace over the blue Mediterranean. At the end of the drive, before a loggia of white stone, Druten brought the car to a standstill and helped his wife to get out. They were both a little stiff, but neither of them noticed it; like Fu Lin, they were filled with a deep, an almost sacred emotion. They gazed on the white stone walls, and their hearts thumped within them; for this was their ancestral home that had been in the family for two generations, and it contained, besides the famous picture gallery, an heirloom of such extraordinary interest and value that the Drutens went straight off to look for it before even glancing at the Rembrandts.

For the Rembrandts proved merely what everyone knew already – that Old Man Druten had made money; whereas the cross carved in the stone proved something known to hardly anyone at all – namely, that Old Man Druten had had a redeeming feature.

Of Old Man Druten's early life – until he fetched up East, that is, and married a wife out of the First Four Thousand – the undisputed

facts amounted to no more than these: that between the ages of thirty
and forty he made money in San Francisco, in which city four young
Chinamen, otherwise of good character, made four separate attempts
to assassinate him. All the rest (as his wife's family pointed out) was
mere rumour. With a fine contempt for gossip, Old Man Druten hired
a bodyguard and went on making money. He made it out of drugstores,
at about the same time that the republics of South America were beginning to acquire their taste for Chinese women. The rumours increasing,
Old Man Druten strengthened his bodyguard and opened a new drugstore; but ill-luck was dogging him, for on the very day of opening an
aged Chinaman, said to be grieving for the loss of a daughter, went
and committed suicide on the new marble floor. It was at this point
that Druten showed his mettle. He went straight to the old man's son
and offered him the post of valet and body-servant at an extremely
adequate salary. The son mused a while in filial piety, consulted his
gods, and made a number of stipulations, among them being this, that
he should bring along with him his own infant son and heir, a small
boy of two years, yellow as butter and answering, like his sire, to the
name of Fu Lin. Druten agreed: he would have agreed to anything.
Fu Lin pondered again, pushed up the salary by one hundred per cent,
and finally accepted.

   With such an answer to slanderous tongues – the son of the dead man
his most trusted servant – Old Druten spent six months longer in San
Francisco; but though no more attempts were made on his life, the time
was spent chiefly in winding up his various businesses. This he did very
successfully, retiring on an income which placed him well up in the
second flight of American millionaires. He wasn't a Rockefeller, but he
could give his wife Rembrandts. After the marriage, curiously enough
– for Old Druten was scarcely a man of cosmopolitan culture – they
settled in Europe, buying a large, rather beautiful villa on the shores
of the Mediterranean. It had gardens on three sides and at the back
a wide stone terrace, from the end of which a short steep flight of steps
– the second, in those days, unmarked by any cross – ran straight down
to the water. Here Mrs Druten hung her pictures, received the local
aristocracy, and in due course gave birth to a son; and here, after an
uncommonly checkered career, Old Man Druten managed to die, if not
actually in his bed, at any rate in a thoroughly domestic and affecting
manner.

   It happened in this way, that descending the terrace steps late one
night – he was fond of being rowed about when all was still, over the
black and silver waters – his old man's foot slipped on the second stair
and he slid quietly as a fish into the deep of the bay. Fu Lin, who was
already standing in the boat, instantly dived after, crying out as he did
so to arouse the house. His call carried far across the water; a second

later, from both house and village, lights flared suddenly and a confusion
of voices cried from one to the other. Fishing-boats put out, and all night
long Fu Lin dived again and again, until in the early morning he had
to be carried bodily to his bed. He was fainting with exhaustion, but
they had to lock his door; the first time they left him he came dragging
himself forth and prepared to dive again.

But not until three days later was the body found. Nor in the end
did Fu Lin find it, but a lad from a strange fishing-boat who came fresh
and strong and spent one whole afternoon diving from the terrace wall.
He found, not a couple of yards from the foot of the steps, a deep and
unsuspected gully in the rock; and in this gully the body had lain wedged
while the boats passed above and Fu Lin cleft open water. They hauled
Old Man Druten up and buried him under marble in the nearest
Protestant cemetery; and a month later Fu Lin was dead too. He had
done his work, he said, and saw no reason to go on living; but before
he died he sat two consecutive days at the bottom of the terrace stairs,
there carving out, on the second step, a big Christian cross in memory
of his master.

'There it is, James,' said Mrs Druten softly.

They stared down in silence. They had expected it, yet not expected
it, and now there it was, greened over a little by seaweed, but yet an
unmistakable cross cut deep into the rock.

'And if a man's valet doesn't know the truth, who does?' asked Stella
Druten. 'To inspire a devotion like that, James – it just proves he was
good at heart.'

Young Druten drew a long breath. 'I believe I remember it,' he said.
'Anyway, I remember Mother bringing me here, and seeing old Fu Lin
squatted below, and then a day or two later her telling me that he'd
gone away ...' Druten cleared his throat and, reaching up to a big stone
urn, broke off a couple of sprays of sweet geranium. 'What they used
to call a broken heart, I suppose. At any rate the doctors couldn't find
anything wrong. But he died all the same, and his body went back home
in a first-class coffin.'

In the long pause that followed they heard for the first time the light,
regular lapping of the green water. It sounded peaceful, friendly; it
belonged with the still sunlight and the smell of flowers.

Stella Druten slipped her hand through her husband's arm and pressed
it softly. 'As soon as Jimmy's old enough we must tell him too. It's
strange, isn't it? – your father and Fu Lin's, then you and our Fu Lin
himself, and now Jimmy and little Charles ... I wish they'd called him
Fu Lin as well. That makes three generations, James.'

Young Druten nodded. 'I guess it's just how the Southerners must
feel about their old darkies. They look on them as part of the family,
and the darkies feel it too. They – I don't know how it is – they sort

of keep up the family traditions, and Fu Lin's the same. This place, for instance, he loves as though it were his own home; if it hadn't been for him I might never have come back here, but he used to talk about it and remind me of it till he made me homesick too. Mother used to tell me that when she shut up the house and went home he was so broken-hearted that she offered to leave him behind with the caretaker; and he'd have jumped at it, I guess, if he hadn't had me to look after.'

His wife smiled back at him. 'Just how old were you both, honey?'

'I was six and Fu Lin was eight. But he took himself very seriously. His father had told him to look after me, you see, and he was sure going to do it. He did it for the next twelve years at a stretch, right until I went to college; and then as they didn't encourage valets at Harvard, he seized the opportunity to go back to 'Frisco, marry a wife, and beget a son. The day I graduated, back he came, bringing the two-year-old with him, and though he didn't actually put it into words, I gathered that I now had his permission to marry as soon as I liked.'

The pressure of his arm tightened. 'But what about *his* wife?' asked Mrs Druten. 'Didn't she mind being left?'

'I have an idea she died when Charles was born. But somehow their women didn't seem to bother them,' said young Druten simply. 'As long as they have us to look after nothing else counts. We don't deserve it, of course, but there it is; and as an awful consequence, darling, I've an inherited tendency to quote Gunga Din.'

He spoke lightly, but the tale had moved him nevertheless; and as they turned to go he dropped back a moment and with a swift, half-furtive gesture tossed a spray of sweet geranium on to the still water.

Like many other Americans of the same age, class, and fortune, the Drutens had early turned their backs on the land of their fathers. Their true, their spiritual home was Europe, and it was with a genuine sensation of relief that they unpacked their trunks and settled down for life at the Villa Caterina. During the first six months there they made only two excursions, one to Oberammergau and one to Bayreuth: the villa, they said, was too delicious to leave; and all their guests agreed with them. For there were guests by the dozen, many of them French or Italian, but many more from the States; and whereas the French and Italians were always led straight to the picture gallery, the Americans, especially those in a hurry, were swiftly shepherded towards the terrace steps. Old Man Druten was still pretty widely remembered, but the sight of the cross and the tale of his servant's devotion never failed to make their effect. The story would be passed on in Paris, repeated on the boat, and finally spread far and wide through every State in the Union; and of all the visiting troop not one failed to remark on the intriguingly feudal atmosphere provided by Fu Lin and his son.

And indeed, without in any way obtruding themselves, the grave young Chinaman and the little yellow boy attracted at least as much attention as either of the Rembrandts. They shared in Old Druten's romantic history, and indeed were often to be seen during the hour of the siesta, standing side by side at the top of the terrace steps; the boy gazing solemnly downward, and his father explaining, in slow guttural phrases, the meaning of the carved cross. For they still spoke to each other in Chinese, and the Drutens, without understanding a syllable, thoroughly appreciated the exotic effect. Their son, they hoped, might possibly pick up a word or two, for like a royal whipping-boy, little Chinese Charles did lessons with Jimmy Druten, played with him in the garden, and slept next door to the nursery as Fu Lin himself slept next to Jimmy's father. The child was a body-servant in the making, and followed in the steps of his fathers with true Oriental piety.

'The way he just worships Jimmy is getting too ridiculous,' Mrs Druten used to say laughingly; and visitor after visitor, glancing out from the window, would see a little white boy hitting a ball while a little yellow boy scrambled after.

At games in general Charles was stupid and clumsy, his only athletic talent lying in the pitching of stones. He could pitch a smooth round pebble plumb on to a five-franc piece at a distance of thirty paces, and Druten now and then had thoughts that as the lad grew older he might be trained as a bowler and play for the M.C.C. For Druten, unlike his wife, who remained faithful to the Continent, had quickly got past being cosmopolitan and was now inclined to the exclusively British.

The boys also did lessons together, and in the schoolroom too, young Charles moved at a respectful distance behind his companion. Only his hands were clever: with pen or brush he could do anything he pleased, write a flowing Italian script or draw big black ideographs on a scroll of silky paper. His hands then were beautiful, moving with calm, delicate assurance, and handling almost with tenderness the materials of his art. Nor was the tenderness a matter of seeming only, for when, one day towards the end of the fifth month, there was found on the terrace a sea bird with a broken wing, the thin yellow fingers dropped scroll and brushes and worked like magic over the shattered bone. With his father's help little Charles made splints half a match long and bandages a centimetre wide; and presently the bird could walk about the terrace and preen its sound wing. For seven days the improvement continued, but on the eighth, while the boys were at their lessons a rat found and killed it.

So after that Charles had an enemy, and the throwing-stones whizzed vainly two or three times a day.

Thus the pleasant life went on, unique (said the visitors) in its mingling of cosmopolitan culture and the joys of domesticity, until one afternoon an odd thing happened.

It was the hour of the siesta, but Druten, though stretched out on a couch, found himself unable to rest. He got up, drank some water, and went to the window which, like those of all the other principal rooms, looked out over the sea. For perhaps five minutes he stood there, blinking at the sun on the water and wondering whether to lie down again; and then, on the terrace below, something caught his attention.

Impervious as ever to the midday heat, little yellow-skinned Charles had come out of the passage door and was lying in wait for his enemy the rat. He had with him his favourite throwing-stones, a pair of big yellowish pebbles polished and rounded by the sea: and as Druten watched, the boy settled himself in the shadow, motionless as a statue, his eyes roving from edge to edge of the sun-dried shrubs.

He had not long to wait. Almost at once, on the far side of the terrace, a bunch of foliage quivered slightly. It made a compact blot of shadow, vandyked at the edge to a pattern of leaves; and as Druten and the boy watched, the blot began slowly to change shape. One of the leaf-points was stretching itself out, it was whiskered on either side, it had two bright eyes; and soon a whole separate and complete outline had detached itself from the first. The rat was abroad and careless in the noonday sun.

Hardly daring to move, lest the beast should hear and take warning, Druten turned his eyes on the other shadow, till then still motionless as the wall behind it; and in that moment a hand flicked up and the pebble flew. The rat writhed once over and then lay still, while from its broken head a small red blotch crept out over the stone.

'Hough!' grunted Charles.

And Druten, with lips half-open to shout applause, closed them again and held his peace; for there was something in the child's demeanour that seemed to show that the business was not yet finished. Without any sign of triumph the boy came slowly across the terrace, picked up the creature by the tail, and flung it contemptuously into the sea: then squatting down by the bloodstain took out a big single-bladed pocket-knife and began scraping at the stone. For half an hour, never raising his head, he scraped and scraped at the patch between his knees; and when he had finished there was a big Christian cross scratched deep into the rock.

This incident Druten found curiously disturbing. It started during the next few days all sorts of odd speculations, which, because he did not share them with anyone, gradually took possession of his mind. It bothered him, for instance, that the same symbol should have been used to commemorate both friend and enemy, and turning this problem idly in his head, he presently found himself embarked on a second train of thought at least as disturbing as the first. He began to recollect certain vague but unsavoury rumours, which in San Francisco at any rate

seemed still to cling about his father's name. Young Druten had visited
that city but once when, at his mother's wish, he set up the Druten
Memorial Fountain; and on account of those same malicious whispers
he had not enjoyed his stay. Sheer rumour, of course; but there was
also the witnessed fact of those four attempts on Old Man Druten's life:
which would seem to show that the Chinese population at any rate took
rumour rather seriously. . . .

'Only – the whole thing's fantastic!' said Druten aloud.

It was nearly two in the morning; for once, sitting alone in the big
lounge, he had heard all the household go off to bed. Directly overhead
his wife's footsteps passed gently down the corridor, she was going her
rounds, looking first into the night-nursery, where Jimmy slept, then
into Charles's room next door. Neither boy was awake tonight, for the
footsteps passed on with hardly a pause; and the gentle shutting of her
own door was the last sound in the house.

In the moments that passed while he listened young Druten's thoughts
seemed suddenly to have raced ahead. He had left off at a general
consideration of the San Francisco rumours and now found himself faced
(with no intermediate step that he could remember) by a question so
cut-and-dried in its brutality as to seem more like the fruit of a lifelong
suspicion than a three-days' doubt. The question was this: Given that
Fu Lin the first had entered Old Druten's service with the deliberate
intention of murdering him, why had he waited? Why not have done
it at once, in San Francisco?

Answer: Because in San Francisco Old Druten still had a bodyguard;
because in San Francisco his death would at once have cast suspicion
on the whole Chinese community. Because – more slowly, more reluctantly, the third reason presented itself – because at that time Old Druten
had not yet begotten a son.

'I'm going crazy,' young Druten assured himself. 'I've got a touch
of the sun. . . .'

In the hall outside a clock chimed the hour. Grateful as at the lifting
of a spell, he pulled himself out of the chair, loosened his shoulders,
and with a conscious effort directed his mind to the tidying of the room.
Two o'clock in the morning – just the time for wild imaginings! He
plumped up a cushion, straightened a chair: the servants in the morning
would be surprised at such neatness.

But his mind was not to be controlled by the folding of a paper; it
had wandered twenty-odd years back, to the night on the terrace when
Old Druten met his end. An impressive scene it was, with lights and
outcry and a faithful servant hurling himself again and again into the
waters of the bay; but for its earliest and most crucial moments – for
what really happened first on the steps and then under water, where
Fu Lin could swim like a fish – for all that there was only Fu Lin's

own word. No one had doubted it; no one had asked, for example, any questions about times; and with a margin of no more than a few minutes, the old man might have been drowned and dead and wedged into the gully before even the alarm was sounded.

'Fantastic!' said young Druten again.

He picked up a handkerchief of his wife's, a picture-book of Jimmy's: from the handkerchief came a faint smell of chypre, but for the first time since his marriage the perfume brought no thought of Stella. At last all was neat, and with a final look behind him, Druten went out into the hall and closed the door. In the extreme stillness the clock ticked heavily. It now showed a quarter past: but instead of going upstairs, he took a lantern in his hand and went down the passage to the terrace door.

Outside it was silent too, and so dark that Druten's lantern seemed to cast no more light than a Christmas candle. The smell of the sea, however, came strong and fresh, clearing his brain and sharpening his senses; and almost as readily as in broad daylight, he crossed the terrace to the head of the stairs. Half-way down he stopped and, leaning a little forward, swung a yellow disk of light over the last two steps. The last of them, water-lapped, showed green with seaweed; and on the second Fu Lin's cross sprawled like a scar.

Irrationally, yet with increasing force, he had felt as though an actual view of the thing would help to settle his mind; and in this his instinct had been right, for suddenly, as he stood there, all doubts were removed, and as surely as though he had seen it he knew now what had passed. The old man fumbling at the step, Fu Lin not in the boat, as he had said, but following behind: and then the single broad ripple, the single parting of the water, as two bodies intertwined slid gently into its depths....

He must have known about that gully before, thought young Druten presently.

And after a little interval – for his mind was as though numbed – another thought came to him: that there was still in the house Fu Lin the second, and not only Fu Lin, but Fu Lin's son, little Christian Charles, who slept in the room next to Jimmy....

I must go back and give warning, thought Druten quickly.

The faintest of sounds made him turn his head. On the topmost step, between him and the house, a Chinaman was standing.

The Case of Arnold Schuttringer

Georges Simenon

The examining magistrate M. Froget sat behind his desk in a most uncomfortable-looking attitude, one shoulder higher than the other, his head hunched forward.

As always, he was all black and white – the white of his skin, of his hair, and of his meticulously ironed linen; the black of his formally cut suit.

It must be admitted that he appeared rather dated. People often wondered if he had not yet reached the age limit; he had seemed sixty for a good five years now.

I have been a guest in his home on the Champ de Mars, and I should like to attempt a personal impression. No man has ever more thoroughly crushed me, more completely undermined my opinion of myself, than M. Froget.

I would tell him a story. He would look at me in a manner that one might take for encouraging. I would finish. I would wait for a remark, a comment, a smile.

He would contemplate me as he might contemplate a landscape or Exhibit A, and at last he would let out a very small sigh. I swear it's enough to make you humble for the rest of your days. Nothing but a sigh! A bit of air! And the free translation would run, 'So you went to all this trouble to tell me that!'

Just so now he contemplated the prisoner, Arnold Schuttringer.

'First of all, Monsieur le Juge, I wish to state—'

'Nothing! You will answer my questions.'

M. Froget uttered these words with a terrible calm. Throughout the questioning he was to remain motionless, his left shoulder hunched higher than his right. His forehead rested on his hand. It was a white hand, almost like wax.

Arnold Schuttringer never took his large bulging eyes off the magistrate. They inspired dislike, those eyes, even a strange revulsion.

Age, thirty. Height, one metre eighty centimetres. Too well fed, or more exactly, bloated. The lips were characteristic. Their edges were thick and firm. They looked like fruit ripe to bursting.

There was nonetheless something unhealthy about the flesh of his face. It was too white, in spite of the red on the cheeks, which suggested make-up.

Hair blond, cut very short. Sparse eyebrows. A grey suit tailored too tight, fitting closely all over and making his muscles stand out as though padded.

M. Froget spoke, leaning over his papers. He sounded as though he read a meticulously studied lesson.

'You were born at Zurich, were you not, of a German father and an Austrian mother? Do not stop me unless I make a mistake. At first you studied chemistry at the University of Nuremberg. At twenty-three you changed your mind and began the medical course at Bonn. Why did you suddenly decide to continue your studies at Paris?'

'Because at Bonn, which is exclusively a university town, it was hard to earn my living while I studied.'

'Your parents never sent you money?'

'My father died ten years ago. My mother is governess with an English family; she earns only enough to keep herself.'

'What made you decide to take up medicine?'

'Personal taste.'

'You have stated in previous depositions that you did not intend to practise.'

'Quite correct. I'm a laboratory man.'

'And you volunteered to do preparation for the amphitheatre. In other words, it is you who cut up the bodies to be dissected.'

'Still correct.'

'For two years you have been employed in the Pharmacie Centrale in the Place Blanche. You start work at eight in the evening and leave at eight in the morning. It is an all-night drugstore. You rarely appear in the shop itself. You use a small office with a couch. When an urgent prescription is handed in, the sales clerk wakes you and you fill it in the laboratory. Why should the proprietor of the drugstore have employed you rather than a licensed pharmacist and a Frenchman?'

'Because I was willing to take half the regular salary. For that consideration, it was understood that I could study while I was on duty and use the lab for my own experiments.'

'From eight to eight, you were alone on the premises with Mme Joly, whose place was in the shop. Around one in the morning, she would prepare coffee for you and serve it in your office. You were her lover.'

'So they say.'

'One of the cleaning women arrived early one morning and surprised you *in flagrante*.'

'If you insist.'

'Mme Joly was thirty-five. Her husband was and still is surveyor

for an architect. He is a man of violent disposition. He was very jealous
and had for some time suspected the truth. In the last few weeks he
has several times appeared unexpectedly at night. Is this correct?'

'So you say.'

'At other times Mme Joly has seen him in the street, spying about.
He has told his colleagues that eventually the affair must end by the
death of both of you.'

'I know nothing of that.'

'The night of the fourth to fifth, you and Mme Joly were on duty
as usual. From evening to morning, there were exactly thirteen
customers. The cash register bears witness to that. Twice you were called
to fill prescriptions. At eleven-thirty Joly, who had been to the movies,
came to see his wife and noticed you through the open door of the office.
He did not speak to you. At two in the morning, a dancer from a cabaret
in the Rue Pigalle appeared and waited for several minutes alone in
the shop. She states that the shop girl, when she finally arrived, was
dishevelled and highly flushed.'

Schuttringer drew his fleshy lips into a scornful smile. 'Is that all?'
he asked.

Usually Mme Joly left around seven, so that she would be home
before her husband awoke. You would stay there alone for a quarter
of an hour until the cleaning women came. On the fifth, Mme Joly
waited for the day staff and did not leave the drugstore until eight
o'clock. You were lying down in the office. When someone opened the
door, you pretended to rouse yourself from a deep sleep.'

'I appreciate that "pretended"!' Schuttringer was sarcastic. 'I suppose
you have established that fact by strict scientific method?'

'When the day staff arrived, Mme Joly was already wearing her
street coat. She left on foot, headed for the Place Clichy where she regularly took the streetcar. You waited for your employer. After ex-
changing a few words with him, you went to your room in the Rue
Monsieur-le-Prince, and then to the dissecting room.'

It was all flat monotony. No emotion. No sensation of combat. On
the one hand M. Froget coldly reciting his lesson. On the other
Schuttringer never taking his large suspicious eyes off the magistrate.

'At nine, M. Joly came to the drugstore. His wife had not come home,
and he demanded your address. The proprietor, thinking him too
excited, did not dare give it to him. Despairingly, the surveyor spent
the morning hunting for you all over the medical college. A laboratory
assistant warned you in time, and you left by a side door, warning him
not to give out your address. You admit this?'

Schuttringer shrugged his shoulders.

'At five in the afternoon, the drugstore received an unexpected order and one of the clerks had to go down into the basement. Not finding what he wanted, he went on into the "reserve," a basement compartment smaller than the others where they keep dangerous items, particularly acids. Behind a pile of candy boxes, he saw some sacks that were out of place. He went to pick them up and let out a cry of pain. The sacking was soaked with vitriol. A little later, after an alarm had been given, they found under the sacks the body of a woman, cut into three pieces, and already badly eaten away by sulphuric acid.

'You know the results of the autopsy. Death less than twenty-four hours previously. The scraps of clothing that were left tallied with the clothes which Mme Joly had worn the preceding night. Same age. Same height. Same figure. M. Joly identified the remains. He accused you without hesitation, and if the police had not protected you, he would have killed you when you were confronted with him.'

'The drugstore has only one entrance, hasn't it?' said Arnold Schuttringer slowly. 'Allow me to point out to you, moreover, that I had no motive for killing Mme Joly. There's one thing, among various others, that your investigation hasn't brought out: From her percentage on the sales, she gave me about two hundred francs a month.' He said this calmly. Not a trace of embarrassment or self-reproach.

As though he had not heard these last remarks, M. Froget replied, 'True, there is only one door. And from eight o'clock in the morning on, there was always someone in the drugstore. Besides, we have reconstructed your actions on the fifth, and it is established that you did not return to the Place Blanche.'

'Which proves—' the prisoner began. He was becoming aggressive.

But at the answer, cold and strong as falling hail, he lost his assurance.

'Which proves nothing!'

No words could do justice to the detachment of M. Froget.

Most examining magistrates pile up question upon question, deafening the prisoner until he finally blurts forth some phrase that constitutes a confession.

M. Froget, on the contrary, left the prisoner time to reflect, and even time to reflect too much. His silences lasted many minutes, his questions hardly as many seconds.

This five-minute silence seemed like an intermission. And when the curtain went up again, Arnold Schuttringer was less sure of himself.

M. Froget's attitude had likewise changed. His voice was more biting. His hands held an ivory paper cutter which he kept bending so far that the other mechanically watched for the moment when it would snap.

'You will please reply "yes" or "no" to the remaining questions. At Bonn you were involved in a scandal which has never been cleared up and which cost the lives of a young man of seventeen and a girl of sixteen. Is this true?'

'One fourth of the faculty were likewise involved. There were doubtless good reasons for hushing up the affair.'

'You stated several months ago to a girl newly employed in the drugstore that a woman who had once known you could not do without you.'

Schuttringer blushed imperceptibly and tried to smile, but achieved only a strained grimace.

'Mme Joly has boasted that thanks to you she learned to take cocaine.'

'There are thirty or forty thousand of us here in Paris who—'

'I am not questioning your morals, only your actions. Did you serve one or more customers on the night of the fourth to fifth?'

'I filled two prescriptions.'

'Did you go into the shop proper?'

'No!'

'Then you did not ring up any sales? And all figures on the cash register were recorded by Mme Joly?'

Schuttringer was silent – puzzled, defiant, vaguely disquieted.

'Thirteen sales gave a registered total of ninety-six francs, twenty-five centimes. Two of these sales were the prescriptions which you filled. Ten others represent sales across the counter. The thirteenth . . .'

There was a silence. Schuttringer did not move. He frowned, and his eyes bulged more than ever. You could see that he was vainly trying to understand.

'The thirteenth item registered is five francs, seventy-five centimes. This sum, according to the formal testimony of the proprietor, can refer only to a box of absorbent cotton B. There is no other merchandise in the shop that costs five seventy-five.'

Another silence, M. Froget moved his papers about.

'Did you sell any absorbent cotton?'

'I never set foot in the shop.'

'Not one box of cotton left the shelves that night. This is all the easier to check because a carton was opened the day before, and all the boxes are still there.'

'Which proves . . . ?'

'That on the morning of the fifth there was five seventy-five too much in the cash register. That is all. Five francs, seventy-five centimes which had been rung up on the machine, which had been put in the cash drawer, but which did not represent any sale of merchandise.'

Schuttringer shifted about on his chair.

M. Froget's voice was dry, his attitude so stern and cutting that the prisoner lost all assurance.

'The body could not have reached the basement without your knowledge and consent. Only one door, as you yourself emphasized. During the day, many people constantly in the shop which one would have to cross. At night, only you and Mme Joly, who belongs to you body and soul.

'Therefore, crime or complicity on your part. At any rate, a strong presumption thereof.'

The rest was short. M. Froget recognized that his adversary was intelligent enough to lose no link of an extremely condensed chain of reasoning.

'On the fifth, Mme Joly waits for the day staff before leaving. This is still under the heading of presumptions. She waits only because she needs to be seen. Or rather, you need to have her seen. After that, it will seem mathematically impossible to convict you.

'The crime has already been committed. The body is in the basement, soaked in vitriol. On the evening of that same day, the experts place the time of death as almost twenty-four hours previously.

'Conclusion: the body is not that of Mme Joly.

'Five seventy-five too much in the cash register. Now neither you nor your mistress had any reason to go putting money in there, simply to create a confusing anomaly.

'*There had been a purchase. But the article was not taken out of the shop.*

'It must be the absorbent cotton. A young woman comes into the shop, receives her merchandise, and pays for it. She is then lured into the back room, killed, cut apart, and stowed away in the basement under sacks soaked in acid.

'But Mme Joly makes the slip of putting the cotton back on the shelf, that cotton which has been bought but which still has not left the shop, because the purchaser herself has not left.

'Which might be called a mechanical proof.'

With a vulgar gesture Schuttringer rubbed his hand along his thick and greasy neck and said, 'Some head you've got there! You must be proud.'

But M. Froget was no longer listening. He was writing in his tensous notebook, with a pen so fine that, guided by any hand other than his, it might have torn the paper.

'Joly jealous, and become dangerous. Hard to kill him without risks. And the lovers, for obscure reasons, need each other.

'So instead Mme Joly shall apparently die. They wait until, when they are alone at night, a customer turns up whose appearance corresponds more or less with hers. Murder. Change of clothing. Vitriol.

'At eight Mme Joly waits for the day staff *in her street coat*, to hide the dress that is not hers.

'She disappears and waits for her lover at some prearranged rendezvous.'

Across these lines I have read a note written later in red ink:
'Died at Salpêtrière Hospital of general paresis, a year after acquittal for lack of criminal responsibility.'

The People Next Door

Pauline C. Smith

'Well, how are you getting along with your new neighbour?' Ed asked.

Evelyn looked down at the knitting in her lap. 'All right,' she said.

'I talked with her a few minutes before dinner, while I was out in the yard. They used to live in California, she said. Seemed like a nice, ordinary woman.'

Evelyn held up the wool, inspected it. 'She did?'

'You like her all right, don't you?'

'I guess so.'

'It gives you someone for company during the day. Keeps you from thinking about yourself too much,' he persisted.

'I don't see her much. Sometimes I talk to her when she's hanging the wash on the line.'

'Well, it's good for you,' he said briskly, the clinical look taking over his face.

Evelyn picked up the wool again and clicked the needles. The knitting was a form of prescription.

'She hangs out her washing as if she was angry at it,' she said. 'She puts the clothespins on the shirts as if she were stabbing them.'

'Evie!' His tone was sharp.

'Well, she does,' Evelyn persisted. 'Maybe it's because there's so many shirts. Fourteen of them. Two clean shirts every day. Perhaps her husband has a phobia about clean shirts.'

Ed rattled his newspaper as he lowered it.

'Evie,' he said, 'you mustn't imagine things! You mustn't try to find phobias and neuroses in everything anybody does. It isn't healthy. I should think you'd have had enough of analysing and being analysed all this last year since your breakdown.'

Evie thought of the washing erupting convulsively on to the line as the woman next door hung up each garment with controlled violence.

'Maybe she's tired of washing and ironing so many shirts every week,' she said. 'Maybe she's sick to death of it. Maybe that's why she seems to be stabbing the shirts with the clothespins.'

'Evie, you're almost well now!' Ed was speaking with forced calm. 'You can't afford to let your imagination run away about every simple little thing. It isn't healthy. You'll have a relapse.'

'I'm sorry, Ed.' She picked up the wool again. 'I won't imagine things.'

'That's a good girl.' He relaxed. 'She tell you what her husband does?'

'He's a salesman,' Evelyn said, needles clicking. 'He sells cutlery to restaurants – knives and cleavers and things.'

'You see?' Ed remarked. 'Salesmen have to be neat. That's why he wears so many shirts.'

'Is it?' Evelyn studied the sweater. The grey wool was very unexciting. She decided she would work a little pattern into it – red, maybe. 'Have you ever seen him?'

'No.' Ed removed his glasses and polished them. 'Have you?'

'Every morning. He leaves for work a little while after you do. His car is parked in their driveway, right by our kitchen window. I see him while I'm doing the breakfast dishes.'

Ed turned the pages of his newspaper to the sport section. 'What's he like?'

'He's very tall and thin. His mouth is thin, like a knife. He wears grey all the time. He makes me think of a grey snake.'

'Evie!' Ed's voice was angry now. 'Stop that!'

'All right.' She stood up. 'I guess I'll go to bed now.'

In her bedroom, she stood for a moment at the window. There was a light on next door – one window was an orange oblong. She got into bed, took a nembutal, and fell asleep.

Over the clean suds of dishwater each morning she saw the man next door appear, stride quickly to his car, and get in with his sample case – tall, his features as sharp as the knives he sold, his eyes hooded. Then the car would start, rattle off, and he would be gone.

Through her brief appearances in the backyard, Evelyn grew to know the woman; by her long strides to the refuse can where she would clatter the lid off, throw in her paper-wrapped bundle with an over-arm motion, clang the lid back; by her short, fierce tussle with a garment on the clothesline; by her soliloquy as she talked to herself, the words inaudible but the tone clear – sometimes a grumbling complaint and sometimes a violently fierce monologue. Evelyn grew to know her, she felt quite well. And sometimes at night she would hear sounds from next door. Not very loud sounds; not conversation. Muffled sounds. You would have to use imagination to say they were sounds of anger, or perhaps of pain. And she had promised Ed not to let herself imagine things ...

When the car had been sitting in the driveway for two days, she mentioned it to Ed. He lowered his paper.

'Oh?' he said politely. 'Is he sick?'

'Maybe he is. I haven't seen her either.'

'You'd better go over, hadn't you? Maybe they're both sick.'

'No. I don't want to go over there.'

He glanced at his paper, then at his wife. 'Why not? You've talked to her. It would be the kind thing to do.'

Evelyn bent over her occupational therapy, the knitting on her lap. 'She might think I was snooping.'

Aggravation and indulgence struggled in Ed's face. At last, he said mildly. 'I don't think she'd think that.'

'She might.'

Through one more day without backyard clangour, Evelyn listened and watched while the house next door slept.

On the next day the woman next door emerged to hang out her washing. She no longer moved with a controlled fury. She handled the pieces of wash, even the shirts, as if they were fabric, inanimate and impersonal – no longer as if she wrestled a hated opponent.

Stepping to the dividing fence, Evelyn rested her hands on the palings. She leaned over. 'I see your husband's car in the driveway . . .' she began.

The words seemed to filter slowly through the other woman's mind, to arrange themselves in her brain to make a sense which startled her. She looked at the car, then back at Evelyn.

'He took a trip.' Her expression was suddenly veiled and withdrawn. She wet her lips with the tip of her tongue. 'He's gone off to a convention. It was too far to drive. He took the train and left the car for me.'

'Oh, that's it,' Evie said politely. 'We were afraid he was sick.'

'No, he's not sick. He's not sick at all.'

Abruptly the woman backed away, spare-lipped mouth moving as if to utter further words of explanation that would reduce the unusual to the commonplace. Then she turned, stepped through her back door and locked it behind her.

'The man next door is out of town,' Evelyn told Ed that evening.

He smiled. 'So you went over, after all.'

'No.'

'Oh? You talked to her, though?'

'Yes. I talked to her.' Evelyn bent over her knitting. 'She took the car and went away this afternoon.'

Rustling the paper, Ed settled to read.

'She wasn't gone long. When she came back, she had two big dogs in the car with her.'

He lowered the paper. 'She did?'

'Two big thin dogs,' described Evelyn. 'She tied them in the backyard using the clothesline to tie them to the clothes pole. She had a big wash this morning and after it dried, she went and got the dogs and tied them with the clothesline.'

'Maybe she's scared while her husband's gone. And she got them for watchdogs.'

'Maybe.'

Now Evelyn felt ready to give up the nembutal she had used to get her to sleep all these months. Pushing the little bottle of sleeping tablets far back on the bedside table, she lay down. She thought of the woman next door, the dogs, and the car in the driveway ... the woman, the dogs, and the car ...

At last, she rose to pace through the darkened house.

Standing at the kitchen window, she looked out at the night to see a button of light cross the yard next door. Her eyes followed it. She heard a plop, a snarl, and a growl – then the gulping, snuffling sound of hunger being satisfied. The light made an arc and moved back to the house and was lost.

For a long time she stood at the window, then she went to her bedroom, took a nembutal, and fell asleep ...

'She doesn't like the dogs,' Evelyn told Ed several days later.

'She doesn't have to. They're watchdogs, not pets.'

'She walks them every day. She unties their ropes from the clothes pole and goes off with them. When she comes back, she's tired and the dogs are tired. Then after dark she gives them a big dinner.'

Evie thought of them, the slip-slap drag of the animals, their lolling tongues – the fatigued tread of the woman, her face drained of everything but lassitude. Of the way she retied them to the clothes pole, knotting, knotting, and reknotting the ropes while they lay, eyes closed, panting, satiated.

'What does she say about her husband? Seems to me that convention is lasting awfully long.'

'She doesn't say anything. She just walks the dogs. Walks them and feeds them.'

Ed laid down his paper. 'Evie,' he said, 'don't you talk with her any more?'

Holding the needles tightly, Evelyn looked at him. 'I don't see her to talk with her. She just walks the dogs. She doesn't hang anything on her line any more because she doesn't have any line. She doesn't seem to do anything in the yard except untie the dogs and tie them up again.'

'Well, that's too bad. I wanted you to have some company. Maybe you could walk ...'

'No! I don't want to walk with her or the dogs.' Evelyn dropped the knitting on the chair as she left for bed ...

Filled with torpor, the dogs were quiet now, lazy, growing fat as they

502 Pauline C. Smith

ambled reluctantly at the end of their rope leashes, to crawl back and lie somnolent.

Eveyln was knitting quietly. The sweater was almost finished; the drab, uninteresting sweater with the bright little pattern of scarlet she had added. 'She took the dogs away in the car today,' she told Ed on Friday.

Ed looked at her óver his glasses. 'She did?'

'And she came back alone. Then she went in the house, got two suitcases, came out, put them in the car, and drove off.'

'Maybe that's why she took the dogs away – she's going on a trip.'

'She's going on a trip all right.'

'Or perhaps the upkeep was too high.' Ed yawned, and polished his glasses, fitted them carefully on his nose. 'She shouldn't have exercised them so much. It made them too hungry.' He opened his paper and placed it across his knees. 'Must have cost her plenty to feed the brutes.'

Evie pulled the needles from the yarn and folded the sweater. She stood. The thing was a pattern, its design all finished.

'I don't think it did,' she said. 'I don't think it cost her hardly anything at all.'

The King of Spades

Nancy Spain

Mind you, I don't think the tennis court was haunted, or any thing soppy like that. No, the court was an ordinary court, promise you: the club, an ordinary club. But that, to my way of thinking, makes it even more horrible. This, as you will understand, is a private matter between me and Doreen. I'm not sure that I ought to tell it. But now that the war is over it has got much, much worse. And I cannot keep it to myself a moment longer.

I was a bank clerk, with prospects, when it all started. I never quite know what prospects *are*, but my Mum was always on about them to my Uncle Henry whenever she went up to London to have lunch with him. Uncle Henry is Mum's rich brother, and he is the only one of our family who is remotely well off. In a way it was he who got me involved in this thing, so you'd better know about Uncle Henry.

It was Uncle Henry who paid for me to go to the Grammar, for example. It was he who took Mum and me away to the seaside after we both had such shocking chest colds that winter when Dad died. And when Mum died it was he who paid for the funeral and everything. And when I married Doreen he gave the bride away. Although he didn't like her much; I never knew why.

So naturally when I turned out to play tennis not so dustily it was Uncle Henry who bought me my flannels and things. Oh, and a new racket before I discovered all the dodgy ways one can get rackets on the cheap. Uncle Henry was mother's favourite brother. And he was proud of his nephew. Ronnie-Boy. That was what he called me, on account of my father having been called Ronnie too.

Well, Uncle Henry had great hopes of me and The Wimbledon, as he called it. I never discovered quite what he did for a living. He was some sort of bookmaker, I think. Anyway, he was mad keen on sport, and my winning a few little potty tournaments decided him. Other young men went around playing in tournaments all over England, did they? So should Ronnie-Boy. I was at a bit of a loose end when mother died and the idea was it would take me out of myself.

I was about eighteen at the time and I'd like to know what kid of that age could withstand an offer like that? A real old ego-booster Uncle Henry was, I assure you. But it was while I was away, playing in Hampshire and Sussex and Cornwall and Scarborough and such places, that I met Janice. That was the trouble.

Until I met Janice there had never been any girl in my life other than Doreen. We lived in houses side by side (that was before the war and the doodle-bugs destroyed that little row of semi-detached up there by the golf course), and we went to the pictures together. She even mothered me and darned my socks and gave me the best bits of the chicken etcetera. For I always ate with her (she was an only child, too) and she was a super cook in those days. The only thing Doreen and I didn't do together was play tennis. She was hopeless at all sports, as a matter of fact, except swimming. She was a very good swimmer, Doreen. But we shared all our secrets, and did all our prep together when we were kids. She was jolly good at some things, maths, for example. And we both got jobs in this branch of the bank together. Travelled up to town by the same train every morning. Lunched together. And by good luck (for me, I mean) worked on the same ledger.

For of course she didn't get all the time off that I got off; and when I was away 'gallivanting' on the tennis court (the manager's word, not mine) she would do double work, hers and mine. So no-one ever knew how hopeless I was at it ... I suppose I had been taking advantage of Doreen's affection for me *and* taking it for granted for a long time before I met Janice.

I met Janice at Scarborough and we played together there quite by chance. She was a rich girl. Rich, that is, in that she had £500 a year of her own and a dirty great car. (It was quite a small car, really, but when you have hardly got the price of a third-class railway fare to the next tournament every car is a dirty great car.) We won at Scarborough. So what could be more natural than that she should give me a lift to the next tournament? To save my rail fare, of course. And she wouldn't let me pay my share of the petrol either. A most domineering, un-domesticated, fascinating personality: Janice.

I don't remember the colour of her hair, or her eyes, and anyway what does it matter? that's not what boys find attractive in girls.

She was jolly good fun, although she had an awful temper. And she was a magnificent tennis player. And sexy. Why, she couldn't walk into a milk bar without the milk addicts getting intoxicated. It's no wonder, really, I was infatuated with Janice. I never loved her. I swear I didn't. I loved Doreen all through.

Well, the trouble started when Janice came to stay for Wimbledon. It was considered improper in our suburb for her to stay in *my* house, so she stayed with Doreen, which was an awful bore as we kept on having to go out in the evenings as a threesome and the two of them just didn't *mix*. Doreen was obviously pleased that my tennis was so good and that Janice and I had won so many events together, but she was downright rude to Janice over tea one evening. She had taken it very hard, I gather, when Janice leant back and lit a cigarette and allowed her to clear away and wash up without doing a hand's turn. Janice simply said 'Come on, Ronald' (that was another thing, Janice always called me Ronald whereas Doreen called me Ron or Ronnie). 'Just time for a knock before the light goes.' Naturally I got up and got my things. Doreen didn't call me either Ron or Ronnie when she ticked me off about my bad manners that week. She was quite right, of course, but I hardly listened, I was so full of tennis practice and Janice. Hard to say which I was keenest on really, Janice or my backhand. We had qualified for Wimbledon, you see, and Uncle Henry was ever so pleased, and you know how something like that at that age *is* your whole life? I am twenty-four now, and of course I think differently.

Perhaps you remember that match of ours against Perry and Miss Round in the third day of Wimbledon? Oh. Well, you ought to. I always forget lots of people don't give a damn about tennis. We didn't beat Perry and Miss Round, of course, but we held them to twenty all in the final set, and the light was getting so bad that the referee asked us to stop and play it off in the morning. Which meant of course we'd be beaten. 'Ah well.' Janice shrugged her lovely golden-brown shoulders. 'Play one game in your life like that and die,' she said. And we all agreed. Everyone remembered her making the remark at the time. It even came out at the inquest. That was why I thought you ought to remember. Because we didn't play it off in the morning. We couldn't. Janice was dead.

Headlines in all the evening papers. She was found drowned in the swimming pool at the King of Spades. She had a big bruise on the side of her head. It was thought she must have dived in and hit her head on something, for her lungs were full of water and she'd drowned. The funny thing is I didn't know she was a bit keen on swimming. But it was a bit hot that evening and she must have gone to get her costume and cool down without a word to anyone. I waited about a bit on the dance floor, but I felt a fool. After a time I got sick of hanging about and I went home. As I had had this argument with Doreen recently about manners I felt I might have done something wrong without knowing it. But I knew nothing until the morning.

Everybody had hysterics except Doreen. Imagine it, we were due on Court – the Centre Court, too – at two o'clock. Can you wonder I had a sort of nervous breakdown and didn't know what was happening? Doreen seemed to get quieter and quieter, but I was quite washed up. I was in bed for a month or two. When I got up I'd lost stones. I did play tennis once or twice, but all the fun had gone out of it for me. Doreen was in and out looking after me all the time. She was everything I had then. No-one was really surprised when I eventually stopped playing altogether. Uncle Henry was disappointed, but even he could see why I was so upset. After all, it's awful for someone so young and gay and beautiful to die. It was an awful shock.

Well, I was even glad of the bank for a while. At least it was still *there*. My clothes hung on me in folds and the manager found out how bad I was at figures, and I was terribly miserable. But then it was September 1939 and there was the war. I joined the RAF, as much to get away from the bank as anything. And Doreen said we were going to have a baby. And I believed her. So we got married and Uncle Henry gave the bride away, like I said.

But almost directly Doreen stopped cooking properly. She just opened tins and things. But I thought it was the war, I didn't think anything of it, and anyway I mostly ate at camp. I thought she was a bit strange when she came to visit me for my forty-eights. When I went home in the winter it was not too bad. But when I had been in the RAF six months I went home for summer furlough and Doreen suggested we should play tennis. Doreen, who hadn't even got a backhand ... or a racket of her own as far as I knew.

'Did you say go down *to the club*?' I said. I could hardly believe my ears. She *had* changed since I'd been away. (Doreen was always so shy.) 'Oh, come on, Ronald. You always used to be so keen.' I just stared at her. 'Tennis?' I said. 'Why, I haven't touched a racket for months. . . .'

'Exactly so. But all your things are on the bed and your tennis shoes are clean and everyone's expecting us. Oh do come *on*, Ronald. It's Mrs Byers' tea day. She always makes super sponge cakes.'

Maybe you wonder why such a simple remark should send a chill down my spine. Doreen couldn't play tennis worth a darn. Not that that mattered, particularly, perhaps on a chap's summer leave she was just trying to be nice: but surely she should know it gave me the horrors? And she had called me Ronald instead of Ron or Ronnie.

I went upstairs to the bathroom and I sat on the edge of the bath. We had one of those dear little houses with a strip of lawn at the back, and a strip of lawn at the front: and we were deeply attached to Mr and Mrs Byers next door. Uncle Henry had put up the money when we got married, and I was paying the instalments out of my marriage allowance. What was wrong? I just didn't know.

I looked out of the window at the big, fat white clouds sweeping up over Surrey, at the fat mauve blossoms shaking in the wind. And I saw the tubby little sunburnt baby boy, two years old, that belonged to Mr and Mrs Byers' eldest daughter, staggering down their crazy paving to the bottom of the garden. It was as though my heart turned over, I loved him so. He was so alive. Yes, that was what was wrong. I went to the top of the stairs and called her. She answered from the kitchen, very off-hand, but civil. I could see my tennis shoes on the hall chest, stiff with blanco, and a white patch where some had fallen on the carpet, and my two rackets in their presses and a new box of Slazenger tennis balls. And my club sweater.

I knew if I went into our bedroom my flannels would be on the bed. I couldn't bear it. I wanted so much that our baby which was on the way should be something to do with Janice. Now, that *is* soppy, I suppose? But lots of people are as sentimental as that, I assure you ... I sat down with a bump on the top of the stairs and called her again. This time she came out of the kitchen, and I got my second shock. She was wearing a nifty little pair of tennis shorts. She looked slender as a fountain pen.

'You're not going to *play*?' I said. 'Doreen?'

'Why not?' she said. 'I've got much better since you've been away flying your kite.'

Now, there again, there is nothing *in* such a remark, is there? Flying my kite is a phrase I always use about myself. Doreen had picked it up from me in the bank, I suppose. But it wasn't *her*, somehow. And I had been away from home a long time. Six months, at least. Six months. That brought me up with a shock again. I looked at her long and hard where she stood, so dainty and elegant at the bottom of the stairs. That was when I realized she must have lied to me about the baby. I needn't have married her at all. Right. I'd show her.

I got up without saying anything to her and went into the bedroom and changed. I've never been so furious in my life. And I didn't speak all the way to the club, either. Nor did I look at her. I couldn't.

It was a lovely day. The sun was hot. But all the joy had gone out of it for me. And the club seemed different. I saw it all very small, as though I had a telescope the wrong way round. I nodded and cracked a half-hearted grin at the secretary, a dear old boy in shrunken yellow flannels, who was dying to hear all about the RAF. Then I went into the pavilion to change my shoes.

I took hours, I remember, tying and untying my laces in the pavilion, because I didn't want to go out on court and look at my wife make a fool of herself. It was dead, the air in there. No fly buzzed on the pane. Nothing moved. Plastic curtains stuck immovable. I was afraid. Every-one else was out enjoying themselves. Their shouting on the courts was faint, muffled, I suppose, by window-panes. I lifted a corner of the warm, horrid curtain and peered out, unobserved, spying on the people at play.

I could see the secretary and his awkward Edwardian serve, playing with two women, knocking a ball about. They were waiting for their fourth to join them. Me. I couldn't move. For out on the court, hitting the ball as hard as she used to hit it, I thought I saw Janice my love, my angel of wickedness. Janice, my girl.

I rubbed my eyes. It was a trick of the light. Or my eyes, perhaps. But it wasn't my eyes, I tell you. My eyes are perfect. I thought it must be my heart then. I wanted to see her so much, to play tennis with her again. It was an agony, walking down the pavilion steps, across the green to join her. I went in a nightmare.

You know how I felt when I found it was only Doreen all the time.

And then we started to play. It was indeed Doreen. Doreen with Janice's forehand. Doreen with Janice's little tricks of bad behaviour. Hustling the opposition. Serving before they were quite ready. Tut-tutting at me under her breath if I missed a ball. And I frequently did, believe me. Can you blame me? I couldn't take my eyes off her. Every little trick was there: holding three balls for serving, showing off. Playing a stroke over again, if she miss-hit one. (She very, very seldom did *that*.) When we had played and won our set I was beside myself. Doreen had always been so bad at games. How could she possibly have learnt to play like this? Then as we came back to the pavilion and I realized for the one hundredth time that nobody at all had been watching us I wasn't surprised that no-one at the club had noticed. They weren't experts, after all. And then I was suddenly annoyed. For an intelligent, sensitive girl like Doreen to have worked up an imitation of Janice's game seemed to me in the worst possible taste. The cake at tea choked me. I didn't know which was worst . . . home with her and her lies, or to stay and remember the grace like a swallow, now ashes in Putney Vale Crematorium. We got home in the end. It was still light. The sun was low though, near to setting. And when it was that she lit a cigarette and sat waiting for *me* to make her a cup of tea, then this thing really hit me. I was cold up and down my spine as I refused to do it.

'Whatever's come over you?' I said. 'This isn't like you. You used to be such a little homebody.'

'*Homebody*,' she said. Her voice had gone as hard as her eyes. 'How dare you, you jumped-up temporary gentleman from a bank—?'

'What's wrong with a bank?' I said. 'Be reasonable. We used to work on the same ledger, didn't we?'

The look in her eyes was so malevolent that I was afraid again.

'Reasonable,' she said. 'Why should *I* be reasonable?'

She stopped looking at me. She looked out of the window instead. She muttered something that sounded as if it were bad enough to find a body like that and a brain like that, but even she'd got better things to do with them than make cups of tea for me. 'Homebody,' she said, again. It seemed to have got right under her skin, that word. Her face completely changed. Her mouth was a different shape. I supposed it was rage. I'd never seen her in a temper before. But she didn't look like

Doreen in a temper. Her eyes blazed and they seemed to belong to someone else.

'Why, Doreen,' I said. 'You look just like Janice.'

'Janice,' she said, and then she started to speak very fast, but she still spaced her words with terrible, mad care. 'Janice. But she was hit on the head with a brick and held under the water in the swimming-pool at the King of Spades until she drowned.'

Then she stopped and gasped. And her hand flew up to her mouth.

'How did you know that?' I asked her. I was in agony. 'How would you know that if you weren't there?'

She tried to say, but she couldn't. She just nodded. And when I held her in my arms later she was cold and yet she burnt me, as iron does in winter time. I knew she would tell me no more lies. I knew it as certainly as I knew that Doreen had murdered Janice over a year ago in the swimming-pool at the King of Spades.

The Portobello Road

Muriel Spark

One day in my young youth at high summer, lolling with my lovely companions upon a haystack, I found a needle. Already and privately for some years I had been guessing that I was set apart from the common run, but this of the needle attested the fact to my whole public, George, Kathleen, and Skinny. I sucked my thumb, for when I had thrust my idle hand deep into the hay, the thumb was where the needle had stuck.

When everyone had recovered George said, 'She put in her thumb and pulled out a plum.' Then away we were into our merciless hacking-hecking laughter again.

The needle had gone fairly deep into the thumb cushion, and a small red river flowed and spread from the tiny puncture. So that nothing of our joy should lag, George put in quickly:

'Mind your bloody thumb on my shirt.'

Then hac-hec-hoo, we shrieked into the hot Borderland afternoon. Really I should not care to be so young of heart again. That is my thought every time I turn over my old papers and come across the photograph. Skinny, Kathleen, and myself are in the photo atop the haystack. Skinny had just finished analysing the inwards of my find.

'It couldn't have been done by brains. You haven't much brains, but you're a lucky wee thing.'

Everyone agreed that the needle betokened extraordinary luck. As it was becoming a serious conversation, George said:

'I'll take a photo.'

I wrapped my hanky round my thumb and got myself organized. George pointed up from his camera and shouted:

'Look, there's a mouse!'

Kathleen screamed and I screamed, although I think we knew there was no mouse. But this gave us an extra session of squalling hee-hoos. Finally, we three composed ourselves for George's picture. We look lovely, and it was a great day at the time, but I would not care for it all over again. From that day I was known as Needle.

*

One Saturday in recent years I was mooching down the Portobello Road from the Ladbroke Grove end, threading among the crowds of marketers on the narrow pavement, when I saw a woman. She had a haggard, careworn, wealthy look, thin but for the breasts forced-up high like a pigeon's. I had not 'seen her for nearly five years. How changed she was! But I recognized Kathleen my friend; her features had already begun to sink and protrude in the way that mouths and noses do in people destined always to be old for their years. When I had last seen her, nearly five years ago, Kathleen, barely thirty, had said:

'I've lost all my looks; it's in the family. All the women are handsome as girls, but we go off early, we go brown and nosey.'

I stood silently among the people, watching. As you will see, I wasn't in a position to speak to Kathleen. I saw her shoving in her avid manner from stall to stall. She was always fond of antique jewellery and of bargains. I wondered that I had not seen her before in the Portobello Road on my Saturday morning ambles. Her long stiff-crooked fingers pounced to select a jade ring from amongst the jumble of brooches and pendants, onyx, moonstone, and gold, set out on the stall.

'What d'you think of this?' she said.

I saw then who was with her. I had been half conscious of the huge man following several paces behind her, and now I noticed him.

'It looks all right,' he said. 'How much is it?'

'How much is it?' Kathleen asked the vendor.

I took a good look at this man accompanying Kathleen. It was her husband. The beard was unfamiliar, but I recognized beneath it his enormous mouth, the bright, sensuous lips, the large brown eyes for ever brimming with pathos.

It was not for me to speak to Kathleen, but I had a sudden inspiration which caused me to say quietly:

'Hallo, George.'

The giant of a man turned round to face the direction of my voice. There were so many people – but at length he saw me.

'Hallo, George,' I said again.

Kathleen had started to haggle with the stall owner, in her old way, over the price of the jade ring. George continued to stare at me, his big mouth slightly parted so that I could see a wide slit of red lips and white teeth between the fair grassy growths of beard and moustache.

'My God!' he said.

'What's the matter?' said Kathleen.

'Hallo, George!' I said again, quite loud this time and cheerfully.

'Look!' said George. 'Look who's there, over beside the fruit stall.'

Kathleen looked but didn't see.

'Who is it?' she said impatiently.

'It's Needle,' he said. 'She said "Hallo George".'

'*Needle*,' said Kathleen. 'Who do you mean? You don't mean our old friend *Needle* who—'

'Yes. There she is. My God!'

He looked very ill, although when I had said 'Hallo George', I had spoken friendly enough.

'I don't see anyone faintly resembling poor Needle,' said Kathleen, looking at him. She was worried.

George pointed straight at me. 'Look *there*. I tell you that is Needle.'

'You're ill, George. Heavens, you must be seeing things. Come on home. Needle isn't there. You know as well as I do, Needle is dead.'

I must explain that I departed this life nearly five years ago. But I did not altogether depart this world. There were those odd things still to be done which one's executors can never do properly. Papers to be looked over, even after the executors have torn them up. Lots of business except of course on Sundays and Holidays of Obligation, plenty to take an interest in for the time being. I take my recreation on Saturday mornings. If it is a wet Saturday, I wander up and down the substantial lanes of Woolworths as I did when I was young and visible. There is a pleasurable spread of objects on the counters which I now perceive and exploit with a certain detachment, since it suits with my condition of life. Creams, toothpastes, combs and hankies, cotton gloves, flimsy flowering scarves, writing paper and crayons, ice-cream cones and orangeade, screwdrivers, boxes of tacks, tins of paint, of glue, marmalade; I always liked them, but far more now that I have no need of any. When Saturdays are fine I go instead to the Portobello Road, where formerly I would jaunt with Kathleen in our grown-up days. The barrow loads do not change much, of apples and rayon vests in common blues and low-taste mauve, of silver plate, trays, and teapots long since changed hands from the bygone citizens to dealers, from shops to the new flats and breakable homes, and then over to the barrow stalls and the dealers again: Georgian spoons, rings, earrings of turquoise and opal set in the butterfly pattern of true-lovers' knot, patch boxes with miniature paintings of ladies on ivory, snuff boxes of silver with Scotch pebbles inset.

Sometimes as occasion arises on a Saturday morning, my friend Kathleen who is a Catholic has a Mass said for my soul, and then I am in attendance as it were at the church. But most Saturdays I take my delight among the solemn crowds with their aimless purposes, their eternal life not far away, who push past the counters and stalls, who handle, buy, steal, touch, desire and ogle the merchandise. I hear the tinkling tills, I hear the jangle of loose change and tongues and children wanting to hold and have.

That is how I came to be in the Portobello Road that Saturday morning when I saw George and Kathleen. I would not have spoken had I not been inspired to it. Indeed, it is one of the things I can't do now – to speak out, unless inspired. And most extraordinary, on that morning as I spoke a degree of visibility set in. I suppose from poor George's point of view it was like seeing a ghost when he saw me standing by the fruit barrow repeating in so friendly a manner, 'Hallo, George!'

We were bound for the south. When our education, what we could get of it from the north, was thought to be finished, one by one we were sent or sent for to London. John Skinner, whom we called Skinny, went to study more archaeology; George to join his uncle's tobacco firm; Kathleen to stay with her rich connections and to potter intermittently in the Mayfair hat shop which one of them owned. A little later I also went to London to see life, for it was my ambition to write about life, which first I had to see.

'We four must stick together,' George said very often in that yearning way of his. He was always desperately afraid of neglect. We four looked likely to shift off in different directions and George did not trust the other three of us not to forget all about him. More and more as the time came for him to depart for his uncle's tobacco farm in Africa he said:

'We four must keep in touch.'

And before he left he told each of us anxiously:

'I'll write regularly, once a month, we must keep together for the sake of the old times.' He had three prints taken from the negative of that photo on the haystack, wrote on the back of them, "George took this the day that Needle found the needle", and gave us a copy each. I think we all wished he could become a bit more callous.

During my lifetime I was a drifter, nothing organized. It was difficult for my friends to follow the logic of my life. By the normal reckonings I should have come to starvation and ruin, which I never did. Of course I did not live to write about life as I wanted to do. Possibly that is why I am inspired to do so now in these peculiar circumstances.

I taught in a private school in Kensington for almost three months, very small children. I didn't know what to do with them, but I was kept fairly busy escorting incontinent little boys to the lavatory and telling the little girls to use their handkerchiefs. After that I lived a winter holiday in London on my small capital, and when that had run out I found a diamond bracelet in a cinema for which I received a reward of fifty pounds. When it was used up, I got a job with a publicity man, writing speeches for absorbed industrialists, in which the dictionary of quotations came in very useful. So it went on. I got engaged to Skinny, but shortly after that I was left a small legacy, enough to keep me for six months. This somehow decided me that I didn't love Skinny, so I gave him back the ring.

But it was through Skinny that I went to Africa. He was engaged with a party of researchers to investigate King Solomon's mines, that series of ancient workings ranging from the ancient port of Ophir, now called Beira, across Portuguese East Africa and Southern Rhodesia to the mighty jungle-city of Zimbabwe, whose temple walls still stand by the approach to an ancient and sacred mountain, where the rubble of that civilization scatters itself over the surrounding Rhodesian waste. I accompanied the party as a sort of secretary. Skinny vouched for me, he paid my fare, he sympathized by his action with my inconsequential life although when he spoke of it he disapproved. A life like mine annoys most people; they go to their jobs every day, attend to things, give orders, pummel typewriters, and get two or three weeks off every year, and it vexes them to see someone else not bothering to do these things and yet getting away with it, not starving, being lucky as they call it. Skinny, when I had broken off our engagement, lectured me about this but still he took me to Africa knowing I should probably leave his unit within a few months.

We were there a few weeks before we began inquiring for George, who was farming about four hundred miles away to the north. We had not told him of our plans.

'If we tell George to expect us in his part of the world, he'll come rushing to pester us the first week. After all, we're going on business,' Skinny had said.

Before we left, Kathleen told us, 'Give George my love, and tell him not to send frantic cables every time I don't answer his letters right away. Tell him I'm busy in the hat shop and being presented. You would think he hadn't another friend in the world the way he carries on.'

We had settled first at Fort Victoria, our nearest place of access to the Zimbabwe ruins. There we made inquiries about George. It was clear he hadn't many friends. The older settlers were the most tolerant about the half-caste woman he was living with, as we learned, but they were furious about his methods of raising tobacco, which we learned were most unprofessional and in some mysterious way disloyal to the whites. We could never discover how it was that George's style of tobacco farming gave the blacks opinions about themselves, but that's what the older settlers claimed. The newer immigrants thought he was unsociable, and of course his living with that nig made visiting impossible.

I must say I was myself a bit offput by this news about the brown woman. I was brought up in a university town where there were Indian, African, and Asiatic students abounding in a variety of tints and hues. I was brought up to avoid them for reasons connected with local reputation and God's ordinances. You cannot easily go against what you were brought up to do unless you are a rebel by nature.

Anyhow, we visited George eventually, taking advantage of the offer of transport from some people bound north in search of game. He had heard of our arrival in Rhodesia, and though he was glad, almost relieved, to see us, he pursued a policy of sullenness for the first hour.

'We wanted to give you a surprise, George.'

'How were we to know that you'd get to hear of our arrival, George? News here must travel faster than light, George.'

'We did hope to give you a surprise, George.'

We flattered and 'Georged' him until at last he said, 'Well, I must say it's good to see you. All we need now is Kathleen. We four simply must stick together. You find when you're in a place like this, there's nothing like old friends.'

He showed us his drying sheds. He showed us a paddock where he was experimenting with a horse and a zebra mare, attempting to mate them. They were frolicking happily, but not together. They passed each other in their private play time and again, but without acknowledgment and without resentment.

'It's been done before,' George said. 'It makes a fine, strong beast, more intelligent than a mule and sturdier than a horse. But I'm not having any success with this pair; they won't look at each other.'

After a while he said, 'Come in for a drink and meet Matilda.'

She was dark brown, with a subservient hollow chest and round shoulders, a gawky woman, very snappy with the houseboys. We said pleasant things as we drank on the stoep before dinner, but we found George difficult. For some reason he began to rail me for breaking off my engagement to Skinny, saying what a dirty trick it was after all those good times in the old days. I diverted attention to Matilda. I supposed, I said, she knew this part of the country well?

'No,' said she, 'I been a-shellitered my life. I not put out to working. Me nothing to go from place to place is allowed like dirty girls does.' In her speech she gave every syllable equal stress.

George explained. 'Her father was a white magistrate in Natal. She had a sheltered unbringing, different from the other coloureds, you realize.'

'Man, me no black-eyed Susan,' said Matilda, 'no, no.'

On the whole, George treated her as a servant. She was about four months advanced in pregnancy, but he made her get up and fetch for him many times. Soap: that was one of the things Matilda had to fetch. George made his own bath soap, showed it proudly, gave us the recipe which I did not trouble to remember; I was fond of nice soaps during my lifetime, and George's smelt of brilliantine and looked likely to soil one's skin.

'D'you brahn?' Matilda asked me.

George said, 'She is asking if you go brown in the sun.'

'No, I go freckled.'

'I got sister-in-law go freckles.'

She never spoke another word to Skinny nor to me, and we never saw her again.

Some months later I said to Skinny.

'I'm fed up with being a camp follower.'

He was not surprised that I was leaving his unit, but he hated my way of expressing it. He gave me a Presbyterian look.

'Don't talk like that. Are you going back to England or staying?'

'Staying for a while.'

'Well, don't wander too far off.'

I was able to live on the fee I got for writing a gossip column in a local weekly, which wasn't my idea of writing about life, of course. I made friends, more than I could cope with, after I left Skinny's exclusive little band of archaeologists. I had the attractions of being newly out from England and of wanting to see life. Of the countless young men and go-ahead families who purred me along the Rhodesian roads hundred after hundred miles, I only kept up with one family when I returned to my native land. I think that was because they were the most representative, they stood for all the rest; people in those parts are very typical of each other, as one group of standing stones in that wilderness is like the next.

I met George once more in an hotel in Bulawayo. We drank highballs and spoke of war. Skinny's party were just then deciding whether to remain in the country or return home. They had reached an exciting part of their research, and whenever I got a chance to visit Zimbabwe he would take me for a moonlight walk in the ruined temple, and try to make me see phantom Phoenicians flitting ahead of us or along the walls. I had half a mind to marry Skinny; perhaps, I thought, when his studies were finished. The impending war was in our bones; so I remarked to George as we sat drinking highballs on the hotel stoep in the hard, bright, sunny July winter of that year.

George was inquisitive about my relations with Skinny. He tried to pump me for about half an hour, and when at last I said, 'You are becoming aggressive, George,' he stopped. He became quite pathetic. He said, 'War or no war, I'm clearing out of this.'

'It's the heat does it,' I said.

'I'm clearing out, in any case. I've lost a fortune in tobacco. My uncle is making a fuss. It's the other bloody planters; once you get the wrong side of them you're finished in this wide land.'

'What about Matilda?' I asked.

He said, 'She'll be all right. She's got hundreds of relatives.'

I had already heard about the baby girl. Coal black, by repute, with George's features. And another on the way, they said.

'What about the child?'

He didn't say anything to that. He ordered more highballs, and when they arrived he swizzled his for a long time with a stick. 'Why didn't you ask me to your twenty-first?' he said then.

'I didn't have anything special, no party, George. We had a quiet drink among ourselves, George, just Skinny and the old professors and two of the wives and me, George.'

'You didn't ask me to your twenty-first,' he said. 'Kathleen writes to me regularly.'

This wasn't true. Kathleen sent me letters fairly often in which she said, 'Don't tell George I wrote to you, as he will be expecting word from me and I can't be bothered actually.'

'But you,' said George, 'don't seem to have any sense of old friendships, you and Skinny.'

'Oh, George!' I said.

'Remember the times we had,' George said. 'We used to have times.' His large brown eyes began to water.

'I'll have to be getting along,' I said.

'Please don't go. Don't leave me just yet. I've something to tell you.'

'Something nice?' I laid on an eager smile. All responses to George had to be overdone.

'You don't know how lucky you are,' George said.

'How?' I said. Sometimes I got tired of being called lucky by everybody. There were times when, privately practising my writings about life, I knew the bitter side of my fortune. When I failed again and again to reproduce life in some satisfactory and perfect form, I was the more imprisoned, for all my carefree living, within my craving for this satisfaction. Sometimes, in my impotence and need I secreted a venom which infected all my life for days on end, and which spurted out indiscriminately on Skinny or on anyone who crossed my path.

'You aren't bound by anyone,' George said. 'You come and go as you please. Something always turns up for you. You're free, and you don't know your luck.'

'You're a damn sight more free than I am,' I said sharply. 'You've got your rich uncle.'

'He's losing interest in me,' George said. 'He's had enough.'

'Oh well, you're young yet. What was it you wanted to tell me?'

'A secret,' George said. 'Remember we used to have those secrets!'

'Oh yes, we did.'

'Did you ever tell any of mine?'

'Oh no, George.' In reality, I couldn't remember any particular secret out of the dozens we must have exchanged from our schooldays onwards.

'Well, this is a secret, mind. Promise not to tell.'

'Promise.'

'I'm married.'

'Married, George! Oh, who to?'

'Matilda.'

'How dreadful!' I spoke before I could think, but he agreed with me.

'Yes, it's awful, but what could I do?'

'You might have asked my advice,' I said pompously.

'I'm two years older than you are. I don't ask advice from you, Needle, little beast.'

'Don't ask for sympathy, then.'

'A nice friend you are,' he said, 'I must say, after all these years.'

'Poor George,' I said.

'There are three white men to one white woman in this country,' said George. 'An isolated planter doesn't see a white woman, and if he sees one she doesn't see him. What could I do? I needed the woman.'

I was nearly sick. One, because of my Scottish upbringing. Two, because of my horror of corny phrases like 'I needed the woman', which George repeated twice again.

'And Matilda got tough,' said George, 'after you and Skinny came to visit us. She had some friends at the Mission, and she packed up and went to them.'

'You should have let her go,' I said.

'I went after her,' George said. 'She insisted on being married, so I married her.'

'That's not a proper secret, then,' I said. 'The news of a mixed marriage soon gets about.'

'I took care of that,' George said. 'Crazy as I was, I took her to the Congo and married her there. She promised to keep quiet about it.'

'Well, you can't clear off and leave her now, surely,' I said.

'I'm going to get out of this place. I can't stand the woman, and I can't stand the country. I didn't realize what it would be like. Two years of the country and three months of my wife has been enough.'

'Will you get a divorce?'

'No, Matilda's Catholic. She won't divorce.'

George was fairly getting through the highballs, and I wasn't far behind him. His brown eyes floated shiny and liquid as he told me how he had written to tell his uncle of his plight. 'Except of course, I didn't say we were married, that would have been too much for him. He's a prejudiced, hardened old colonial. I only said I'd had a child by a coloured woman and was expecting another, and he perfectly understood. He came at once by plane a few weeks ago. He's made a settlement on her, providing she keeps her mouth shut about her association with me.'

'Will she do that?'

'Oh yes, or she won't get the money.'

'But as your wife she has a claim on you, in any case.'

'If she claimed as my wife, she'd get far less. Matilda knows what she's doing, greedy bitch she is. She'll keep her mouth shut.'

'Only, you won't be able to marry again, will you George?'

'Not unless she dies,' he said. 'And she's as strong as a trek ox.'

'Well, I'm sorry, George,' I said.

'Good of you to say so,' he said. 'But I can see by your chin that you disapprove of me. Even my old uncle understood.'

'Oh, George, I quite understand. You were lonely, I suppose.'

'You didn't even ask me to your twenty-first. If you and Skinny had been nicer to me, I would never have lost my head and married the woman, never.'

'You didn't ask me to your wedding,' I said.

'You're a catty bissom, Needle; not like what you were in the old times when you used to tell us your wee stories.'

'I'll have to be getting along,' I said.

'Mind you keep the secret,' George said.

'Can't I tell Skinny? He would be very sorry for you, George.'

'You mustn't tell anyone. Keep it a secret. Promise.'

'Promise,' I said. I understood that he wished to enforce some sort of bond between us with this secret, and I thought, 'Oh well, I suppose he's lonely. Keeping his secret won't do any harm.'

I returned to England with Skinny's party just before the war.

I did not see George again till just before my death, five years ago.

After the war Skinny returned to his studies. He had two more exams, over a period of eighteen months, and I thought I might marry him when the exams were over.

'You might do worse than Skinny,' Kathleen used to say to me on our Saturday morning excursions to the antique shops and the junk stalls.

She, too, was getting on in years. The remainder of our families in Scotland were hinting that it was time we settled down with husbands. Kathleen was a little younger than me, but looked much older. She knew her chances were diminishing, but at that time I did not think she cared very much. As for myself, the main attraction of marrying Skinny was his prospective expeditions in Mesopotamia. My desire to marry him had to be stimulated by the continual reading of books about Babylon and Assyria; perhaps Skinny felt this, because he supplied the books, and even started instructing me in the art of deciphering cuneiform tables.

Kathleen was more interested in marriage than I thought. Like me she had racketed around a good deal during the war; she had actually been engaged to an officer in the US navy, who was killed. Now she kept an antique shop near Lambeth, was doing very nicely, lived in a Chelsea square, but for all that she must have wanted to be married and have children. She would stop and look into all the prams which the mothers had left outside shops or area gates.

'The poet Swinburne used to do that,' I told her once.

'Really? Did he want children of his own?'

'I shouldn't think so. He simply liked babies.'

Before Skinny's final exam he fell ill and was sent to a sanatorium in Switzerland.

'You're fortunate, after all, not to be married to him,' Kathleen said. 'You might have caught TB.'

I was fortunate, I was lucky . . . so everyone kept telling me on different occasions. Although it annoyed me to hear, I knew they were right, but in a way that was different from what they meant. It took me very small effort to make a living; book reviews, odd jobs for Kathleen, a few months with the publicity man again, still getting up speeches about literature, art, and life for industrial tycoons. I was waiting to write about life, and it seemed to me that the good fortune lay in this whenever it should be. And until then I was assured of my charmed life, the necessities of existence always coming my way, and I with far more leisure than anyone else. I thought of my type of luck after I became a Catholic and was being confirmed. The bishop touches the candidate on the cheek, a symbolic reminder of the sufferings a Christian is supposed to undertake. I thought, how lucky, what a feathery symbol to stand for the hellish violence of its true meaning.

I visited Skinny twice in the two years that he was in the sanatorium. He was almost cured, and expected to be home within a few months. I told Kathleen after my last visit.

'Maybe I'll marry Skinny when he's well again.'

'Make it definite, Needle, and not so much of the maybe. You don't know when you're well off,' she said.

This was five years ago, in the last year of my life. Kathleen and I had become very close friends. We met several times each week, and after our Saturday morning excursions in the Portobello Road very often I would accompany Kathleen to her aunt's house in Kent for a long weekend.

One day in the June of that year I met Kathleen specially for lunch because she had phoned me to say she had news.

'Guess who came into the shop this afternoon,' she said.

'Who?'

'George.'

We had half imagined George was dead. We had received no letters in the past ten years. Early in the war we had heard rumours of his keeping a night club in Durban, but nothing after that. We could have made inquiries if we had felt moved to do so.

At one time, when we discussed him, Kathleen had said:

'I ought to get in touch with poor George. But, then, I think he would write back. He would demand a regular correspondence again.'

'We four must stick together,' I mimicked.

'I can visualize his reproachful limpid orbs,' Kathleen said.

Skinny said, 'He's probably gone native. With his coffee concubine and a dozen mahogany kids.'

'Perhaps he's dead,' Kathleen said.

I did not speak of George's marriage, nor any of his confidences in the hotel at Bulawayo. As the years passed, we ceased to mention him except in passing, as someone more or less dead so far as we were concerned.

Kathleen was excited about George's turning up. She had forgotten her impatience with him in former days; she said:

'It was so wonderful to see old George. He seems to need a friend, feels neglected, out of touch with things.'

'He needs mothering, I suppose.'

Kathleen didn't notice the malice. She declared, 'That's exactly the case with George. It always has been. I can see it now.'

She seemed ready to come to any rapid new and happy conclusion about George. In the course of the morning he had told her of his wartime night club in Durban, his game-shooting expeditions since. It was clear he had not mentioned Matilda. He had put on weight, Kathleen told me, but he could carry it.

I was curious to see this version of George, but I was leaving for Scotland next day and did not see him till September of that year just before my death.

While I was in Scotland I gathered from Kathleen's letters that she was seeing George very frequently, finding enjoyable company in him, looking after him. 'You'll be surprised to see how he has developed.' Apparently he would hang round Kathleen in her shop most days – 'it makes him feel useful' as she maternally expressed it. He had an old relative in Kent whom he visited at weekends; this old lady lived a few miles from Kathleen's aunt, which made it easy for them to travel down together on Saturdays and go for long country walks.

'You'll see such a difference in George,' Kathleen said on my return to London in September. I was to meet him that night, a Saturday. Kathleen's aunt was abroad, the maid on holiday, and I was to keep Kathleen company in the empty house.

George had left London for Kent a few days earlier. 'He's actually helping with the harvest down there!' Kathleen told me lovingly.

Kathleen and I had planned to travel down together, but on that Saturday she was unexpectedly delayed in London on some business. It was arranged that I should go ahead of her in the early afternoon to see to the provisions for our party; Kathleen had invited George to dinner at her aunt's house that night.

'I should be with you by seven,' she said. 'Sure you won't mind the empty house? I hate arriving at empty houses myself.'

I said no, I liked an empty house.

So I did, when I got there. I had never found the house more likeable. A large Georgian vicarage in about eight acres, most of the rooms shut and sheeted, there being only one servant. I discovered that I wouldn't need to go shopping, Kathleen's aunt had left many and delicate supplies with notes attached to them: 'Eat this up please do, see also fridge', and 'A treat for three hungry people, see also 2 bttles beaune for yr party on back kn table.' It was like a treasure hunt as I followed clue after clue through the cool, silent domestic quarters. A house in which there are no people – but with all the signs of tenancy – can be a most tranquil, good place. People take up space in a house out of proportion to their size. On my previous visits I had seen the rooms overflowing as it seemed, with Kathleen, her aunt, and the little fat maidservant; they were always on the move. As I wandered through that part of the house which was in use, opening windows to let in the pale yellow air of September, I was not conscious that I, Needle, was taking up any space at all, I might have been a ghost.

The only thing to be fetched was the milk. I waited till after four when the milking should be done, then set off for the farm which lay across two fields at the back of the orchard. There, when the byreman was handing me the bottle, I saw George.

'Hallo, George,' I said.

'Needle! What are you doing here?' he said.

'Fetching milk,' I said.

'So am I. Well, it's good to see you, I must say.'

As we paid the farmhand, George said, 'I'll walk back with you part of the way. But I mustn't stop, my old cousin's without any milk for her tea. How's Kathleen?'

'She was kept in London. She's coming on later, about seven, she expects.'

We had reached the end of the first field. George's way led to the left and on to the main road.

'We'll see you tonight, then?' I said.

'Yes, and talk about old times.'

'Grand,' I said.

But George got over the stile with me.

'Look here,' he said. 'I'd like to talk to you, Needle.'

'We'll talk tonight, George. Better not keep your cousin waiting for the milk.' I found myself speaking to him almost as if he were a child.

'No, I want to talk to you alone. This is a good opportunity.'

We began to cross the second field. I had been hoping to have the house to myself for a couple more hours, and I was rather petulant.

'See,' he said suddenly, 'that haystack.'

'Yes,' I said absently.

'Let's sit there and talk. I'd like to see you up on a haystack again. I still keep that photo. Remember that time when—'

'I found the needle,' I said very quickly, to get it over.

But I was glad to rest. The stack had been broken up, but we managed to find a nest in it. I buried my bottle of milk in the hay for coolness. George placed his carefully at the foot of the stack.

'My old cousin is terribly vague, poor soul. A bit hazy in her head. She hasn't the least sense of time. If I tell her I've only been gone ten minutes, she'll believe it.'

I giggled and looked at him. His face had grown much larger, his lips full, wide, and with a ripe colour that is strange in a man. His brown eyes were abounding as before with some inarticulate plea.

'So you're going to marry Skinny after all these years?'

'I really don't know, George.'

'You played him up properly.'

'It isn't for you to judge. I have my own reasons for what I do.'

'Don't get sharp,' he said, 'I was only funning.' To prove it, he lifted a tuft of hay and brushed my face with it.

'D'you know,' he said next, 'I didn't think you and Skinny treated me very decently in Rhodesia.'

'Well, we were busy, George. And we were younger then; we had a lot to do and see. After all, we could see you any other time, George.'

'A touch of selfishness,' he said.

'I'll have to be getting along, George.' I made to get down from the stack.

He pulled me back. 'Wait, I've got something to tell you.'

'OK, George, tell me.'

'First promise not to tell Kathleen. She wants it kept a secret so that she can tell you herself.'

'All right. Promise.'

'I'm going to marry Kathleen.'

'But you're already married.'

Sometimes I heard news of Matilda from the one Rhodesian family with whom I still kept up. They referred to her as 'George's Dark Lady', and of course they did not know he was married to her. She had apparently made a good thing out of George, they said, for she minced around all tarted up, never did a stroke of work, and was always unsettling the respectable coloured girls in their neighbourhood. According to accounts, she was a living example of the folly of behaving as George did.

'I married Matilda in the Congo,' George was saying.

'It would still be bigamy,' I said.

He was furious when I used that word bigamy. He lifted a handful of hay as if he would throw it in my face, but controlling himself mean-while, he fanned it at me playfully.

'I'm not sure that the Congo marriage was valid,' he continued. 'Anyway, as far as I'm concerned, it isn't.'

'You can't do a thing like that,' I said.

'I need Kathleen. She's been decent to me. I think we were always meant for each other, me and Kathleen.'

'I'll have to be going,' I said.

But he put his knee over my ankles so that I couldn't move. I sat still and gazed into space.

He tickled my face with a wisp of hay.

'Smile up, Needle,' he said; 'let's talk like old times.'

'Well?'

'No one knows about my marriage to Matilda except you and me.'

'And Matilda,' I said.

'She'll hold her tongue so long as she gets her payments. My uncle left an annuity for the purpose; his lawyers see to it.'

'Let me go, George.'

'You promised to keep it a secret,' he said, 'you promised.'

'Yes, I promised.'

'And now that you're going to marry Skinny, we'll be properly coupled off as we should have been years ago. We should have been, but youth – our youth – got in the way, didn't it?'

'Life got in the way,' I said.

'But everything's going to be all right now. You'll keep my secret, won't you? You promised.' He had released my feet. I edged a little farther from him.

I said, 'If Kathleen intends to marry you, I shall tell her that you're already married.'

'You wouldn't do a dirty trick like that, Needle? You're going to be happy with Skinny, you wouldn't stand in the way of my—'

'I must, Kathleen's my best friend,' I said swiftly.

He looked as if he would murder me, and he did; he stuffed hay into my mouth until it could hold no more, kneeling on my body to keep it prone, holding both my wrists tight in his huge left hand. I saw the red full lines of his mouth, and the white slit of his teeth last thing on earth. Not another soul passed by as he pressed my body into the stack, as he made a deep nest for me, tearing up the hay to make a groove the length of my corpse, and finally pulling the warm dry stuff in a mound over his concealmeant, so natural looking in a broken haystack. Then George climbed down, took up his bottle of milk and went his way. I suppose that was why he looked so unwell when I stood, nearly five years later, by the barrow in the Portobello Road and said in easy tones, 'Hallo, George!'

The Haystack Murder was one of the notorious crimes of that year.
My friends said, 'A girl who had everything to live for.'

After a search that lasted twenty hours, when my body was found,
the evening papers said, ' "Needle" is found: in haystack!'

Kathleen, speaking from that Catholic point of view which takes some
getting used to said, 'She was at Confession only the day before she died
– wasn't she lucky?'

The poor byrehand who sold us the milk was grilled for hour after
hour by the local police, and later by Scotland Yard. So was George.
He admitted walking as far as the haystack with me, but he denied
lingering there.

'You hadn't seen your friend for ten years?' the inspector asked him.

'That's right,' said George.

'And you didn't stop to have a chat?'

'No. We'd arranged to meet later at dinner. My cousin was waiting
for the milk, I couldn't stop.'

The old soul, his cousin, swore that he hadn't been gone more than
ten minutes in all, and she believed it to the day of her death a few
months later. There was the microscopic evidence of hay on George's
jacket, of course, but the same evidence was on every man's jacket in
the district that fine harvest year. Unfortunately, the byreman's hands
were even brawnier and mightier than George's. The marks on my wrists
had been done by such hands, so the laboratory charts indicated when
my postmortem was all completed. But the wristmarks weren't enough
to pin down the crime to either man. If I hadn't been wearing my long-
sleeved cardigan, it was said, the bruises might have matched up properly
with someone's fingers.

Kathleen, to prove that George had absolutely no motive, told the
police that she was engaged to him. George thought this a little foolish.
They checked up on his life in Africa, right back to his living with
Matilda. But the marriage didn't come out – who would think of looking
up registers in the Congo? Not that this would have proved any motive
for murder. All the same, George was relieved when the inquiries were
over without the marriage to Matilda being disclosed. He was able to
have his nervous breakdown at the same time as Kathleen had hers,
and they recovered together and got married, long after the police had
shifted their inquiries to an Air Force camp five miles from Kathleen's
aunt's home. Only a lot of excitement and drinks came of those investigations. The Haystack Murder was one of the unsolved crimes that
year.

Shortly afterwards the byrehand emigrated to Canada to start afresh,
with the help of Skinny who felt sorry for him.

After seeing George taken away home by Kathleen that Saturday in the Portobello Road, I thought that perhaps I might be seeing more of him in similar circumstances. The next Saturday I looked out for him, and at last there he was, without Kathleen, half worried, half hopeful.

I dashed his hopes, I said, 'Hallo, George!'

He looked in my direction, rooted in the midst of the flowing market mongers in that convivial street. I thought to myself, 'He looks as if he had a mouthful of hay.' It was the new bristly maize-coloured beard and moustache surrounding his great mouth suggested the thought, gay and lyrical as life.

'Hallo, George!' I said again.

I might have been inspired to say more on that agreeable morning, but he didn't wait. He was away down a side street and along another street and down one more, zigzag, as far and as devious as he could take himself from the Portobello Road.

Nevertheless, he was back again next week. Poor Kathleen had brought him in her car. She left it at the top of the street, and got out with him, holding him tight by the arm. It grieved me to see Kathleen ignoring the spread of scintillations on the stalls. I had myself seen a charming Battersea box quite to her taste, also a pair of enamelled silver earrings. But she took no notice of these wares, clinging close to George, and, poor Kathleen – I hate to say how she looked.

And George was haggard. His eyes seemed to have got smaller as if he had been recently in pain. He advanced up the road with Kathleen on his arm, letting himself lurch from side to side with his wife bobbing beside him, as the crowds asserted their rights of way.

'Oh, George!' I said. 'You don't look at all well, George.'

'Look!' said George. 'Over there by the hardwear barrow. That's Needle.'

Kathleen was crying. 'Come back home, dear,' she said.

'Oh, you don't look well, George!' I said.

They took him to a nursing home. He was fairly quiet, except on Saturday mornings when they had a hard time of it to keep him indoors and away from the Portobello Road.

But a couple of months later he did escape. It was a Monday.

They searched for him in the Portobello Road, but actually he had gone off to Kent to the village near the scene of the Haystack Murder. There he went to the police and gave himself up, but they could tell from the way he was talking that there was something wrong with the man.

'I saw Needle in the Portobello Road three Saturdays running,' he explained, 'and they put me in a private ward, but I got away while the nurses were seeing to the new patient. You remember the murder of Needle – well, I did it. Now you know the truth, and that will keep bloody Needle's mouth shut.'

Dozens of poor mad fellows confess to every murder. The police obtained an ambulance to take him back to the nursing home. He wasn't there long. Kathleen gave up her shop, and devoted herself to looking after him at home. But she found that the Saturday mornings were a strain. He insisted on going to see me in the Portobello Road, and would come back to insist that he'd murdered Needle. Once he tried to tell her something about Matilda, but Kathleen was so kind and solicitous, I don't think he had the courage to remember what he had to say.

Skinny had always been rather reserved with George since the murder. But he was kind to Kathleen. It was he who persuaded them to emigrate to Canada so that George should be well out of reach of the Portobello Road.

George has recovered somewhat in Canada, but of course he will never be the old George again, as Kathleen writes to Skinny. 'That Haystack tragedy did for George,' she writes. 'I feel sorrier for George sometimes than I am for poor Needle. But I do often have Masses said for Needle's soul.'

I doubt if George will ever see me again in the Portobello Road. He broods much over the crumpled snapshot he took of us on the haystack. Kathleen does not like the photograph. I don't wonder. For my part, I consider it quite a jolly snap, but I don't think we were any of us so lovely as we look in it, gazing blatantly over the ripe cornfields – Skinny with his humorous expression, I secure in my difference from the rest, Kathleen with her head prettily perched on her hand, each reflecting fearlessly in the face of George's camera the glory of the world, as if it would never pass.

Blue Murder

Wilbur Daniel Steele

At Mill Crossing it was already past sunset. The rays, redder for what autumn leaves were left, still laid fire along the woods crowning the stony slopes of Jim Bluedge's pastures; but then the line of the dusk began and from that level it filled the valley, washing with transparent blue the buildings scattered about the bridge, Jim's house and horse sheds and hay barns, Frank's store, and Camden's blacksmith shop.

The mill had been gone fifty years, but the falls which had turned its wheel still poured in the bottom of the valley, and when the wind came from the Footstool way their mist wet the smithy, built of the old stone on the old foundations, and their pouring drowned the clink of Camden's hammer.

Just now they couldn't drown Camden's hammer, for he wasn't in the smithy; he was at his brother's farm. Standing inside the smaller of the horse paddocks behind the sheds he drove in stakes, one after another, cut green from saplings, and so disposed as to cover the more glaring of the weaknesses in the five foot fence. From time to time, when one was done and another to do, he rested the head of his sledge in the pocket of his leather apron (he was never without it; it was as though it had grown on him, lumpy with odds and ends of his trade – bolts and nails and rusty pliers and old horseshoes) and, standing so, he mopped the sweat from his face and looked up at the mountain.

Of the three brothers he was the dumb one. He seldom had anything to say. It was providential (folks said) that of the three enterprises at the Crossing one was a smithy; for while he was a strong, big, hungry-muscled fellow, he never would have had the shrewdness to run the store or the farm. He was better at pounding – pounding while the fire reddened and the sparks flew, and thinking, and letting other people wonder what he was thinking of.

Blossom Bluedge, his brother's wife sat perched on the top bar of the paddock gate, holding her skirts around her ankles with a trifle too much care to be quite unconscious, and watched him work. When he looked at the mountain he was looking at the mares, half a mile up the slope, grazing in a line as straight as soldiers, their heads all one way. But Blossom thought it was the receding light he was thinking of, and her own sense of misgiving returned and deepened.

'You'd have thought Jim would be home before this, wouldn't you, Cam?'

Her brother-in-law said nothing.

'Cam, look at me!'

It was nervousness, but it wasn't all nervousness – she was the prettiest in the valley; a small part of it was mingled coquetry and pique.

The smith began to drive another stake, swinging the hammer from high overhead, his muscles playing in fine big rhythmical convulsions under the skin of his arms and chest, covered with short blond down. Studying him cornerwise, Blossom muttered, 'Well, *don't* look at me, then!'

He was too dumb for any use. He was dumb as this: when all three of the Bluedge boys were after her a year ago, Frank, the storekeeper, had bought her candy: chocolates wrapped in silver foil in a two-pound Boston box. Jim had laid before her the Bluedge farm and with it the dominance of the valley. And Camden! To the daughter of Ed Beck, the apple grower, Camden brought a *box of apples*! – and been bewildered too, when, for all she could help it, she had had to clap a hand over her mouth and run into the house to have her giggle.

A little more than just bewildered, perhaps. Had she, or any of them, ever speculated about that? ... He had been dumb enough before; but that was when he started being as dumb as he was now.

Well, if he wanted to be dumb let him be dumb. Pouting her pretty lips and arching her fine brows, she forgot the unimaginative fellow and turned to the ridge again. And now, seeing the sun was quite gone, all the day's vague worries and dreads – held off by this and that – could not be held off longer. For weeks there had been so much talk, so much gossip and speculation and doubt.

'Camden,' she reverted suddenly. 'Tell me one thing; did you hear—'

She stopped there. Some people were coming into the kitchen yard, dark forms in the growing darkness. Most of them lingered at the porch, sitting on the steps and lighting their pipes. The one that came out was Frank, the second of her brothers-in-law. She was glad. Frank wasn't like Camden; he would talk. Turning and taking care of her skirts, she gave him a bright and sisterly smile.

'Well, Frankie, what's the crowd?'

Far from avoiding the smile, as Camden's habit was, the storekeeper returned it with a brotherly wink for good measure. 'Oh, they're tired of waiting down the road, so they come up here to see the grand arrival.' He was something of a man of the world; in his calling he acquired a fine turn for scepticism. 'Don't want to miss being on hand to see what flaws they can pick in "Jim's five hundred dollar's worth of experiment".'

'Frank, ain't you the least bit worried over Jim? So late?'

'Don't see why.'

'All the same, I wish either you or Cam could've gone with him.'

'Don't see why. Had all the men from Perry's stable there in Twinshead to help him get the animal off the freight, and he took an extra rope and the log-chain and the heavy wagon, so I guess no matter how wild and woolly the devil is he'll scarcely be climbing over the tailboard. Besides, them Western horses ain't such a big breed; even a stallion.'

'All the same – (look the other way, Frankie).' Flipping her ankles over the rail, Blossom jumped down beside him. 'Listen, Frank, tell me something; did you hear – did you hear the reason Jim's getting him cheap was because he killed a man out West there, what's-its-name, Wyoming?'

Frank was taking off his sleeve protectors, the pins in his mouth. It was Camden, at the bars, speaking in his sudden deep rough way, 'Who the hell told you that?'

Frank got the pins out of his mouth. 'I guess what it is, Blossie, what's mixed you up is having that name "Blue Murder".'

'No sir! I got some sense and some ears. You don't go fooling me.'

Frank laughed indulgently and struck her shoulder with a light hand. 'Don't worry. Between two horsemen like Jim and Cam—'

'Don't *Cam* me! He's none of *my* horse. I told Jim once—' Breaking off, Camden hoisted his weight over the fence and stood outside, his feet spread and his hammer in both hands, an attitude that would have looked a little ludicrous had anyone been watching him.

Jim had arrived. With a clatter of hoofs and a rattle of wheels he was in the yard and come to a standstill, calling aloud as he threw the lines over the team, 'Well, friends, here we are.'

The curious began to edge around, closing a cautious circle. The dusk had deepened so that it was hard to make anything at any distance of Jim's 'experiment' but a blurry silhouette anchored at the wagon's tail. The farmer put an end to it, crying from his eminence, 'Now, now, clear out and don't worry him; give him some peace tonight, for Lord's sake! Git!' He jumped to the ground and began to whack his arms, chilled with driving, only to have them pinioned by Blossom's without warning.

'Oh, Jim, I'm so glad you come. I been so worried; gi' me a kiss!'

The farmer reddened, eyeing the cloud of witnesses. He felt awkward and wished she could have waited. 'Get along, didn't I tell you fellows?' he cried with a trace of the Bluedge temper. 'Go and wait in the kitchen then; I'll tell you all about everything soon's I come in. . . . Well now – wife—'

'What's the matter?' she laughed, an eye over her shoulder. 'Nobody's looking that matters. I'm sure Frank don't mind. And as for Camden—'

Camden wasn't looking at them. Still standing with his hammer two-fisted and his legs spread, his chin down and his thoughts to himself (the dumb head) he was looking at Blue Murder, staring at that other dumb head, which, raised high on the motionless column of the stallion's neck, seemed hearkening with an exile's doubt to the sounds of this new universe, testing with wide nostrils the taint in the wind of equine strangers, and studying with eyes accustomed to far horizons these dark pastures that went up in the air.

Whatever the smith's cogitations, presently he let the hammer down and said aloud, 'So you're him, eh?'

Jim put Blossom aside, saying, 'Got supper ready? I'm hungry!' Excited by the act of kissing and the sense of witnesses to it, she fussed her hair and started kitchenwards as he turned to his brothers.

'Well, what do you make of him?'

'Five hundred dollars,' said Frank. 'However, it's your money.'

Camden was shorter. 'Better put him in.'

'All right; let them bars down while I and Frank lead him around.'

'No thanks!' the storekeeper kept his hands in his pockets. 'I just cleaned up, thanks. Cam's the boy for horses.'

'He's none o' my horse!' Camden wet his lips, shook his shoulders, and scowled. 'Be damned, no!' He never had the right words, and it made him mad. Hadn't he told Jim from the beginning that he washed his hands of this fool Agricultural College squandering, 'and a man-killer to the bargain?'

'Unless,' Frank put in slyly, 'unless Cam's scared.'

'Oh, is Cam scared?'

'Scared?' And still to the brothers' enduring wonder, the big dense fellow would rise to that boyhood bait. 'Scared? The hell I'm scared of any horse ever wore a shoe! Come on, I'll show you! I'll show you!'

'Well, be gentle with him, boys, he may be brittle.' As Frank sauntered off around the shed he whistled the latest tune.

In the warmth and light of the kitchen he began to fool with his pretty sister-in-law, feigning princely impatience and growling with a wink at the assembled neighbours, 'When do we eat?'

But she protested, 'Land, I had everything ready since five, ain't I? And now if it ain't you it's them to wait for. I declare for men!'

At last one of the gossips got in a word.

'What you make of Jim's purchase, Frank?'

'Well, it's Jim's money, Darred. If I had the running of this farm—' Frank began drawing up chairs noisily, leaving it at that.

Darred persisted. 'Don't look to me much like an animal for women and children to handle, not yet awhile.'

'Cowboys han'les 'em, pa.' That was Darred's ten-year-old, big-eyed.

Blossom put the kettle back, protesting, 'Leave off, or you'll get me worried to death; all your talk ... I declare, where *are* those bad boys?' opening the door she called into the dark, 'Jim! Cam! Land's sake!'

Subdued by distance and the intervening sheds, she could hear them at their business – sounds muffled and fragmentary, soft thunder of hoofs, snorts, puffings, and the short words of men in action: 'Aw, leave him be in the paddock tonight.' ... 'With them mares there, you damn fool?' ... 'Damn fool, eh? Try getting him in at that door and see who's the damn fool!' ... 'Come on, don't be so scared' ... 'Scared, eh? Scared?' ...

Why was it she always felt that curious tightening of all her powers of attention when Camden Bluedge spoke? Probably because he spoke so rarely, and then so roughly, as if his own thickness made him mad. Never mind.

'Last call for supper in the dining-car, boys!' she called and closed the door. Turning back to the stove she was about to replace the tea water for the third time, when, straightening up she said, 'What's that?'

No one else had heard anything. They looked at one another.

'Frank, go – go see what – go tell the boys come in.'

Frank hesitated, feeling foolish, then went to the door.

Then everyone in the room was out of his chair.

There were three sounds. The first was human and incoherent. The second was incoherent too, but it wasn't human. The third was a crash, a ripping and splintering of wood.

When they got to the paddock they found Camden crawling from beneath the wreckage of the fence where a gap was opened on the pasture side. He must have received a blow on the head, for he seemed dazed. He didn't seem to know they were there. At a precarious balance – one hand at the back of his neck – he stood facing up the hill, gaping after the diminuendo of floundering hoofs, invisible above.

So seconds passed. Again the beast gave tongue, a high wild horning note, and on the black of the stony hill to the right of it a faint shower of sparks blew like fireflies where the herding mares wheeled. It seemed to waken the dazed smith. He opened his mouth *'Almighty God!'* Swinging, he flung his arms towards the shed. *'There! There!'*

At last someone brought a lantern. They found Jim Bluedge lying on his back in the corner of the paddock near the door to the shed. In the lantern light, and still better in the kitchen when they had carried him in, they read the record of the thing which Camden, dumb in good earnest now, seemed unable to tell them with anything but his strange unfocused stare.

The bloody offence to the skull would have been enough to kill the man, but it was the second, full on the chest above the heart, that told the tale. On the caved grating of the ribs, already turning blue under the yellowish down, the iron shoe had left its mark; and when, laying back the rag of shirt, they saw that the toe of the shoe was upward and the cutting calkends down they knew all they wanted to know of that swift, black, crushing episode.

No outlash of heels in fright. Here was a forefoot. An attack aimed and frontal; an onslaught reared, erect; beast turned biped; red eyes mad to white aghast.... And only afterwards, when it was done, the blood-fright that serves the horse for conscience; the blind rush across the enclosure; the fence gone down....

No one had much to say. No one seemed to know what to do.

As for Camden, he was no help. He simply stood propped on top of his logs of legs where someone had left him. From the instant when with his *'Almighty God!'* he had been brought back to memory, instead of easing its hold as the minutes passed, the event to which he remained the only living human witness seemed minute by minute to tighten its grip. It set its sweat-beaded stamp on his face, distorted his eyes, and tied his tongue. He was no good to anyone.

As for Blossom, even now – perhaps more than ever now – her dependence on physical touch was the thing that ruled her. Down on her knees beside the lamp they had set on the floor, she plucked at one of the dead man's shoes monotonously, and as it were idly, swaying the toe like an inverted pendulum from side to side. That was all. Not a word. And when Frank, the only one of the three with any sense, got her up finally and led her away to her room, she clung to *him.*

It was lucky that Frank was a man of affairs. His brother was dead, and frightfully dead, but there was tomorrow for grief. Just now there were many things to do. There were people to be gotten rid of. With short words and angry gestures he cleared them out, all but Darred and a man named White, and to these he said, 'Now first thing, Jim can't stay here.' He ran and got a blanket from a closet. 'Give me a hand and we'll lay him in the ice house overnight. Don't sound so good, but it's best, poor fellow. Cam, came along!'

He waited a moment, and as he studied the wooden fool the blood poured back into his face. 'Wake up, Cam! You great big scared stiff, you!'

Camden brought his eyes out of nothingness and looked at his brother. A twinge passed over his face, convulsing the mouth muscles. 'Scared?'

'Yes, you're scared!' Frank's lip lifted, showing the tips of his teeth. 'And I'll warrant you something: if you wasn't the scared stiff you was, this hellish damn thing wouldn't have happened, maybe. Scared! You a blacksmith! Scared of a horse!'

'Horse!' Again that convulsion of the mouth muscles, something between irony and an idiot craft. 'Why don't you go catch 'im?'

'Hush it! Don't waste time by going loony now, for God's sake. Come!'

'My advice to anybody—' Camden looked crazier than ever, knotting his brows. 'My advice to anybody is to let somebody else go catch that – that—' Opening the door he faced out into the night, his head sunk between his shoulders and the fingers working at the ends of his hanging arms; and before they knew it he began to swear. They could hardly hear because his teeth were locked and his breath soft. There were all the vile words he had ever heard in his life, curses and threats and abominations, vindictive, violent, obscene. He stopped only when at a sharp word from Frank he was made aware that Blossom had come back into the room. Even then he didn't seem to comprehend her return but stood blinking at her, and at the rifle she carried, with his distraught bloodshot eyes.

Frank comprehended. Hysteria had followed the girl's blankness. Stepping between her and the body on the floor, he spoke in a persuasive, unhurried way. 'What are you doing with that gun, Blossie? Now, now, you don't want that gun, you know you don't.'

It worked. Her rigidity lessened appreciably. Confusion gained.

'Well, but – oh, Frank – well, but when we going to shoot him?'

'Yes, yes, Blossie – now, yes – only you best give me that gun, that's the girlie.' When he had got the weapon he put an arm around her shoulders. 'Yes, yes, course we're going to shoot him; what you think? Don't want an animal like that running round. Now first thing in the morning—'

Hysteria returned. With its strength she resisted his leading.

'No, now! *Now!*'

'He's gone and killed Jim! Killed my husband! I won't have him left alive another minute! I won't! *Now!* No sir, I'm going myself, I am! Frank, I am! *Cam!*'

At his name, appealed to in that queer screeching way, the man in the doorway shivered all over, wet his lips, walked out into the dark.

'There, you see?' Frank was quick to capitalize anything. 'Cam's gone to do it. Cam's gone, Blossie! . . . Here, one of you – Darred, take this gun and run give it to Camden, that's the boy.'

'You sure he'll kill him, Frank? you *sure?*'

'Sure as daylight. Now you come along back to your room like a good girl and get some rest. Come, I'll go with you.'

When Frank returned to the kitchen ten minutes later, Darred was back.

'Well, now, let's get at it and carry out poor Jim; he can't lay here. . . . Where's Cam gone *now*, damn him!'

'Cam? Why, he's gone and went.'

'Went where?'

'Up the pasture, like you said.'

'Like I—' Frank went an odd colour. He walked to the door.

Between the light on the sill and the beginnings of the stars where the
woods crowned the mountain was all one blackness. One stillness too.
He turned on Darred. 'But look, you never gave him that gun, even.'

'He didn't want it.'

'Lord's sake; what did he say?'

'Said nothing. He'd got the log-chain out of the wagon and when I
caught him he was up hunting his hammer in under that wreck at the
fence. Once he found it he started off up. "Cam", says I, "here's a gun,
want it?" He seem not to. Just went on walking up.'

'How'd he look?'

'Look same's you seen him looking. Sick.'

'The damned fool!' . . .

Poor dead Jim! Poor fool Camden! As the storekeeper went about his
business, and afterward when, the ice house door closed on its tragic
tenant and White and Darred gone off home, he roamed the yard,
driven here and there, soft-footed, waiting, hearkening – his mind was
for a time not on his own property but the plaything of thoughts diverse
and wayward. Jim his brother, so suddenly and so violently gone. The
stallion. That beast that had kicked him to death. With anger and hate
and pitiless impatience of time he thought of the morrow, when they
would catch him and take their revenge with guns and clubs.
Behind these speculations, covering the background of his consciousness
and stringing his nerves to endless vigil, spread the wall of the mountain:
silent from instant to instant but devising under its black silence (who-
could-know-what instant to come) a neigh, a yell, a spark-line of iron
hoofs on rolling flints, a groan. And still behind that and deeper into the
borders of the unconscious, the storekeeper thought of the farm that had
lost its master, the rich bottoms, the broad, well-stocked pastures, the
fat barns, and the comfortable house whose chimneys and gable ends
fell into changing shapes of perspective against the stars as he wandered
here and there. . . .

Jim gone. . . . And Camden, at any moment. . . .

His face grew hot. An impulse carried him a dozen steps. 'I ought to
go up. Ought to take the gun and go up.' But there shrewd sanity put
on the brakes. 'Where's the use? Couldn't find him in this dark. Besides
I oughtn't to leave Blossom here alone.'

With that he went around towards the kitchen, thinking to go in.
But the sight of the lantern, left burning out near the sheds, sent his ideas
off on another course. At any rate it would give his muscles and nerves
something to work on. Taking the lantern and entering the paddock, he
fell to patching the gap into the pasture, using broken boards from the
wreck. As he worked his eyes chanced to fall on footprints in the dung-
mixed earth – Camden's footprints, leading away beyond the little ring
of light. And beside them, taking off from the landing-place of that

prodigious leap, he discerned the trail of the stallion. After a moment he got down on his knees where the earth was softest, holding the lantern so that its light fell full.

He gave over his fence building. Returning to the house his gait was no longer that of the roamer; his face, caught by the periodic flare of the swinging lantern, was the face of another man. In its expression there was a kind of fright and a kind of calculating eagerness. He looked at the clock on the kitchen shelf, shook it, and read it again. He went to the telephone and fumbled at the receiver. He waited till his hand quit shaking, then removed it from the hook.

'Listen, Darred,' he said, when he had got the farmer at last, 'get White and whatever others you can and come over first thing it's light. Come a-riding and bring your guns. No, Cam ain't back.'

He heard Blossom calling. Outside her door he passed one hand down over his face, as he might have passed a wash rag to wipe off what was there. Then he went in.

'What's the matter, Blossie? Can't sleep?'

'No, I can't sleep. Can't think. Can't sleep. Oh, Frankie!'

He sat down beside the bed.

'Oh, Frankie, Frankie, *hold my hand*!'

She looked almost homely, her face bleached out and her hair in a mess on the pillow. But she would get over that. And the short sleeve of the nightgown on the arm he held was edged with pretty lace.

'Got your watch here?' he asked. She gave it to him from under the pillow. This too he shook as if he couldn't believe it was going.

Pretty Blossom Beck. Here for a wonder he sat in her bedroom and held her hand. One brother was dead and the other was on the mountain.

But little by little, as he sat and dreamed so, nightmare crept over his brain. He had to arouse and shake himself. He had to set his thoughts resolutely in other roads.... Perhaps there would be even the smithy. The smithy, the store, the farm. Complete. The farm, the farmhouse, the room in the farmhouse, the bed in the room, the wife in the bed. Complete beyond belief. If.... Worth dodging horror for. If....

'Frank, has Cam come back?'

'Cam? Don't worry about Cam.... Where's that watch again?..'

Far from rounding up their quarry in the early hours after dawn, it took the riders, five of them, till almost noon simply to make certain that he wasn't to be found – not in any of the pastures. Then when they discovered the hole in the fence far up in the woods beyond the crest where Blue Murder had led the mares in a break for the open country of hills and ravines to the south, they were only beginning.

The farmers had left their work undone at home and, as the afternoon lengthened and with it the shadows in the hollow places, they began to eye one another behind their leader's back. Yet they couldn't say it;

there was something in the storekeeper's air today, something zealous and pitiless and fanatical, that shut them up and pulled them plodding on.

Frank did the trailing. Hopeless of getting anywhere before sundown in that unkempt wilderness of a hundred square miles of scrub, his companions slouched in their saddles and rode more and more mechanically, knee to knee, and it was he who made the casts to recover the lost trail and, dismounting to read the dust, cried back, 'He's still with 'em,' and with gestures of imperious excitement beckoned them on.

'Which you mean?' Darred asked him once. 'Cam or the horse?'

Frank wheeled his beast and spurred back at the speaker. It was extraordinary. 'You don't know what you're talking about!' he cried, with a causelessness and a disordered vehemence that set them first staring, then speculating. 'Come on, you dumb heads; don't talk – *ride!*'

By the following day, when it was being told in all the farmhouses, the story might vary in details and more and more as the tellings multiplied, but in its fundamentals it remained the same. In one thing they certainly all agreed: they used the same expression – 'It was like Frank was drove. Drove in a race against something, and not sparing the whip.'

They were a good six miles to the south of the fence. Already the road back home would have to be followed three parts in the dark.

Darred was the spokesman. 'Frank, I'm going to call it a day.'

The others reined up with him but the man ahead rode on. He didn't seem to hear. Darred lifted his voice. 'Come on, call it a day, Frank. Tomorrow, maybe. But you see we've run it out and they're not here.'

'Wait,' said Frank over his shoulder, still riding on into the pocket.

White's mount, a mare, laid back her ears, shied, and stood trembling. After a moment she whinnied.

It was as if she had whinnied for a dozen. A crashing in the woods above them to the left and the avalanche came – down streaming, erupting, wheeling, wheeling away with volleying snorts, a dark rout.

Darred, reining his horse, began to shout, 'Here they go this way, Frank!' But Frank was yelling, 'Up here boys! This way, quick!'

It was the same note, excited, feverish, disordered, breaking like a child's. When they neared him they saw he was off his horse, rifle in hand, and down on his knees to study the ground where the woods began. By the time they reached his animal the impetuous fellow had started up into the cover, his voice trailing, 'Come on; spread out and come on!'

One of the farmers got down. When he saw the other three keeping their saddles he swung up again.

White spoke this time. 'Be darned if I do!' He lifted a protesting hail. 'Come back here, Frank! You're crazy! It's getting dark!'

It was Frank's own fault. They told him plainly to come back and he wouldn't listen.

For a while they could hear his crackle in the mounting underbrush. Then that stopped, whether he had gone too far for their ears or whether he had come to a halt to give his own ears a chance. . . . Once, off to the right, a little higher up under the low ceiling of the trees that darkened moment by moment with the rush of night, they heard another movement, another restlessness of leaves and stones. Then that was still, and everything was still.

Darred ran a sleeve over his face and swung down. 'God alive, boys!'

It was the silence. All agreed there – the silence and the deepening dusk.

The first they heard was the shot. No voice. Just the one report. Then after five breaths of another silence a crashing of growth, a charge in the darkness under the withered scrub, continuous and diminishing.

They shouted 'Frank!' No answer. They called, *'Frank Bluedge!'*

Now, since they had to, they did. Keeping contact by word, and guided partly by directional memory (and mostly in the end by luck), after a time they found the storekeeper in a brake of ferns, lying across his gun.

They got him down to the open, watching behind them all the while. Only then, by the flares of successive matches, under the noses of the snorting horses, did they look for the damage done.

They remembered the stillness and the gloom; it must have been quiet back in there. The attack had come from behind – equine and pantherine at once, and planned and cunning. A deliberate lunge with a forefoot again: the shoe which had crushed the backbone between the shoulder blades was a fore shoe; that much they saw by the match flares in the red wreck.

They took no longer getting home than they had to, but it was longer than they wished. With Frank across his own saddle, walking their horses and with one or another ahead to pick the road (it was going to rain, and even the stars were lost), they made no more than a creeping speed.

None of them had much to say on the journey. Finding the break in the boundary fence and feeling through the last of the woods, the lights of their farms began to show in the pool of blackness below, and Darred uttered a part of what had lain in their minds during the return.

'Well, that leaves Cam.'

None followed it up. None cared to go any closer than he was to the real question. Something new, alien, menacing and pitiless had come into the valley of their lives with that beast they had never really seen; they felt its oppression, every one, and kept the real question back in their minds: *'Does* it leave Cam?'

It answered itself. Camden was at home when they got there.

He had come in a little before them, empty-handed. Empty-headed too. When Blossom, who had waited all day, part of the time with neighbour women who had come in and part of the time alone to the point of going mad – when she saw him coming down the pasture, his feet stumbling and his shoulders dejected, her first feeling was relief. Her first words, however were, 'Did you get him, Cam?' And all he would answer was, 'Gi' me something to eat, can't you? Gi' me a few hours' sleep, can't you? Then wait!'

He looked as if he would need more than a few hours' sleep. Propped on his elbows over his plate, it seemed as though his eyes would close before his mouth would open.

His skin was scored by thorns and his shirt was in ribbons under the straps of his iron-sagged apron; but it was not by these marks that his twenty-odd hours showed: it was by his face. While yet his eyes were open and his wits still half awake, his face surrendered. The flesh relaxed into lines of stupor, a putty-formed, putty-coloured mask of sleep.

Once he let himself be aroused. This was when, to an abstracted query as to Frank's whereabouts, Blossom told him Frank had been out with four others since dawn. He heaved clear of the table and opened his eyes at her, showing the red around the rims.

He spoke with the thick tongue of the drunkard. 'If anybody but me lays hand on that stallion I'll kill him. I'll wring his neck.'

Then he relapsed into his stupidity, and not even the arrival of the party bringing his brother's body home seemed able to shake him so far clear of it again.

At first, when they had laid Frank on the floor where on the night before they had laid Jim, he seemed hardly to comprehend.

'What's wrong with Frank?'

'Some more of Jim's "experiment".'

'Frank see him? He's scared, Frank is. Look at his face there.'

'He's dead, Cam.'

'Dead, you say? Frank dead? Dead of fright; is that it?'

Even when, rolling the body over they showed him what was what, he appeared incapable of comprehension, of amazement, of passion, or of any added grief. He looked at them all with a kind of befuddled protest. Returning to chair and his plate, he grumbled, 'Le' me eat first can't you? Can't you gi' me a little time to sleep?'

'Well, you wouldn't do much tonight anyway, I guess.'

At White's words Blossom opened her mouth for the first time.

'No, nothing tonight, Cam. Cam! *Camden*! Say! Promise!'

'And then tomorrow, Cam, what we'll do is to get every last man in the valley, and we'll go at this right. We'll lay hand on that devil—'

Camden swallowed his mouthful of cold steak with difficulty. His obsession touched, he showed them the rims of his eyes again.

'You do and I'll wring your necks. The man that touches that animal before I do gets his neck wrang. That's all you need to remember.'

'Yes, yes – no – that is—' Poor Blossom. 'Yes, Mr White, thanks; no, Cam's not going out tonight.... No, Cam, nobody's going to inter-fere – nor nothing. Don't you worry there....'

Again poor Blossom! Disaster piled too swiftly on disaster; no discipline but instinct left. Caught in fire and flood and earthquake and not know-ing what to come, and no creed but 'save him who can!' – by hook or crook of wile or smile. With the valley of her life emptied out and its emptiness repeopled monstrously and pressing down black on the roof under which (now that Frank was gone to the ice house too and the farmers back home) one brother was left of three – she would tread softly, she would talk or she would be dumb, as her sidelong glimpses of the awake-asleep man's face above the table told her was the instant's need; or if he would eat, she would magic out of nothing something, anything; or if he would sleep, he could sleep, so long as he slept in that house where she could know he was sleeping.

Only one thing. If she could touch him. If she could touch and cling.

Lightning filled the windows. After a moment the thunder came avalanching down the pasture and brought up against the clapboards of the house. At this she was behind his chair. She put out a hand. She touched his shoulder. The shoulder was bare, the shirt ripped away; it was caked with sweat and with the blackening smears of scratches, but for all its exhaustion it was flesh alive – a living man to touch.

Camden blundered up. 'What the hell!' He started off two steps and wheeled on her. 'Why don't you get off to bed for Goll sake!'

'Yes, Cam, yes – right off, yes.'

'Well, I'm going, I can tell you. For Goll sake, I need some sleep!'

'Yes, that's right, yes, Cam, good night, Cam – only – only you promise – promise you won't go out – nowheres.'

'Go out? Not likely I won't! Not likely! Get along.'

It took her no time to get going then – quick and quiet as a mouse.

Camden lingered to stand at one of the windows where the lightning came again, throwing the black barns and paddocks at him from the white sweep of the pastures crowned by woods.

As it had taken her no time to go, it took Blossom no time to undress and get in bed. When Camden was on his way to his room he heard her calling, 'Cam! Just a second, Cam!'

In the dark outside her door he drew one hand down over his face, wiping off whatever might be there. Then he entered.

'Yes? What?'

'Cam, sit by me a minute, won't you? And Cam, oh Cam, hold my hand.'

As he slouched down, his fist enclosing her fingers, thoughts awakened and ran and fastened on things. They fastened, tentatively at first, upon the farm. Jim gone. Frank gone. The smithy, the store, and the farm. The whole of Mill Crossing. The trinity. The three in one . . .

'Tight, Cam, for pity's sake! Hold it tight!'

His eyes, falling to his fist, strayed up along the arm it held. The sleeve, rumpled near the shoulder, was trimmed with pretty lace . . .

'Tighter, Cam!'

A box of apples. That memory hidden away in the cellar of his mind. Hidden away, clamped down in the dark, till the noxious vapours, the murderous vapours of its rotting had filled the shut-up house he was . . . A box of red apples for the apple grower's girl . . . the girl who sniggered and ran away from him to laugh at him . . .

And here, by the unfolding of a devious destiny, he sat in that girl's bedroom, holding that girl's hand. Jim who had got her, Frank who had wanted her lay side by side out there in the ice house under the lightning. While he, the 'dumb one' – the last to be thought of with anything but amusement and the last to be feared – his big hot fist enclosing her imprecating hand now, and his eyes on the pretty lace at her shoulder. He jumped up with a gulp and a clatter of iron.

'What the –' He flung her hand away. 'What the – hell!' He swallowed. 'Damn you, Blossie Beck!' He stared at her with repugnance and mortal fright. 'Why, you – you – you –'

He moderated his voice with an effort, wiping his brow, 'Good night. You must excuse me, Blossie; I wasn't meaning – I mean – I hope you sleep good. *I* shall . . . Good night!'

In his own brain was the one word, 'Hurry!'

She lay and listened to his boots going along the hall and heard the closing of his door. She ought to have put out the lamp. But even with the shades drawn, the lightning around the edges of the window unnerved her; in the dark alone it would have been more than she could bear.

She lay so still she felt herself nearing exhaustion from the sustained rigidity of her limbs. Rain came and with the rain, wind. Around the eaves it neighed like wild stallions; down the chimneys it moaned like men.

Slipping out of bed and pulling on a bathrobe she ran from her room, barefooted, and along the hall to Camden's door. 'Cam!' she called. 'Oh, Cam!' she begged, 'Please, please!'

And now he wouldn't answer her.

New lightning, diffused through all the sky by the blown rain, ran at her along the corridor. She pushed the door open. The lamp was burning on the bureau but the room was empty and the bed untouched.

Taking the lamp she skittered down to the kitchen. No one there . . .

*

'*Hurry!*'

Camden had reached the woods when the rain came. Lighting the lantern he had brought, he made his way on to the boundary fence. There, about a mile to the east of the path the others had taken that day, he pulled the rails down and tumbled the stones together in a pile. Then he proceeded another hundred yards, holding the lantern high and peering through the streaming crystals of the rain.

Blue Murder was there. Neither the chain nor the sapling had given way. The lantern and, better than the lantern, a globe of lightning, showed the tethered stallion glistening and quivering, his eyes all whites at the man's approach.

'Gentle, boy; steady, boy!' Talking all the while in the way he had with horses, Camden put a hand on the taut chain and bore with a gradually progressive weight, bringing the dark head nearer. 'Steady, boy; gentle there, damn you; gentle!'

Was he afraid of horses? Who said he was afraid of horses?

The beast's head was against the man's chest, held there by an arm thrown over the bowed neck. As he smoothed the forehead and fingered the nose with false caresses, Camden's 'horse talk' ran on – the cadence one thing, the words another.

'Steady, Goll damn you; you're going to get yours. Cheer up, cheer up, the worst is yet to come. Come now! Come easy! Come along!'

When he had unloosed the chain he felt for and found with his free hand his hammer hidden behind the tree. Throwing the lantern into the brush where it flared for an instant before dying, he led the stallion back as far as the break he had made in the fence. Taking a turn with the chain around the animal's nose, like an improvised hackamore, he swung from the stone pile to the slippery back. A moment's shying, a sliding caracole of amazement and distrust, a crushing of knees, a lash of the chain end, and that was all there was to that. Blue Murder had been ridden before . . .

In the smithy, chambered in the roaring of the falls and the swish and shock of the storm, Camden sang as he pumped his bellows, filling the cave beneath the rafters with red. The air was nothing, the words were mumbo-jumbo, but they swelled his chest. His eyes, cast from time to time at his wheeling prisoner had lost their look of helplessness and surly distraction.

Scared? He? No, no, no! Now that he wasn't any longer afraid of time, he wasn't afraid of anything on earth.

'Shy, you devil!' He wagged his exalted head. 'Whicker, you hellion! Whicker all you want to, stud horse! Tomorrow they're going to get you, the numb fools! Tomorrow they can have you. *I* got you *tonight!*'

He was more than other men; he was enormous. Fishing an iron shoe from that inseparable apron pocket of his, he thrust it into the coals and blew and blew. He tried it and it was burning red. He tried it again and it was searing white. Taking it out on the anvil he began to beat it, swinging his hammer one-handed, gigantic. So in the crimson light, irradiating iron sparks, he was at his greatest. Pounding, pounding. A man in the dark of night with a hammer about him can do wonders; with a horseshoe about him he can cover up a sin. And if the dark of night in a paddock won't hold it, then the dark of undergrowth on a mountainside will . . .

Pounding, pounding; thinking, thinking, in a great halo of hot stars. Feeding his hungry, his insatiable muscles.

'Steady now, you blue bastard! Steady boy!'

What he did not realize in his feverish exhaustion was that his muscles were not insatiable. In the thirty-odd hours past they had had a feast spread before them and they had had their fill . . . More than their fill.

As with the scorching iron in his tongs he approached the stallion, he had to step over the nail box he had stepped over five thousand times in the routine of every day.

A box of apples, eh? Apples to snigger at, eh? But whose girl are you now? . . . Scared, eh?

His foot was heavier of a sudden than it should have been. This five thousand and first time, by the drag of the tenth of an inch, the heel caught the lip of the nail box.

He tried to save himself from stumbling. At the same time, instinctively, he held the iron flame in his tongs away.

There was a scream out of a horse's throat; a whiff of hair and burnt flesh.

There was a lash of something in the red shadows. There was another sound and another wisp of stench . . .

When, guided by the stallion's whinnying, they found the smith next day, they saw by the cant of his head that his neck was broken, and they perceived that he too had on him the mark of a shoe. It lay up on one side of his throat and the broad of a cheek. It wasn't blue, this time, however – it was red. It took them some instants in the sunshine pouring through the wide door to comprehend this phenomenon. It wasn't sunk in by a blow this time; it was burned in, a brand.

Darred called them to look at the stallion, chained behind the forge.

'Almighty God!' The words sounded funny in his mouth. They sounded the funnier in that they were the same ones the blundering smith had uttered when, staring uphill from his clever wreckage of the paddock fence, he had seen the mares striking sparks from the stones where the stallion struck none. And he, of all men, a smith!

'Almighty God!' called Darred. 'What do you make of these here feet?'

One fore hoof was freshly pared for shoeing; the other three hoofs were as virgin as any yearling's on the plains. Blue Murder had never yet been shod . . .

The Murder

John Steinbeck

This happened a number of years ago in Monterey County, in central California. The Cañon del Castillo is one of those valleys in the Santa Lucia range which lie between its many spurs and ridges. From the main Cañon del Castillo a number of little arroyos cut back into the mountains, oak-wooded canyons, heavily brushed with poison-oak and sage. At the head of the canyon there stands a tremendous stone castle, buttressed and towered like those strongholds the Crusaders put up in the path of their conquests. Only a close visit to the castle shows it to be a strange accident of time and water and erosion working on soft, stratified sandstone. In the distance the ruined battlements, the gates, the towers, even the arrow slits require little imagination to make out.

Below the castle, on the nearly level floor of the canyon, stand an old ranch house, a weathered and mossy barn, and a warped feeding shed for cattle. The house is empty and deserted; the doors, swinging on rusted hinges, squeal and bang on nights when the wind courses down from the castle. Not many people visit the house. Sometimes a crowd of boys tramp through the rooms, peering into empty closets and loudly defying the ghosts they deny.

Jim Moore, who owns the land, does not like to have people about the house. He rides up from his new house, farther down the valley, and chases the boys away. He has put NO TRESPASSING signs on his fences to keep curious and morbid people out. Sometimes he thinks of burning the old house down, but then a strange and powerful relation with the swinging doors, the blind and desolate windows forbids the destruction. If he should burn the house he would destroy a great and important piece of his life. He knows that when he goes to town with his plump and still-pretty wife, people turn and look at his retreating back with awe and some admiration.

Jim Moore was born in the old house and grew up in it. He knew every grained and weathered board of the barn, every smooth, worn manger rack. His mother and father were both dead when he was thirty. He celebrated his majority by raising a beard. He sold the pigs and decided never to have any more. At last he bought a fine Guernsey bull to improve his stock, and he began to go to Monterey on Saturday nights, to get drunk and talk with the noisy girls of the Three Star.

Within a year Jim Moore married Jelka Šepić, a Yugoslav girl, daughter of a heavy and patient farmer of Pine Canyon. Jim was not proud of her foreign family, of her many brothers and sisters and cousins, but he delighted in her beauty. Jelka had eyes as large and questioning as a doe's eyes. Her nose was thin and sharply faceted, and her lips were deep and soft. Jelka's skin always startled Jim, for between night and night he forgot how beautiful it was. She was so smooth and quiet and gentle, such a good housekeeper, that Jim often thought with disgust of her father's advice on the wedding day. The old man, bleary and bloated with festival beer, elbowed Jim in the ribs and grinned suggestively, so that his little dark eyes almost disappeared behind puffed and wrinkled lids.

'Don't be big fool now,' he said. 'Jelka is Slav girl. He's not like American girl. If he is bad, beat him. If he's good too long, beat him too. I beat his mama. Papa beat my mama. Slav girl! He's not like a man that don't beat hell out of him.'

'I wouldn't beat Jelka,' Jim said.

The father giggled and nudged him again with his elbow. 'Don't be big fool,' he warned. 'Sometimes you see.' He rolled back to the beer barrel.

Jim found soon enough that Jelka was not like American girls. She was very quiet. She never spoke first, but only answered his questions, and then with soft short replies. She learned her husband as she learned passages of Scripture. After they had been married a while, Jim never wanted for any habitual thing in the house but Jelka had it ready for him before he could ask. She was a fine wife, but there was no companionship in her. She never talked. Her great eyes followed him, and when he smiled, sometimes she smiled too, a distant and covered smile. Her knitting and mending and sewing were interminable. There she sat, watching her wise hands, and she seemed to regard with wonder and pride the little white hands that could do such nice and useful things. She was so much like an animal that sometimes Jim patted her head and neck under the same impulse that made him stroke a horse.

In the house Jelka was remarkable. No matter what time Jim came in from the hot dry range or from the bottom farmland, his dinner was exactly, steamingly ready for him. She watched while he ate, and pushed the dishes close when he needed them, and filled his cup when it was empty.

Early in the marriage he told her things that happened on the farm, but she smiled at him as a foreigner does who wishes to be agreeable even though he doesn't understand.

'The stallion cut himself on the barbed wire,' he said.

And she replied, 'Yes,' with a downward inflection that held neither question nor interest.

He realized before long that he could not get in touch with her in any way. If she had a life apart, it was so remote as to be beyond his reach. The barrier in her eyes was not one that could be removed, for it was neither hostile nor intentional.

At night he stroked her straight black hair and her unbelievably smooth golden shoulders, and she whimpered a little with pleasure. Only in the climax of his embrace did she seem to have a life apart and fierce and passionate. And then immediately she lapsed into the alert and painfully dutiful wife.

'Why don't you ever talk to me?' he demanded. 'Don't you want to talk to me?'

'Yes,' she said. 'What do you want me to say?' She spoke the language of his race out of a mind that was foreign to his race.

When a year had passed, Jim began to crave the company of women, the chattery exchange of smalltalk, the shrill pleasant insults, the shame-sharpened vulgarity. He began to go again to town, to drink and to play with the noisy girls of the Three Star. They liked him there for his firm, controlled face and for his readiness to laugh.

'Where's your wife?' they demanded.

'Home in the barn,' he responded. It was a never-failing joke.

Saturday afternoons he saddled a horse and put a rifle in the scabbard in case he should see a deer. Always he asked, 'You don't mind staying alone?'

'No I don't mind.'

And once he asked, 'Suppose someone should come?'

Her eyes sharpened for a moment, and then she smiled. 'I would send them away,' she said.

'I'll be back about noon tomorrow. It's too far to ride in the night.' He felt that she knew where he was going, but she never protested nor gave any sign of disapproval. 'You should have a baby,' he said.

Her face lighted up. 'Some time God will be good,' she said eagerly.

He was sorry for her loneliness. If only she visited with the other women of the canyon she would be less lonely, but she had no gift for visiting. Once every month or so she put horses to the buckboard and went to spend an afternoon with her mother, and with the brood of brothers and sisters and cousins who lived in her father's house.

'A fine time you'll have,' Jim said to her. 'You'll gabble your crazy language like ducks for a whole afternoon. You'll giggle with that big grown cousin of yours with the embarrassed face. If I could find any fault with you, I'd call you a damn foreigner.' He remembered how she blessed the bread with the sign of the cross before she put it in the oven, how she knelt at the bedside every night, how she had a holy picture tacked to the wall in the closet.

On Saturday of a hot dusty June, Jim mowed the farmflat. The day was long. It was after six o'clock when the mower tumbled the last band of oats. He drove the clanking machine up into the barnyard and backed it into the implement shed, and there he unhitched the horses and turned them out to graze on the hills over Sunday. When he entered the kitchen Jelka was just putting his dinner on the table. He washed his hands and face, and sat down to eat.

'I'm tired,' he said, 'but I think I'll go to Monterey anyway. There'll be a full moon.'

Her soft eyes smiled.

'I'll tell you what I'll do,' he said. 'If you would like to go, I'll hitch up a rig and take you with me.'

She smiled again and shook her head. 'No, the stores would be closed. I would rather stay here.'

'Well, all right, I'll saddle a horse then. I didn't think I was going. The stock's all turned out. Maybe I can catch a horse easy. Sure you don't want to go?'

'If it was early, and I could go to the stores – but it will be ten o'clock when you get there.'

'Oh, no – well, anyway, on horseback I'll make it a little after nine.'

Her mouth smiled to itself, but her eyes watched him for the development of a wish. Perhaps because he was tired from the long day's work, he demanded, 'What are you thinking about?'

'Thinking about? I remember, you used to ask that nearly every day when we were first married.'

'But what are you?' he insisted irritably.

'Oh – I'm thinking about the eggs under the black hen.' She got up and went to the big calendar on the wall. 'They will hatch tomorrow or maybe Monday.'

It was almost dusk when he had finished shaving and putting on his blue serge suit and his new boots. Jelka had the dishes washed and put away. As Jim went through the kitchen he saw that she had taken the lamp to the table near the window, and that she sat beside it knitting a brown wool sock.

'Why do you sit there tonight?' he asked. 'You always sit over here. You do funny things sometimes.'

Her eyes arose slowly from her flying hands. 'The moon,' she said quietly. 'You said it would be full tonight. I want to see the moon rise.'

'But you're silly. You can't see it from that window. I thought you knew direction better than that.'

She smiled remotely. 'I will look out of the bedroom window then.'

Jim put on his black hat and went out. Walking through the dark empty barn, he took a halter from the rack. On the grassy sidehill he whistled high and shrill. The horses stopped feeding and moved slowly in towards him, and stopped twenty feet away. Carefully he approached his bay gelding and moved his hand from its rump along its side and up and over its neck. The halterstrap clicked in its buckle. Jim turned and led the horse back to the barn. He threw his saddle on and cinched it tight, put his silver-bound bridle over the stiff ears, buckled the throat latch, knotted the tie-rope about the gelding's neck and fastened the neat coil-end to the saddle-string. Then he slipped the halter and led the horse to the house. A radiant crown of soft red light lay over the eastern hills. The full moon would rise before the valley had completely lost the daylight.

In the kitchen Jelka still knitted by the window. Jim strode to the corner of the room and took up his 30-30 carbine. As he rammed shells into the magazine, he said, 'The moon glow is on the hills. If you are going to see it rise, you better go outside now. It's going to be a good red one at rising.'

'In a moment,' she replied, 'when I come to the end here.' He went to her and patted her sleek head.

'Goodnight. I'll probably be back by noon tomorrow.' Her dusty black eyes followed him out of the door.

Jim thrust the rifle into his saddle-scabbard, and mounted and swung his horse down the canyon. On his right, from behind the blackening hills, the great red moon slid rapidly up. The double light of the day's last afterglow and the rising moon thickened the outlines of the trees and gave a mysterious new perspective to the hills. The dusty oaks shimmered and glowed, and the shade under them was black as velvet. A huge, long-legged shadow of a horse and half a man rode to the left and slightly ahead of Jim. From the ranches near and distant came the sound of dogs tuning up for a night of song. And the roosters crowed, thinking a new dawn had come too quickly. Jim lifted the gelding to a trot. The spattering hoofsteps echoed back from the castle behind him. He thought of blonde May at the Three Star in Monterey, 'I'll be late. Maybe someone else'll have her,' he thought. The moon was clear of the hills now.

Jim had gone a mile when he heard the hoofbeats of a horse coming towards him. A horseman cantered up and pulled to a stop. 'That you, Jim?'

'Yes. Oh, hello, George.'

'I was just riding up to your place. I want to tell you – you know the springhead at the upper end of my land?'

'Yes, I know.'

'Well, I was up there this afternoon. I found a dead campfire and a calf's head and feet. The skin was in the fire, half burned, but I pulled it out and it had your brand.'

'The hell,' said Jim. 'How old was the fire?'

'The ground was still warm in the ashes. Last night, I guess. Look, Jim, I can't go up with you. I've got to go to town, but I thought I'd tell you, so you could take a look around.'

Jim asked quietly, 'Any idea how many men?'

'No. I didn't look close.'

'Well, I guess I better go up and look. I was going to town too. But if there are thieves working, I don't want to lose any more stock. I'll cut up through your land if you don't mind, George.'

'I'd go with you, but I've got to go to town. You got a gun with you?'

'Oh yes, sure. Here under my leg. Thanks for telling me.'

'That's all right. Cut through any place you want. Goodnight.' The neighbour turned his horse and cantered back in the direction from which he had come.

For a few moments Jim sat in the moonlight, looking down at his stilted shadow. He pulled his rifle from its scabbard, levered a shell into the chamber, and held the gun across the pommel of his saddle. He turned left from the road, went up the little ridge, through the oak grove, over the grassy hog-back and down the other side into the next canyon.

In half an hour he had found the deserted camp. He turned over the heavy, leathery calf's head and felt its dusty tongue to judge by the dryness how long it had been dead. He lighted a match and looked at his brand on the half-burned hide. At last he mounted his horse again, rode over the bald grassy hills and crossed into his own land.

A warm summer wind was blowing on the hilltops. The moon, as it quartered up the sky, lost its redness and turned the colour of strong tea. Among the hills the coyotes were singing, and the dogs at the ranch houses below joined them with broken-hearted howling. The dark green oaks below and the yellow summer grass showed their colours in the moonlight.

Jim followed the sound of the cowbells to his herd, and found them eating quietly, and a few deer feeding with them. He listened long for the sound of hoofbeats or the voices of men on the wind.

It was after eleven when he turned his horse towards home. He rounded the west tower of the sandstone castle, rode through the shadow and out into the moonlight again. Below, the roofs of his barn and house shone dully. The bedroom window cast back a streak of reflection.

The feeding horses lifted their heads as Jim came down through the pasture. Their eyes glinted redly when they turned their heads.

Jim had almost reached the corral fence – he heard a horse stamping in the barn. His hand jerked the gelding down. He listened. It came again, the stamping from the barn. Jim lifted his rifle and dismounted silently. He turned his horse loose and crept towards the barn.

In the blackness he could hear the grinding of the horse's teeth as it chewed hay. He moved along the barn until he came to the occupied stall. After a moment of listening he scratched a match on the butt of his rifle. A saddled and bridled horse was tied in the stall. The bit was slipped under the chin and the cinch loosened. The horse stopped eating and turned its head towards the light.

Jim blew out the match and walked quickly out of the barn. He sat on the edge of the horse trough and looked into the water. His thoughts came so slowly that he put them into words and said them under his breath.

'Shall I look through the window? No. My head would throw a shadow in the room.'

He regarded the rifle in his hand. Where it had been rubbed and handled, the black gun-finish had worn off, leaving the metal silvery.

At last he stood up with decision and moved towards the house. At the steps, an extended foot tried each board tenderly before he put his weight on it. The three ranch dogs came out from under the house and shook themselves, stretched and sniffed, wagged their tails and went back to bed.

The kitchen was dark, but Jim knew where every piece of furniture was. He put out his hand and touched the corner of the table, a chair-back, the towel hanger, as he went along. He crossed the room so silently that even he could hear only his breath and the whisper of his trouser-legs together, and the beating of his watch in his pocket. The bedroom door stood open and spilled a patch of moonlight on the kitchen floor. Jim reached the door at last and peered through.

The moonlight lay on the white bed. Jim saw Jelka lying on her back, one soft bare arm flung across her forehead and eyes. He could not see who the man was, for his head was turned away. Jim watched, holding his breath. Then Jelka twitched in her sleep and the man rolled his head and sighed – Jelka's cousin, her grown, embarrassed cousin.

Jim turned and quickly stole back across the kitchen and down the back steps. He walked up the yard to the water trough again, and sat down on the edge of it. The moon was white as chalk, and it swam in the water, and lighted the straws and barley dropped by the horses' mouths. Jim could see the mosquito wigglers, tumbling up and down, end over end, in the water, and he could see a newt lying in the sunmoss in the bottom of the trough.

He cried a few, dry, hard, smothered sobs, and wondered why, for his thought was of the grassed hilltops and of the lonely summer wind whisking along.

His thought turned to the way his mother used to hold a bucket to catch the throat-blood when his father killed a pig. She stood as far away as possible and held the bucket at arm's length to keep her clothes from getting spattered.

Jim dipped his hand into the trough and stirred the moon to broken, swirling streams of light. He wetted his forehead with his damp hands and stood up. This time he did not move so quietly, but he crossed the kitchen on tiptoe and stood in the bedroom door. Jelka moved her arm and opened her eyes a little. Then the eyes sprang wide, then they glistened with moisture. Jim looked into her eyes; her face was blank of expression. A little drop ran out of Jelka's nose and lodged in the hollow of her upper lip. She stared back at him.

Jim cocked the rifle. The steel click sounded through the house. The man on the bed stirred uneasily in his sleep. Jim's hands were quivering. He raised the gun to his shoulder and held it tightly to keep from shaking. Over the sights he saw the little white square between the man's brows and hair. The front sight wavered a moment and then came to rest.

The gun crash tore the air. Jim, still looking down the barrel, saw the whole bed jolt under the blow. A small, black bloodless hole was in the man's forehead. But behind, the hollow-point bullet took brain and bone and splashed them on the pillow.

Jelka's cousin gurgled in his throat. His hands came crawling out from under the covers like big white spiders, and they walked for a moment, then shuddered and fell quiet.

Jim looked slowly back at Jelka. Her nose was running. Her eyes had moved from him to the end of the rifle. She whined softly, like a cold puppy.

Jim turned in panic. His boot-heels beat on the kitchen floor, but outside he moved slowly towards the watering trough again. There was a taste of salt in his throat, and his heart heaved painfully. He pulled his hat off and dipped his head into the water, then he leaned over and vomited on the ground. In the house he could hear Jelka moving about. She whimpered like a puppy. Jim straightened up, weak and dizzy.

He walked tiredly through the corral and into the pasture. His saddled horse came at his whistle. Automatically he tightened the cinch, mounted and rode away, down the road to the valley. The squat black shadow travelled under him. The moon sailed high and white. The uneasy dogs barked monotonously.

At daybreak a buckboard and pair· trotted up to the ranch yard, scattering the chickens. A deputy sheriff and a coroner sat in the seat. Jim Moore half reclined against his saddle in the wagon-box. His tired gelding followed behind. The deputy sheriff set the brake and wrapped the lines around it. The men dismounted.

Jim asked, 'Do I have to go in? I'm too tired and wrought up to see it now.'

The coroner pulled his lips and studied. 'Oh, I guess not. We'll tend to things and look around.'

Jim sauntered away towards the watering trough. 'Say,' he called, 'kind of clean up a little, will you? You know.'

The men went on into the house.

In a few minutes they emerged, carrying the stiffened body between them. It was wrapped up in a comforter. They eased it up into the wagon-box. Jim walked back towards them. 'Do I have to go in with you now?'

'Where's your wife, Mr Moore?' the deputy sheriff demanded.

'I don't know,' he said wearily. 'She's somewhere around.'

'You're sure you didn't kill her too?'

'No. I didn't touch her. I'll find her and bring her in this afternoon. That is, if you don't want me to go in with you now.'

'We've got your statement,' the coroner said. 'And by God, we've got eyes, haven't we, Will? Of course there's a technical charge of murder against you, but it'll be dismissed. Always is in this part of the country. Go kind of light on your wife, Mr Moore.'

'I won't hurt her,' said Jim.

He stood and watched the buckboard jolt away. He kicked his feet reluctantly in the dust. The hot June sun showed its face over the hills and flashed viciously on the bedroom window.

Jim went slowly into the house, and brought out a nine-foot, loaded bull-whip. He crossed the yard and walked into the barn. And as he climbed the ladder to the hayloft, he heard the high, puppy whimpering start.

When Jim came out of the barn again, he carried Jelka over his shoulder. By the watering trough he set her tenderly on the ground. Her hair was littered with bits of hay. The back of her shirtwaist was streaked with blood.

Jim wetted his bandanna at the pipe and washed her bitten lips, and washed her face and brushed back her hair. Her dusty black eyes followed every move he made.

'You hurt me,' she said. 'You hurt me bad.'

He nodded gravely. 'Bad as I could without killing you.'

The sun shone hotly on the ground. A few blowflies buzzed about, looking for the blood.

Jelka's thickened lips tried to smile. 'Did you have any breakfast at all?'

'No,' he said. 'None at all.'

'Well, then I'll fry you up some eggs.' She struggled painfully to her feet.

'Let me help you,' he said. 'I'll help you get your waist off. It's drying stuck to your back. It'll hurt.'

'No. I'll do it myself.' Her voice had a peculiar resonance in it. Her dark eyes dwelt warmly on him for a moment, and then she turned and limped into the house.

Jim waited, sitting on the edge of the watering trough. He saw the smoke start up out of the chimney and sail straight up into the air. In a very few moments Jelka called him from the kitchen door.

'Come, Jim. Your breakfast.'

Four fried eggs and four thick slices of bacon lay on a warmed plate for him. 'The coffee will be ready in a minute,' she said.

'Won't you eat?'

'No. Not now. My mouth's too sore.'

He ate his eggs hungrily and then looked up at her. Her black hair was combed smooth. She had on a fresh white shirtwaist. 'We're going to town this afternoon,' he said. 'I'm going to order lumber. We'll build a new house farther down the canyon.'

Her eyes darted to the closed bedroom door and then back to him. 'Yes,' she said. 'That will be good.' And then after a moment, 'Will you whip me any more – for this?'

'No, not any more, for this.'

Her eyes smiled. She sat down on a chair beside him, and Jim put out his hand and stroked her hair, and the back of her neck.

Markheim

Robert Louis Stevenson

'Yes,' said the dealer, 'our windfalls are of various kinds. Some customers are ignorant, and then I touch a dividend on my superior knowledge. Some are dishonest,' and here he held up the candle, so that the light fell strongly on his visitor, 'and in that case,' he continued, 'I profit by my virtue.'

Markheim had but just entered from the daylight streets, and his eyes had not yet grown familiar with the mingled shine and darkness in the shop. At these pointed words, and before the near presence of the flame, he blinked painfully and looked aside.

The dealer chuckled. 'You come to me on Christmas Day,' he resumed, 'when you know that I am alone in my house, put up my shutters, and make a point of refusing business. Well, you will have to pay for that; you will have to pay for my loss of time, when I should be balancing my books; you will have to pay, besides, for a kind of manner that I remark in you today very strongly. I am the essence of discretion, and ask no awkward questions; but when a customer cannot look me in the eye, he has to pay for it.' The dealer once more chuckled; and then, changing to his usual business voice, though still with a note of irony, 'You can give, as usual, a clear account of how you came into the possession of the object?' he continued. 'Still your uncle's cabinet? A remarkable collector, sir!'

And the little pale, round-shouldered dealer stood almost on tiptoe, looking over the top of his old spectacles, and nodding his head with every mark of disbelief. Markheim returned his gaze with one of infinite pity, and a touch of horror.

'This time,' said he, 'you are in error. I have not come to sell, but to buy. I have no curios to dispose of; my uncle's cabinet is bare to the wainscot; even were it still intact, I have done well on the Stock Exchange, and should more likely add to it than otherwise, and my errand today is simplicity itself. I seek a Christmas present for a lady,' he continued, waxing more fluent as he struck into the speech he had prepared; 'and certainly I owe you every excuse for thus disturbing you upon so small a matter. But the thing was neglected yesterday; I must produce my little compliment at dinner; and as you very well know, a rich marriage is not a thing to be neglected.'

There followed a pause, during which the dealer seemed to weigh this statement incredulously. The ticking of many clocks among the curious lumber of the shop, and the faint rushing of the cabs in a near thoroughfare, filled up the interval of silence.

'Well, sir,' said the dealer, 'be it so. You are an old customer after all; and if, as you say, you have the chance of a good marriage, far be it from me to be an obstacle. Here is a nice thing for a lady now,' he went on, 'this hand glass – fifteenth century, warranted; comes from a good collection, too; but I reserve the name, in the interests of my customer, who was just like yourself, my dear sir, the nephew and sole heir of a remarkable collector.'

The dealer, while he thus ran on in his dry and biting voice, had stooped to take the object from its place; and, as he had done so, a shock had passed through Markheim, a start both of hand and foot, a sudden leap of many tumultuous passions to the face. It passed as swiftly as it came, and left no trace beyond a certain trembling of the hand that now received the glass.

'A glass,' he said hoarsely, and then paused, and repeated it more clearly. 'A glass? For Christmas? Surely not?'

'And why not?' cried the dealer. 'Why not a glass?'

Markheim was looking upon him with an indefinable expression. 'You ask me why not?' he said. 'Why, look here – look in it – look at yourself! Do you like to see it? No! nor I – nor any man.'

The little man had jumped back when Markheim had so suddenly confronted him with the mirror; but now, perceiving there was nothing worse on hand, he chuckled. 'Your future lady, sir, must be pretty hard favoured,' said he.

'I ask you,' said Markheim, 'for a Christmas present, and you give me this – this damned reminder of years, and sins, and follies – this hand-conscience! Did you mean it? Had you a thought in your mind? Tell me. It will be better for you if you do. Come, tell me about yourself. I hazard a guess now, that you are in secret a very charitable man?'

The dealer looked closely at his companion. It was very odd, Markheim did not appear to be laughing; there was something in his face like an eager sparkle of hope, but nothing of mirth.

'What are you driving at?' the dealer asked.

'Not charitable?' returned the other gloomily. 'Not charitable; not pious; not scrupulous; unbeloved; a hand to get money, a safe to keep it. Is that all? Dear God, man, is that all?'

'I will tell you what it is,' began the dealer with some sharpness, and then broke off again into a chuckle. 'But I see this is a love match of yours, and you have been drinking the lady's health.'

'Ah!' cried Markheim, with a strange curiosity. 'Ah, have you been in love? Tell me about that.'

'I,' cried the dealer. 'I in love! I never had the time, nor have I the time today for all this nonsense. Will you take the glass?'

'Where is the hurry?' returned Markheim. 'It is very pleasant to stand here talking; and life is so short and insecure that I would not hurry away from any pleasure – no, not even from so mild a one as this. We should rather cling, cling to what little we can get, like a man at a cliff's edge. Every second is a cliff, if you think upon it – a cliff a mile high – high enough, if we fall, to dash us out of every feature of humanity. Hence it is best to talk pleasantly. Let us talk of each other: why should we wear this mask? Let us be confidential. Who knows, we might become friends?'

'I have just one word to say to you,' said the dealer. 'Either make your purchase, or walk out of my shop!'

'True, true,' said Markheim. 'Enough fooling. To business. Show me something else.'

The dealer stooped once more, this time to replace the glass upon the shelf, his thin blond hair falling over his eyes as he did so. Markheim moved a little nearer, with one hand in the pocket of his greatcoat; he drew himself up and filled his lungs; at the same time many different emotions were depicted together on his face – terror, horror, and resolve, fascination and a physical repulsion; and through a haggard lift of his upper lip, his teeth looked out.

'This, perhaps, may suit,' observed the dealer: and then, as he began to re-arise, Markheim bounded from behind upon his victim. The long, skewerlike dagger flashed and fell. The dealer struggled like a hen, striking his temple on the shelf, and then tumbled on the floor in a heap.

Time had some score of small voices in that shop, some stately and slow as was becoming to their great age; others garrulous and hurried. All these told out the seconds in an intricate chorus of tickings. Then the passage of a lad's feet, heavily running on the pavement, broke in upon these smaller voices and startled Markheim into the consciousness of his surroundings. He looked about him awfully. The candle stood on the counter, its flame solemnly wagging in a draught; and by that inconsiderable movement, the whole room was filled with noiseless bustle and kept heaving like a sea: the tall shadows nodding, the gross blots of darkness swelling and dwindling as with respiration, the faces of the portraits and the china gods changing and wavering like images in water. The inner door stood ajar, and peered into that leaguer of shadows with a long slit of daylight like a pointing finger.

From these fear-stricken rovings, Markheim's eyes returned to the body of his victim, where it lay both humped and sprawling, incredibly small and strangely meaner than in life. In these poor, miserly clothes, in that ungainly attitude, the dealer lay like so much sawdust. Markheim had feared to see it, and, lo! it was nothing. And yet, as he gazed, this bundle of old clothes and pool of blood began to find eloquent voices. There it must lie; there was none to work the cunning hinges or direct the miracle of locomotion – there it must lie till it was found. Found! aye, and then? Then would this dead flesh lift up a cry that would ring over England, and fill the world with the echoes of pursuit. Aye, dead or not, this was still the enemy. 'Time was that when the brains were out,' he thought; and the first word struck into his mind. Time, now that the deed was accomplished – time, which had closed for the victim, had become instant and momentous for the slayer.

The thought was yet in his mind, when, first one and then another, with every variety of pace and voice – one deep as the bell from a cathedral turret, another ringing on its treble notes the prelude of a waltz – the clocks began to strike the hour of three in the afternoon.

The sudden outbreak of so many tongues in that dumb chamber staggered him. He began to bestir himself, going to and fro with the candle, beleaguered by moving shadows, and startled to the soul by chance reflections. In many rich mirrors, some of home design, some from Venice or Amsterdam, he saw his face repeated and repeated, as it were an army of spies; his own eyes met and detected him; and the sound of his own steps, lightly as they fell, vexed the surrounding quiet. And still, as he continued to fill his pockets, his mind accused him with a sickening iteration, of the thousand faults of his design. He should have chosen a more quiet hour; he should have prepared an alibi; he should not have used a knife; he should have been more cautious, and only bound and gagged the dealer, and not killed him; he should have been more bold, and killed the servant also; he should have done all things otherwise: poignant regrets, weary, incessant toiling of the mind to change what was unchangeable, to plan what was now useless, to be the architect of the irrevocable past. Meanwhile, and behind all this activity, brute terrors, like the scurrying of rats in a deserted attic, filled the more remote chambers of his brain with riot; the hand of the constable would fall heavy on his shoulder, and his nerves would jerk like a hooked fish; or he beheld, in galloping defile, the dock, the prison, the gallows, and the black coffin.

Terror of the people in the street sat down before his mind like a besieging army. It was impossible, he thought, but that some rumour of the struggle must have reached their ears and set on edge their curiosity; and now, in all the neighbouring houses, he divined them sitting motionless and with uplifted ear – solitary people, condemned to spend Christmas dwelling alone on memories of the past, and now startlingly recalled from that tender exercise; happy family parties, struck into silence round the table, the mother still with raised finger: every degree and age and humour, but all, by their own hearths, prying and hearkening and weaving the rope that was to hang him. Sometimes it seemed to him he could not move too softly; the clink of the tall Bohemian goblets rang out loudly like a bell; and alarmed by the bigness of the ticking, he was tempted to stop the clocks. And then, again, with a swift transition of his terrors, the very silence of the place appeared a source of peril, and a thing to strike and freeze the passer-by; and he would step more boldly, and bustle aloud among the contents of the shop, and imitate, with elaborate bravado, the movements of a busy man at ease in his own house.

But he was now so pulled about by different alarms that, while one portion of his mind was still alert and cunning, another trembled on the brink of lunacy. One hallucination in particular took a strong hold on his credulity. The neighbour hearkening with white face beside his window, the passer-by arrested by a horrible surmise on the pavement – these could at worst suspect, they could not know; through the brick walls and shuttered windows only sounds could penetrate. But here, within the house, was he alone? He knew he was; he had watched the servant set forth sweethearting, in her poor best, 'out for the day' written in every ribbon and smile. Yes, he was alone, of course; and yet, in the bulk of empty house above him, he could surely hear a stir of delicate footing – he was surely conscious, inexplicably conscious of some presence. Aye, surely; to every room and corner of the house his imagination followed it; and now it was a faceless thing, and yet had eyes to see with; and again it was a shadow of himself; and yet again behold the image of the dead dealer, reinspired with cunning and hatred.

At times, with a strong effort, he would glance at the open door which still seemed to repel his eyes. The house was tall, the skylight small and dirty, the day blind with fog; and the light that filtered down to the ground story was exceedingly faint, and showed dimly on the threshold of the shop. And yet, in that strip of doubtful brightness, did there not hang wavering a shadow?

Suddenly, from the street outside, a very jovial gentleman began to beat with a staff on the shop-door, accompanying his blows with shouts and railleries in which the dealer was continually called upon by name. Markheim, smitten into ice, glanced at the dead man. But no! he lay quite still; he was fled away far beyond earshot of these blows and shoutings; he was sunk beneath seas of silence; and his name, which would once have caught his notice above the howling of a storm, had become an empty sound. And presently the jovial gentleman desisted from his knocking and departed.

Here was a broad hint to hurry what remained to be done, to get forth from this accusing neighbourhood, to plunge into a bath of London multitudes, and to reach, on the other side of day, that haven of safety and apparent innocence – his bed. One visitor had come: at any moment another might follow and be more obstinate. To have done the deed, and yet not to reap the profit, would be too abhorrent a failure. The money, that was now Markheim's concern; and as a means to that, the keys.

He glanced over his shoulder at the open door, where the shadow was still lingering and shivering; and with no conscious repugnance of the mind, yet with a tremor of the belly, he drew near the body of his victim. The human character had quite departed. Like a suit half-stuffed with bran, the limbs lay scattered, the trunk doubled, on the floor; and yet the thing repelled him. Although so dingy and inconsiderable to the eye, he feared it might have more significance to the touch. He took the body by the shoulders, and turned it on its back. It was strangely light and supple, and the limbs, as if they had been broken, fell into the oddest postures. The face was robbed of all expression; but it was as pale as wax, and shockingly smeared with blood about one temple. That was, for Markheim, the one displeasing circumstance. It carried him back, upon the instant, to a certain fair-day in a fishers' village: a grey day, a piping wind, a crowd upon the street, the blare of brasses, the booming of drums, the nasal voice of a ballad singer; and a boy going to and fro, buried over head in the crowd and divided between interest and fear, until, coming out upon the chief place of concourse, he beheld a booth and a great screen with pictures, dismally designed, garishly coloured: Brownrigg with her apprentice; the Mannings with their murdered guest; We are in the death-grip of Thurtell; and a score besides of famous crimes. The thing was as clear as an illusion; he was once again that little boy; he was looking once again, and with the same sense of physical revolt, at these vile pictures; he was still stunned by the thumping of the drums. A bar of that day's music returned upon his memory; and at that, for the first time, a qualm came over him, a breath of nausea, a sudden weakness of the joints, which he must instantly resist and conquer.

He judged it more prudent to confront than to flee from these considerations; looking the more hardily in the dead face, bending his mind to realize the nature and greatness of his crime. So little a while ago that face had moved with every change of sentiment, that pale mouth had spoken, that body had been all on fire with governable energies; and now, and by his act, that piece of life had been arrested, as the horologist, with interjected finger, arrests the beating of the clock. So he reasoned in vain; he could rise to no more remorseful consciousness; the same heart which had shuddered before the painted effigies of crime, looked on its reality unmoved. At best, he felt a gleam of pity for one who had been endowed in vain with all those faculties that can make the world a garden of enchantment, one who had never lived and who was now dead. But of penitence, no, not a tremor.

With that, shaking himself clear of these considerations, he found the keys and advanced towards the open door of the shop. Outside, it had begun to rain smartly; and the sound of the shower upon the roof had banished silence. Like some dripping cavern, the chambers of the house were haunted by an incessant echoing, which filled the ear and mingled with the ticking of the clocks. And, as Markheim approached the door, he seemed to hear, in answers to his own cautious tread, the steps of another foot withdrawing up the stair. The shadow still palpitated loosely on the threshold. He threw a ton's weight of resolve upon his muscles, and drew back the door.

The faint, foggy daylight glimmered dimly on the bare floor and stairs; on the bright suit of armour posted, halbert in hand, upon the landing; and on the dark wood-carvings, and framed pictures that hung against the yellow panels of the wainscot. So loud was the beating of the rain through all the house that, in Markheim's ears, it began to be distinguished into many different sounds. Footsteps and sighs, the tread of regiments marching in the distance, the chink of money in the counting, and the creaking of doors held stealthily ajar, appeared to mingle with the patter of the drops upon the cupola and the gushing of the water in the pipes. The sense that he was not alone grew upon him to the verge of madness. On every side he was haunted and begirt by presences. He heard them moving in the upper chambers; from the shop, he heard the dead man getting to his legs; and as he began with a great effort to mount the stairs, feet fled quietly before him and followed stealthily behind. If he were but deaf, he thought, how tranquilly he would possess his soul! And then again, and hearkening with every fresh attention, he blessed himself for that unresting sense which held the outposts and stood a trusty sentinel upon his life. His head turned continually on his neck; his eyes, which seemed starting from their orbits, scouted on every side, and on every side were half-rewarded as with the tail of something nameless vanishing. The four-and-twenty steps to the first floor were four-and-twenty agonies.

On that first storey, the doors stood ajar, three of them like three ambushes, shaking his nerves like the throats of cannon. He could never again, he felt, be sufficiently immured and fortified from men's observing eyes; he longed to be home, girt in by walls, buried among bedclothes, and invisible to all but God. And at that thought he wondered a little, recollecting tales of other murderers and the fear they were said to entertain of heavenly avengers. It was not so, at least, with him. He feared the laws of nature, lest, in their callous and immutable procedure, they should preserve some damning evidence of his crime. He feared tenfold more, with a slavish, superstitious terror, some scission in the continuity of man's experience, some wilful illegality of nature. He played a game of skill, depending on the rules, calculating consequence from cause; and what if nature, as the defeated tyrant overthrew the chess-board, should break the mould of their succession? The like had befallen Napoleon (so writers said) when the winter changed the time of its appearance. The like might befall Markheim: the solid walls might become transparent and reveal his doings like those of bees in a glass hive; the stout planks might yield under his foot like quicksands and detain him in their clutch; aye, and there were soberer accidents that might destroy him: if, for instance, the house should fall and imprison him beside the body of his victim; or the house next door should fly on fire, and the firemen invade him from all sides. These things he feared; and, in a sense, these things might be called the hands of God reached forth against sin. But about God Himself he was at ease; his act was doubtless exceptional, but so were his excuses, which God knew; it was there, and not among men, that he felt sure of justice.

When he had got safe into the drawing-room, and shut the door behind him, he was aware of a respite from alarms. The room was quite dismantled, uncarpeted besides, and strewn with packing cases and incongruous furniture; several great pier-glasses, in which he beheld himself at various angles, like an actor on a stage; many pictures, framed and unframed, standing, with their faces to the wall; a fine Sheraton sideboard, a cabinet of marquetry, and a great old bed, with tapestry hangings. The windows opened to the floor; but by great good fortune the lower part of the shutters had been closed, and this concealed him from the neighbours. Here, then, Markheim drew in a packing case before the cabinet, and began to search among the keys. It was a long business, for there were many; and it was irksome, besides; for, after all, there might be nothing in the cabinet, and time was on the wing. But the closeness of the occupation sobered him. With the tail of his eye he saw the door – even glanced at it from time to time directly, like a besieged commander pleased to verify the good estate of his defences. But in truth he was at peace. The rain falling in the street sounded natural and pleasant. Presently, on the other side, the notes of a piano were wakened to the music of a hymn, and the voices of many children took up the air and words. How stately, how comfortable was the melody! How fresh the youthful voices! Markheim gave ear to it smilingly, as he sorted out the keys; and his mind was thronged with answerable ideas and images; church-going children and the pealing of the high organ; children afield, bathers by the brookside, ramblers on the brambly common, kite-flyers in the windy and cloud-navigated sky; and then, at another cadence of the hymn, back again to church,

and the somnolence of summer Sundays, and the high genteel voice of
the parson (which he smiled a little to recall) and the painted Jacobean
tombs, and the dim lettering of the Ten Commandments in the chancel.

And as he sat thus, at once busy and absent, he was startled to his
feet. A flesh of ice, a flash of fire, a bursting gush of blood, went over
him, and then he stood tranfixed and thrilling. A step mounted the stair
slowly and steadily, and presently a hand was laid upon the knob, and
the lock clicked, and the door opened.

Fear held Markheim in a vice. What to expect he knew not, whether
the dead man walking, or the official ministers of human justice, or some
chance witness blindly stumbling in to consign him to the gallows. But
when a face was thrust into the aperture, glanced round the room, looked
at him, nodded and smiled as if in friendly recognition, and then withdrew again, and the door closed behind it, his fear broke loose from
his control in a hoarse cry. At the sound of this the visitant returned.

'Did you call me?' he asked pleasantly, and with that he entered the
room and closed the door behind him.

Markheim stood and gazed at him with all his eyes. Perhaps there
was a film upon his sight, but the outlines of the new-comer seemed
to change and waver like those of the idols in the wavering candlelight
of the shop; and at times he thought he knew him; and at times he thought
he bore a likeness to himself; and always, like a lump of living terror,
there lay in his bosom the conviction that this thing was not of the earth
and not of God.

And yet the creature had a strange air of the commonplace, as he
stood looking on Markheim with a smile; and when he added: 'You
are looking for the money, I believe?' it was in the tones of everyday
politeness.

Markheim made no answer.

'I should warn you,' resumed the other, 'that the maid has left her
sweetheart earlier than usual and will soon be here. If Mr Markheim
be found in this house, I need not describe to him the consequences.'

'You know me?' cried the murderer.

The visitor smiled. 'You have long been a favourite of mine,' he said;
'and I have long observed and often sought to help you.'

'What are you?' cried Markheim: 'the devil?'

'What I may be,' returned the other, 'cannot affect the service I
propose to render you.'

'It can,' cried Markheim; 'it does! Be helped by you? No, never; not
by you! You do not know me yet; thank God, you do not know me!'

'I know you,' replied the visitant, with a sort of kind severity or rather
firmness. 'I know you to the soul.'

'Know me!' cried Markheim. 'Who can do so? My life is but a travesty
and slander on myself. I have lived to belie my nature. All men do;

all men are better than this disguise that grows about and stifles them. You see each dragged away by life, like one whom bravos have seized and muffled in a cloak. If they had their own control – if you could see their faces, they would be altogether different, they would shine out for heroes and saints! I am worse than most; myself is more overlaid; my excuse is known to me and God. But, had I the time, I could disclose myself.'

'To me?' inquired the visitant.

'To you before all,' returned the murderer. 'I supposed you were intelligent. I thought – since you exist – you would prove a reader of the heart. And yet you would propose to judge me by my acts! Think of it; my acts! I was born and I have lived in a land of giants; giants have dragged me by the wrists since I was born out of my mother – the giants of circumstance. And you would judge me by my acts! But can you not look within? Can you not understand that evil is hateful to me? Can you not see within me the clear writing of conscience, never blurred by any wilful sophistry, although too often disregarded? Can you not read me for a thing that surely must be common as humanity – the unwilling sinner?'

'All this is very feelingly expressed,' was the reply, 'but it regards me not. These points of consistency are beyond my province, and I care not in the least by what compulsion you may have been dragged away, so as you are but carried in the right direction. But times flies; the servant delays, looking in the faces of the crowd and at the pictures on the hoardings, but still she keeps moving nearer; and remember, it is as if the gallows itself was striding towards you through the Christmas streets! Shall I help you; I, who know all? Shall I tell you where to find the money?'

'For what price?' asked Markheim.

'I offer you the service for a Christmas gift,' returned the other.

Markheim could not refrain from smiling with a kind of bitter triumph. 'No,' said he, 'I will take nothing at your hands; if I were dying of thirst, and it was your hand that put the pitcher to my lips, I should find the courage to refuse. It may be credulous, but I will do nothing to commit myself to evil.'

'I have no objection to a deathbed repentance,' observed the visitant.

'Because you disbelieve their efficacy!' Markheim cried.

'I do not say so,' returned the other; 'but I look on these things from a different side, and when the life is done my interest falls. The man has lived to serve me, to spread black looks under colour of religion, or to sow tares in the wheat-field, as you do, in a course of weak compliance with desire. Now that he draws so near to his deliverance, he can add but one act of service – to repent, to die smiling, and thus to build up in confidence and hope the more timorous of my surviving followers. I am not so hard a master. Try me. Accept my help. Please yourself in life as you have done hitherto; please yourself more amply, spread your elbows at the board; and when the night begins to fall and the curtains to be drawn, I tell you, for your greater comfort, that you will find it even easy to compound your quarrel with your conscience, and to make a truckling peace with God. I came but now from such a deathbed, and the room was full of sincere mourners, listening to the man's last words: and when I looked into that face, which had been set as a flint against mercy, I found it smiling with hope.'

'And do you, then, suppose me such a creature?' asked Markheim. 'Do you think I have no more generous aspirations than to sin, and sin, and sin, and, at the last, sneak into heaven? My heart rises at the thought. Is this, then, your experience of mankind? or is it because you find me with red hands that you presume such baseness? and is this crime of murder indeed so impious as to dry up the very springs of good?'

'Murder is to me no special category,' replied the other. 'All sins are murder, even as all life is war. I behold your race, like starving mariners on a raft, plucking crusts out of the hands of famine and feeding on each other's lives. I follow sins beyond the moment of their acting; I find in all that the last consequence is death; and to my eyes, the pretty maid who thwarts her mother with such taking graces on a question of a ball, drips no less visibly with human gore than such a murderer as yourself. Do I say that I follow sins? I follow virtues also; they differ not by the thickness of a nail, they are both scythes for the reaping angel of Death. Evil, for which I live, consists not in action but in character. The bad man is dear to me; not the bad act, whose fruits, if we could follow them far enough down the hurtling cataract of the ages, might yet be found more blessed than those of the rarest virtues. And it is not because you have killed a dealer, but because you are Markheim, that I offer to forward your escape.'

'I will lay my heart open to you,' answered Markheim. 'This crime on which you find me is my last. On my way to it I have learned many lessons; itself is a lesson, a momentous lesson. Hitherto I have been driven with revolt to what I would not; I was a bond-slave to poverty, driven and scourged. There are robust virtues that can stand in these temp-tations; mine was not so: I had a thirst of pleasure. But today, and out of this deed, I pluck both warning and riches – both the power and a fresh resolve to be myself. I become in all things a free actor in the world; I begin to see myself all changed, these hands the agents of good, this heart at peace. Something comes over me out of the past; something of what I have dreamed on Sabbath evenings to the sound of the church organ, of what I forecast when I shed tears over noble books, or talked, an innocent child, with my mother. There lies my life; I have wandered a few years, but now I see once more my city of destination.'

'You are to use this money on the Stock Exchange, I think?' remarked the visitor; 'and there, if I mistake not, you have already lost some thousands?'

'Ah,' said Markheim, 'but this time I have a sure thing.'

'This time, again, you will lose,' replied the visitor quietly.

'Ah, but I keep back the half!' cried Markheim.

'That also you will lose,' said the other.

The sweat started upon Markheim's brow. 'Well, then, what matter?' he exclaimed. 'Say it be lost, say I am plunged again in poverty, shall one part of me, and that the worse, continue until the end to override the better? Evil and good run strong in me, haling me both ways. I do not love the one thing, I love all. I can conceive great deeds, renunciations, martyrdoms; and though I be fallen to such a crime as murder, pity is no stranger to my thoughts. I pity the poor; who knows their trials better than myself? I pity and help them; I prize love, I love honest laughter; there is no good thing nor true thing on earth but I love it from my heart. And are my vices only to direct my life, and my virtues to lie without effect, like some passive lumber of the mind? Not so; good, also is a spring of acts.'

But the visitant raised his finger. 'For six-and-thirty years that you have been in this world,' said he, 'through many changes of fortune and varieties of humour, I have watched you steadily fall. Fifteen years ago you would have started at a theft. Three years back you would have blenched at the name of murder. Is there any crime, is there any cruelty or meanness, from which you still recoil? – five years from now I shall detect you in the fact! Downward, downward, lies your way; nor can anything but death avail to stop you.'

'It is true,' Markheim said huskily, 'I have in some degree complied with evil. But it is so with all: the very saints, in the mere exercise of living, grow less dainty, and take on the tone of their surroundings.'

'I will propound to you one simple question,' said the other; 'and as you answer, I shall read to you your moral horoscope. You have grown in many things more lax; possibly you do right to be so; and at any account, it is the same with all men. But granting that, are you in any one particular, however trifling, more difficult to please with your own conduct, or do you go in all things with a looser rein?'

'In any one?' repeated Markheim, with an anguish of consideration. 'No,' he added, with despair, 'in none! I have gone down in all.'

'Then,' said the visitor, 'content yourself with what you are, for you will never change; and the words of your part on this stage are irrevocably written down.'

Markheim stood for a long while silent, and indeed it was the visitor who first broke the silence. 'That being so,' he said, 'shall I show you the money?'

'And grace?' cried Markheim.

'Have you not tried it?' returned the other. 'Two or three years ago, did I not see you on the platform of revival meetings, and was not your voice the loudest in the hymn?'

'It is true,' said Markheim; 'and I see clearly what remains for me by way of duty. I thank you for these lessons from my soul; my eyes are opened, and I behold myself at last for what I am.'

At this moment, the sharp note of the door-bell rang through the house; and the visitant, as though this were some concerted signal for which he had been waiting, changed at once in his demeanour.

'The maid!' he cried. 'She has returned, as I forewarned you, and there is now before you one more difficult passage. Her master, you must say, is ill; you must let her in, with an assured but rather serious countenance – no smiles, no overacting, and I promise you success! Once the girl within, and the door closed, the same dexterity that has already rid you of the dealer will relieve you of this last danger in your path. Thenceforward you have the whole evening – the whole night, if needful – to ransack the treasures of the house and to make good your safety. This is help that comes to you with the mask of danger. Up!' he cried; 'up, friend; your life hangs trembling in the scales: up, and act!'

Markheim steadily regarded his counsellor. 'If I be condemned to evil acts,' he said, 'there is still one door of freedom open – I can cease from action. If my life be an ill thing, I can lay it down. Though I be, as you say truly, at the beck of every small temptation, I can yet, by one decisive gesture, place myself beyond the reach of all. My love of good is damned to barrenness; it may, and let it be! But I have still my hatred of evil; and from that, to your galling disappointment, you shall see that I can draw both energy and courage.'

The features of the visitor began to undergo a wonderful and lovely change: they brightened and softened with a tender triumph, and, even as they brightened, faded and dislimned. But Markheim did not pause to watch or understand the transformation. He opened the door and went downstairs very slowly, thinking to himself. His past went soberly before him; he beheld it as it was, ugly and strenuous like a dream, random as chance-medley – a scene of defeat. Life, as he thus reviewed it, tempted him no longer; but on the farther side he perceived a quiet haven for his bark. He paused in the passage, and looked into the shop, where the candle still burned by the dead body. It was strangely silent. Thoughts of the dealer swarmed into his mind, as he stood gazing. And then the bell once more broke out into impatient clamour.

He confronted the maid upon the threshold with something like a smile.

'You had better go for the police,' said he: 'I have killed your master.'

The Secret of the Growing Gold

Bram Stoker

When Margaret Delandre went to live at Brent's Rock the whole neigh-bourhood awoke to the pleasure of an entirely new scandal. Scandals in connection with either the Delandre family or the Brents of Brent's Rock, were not few; and if the secret history of the county had been written in full both names would have been found well represented. It is true that the status of each was so different that they might have belonged to different continents – or to different worlds for the matter of that – for hitherto their orbits had never crossed. The Brents were accorded by the whole section of the country a unique social dominance, and had ever held themselves as high above the yeoman class to which Margaret Delandre belonged, as a blue-blooded Spanish hidalgo out-tops his peasant tenantry.

The Delandres had an ancient record and were proud of it in their way as the Brents were of theirs. But the family had never risen above yeomanry; and although they had been once well-to-do in the good old times of foreign wars and protection, their fortunes had withered under the scorching of the free trade sun and the 'piping times of peace'. They had, as the elder members used to assert, 'stuck to the land', with the result that they had taken root in it, body and soul. In fact, they, having chosen the life of vegetables, had flourished as vegetation does – blossomed and thrived in the good season and suffered in the bad. Their holding, Dander's Croft, seemed to have been worked out, and to be typical of the family which had inhabited it. The latter had declined generation after generation, sending out now and again some abortive shoot of unsatisfied energy in the shape of a soldier or sailor, who had worked his way to the minor grades of the services and had there stopped, cut short either from unheeding gallantry in action or from that destroy-ing cause to men without breeding or youthful care – the recognition of a position above them which they feel unfitted to fill. So, little by little, the family dropped lower and lower, the men brooding and dis-satisfied, and drinking themselves into the grave, the women drudging at home, or marrying beneath them – or worse. In process of time all disappeared, leaving only two in the Croft, Wykham Delandre and his sister Margaret. The man and woman seemed to have inherited in masculine and feminine form respectively the evil tendency of their race, sharing in common the principles, though manifesting them in different ways, of sullen passion, voluptuousness and recklessness.

The history of the Brents had been something similar, but showing the causes of decadence in their aristocratic and not their plebeian forms. They, too, had sent their shoots to the wars; but their positions had been different, and they had often attained honour – for without flaw they were gallant, and brave deeds were done by them before the selfish dissipation which marked them had sapped their vigour.

The present head of the family – if family it could now be called when one remained of the direct line – was Geoffrey Brent. He was almost a type of a wornout race, manifesting in some ways its most brilliant qualities, and in others its utter degradation. He might be fairly compared with some of those antique Italian nobles whom the painters have preserved to us with their courage, their unscrupulousness, their refinement of lust and cruelty – the voluptuary actual with the fiend potential. He was certainly handsome, with that dark, aquiline, commanding beauty which women so generally recognize as dominant. With men he was distant and cold; but such a bearing never deters womankind. The inscrutable laws of sex have so arranged that even a timid woman is not afraid of a fierce and haughty man. And so it was that there was hardly a woman of any kind or degree, who lived within view of Brent's Rock, who did not cherish some form of secret admiration for the handsome wastrel. The category was a wide one, for Brent's Rock rose up steeply from the midst of a level region and for a circuit of a hundred miles it lay on the horizon, with its high old towers and steep roofs cutting the level edge of wood and hamlet, and far scattered mansions.

So long as Geoffrey Brent confined his dissipations to London and Paris and Vienna – anywhere out of sight and sound of his home – opinion was silent. It is easy to listen to far off echoes unmoved, and we can treat them with disbelief, or scorn, or disdain, or whatever attitude of coldness may suit our purpose. But when the scandal came close home it was another matter; and the feeling of independence and integrity which is in people of every community which is not utterly spoiled, asserted itself and demanded that condemnation should be expressed. Still there was a certain reticence in all, and no more notice was taken of the existing facts than was absolutely necessary. Margaret Delandre bore herself so fearlessly and so openly – she accepted her position as the justified companion of Geoffrey Brent so naturally that people came to believe that she was secretly married to him, and therefore thought it wiser to hold their tongues lest time should justify her and also make her an active enemy.

The one person who, by his interference, could have settled all doubts was debarred by circumstances from interfering in the matter. Wykham Delandre had quarrelled with his sister – or perhaps it was that she had quarrelled with him – and they were on terms not merely of armed neutrality but of bitter hatred. The quarrel had been antecedent to Margaret going to Brent's Rock. She and Wykham had almost come to blows. There had certainly been threats on one side and on the other; and in the end Wykham, overcome with passion, had ordered his sister to leave his house. She had risen straightway, and, without waiting to pack up even her own personal belongings, had walked out of the house. On the threshold she had paused for a moment to hurl a bitter threat at Wykham that he would rue in shame and despair to the last hour of his life his act of that day. Some weeks had since passed; and it was understood in the neighbourhood that Margaret had gone to London, when she suddenly appeared driving out with Geoffrey Brent, and the entire neighbourhood knew before nightfall that she had taken up her abode at the Rock. It was no subject of surprise that Brent had come back unexpectedly, for such was his usual custom. Even his own servants never knew when to expect him, for there was a private door, of which he alone had the key, by which he sometimes entered without anyone in the house being aware of his coming. This was his usual method of appearing after a long absence.

Wykham Delandre was furious at the news. He vowed vengeance – and to keep his mind level with his passion drank deeper than ever. He tried several times to see his sister, but she contemptuously refused to meet him. He tried to have an interview with Brent and was refused by him also. Then he tried to stop him in the road, but without avail, for Geoffrey was not a man to be stopped against his will. Several actual encounters took place between the two men, and many more were threatened and avoided. At last Wykham Delandre settled down to a morose, vengeful acceptance of the situation.

Neither Margaret nor Geoffrey was of a pacific temperament, and it was not long before there began to be quarrels between them. One thing would lead to another, and wine flowed freely at Brent's Rock. Now and again the quarrels would assume a bitter aspect, and threats would be exchanged in uncompromising language that fairly awed the listening servants. But such quarrels generally ended where domestic altercations do, in reconciliation, and in a mutual respect for the fighting qualities proportionate to their manifestation. Fighting for its own sake is found by a certain class of persons, all the world over, to be a matter of absorbing interest, and there is no reason to believe that domestic conditions minimize its potency. Geoffrey and Margaret made occasional absences from Brent's Rock, and on each of these occasions Wykham Delandre also absented himself; but as he generally heard of the absence too late to be of any service, he returned home each time in a more bitter and discontented frame of mind than before.

At last there came a time when the absence from Brent's Rock became longer than before. Only a few days earlier there had been a quarrel, exceeding in bitterness anything which had gone before; but this, too, had been made up, and a trip on the Continent had been mentioned before the servants. After a few days Wykham Delandre also went away, and it was some weeks before he returned. It was noticed that he was full of some new importance – satisfaction, exaltation – they hardly knew how to call it. He went straightway to Brent's Rock, and demanded to see Geoffrey Brent, and on being told that he had not yet returned, said, with a grim decision which the servants noted:

'I shall come again. My news is solid – it can wait!' and turned away. Week after week went by, and month after month; and then there came a rumour, certified later on, that an accident had occurred in the Zermatt valley. Whilst crossing a dangerous pass the carriage containing an English lady and the driver had fallen over a precipice, the gentleman of the party, Mr Geoffrey Brent, having been fortunately saved as he had been walking up the hill to ease the horses. He gave information, and search was made. The broken rail, the excoriated roadway, the marks where the horses had struggled on the decline before finally pitching over into the torrent – all told the sad tale. It was a wet season, and there had been much snow in the winter, so that the river was swollen beyond its usual volume, and the eddies of the stream were packed with ice. All search was made, and finally the wreck of the carriage and the body of one horse were found in an eddy of the river. Later on, the body of the driver was found on the sandy, torrent-swept waste near Täsch; but the body of the lady, like that of the other horse, had quite disappeared, and was – what was left of it by that time – whirling amongst the eddies of the Rhone on its way down to the Lake of Geneva.

Wykham Delandre made all the enquiries possible, but could not find any trace of the missing woman. He found, however, in the books of the various hotels the name of 'Mr and Mrs Geoffrey Brent'. And he had a stone erected at Zermatt to his sister's memory, under her married name, and a tablet put up in the church at Bretten, the parish in which both Brent's Rock and Dander's Croft were situated.

There was a lapse of nearly a year, after the excitement of the matter had worn away, and the whole neighbourhood had gone on its accustomed way. Brent was still absent, and Delandre more drunken, more morose, and more revengeful than before.

Then there was a new excitement. Brent's Rock was being made ready for a new mistress. It was officially announced by Geoffrey himself in a letter to the Vicar, that he had been married some months before to an Italian lady, and that they were then on their way home. Then a small army of workmen invaded the house; and hammer and plane sounded, and a general air of size and paint pervaded the atmosphere. One wing of the old house, the south, was entirely re-done; and then the great body of the workmen departed, leaving only materials for the doing of the old hall when Geoffrey Brent should have returned, for he had directed that the decoration was only to be done under his own eyes. He had brought with him accurate drawings of a hall in the house of his bride's father, for he wished to reproduce for her the place to which she had been accustomed. As the moulding had all to be re-done, some scaffolding poles and boards were brought in and laid on one side of the great hall, and also a great wooden tank or box for mixing the lime, which was laid in bags beside it.

When the new mistress of Brent's Rock arrived the bells of the church rang out, and there was a general jubilation. She was a beautiful creature, full of the poetry and fire and passion of the South; and the few English words which she had learned were spoken in such a sweet and pretty broken way that she won the hearts of the people almost as much by the music of her voice as by the melting beauty of her dark eyes.

Geoffrey Brent seemed more happy than he had ever before appeared; but there was a dark, anxious look on his face that was new to those who knew him of old, and he started at times as though at some noise that was unheard by others.

And so months passed and the whisper grew that at last Brent's Rock was to have an heir. Geoffrey was very tender to his wife, and the new bond between them seemed to soften him. He took more interest in his tenants and their needs than he had ever done; and works of charity on his part as well as on his sweet young wife's were not lacking. He seemed to have set all his hopes on the child that was coming, and as he looked deeper into the future the dark shadow that had come over his face seemed to die gradually away.

All the time Wykham Delandre nursed his revenge. Deep in his heart had grown up a purpose of vengeance which only waited an opportunity to crystallize and take a definite shape. His vague idea was somehow centred in the wife of Brent, for he knew that he could strike him best through those he loved, and the coming time seemed to hold in its womb the opportunity for which he longed. One night he sat alone in the living-room of his house. It had once been a handsome room in its way, but time and neglect had done their work and it was now little better than a ruin, without dignity or picturesqueness of any kind. He had been drinking heavily for some time and was more than half stupefied. He thought he heard a noise as of someone at the door and looked up. Then he called half savagely to come in; but there was no response.

With a muttered blasphemy he renewed his potations. Presently he forgot all around him, sank into a daze, but suddenly awoke to see standing before him someone or something like a battered, ghostly edition of his sister. For a few moments there came upon him a sort of fear. The woman before him, with distorted features and burning eyes seemed hardly human, and the only thing that seemed a reality of his sister, as she had been, was her wealth of golden hair, and this was now streaked with grey. She eyed her brother with a long, cold stare; and he, too, as he looked and began to realize the actuality of her presence, found the hatred of her which he had had, once again surging up in his heart. All the brooding passion of the past year seemed to find a voice at once as he asked her:—

'Why are you here? You're dead and buried.'

'I am here, Wykham Delandre, for no love of you, but because I hate another even more than I do you!' A great passion blazed in her eyes.

'Him?' he asked, in so fierce a whisper that even the woman was for an instant startled till she regained her calm.

'Yes, him!' she answered. 'But make no mistake, my revenge is my own; and I merely use you to help me to it.'

Wykham asked suddenly:

'Did he marry you?'

The woman's distorted face broadened out in a ghastly attempt at a smile. It was a hideous mockery, for the broken features and seamed scars took strange shapes and strange colours, and queer lines of white showed out as the straining muscles pressed on the old cicatrices.

'So you would like to know! It would please your pride to feel that your sister was truly married! Well, you shall not know. That was my revenge on you, and I do not mean to change it by a hair's breadth. I have come here tonight simply to let you know that I am alive, so that if any violence be done me where I am going there may be a witness.'

'Where are you going?' demanded her brother.

'That is my affair! And I have not the least intention of letting you know!' Wykham stood up, but the drink was on him and he reeled and fell. As he lay on the floor he announced his intention of following his sister; and with an outburst of splenetic humour told her that he would follow her through the darkness by the light of her hair, and of her beauty. At this she turned on him, and said that there were others beside him that would rue her hair and her beauty too. 'As he will,' she hissed; 'for the hair remains though the beauty be gone. When he withdrew the linchpin and sent us over the precipice into the torrent, he had little thought of my beauty. Perhaps his beauty would be scarred like mine were he whirled, as I was, among the rocks of the Visp, and frozen on the ice pack in the drift of the river. But let him beware! His time

is coming!' and with a fierce gesture she flung open the door and passed
out into the night.

Later on that night, Mrs Brent, who was but half-asleep, became
suddenly awake and spoke to her husband:

'Geoffrey, was not that the click of a lock somewhere below our
window?'

But Geoffrey – though she thought that he, too, had started at the
noise – seemed sound asleep, and breathed heavily. Again Mrs Brent
dozed; but this time awoke to the fact that her husband had arisen and
was partially dressed. He was deadly pale, and when the light of the
lamp which he had in his hand fell on his face, she was frightened at
the look in his eyes.

'What is it, Geoffrey? What dost thou?' she asked.

'Hush! little one,' he answered, in a strange, hoarse voice. 'Go to
sleep. I am restless, and wish to finish some work I left undone.'

'Bring it here, my husband,' she said; 'I am lonely and I fear when
thou art away.'

For reply he merely kissed her and went out, closing the door behind
him. She lay awake for a while, and then nature asserted itself, and
she slept.

Suddenly she started broad awake with the memory in her ears of
a smothered cry from somewhere not far off. She jumped up and ran
to the door and listened, but there was no sound. She grew alarmed
for her husband, and called out: 'Geoffrey! Geoffrey!'

After a few moments the door of the great hall opened, and Geoffrey
appeared at it, but without his lamp.

'Hush!' he said, in a sort of whisper, and his voice was harsh and
stern. 'Hush! Get to bed! I am working and must not be disturbed.
Go to sleep, and do not wake the house!'

With a chill in her heart – for the harshness of her husband's voice
was new to her – she crept back to bed and lay there trembling, too
frightened to cry, and listened to every sound. There was a long pause
of silence, and then the sound of some iron implement striking muffled
blows! Then there came a clang of a heavy stone falling, followed by
a muffled curse. Then a dragging sound, and then more noises of stone
on stone. She lay all the while in an agony of fear, and her heart beat
dreadfully. She heard a curious sort of scraping sound; and then there
was silence. Presently the door opened gently, and Geoffrey appeared.
His wife pretended to be asleep; but through her eyelashes she saw him
wash from his hands something white that looked like lime.

In the morning he made no allusion to the previous night, and she
was afraid to ask any question.

From that day there seemed some shadow over Geoffrey Brent. He neither ate nor slept as he had been accustomed, and his former habit of turning suddenly as though someone were speaking from behind him revived. The old hall seemed to have some kind of fascination for him. He used to go there many times in the day, but grew impatient if anyone, even his wife, entered it. When the builder's foreman came to enquire about continuing his work Geofrrey was out driving; the man went into the hall, and when Geoffrey returned the servant told him of his arrival and where he was. With a frightful oath he pushed the servant aside and hurried up to the old hall. The workman met him almost at the door; and as Geoffrey burst into the room he ran against him. The man apologized:

'Beg pardon, sir, but I was just going out to make some enquiries. I directed twelve sacks of lime to be sent here, but I see there are only ten.'

'Damn the ten sacks and the twelve too!' was the ungracious and incomprehensible rejoinder.

The workman looked surprised, and tried to turn the conversation.

'I see, sir, there is a little matter which our people must have done; but the governor will of course see it set right at his own cost.'

'What do you mean?'

'That 'ere 'arth-stone, sir. Some idiot must have put a scaffold pole on it and cracked it right down the middle, and it's thick enough you'd think to stand hanythink.' Geoffrey was silent for quite a minute, and then said in a constrained voice and with much gentler manner:

'Tell your people that I am not going on with the work in the hall at present. I want to leave it as it is for a while longer.'

'All right, sir. I'll send up a few of our chaps to take away these poles and lime bags and tidy the place up a bit.'

'No! No!' said Geoffrey. 'Leave them where they are. I shall send and tell you when you are to get on with the work.' So the foreman went away, and his comment to his master was:

'I'd send in the bill, sir, for the work already done. 'Pears to me that money's a little shaky in that quarter.'

Once or twice Delandre tried to stop Brent on the road, and, at last, finding that he could not attain his object, rode after the carriage, calling out:

'What has become of my sister, your wife?' Geoffrey lashed his horses into a gallop, and the other, seeing from his white face and from his wife's collapse almost into a faint that his object was attained, rode away with a scowl and a laugh.

That night when Geoffrey went into the hall he passed over to the great fireplace, and all at once started back with a smothered cry. Then with an effort he pulled himself together and went away, returning with a light. He bent down over the broken hearth-stone to see if the moonlight falling through the storied window had in any way deceived him. Then with a groan of anguish he sank to his knees.

There, sure enough, through the crack in the broken stone were protruding a multitude of threads of golden hair just tinged with grey!

He was disturbed by a noise at the door, and looking round, saw his wife standing in the doorway. In the desperation of the moment he took action to prevent discovery, and lighting a match at the lamp, stooped down and burned away the hair that rose through the broken stone. Then rising nonchalantly as he could, he pretended surprise at seeing his wife beside him.

For the next week he lived in an agony; for, whether by accident or design, he could not find himself alone in the hall for any length of time. At each visit the hair had grown afresh through the crack, and he had to watch it carefully lest his terrible secret should be discovered. He tried to find a receptacle for the body of the murdered woman outside the house, but someone always interrupted him; and once, when he was coming out of the private doorway, he was met by his wife, who began to question him about it, and manifested surprise that she should not have before noticed the key which he now reluctantly showed her. Geoffrey dearly and passionately loved his wife, so that any possibility of her discovering his dread secrets, or even of doubting him, filled him with anguish; and after a couple of days had passed, he could not help coming to the conclusion that, at least, she suspected something.

That very evening she came into the hall after her drive and found him there sitting moodily by the deserted fireplace. She spoke to him directly.

'Geoffrey, I have been spoken to by that fellow Delandre, and he says horrible things. He tells to me that a week ago his sister returned to his house, the wreck and ruin of her former self, with only her golden hair as of old, and announced some fell intention. He asked me where she is – and oh, Geoffrey, she is dead, she is dead! So how can she have returned? Oh! I am in dread, and I know not where to turn!'

For answer, Geoffrey burst into a torrent of blasphemy which made her shudder. He cursed Delandre and his sister and all their kind, and in especial he hurled curse after curse on her golden hair.

'Oh, hush! Hush!' she said, and was then silent, for she feared her husband when she saw the evil effect of his humour. Geoffrey in the torrent of his anger stood up and moved away from the hearth; but suddenly stopped as he saw a new look of terror in his wife's eyes. He followed their glance, and then he, too, shuddered – for there on the broken hearth-stone lay a golden streak as the points of the hair rose through the crack.

'Look, look!' she shrieked. 'Is it some ghost of the dead? Come away

– come away!' and seizing her husband by the wrist with the frenzy of madness, she pulled him from the room.

That night she was in a raging fever. The doctor of the district attended her at once, and special aid was telegraphed for to London. Geoffrey was in despair, and in his anguish at the danger of his young wife almost forgot his own crime and its consequences. In the evening the doctor had to leave to attend to others; but he left Geoffrey in charge of his wife. His last words were:

'Remember, you must humour her till I come in the morning, or till some other doctor has her case in hand. What you have to dread is another attack of emotion. See that she is kept warm. Nothing more can be done.'

Late in the evening, when the rest of the household had retired, Geoffrey's wife got up from her bed and called to her husband.

'Come!' she said. 'Come to the old hall! I know where the gold comes from! I want to see it grow!'

Geoffrey would fain have stopped her, but he feared for her life or reason on the one hand, and lest in a paroxysm she should shrink out her terrible suspicion, and seeing that it was useless to try to prevent her, wrapped a warm rug around her and went with her to the old hall. When they entered, she turned and shut the door and locked it.

'We want no strangers amongst us three tonight!' she whispered with a wan smile.

'We three! Nay we are but two,' said Geoffrey with a shudder; he feared to say more.

'Sit here,' said his wife as she put out the light. 'Sit here by the hearth and watch the gold growing. The silver moonlight is jealous! See it steals along the floor towards the gold – our gold!' Geoffrey looked with growing horror, and saw that during the hours that had passed the golden hair had protruded further through the broken hearth-stone. He tried to hide it by placing his feet over the broken place; and his wife, drawing her chair beside him, leant over and laid her head on his shoulder.

'Now do not stir, dear,' she said; 'let us sit still and watch. We shall find the secret of the growing gold!' He passed his arm round her and sat silent; and as the moonlight stole along the floor she sank to sleep.

He feared to wake her; and so sat silent and miserable as the hours stole away.

Before his horror-struck eyes the golden hair from the broken stone grew and grew; and as it increased, so his heart got colder and colder, till at last he had not power to stir, and sat with eyes full of terror watching his doom.

In the morning when the London doctor came, neither Geoffrey nor his wife could be found. Search was made in all the rooms, but without avail. As a last resource the great door of the old hall was broken open, and those who entered saw a grim and sorry sight.

There by the deserted hearth Geoffrey Brent and his young wife sat cold and white and dead. Her face was peaceful, and her eyes were closed in sleep; but his face was a sight that made all who saw it shudder, for there was on it a look of unutterable horror. The eyes were open and stared glassily at his feet, which were twined with tresses of golden hair, streaked with grey, which came through the broken hearth-stone.

A Theme for Hyacinth

Julian Symons

Happiness, Robin Edgley thought as he felt the sun on his chest and stomach and legs, seeping through the epidermis to irradiate the blood and sinew and, yes, heart beneath; it is by pure chance that I have discovered happiness for the first time in my life. If Felix had not been laid low by influenza and been delayed leaving England for a week, Gerda would never have spoken to me and this would have been simply another holiday. Instead, it was a revelation to himself of his inmost nature.

Happiness, happiness! It was a golden body that you held in your hands on a green island beside a blue sea, but it was also – to move beyond that rather seaside-posterish conception – the inward reassurance given by his love for Gerda, the feeling of merging his identity with that of another human being, something that went beyond the possibilities of words.

Pleasurable warmth was turning into heat. Perhaps his front had been cooked sufficiently. He removed the bandage from his eyes, glanced round, and saw that he shared the terrace beside the sea with half a dozen old men and women; he turned onto his stomach and picked up the poetry anthology he had been reading. One poem, 'Le Monocle de Mon Oncle,' by Wallace Stevens, fascinated him. It was a middle-aged man's reflections on love:

> In the high west there burns a furious star.
> It is for fiery boys that star was set
> And for sweet-smelling virgins close to them.
> The measure of the intensity of love
> Is measure, also, of the verve of earth.

True, he thought. He felt in himself a sharpening of the senses, a deepened awareness of everything about him. But the next verse provoked disagreement.

When amorists grow bald, then amours shrink
Into the compass and curriculum
Of introspective exiles lecturing.
It is a theme for Hyacinth alone.

No, no, he cried silently. His head was silvered and not bald, but the point was that love between a mature man and a young woman could contain everything felt by those 'fiery boys' – and more, much more. Was the poem not proved untrue by almost the first words Gerda had spoken to him?

He was wondering at that time, three days ago, why he had ever come. He had succumbed to the boyish eagerness of his cousin Felix, and had regretted it almost immediately. Looking sideways at him out of those dark eyes that were absurdly long-lashed for a man's, Felix had said he was going away and asked why Nunky – which was his name for Robin, although they were not blood relations – didn't come too.

'I'm fed up with bloody agents, bloody producers, bloody theatre. Getting out of it, Nunky, going to look for the sun. Let them bloody ring my flat and not find me; they'll be keener when I come back. Since you're a man of leisure, why not make it a twosome? Where was he going? He didn't know, but it turned out to be Yugoslavia, the Adriatic coast, Dubrovnik. 'Boiling hot, wonderful swimming, fishing, and cheap. Not that that matters to you, but it does to me. And we might find a couple of birds. If you're so inclined.'

Again that sideways glance from the fine eyes that – he could admit it frankly now – always disturbed him. The disturbance came from the doubts about himself raised by such glances and by the impulse he felt at times to put an arm round the young man's shoulders, to push him playfully over onto a sofa when they had an argument. It was five years since Mary's death, and he had neither remarried nor even engaged in a love affair since then. Was there something wrong with him?

Thinking of his own fastidiousness, of the care he took about the colour and fit of clothes, of his liking for picking up nice little pieces of bric-a-brac and of putting them in just the right spot in his flat, he wondered whether he could possibly be (a word he disliked using, disliked even the thought of) queer? Or was it just that the rackety life Felix lived fascinated him, shifting quarterly from flat to flat, often out of work and sometimes tremendously hard up? Occasionally Robin had lent him small sums of money, which had always been returned, but he had worried even about these. Was he trying to buy affection?

He could admit all this now, since Gerda had proved that there was nothing queer about him.

So much for Felix, who had done him the best turn of his life by contracting influenza and by telephoning, in a woebegone voice about

which there was as always a hint of self-mockery, to say that he would
come out as soon as he felt better. But these had not been Robin's
thoughts as he took a hot bath, changed into a dashing maroon dinner
jacket, and sat down to dinner alone on that first night in the hotel.
Afterward he stood on the terrace leaning on his silver-headed malacca
cane, and stared gloomily at the lights of the old city. He felt a touch
on his arm.

'You will forgive me if I speak to you,' the girl said. 'But I could
not help looking at you in the restaurant. You were the most attractive
man in the room.' She paused and made a careful amendment. 'That
is not quite right. I should have said the most *interesting* man.'

That made it easier for him to say, 'Thank you.'

'My name is Gerda.'

'Robin Edgley.' She was young, blonde, beautiful. He felt a moment's
panic. 'Shall we sit down? Would you like a drink?'

When they were sitting in chairs that overlooked the bay, drinks by
their sides, he felt a little more comfortable. 'You took my breath away.
Do you often say that kind of thing to a strange man?'

'Never before. Please believe me.' She spoke gravely, and he did
believe her. She was not, he now saw, quite the dazzling beauty he had
thought. Her hair was silky and her features fine, but the large mouth
turned down sulkily at the corners and her blue eyes were very wide
apart under their thick blonde brows. The eyes looked cold, but a kind
of warmth came from her, almost as if some fire burned within her.
Her English was perfect, but accented.

He asked if she was German, and she nodded. 'You're a very unusual
girl.'

'Don't talk like that. As if you were my uncle.' She spoke sharply.
'We are the same age, you and I.'

'What nonsense. I might be your uncle. I am forty-five.' In fact, he
was four years older.

'I did not mean in that way. We feel the same emotions. When you
look at this landscape, what do you feel?'

He looked into gathering darkness, and she said impatiently, 'Not
now. When you came.'

'Romantic, I suppose.'

'And subtle.'

'Yes, romantic in a subtle way,' he said, although he had not felt
this at all.

'Young men do not feel such things. They bore me.' Without taking
breath, she asked, 'Shall we go for a walk?'

They walked in the Gradac Park, among old cypress and pine trees,
above the sea. He found himself talking with unusual freedom, telling
her that he had been a partner in a small firm manufacturing a new

kind of air vent for kitchens, and that he had retired from it a couple of years ago. He tried to explain something of his feeling.

'Suddenly it seemed ridiculous, going in to an office every day. I thought, is this all I'm going to do with my life? Of course, when Mary was alive it was different, but she died five years ago.'

'Mary?'

'My wife. I forgot you didn't know her. Isn't that silly?'

'Nothing about you is silly. Yes, there is one thing.' She pointed to the stick. 'Why use that? It is for lame men.'

'Ah, but you don't realize—' With a twist and a flourish he drew the sword from its sheath. 'If I am attacked.'

'I think it is foolish.' In her precise English it sounded very definite. 'What else have you found in life?'

'I don't know. Places – all the places I haven't seen. Poetry – I always liked reading poetry. Meeting people, not just English people.'

'Have you found what you hoped?'

'I don't know. Enough to be glad that I gave up business.'

But as he spoke it seemed to him that something was terribly missing. He asked what she did, and she laughed deep in her throat.

'You will see.' She would say nothing more. On the way back he was very conscious of her physical presence at his side. There was something animal, assured yet stealthy, about the movements of her body. Once he touched her arm and felt an almost irresistible desire to grip her shoulders and turn her to him. Then the moment was over and they were walking along again.

In the hotel lobby he was uncertain whether to suggest a drink in his room. Then that moment also passed. She said good night and was walking away, the golden hair like a cap at the back of her head.

On the following morning he woke in excellent spirits. He ate breakfast on the balcony outside his room and watched tourists going off in coaches to Mostar, the bay of Kotor, and on the Grand Tour of Montenegro. The holiday-makers, mostly brawny Germans and unbecomingly sunburned English, stood about chatting until they were shepherded by energetic guides into the coaches. The voices of the guides rang out like those of schoolteachers gathering children to cross the road.

'Hurry, please. We are already five minutes late.'

There was something familiar about the precision of the tone even as it floated up to him, and he identified her in a blue-and-white sleeveless dress, with a dark-blue peaked cap on the side of her head. She looked up, saw him, touched her fingers to her lips, then jumped into the coach and was gone.

He was in the sun lounge when the travellers returned in the early evening. He assured himself that he was not waiting for her, but the thrill that went through his body at sight of her golden hair under the peaked cap was something he had not felt for years.

She came up to him at once. Beads of moisture marked her upper lip. He asked if she wanted a drink. She shook her head. 'I am not presentable. Those coaches are hot. But in ten minutes I should like a large, *large* gin and tonic.'

He had it waiting for her in the bar. 'So you're a guide.'

'Only for a few days, with this one party. On Sunday my husband comes out. Then, we shall be on holiday.' Her petulant mouth turned down. 'His name is Porter, so that I am Gerda Porter. It sounds ridiculous. He is a travel agent. I thought it would be amusing to play the part of a guide, for just one party, so he arranged it.'

'He sounds nice.'

'Don't let us talk about him. Shall I come to your room now or after dinner?' He stared at her. 'I have shocked you? You do not like women to be frank?'

He went on staring, and she looked back with one thick eyebrow raised, half smiling. 'Now,' he said and then added, with what he felt at the time to be wretched pusillanimity, 'In separate lifts. We must be careful.'

They went up in separate elevators. They did not come down to dinner.

Two days later her party went home. He watched her with them, talking to the men, who asked about playing at the casino, where only foreign currency was permitted, and about making special trips to see what they called 'something of the way people really live here' (as though the Yugoslavs were another species), and with the women, who engaged her in endless chats about what they could buy and what they could take home.

She handled all their queries with efficiency, courtesy, and an apparently endless patience. After seeing them off at the airport, she came back and sat in a chair beside him.

'I'm glad that's over. What a boring lot!'

'You handled them perfectly.'

'Why not? I used to be a travel courier. I was enjoying it. But after meeting you—' She left the sentence unfinished. 'We have three days.'

'Three days?'

'Before my husband arrives.' Her eyes were like blue marbles.

That day they explored Dubrovnik, intoxicated by the pleasure of being in a city sacred to walkers. They wandered from side to side of the plaza looking in the windows of shops that all seemed to sell the same goods, priced head scarfs and rugs in the Gundulic Square market, ate unidentifiable fish at a little restaurant in Ul Siroka, made a circuit of the ramparts. After lunch they drank coffee on the terrace of the Gradska Kafana by the harbour. Then they hired a motorboat with surprising ease, and in the motorboat discovered the island.

The Dalmation coast is full of islands, including Lokrum, less than half a mile from the walled city, which appears to be covered with pine woods but, in fact, contains a park filled with subtropical vegetation and twenty small coves for bathers. Lokrum is a 'trippers' haunt,' but a little beyond it there are a dozen tiny islands, no more than a few hundred yards long, some almost pure rock, others covered by shrubs and dwarf trees, and with natural landing places.

It was one of these that they found, rowing in the last few yards and pulling up the boat into a tiny bay. They took off their clothes, swam naked in the clear blue water, then walked back a few yards from the beacon and made love on the grass. The walls of Dubrovnik were visible less than a mile away, yet they were completely alone. This is unreal, he told himself; it has nothing to do with any life I have ever known. These thoughts were interrupted by Gerda.

'Look at me! I sweat like a pig.' There was moisture on her brow and on her body. 'Disgusting. Not like you – your body is dry.'

'Dry with old age.'

'Don't talk like that; it's stupid. My husband is an old man.'

'Gerda—'

'And I do not wish you to call me Gerda; it is the name he uses. I tell you my secret name – it is Hella. You call me Hel.'

'Hel, you have shown me heaven,' he said inanely. 'Does he look like me, your husband?'

She snorted with laughter. 'You'll see.' With her face half-buried in grass, she told him about her life. Her parents had escaped from East to West Germany, and she had gone from West Germany to England, where she worked as an *au pair* girl. She had no intention of remaining with the family, but she could not get a job without a labour permit. So she forged one and was engaged as a courier by Porter Travel, Ltd.

'And then you married the boss.' He said it lightly, to hide the fact that her calm talk of forgery had shocked him.

'Yes.'

'You say he is – my age. Did he attract you?'

'Yes, but that was not important. He found out that my permit was no good, so it was the only thing to do. When I see something must be done, I do it.'

'You're ruthless.'

'When it is necessary. But if I had known what it would be like—' Again she did not finish the sentence, but stared at him with her brilliant marble eyes. Then she turned and ran down again to the sea. He got up and followed her.

It was on the island, the following day, that he told her he loved her. This was something he had not said to any woman, except to Mary in the early days of their marriage. She made no reply. 'But you don't love me, Hel, do you?'

'I am not sure. Anyway, it does not matter. It is Friday. On Sunday afternoon my husband will arrive.'

'Felix too. I've had a cable.' He had told her about Felix.

'When he is here, it will be all over.'

'I want to marry you.' He had not known that he was going to say these words, but as soon as they were uttered he knew them to be true. She remained silent. 'Did you hear me?'

'I heard you. It is impossible.'

'Why?'

'My husband is a Catholic. He would not divorce me.'

'If you left him, we could live together.' He was astonished to hear himself suggest it.

'He would bring a law case, drag you through the courts. Would you like that, respectable Robin? There is only one way we could be together.'

'How?'

'If he were dead.'

He had closed his eyes. Now he opened them. She had a towel wrapped round her, and she was leaning on one arm looking at him. He realized at once that she meant they should kill her husband in some way. He was not even surprised, for he understood by now the total ruthlessness of her character. But he was a conventional man, and conventional words accurately expressed his reaction. 'You must be mad.'

She made no reply, but began to dress. They went down to the boat in silence. Then she put her arms round him. 'I love you, Robin, but how can I permit myself to do so? What would be the use?'

'If you loved me, you wouldn't talk like that.'

'I love like a German. If I want something, I try to get it. If I cannot get it, I do without and don't complain. You do not have the courage to help me, so we have till Sunday. We can enjoy that much.'

But Robin did not enjoy it, or not in the same way. The sensual grip she exerted on him was very powerful. He had always thought of himself as a less than average sensual man, for he had never experienced with Mary anything like the feelings that Gerda inspired in him. The intensity of his actions and reactions during lovemaking frightened him, just as in a different way he was frightened by the feeling that he existed as an instrument for her satisfaction. He told himself that he loved her, but did he feel anything more than a sexual itch? Lines from another poem came into his head:

> But at my back from time to time I hear
> The sound of horns and motors which shall bring
> Sweeney to Mrs Porter in the spring.

To think of himself as ape-neck Sweeney, the image of mindless sensuality, distressed and worried him. But overriding such feelings was the longing he felt for her that made another part of himself say, 'This is the first happiness you have had in your long dreary life. Are you going to throw it away?'

He held out until Sunday morning. On Saturday they went to the island, but it was not a success, and on Sunday morning neither of them suggested a visit. When they found that two places were vacant on a coach expedition to Cilipi, a few miles away, to see the peasants come to church in local costume, they got in.

The scene as they approached was farcical. Dozens of coaches were drawn up along the roadside. They parked half a mile from the church square. When they reached it, the place was packed with camera-carrying tourists, taking shots of everything in sight. A few locals moved in and out of the throng, the women wearing white nunlike coifs, embroidered blouses, and long black skirts. Tourists snapped cameras within inches of their faces, asked them to hold still, climbed onto cars to get angled shots. A scrawny American with white knees showing below baggy shorts aimed his camera at a fezzed village elder who sat placidly smoking a long clay pipe.

'Excuse it, please.' The American pushed Robin and Gerda aside, dropped to one knee, then suddenly flung himself flat onto the ground and squinted up at the Cilipian, who stared into the distance with imperturbable dignity. Robin looked at Gerda. They both burst out laughing, then walked out of the square and the village down a rough path that led through scrub to nowhere.

'You do not have your cane.' He had left it in his room ever since that first evening. He said curtly she had been right, he did not need it. She glanced at him, said nothing.

'Did you ever see anything so awful as those tourists? The Yugoslavs must think we're all barbarians.'

'But I am a barbarian. You think so.' Her words were like an accusation.

She leaned against a rock. 'You are afraid of everything. If I said to you, take me into that field, make love to me, would you do it?'

'Hel, it wouldn't be—' Two coiffed women came up the stony path. '*Dobar dan,*' he said.

'*Dobar dan.*' They passed on.

She said ironically, as he stumbled on a rock, 'You need your cane. I think you should carry it.' She wore dark glasses, but he knew that behind them her blue eyes would be cold. He could not bear the thought of losing her. 'Hel, tell me what you want.'

'It must be what *we* want.'

'What we want.' When he put his hand on her arm, it seemed to burn him.

She told him in her precise English, speaking in a rapid, low voice. She used sleeping tablets and would put two of them into her husband's coffee one day after lunch. Robin would take him out in the boat. In half an hour her husband would be asleep. Near the island the boat would overturn, and the sleeping man would drown. Robin was a strong swimmer, he could easily reach the island. There he would wait until a boat saw him, or an expedition came looking for them from Dubrovnik.

'It would be murder.'

'He would know nothing.'

'I should be suspected. People have seen us together.'

'Do you think the Yugoslav police will trouble about that? They are peasants, like the people here. It is obviously an accident. Probably they do not find the body. And if they do—' The sulky mouth curved upward in a smile. 'I will tell you something. He cannot swim.'

' "La Belle Dame sans Merci," ' he said.

'What is that?'

'A poem. It means you are ruthless. And I am in thrall to you.'

'I do not understand.'

'Yes. It means that I say yes.'

She did not reply, did not take off the dark glasses, merely looked at him and nodded. Then she took his hand and led him into the field. The pleasure that followed was intense, and almost painful.

'You're looking uncommonly fit, Nunky,' Felix said. 'A fine bronzed figure of an Englishman. You bear every sign of not having missed me. Discovered any female talent?'

'Don't be absurd.'

'Most of them look over the age of consent to me.'

'I have been out once or twice with Mrs Porter. Her husband was on your plane. They're staying at this hotel.'

'Little fat chap – I remember him meeting her. A blonde piece, a bit too Nordic for me.'

'She is of German origin,' he said with what he knew to be ridiculous stiffness.

Felix looked at him and whistled. 'You sound as if you've fallen for the fair Nordic lady. I shall have to look after you, Nunky, I can see that.'

He went out with Felix in the boat that afternoon, and landed on the island. They both swam, and then Felix put on his skindiving equipment and disappeared for three-quarters of an hour while Robin lay on the beach and thought about Hel. Her absence ached in him like a tooth, and when Felix reappeared and talked enthusiastically about the marvellous clarity of the water, so that he could see fish swimming fifty feet below him, and said it would be quite easy to swim from the island to Dubrovnik, he heard himself becoming unreasonably snappish.

The old relationship with Felix, in which he had responded eagerly to his young cousin's coquettish facetiousness, had been replaced by a feeling of irritation. He no longer wished to be called Nunky and felt no inclination to indulge in pseudo-boyish horseplay. When the young man took out a mirror and began carefully to comb his hair, he felt a faint stirring of distaste.

Closing his eyes, he immediately saw Hel in bed with her fat stumpy husband, forced to accept his lovemaking or – worse still – welcoming it. He got up, walked to the water's edge, began to throw stones into the sea. Felix watched him with a smiling mouth and inquisitive eyes.

She introduced him to Porter that evening. Good Heavens, Robin thought as he looked at the squat paunchy little man who shook hands with him, he's *old*! However did she bring herself to marry him? It was a shock to remember that Porter was no more than two or three years older than himself, but then there was the difference between them of a man who had kept his body in trim and one who had let it go to seed.

'Hear you've been squiring Gerda around, Mr Edgley. I appreciate that. Not that she's had much spare time, with this crazy idea she had of being guide to one of my parties. Had to indulge her – I'm an indulgent man, isn't that so, my dear?' He patted her hand.

'From what I saw, she was a most efficient guide.'

'Should be. Used to do it for a living; now it's for fun. I tell you what I'd like, Robin – don't mind if I call you that; I know Gerda does – what I'd like is for you and your friend to be my guests this evening. Let's go and paint this little old Communist town red.'

'Norman knows all the best places,' Gerda said without smiling.

'I should, my dear, I should. The food at this place is – well, it's hotel food, and that's all you can say for it. But I know a little place where – well, you leave it to me.' He winked one eye.

It was a terrible evening. They ate a special Montenegrin dinner, which began with smoked ham, followed by red mullet and *raznici*, which proved to be a brother to *kebab*, meat grilled on a skewer. The restaurant was set in a garden, just outside the city walls.

Porter – or as he insisted on being called, Norman – talked Serbo-Croat to waiters who responded in English. They drank slivovitz to begin with, continued with several bottles of full red Yugoslav wine, and ended with more slivovitz. Norman sent back one bottle of slivovitz with what

sounded like a flow of objectionable remarks in Serbo-Croat. When the
waiter shrugged and brought a bottle of another make, he said triumphantly, 'You see. You have to know to get the right stuff.'

There was a band and all three of them danced with Gerda. When
Robin moved round, feeling the hard warmth of her body beneath his
hand, he found the sensation almost intolerable. 'You see what he is
like,' she said. 'An old man. Disgusting.'

'Not much older than I am.'

'Do not be stupid. It is not at all the same.'

'Hel, I have to see you, talk to you.'

'We cannot,' she said crisply. 'This I told you.'

'I just have to see you alone.'

'Impossible. Besides, what is there to talk about? Today is Sunday.
Tomorrow after lunch.'

The dance was almost finished before he said, 'Yes.'

Felix danced with Gerda, holding her as lightly as possible, his arched
nostrils slightly distended, his head held high in the manner of a horse
ready to shy at what he may meet round the next corner. They seemed
to exchange little conversation. Norman drank another glass of slivovitz,
belched slightly.

'After this, I want you to be my guests at the casino.'

'Very kind of you, but—' Robin protested.

'Won't take but for an answer. Beautiful, isn't she?'

An alarming remark. Robin did not know what to say. 'Very charming.'

'Some men would be jealous. Not me. I like it, like her to have other
friends. I understand.' He drummed with his fingers on the table. Robin
realized that his host was drunk. 'I've never regretted anything – want
you to know that. No regrets, no heel taps. Loveliest girl I ever saw,
married her. What d'you say to that?'

Robin had no desire to say anything to it. When Gerda and Felix
came back, Porter rose a little unsteadily. 'May I have the pleasure?'

She said nothing, but moved into his arms. Felix seemed about to
speak, then did not. Robin watched them dancing. Porter's arm was
on her bare back, and he seemed to be talking continuously.

Felix, like a man who has come to a decision, said, 'Nunky.'

Irritation spilled over. 'Once and for all, will you please understand
that I do not want to be called by that ridiculous name!'

'Sorry.'

There was a disturbance among the dancers. Gerda emerged from
it, half-supporting her husband. Porter sat down heavily, closed his eyes,
and opened them again. He insisted they must all go on to the casino,
but with the headwaiter's help they got a taxi and returned to the hotel.
During the taxi ride Porter began to snore. At the hotel Felix and Robin

each took an arm to get him into the elevator. In the bedroom Gerda removed his jacket and waved them away.

'I can put him to bed, thank you. I have done it before.'

Alone in his room, Robin looked at himself in the glass. Below the abundant white hair, his face was youthful. Calves and thighs were slightly withered, but his body was supple, his stomach flat.

'With this body I thee worship,' he said aloud. He picked up the malacca walking stick, drew the sword from it, made a few passes at an imaginary enemy. Perhaps he too was a little drunk, he thought as he carried on a dialogue with himself while staring into the glass.

Robin Edgley, he said, retired director of a firm manufacturing fan ventilators, you are reaching out for happiness, and there is only one way to obtain it. Make up your mind to that. But what you are about to do is crazy, another part of himself said; you are thinking of forever, but she is thinking of today and tomorrow and perhaps next year. And not only is it crazy, but it is wrong, opposed to all the instincts you have lived by since youth. How can you imagine that after doing wrong you will be happy? What does that matter, the first voice said, when I have been given a glimpse of eternity. . . .

It was a long time before he fell asleep, and when he slept he dreamed. He was in the sea and Porter was with him, the boat overturned; he was holding Porter under the water, but instead of submitting quietly, the man flailed and twisted like a fish. Then Robin gripped a throat which was smooth, young, and white instead of the swollen wrinkled column he was expecting, and it was Hel's throat he was squeezing, her face that was gaspingly lifted to his own before he too started to gasp and thrash about, conscious that life was being pressed out of him—

He woke with the sheet twisted round his body. The dream disturbed him. There was some element in it that he could not recall; something had happened that his conscious mind refused to register. He looked at his watch and saw that it was only two o'clock. He did not sleep again until four. . . .

In the morning Porter looked pale but cheerful. At eleven o'clock he was drinking a champagne cocktail on the terrace. 'Hear you put me to bed last night, old man; very nice of you. Sort of thing that's liable to happen, you know, first night.' He spoke like the victim of some natural disaster.

'How do you feel now?'

'I'm okay. Champagne with cognac always puts me right. Though, mind you, it's got to be cognac, not this filthy local brandy. You're a fisherman, Gerda tells me.'

'I do fish, yes.'

'How about taking a boat after lunch, the two of us, eh?'

'I'm really not at all expert.'

'That's all right, neither am I. We'll just trawl for mullet and bream – what do they call 'em here, *dentex*? That's a hell of a name to give a fish.

'What about your wife?'

'She wants to go to Lokrum, going to show it to that cousin of yours. I've been out half a dozen times myself, sooner do a bit of fishing. Bores Gerda; I know it does. Anyway, I want to have a quiet natter.'

'All right, let's go fishing.'

Later, walking round Dubrovnik with Felix, he learned a little more about the intended expedition to Lokrum. Sitting between the coupled columns in the elegant cloister of the Franciscan monastery, swinging a leg clad in tight sky-blue slacks, Felix calmly admitted that he had deliberately arranged it.

'Let's be frank about it; Porter's a slob, but Hel's poison. You don't want to be mixed up with her.'

'I am not mixed up, as you put it.'

'Oh, come *on*.' Felix could not help posing, whatever his surroundings, and now he turned away from Robin so that his fine profile was outlined against the grey stone like the head on a coin. 'You follow her with your eyes wherever she goes, you treat her as though she were made of china. And believe me, she's not; she's tough as old boots. I know her kind.' Robin made no reply. Felix went on. 'Even old slob Porter must spot it soon. So I thought I'd remove you from temptation this afternoon. And for the rest of the time we're here – well, they tell me there are lots of perfectly fascinating places to see on guided tours.'

'Thank you.' He knew how much Felix disliked guided tours.

'Think nothing of it. And now, shall we go and look at the Museum of the Socialist Revolution? You know, I've been longing to do that ever since I got here.'

They visited the museum and then went round the ramparts. Coming away from them down the narrow steps, Felix slipped and fell. He got up and grimaced. He had twisted his ankle. After hobbling back to the hotel, he borrowed Robin's stick. 'If I'm going to hobble, I'll do it in style, look like a man of distinction.'

He was with Gerda alone for a few minutes before lunch. She wore an 'op-art' dress in zigzags that drew a great many eyes to her. Catching a brief glimpse of them both in a glass and admiring his own dark-blue linen shirt and pale trousers, he could not help thinking they made a handsome couple. She let him buy her a drink in the bar. She spoke rapidly.

'This afternoon your cousin takes me to Lokrum, so I shall be out of the way. You will drink coffee with us after lunch.'

'Hel, I don't know.'

'What?' she said sharply. 'What do you not know?'

'Whether I can go through with it.'

She finished her drink, turned on her heel, and left him.

After lunch it was Porter who stopped by their table and suggested that they all have coffee together. Really, Robin thought, if ever a man could be called the architect of his own destruction, it was Porter – but no doubt Hel had put him up to it. She smiled briefly as she waited for them at the table, with coffee already poured. Porter was jovial.

'You know what made me marry Gerda? Because she's the most honest woman I ever met.'

'Is that so?' Felix made the question sound like an insult.

'You know, she worked for me as a courier, and I found she had a phony work permit. So when I said marry me, she said, "I might consider it; this way at least I won't have to worry about a permit." '

'The kind of thing that other people think I am prepared to say.' Gerda spoke with a touch of complacency.

'And would you believe it, she made another condition. A girl in her position, making conditions with me!' He roared with laughter. 'You're more than twice my age, she says; you'll have the best years of my life. So what happens to me when you die? She actually *said* that, mind you. So I told her I'd look after her and I have.'

'Very rash.' Felix murmured the words so that Porter did not hear them, but Gerda did.

'I am a German, and Germans are realistic.' Her glance at Felix was hostile. It seemed likely to be an uncomfortable afternoon for them both on Lokrum. 'We will walk down to the boat with you. If you can manage that,' she said to Felix.

'I'm improving rapidly.' Certainly he limped much less as they went down to the harbour. Porter was carrying some fishing tackle in case, as he said, he had a chance to use it. Robin changed into clean shorts. The crisp elegance of his appearance contrasted favourably, he thought, with Porter's sweat-stained shirt and general grubbiness.

The slick young man who rented the boat indicated with a slightly contemptuous air the trawling lines fixed to it, and Porter nodded and waved his hand to indicate that he did not need to be told. He climbed in, complete with fishing tackle. Robin, in the stern, started the outboard, and they were away. Felix and Gerda waved from the harbour.

They skirted Lokrum and moved into the open water beyond. Porter dropped his lines, lighted a pipe, and sat back. He looked what he was – a prosperous businessman carrying too much weight. Robin stared at him, unable to believe what he was going to do.

'Tell me something.' Porter's next words were inaudible. Robin almost closed the throttle, so that the boat jogged up and down on the blue water.

'What's that?'

'I like you, Robin, so I thought I ought to—' His next words were again inaudible. 'Gerda,' he ended.

'I can't hear properly.' He closed the throttle completely, so that the motor cut out. They drifted slowly towards the island, his island, only a few hundred yards away. Porter's voice came through the stillness.

'Gerda likes to be with me. I don't say she's happy, because she's not a contented person, never would be. But don't get the wrong idea.'

'I don't know what you mean.'

'She likes me. She thinks of crazy things, does them sometimes. Ran away from me once, came back after a couple of weeks, no money. She needs money; that's her motive power, like the engine that runs this boat. So she always comes back.'

'Why are you telling me this?' There was something wrong in the boat.

'Just wanted you to understand. I'm not a fool, Robin – I may look it, but I'm not. Why do you think I let her do this crazy little job out here? Think I haven't got other couriers? I knew she wanted an affair, wanted to let off steam.'

With a feeling of disbelief he saw that his cane lay just below Porter's fishing tackle. 'How did that get there?' he cried.

'What? Oh, the cane. Your cousin asked me to slip it in with my tackle; thought you might need it. In case the rocks were slippery, he said. He's a bit of a joker, that boy.'

'I don't understand.'

'About Gerda, now; don't get the wrong idea; that's all. You were just a pebble who happened to be on the beach. She doesn't like men of our age. I ought to know.' Porter knocked out his pipe. 'Okay, start her up again.'

Robin tugged savagely at the cord, and the outboard sprang to life. They roared through the water with the throttle wide open. When will it happen, he thought, when are the pills going to work? I can't stand much more of this. He felt weary himself, a weariness that sprang from the bad dreams and restlessness of the night.

Porter's voice seemed to come from far away, and he ignored it. The island loomed larger, and momentarily he lost his grip on the tiller. Porter was scrambling towards him, his face alarmed. The boat rocked. Robin began to laugh.

'Better not upset the boat when you can't swim,' Robin warned.

'Who the hell told you I couldn't swim? All fat men can swim. Here, give me the tiller; I'll take the boat in. Are you ill?'

He wanted to say that he had the situation under control and that Porter's own wife had said he was a non-swimmer; but suddenly he was too tired to speak. *She's made a mess of it*, he thought as Porter leaned over him, pushing him to the bottom of the boat in his anxiety to steer.

She put the pills in the wrong cup. Then he could no longer keep his eyes open.

He was in the middle of a dream which was both pleasurable and disturbing. Pleasurable because he was not fighting for breath as he had been last night, nor involved in any kind of struggle. He lay on the island beach, just a few yards from the sea, the sun burning down. Concern about the boat was removed by the sight of it carefully drawn up onto the beach.

Good old Porter! All that nonsense about the boat overturning – it must have been nonsense, because Porter could swim. It had been a figment of his imagination. 'Figment,' he said happily, but could not hear the word. When he felt more energetic, he would go into the sea.

Why was he disturbed, then? Well, first of all, was he dreaming or not? 'Do I wake or sleep?' he asked, but again could hear no words spoken. But that was not the main thing. The main thing was that in his dream he had heard a cry. Perhaps the cry of a bird, but no bird was visible. Had the cry wakened him, or was he still dreaming?

He found it difficult to focus. The boat, like everything else, looked hazy. And now a monster appeared in the sea, vanished, reappeared briefly, then sank under the waves. What kind of monster? Dark and with nothing very distinguishable in the way of a head; a strange dark monster that writhed and splashed and vanished. The sea snake of Dubrovnik?

But surely sea snakes did not exist. I refuse to believe in you, monster, he thought, you are part of my dream. And sure enough, the monster had gone – he *was* dreaming. He closed his eyes again.

When they reopened the sun was low in the sky and had lost its power. He felt cold, he knew that he was awake, and his uneasiness had increased. Where was Porter? Asleep somewhere else? It was still an effort to move, and a greater effort to think.

Had Porter gone back to Dubrovnik? There was something wrong with this idea, and he worked out what it was. Porter could not have gone to Dubrovnik or the boat would not still be on the beach.

Something else worried him, something done or said which he must try to remember. Was it perhaps that he had never even attempted what he had set out to do, that whether through his fault or hers he had failed? Oh, hell, he thought, oh, hell, oh, Hel, what is there left for us now?

And then he traced the origin of this particular uneasiness. Hel, she had said, was a special name, one that even her husband never used, and that he himself must never use in public. He had not done so. How did it happen that Felix knew the name? He remembered the conversation, which seemed long ago, although it was only this morning; he even remembered the words: 'Porter's just a slob, but Hel's poison.'

Desperately, like a man submerged trying to reach the surface, he
strove to understand this but failed.

At the far end of the beach, jewels glittered. Were they diamonds?
Through the haze of his mind came the thought that jewels are not
found on beaches. If he was lying on jewels, it would be proof that he
was dreaming. He picked up a handful of sand, looked at it, saw that
it was the characteristic powdery shingle of the coast. It did not shine,
so why were diamonds flashing less than a hundred yards away?

Collect them, he thought, sell them, and he would be rich. He tried
to get up, dropped on his knees again dizzily, and then managed it.
Tottering like an invalid, he approached the thing that shone. Half a
dozen yards away he identified it. His swordstick, removed from its
walking-stick sheath, was what glittered in the setting sun.

But that was not surprising – the sun always glittered on metal. But
what was it doing here, and why did one end of it look dull? At the
same time he noticed dark smears on his shirt.

He ran down to the sea, dipped the blade in the water. The stick
itself lay a little farther back up the beach. He stared at it, stared again
at the blade, began to shiver. The putt-putt of an engine came into
his consciousness, and looking out to sea, he saw a motor launch making
for the island. A man in uniform stood in the bow, blasts sounded on a
hooter.

Robin Edgley dropped to his knees and prayed that what he saw and
felt might still be a dream. . . .

The young Yugoslav lieutenant of police and his assistant found the
woman's husband without difficulty. The body lay a few yards back
from the beach in a hollow, with stab wounds through the chest. The
weapon was present, the sword stick which the man Edgley had been
cleaning in the water.

As for the motive, the woman herself had admitted behaving badly
with Edgley when she called on them to ask for police help because
she was worried that the boat had not returned. The lieutenant found
the situation both ridiculous and disgusting. One would not have supposed – this was the only surprise – that so fussy a man as this Englishman
would have been capable of so vigorous a reaction.

He offered no resistance when the lieutenant handcuffed him. They
put the dead man into the other boat, and his assistant brought it back.
On the return journey the lieutenant, who was proud of the English
he had learned as a second language at school, tried without success
to make conversation. The Englishman said almost nothing, except when
they passed Lokrum. Then he made the suggestion that a man wearing
skindiving equipment could have swum from Lokrum to the island.

'It would be possible,' said the lieutenant. 'But what man? And my dear Mr Edgley, how would he have obtained your sword? And why were you cleaning the sword when we came?'

'It is hopeless,' Edgley said, and then after a pause, 'It was all planned, of course.'

Was this a kind of religious determinism, a reference to the God in whom Edgley no doubt believed? The lieutenant decided to make the situation clear. 'It is hopeless to attempt to deceive. But it was a crime of passion. You will find that we understand such things. You will perhaps be only five years in prison.'

The Englishman made no reply. He said only one more thing, just before they tied up in Dubrovnik harbour. The woman waited there, her gold hair visible in the dusk. A man whom the lieutenant knew to be Edgley's cousin waited with her. Edgley then said something which the lieutenant, in spite of his excellent English, did not understand. 'Will you please repeat that?' he asked, a little annoyed.

'A theme for Hyacinth,' Edgley said. 'It is a theme for Hyacinth alone.'

It made no better sense the second time.

Miss Smith

William Trevor

One day Miss Smith asked James what a baby horse was called, and
James couldn't remember. He blinked and shook his head. He knew,
he explained, but he just couldn't remember. Miss Smith said:

'Well, well; James Machen doesn't know what a baby horse is called.'

She said it loudly so that everyone in the class-room heard. James
became very confused. He blinked and said:

'Pony, Miss Smith?'

'Pony! James Machen says a baby horse is a pony! Hands up everyone
who knows what a baby horse is.'

All the right arms in the room, except James's and Miss Smith's, shot
upwards. Miss Smith smiled at James.

'Everyone knows,' she said. 'Everyone knows what a baby horse is
called except James.'

James thought: I'll run away. I'll join the tinkers and live in a tent.

'What's a baby horse called?' Miss Smith asked the class, and the
class shouted:

'Foal, Miss Smith.'

'A foal, James,' Miss Smith repeated. 'A baby horse is a foal, James dear.'

'I knew, Miss Smith. I knew but...'

Miss Smith laughed and the class laughed, and afterwards nobody
would play with James because he was so silly to think that a baby
horse was a pony.

James was an optimist about Miss Smith. He thought it might be
different when the class went on the summer picnic or sat tightly together
at the Christmas party, eating cake and biscuits and having their mugs
filled from big enamel jugs. But it never was different. James got left
behind when everyone was racing across the fields at the picnic, and
Miss Smith had to wait impatiently, telling the class that James would
have to have his legs stretched. And at the party she heaped his plate
with seed cake, because she imagined so she said, that he was the kind
of child who enjoyed such fare.

Once James found himself alone with Miss Smith in the class-room.

She was sitting at her desk correcting some homework. James was staring in front of him, admiring a fountain pen that the day before his mother had bought for him. It was a small fountain pen, coloured purple and black and white. James believed it to be elegant.

It was very quiet in the class-room. Soundlessly, Miss Smith's red pencil ticked and crossed and underlined. Without looking up, she said: 'Why don't you go out and play?'

'Yes, Miss Smith,' said James. He walked to the door, clipping his pen into his pocket. As he turned the handle he heard Miss Smith utter a sound of irritation. He turned and saw that the point of her pencil had broken. 'Miss Smith, you may borrow my pen. You can fill it with red ink. It's quite a good pen.'

James crossed the room and held out his pen. Miss Smith unscrewed the cap and prodded at the paper with the nib. 'What a funny pen, James!' she said. 'Look, it can't write.'

'There's no ink in it,' James explained. 'You've got to fill it with red ink, Miss Smith.'

But Miss Smith smiled and handed the pen back. 'What a silly boy you are to waste your money on such a poor pen!'

'But I didn't . . .'

'Come along now, James, aren't you going to lend me your pencil sharpener?'

'I haven't got a pencil sharpener, Miss Smith.'

'No pencil sharpener? Oh James, James, you haven't got anything, have you?'

When Miss Smith married, James imagined he had escaped her for ever. But the town they lived in was a small one and they often met in the street or in a shop. And Miss Smith, who at first found marriage rather boring, visited the school quite regularly. 'How's James?' she would say, smiling alarmingly at him. 'How's my droopy old James?'

Then, when Miss Smith had been married for about a year she gave birth to a son, which occupied her a bit. He was a fine child, eight pounds six ounces, with a good long head and blue eyes. Miss Smith was delighted with him, and her husband, a solicitor, complimented her sweetly and bought cigars and drinks for all his friends. In time, mother and son were seen daily taking the air: Miss Smith on her trim little legs and the baby in his frilly pram. James, meeting the two, said: 'Miss Smith, may I see the baby?' But Miss Smith laughed and said that she was not Miss Smith any more. She wheeled the pram rapidly away, as though the child within it might be affected by the proximity of the other.

'What a dreadful little boy that James Machen is!' Miss Smith reported to her husband. 'I feel so sorry for the parents.'

'Do I know him? What does the child look like?'

'Small, dear, like a weasel wearing glasses. He quite gives me the creeps.'

Almost without knowing it, James developed a compulsion about Miss Smith. At first it was quite a simple compulsion: just that James had to talk to God about Miss Smith every night before he went to sleep, and try to find out from God what it was about him that Miss Smith so despised. Every night he lay in bed and had his conversation, and if once he forgot it James knew that the next time he met Miss Smith she would probably say something that might make him drop down dead.

After about a month of conversation with God James discovered that he had found the solution. It was so simple that he marvelled he had never thought of it before. He began to get up very early in the morning and pick bunches of flowers. He would carry them down the street to Miss Smith's house and place them on a window-sill. He was careful not to be seen, by Miss Smith or by anyone else: he knew that if anyone saw him the plan couldn't work. When he had picked all the flowers in his own garden he started to pick them from other people's garden. He became rather clever at moving silently through the gardens, picking flowers for Miss Smith.

Unfortunately, though, on the day that James carried his thirty-first bunch of blooms to the house of Miss Smith he was observed. He saw the curtains move as he reached up to lay the flowers on the window-sill. A moment later Miss Smith, in her dressing-gown, had caught him by the shoulder and pulled him into the house.

'James Machen! It would be James Machen, wouldn't it? Flowers from the creature, if you please! What are you up to, you dozey James?'

James said nothing. He looked at Miss Smith's dressing-gown and thought it was particularly pretty: blue and woolly, with an edging of silk.

'You've been trying to get us into trouble,' cried Miss Smith. 'You've been stealing flowers all over the town and putting them at our house. You're an underhand child, James.'

James stared at her, and then ran away.

After that, James thought of Miss Smith almost all the time. He thought of her face when she caught him with the flowers, and how she had afterwards told his father and nearly everyone else in the town. He thought of how his father had had to say he was sorry to Miss Smith, and how his mother and father had quarrelled about the affair. He counted up all the things Miss Smith had ever said to him, and all the things she had ever done to him, like giving him seed cake at the Christmas party. He hadn't meant to harm Miss Smith as she said he had. Giving people flowers wasn't unkind; it was to show them you liked them and wanted them to like you.

'When somebody hurts you,' James said to the man who came to cut the grass, 'what do you do about it?'

'Well,' said the man, 'I suppose you hurt them back.'

'Supposing you can't,' James argued.

'Oh, but you always can. It's easy to hurt people.'

'It's not, really,' James said.

'Look,' said the man, 'all I've got to do is to reach out and give you a clip on the ear. That'd hurt you.'

'But I couldn't do that to you. Because you're too big. How d'you hurt someone who's bigger than you?'

'It's easier to hurt people who are weaker. People who are weaker are always the ones who get hurt.'

'Can't you hurt someone who is stronger?'

The grass-cutter thought for a time. 'You have to be cunning to do that. You've got to find the weak spot. Everyone has a weak spot.'

'Have you got a weak spot?'

'I suppose so.'

'Could I hurt you on your weak spot?'

'You don't want to hurt me, James.'

'No, but just could I?'

'Yes, I suppose you could.'

'Well then?'

'My little daughter's smaller than you. If you hurt her, you see, you'd be hurting me. It'd be the same, you see.'

'I see,' said James.

All was not well with Miss Smith. Life, which had been so happy when her baby was born, seemed now to be directed against her. Perhaps it was that the child was becoming difficult, going through a teething phase that was pleasant for no one; or perhaps it was that Miss Smith recognized in him some trait she disliked and knew that she would be obliged to watch it develop, powerless to intervene. Whatever the reason, she felt depressed. She often thought of her teaching days, of the big square schoolroom with the children's models on the shelves and the pictures of kings on the walls. Nostalgically, she recalled the feel of frosty air on her face as she rode her bicycle through the town, her mind already practising the first lesson of the day. She had loved those winter days: the children stamping their feet in the playground, the stove groaning and cracking, so red and so fierce that it had to be penned off for safety's sake. It had been good to feel tired, good to bicycle home, shopping a bit on the way – home to tea and the wireless and an evening of reading by the fire. It wasn't that she regretted anything; it was just that now and again, for a day or two, she felt she would like to return to the past.

*

'My dear,' Miss Smith's husband said, 'you really will have to be more careful.'

'But I am. Truly I am. I'm just as careful as anyone can be.'

'Of course you are. But it's a difficult age. Perhaps, you know, you need a holiday.'

'But I've had difficult ages to deal with for years . . .'

'Now now, my dear, it's not quite the same, teaching a class of kids.'

'But it shouldn't be as difficult. I don't know . . .'

'You're tired. Tied to a child all day long, every day of the week, it's no joke. We'll take an early holiday.'

Miss Smith did feel tired, but she knew that it wasn't tiredness that was really the trouble. Her baby was almost two, and for two years she knew she had been making mistakes with him. Yet somehow she felt that they weren't her mistakes. It was as though some other person occasionally possessed her: a negligent worthless kind of person, who was cruel, almost criminal, in her carelessness. Once she discovered the child crawling on the pavement beside his pram: she had apparently forgotten to attach his harness to the pram hooks. Once there had been beads in his pram, hundreds of them, small and red and made of glass. A woman had drawn her attention to the danger, regarding curiously the supplier of so unsuitable a plaything. 'In his nose he was putting one, dear. And may have swallowed a dozen already. It could kill a mite, you know.' The beads were hers, but how the child had got them she could not fathom. Earlier, when he had been only a couple of months, she had come into his nursery to find an excited cat scratching at the clothes of his cot; and on another occasion she had found him eating a turnip. She wondered if she might be suffering from some kind of serious absentmindedness, or blackouts. Her doctor told her, uncomfortingly, that she was a little run down.

'I'm a bad mother,' said Miss Smith to herself; and she cried as she looked at her child, warm and pretty in his sleep.

But her carelessness continued, and people remarked that it was funny in a teacher. Her husband was upset and unhappy, and finally suggested that they should employ someone to look after the child. 'Someone else?' said Miss Smith. 'Someone *else*? Am I then incapable? Am I so wretched and stupid that I cannot look after my own child? You speak to me as though I were half crazy.' She felt confused and sick and miserable: The marriage teetered beneath the tension, and there was no question of further children.

Then there were two months without incident. Miss Smith began to feel better; she was getting the hang of things; once again she was in control of her daily life. Her child grew and flourished. He trotted nimbly beside her, he spoke his own language, he was wayward and irresponsible, and to Miss Smith and her husband he was intelligent and full of charm. Every day Miss Smith saved up the sayings and doings of this child and duly reported them to her husband. 'He is quite intrepid,' Miss Smith said, and she told her husband how the child would tumble about the room, trying to stand on his head. 'He has an aptitude for athletics,' her husband remarked. They laughed that they, so un-athletic in their ways, should have produced so physically lively an offspring.

'And how has our little monster been today?' Miss Smith's husband asked, entering the house one evening at his usual time.

Miss Smith smiled, happy after a good, quiet day. 'Like gold,' she said.

Her husband smiled too, glad that the child had not been a nuisance to her and glad that his son, for his own sake, was capable of adequate behaviour. 'I will just take a peep at him,' he announced, and he ambled off to the nursery.

He sighed with relief as he climbed the stairs, thankful that all was once again well in the house. He was still sighing when he opened the nursery door and smelt gas. It hissed insidiously from the unlit fire. The room was sweet with it. The child, sleeping, sucked it into his lungs.

The child's face was blue. They carried him from the room, both of them helpless and inadequate in the situation. And then they waited, without speaking, while his life was recovered, until the moment when the doctor, white-coated and stern, explained that it had been a nearer thing than he would wish again to handle.

'This is too serious,' Miss Smith's husband said. 'We cannot continue like this. Something must be done.'

'I cannot understand . . .'

'It happens too often. The strain is too much for me, dear.'

'I cannot understand it.'

Every precaution had been taken with the gas fire in the nursery. The knob that controlled the gas pressure was a key and the key was removable. Certainly, the control point was within the child's reach, but one turned it on or off, slipped the key out of its socket, and placed it on the mantelpiece. That was the simple rule.

'You forgot to take out the key,' Miss Smith's husband said. In his mind an idea took on a shape that frightened him. He shied away, watching it advance, knowing that he possessed neither the emotional nor the mental equipment to fight it.

'No, no, no,' Miss Smith said. 'I never forget it. I turned the fire off and put the key on the mantelpiece. I remember distinctly.'

He stared at her, drilling his eyes into hers, hopelessly seeking the truth. When he spoke his voice was dry and weary.

'The facts speak for themselves. You cannot suggest there's another solution?'

'But it's absurd. It means he got out of his cot, turned the key, returned to bed and went to sleep.'

'Or that you turned off the fire and idly turned it on again.'

'I couldn't have; how could I?'

Miss Smith's husband didn't know. His imagination, like a pair of calipers, grasped the ugly thought and held it before him. The facts were on its side, he could not ignore them: his wife was deranged in her mind; consciously or otherwise, she was trying to kill their child.

'The window,' Miss Smith said. 'It was open when I left it. It always is, for air. Yet you found it closed.'

'The child certainly could not have done that. I cannot see what you are suggesting.'

'I don't know. I don't know what I am suggesting. Except that I don't understand.'

'He is too much for you, dear, and that's all there is to it. You must have help.'

'We can't afford it.'

'Be that as it may, we must. We have the child to think of, if not ourselves.'

'But one child! One child cannot be too much for anyone. Look, I will be extra careful in future. After all, it is the first thing like this that has happened for ages.'

'I'm sorry, dear. We must advertise for a woman.'

'Please...'

'Darling, I'm sorry. It's no use talking. We have talked enough, and it has got us nowhere. This is something to be sensible about.'

'Please let's try again.'

'And in the meanwhile? In the meanwhile our child's life must be casually risked day in day out?'

'No, no.'

Miss Smith pleaded, but her husband said nothing further. He pulled hard on his pipe, biting it between his jaws, unhappy and confused in his mind.

Miss Smith's husband did indeed advertise for a women to see to the needs of their child, but it was, in fact, unnecessary in the long run to employ one. Because on his second birthday, late in the afternoon, the child disappeared. Miss Smith had put him in the garden. It was a perfectly safe garden: he played there often. Yet when she called him for his tea he did not come; and when she looked for the reason she found that he was not there. The small gate that led to the fields at the back of the house was open. She had not opened it; she rarely used it. Distractedly, she thought he must have managed to release the catch himself. 'That's quite impossible,' her husband said. 'It's too high and too stiff.' He looked at her oddly, confirmed in his mind that she wished to be rid of her child. Together they tramped the fields with the police, but although they covered a great area and were out for most of the night, they were utterly unsuccessful.

When the search continued in the light of the morning it was a search without hope, and the hopelessness in time turned into the fear of what discovery would reveal. 'We must accept the facts,' Miss Smith's husband said, but she alone continued to hope. She dragged her legs over the wide countryside, seeking a miracle, but finding neither trace nor word of the direction of her child's wanderings.

A small boy, so quiet she scarcely noticed him, stopped her once by a sawmill. He spoke some shy salutation, and when she blinked her eyes at his face she saw that he was James Machen. She passed him by, thinking only that she envied him his life, that for him to live and her child to die was proof indeed of a mocking Providence. She prayed to this Providence, promising a score of resolutions if only all would be well.

But nothing was well, and Miss Smith brooded on the thought that her husband had not voiced. *I released the gate myself. For some reason I have not wanted this child. God knows I loved him, and surely it wasn't too weak a love? Is it that I've loved so many other children that I have none left that is real enough for my own?* Pathetic, baseless theories flooded into Miss Smith's mind. Her thoughts floundered, and collapsed into wretched chaos.

'Miss Smith,' James said, 'would you like to see your baby?'

He stood at her kitchen door, and Miss Smith, hearing the words, was incapable immediately of grasping their meaning. The sun, reflected in the kitchen, was mirrored again in the child's glasses. He smiled at her, more confidently than she remembered, revealing a silvery wire stretching across his teeth.

'What did you say?' Miss Smith asked.

'I said, would you like to see your baby?'

Miss Smith had not slept for a long time. She was afraid to sleep because of the nightmares. Her hair hung lank about her shoulders, her eyes were dead and seemed to have fallen deeper into her skull. She stood listening to this child, nodding her head up and down, very slowly, in a mechanical way. Her left hand moved gently back and forth on the smooth surface of her kitchen table.

'My baby?' Miss Smith said, 'My baby?'

'You have lost your baby,' James reminded her.

Miss Smith nodded a little faster.

'I will show you,' James said.

He caught her hand and led her from the house, through the garden and through the gate into the fields. Hand in hand, they walked through the grass, over the canal bridge and across the warm, ripe meadows.

'I will pick you flowers,' James said, and he ran to gather poppies and cow parsley and blue, beautiful cornflowers.

'You give people flowers,' James said, 'because you like them and you want them to like you.'

She carried the flowers, and James skipped and danced beside her, hurrying her along. She heard him laughing; she looked at him and saw his small weasel face twisted into a merriment that frightened her.

The sun was fierce on her neck and shoulders. Sweat gathered on her forehead and ran down her cheeks. She felt it on her body tightening her clothes to her back and thighs. Only the child's hand was cool, and beneath her fingers she assessed its strength, wondering about its history. Again the child laughed.

On the heavy air his laughter rose and fell; it quivered through his body, and twitched lightly in his hand. It came as a giggle, then a breathless spasm; it rose like a storm from him; it rippled to gentleness; and it pounded again like the firing of guns in her ear. It would not stop. She knew it would not stop. As they walked together on this summer's day the laughter would continue until they arrived at the horror, until the horror was complete.

The Treasure Hunt

Edgar Wallace

There is a tradition in criminal circles that even the humblest of detective officers is a man of wealth and substance, and that his secret hoard was secured by thieving, bribery and blackmail. It is the gossip of the fields, the quarries, the tailor's shop, the laundry and the bake-house of fifty county prisons and three convict establishments, that all highly placed detectives have by nefarious means laid up for themselves sufficient earthly treasures to make work a hobby and their official pittance the most inconsiderable portion of their incomes.

Since Mr J. G. Reeder had for more than twenty years dealt exclusively with bank robbers and forgers, who are the aristocrats and capitalists of the underworld, legend credited him with country houses and immense secret reserves. Not that he would have a great deal of money in the bank. It was admitted that he was too clever to risk discovery by the authorities. No, it was hidden somewhere: it was the pet dream of hundreds of unlawful men that they would some day discover the hoard and live happily ever after. The one satisfactory aspect of his affluence (they all agreed) was that, being an old man – he was over fifty – he couldn't take his money with him, for gold melts at a certain temperature and gilt-edged stock is seldom printed on asbestos paper.

The Director of Public Prosecutions was lunching one Saturday at his club with a judge of the King's Bench – Saturday being one of the two days in the week when a judge gets properly fed. And the conversation drifted to a certain Mr J. G. Reeder, the chief of the Director's sleuths.

'He's capable,' he confessed reluctantly, 'but I hate his hat. It is the sort that So-and-so used to wear,' he mentioned by name an eminent politician; 'and I loathe his black frockcoat – people who see him coming into the office think he's a coroner's officer – but he's capable. His side whiskers are an abomination, and I have a feeling that, if I talked rough to him, he would burst into tears – a gentle soul. Almost too gentle for my kind of work. He apologizes to the messenger every time he rings for him!'

The judge, who knew something about humanity, answered with a frosty smile.

'He sounds rather like a potential murderer to me,' he said cynically.

Here, in his extravagance, he did Mr J. G. Reeder an injustice, for Mr Reeder was incapable of breaking the law – quite. At the same time there were many people who formed an altogether wrong conception of J. G.'s harmlessness as an individual. And one of these was a certain Lew Kohl, who mixed counterfeiting with elementary burglary.

Threatened men live long, a trite saying but, like most things trite, true. In a score of cases, where Mr J. G. Reeder had descended from the witness stand, he had met the baleful eye of the man in the dock and had listened with mild interest to colourful promises as to what would happen to him in the near future. For he was a great authority on forged banknotes and he had sent many men to penal servitude.

Mr Reeder, that inoffensive man, had seen prisoners foaming at the mouth in their rage, he had seen them white and livid, he had heard their howling execrations and he had met these men after their release from prison and had found them amiable souls half ashamed and half amused at their nearly forgotten outbursts and horrific threats.

But when, in the early part of 1914, Lew Kohl was sentenced for ten years, he neither screamed his imprecations nor registered a vow to tear Mr Reeder's heart, lungs, and important organs from his frail body.

Lew just smiled and his eyes caught the detective's for the space of a second – the forger's eyes were pale blue and speculative, and they held neither hate nor fury. Instead, they said in so many words:

'At the first opportunity I will kill you.'

Mr Reeder read the message and sighed heavily, for he disliked fuss of all kinds, and resented, in so far as he could resent anything, the injustice of being made personally responsible for the performance of a public duty.

Many years had passed, and considerable changes had occurred in Mr Reeder's fortune. He had transferred from the specialized occupation of detecting the makers of forged banknotes to the more general practice of the Public Prosecutor's bureau, but he never forgot Lew's smile.

The work in Whitehall was not heavy and it was very interesting. To Mr Reeder came most of the anonymous letters which the Director received in shoals. In the main they were self-explanatory, and it required no particular intelligence to discover their motive. Jealousy, malice, plain mischief-making, and occasionally a sordid desire to benefit financially by the information which was conveyed, were behind the majority. But occasionally:

Sir James is going to marry his cousin, and it's not three months since his poor wife fell overboard from the Channel steamer crossing to Calais. There's something very fishy about this business. Miss Margaret doesn't like him, for she knows he's after her money. Why was I sent away to London that night? He doesn't like driving in the dark, either. It's strange that he wanted to drive that night when it was raining like blazes.

This particular letter was signed 'A Friend'. Justice has many such friends.

'Sir James' was Sir James Tithermite, who had been a director of some new public department during the war and had received a baronetcy for his services.

'Look it up,' said the Director when he saw the letter. 'I seem to remember that Lady Tithermite was drowned at sea.'

'On the nineteenth of December last year,' said Mr Reeder solemnly. 'She and Sir James were going to Monte Carlo, breaking their journey in Paris. Sir James, who has a house near Maidstone, drove to Dover, garaging the car at the Lord Wilson Hotel. The night was stormy and the ship had a rough crossing – they were halfway across when Sir James came to the purser and said that he had missed his wife. Her baggage was in the cabin, her passport, rail ticket, and hat, but the lady was not found, indeed was never seen again.'

The Director nodded.

'I see you've read up the case.'

'I remember it,' said Mr Reeder. 'The case is a favourite speculation of mine. Unfortunately, I see evil in everything and I have often thought how easy – but I fear that I take a warped view of life. It is a horrible handicap to possess a criminal mind.'

The Director looked at him suspiciously. He was never quite sure whether Mr Reeder was serious. At that moment, his sobriety was beyond challenge.

'A discharged chauffeur wrote that letter of course,' he began.

'Thomas Dayford, of 179, Barrack Street, Maidstone,' concluded Mr Reeder. 'He is at present in the employ of the Kent Motor-Bus Company, and has three children, two of whom are twins and bonny little rascals.'

The Chief laughed helplessly.

'I'll take it that you know!' he said. 'See what there is behind the letter. Sir James is a big fellow in Kent, a Justice of the Peace, and he has powerful political influences. There is nothing in this letter, of course. Go warily, Reeder – if any kick comes back to this office, it goes on to you – doubled!'

Mr Reeder's idea of walking warily was peculiarly his own. He travelled down to Maidstone the next morning, and finding a bus that passed the lodge gates to Elfreda Manor, he journeyed comfortably and economically, his umbrella between his knees. He passed through the lodge gates, up a long and winding avenue of poplars, and presently came within sight of the grey manor house.

In a deep chair on the lawn he saw a girl sitting, a book on her knees, and evidently she saw him, for she rose as he crossed the lawn and came towards him eagerly.

'I'm Miss Margaret Letherby – are you from –?' She mentioned the name of a well-known firm of lawyers, and her face fell when Mr Reeder regretfully disclaimed connection with those legal lights. She was as pretty as a perfect complexion and a round, not too intellectual face could, in combination, make her.

'I thought – do you wish to see Sir James? He is in the library. If you ring, one of the maids will take you to him.'

Had Mr Reeder been the sort of man who could be puzzled by anything, he would have been puzzled by the suggestion that any girl with money of her own should marry a man much older than herself against her own wishes. There was little mystery in the matter now. Miss Margaret would have married any strong-willed man who insisted.

'Even me,' said Mr Reeder to himself, with a certain melancholy pleasure.

There was no need to ring the bell. A tall, broad man in a golfing suit stood in the doorway. His fair hair was long and hung over his forehead in a thick flat strand; a heavy tawny moustache hid his mouth and swept down over a chin that was long and powerful.

'Well?' he asked aggressively.

'I'm from the Public Prosecutor's office,' murmured Mr Reeder. 'I have had an anonymous letter.'

His pale eyes did not leave the face of the other man.

'Come in,' said Sir James gruffly.

As he closed the door he glanced quickly first towards the girl and then towards the poplar avenue.

'I'm expecting a fool of a lawyer,' he said, as he flung open the door of what was evidently the library.

His voice was steady; not by a flicker of eyelash had he betrayed the slightest degree of anxiety when Reeder had told his mission.

'Well – what about this anonymous letter? You don't take much notice of that kind of trash, do you?'

Mr Reeder deposited his umbrella and flatcrowned hat on a chair before he took a document from his pocket and handed it to the baronet, who frowned as he read. Was it Mr Reeder's vivid imagination, or did the hard light in the eyes of Sir James soften as he read?

'This is a cock and bull story of somebody having seen my wife's jewellery on sale in Paris,' he said. 'There is nothing in it. I can account for every one of my poor wife's trinkets. I brought back the jewel case after that awful night. I don't recognize the handwriting: who is the lying scoundrel who wrote this?'

Mr Reeder, who had thought it best to prepare an entirely new letter to show Sir James, had never before been called a lying scoundrel, but he accepted the experience with admirable meekness.

'I thought it untrue,' he said, shaking his head. 'I followed the details of the case very thoroughly. You left here in the afternoon—'

'At night,' said the other brusquely. He was not inclined to discuss the matter, but Mr Reeder's appealing look was irresistible. 'It was only eighty minutes' run to Dover. We got to the pier at eleven o'clock, about the same time as the boat train, and we went on board at once. I got my cabin key from the purser and put her ladyship and her baggage inside.'

'Her ladyship was a good sailor?'

'Yes, a very good sailor; she was remarkably well that night. I left her in the cabin dozing, and went for a stroll on the deck –'

'Raining very heavily and a strong sea running,' nodded Reeder, as though in agreement with something the other man had said.

'Yes – I'm a pretty good sailor – anyway, that story about my poor wife's jewels is utter nonsense. You can tell the Director that, with my compliments.'

He opened the door for his visitor, and Mr Reeder was some time replacing the letter and gathering his belongings.

'You have a beautiful place here, Sir James – a lovely place. An extensive estate?'

'Three thousand acres.' This time he did not attempt to disguise his impatience. 'Good afternoon.'

Mr Reeder went slowly down the drive, his remarkable memory at work.

He missed the bus, which he could easily have caught, and pursued an apparently aimless way along the winding road which marched with the boundaries of the baronet's property. A walk of a quarter of a mile brought him to a lane shooting off at right angles from the main road, and marking, he guessed, the southern boundary. At the corner stood an old stone lodge, on the inside of a forbidding iron gate. The lodge was in a pitiable state of neglect and disrepair. Tiles had been dislodged from the roof, the windows were grimy or broken, and the little garden was overrun with rocks and thistles. Beyond the gate was a narrow, weed-covered drive that trailed out of sight into a distant plantation.

Hearing the clang of a mailbox closing, he turned to see a postman mounting his bicycle.

'What place is this?' asked Mr Reeder, arresting the postman's departure.

'South Lodge – Sir James Tithermite's property. It's never used now. Hasn't been used for years – I don't know why; it's a short cut if they happen to be coming this way.'

Mr Reeder walked with him towards the village. He was a skilful pumper of wells, however dry, and the postman was not dry by any means.

'Yes, poor lady! She was very frail – one of those sort of invalids that last out many a healthy man.'

Mr Reeder put a question at random and scored most unexpectedly.

'Yes, her ladyship was a bad sailor. I know, because every time she went abroad she used to get a bottle of that stuff people take for seasickness. I've delivered many a bottle till Raikes, the chemist, stocked it – "Pickers' Travellers' Friend", that's what it was called. Mr Raikes was only saying to me the other day that he'd got half a dozen bottles on hand, and he didn't know what to do with them. Nobody in Climbury ever goes to sea.'

Mr Reeder went on to the village and idled his precious time in most unlikely places. At the chemist's, at the blacksmith shop, at the modest lumber yard. He caught the last bus back to Maidstone, and by great good luck the last train to London.

And, in his vague way, he answered the Director's query the next day with: 'Yes, I saw Sir James: a very interesting man.'

This was on Friday. All day Saturday he was busy. The Sabbath brought him a new interest.

On this bright Sunday morning, Mr Reeder, attired in a flowered dressing-gown, his feet encased in black velvet slippers, stood at the window of his house in Brockley Road and surveyed the deserted thoroughfare. The bell of a local church had rung for early Mass, and there was nothing living in sight except a black cat that lay asleep in a patch of sunlight on the top step of the house opposite. The hour was seven-thirty, and Mr Reeder had been at his desk since six, working by artificial light, the month being October towards the close.

From the half-moon of the window bay he regarded a section of the Lewisham High Road and as much of Tanners Hill as can be seen before it dips past the railway bridge into sheer Deptford.

Returning to his table, he opened a carton of the cheapest cigarettes and, lighting one, puffed in an amateurish fashion. He smoked cigarettes rather like a woman who detests them but feels that it is the correct thing to do.

'Dear me,' said Mr Reeder feebly.

He was back at the window, and he had seen a man turn out of Lewisham High Road. He had crossed the road and was coming straight to Daffodil House – which frolicsome name appeared on the door posts of Mr Reeder's residence. A tall, straight man, with a sombrely brown face, he came to the front gate, passed through and beyond the watcher's range of vision.

'Dear me!' said Mr Reeder, as he heard the tinkle of a bell.

A few minutes later his housekeeper tapped on the door.

'Will you see Mr Kohl, sir?' she asked.

Mr J. G. Reeder nodded.

Lew Kohl walked into the room to find a middle-aged man in a flamboyant dressing-gown sitting at his desk, a pair of pince-nez set crookedly on his nose.

'Good morning, Kohl.'

Lew Kohl looked at the man who had sent him to seven and a half years of hell, and the corners of his thin lips curled.

''Morning, Mr Reeder.' His eyes flashed across the almost bare surface of the writing desk on which Reeder's hands were lightly clasped. 'You didn't expect to see me, I guess?'

'Not so early,' said Reeder in his hushed voice, 'but I should have remembered that early rising is one of the good habits which are inculcated by penal servitude.'

He said this in the manner of one bestowing praise for good conduct.

'I suppose you've got a pretty good idea of why I have come, eh? I'm a bad forgetter, Reeder, and a man in Dartmoor has time to think.'

The older man lifted his sandy eyebrows, the steel-rimmed glasses on his nose slipped farther askew.

'That phrase seems familiar,' he said, and the eyebrows lowered in a frown. 'Now let me think – it was in a melodrama, of course, but was it "Souls in Harness" or "The Marriage Vow"?'

He appeared genuinely anxious for assistance in solving this problem.

'This is going to be a different kind of play,' said the long-faced Lew through his teeth. 'I'm going to get you, Reeder – you can go along and tell your boss, the Public Prosecutor. But I'll get you sweet! There will be no evidence to swing me. And I'll get that nice little stocking of yours, Reeder!'

The legend of Reeder's fortune was accepted even by so intelligent a man as Kohl.

'You'll get my stocking! Dear me, I shall have to go barefooted,' said Mr Reeder, with a faint show of humour.

'You know what I mean – think that over. Some hour and day you'll go out, and all Scotland Yard won't catch me for the killing! I've thought that out—'

'One has time to think in Dartmoor,' murmured Mr J. G. Reeder encouragingly. 'You're becoming one of the world's thinkers, Kohl. Do you know Rodin's masterpiece – a beautiful statue throbbing with life—'

'That's all.' Lew Kohl rose, the smile still trembling at the corner of his mouth. 'Maybe you'll turn this over in your mind, and in a day or two you won't be feeling so gay.'

Reeder's face was pathetic in its sadness. His untidy sandy-grey hair seemed to be standing on end; the large ears, that stood out at right angles to his face, gave the illusion of quivering movement.

Lew Kohl's hand was on the door knob.

Womp!

It was the sound of a dull weight striking a board; something winged past his cheek, before his eyes a deep hole showed in the wall, and his face was stung by flying grains of plaster. He spun round with a whine of rage.

Mr Reeder had a long-barrelled Browning in his hand, with a barrel-shaped silencer over the muzzle, and he was staring at the weapon open-mouthed.

'Now how on earth did that happen?' he asked in wonder.

Lew Kohl stood trembling with rage and fear, his face yellow-white.

'You – you swine!' he breathed. 'You tried to shoot me!'

Mr Reeder stared at him over his glasses.

'Good gracious – you think that? Still thinking of killing me, Kohl?'

Kohl tried to speak but found no words, and flinging open the door, he strode down the stairs and through the front entrance. His foot was on the first step when something came hurtling past him and crashed to fragments at his feet. It was a large stone vase that had decorated the window sill of Mr Reeder's bedroom. Leaping over the debris of stone and flower mould, he glared up into the surprised face of Mr J. G. Reeder.

'I'll get you!' he spluttered.

'I hope you're not hurt?' asked the man at the window in a tone of concern. 'These things happen. Some day and some hour—'

As Lew Kohl strode down the street, the detective was still talking.

Mr Stan Bride, late of Dartmoor, was at his morning ablutions when his friend and sometime prison associate came into the little room that overlooked Fitzroy Square.

Stan Bride, who bore no resemblance to anything virginal, being a stout and stumpy man with a huge red face and many chins, stopped in the act of drying himself and gazed over the edge of the towel.

'What's the matter with you?' he asked sharply. 'You look as if you'd been chased by a cop. What did you go out so early for?'

Lew told him, and the jovial countenance of his roommate grew longer and longer.

'You poor fish!' he hissed. 'To go after Reeder with that stuff! Don't you think he was waiting for you? Do you suppose he didn't know the very moment you left the Moor?'

'I've scared him, anyway,' said the other, and Mr Bride laughed.

'Good scout!' he sneered. 'If he's as white as you, he *is* scared! But he's not. Of course he shot past you – if he'd wanted to shoot you, you'd be stiff by now. But he didn't. Thinker, he – he's given you somep'n' to think about.'

'Where that gun came from I don't—'

There was a knock at the door and the two men exchanged glances.

'Who's there?' asked Bride, and a familiar voice answered.

'It's that dick from the Yard,' whispered Bride, and opened the door.

The 'dick' was Sergeant Allford, CID, an affable and portly man and a detective of some promise.

''Morning, boys – not been to church, Stan?'

Stan grinned politely.

'How's trade, Lew?'

'Not so bad.' The forger was alert, suspicious.

'Come to see you about a gun – got an idea you're carrying one, Lew – Colt automatic R.7/94318. That's not right, Lew – guns don't belong to this country.'

'I've got no gun,' said Lew sullenly.

Bride had suddenly become an old man, for he also was a convict on parole, and the discovery might send him back to serve his unfinished sentence.

'Will you take a little walk to the station, or will you let me go over you?'

'Go over me,' said Lew, and put out his arms stiffly while the detective frisked him.

'I'll have a look around,' said the detective, and his 'look around' was very thorough.

'Must have been mistaken,' said Sergeant Allford. And then, suddenly: 'Was that what you chucked into the river as you were walking along the Embankment?'

Lew started. It was the first intimation he had received that he had been tailed that morning.

Bride waited till the detective was visible from the window crossing Fitzroy Square; then he turned in a fury on his companion.

'Clever, ain't you! That old hound knew you had a gun – knew the number. And if Allford had found it you'd have been pulled in, and me too!'

'I threw it in the river,' said Lew sulkily.

'Brains – not many but some!' said Bride, breathing heavily 'You lay off Reeder – he's poison, and if you don't know it you're deaf! Scared

him! You big stiff! He'd cut your throat and write a hymn about
it.'

'I didn't know they were tailing me,' growled Kohl, 'but I'll get him!
And his money too.'

'Get him from another lodging,' said Bride curtly. 'A crook I don't
mind, a murderer I don't mind, but a talking jackass makes me sick.
Get his stuff if you can – I'll bet it's all invested in real estate, and
you can't lift houses – but don't talk about it. I like you, Lew, up to
a point; you're miles before the point and out of sight. I don't like
Reeder – I don't like snakes, but I keep away from the Zoo.'

So Lew Kohl went into new lodgings on the top floor of a house in
Dean Street, and here he had leisure and inclination to brood upon
his grievances and to plan afresh the destruction of his enemy. And new
plans were needed, for the schemes which had seemed so watertight
in the quiet of a Devonshire cell showed daylight through many crevices.

Lew's homicidal urge had undergone considerable modification. He
had been experimented upon by a very clever psychologist – though
he never regarded Mr Reeder in this light, and, indeed, had the vaguest
idea as to what the word meant. But there were other ways of hurting
Reeder, and his mind fell constantly back to the dream of discovering
the detective's hidden treasure.

It was nearly a week later that Mr Reeder invited himself into the
Director's private office, and the great official listened spellbound while
his subordinate offered his outrageous theory about Sir James Tithermite
and his dead wife. When Mr Reeder had finished, the Director pushed
back his chair from the table.

'My dear man,' he said, a little irritably, 'I can't possibly give a
warrant on the strength of your surmises – not even a search warrant.
The story is so fantastic, so incredible, that it would be more at home
in the pages of a sensational story than in a Public Prosecutor's report.'

'It was a wild night, and yet Lady Tithermite was not ill,' suggested
the detective gently. 'That is a fact to remember, sir.'

The Director shook his head.

'I can't do it – not on the evidence,' he said. 'I should raise a storm
that'd swing me into Whitehall. Can't you do anything – unofficially?'

Mr Reeder shook his head.

'My presence in the neighbourhood has been remarked,' he said
primly. 'I think it would be impossible to – er – cover up my traces.
And yet I have located the place, and could tell you within a few inches—'

Again the Director shook his head.

'No, Reeder,' he said quietly, 'the whole thing is sheer deduction on
your part. Oh, yes, I know you have a criminal mind – I think you
have told me that before. And that is a good reason why I should not

issue a warrant. You're simply crediting this unfortunate man with your ingenuity. Nothing doing!'

Mr Reeder sighed and went back to his bureau, not entirely despondent, for there had intruded a new element into his investigations.

Mr Reeder had been to Maidstone several times during the week, and he had not gone alone; though seemingly unconscious of the fact that he had developed a shadow, for he had seen Lew Kohl on several occasions, and had spent an uncomfortable few minutes wondering whether his experiment had failed.

On the second occasion an idea had developed in the detective's mind, and if he were a laughing man he would have chuckled aloud when he slipped out of Maidstone station one evening and, in the act of hiring a cab, had seen Lew Kohl negotiating for another.

Stan Bride was engaged in the tedious but necessary practice of so cutting a pack of cards that the ace of diamonds remained at the bottom, when his former co-lodger burst in upon him, and there was a light of triumph in Lew's cold eye which brought Mr Bride's heart to his boots.

'I've got him!' said Lew.

Bride put aside the cards and stood up.

'Got who?' he asked coldly. 'And if it's killing, you needn't answer, but get out!'

'There's no killing.'

Lew sat down squarely at the table, his hands in his pockets, a real smile on his face.

'I've been trailing Reeder for a week, and that fellow wants some trailing!'

'Well?' asked the other, when he paused dramatically.

'I've found where he hides his cash.'

Bride scratched his chin, and was half convinced.

'You have?'

Lew nodded.

'He's been going to Maidstone a lot lately, and driving to a little village about five miles out. There I always lost him. But the other night, when he came back to the station to catch the last train, he slipped into the waiting-room and I found a place where I could watch him. What do you think he did?'

Mr Bride hazarded no suggestion.

'He opened his bag,' said Lew impressively, 'and took out a wad of notes as thick as that! He'd been drawing on his private bank! I trailed him up to London. There's a restaurant in the station and he went in to get a cup of coffee, with me keeping well out of his sight. As he came out of the restaurant he took out his handkerchief and wiped his mouth. He didn't see the little book that dropped, but I did. I was scared sick that somebody else would see it, or that he'd wait long enough to find it himself. But he went out of the station and I got that book before you could say "knife". Look!'

It was a well-worn little notebook, covered with faded red morocco. Bride put out his hand to take it.

'Wait a bit,' said Lew. 'Are you in this with me fifty-fifty, because I want some help?'

Bride hesitated.

'If it's just plain thieving, I'm with you,' he said.

'Plain thieving – and sweet,' said Lew exultantly, and pushed the book across the table.

For the greater part of the night they sat together talking in low tones, discussing impartially the methodical book-keeping of Mr J. G. Reeder and his exceeding dishonesty.

The Monday night was wet. A storm blew up from the south-west, and the air was filled with falling leaves as Lew and his companion footed the five miles which separated them from the village. Neither carried any impedimenta that was visible, yet under Lew's waterproof coat was a kit of tools of singular ingenuity, and Mr Bride's coat pockets were weighted down with the sections of a powerful jemmy.

The met nobody in their walk, and the church bell was striking eleven when Lew gripped the bars of the South Lodge gates, on the estate of Sir James Tithermite, pulled himself up to the top and dropped lightly on the other side. He was followed by Mr Bride, who, in spite of his bulk, was a singularly agile man. The ruined lodge showed in the darkness, and they passed through the creaking gates to the door and Lew flashed his lantern upon the keyhole before he began manipulation with the implements which he had taken from his kit.

The door was opened in ten minutes and a few seconds later they stood in a low-roofed little room, the principal feature of which was a deep, grateless fireplace. Lew took off his mackintosh and stretched it over the window before he spread the light in his lamp and, kneeling down, brushed the debris from the hearth, examining the joints of the big stone carefully.

'This work's been botched,' he said. 'Anybody could see that.'

He put the claw of the jemmy into a crack and levered up the stone, and it moved slightly. Stopping only to dig a deeper crevice with a chisel and hammer, he thrust the claw of the jemmy farther down. The stone came up above the edge of the floor and Bride slipped the chisel underneath.

'Now together,' grunted Lew.

They got their fingers beneath the hearthstone and with one heave hinged it up. Lew picked up the lamp and, kneeling down, flashed a light into the dark cavity. And then:

'Oh, my God!' he shrieked.

A second later two terrified men rushed from the house into the drive. And a miracle had happened, for the gates were open and a dark figure stood squarely before them.

'Put up your hands, Kohl!' said a voice, and, hateful as it was to Lew Kohl, he could have fallen on the neck of Mr Reeder.

At twelve o'clock that night Sir James Tithermite was discussing matters with his bride-to-be: the stupidity of her lawyers, who wished to safeguard her fortune, and his own cleverness and foresight in securing complete freedom of action for the girl who was to be his wife.

'These blackguards think of nothing but their fees,' he began, when his footman came in unannounced, and behind him the Chief Constable of the county and a man he remembered seeing before.

'Sir James Tithermite?' said the Chief Constable unnecessarily, for he knew Sir James very well.

'Yes, Colonel, what is it?' asked the baronet, his face twitching.

'I am taking you into custody on a charge of wilfully murdering your wife, Eleanor Mary Tithermite.'

'The whole thing turned upon the question as to whether Lady Tithermite was a good or a bad sailor,' explained J. G. Reeder to his chief. 'If she were a bad sailor, it was unlikely that she would be on the ship, even for five minutes, without calling for the stewardess. The stewardess did not see her ladyship, nor did anybody on board, for the simple reason that she was not on board!

'She was murdered within the grounds of the Manor; her body was buried beneath the hearthstone of the old lodge, and Sir James continued his journey by car to Dover, handing over his packages to a porter and telling him to take them to his cabin before he turned to put the car into the hotel garage. He had timed his arrival so that he passed on board with a crowd of passengers from the boat train, and nobody knew whether he was alone or whether he was accompanied, and, for the matter of that, nobody cared.

'The purser gave him his key, and he put the baggage, including his wife's hat, into the cabin, paid the porter and dismissed him. Officially, Lady Tithermite was on board, for he surrendered her ticket to the collector and received her landing voucher. And then he discovered she had disappeared. The ship was searched, but of course the unfortunate lady was not found. As I remarked before—'

'You have a criminal mind,' said the Director good-humouredly. 'Go on, Reeder.'

'Having this queer and objectionable trait, I saw how very simple a matter it was to give the illusion that the lady was on board, and I decided that, if the murder was committed, it must have been within

a few miles of the house. And then the local builder told me that he
had given Sir James a little lesson in the art of mixing mortar. And
the local blacksmith told me that the gate had been damaged, presumably by Sir James's car – I had seen the broken rods and all I wanted
to know was when the repairs were made. That she was beneath the
fireplace hearth in the lodge I was certain. Without a search warrant
it was impossible to prove or disprove my theory, and I myself could
not conduct a private investigation without risking the reputation of
our department – if I may say "our",' he said apologetically.

The Director was thoughtful.
'Of course, you induced this man Kohl to dig up the hearth by pretending you had money buried there. I presume you revealed that fact
in your notebook? But why on earth did he imagine that you had a
hidden treasure?'
Mr Reeder smiled sadly.
'The criminal mind is a peculiar thing,' he said, with a sigh. 'It har-
bours illusions and fairy stories. Fortunately, I understand that mind.
As I have often said . . .'

The Snow

Hugh Walpole

The second Mrs Ryder was a young woman not easily frightened, but now she stood in the dusk of the passage leaning back against the wall, her hand on her heart, looking at the grey-faced window beyond which the snow was steadily falling against the lamp-light.

The passage where she was, led from the study to the dining-room, and the window looked out on to the little paved path that ran at the edge of the Cathedral green. As she stared down the passage she couldn't be sure whether the woman were there or no. How absurd of her! She knew the woman was not there. But if the woman was not, how was it that she could discern so clearly the old-fashioned grey cloak, the untidy grey hair, and the sharp outline of the pale cheek and pointed chin? Yes, and more than that, the long sweep of the grey dress, falling in folds to the ground, the flash of a gold ring on the white hand. No. No. No. This was madness. There was no one and nothing there. Hallucination ...

Very faintly a voice seemed to come to her: 'I warned you. This is for the last time....'

The nonsense! How far now was her imagination to carry her? Tiny sounds about the house, the running of a tap somewhere, a faint voice from the kitchen, these and something more had translated themselves into an imagined voice. 'The last time ...'

But her terror was real. She was not normally frightened by anything. She was young and healthy and bold, fond of sport, hunting, shooting, taking any risk. Now she was truly *stiffened* with terror – she could not move, could not advance down the passage as she wanted to and find light, warmth, safety in the dining-room. All the time the snow fell steadily, stealthily, with its own secret purpose, maliciously, beyond the window in the pale glow of the lamplight.

Then, unexpectedly, there was noise from the hall, opening of doors, a rush of feet, a pause, and then in clear, beautiful voices the well-known strains of 'Good King Wenceslas.' It was the Cathedral choir-boys on their regular Christmas round. This was Christmas Eve. They always came just at this hour on Christmas Eve.

With an intense, almost incredible relief she turned back into the hall. At the same moment her husband came out of the study. They stood together, smiling at the little group of mufflered, becoated boys who were singing, heart and soul in the job, so that the old house simply rang with their melody.

Reassured by the warmth and human company, she lost her terror. It had been her imagination. Of late she had been none too well. That was why she had been so irritable. Old Dr Bernard was no good: he didn't understand her case at all. After Christmas she would go to London and have the very best advice. . . .

Had she been well she could not, half an hour ago, have shown such miserable temper over nothing. She knew that it was over nothing, and yet the knowledge did not make it any easier for her to restrain herself. After every bout of temper she told herself that there should never be another – and then Herbert said something irritating, one of his silly, muddle-headed stupidities, and she was off again!

She could see now as she stood beside him at the bottom of the staircase that he was still feeling it. She had certainly half an hour ago said some abominably rude personal things – things that she had not meant at all – and he had taken them in his meek, quiet way. Were he not so meek and quiet, did he only pay her back in her own coin, she would never lose her temper. Of that she was sure.

But who wouldn't be irritated by that meekness and by the only re-proachful thing that he ever said to her: 'Elinor understood me better, my dear'? To throw the first wife up against the second! Wasn't that the most tactless thing that a man could possibly do? And Elinor, that worn, elderly woman, the very opposite of her own gay, bright, amusing self? That was why Herbert had loved her, because she was gay and bright and young. It was true that Elinor had been devoted, that she had been so utterly wrapped up in Herbert that she lived only for him. People were always recalling her devotion, which was sufficiently rude and tactless of them.

Well, she could not give anyone that kind of old-fashioned sugary devotion; it wasn't in her, and Herbert knew it by this time.

Nevertheless, she loved Herbert in her own way, as he must know, know it so well that he ought to pay no attention to the bursts of temper. She wasn't well. She would see a doctor in London. . . .

The little boys finished their carols, were properly rewarded, and tumbled like feathery birds out into the snow again. They went into the study, the two of them, and stood beside the big open log-fire. She put her hand up and stroked his thin, beautiful cheek.

'I'm so sorry to have been cross just now, Bertie. I didn't mean half I said, you know.'

But he didn't, as he usually did, kiss her and tell her that it didn't matter. Looking straight in front of him, he answered:

'Well, Alice, I do wish you wouldn't. It hurts, horribly. It upsets me more than you think. And it's growing on you. You make me miserable. I don't know what to do about it. And it's all about nothing.'

Irritated at not receiving the usual commendation for her sweetness in making it up again, she withdrew a little and answered:

'Oh, all right. I've said I'm sorry. I can't do any more.'

'But tell me,' he insisted, 'I want to know. What makes you so angry, so suddenly – and about nothing at all?'

She was about to let her anger rise, her anger at his obtuseness, obstinacy, when some fear checked her, a strange, unanalysed fear, as though someone had whispered to her, 'Look you! This is the last time!'

'It's not altogether my own fault,' she answered, and left the room.

She stood in the cold hall, wondering where to go. She could feel the snow falling outside the house and shivered. She hated the snow, she hated the winter, this beastly cold, dark English winter, that went on and on, only at last to change into a damp, soggy English spring.

When she urged Herbert to winter abroad – which he could quite easily do – he answered her impatiently; he had the strongest affection for this poky dead-and-alive Cathedral town. The Cathedral seemed to be precious to him; he wasn't happy if he didn't go and see it every day! She wouldn't wonder if he didn't think more of the Cathedral than he did of herself. Elinor had been the same; she had even written a little book about the Cathedral, about the Black Bishop's Tomb and the stained glass and the rest. . . .

What was the Cathedral after all? Only a building!

She was standing in the drawing-room looking out over the dusky ghostly snow to the great hulk of the Cathedral that Herbert said was like a flying ship, but to herself was more like a crouching beast licking its lips over the miserable sinners that it was for ever devouring.

As she looked and shivered, feeling that in spite of herself her temper and misery were rising so that they threatened to choke her, it seemed to her that her bright and cheerful firelit drawing-room was suddenly open to the snow. It was exactly as though cracks had appeared every-where, in the ceiling, the walls, the windows, and that through these cracks the snow was filtering, dribbling in little tracks of wet down the walls, already perhaps making pools of water on the carpet.

This was, of course, imagination, but it was a fact that the room was most dreadfully cold, although a great fire was burning and it was the cosiest room in the house.

Then, turning, she saw the figure standing by the door. This time there could be no mistake. It was a grey shadow, and yet a shadow with form and outline – the untidy grey hair, the pale face like a moon-lit leaf, the long grey clothes, and something obstinate, vindictive, terribly menacing in its pose.

She moved and the figure was gone; there was nothing there and the room was warm again, quite hot, in fact. But young Mrs Ryder, who had never feared anything in all her life, save the vanishing of her youth, was trembling so that she had to sit down, and even then her trembling did not cease. Her hand shook on the arm of her chair.

She had created this thing out of her imagination of Elinor's hatred of her and her own hatred of Elinor.

It was true that they had never met, but who knew but that the spiritualists were right, and Elinor's spirit, jealous of Herbert's love for her, had been there driving them apart, forcing her to lose her temper and then hating her for losing it? Such things might be! But she had not much time for speculation. She was preoccupied with her fear. It was a definite, positive fear, the kind of fear that one has just before one goes under an operation. Someone or something was threatening her. She clung to her chair as though to leave it were to plunge into disaster.

She longed for Herbert to come and protect her. She felt most kindly to him. She would never lose her temper with him again – and at that same moment some cold voice seemed to whisper in her ear: 'You had better not. It will be for the last time.'

At length she found courage to rise, cross the room and go up to dress for dinner. In her bedroom courage came to her once more. It was certainly cold, and the snow, as she could see when she looked between her curtains, was falling more heavily than ever, but she had a warm bath, sat in front of her fire and was sensible again.

For many months this odd sense that she was watched and accompanied by someone hostile to her had been growing. It was stronger perhaps because of the things that Herbert told her about Elinor; she was the kind of woman, he said, who, once she loved anyone, would never relinquish her grasp; she was utterly faithful. He implied that her tenacious fidelity had been at times a little difficult.

'She always said,' he added once, 'that she would watch over me until I rejoined her in the next world. Poor Elinor!' he sighed. 'She had a fine religious faith, stronger than mine, I fear.'

It was always after one of her tantrums that young Mrs Ryder had been most conscious of this hallucination, this dreadful discomfort of feeling that someone was near you who hated you – but it was only during the last week that she began to fancy that she actually saw anyone, and with every day her sense of this figure had grown stronger.

It was, of course, only nerves, but it was one of those nervous afflictions that became tiresome indeed if you did not rid yourself of it. Mrs Ryder, secure now in the warmth and intimacy of her bedroom, determined that henceforth everything should be sweetness and light. No more tempers! Those were the things that did her harm.

Even though Herbert were a little trying, was not that the case with every husband in the world? And was it not Christmas time? Peace and Good Will to men! Peace and Good Will to Herbert!

They sat down opposite to one another in the pretty little dining-room hung with Chinese woodcuts, the table gleaming and the amber curtains richly dark in the firelight.

But Herbert was not himself. He was still brooding, she supposed, over their quarrel of the afternoon. Weren't men children? Incredible the children that they were!

So when the maid was out of the room she went over to him, bent down and kissed his forehead.

'Darling ... you're still cross. I can see you are. You mustn't be. Really, you mustn't. It's Christmas time, and if I forgive you, you must forgive me.'

'You forgive me?' he asked, looking at her in his most aggravating way. 'What have you to forgive me for?'

Well, that was really too much. When she had taken all the steps, humbled her pride.

She went back to her seat, but for a while could not answer him because the maid was there. When they were alone again, she said, summoning all her patience:

'Bertie, dear, do you really think that there's anything to be gained by sulking like this? It isn't worthy of you. It isn't really.'

He answered her quietly:

'Sulking? No, that's not the right word. But I've got to keep quiet. If I don't I shall say something I'm sorry for.' Then, after a pause, in a low voice, as though to himself: 'These constant rows are awful.'

Her temper was rising again, another self that had nothing to do with her real self, a stranger to her and yet a very old familiar friend.

'Don't be so self-righteous,' she answered, her voice trembling a little. 'These quarrels are entirely my own fault, aren't they?'

'Elinor and I never quarrelled,' he said, so softly that she scarcely heard him.

'No! Because Elinor thought you perfect. She adored you. You've often told me. I don't think you perfect. I'm not perfect either. But we've both got faults. I'm not the only one to blame.'

'We'd better separate,' he said suddenly, looking up. 'We don't get on now. We used to. I don't know what's changed everything. But, as things are, we'd better separate.'

She looked at him and knew that she loved him more than ever, but because she loved him so much she wanted to hurt him, and because he had said that he thought he could get on without her she was so angry that she forgot all caution. Her love and her anger helped one another. The more angry she became the more she loved him.

'I know why you want to separate,' she said. 'It's because you're in love with someone else. ('How funny,' something inside her said. 'You don't mean a word of this.') You've treated me as you have, and then you leave me.'

'I'm not in love with anyone else,' he answered her steadily, 'and you know it. But we are so unhappy together that it's silly to go on ... silly. The whole thing has failed.'

There was so much unhappiness, so much bitterness, in his voice that she realized that at last she had truly gone too far. She had lost him. She had not meant this. She was frightened and her fear made her so angry that she went across to him.

'Very well, then ... I'll tell everyone ... what you've been. How you've treated me.'

'Not another scene.' he answered wearily. 'I can't stand any more. Let's wait. To-morrow is Christmas Day ...'

He was so unhappy that her anger with herself maddened her. She couldn't bear his sad, hopeless disappointment with herself, their life together, everything.

In a fury of blind temper she struck him; it was as though she were striking herself. He got up and without a word left the room. There was a pause, and then she heard the hall door close. He had left the house.

She stood there, slowly coming to her control again. When she lost her temper it was as though she sank under water. When it was all over she came once more to the surface of life, wondering where she'd been and what she had been doing. Now she stood there, bewildered, and then at once she was aware of two things, one that the room was bitterly cold and the other that someone was in the room with her.

This time she did not need to look around her. She did not turn at all, but only stared straight at the curtained windows, seeing them very carefully, as though she were summing them up for some future analysis, with their thick amber folds, gold rod, white lines – and beyond them the snow was falling.

She did not need to turn, but, with a shiver of terror, she was aware that that grey figure who had, all these last weeks, been approaching ever more closely, was almost at her very elbow. She heard quite clearly: 'I warned you. That was the last time.'

At the same moment Onslow the butler came in. Onslow was broad, fat, and rubicund – a good faithful butler with a passion for church music.

He was undisturbed, his ceremonial complacency clothed him securely.

'Mr Ryder has gone out,' she said firmly. Oh, surely he must see something, feel something.

'Yes, madam!' Then smiling rather grandly: 'It's snowing hard. Never seen it harder here. Shall I build up the fire in the drawing-room, madam?'

'No, thank you. But Mr Ryder's study . . .'

'Yes, madam. I only thought that as this room was so warm you might find it chilly in the drawing-room.'

This room warm, when she was shivering from head to foot; but holding herself lest he should see . . . She longed to keep him there, to implore him to remain; but in a moment he was gone, softly closing the door behind him.

Then a mad longing for flight seized her, and she could not move. She was rooted there to the floor, and even as, wildly trying to cry, to scream, to shriek the house down, she found that only a little whisper would come, she felt the cold touch of a hand on hers.

She did not turn her head: her whole personality, all her past life, her poor little courage, her miserable fortitude were summoned to meet this sense of approaching death, which was as unmistakable as a certain smell, or the familiar ringing of a gong. She had dreamt in nightmares of approaching death, and it had always been like this, a fearful con-striction of the heart, a paralysis of the limbs, a choking sense of disaster like an anaesthetic.

'You were warned,' something said to her again.

She knew that if she turned she would see Elinor's face, set, white, remorseless. The woman had always hated her, been vilely jealous of her, protecting her wretched Herbert.

A certain vindictiveness seemed to release her. She found that she could move, her limbs were free.

She passed to the door, ran down the passage into the hall. Where would she be safe? She thought of the Cathedral, where tonight there was a carol service. She opened the hall door and, just as she was, meeting the thick, involving, muffling snow, she ran out.

She started across the green towards the Cathedral door. Her thin black slippers sank in the snow. Snow was everywhere – in her hair, her eyes, her nostrils, her mouth, on her bare neck between her breasts.

'Help! Help! Help!' she wanted to cry, but the snow choked her. Lights whirled about her. The Cathedral rose like a huge black eagle and flew towards her.

She fell forward, and even as she fell, a hand, far colder than the snow, caught her neck. She lay struggling in the snow, and as she struggled there two hands of an icy fleshless chill closed about her throat.

Her last knowledge was the hard outline of a ring pressing into her neck. Then she lay still, her face in the snow, and the flakes eagerly, savagely covered her.

The Cone

H. G. Wells

The night was hot and overcast, the sky red-rimmed with the lingering sunset of mid-summer. They sat at the open window, trying to fancy
the air was fresher there. The trees and shrubs of the garden stood stiff
and dark; beyond in the roadway a gas-lamp burnt, bright orange against
the hazy blue of the evening. Farther were the three lights of the railway
signal against the lowering sky. The man and woman spoke to one
another in low tones.

'He does not suspect?' said the man, a little nervously.

'Not he,' she said peevishly, as though that too irritated her. 'He thinks
of nothing but the works and the prices of fuel. He has no imagination,
no poetry.'

'None of these men of iron have,' he said sententiously. 'They have
no hearts.'

'*He* has not,' she said. She turned her discontented face towards the
window. The distant sound of a roaring and rushing drew nearer and
grew in volume; the house quivered; one heard the metallic rattle of
the tender. As the train passed, there was a glare of light above the
cutting and a driving tumult of smoke, one, two, three, four, five, six,
seven, eight black oblongs – trucks – passed across the dim grey of the
embankment, and were suddenly extinguished one by one in the throat
of the tunnel, which, with the last, seemed to swallow down train, smoke,
and sound in one abrupt gulp.

'This country was all fresh and beautiful once,' he said; 'and now
– it is Gehenna. Down that way – nothing but pot-banks and chimneys
belching fire and dust into the face of heaven . . . But what does it matter?
An end comes, an end to all this cruelty . . . *Tomorrow*.' He spoke the
last word in a whisper.

'*Tomorrow*,' she said, speaking in a whisper too, and still staring out
of the window.

'Dear!' he said, putting his hand on hers.

She turned with a start, and their eyes searched one another's. Hers
softened to his gaze. 'My dear one!' she said, and then: 'It seems so

strange – that you should come into my life like this – to open—' She paused.

'To open?' he said.

'All this wonderful world' – she hesitated, and spoke still more softly – 'this world of *love* to me.'

Then suddenly the door clicked and closed. They turned their heads, and he started violently back. In the shadow of the room stood a great shadowy figure – silent. They saw the face dimly in the half-light, with unexpressive dark patches under the penthouse brows. Every muscle in Raut's body suddenly became tense. When could the door have opened? What had he heard? Had he heard all? What had he seen? A tumult of questions.

The newcomer's voice came at last, after a pause that seemed interminable. 'Well?' he said.

'I was afraid I had missed you, Horrocks,' said the man at the window, gripping the window-ledge with his hands. His voice was unsteady.

The clumsy figure of Horrocks came forward out of the shadow. He made no answer to Raut's remark. For a moment he stood above them.

The woman's heart was cold within her. 'I told Mr Raut it was just possible you might come back,' she said in a voice that never quivered.

Horrocks, still silent, sat down abruptly in the chair by her little work-table. His big hands were clenched; one saw now the fire of his eyes under the shadow of his brows. He was trying to get his breath. His eyes went from the woman he had trusted to the friend he had trusted, and then back to the woman.

By this time and for the moment all three half understood one another. Yet none dared say a word to ease the pent-up things that choked them.

It was the husband's voice that broke the silence at last.

'You wanted to see me?' he said to Raut.

Raut started as he spoke. 'I came to see you,' he said, resolved to lie to the last.

'Yes,' said Horrocks.

'You promised,' said Raut, 'to show me some fine effects of moonlight and smoke.'

'I promised to show you some fine effects of moonlight and smoke,' repeated Horrocks in a colourless voice.

'And I thought I might catch you tonight before you went down to the works,' proceeded Raut, 'and come with you.'

There was another pause. Did the man mean to take the thing coolly? Did he after all know? How long had he been in the room? Yet even at the moment when they heard the door, their attitudes ... Horrocks glanced at the profile of the woman, shadowy pallid in the half-light. Then he glanced at Raut, and seemed to recover himself suddenly. 'Of course,' he said, 'I promised to show you the works under their proper dramatic conditions. It's odd how I could have forgotten.'

'If I am troubling you—' began Raut.

Horrocks started again. A new light had suddenly come into the sultry gloom of his eyes. 'Not in the least,' he said.

'Have you been telling Mr Raut of all these contrasts of flame and shadow you think so splendid?' said the woman, turning now to her husband for the first time, her confidence creeping back again, her voice just one half-note too high. 'That dreadful theory of yours that machinery is beautiful, and everything else in the world ugly. I thought he would not spare you, Mr Raut. It's his great theory, his one discovery in art.'

'I am slow to make discoveries,' said Horrocks grimly, damping her suddenly. 'But what I discover . . .' He stopped.

'Well?' she said.

'Nothing,' and suddenly he rose to his feet.

'I promised to show you the works,' he said to Raut, and put his big, clumsy hand on his friend's shoulder. 'And you are ready to go?'

There was another pause. Each of them peered through the indistinctness of the dusk at the other two. Horrocks's hand still rested on Raut's shoulder. Raut half fancied still that the incident was trivial after all. But Mrs Horrocks knew her husband better, knew that grim quiet in his voice, and the confusion in her mind took a vague shape of physical evil. 'Very well,' said Horrocks, and, dropping his hand, turned towards the door.

'My hat?' Raut looked round in the half-light.

'That's my work-basket,' said Mrs Horrocks with a gust of hysterical laughter. Their hands came together on the back of the chair. 'Here it is!' he said. She had an impulse to warn him in an undertone, but she could not frame a word. 'Don't go!' and 'Beware of him!' struggled in her mind, and the swift moment passed.

'Got it?' said Horrocks, standing with the door half-open.

Raut stepped towards him. 'Better say good-bye to Mrs Horrocks,' said the ironmaster, even more grimly quiet in his tone than before.

Raut started and turned. 'Good evening, Mrs Horrocks,' he said, and their hands touched.

Horrocks held the door open with a ceremonial politeness unusual in him towards men. Raut went out, and then, after a wordless look at her, her husband followed. She stood motionless while Raut's light footfall and her husband's heavy tread, like bass and treble, passed down the passage together. The front door slammed heavily. She went to the window, moving slowly, and stood watching – leaning forward. The two men appeared for a moment at the gateway in the road, passed under the street lamp, and were hidden by the black masses of the shrubbery. The lamplight fell for a moment on their faces, showing only unmeaning pale patches, telling nothing of what she still feared, and doubted, and craved vainly to know. Then she sank down into a crouching attitude in the big arm-chair, her eyes wide open and staring out at the red lights from the furnaces that flickered in the sky. An hour after she was still there, her attitude scarcely changed.

The oppressive stillness of the evening weighed heavily upon Raut. They went side by side down the road in silence, and in silence turned into the cinder-made by-way that presently opened out the prospect of the valley.

A blue haze, half dust, half mist, touched the long valley with mystery. Beyond were Hanley and Etruria, grey and black masses, outlined thinly by the rare golden dots of the street-lamps, and here and there a gaslit window, or the yellow glare of some late-working factory or crowded public-house. Out of the masses, clear and slender against the evening sky, rose a multitude of tall chimneys, many of them reeking, a few smokeless during a season of 'play'. Here and there a pallid patch and ghostly stunted beehive shapes showed the position of a pot-bank, or a wheel, black and sharp against the hot lower sky, marked some colliery where they raise the iridescent coal of the place. Nearer at hand was the broad stretch of railway, and half invisible trains shunted – a steady puffing and rumbling, with every now and then a ringing concussion and a series of impacts, and a passage of intermittent puffs of white steam across the further view. And to the left, between the railway and the dark mass of the low hill beyond, dominating the whole view, colossal, inky-black, and crowned with smoke and fitful flames, stood the great cylinders of the Jeddah Company Blast Furnaces, the central edifices of the big ironworks of which Horrocks was the manager. They stood heavy and threatening, full of an incessant turmoil of flames and seething molten iron, and about the feet of them rattled the rolling-mills, and the steam-hammer beat heavily and splashed the white iron sparks hither and thither. Even as they looked, a truckful of fuel was shot into one of the giants, and the red flames gleamed out, and a confusion of smoke and black dust came boiling upwards towards the sky.

'Certainly you get some fine edifices of colour with your furnaces,' said Raut, breaking a silence that had become apprehensive.

Horrocks grunted. He stood with his hands in his pockets, frowning down at the dim steaming railway and the busy ironworks beyond, frowning as if he were thinking out some knotty problem.

Raut glanced at him and away again. 'At present your moonlight effect is hardly ripe,' he continued, looking upward; 'the moon is still smothered by the vestiges of daylight.'

Horrocks stared at him with the expression of a man who has suddenly awakened. 'Vestiges of daylight? ... Of course, of course.' He too looked up at the moon, pale still in the midsummer sky. 'Come along,' he said suddenly, and gripping Raut's arm in his hand, made a move towards the path that dropped from them to the railway.

Raut hung back. Their eyes met and saw a thousand things in a moment that their lips came near to say. Horrocks's hand tightened and then relaxed. He let go, and before Raut was ware of it, they were arm in arm, and walking, one unwillingly enough, down the path.

'You see the fine effects of the railway signals towards Burslem,' said Horrocks, suddenly breaking into loquacity, striding fast and tightening the grip of his elbow the while. 'Little green lights and red and white lights, all against the haze. You have an eye for effect, Raut. It's a fine effect. And look at those furnaces of mine, how they rise upon us as we come down the hill. That to the right is my pet – seventy feet of him. I packed him myself, and he's boiled away cheerfully with iron in his guts for five long years. I've a particular fancy for *him*. That line of red there – a lovely bit of warm orange you'd call it, Raut – that's the puddlers' furnaces, and there, in the hot light, three black figures – did you see the white splash of the steam-hammer then? – that's the rolling-mills. Come along! Clang, clatter, how it goes rattling across the floor! Sheet tin, Raut – amazing stuff. Glass mirrors are not in it when that stuff comes from the mill. And, squelch! – there goes the hammer again. Come along!'

He had to stop talking to catch his breath. His arm twisted into Raut's with benumbing tightness. He had come striding down the black path towards the railway as though he was possessed. Raut had not spoken a word, had simply hung back against Horrocks's pull with all his strength.

'I say,' he said now, laughing nervously, but with an undertone of snarl in his voice, 'why on earth are you nipping my arm off, Horrocks, and dragging me along like this?'

At length Horrocks released him. His manner changed again. 'Nipping your arm off?' he said. 'Sorry. But it's you taught me the trick of walking in that friendly way.'

'You haven't learnt the refinements of it yet then,' said Raut, laughing artificially again. 'By Jove! I'm black and blue.' Horrocks offered no apology. They stood now near the bottom of the hill, close to the fence that bordered the railway. The ironworks had grown larger and spread out with their approach. They looked up to the blast furnaces now instead of down; the further view of Etruria and Hanley had dropped out of sight with their descent. Before them, by the stile, rose a notice-board, bearing, still dimly visible, the words 'BEWARE OF THE TRAINS', half hidden by splashes of coaly mud.

'Fine effects,' said Horrocks, waving his arm. 'Here comes a train. The puffs of smoke, the orange glare, the round eye of light in front of it, the melodious rattle. Fine effects! But these furnaces of mine used to be finer, before we shoved cones in their throats, and saved the gas.'

'How!' said Raut. 'Cones?'

'Cones, my man, cones. I'll show you one nearer. The flames used to flare out of the open throats, great – what is it? – pillars of cloud by day, red and black smoke, and pillars of fire by night. Now we run it off in pipes, and burn it to heat the blast, and the top is shut by a cone. You'll be interested in that cone.'

'But every now and then,' said Raut, 'you get a burst of fire and smoke up there.'

'The cone's not fixed, it's hung by a chain from a lever, and balanced by an equipoise. You shall see it nearer. Else, of course, there'd be no way of getting fuel into the thing. Every now and then the cone dips, and out comes the flare.'

'I see,' said Raut. He looked over his shoulder. 'The moon gets brighter,' he said.

'Come along,' said Horrocks abruptly, gripping his shoulder again, and moving him suddenly towards the railway crossing. And then came one of those swift incidents, vivid, but so rapid that they leave one doubtful and reeling. Half-way across, Horrocks's hand suddenly clenched upon him like a vice, and swung him backward and through a half-turn, so that he looked up the line. And there a chain of lamp-lit carriage-windows telescoped swiftly as it came towards them, and the red and yellow lights of an engine grew larger and larger, rushing down upon them. As he grasped what this meant, he turned his face to Horrocks, and pushed with all his strength against the arm that held him back between the rails. The struggle did not last a moment. Just as certain as it was that Horrocks held him there, so certain was it that he had been violently lugged out of danger.

'Out of the way,' said Horrocks, with a gasp, as the train came rattling by, and they stood panting by the gate into the ironworks.

'I did not see it coming,' said Raut, still, even in spite of his own apprehensions, trying to keep up an appearance of ordinary intercourse.

Horrocks answered with a grunt. 'The cone,' he said, and then, as one who recovers himself, 'I thought you did not hear.'

'I didn't,' said Raut.

'I wouldn't have had you run over then for the world,' said Horrocks.

'For a moment I lost my nerve,' said Raut.

Horrocks stood for half a minute, then turned abruptly towards the ironworks again. 'See how fine these great mounds of mine, these clinker-heaps, look in the night! That truck yonder, up above there! Up it goes, and out-tilts the slag. See the palpitating red stuff go sliding down the slope. As we get nearer, the heap rises up and cuts the blast furnaces. See the quiver up above the big one. Not that way! This way, between the heaps. That goes to the puddling furnaces, but I want to show you the canal first.' He came and took Raut by the elbow, and so they went along side by side. Raut answered Horrocks vaguely. What, he asked himself, had really happened on the line? Was he deluding himself with his own fancies, or had Horrocks actually held him back in the way of the train? Has he just been within an ace of being murdered?

Suppose this slouching, scowling monster *did* know anything? For a minute or two then Raut was really afraid for his life, but the mood passed as he reasoned with himself. After all, Horrocks might have heard nothing. At any rate, he pulled him out of the way in time. His odd manner might be due to the mere vague jealousy he had shown once before. He was talking now of the ash-heaps and the canal. 'Eigh?' said Horrocks.

'What?' said Raut. 'Rather! The haze in the moonlight. Fine!'

'Our canal,' said Horrocks, stopping suddenly. 'Our canal by moonlight and firelight is an immense effect. You've never seen it? Fancy that! You've spent too many of your evenings philandering up in Newcastle there. I tell you, for real florid effects – But you shall see. Boiling water . . .'

As they came out of the labyrinth of clinker-heaps and moulds of coal and ore, the noises of the rolling-mill sprang upon them suddenly, loud, near, and distinct. Three shadowy workmen went by and touched their caps to Horrocks. Their faces were vague in the darkness. Raut felt a futile impulse to address them, and before he could frame his words, they passed into the shadows. Horrocks pointed to the canal close before them now; a weird-looking place it seemed, in the blood-red reflections of the furnaces. The hot water that cooled the tuyères came into it, some fifty yards up – a tumultuous, almost boiling affluent, and the steam rose up from the water in silent white wisps and streaks, wrapping damply about them, an incessant succession of ghosts coming up from the black and red eddies, a white uprising that made the head swim. The shining black tower of the larger blast-furnace rose overhead out of the mist, and its tumultuous riot filled their ears. Raut kept away from the edge of the water, and watched Horrocks.

'Here it is red,' said Horrocks, 'blood-red vapour as red and hot as sin; but yonder there, where the moonlight falls on it, and it drives across the clinker-heaps, it is as white as death.'

Raut turned his head for a moment, and then came back hastily to his watch on Horrocks. 'Come along to the rolling-mills,' said Horrocks. The threatening hold was not so evident that time, and Raut felt a little reassured. But all the same, what on earth did Horrocks mean about 'white as death' and 'red as sin'? Coincidence, perhaps.

They went and stood behind the puddlers for a little while, and then through the rolling-mills, where amidst an incessant din the deliberate steam-hammer beat the juice out of the succulent iron, and black, half-naked Titans rushed the plastic bars, like a hot sealing-wax, between the wheels. 'Come on,' said Horrocks in Raut's ear, and they went and peeped through the little glass hole behind the tuyères and saw the tumbled fire writhing in the pit of the blast-furnace. It left one eye blinded for a while. Then, with green and blue patches dancing across the dark, they went to the lift by which the trucks of ore and fuel and lime were raised to the top of the big cylinder.

And out upon the narrow rail that overhung the furnace Raut's doubts came upon him again. Was it wise to be here? If Horrocks did know – everything! Do what he would, he could not resist a violent trembling. Right under foot was a sheer depth of seventy feet. It was a dangerous place. They pushed by a truck of fuel to get to the railing that crowned the place. The reek of the furnace, a sulphurous vapour streaked with pungent bitterness, seemed to make the distant hillside of Hanley quiver. The moon was riding out now from among a drift of clouds, half-way up the sky above the undulating wooded outlines of Newcastle. The steaming canal ran away from below them under an indistinct bridge, and vanished into the dim haze of the flat fields towards Burslem.

'That's the cone I've been telling you of,' shouted Horrocks; 'and, below that, sixty feet of fire and molten metal, with the air of the blast frothing through it like gas in soda-water.'

Raut gripped the hand-rail tightly, and stared down at the cone. The heat was intense. The boiling of the iron and the tumult of the blast made a thunderous accompaniment to Horrocks's voice. But the thing had to be gone through now. Perhaps after all . . .

'In the middle,' bawled Horrocks, 'temperature near a thousand degrees. If *you* were dropped into it . . . flash into flame like a pinch of gunpowder in a candle. Put your hand out and feel the heat of his breath. Why, even up here I've seen the rain-water boiling off the trucks. And that cone there. It's a damned sight too hot for roasting cakes. The top side of it's three hundred degrees.'

'Three hundred degrees?' said Raut.

'Three hundred centigrade, mind!' said Horrocks. 'It will boil the blood out of you in no time.'

'Eigh?' said Raut, and turned.

'Boil the blood out of you in . . . No, you don't!'

'Let me go!' screamed Raut. 'Let go my arm!'

With one hand he clutched at the hand-rail, then with both. For a moment the two men stood swaying. Then suddenly, with a violent jerk, Horrocks had twisted him from his hold. He clutched at Horrocks and missed, his foot went back into empty air; in mid-air he twisted himself, and then cheek and shoulder and knee struck the hot cone together.

He clutched the chain by which the cone hung, and the thing sank an infinitesimal amount as he struck it. A circle of glowing red appeared about him, and a tongue of flame, released from the chaos within, flickered up towards him. An intense pain assailed him at the knees, and he could smell the singeing of his hands. He raised himself to his feet, and tried to climb up the chain, and then something struck his head. Black and shining with the moonlight, the throat of the furnace rose about him.

Horrocks, he saw, stood above him by one of the trucks of fuel on the rail. The gesticulating figure was bright and white in the moonlight and shouting, 'Fizzle, you fool! Fizzle, you hunter of women! You hot-blooded hound! Boil! boil! boil!'

Suddenly he caught up a handful of coal out of the truck, and flung it deliberately, lump after lump, at Raut.

'Horrocks!' cried Raut. 'Horrocks!'

He clung crying to the chain, pulling himself up from the burning of the cone. Each missile Horrocks flung hit him. His clothes charred and glowed, and as he struggled the cone dropped, and a rush of hot suffocating gas whooped out and burned round him in a swift breath of flame.

His human likeness departed from him. When the momentary red had passed, Horrocks saw a charred, blackened figure, its head streaked with blood, still clutching and fumbling with the chain, and writhing in agony – a cindery animal, an inhuman, monstrous creature that began a sobbing, intermittent shriek.

Abruptly, at the sight, the ironmaster's anger passed. A deadly sickness came upon him. The heavy odour of burning flesh came drifting up to his nostrils. His sanity returned to him.

'God have mercy upon me!' he cried. 'O God! what have I done?'

He knew the thing below him, save that it still moved and felt, was already a dead man – that the blood of the poor wretch must be boiling in his veins. An intense realization of that agony came to his mind, and overcame every other feeling. For a moment he stood irresolute, and then, turning to the truck, he hastily tilted its contents upon the struggling thing that had once been a man. The mass fell with a thud, and went radiating over the cone. With the thud the shriek ended, and a boiling confusion of smoke, dust, and flame came rushing up towards him. As it passed, he saw the cone clear again.

Then he staggered back, and stood trembling, clinging to the rail with both hands. His lips moved, but no words came to them.

Down below was the sound of voices and running steps. The clangour of rolling in the shed ceased abruptly.

In the Fog

Dennis Wheatley

The fog came down quite suddenly; otherwise I would not have been out in it. I mean I would not have been walking in it, but would have had the porter get me a taxi to take me to my luncheon appointment. For a long time now I've had a horror of fog, as it was in one that I squared accounts with Eric Martin.

When I left my office on the far side of Regent Street there was no more than the grey mist that so often blurs the outlines of London's buildings on a November morning, and I had felt that the walk across to the lower end of Piccadilly would do me good; but by the time I crossed Hanover Square the mist had thickened and taken on a yellowish tinge. When I reached Bond Street the drivers of motor vehicles were having to switch on their headlights.

There was a time when I enjoyed walking in a fog in the West End of London. In those days nearly all the mansions in Mayfair were still occupied as private houses. The servants rarely troubled to draw the heavy brocaded curtains and often the lights were on, so one could see into the downstairs rooms. It was fun to glance in passing at the gracious interiors with their Adam mantelpieces and Chippendale furniture. Sometimes a footman would be laying a table and one could speculate with a shade of envy on the well-dressed men and lovely women who would soon be sitting there enjoying an epicurean lunch.

But now that glamorous Mayfair depicted by Michael Arlen was no more. The mansions had been converted into offices or shops; and as I turned into Grosvenor Street I had no inclination to look into them. The fog was now billowing down in thick, sluggish waves from the direction of the Park, and it aroused in me again those awful memories of my last walk with Eric.

It was while I was at the Ministry of Economic Warfare that I met him. He was about thirty then; a tall, broad-shouldered man with rather a pleasant face but eyes that were hard as agates; and as soon as one got to know him well, one realized that those hard, unsmiling eyes were the key to his personality. He was the most cynical and ruthless man I have ever met.

No doubt it was those qualities which made him so successful at his job, for he was a saboteur. Not the ordinary kind, who starts fires in ships and leaves sticks of gelignite in factories, but on a much higher level. He was a scholar of considerable attainments, and spoke several Near-Eastern languages fluently. His job was the bringing to grief, by fair means or foul, of politicians and big industrialists in the Moham-medan world who were helping the Nazis.

My memories of him were so vivid that, by the time I was approaching Berkeley Square, I could almost feel his presence. It was a horribly unnerving sensation and I tried to rid myself of it; but my brain rejected every train of thought except that which had led up to my impulse to kill him.

He had returned to London only to report, but a series of minor operations on his nose kept him here for nearly four months. Quite early in his stay I invited him home and introduced him to my family circle. I little thought then of the price we should have to pay for his amusing conversation; and until it was too late I had not even an idea that there was anything between him and Mary.

She was a cousin of mine, a lovely young thing of eighteen who had just gone into the W.R.N.S., and was doing her initial training at Golden Square. Her boyfriends up till then had been jolly youngsters little older than herself and I suppose it was Eric's polished man-of-the-world manner that carried her off her feet. Anyhow, he was fit again and shortly about to return to Palestine when she came to see me one evening and confided in a flood of tears that she was going to have a baby by him.

At first I was more surprised than angry, because having known Mary from her childhood I still thought of her as too young even to think of going to bed with a man. But as the full realization of what had happened came home to me, that very fact made Eric's seduction of her more unforgivable.

The next night I went to see him, told him what I thought of him and asked what he meant to do about it.

'Nothing,' he replied cynically. 'She should have taken the trouble to look after herself. Any girl old enough to go into one of the Services is perfectly fair game; and if it hadn't been me, it would soon have been someone else.'

I lost my temper then, but he only laughed and began to poke fun at me. He said that had it been any other girl I wouldn't have given it a second thought; that my indignation was due simply to jealousy and my belated realization that I had been too slow-witted or hidebound by convention to seduce her myself. That was untrue, but it shook me, because he was right about my being in love with her. Positively choking with fury, I slammed the door and rushed out of the house.

Next morning the two of us had to interview an Arab potentate who was staying at the Dorchester. It was a foggy November morning, and after we left the office we followed the same route out of Berkeley Square as that which I was taking now. As we walked up Hill Street I tackled him again. But he was adamant and quoted some Arab proverb to the effect that God had made women for the recreation of man.

It must have been the fog that caused us to turn along South Audley Street instead of crossing it, and take the slightly longer way up Stanhope Street to Park Lane. As we reached the corner it was so thick that we could barely make out the kerb of the pavement, let alone see across the road. For a moment we paused there, still wrangling. Perhaps it was old-fashioned of me, but I insisted that if he would not make any attempt to help her get out of her trouble, it was up to him to save her from disgrace by marrying her.

Stepping off the pavement we began to cross the open space towards the Dorchester. The murk was faintly broken by the dull yellow head-lights of a bus as it rumbled towards us from the direction of Oxford Street. Suddenly, Eric exclaimed:

'Oh, go to hell! If you're so anxious to protect her good name, marry her yourself.'

In that unnatural night we seemed as utterly cut off from the world as if we had been at the bottom of a coal mine. At his words something seemed to snap inside my brain.

'All right!' I cried. 'If she'll have me, I will. But it's you who are going to hell!' Then I gave him a violent push and sent him reeling under the oncoming bus.

Swerving away, I bolted into the fog. Some minutes later, I managed to get my bearings and found that I was in Grosvenor Square. With pounding heart I realized that unless I kept my head I stood a good chance of being hanged for murder; so I made my way back to the Dorchester, interviewed the Arab, then returned to the Ministry and reported that soon after leaving it with me, Eric had said that he felt ill, and decided to go home.

Next morning, I scanned the papers frantically. There was nothing about Eric. But the following day there was a short paragraph reporting that the body of a man who had died from fatal injuries had been picked up in Park Lane and later identified as his. I could breathe again without fear of arrest, but it did nothing to lessen my horror at the awful thing I had done.

For months I was oppressed by a terrible sense of guilt; then for quite long periods I began to forget my crime. But the sight of fog always brings it back to me and now, as I turned up Hill Street, I was filled with a grim foreboding that I should yet be called on to pay for it in some way.

Perhaps that was caused by the unnerving knowledge that I was being followed. Fog deadens all sound and gives even passing traffic a ghostly appearance. The busy streets seemed to have become almost empty and strangely silent; but I could distinctly hear footsteps behind me and the awful thing was that I thought I knew whose they were.

I attempted to increase my pace, but found I couldn't. When I reached the corner of Queen Street, the footsteps were right on my heels. To get to the Club where I was lunching I ought to have turned left there and gone through Shepherds Market, but some influence that it was beyond my power to combat forced me to go straight on – just as I had done with Eric.

A moment later, a tall figure loomed up beside me. I knew for certain then that there was good reason for my terror. It *was* Eric. Yet it could not be Eric in the flesh. It was his ghost that had returned to claim me.

Falling into step with me, it said – or I thought it said: 'Hello, Reeves. I could have identified you fifty yards away by that old smoker's cough of yours. How's the world using you?'

I was sweating with fear, yet felt impelled to reply: 'All right, thanks. Since the war, I've done very well for myself.'

'So I gather,' said my sinister companion. 'I hear, too, that you married Mary. How has that turned out?'

I knew that it could only be my guilty conscience causing me to imagine things, so I closed my eyes for a moment and made a desperate attempt to force my mind back into normal channels. But when I opened them again, he was still there and I heard myself mutter:

'We've been very happy. She has two sons now.'

The cynical voice came again. 'You're a lucky fellow, Reeves, to have made money, married the girl you loved and got away with murder.'

The way he said it sent cold shivers down my spine. It was so obvious that he had waited all this time, till I had little left to wish for, before returning to destroy me.

With the fog swirling about us, we had turned along South Audley Street and up Stanhope Street. I was half fainting with terror at the awful thought of what was about to happen. I felt certain that the sands of my life were running out. When we reached Park Lane he meant to force me – just as he had forced me to walk past Queen Street – to throw myself under a bus.

I made an effort to turn and run, but could not. I tried to shout for help, but no sound came from my throat. We arrived side by side on the fatal corner. The yellow headlamps of an approaching bus were visible only twenty feet away. It was bearing down on us inexorably. As though thrust by invisible hands, I lurched forward.

Suddenly my arm was grasped and I was jerked back. In a daze I heard Eric say: 'What the hell are you playing at? D'you want to kill yourself? You might not have the luck that I had of falling flat between the wheels. And I don't bear you any malice for that push, you know. It gave me the idea of having myself reported dead by our Ministry. As several people were after my blood, a change of identity suited me very well, just then. I've been in Turkistan, most of the time since. Come to the Club for a drink and I'll tell you what I've been up to all these years.'

The Cyprian Bees

Anthony Wynne

Inspector Biles, of Scotland Yard, placed a small wooden box on the table in front of Dr Hailey.

'There,' he remarked in cheerful tones, 'is a mystery which even you, my dear doctor, will scarcely be able to solve.'

Dr Hailey bent his great head, and examined the box with minute care. It was merely a hollowed-out block of wood, to which a lid, also of wood, was attached at one point by a nail. The lid rotated on this nail. He put out his hand to open it, but Biles checked that intention immediately.

'Take care!' he exclaimed; 'there are three live bees in that box.' He added, 'There were four of them originally, but one stung a colleague of mine, who was incautious enough to pull the lid open without first finding out what it covered.'

He leaned back in his chair, and drew a long whiff of the excellent cigar with which Dr Hailey had supplied him. He remained silent, while a heavy vehicle went lumbering down Harley Street. Then he said:

'Last night, one of my men found the box lying in the gutter in Piccadilly Circus, just opposite the Criterion Theatre. He thought it looked peculiar, and brought it down to the Yard. We have a beekeeper of some distinction on the strength, and he declares that these insects are all workers, and that only a lunatic would carry them about in this fashion. Queens, it appears, are often transported in boxes.'

Dr Hailey raised his eyeglass and set it in his eye.

'So I have heard.' He opened his snuff-box, and took a large pinch. 'You know, of course, my dear Biles,' he added, 'what this particular box contained before the bees were put into it?'

'No – I don't.'

'Serum – either anti-diphtheria serum or one of the other varieties. Practically every manufacturer of these products uses this type of receptacle for them.'

'H'm!' Biles leaned forward in his chair. 'So that means that, in all probability, the owner of the bees is a doctor. How very interesting!'

Dr Hailey shook his head.

'It doesn't follow,' he remarked. 'The box was perhaps left in a patient's house after its contents had been used. The patient may have employed it for its present purpose.'

Biles nodded. He appeared to hesitate a moment; then he said:

'The reason why I troubled you was that, last night, a woman was found dead at the wheel of a motor car – a closed coupé – in Leicester Square. She had been stung by a bee just before her death.'

He spoke in quiet tones, but his voice nevertheless revealed the fact that the disclosure he was making had assumed great importance in his mind. He added:

'The body was examined by a doctor almost immediately. He observed the sting, which was in her forehead. The dead bee was recovered later, from the floor of the car.'

As he spoke he took another box from his pocket and opened it. He held it out to the doctor.

'You will notice that there are rather unusual markings on the bee's body – these yellow rings. Our expert says that they indicate a special breed, the Cyprian, and that these insects are notoriously very ill-natured. The peculiar thing is that the bees in the wooden box are also Cyprian bees.'

Dr Hailey picked up a large magnifying glass which lay on the table beside him, and focused it on the body of the insect. His knowledge of bees was not extensive, but he recognized that this was not the ordinary brown English type. He set the glass down again, and leaned back in his chair.

'It is certainly very extraordinary,' he declared. 'Have you any theory?'

Biles shook his head. 'None, beyond the supposition that the shock caused by the sting was probably the occasion for the woman's sudden collapse. She was seen to pull quickly to the side of the road, and stop the car, so she must have had a presentiment of what was coming. I suppose heart-failure might be induced by a sting?'

'It is just possible.' Dr Hailey took more snuff. 'Once, long ago,' he said, 'I had personal experience of a rather similar case – that of a bee-keeper who was stung some years after he had given up his own apiary. He died in about five minutes. But that was a clear case of anaphylaxis.'

'I don't understand.'

Dr Hailey thought a moment. 'Anaphylaxis,' he explained, 'is the name given to one of the most amazing phenomena in the whole of medical science. If a human being receives an injection of serum or blood, or any extract or fluid from the animal body, a tremendous sensitiveness is apt to develop, afterwards, towards that particular sub-stance. For example, an injection of the white of a duck's egg will, after the lapse of a week or so, render a man so intensely sensitive to this particular egg-white that, if a further injection is given, instant death may result.'

'Even if a duck's egg is eaten, there may be violent sickness and collapse, though hen's eggs will cause no ill effect. Queerly enough, however, if the injection is repeated within, say, a day of its first administration no trouble occurs. For the sensitiveness to develop, it is essential that time should elapse between the first injection and the second one. Once the sensitiveness has developed, it remains active for years. The beekeeper, whose death I happened to witness, had often been stung before: but he had not been stung for a very long time.'

'Good God!' Biles's face wore an expression of new interest. 'So it is possible that this may actually be a case of – *murder*!'

He pronounced the word in tones of awe. Dr Hailey saw that already his instincts as a man-hunter were quickening.

'It is just possible. But do not forget, my dear Biles, that the murderer using this method would require to give his victim a preliminary dose – by inoculation – of bee-poison, because a single sting would scarcely be enough to produce the necessary degree of sensitiveness. That is to say, he would require to exercise an amount of force which would inevitably defeat his purpose – *unless he happened to be a doctor.*'

'Ah! the wooden serum-box!' The detective's voice thrilled.

'Possibly. A doctor undoubtedly could inject bee-poison, supposing he possessed it, instead of ordinary serum, or of an ordinary vaccine. It would hurt a good deal – but patients expect inoculation to hurt them.'

Biles rose. 'There is no test, is there,' he asked, 'by which it would be possible to detect the presence of this sensitiveness you speak of in a dead body?'

'None.'

'So we can only proceed by means of circumstantial evidence.' He drew a sharp breath. 'The woman has been identified as the widow of an artist named Bardwell. She had a flat – a luxurious one – in Park Mansions, and seems to have been well off. But we have not been able to find any of her relations so far.' He glanced at his watch. 'I am going there now. I suppose I couldn't persuade you to accompany me?'

Dr Hailey's rather listless eyes brightened. For answer he rose, towering above the detective in that act.

'My dear Biles, you know that you can always persuade me.'

The flat in Park Mansions was rather more, and yet rather less, than luxurious. It bespoke prodigality, but it bespoke also restlessness of mind – as though its owner had felt insecure in her enjoyment of its comforts. The rooms were too full, and their contents were saved from vulgarity only by sheer carelessness of their bestowal. This woman seemed to have bought anything, and to have cared for nothing. Thus, in her dining-room, an exquisite Queen Anne sideboard was set cheek by jowl with a most horrible Victorian armchair made of imitation walnut. In the drawing-room there were flower-glasses of the noblest period of Venetian craftmanship, in which beauty was held captive in wonderful strands of gold, and beside these, shocking and obscene examples of 'golden glass' ware from some third-rate Bohemian factory.

Dr Hailey began to form a mental picture of the dead woman. He saw her, changeable, greedy, gaudy, yet with a certain instinctive charm – the kind of woman who, if she is young and beautiful, gobbles a man up. Women of that sort, his experience had shown him, were apt to drive their lovers to despair with their extravagances or their infidelities. Had the owner of the bees embarked on his terrible course in order to secure himself against the mortification of being supplanted by some more attractive rival? Or was he merely removing from his path a woman of whom he had grown tired? In any case, if the murder theory was correct, he must have stood in the relationship to the dead girl of doctor to patient, and he must have possessed an apiary of his own.

A young detective, whom Biles introduced as Tadcaster, had already made a careful examination of the flat. He had found nothing, not even a photograph. Nor had the owners of neighbouring flats been able to supply any useful information. Mrs Bardwell, it appeared, had had men friends who had usually come to see her after dark. They had not, apparently, been in the habit of writing to her, or, if they had, she had destroyed all their letters. During the last few weeks, she seemed to have been without a servant.

'So you have found nothing?' Biles's tones were full of disappoint-ment.

'Nothing, sir – unless, indeed, this is of any importance.'

Tadcaster held out a crumpled piece of paper. It was a shop receipt, bearing the name of *The Times* Book Club, for a copy of *The Love-Songs of Robert Browning*. There was no name on it.

Biles handed it to Dr Hailey, who regarded it for a few moments in silence, and then asked:

'Where did you find this?'

'In the fireplace of the bedroom.'

The doctor's eyes narrowed.

'It does not strike me,' he said, 'that such a collection of poems would be likely to interest the owner of this flat.'

He folded the slip, and put it carefully into his pocket-book. He added:

'On the other hand, Browning's love-songs do appeal very strongly to some women.' He fixed his eyeglass and regarded the young detective. 'You have not found the book itself, have you?'

'No, sir. There are a few novels in the bedroom, but no poetry of any kind.'

Dr Hailey nodded. He asked to be shown the collection, and made a detailed examination of it. The novels were all of the lurid, sex type. It was as he had anticipated. He opened each of the books, and glanced at the fly-leaves. They were all blank. He turned to Biles.

'I am ready to bet that Mrs Bardwell did not pay that bill at the Book Club,' he declared. 'And I am ready to bet also that this book was not bought for her.'

The detective shrugged his shoulders.

'Probably not,' he said unconcernedly.

'Then, why should the receipt for it be lying in this room?'

'My dear doctor, how should I know? I suppose, because the man who possessed it chose to throw it away here.'

The doctor shook his head.

'Men do not buy collections of love-songs for themselves, nor, for that matter, do women. They buy them – almost invariably – to give to people they are interested in. Everybody, I think, recognizes that.'

He broke off. A look of impatience came into Biles's face.

'Well?'

'Therefore, a man does not, as a rule, reveal to one woman the fact that he has made such a purchase on behalf of another. I mean, it is difficult to believe that any man on intimate terms with Mrs Bardwell would have invited her jealousy by leaving such plain evidence of his interest in another woman lying about in her rooms. I assume, you see, that no man would give that poor lady this particular book.'

Biles shrugged his shoulders. The point seemed to him immaterial. He glanced round the bedroom with troubled eyes.

'I wish,' he declared, 'that we had something to go on – something definite, leading towards some individual.'

His words were addressed impartially to his subordinate and to Dr Hailey. The former looked blank, but the doctor's expression was almost eager. He raised his eyeglass, and put it into his eye.

'My dear Biles,' he said, 'we have something definite to go on. I was about to suggest to you when you interrupted me that the receipt for the book probably fell from the pocket of the purchaser through a hole in that pocket. Just as the little box containing the additional bees, which he had not found it necessary to release, was destined to fall later, when the man, having assured himself that an insect of unimpaired vigour was loose and on the wing, descended in Piccadilly Circus from Mrs Bardwell's car.'

He paused. The detective had turned to him, interested once more. The thought crossed Dr Hailey's mind that it was a pity Biles had not been gifted by Providence with an appreciation of human nature as keen as his grasp of material circumstances. He allowed his eyeglass to drop, in a manner which proclaimed that he had shot his bolt. He asked:

'You have not, perhaps, taken occasion to watch a man receiving a shop receipt for goods he has just bought and paid for? Believe me, a spectacle full of instruction in human nature. The receipt is handed, as a rule, by a girl, and the man, as a rule, pushes it into his nearest pocket, because he does not desire to be so rude or so untidy as to drop it on the floor. Shyness, politeness, and tidiness, my dear Biles, are all prominent elements in our racial character.'

Again he broke off, this time to take a pinch of snuff. The two detectives watched that process with some impatience.

'A man with a hole in his coat-pocket – a hole not very large, yet large enough to allow a piece of crumpled paper to work its way out as the wearer of the coat strode up and down the floor of the room – is not that a clue? A doctor, perhaps, with, deep in his soul, the desire for such women as Mrs Bardwell – cheap, yet attractive women—'

'I thought you expressed the opinion that he bought the love-songs for some other woman!' Biles snapped.

'Exactly. Some other woman sufficiently like Mrs Bardwell to attract him, though evidently possessed of a veneer of education to which Mrs Bardwell could lay no claim.' Dr Hailey's large kindly face grew thoughtful. 'Has it not struck you,' he asked, 'that, though a man may not be faithful to any one woman, he is almost always faithful to a type? Again and again I have seen in first and second wives the same qualities of mind and appearance, both good and bad. Indeed, I would go so far as to say that our first loves and our last are kindred spirits, recognized and chosen by needs and desires which do not change, or change but little, throughout the course of life.'

'Even so, my dear Hailey.'

Biles's look of perplexity had deepened. The doctor, however, was too eager to be discouraged.

'If Mrs Bardwell was, in fact, murdered,' he continued, 'the figure of her murderer is not, I think, very difficult to visualize: a doctor in early middle life – because the dead woman is at least thirty – with a practice in the country, but the tastes of a townsman; a trifle careless of his clothes, since he tolerates holes in his pockets, a sentimental egoist, since he buys Browning's love-songs while plans of murder are turning over in his mind—' He broke off, and thought a moment. 'It is probable that Mrs Bardwell was an expensive luxury. Such women, too, fight like tigers for the possession of the men they rely on. Yet, though she had undoubtedly obtained a great, perhaps a terrible, hold on him, she had failed to make him marry her.'

He turned to Biles, and readjusted his eyeglass.

'Why do you suppose,' he asked, 'Mrs Bardwell failed to make this doctor marry her?'

'I have no idea.' The detective's tones were crisp, almost to the point of abruptness.

Dr Hailey moved across the room to a writing-table which stood near the window. He took a sheet of paper, and marked a small circle on it. Around this he drew a much larger circle. He returned to the detectives, who stood watching him.

'Here is London,' he said, pointing to the small circle, 'and here is the country round it up to a distance of forty miles – that is to say, up to a two-hour journey by motor-car. As our doctor seems to make frequent visits to town, that is not, I think, too narrow a radius. Beyond about forty miles, London is no longer within easy reach.'

He struck his pencil at two places through the circumference of the larger circle, marking off a segment.

'Here,' he went on, 'are the Surrey highlands, the area, within our district, where heather grows, and where, in consequence, almost everyone keeps bees.'

He raised his head, and faced the two men, whose interest he seemed to have recaptured.

'It should not,' he suggested, 'be impossible to discover whether or not, within this area, there is a doctor in practice who keeps Cyprian bees, is constantly running up to London, wears an overcoat with a hole in one of the pockets, and lives apart from his wife.'

'Good heavens!' Biles drew his breath sharply. His instincts as a man-hunter had reasserted themselves. He glanced at the doctor with an enthusiasm which lacked nothing of generosity. The younger detective, however, retained his somewhat critical expression.

'Why should the doctor be living apart from his wife?' he asked.

'Because, had she not left him as soon as he tired of her, he would probably have killed her long ago; and, in that case, he would almost certainly have married Mrs Bardwell during the first flush of his devotion to her. I know these sensualists, who are also puffed up with literary vanity. Marriage possesses for them an almost incredible attractiveness.'

He glanced at his watch as he spoke. The recollection of a professional appointment had come suddenly to his memory.

'If you are to follow up the clue, my dear Biles,' he remarked, as he left the flat, 'I hope you will let me know the result. *The Medical Directory* should serve as a useful starting-point.'

Dr Hailey was kept fully occupied during the next day, and was unable, in consequence, to pursue the mystery of the Cyprian bees any further. In the late afternoon, however, he rang up Inspector Biles at Scotland Yard. A voice, the tones of which were sufficiently dispirited, informed him that the whole of the home counties did not contain a doctor answering the description with which he had furnished the police.

'Mrs Bardwell,' Biles added, 'kept a maid, who has been on holiday. She returned last night, and has now told us that her mistress received very few men at her flat, and that a doctor was not among the number. Of course, it is possible that a doctor may have called during the last fortnight, in the girl's absence. But, in the circumstances, I'm afraid we must look on the murder theory as rather far-fetched. After all, the dead woman possessed a car, and may have been in the country herself on the morning on which she was stung. Bees often get trapped in cars.'

Dr Hailey hung up the receiver, and took a pinch of snuff. He sat down in his big armchair, and closed his eyes that he might pass, in fresh review, the various scraps of evidence he had collected. If the dead woman had not received the doctor at her house, then the idea that they were on intimate terms could scarcely be maintained. In that case, the whole of his deductions must be invalidated. He got up and walked down Harley Street to *The Times* Book Club. He showed the receipt which he had retained, and asked if he might see the assistant who had conducted the sale. The girl remembered the incident clearly. It had occurred about a week earlier. The man who had bought the volume of poems was accompanied by a young woman.

'Did you happen to notice,' Dr Hailey asked, 'what his companion looked like?'

'I think she was very much "made up." She had fair hair; but I can't say that I noticed her carefully.'

'And the man?'

The girl shrugged her shoulders. 'I'm afraid I don't remember him clearly. A business man, perhaps.' She thought a moment. 'He was a good deal older than she was, I should say.'

Dr Hailey left the shop, and walked back towards Harley Street. On one point, at least, he had not been mistaken. The purchaser of the *Love-Songs* was a man, and he had bought them for a woman who was not Mrs Bardwell. Biles had mentioned that this lady had auburn hair. Why should the man have visited Mrs Bardwell so soon after making this purchase? He sighed. After all, why not? Biles was quite right in thinking that no jury in the world would listen to evidence the only basis of which was character-reading at second hand. He reached his door, and was about to let himself into the house when a cab drew up beside him. The young detective, Tadcaster, to whom Biles had introduced him at Park Mansions, got out.

'Can I see you a moment, doctor?' he asked.

They entered the house together, Tadcaster produced a letter from his pocket, and handed it to Dr Hailey. It was a prescription, written on Mrs Bardwell's notepaper, and signed only with initials, which were nearly indecipherable.

'I found it after you had gone,' the young man explained. 'It was dispensed, as you can see, by a local chemist. Today I have seen him, and he says he has had other similar prescriptions to dispense. But he has no idea who the writer is. Mrs Bardwell had the medicine a few days ago.'

Dr Hailey read the prescription, which was a simple iron tonic. The signature was illegible. He shook his head.

'This does not carry us much further, I'm afraid,' he declared.

'You can't tell from the initials who the doctor is.'

'No.'

'In that case, I think we shall have to throw our hands in.' Tadcaster's voice expressed considerable disappointment. It was obvious that he had hoped to make reputation out of the solution of the mystery. 'Your reasoning yesterday,' he added, 'impressed me very much, sir, if I may say so.'

Dr Hailey inclined his head, but his eyes were vacant. So a doctor had called on the dead woman recently – and also, apparently, made earlier visits – a doctor, too, whose prescriptions were unfamiliar to the local chemist. He turned to the young detective.

'I have just heard from Biles,' he said, 'that the maid has come back. Do you happen to know if she has any recollection of these professional visits?'

'I asked her that myself. She says that she knows nothing about them.'

Again the far-away look came to the doctor's eyes. The fact that the prescriptions were written on Mrs Bardwell's notepaper showed that they had been given during an attendance at the flat. For what reason had the dead woman been at pains to hide her doctor's visits from her maid?

'Should I be troubling you very much,' he said, 'if I asked you to take me back to Park Mansions? I confess that I would like to ask that girl a few questions. A doctor can obtain information which is not likely to be imparted to any layman.'

As they drove through the crowded streets, Dr Hailey asked himself again the question which had caused him to embark on this fresh investigation. What reason had Mrs Bardwell for hiding her need of medical attendance from her maid? Even supposing that her doctor was also her lover there seemed to be no sense in such a concealment. He opened his eyes and saw the stream of London's home-going population surging around the cab. Sweet-faced girls and splendid youths, mingled with women whose eyes told their story of disappointment, and men who wore pressing responsibility as an habitual expression. No wonder the police despaired of finding any one nameless human being in this vast tide of humanity, of hopes and fears, of desires and purposes!

The cab stopped. They entered the lift and came to the door of the flat. Tadcaster rang the bell. A moment later the door was opened by a young girl, who invited them to enter in tones which scarcely disguised the anxiety she apparently felt at the return of the police. She closed the door, and then led the way along the dim entrance corridor. She opened the door of the drawing-room.

As the light from the windows fell on her face, Dr Hailey repressed an exclamation of amazement. He started, as though a new idea had sprung to his mind. A slight flush mounted to his cheeks. He raised his eyeglass and inserted it quickly in his eye.

'I have troubled you,' he said to the girl, 'because there are a few points about Mrs Bardwell's health, before her fatal seizure, which I think you can help us to understand. I may say that I am a doctor, assisting the police.'

'Oh, yes!'

The girl's voice was low. Her pretty, heavily powdered face seemed drawn with anxiety, and her eyes moved restlessly from one man to the other. She raised her hand in a gesture of uneasiness, and clasped her brow, seeming to press her golden curls into the white flesh.

'Perhaps it might be better if I spoke to you alone?'

Dr Hailey's tones were very gentle. He looked at Tadcaster as he spoke, and the detective immediately got up and left the room. Then he turned to the girl.

'Your mistress,' he asked, 'discharged you from her employment a fortnight ago?'

The girl started violently, and all the blood seemed to ebb from her cheeks. Wild fear stared at him from her big, lustrous eyes.

'No!'

'My dear girl, if I may say so, you have everything to gain, nothing to lose, by telling the truth.'

He spoke coldly, yet there was a reassuring note in his voice. He saw fear give place a little to that quality of weakness which he had expected to find in her character – the quality which had attracted Mrs Bardwell's lover, and which explained, in some subtle fashion, the gift of the *Love-Songs*. He repeated his question. The girl hung her head. She consented. He let his eyeglass fall.

'Because of your intimacy with a man she had been accustomed to look on as her own particular friend.'

'Oh, no, no! It is not true!'

Again her eyes challenged him; she had thrown back her head, revealing the full roundness of her throat. The light gleamed among her curls. No wonder that this beauty had been able to dispossess her mistress!

'Listen to me.' Dr Hailey's face had grown stern. 'You have denied that any doctor came to this flat – at least, so far as you know. As it happens, however, a number of prescriptions were dispensed for Mrs Bardwell by the local chemist; so that, either she took great pains to hide from you the fact that she was calling in a doctor, or – you have not been speaking the truth.'

'She did not tell me.'

He raised his hand. 'It will be easy,' he said, 'to get an answer to that question. If your mistress was really hiding her doctor's visits from you, she must have taken her prescriptions herself, personally, to the chemist. I shall find out from him later on whether or not that is so.'

Again the girl's mood changed. She began to whimper, pressing a tiny lace handkerchief to her eyes in coquettish fashion.

Dr Hailey drew a deep breath. He waited a moment before framing his next remark. Then he said:

'You realize, I suppose, that if a girl helps a man to commit a crime, she is as guilty as he is, in the eyes of the law.'

'What do you mean?'

All her defences now were abandoned. She stood before him, abject in her terror, with staring eyes and trembling lips.

'That your presence here today proves you have had a share in this business. Why did you return to the flat?'

'Because – because—'

'Because he – the man you are shielding – wanted to find out what the police were doing in the place?'

She tottered towards him, and laid her hands on his arm.

'Oh, God, I am so frightened,' she whispered.

'You have reason – to be frightened.'

He led her to a chair, but suddenly she seemed to get her strength anew. Her grasp on his arm tightened.

'I didn't want him to do it,' she cried, in tones of anguish. 'I swear that I didn't. And I swear that I have no idea, even yet, what he did do. We were going to be married – immediately.'

'Married!' His voice seemed to underline the word.

'I swear that. It was honest and above board, only he had her on his hands, and she had wasted so much of his money.'

For the first time her voice rang true. She added:

'His wife cost a lot, too, though she was not living with him. She died a month ago.'

They stood facing one another. In the silence of the room, the ticking of an ornate little clock on the mantelshelf was distinctly audible.

Dr Hailey leaned forward.

'His name?' he asked.

'No, I shall not tell you.'

She had recaptured her feeble courage. It gleamed from her eyes, for an instant transforming even her weakness. The vague knowledge that she loved this man in her paltry, immoral way, came to him. He was about to repeat his demand, when the door of the room opened. Tadcaster came in with a small, leather-bound volume in his hand.

The girl uttered a shrill cry and sprang towards him; but Dr Hailey anticipated that move. He held her firmly.

'It is the collection of Browning's *Love-Songs*,' the detective said. 'I found it lying open in the next room. There is an inscription signed. "Michael Cornwall."'

He held the book out for the doctor's inspection, but Dr Hailey's face had grown as pale, almost, as that of the girl by his side.

He repeated the name – 'Michael Cornwall' – almost like a man in a dream.

The place was hidden among its trees. Dr Hailey walked up the avenue with slow steps. The thought of the mission which had brought him to this lovely Hampstead house lay – as it had lain through all the hours of the night – like death on his spirits. Michael Cornwall, the well-known Wimpole Street bacteriologist, and he had been boys together at Uppingham. They were still acquaintances.

He came to the front door, and was about to ring the bell when the man he was looking for appeared round the side of the house, accompanied by an old man and a girl.

'Hailey – well I'm dashed!'

Dr Cornwall advanced with outstretched hand. His deep, rather sinister eyes welcomed his colleague with an enthusiasm which was entirely unaffected. He introduced: 'My uncle, Colonel Cornwall, and my cousin, Miss Patsy Cornwall, whom you must congratulate on having just become engaged,' in his quick, staccato manner.

'We're just going round the garden,' he explained, 'and you must accompany us. And, after that, to luncheon. Whereupon, my dear Hailey, if you have – as I feel you have – great business to discuss with me, we shall discuss it.'

His bantering tones accorded well with his appearance, which had changed but little in the years. He was the same astute, moody, inordinately vain fellow who had earned for himself, once upon a time, the nickname of 'The Lynx.'

They strolled across the lawn, and came to a brick wall of that rich russet hue which only time and the seasons can provide. Dr Cornwall opened a door in the wall, and stood back for his companions to enter.

A sight of entrancing beauty greated them, lines of fruit-trees in full blossom, as though the snows of some Alpine sunset had been spread, in all their glowing tints, on this English garden. Dr Hailey, however, had no eyes for this loveliness. His gaze was fixed on a row of white-

painted beehives which gleamed in the sunlight under the distant wall.
Patsy Cornwall exclaimed in sheer wonder. Then a new cry of delight
escaped her, as she detected, in a large greenhouse which flanked the
wall, a magnificent display of scarlet tulips. She took Dr Hailey, in whose
eyes the melancholy expression seemed to have deepened, to inspect
these, while her father and cousin strolled on up the garden path. She
stood with him in the narrow gangway of the greenhouse, and feasted
ecstatic eyes on the wonderful blossoms.

'Don't they make you wish to gather them all and take them away
somewhere where there are no flowers?'

She turned to him, but he had sprung away from her side.

A cry, shrill and terrible, pierced the lazy silence of the morning.
She saw her father and cousin fleeing back, pursued by an immense
swarm of winged insects, towards the garden gate.

Blindly, frantically, they sought to ward off the dreadful onslaught.
The old man stumbled, and would have fallen, had not his nephew
caught him in his arms. She had a momentary glimpse of his face; it
was as though she had looked on the face of Death.

'*The bees!*'

The words broke from Dr Hailey's lips as a moan of despair. He had
come to the closed door of the greenhouse, and seemed to be about
to open it; but at the same moment one of the infuriated insects in
delirious flight struck the glass pane beside him. Then another – and
another – and another. He came reeling back towards the girl.

'Lie down on the gangway!' he shouted, at the highest pitch of his
voice. 'There may be a broken pane somewhere.'

She turned her horror-stricken eyes to him.

'My father – oh, God!'

'Lie down for your life!'

He stood beside her, watching, ready to strike if one of the bees
succeeded in entering the greenhouse. Only once did he remove his
straining eyes from this task. The sight which then greeted them wrought
a fresh cry of horror from his lips.

The terrible swarm hung like a dust-cloud in the air above the garden-
gate, rising and falling in swift undulations, which caused the light to
flash and scintillate on a myriad gilded bodies and shining wings. A
faint, shrill piping came to his ears across the silence. The door in the
wall was open, and the garden now quite empty.

Biles leaned forward.

'Mrs Bardwell's maid has confessed that she rang up Dr Cornwall
immediately before luncheon this morning,' he said. 'She tried to communicate with him before, but he had gone to the country, to a case,
overnight. He got her warning that the police suspected him of being

responsible for her mistress's death, just after he had carried his second victim, his uncle, in a dying condition, from the garden.'

The detective struck a match, and relit his cigar. Dr Hailey sat watching him with sorrowful eyes.

'Ten minutes later, as you know,' he went on, 'Cornwall blew his brains out. He had the wit to see that the game was up. He had been badly stung, of course, but his long experience of the bees made this a less serious matter than it would have been in the case of an ordinary outsider. In any case, moreover, he had to accept that risk if his plan was to succeed.'

Silence fell in the big consulting-room. Then the doctor remarked:

'Miss Cornwall has recently become engaged to be married?'

'Yes.' Biles drew a long whiff. 'That was the circumstance which made speed essential to her cousin's murderous plan. He was hopelessly in debt, as a result of Mrs Bardwell's extravagance. Only his uncle's money, which is considerable, would have saved him. If Miss Cornwall married he must have lost all hope of obtaining it, and so of marrying the girl on whom he had set his fickle heart. I have ascertained that he insisted on inoculating both father and daughter against spring catarrh a month ago, and that the injections he gave them hurt them terribly. No doubt Mrs Bardwell received a similar injection about the same time. Thus, for each of these three individuals, a single bee-sting, on your showing, meant instant death.'

Dr Hailey inclined his head.

'The moment I saw the swarm, the truth flashed across my mind,' he declared. 'These Cyprian bees, as I have been at pains to find out, and as your bee-keeping friend told you, are exceedingly ill-natured. But no bees, unless they have been previously roused to frenzy, ever attack at sight people who have not even approached their hives. It was all too clear, even in that first terrible moment, that the swarm was part of a carefully prepared plan.'

The detective rose, and held out his hand.

'But for you, my dear friend,' he said, 'Miss Cornwall must inevitably have shared her father's fate, and the most devilish murder of which I have ever so much as heard would, almost certainly, have gone unsuspected and unpunished.'

Acknowledgements

The Editor gratefully acknowledges permission to reprint copyright material to the following: *The Author's Literary Estate, Chatto & Windus Ltd and Paul R. Reynolds, Inc., New York, for* Evidence in Camera, *from 'The Allingham Casebook'; copyright © 1969 by Margery Allingham. The Author and Campbell Thomson & McLaughlin Ltd for* The Case of the Emerald Sky; *© Eric Ambler 1940. The Author for* Acid Test; *copyright © Margot Arnold 1977.* Eyewitness *is copyright © the Estate of Robert Arthur. Campbell Thomson & McLaughlin Ltd and The Society of Authors for* The Avenging Chance *by Anthony Berkeley; copyright © 1928 The Society of Authors. Arkham House Publishers Inc., Sauk City, Wisconsin, U.S.A., for* Sweets to the Sweet *by Robert Bloch; copyright 1947 by Weird Tales, copyright 1960 by Robert Bloch. Scott Meredith Literary Agency, Inc., 845 Third Avenue, New York, N.Y. 10022, for* Nightmare in Yellow *by Fredric Brown. The Author for* Baby, *from 'Dark Companions'; copyright © 1976 by Ramsey Campbell. Hughes Massie Ltd and Harold Ober Associates Inc. for* A Note for the Milkman, *from 'Today's Woman'; copyright © 1950 by Sidney Carroll. Miss D. E. Collins, Cassell & Co. Ltd and Dodd, Mead & Co. Inc., for* The Hammer of God *by G. K. Chesterton, from 'The Father Brown Stories' and 'The Innocence of Father Brown'; copyright 1910, 1911 by The Curtis Publishing Co.; copyright 1911 by Dodd, Mead & Co.; copyright renewed 1938 by Frances B. Chesterton. Hughes Massie Ltd and Dodd, Mead & Co. Inc. for* Accident, *from 'Witness for the Prosecution and Other Stories' by Agatha Christie; copyright 1929, 1943 by Agatha Christie; copyright renewed 1971 by Agatha Christie Mallowan. The Estate of the late John Keir Cross and A. M. Heath & Co. Ltd for* Esmeralda. *Murray Pollinger and Alfred A. Knopf, Inc. for* Lamb to the Slaughter; *© Roald Dahl 1953, from 'Someone Like You' by Roald Dahl, published by Michael Joseph Ltd and Penguin Books Ltd. The Author for* Surprise! Surprise!; *Copyright © Roger F. Dunkley 1978. Curtis Brown Ltd, London, on behalf of John Child-Villiers and Valentine Lamb as literary executors of Lord Dunsany, for* The Two Bottles of Relish. *N. P. V. Fleming and Jonathan Cape Ltd for* The Kill, *from 'A Story to Tell' by Peter Fleming.* Something to Do with Figures *by Miriam Allen de Ford is copyright The Planned Parenthood Association of Alameda, San Francisco, The American Humanist Association and The World Federalists, U.S.A., Inc. A. D. Peters & Co. Ltd for* The Turn of the Tide *by C. S. Forester. Celia Fremlin and Victor Gollancz Ltd for* The Blood on the Innocents *from 'By Horror Haunted'. Robert Graves and A. P. Watt Ltd for* Earth to Earth, *from 'Catacrok'. Arkham House Publishers Inc., Sauk City, Wisconsin, U.S.A., for* Mrs Manifold, *from 'The Girl with the Hungry Eyes' by Stephen Grendon. Hamish Hamilton Ltd for* The Two Vaynes, *from 'The Complete Short Stories of L. P. Hartley'; © The Executors of the Estate of the late L. P. Hartley. J. M. Dent & Sons Ltd for* August Heat, *from 'The Beast with Five Fingers and Other Midnight Tales' by W. F. Harvey. Campbell Thomson & McLaughlin Ltd and The Society of Authors for* Dark Journey *by Francis Iles; copyright © The Society of Authors 1934. The Society of Authors as the literary representative of the Estate of W. W. Jacobs for* The Well. *The Author and Elaine Greene Ltd for* Moment of Power *by P. D. James; copyright © P. D. James 1967 (first published in 1967, subsequently titled 'A Very Commonplace Murder'). The National Trust, Macmillan London Ltd and A. P. Watt Ltd for* The Return of Imray *by Rudyard Kipling. The Macmillan Publishing Co. for* The Lady with the Hatchet, *from 'Eight Strokes of the Clock' by Maurice Leblanc. John Farquharson Ltd for* Homicidal Hiccup; *copyright © 1979 by John D. MacDonald.* The Sound of Murder *by William*